THE POINT OF THE PICK

A Novel of the 20th Century

Curtis Seltzer

Cover photo in public domain available at www.publicdomainpictures.net.
Cover design and text formatting by Thea Klein-Mayer.
Author photo by Molly Seltzer.

Printed in the United States of America
Published 2018

ISBN-13: 978-1983720253
ISBN-10: 1983720259

DISCLAIMER

This is a work of fiction, not reporting. The principal characters are not real people. They are fabricated in whole or, in large part, from the author's imagination. Names, characters and incidents are either the product of the author's imagination or used fictively. A few historical figures have been portrayed accurately to anchor the narrative. Some settings are accurate while others are either fictive or recast. This book is not intended to be a history of labor relations in the American coal industry or the Miners for Democracy movement in the United Mine Workers of America.

I wrote a novel that I would like to read. Maybe it fits into a genre, maybe it doesn't. It was not written for a target market. It was written as a way to think about the consequences of ambitions playing out through choices in different circumstances with different individuals.

I wrote the first drafts in about 18 months, beginning in 1984. I came back to it in September, 2013, when I had time to rewrite and finish it. I was surprised at how much of the book was not as bad as I remembered. Some bones are the same; some joints are replacements; some ligaments are new.

As I rewrote 30 years later, I was consciously and subconsciously adding complexity to most of the characters, particularly the ones who are less appealing. This happens when you've passed 70. I've learned that things never turn out perfectly. People are not consistently good or bad. Good intentions often go awry and are sometimes punished. Bad deeds can bring rewards. There is no cosmic hand of justice, goodness and fairness. And in the middle of life's mess, most of us still try to do the best we can with what we have to work with.

Acknowledgements

A number of people have influenced my writing over the years. I'm grateful to University of Virginia faculty John Casey, the late George Garrett and the late Alan Cheuse. Other writers who took an interest include the late Joseph Mohbat, the late Janet Lembke, Dan Moldea, Lisa Tracy, John Howland, Charles Robb of the late <u>Pittsburgh Point</u> and Don McCaig.

Friends from Peabody High School, '63, who contributed knowingly and unknowingly, to my education include Larry Amber, Robert Anservitz, the late Leslie Barni, Stewart Bleckman, David L. Bloom, John Brewer, Gerry Chait, Edward Childs, Les Chodock, the late William Corso, Al Damus, Elaine Marcus Dines, the late Mark Friedman, Nancy Aronson Gold, the late Gary Henderson, Barbara Hepner, Steve Herman, Jay Leipzig, Jim Levey, Paul Levin, Arlene Glickman Levy, Mia Louik, Art Love, Don Mattes, Marc Pollock, the late Nino Siciliano, the late Charles Siegel, Harold "Hershey" Simon, Mark Simon, Stuart Smith, Robert Stein, Donna Fischer Tyson, Dan Wilson and Ed Wulkan. Other Peabodians who have stirred my pot include Alan Venable and Bob Bornholz. The late Ann Swartz, the late Helen DeFrance and the late Paul Williams were Peabody faculty to whom I'm indebted.

Helen Read Steele of Wonalancet, New Hampshire, has been a friend since college. She graciously commented on an early draft. Beverly Medgaus Jones offered sound advice on two drafts and nudged me along in her inimitable way. Allen Cooperman introduced me to Craig McKay who gave me enough encouragement at a critical point to keep me in the game. Paul Arons has been a good friend and friendly critic since before our days in Miss DeFrance's English class where he was praised and I was not, both deservedly. Nancy Debevoise contributed her quick wit and sharp tongue to my prose. Susan and Morry Heller have offered consistent interest and support. I've known many of these individuals since first grade.

Friends who bore on my subject over the years include Thomas N. Bethell, Beth Bogart, Kelly Branham, Steve Cohen, John David, Bob Dreisin, Patsy Crystal Eisenberg, Harrison Willis Elkins, Elizabeth Lowe Frederick, Leah Goldman, Doug Jones, Karl Kurtz, Sharon Lewis, Jim Loesel, Linda Nelson Lucci, Bebe Nava, the late Frank Powers, Bill Resneck, Clif Rexrode, the late Carl Schoffler, Gail Jorgenson Slaughter, Barbara Ellen Smith, Joan Robinson Titus-Carmel and David Underhill.

Sandi and John Bryant, Lucy and the late Dave Katz, their sons Howard and Jerry, Paul Herrup, the late John Nicholas Falk-Seltzer and my late parents, Robert and Rena, also contributed to this narrative in many ways. My late father-in-law, Carey Dowd, would recognize that I stole one of his favorite observations: "Let's stop pooling our ignorance."

Friends with Blue Grass connections who have been a part of this book are Tom Arbogast, the late Tom Atkeson, Bo and Doris Jean Folks, Steve Good, Nancy and Richard Headifen, Les and Laura LaPrade, Roger Orndorff, Clay Hamilton, Bill Rich, Joerg Schreiner, King Seegar, Carl Hull, Gerald Wells, the late Alice and Bill Will and their sons, William, Joe, Jimmie and Jackie.

Thea Klein-Mayer helped plant 600 trees, designed the cover, formatted the prose and navigated publishing. I could not have completed this work without her talented help.

Coal miners who shared their experiences with me include the late Willie Anderson, the late Clifton Bryant, Mike Burdiss, Danny Burleson, the late Levi Daniel, Fred Decker, Willard Esselstyn, the late Walter Burton Franklin, the late Perk Henry, the late Arnold Miller, Steve Shapiro and Frank Thurmond. My long-time friend, the late Robert Guerrant, would find himself in this book.

Others who informed my thinking were Michael Bernard, the late Bobby Brown, Alan Crane, Don Gasper, William Greider, Betty Justice, the late Lorin E. Kerr, Mike Klein, Kate Long, Sally Ward Maggard, Darrell V. McGraw, the late Carey McWilliams of The Nation, Bill Nye, the late Harry Perry, Steve Plotkin, Jim Ridgeway, the late Robert Tufts and John Williams,

I am indebted to my wife, Melissa Dowd, for her inestimable patience and support, and to our daughter, Molly, for supporting herself.

Journalists Patrick Tyler of The Washington Post, Helen Winternitz and Tim Phelps of The Baltimore Sun investigated the shenanigans at the National Bank of Washington in the early 1980s. Their revelations, I think, took that bank off the Mafia's plate.

Columbia University faculty who shaped my thinking include the late Zbigniew Brzezinski, the late William T.R. Fox, Henry Graff, the late Roger Hilsman, the late Richard Hofstadter, the late Julius Lewin, the late Harvey Mansfield, the late Richard B. Morris, the late Warner Schilling, Bruce L. R. Smith, Hans Spiegel, the late Alan Westin and the late Christopher Wright.

I'm grateful to Steve O'Keefe of Orobora, Inc., for walking me through the marketing process with great patience and deep wisdom.

Each of the individuals I've acknowledged contributed a thought, word, phrase or an experience that found its way into this narrative.

For Molly, a wonder in my book

Chapters

Book One

Book Two

Book Three

Book One

Chapter 1

Kanawha County, W.Va., Thursday, October 2, 1975, 11:55 p.m.

They were driving slowly with a caution that neither liked.

Rt. 119 -- a dollar-starved, two-lane highway -- wound up Lens Creek Mountain from Boone County into Kanawha County and West Virginia's capital, Charleston. Thick fog blocked any light the night sky might have offered. The few cars they passed driving south were crawling down the mountain as slowly as they were creeping up. High beams made visibility worse. High beams reminded them of Western Penitentiary, the maximum-security prison on the Ohio River that was five miles west of downtown Pittsburgh—a place familiar to both men.

George "Bonk" Hyskra and Little Louie Lazarro were arguing about the Pittsburgh Pirates, their hometown team.

"I'm tellin' you Ted Kluzewski could hit 'em farther -- even in 1959 when his young years was behind him -- than Willie Stargell at his best," Bonk claimed.

Little Louie snorted: "The nigger does him better by 30, maybe even 40 feet."

"I seen Klu hit one at Forbes Field off the ivy at the 457-foot sign in center," Bonk said.

"Stargell hit *seven* over the right-field stands. Klu never did that. They were both lefties. If Klu was gooder than Stargell, he'd have hit at least one over the roof."

"Kluzewski was only there two years," Bonk said. "Stargell was there from the end of '62 to '70 when they moved to Three Rivers Stadium— that shit pile on the Ohio."

"Kluzewski coulda hit at least one over the roof in two years," Little Louie said.

Bonk tried to be patient with his partner who was not a reasonable person on certain issues. "Well, Dick Stuart hit one *over* the 457 mark. Mighta been 500 feet or more."

"Kluzewski ain't even no Stuart," Little Louie said, sticking to his point that Stargell was the best of the three first basemen despite his race or because of it.

1

"Well, Klu's best years were in Cincy," Bonk said. "He had him that bad back by the time he got to us. Swung a 40-ounce bat that was bigger than Stargell's."

"Stargell swung a 12-pound sledge hammer in the on-deck circle," Little Louie laughed.

"You're right. But I liked Kluzewski," Bonk said.

"I liked him, too," Little Louie said, "but the long ball is not in the lumber. It's in the wrists. You hunkies think a bat is a caveman's club. Didya see how I did that guy tonight? Light wood, but fast wrists."

"It wasn't like you was hittin' a Koufax curve ball," Bonk said. "He was standing there, still as a flagpole. I'm talking about hittin' a fuckin' baseball, and you're talking about hittin' a fuckin' hillbilly."

Little Louie laughed.

Bonk laughed, too. As he did, he let the Cadillac slide off the edge of the asphalt. "Hard to see the road and find your way home down here," he grumbled.

"Ain't hard to see if you're lookin' at the road and not day-dreamin' about Polack heroes," Little Louie said.

"Keep Polacks out of this. Jeez, these roads are like driving corkscrews."

Little Louie fished an iced Iron City beer from a cooler at his feet. He pulled open the pop top and dropped it in the can. "Here, maybe this'll help your eyes," he said, handing the can to Bonk. "It'll steady your driving." He turned the channel knob on the radio and found Conway Twitty singing "You've Never Been This Far Before."

Bonk peered ahead. "Got my low beams on, and I still can't see this road through all this goop. How much you figure we got to go before we hit Charleston? I hate West Virginia roads. These hillbillies don't believe in painting edge stripes like civilized people. You can kill yourself down here without no one's help."

"They don't paint edge stripes because they can't figure out how to open a paint can. I bet hunkies could open a paint can."

"Drop it," Bonk said.

"It's just after midnight. We got this one bad mountain, and then it's no more than 20 minutes to the motel."

In the white Cadillac with Pennsylvania plates, Bonk slowed but still took the curves too fast. The heavy car -- never nimble in corners -- slid onto the shoulder gravel. Bonk yanked the wheel back to the left, oversteering.

"JESUS CHRIST! Watch what you're doin'! Gimme back that beer."

As he put both hands on the wheel, Bonk spilled beer into his lap.

Little Louie grabbed the can from him. Beer sprayed on them and on Bonk's fedora.

"WATCH MY HAT! PUNK!" Bonk shouted. "Gimme my beer back."

2

"Not on this mountain, I ain't."

"Shit," Bonk cursed.

"Wet yourself, did you?"

"Thanks to you. These curves ain't banked right. Or they ain't banked at all. Can't see shit in this shit."

"So slow down. We don't have to meet no one. We ain't on the run. That motel ain't goin' nowhere."

"The motel nowhere. That's where we're goin'," Bonk insisted.

He slowed the Cadillac to 20 and then 15 as they climbed through the thickening mist. The switchbacks tightened and steepened the higher they went. Bonk slowed to 10 in the curves and hugged the faded center stripe. He saw no lights in front or behind. Little Louie opened his window and hung out in an effort to see the road's edge.

"Take it slow, Bonk. There ain't no guardrail on my side, and I can't hardly see nothin'."

Bonk kept crawling upward. As he passed a short straight section, he noticed headlights come up in his rearview mirror. "Maybe that guy'll pass me, and I can follow his tail lights through this crap."

Bonk slowed the Cadillac to five. The headlights behind him closed.

"That asshole is blindin' me. Back off!"

"He's just piggy-backing on our tail lights like you was gonna do him," Lazarro said. "Pull over and let the fucker pass. Then you follow him. There ain't much room over here before it drops off, so come this way just a couple of feet."

Bonk eased the Cadillac over to the right about halfway off the asphalt and slowed almost to a stop. The headlights behind him came closer, filling his mirror.

George Hyskra and Little Louie Lazarro felt a soft nudge from behind.

"That dumb mutt hit me!" Bonk swore. He looked into his mirror, but the driver behind had cut his lights. Bonk stepped on the brake and then lifted his foot, uncertain about what to do. He put his foot back down on the brake.

Little Louie yanked his .38 out of his shoulder holster and turned in his seat. "We ain't in the business of havin' traffic accidents."

They felt the Cadillac pick up speed. Bonk stomped on the brake. The wheels locked. They felt themselves moving forward and even a little faster. Their tires scraped against the asphalt and gravel. They smelled burning rubber.

Bonk fought to turn the steering wheel toward the highway. The Cadillac started angling toward the slope at the edge of the road.

"STOP BRAKING," Little Louie screamed. "GIVE IT THE GAS AND GET HIM OFF YOUR BUMPER!"

George lifted his foot off the brake pedal. The force from behind caught the opportunity. The Cadillac's front wheels slipped over the edge.

3

Little Louie fired his pistol through the rearview window. Glass exploded. He fired twice more as the Cadillac pitched forward and over.

Bonk and Little Louie felt the Cadillac leave the ground.

The Cadillac slid and somersaulted down the steep slope as it gained speed. Its gasoline tank ruptured. The still-running engine ignited the fuel. A flameball exploded. Their car swiped a tree, then another. It stopped about 100 feet below Rt. 119.

The flames touched off the dry scrub brush that had a foothold in the talus. From the highway, a glow could be seen through the fog and darkness.

Biggie Stover drove north toward Charleston. Just past Marmet, he turned onto a lane-and-a-half blacktop road that wound up Muddlety Creek Holler. He passed the last house and turned into a little-used stub of a dirt road. The farther he drove, the narrower the tunnel of roadside vegetation became.

He stopped the red Jeep at the road's end where his big Chevy Blazer was parked facing out. He cut the engine with the Jeep pointed toward a wall of trees and a berm of random trash. His Blazer was on his left. He switched off the Jeep's headlights and then disconnected the jury-rigged shunt, leaving it dangling.

He sat silently, listening to the darkness. He had always learned a lot from being still and listening to quiet. The Jeep's fluids gradually stopped gurgling. The tiny tip-taps of hot metal cooling faded. He heard the tinkling of low water running over creek rocks. A few amphibians still flirted and challenged each other in the early October morning.

Biggie sat with his eyes closed and listened for the abnormal silence that would tell him that something, someone, was stirring. He sifted the noise through his mind, discarding sounds from the creek. He paid no attention to the slight rustling of dry oak leaves and whippy sumacs. He opened his eyes and glanced at his watch: 1:07 a.m. He scanned the darkness. He realized it had only been seven years since he had sat like this, waiting to ambush a Vietcong patrol.

His eyes adjusted. The fog had lifted a bit. He could make out a ford through the creek, which led into private land. A handful of moonlight speckles reflected off the running water. He saw tall, white sycamores on either streambank. He checked the Jeep's mirrors. He tugged the slack out of his driving gloves.

Biggie opened the door, left it ajar and walked to the driver's side of his Blazer. He moved softly and quietly for a big man. He opened the unlocked door.

"Jesus Christ! You scared the shit out of me," Dicey Shuck said. "I was sleepin'."

"Did you get the stuff?" Biggie asked.

4

"Yeah, boy."

"Go back to sleep," Biggie said. "You done good."

Biggie opened the plastic trash bag. He removed a pair of semi-dressy half-boots that were two sizes too small and jammed them on. Using a flashlight he'd retrieved from under the Blazer's seat, he made sure his own boots had not picked up dirt that might be traced back to this spot. He tapped them together to clear them of dust and reminded himself to scrub them when he got home. He put them on the floor behind his seat. With gloved hands, he took the roll of clear packaging tape from the bag.

He took out his pocket knife. He went into the underbrush and cut small branches that still held leaves. He taped the cut ends together, making two bunches. With string from the bag, he tied the two bunches to his Blazer's back fender, behind each back wheel. He'd stockpiled this trick from Saturday morning television westerns he'd watched as a kid.

He took a bottle of soda from the bag and walked over to the creek. He dumped its contents and filled the bottle with water. He went back to the Jeep and dripped water on the ground next to the driver's-side door. He made sure that he left one good print in the damp earth from each foot.

With a chamois cloth he had in the Blazer, he wiped down the Jeep's interior for threads and lint even though he'd worn gloves. He left the two ignition wires twisted together where he had stripped insulation from each one. But he made sure the bare end of the starter wire was not touching the battery wire, which was how he had sparked the Jeep to life several hours earlier.

As he returned to his Blazer, he picked up two rocks, each weighing about five pounds. He put the rocks, roll of tape, the too-small boots, leftover string, chamois, bottle and driving gloves into the trash bag, which he then slit in several places. He got into the driver seat, nudging Dicey Shuck into the passenger seat.

He put on his own boots.

"I'll drop you in Eskdale," Biggie said to Dicey.

"Sure. I'll catch a ride in with the boy tomorrow. My vehicle's parked near the campaign office. No meter. The boy works custodial up at the Capitol."

"Hey, Dicey. How'd you get your handle?"

"Rollin' the cubes on a troop ship comin' home from Europe. Craps."

"Lucky?"

"Well, you might say that. I used dice that I did a little work on. See, you weight the side opposite from what you want to come up. Take a $1/32^{nd}$ bit and drill into one or even two of the black dots. Then put in a couple of ball bearings from the motor pool. Seal it with wax or a dab of melted plastic. Then color it black with India ink."

"Dicey, you old dog. Ain't never figured you for a gambler."

"I wasn't then and ain't now."

5

"Guess you wasn't after all," Biggie admitted. "Come on, it's late."

Biggie stopped and listened before he turned over the Blazer's motor. He drove out to the main dirt road and then onto the hardtop. He stopped and cut the string holding the two bunches of branches. He threw them off to the side of the road. He put the string into the bag. He looked at his watch: 1:28 a.m.

At 12:47 a.m., Jeep Delucci phoned the Charleston Police Department to report his well-known red Jeep had been stolen. He gave a statement at the station the next morning. He said he'd spent the evening at his campaign headquarters on West Washington Street until about 7 p.m., and then went with friends to Murad's Grill down the block. When he walked back to his apartment on Quarrier Street about 12:15, he noticed his Jeep was not parked where he'd left it locked two nights earlier. He provided names of witnesses, including his campaign manager, Jeffrey Becker, who could testify to his presence at headquarters and then at Murad's.

Biggie Stover drove his Blazer into Kanawha City, across the Kanawha River from Charleston. He drove up the arching two-lane bridge that crossed to the north bank. At its apex, he checked for traffic and stopped. Fog was still dense over the water. He got out, took a few steps away from his Blazer and tossed the plastic bag into the River. He heard the splash. He then made a loop around the Capitol and recrossed the River. He drove through Cabin Creek's necklace of old coal camps -- Dry Branch, Sharon, Miami, Dawes and Ohley -- to Eskdale where he stopped in front of a small house with new siding.

"Go quiet," Biggie whispered to Dicey Shuck.

Biggie continued driving south through Red Warrior and Acme to Kayford 20 miles from the River. Past Kayford the hardtop ended. He stopped, spun his hubs into Lock and shifted into four-wheel drive.

Had he continued south, he would have crossed Kayford Mountain into Raleigh County. Instead, he cut west on a private road, opened a locked gate with a key on his own chain and started winding down the mountain toward his home outside of Orgas in Boone County. He had driven this old logging road many times in the darkness, going or coming from hunting deer.

Thirty minutes after leaving Kayford, Biggie slipped his Blazer into his carport. It was close to 3 a.m. No neighbor saw him arrive, since his was the last house at the upper end of Stover Holler. Outside the kitchen door, he slipped off his boots and hosed them off. He opened the door and went into his bedroom barefoot. He undressed and climbed into bed.

"Where you been, hon?" his wife, Brenda, mumbled as he slid next to her.

"Politickin'."

"Too late for politickin'."

"You're right," Biggie said and kissed her. "Won't happen again."

"You've said that before."

"Thangs come up that gotta be put down," he said.

"Who are you more interested in, me or the campaign?"

"You."

"Too late for gettin' mad," she said. "So, okay. Here I am."

Early the next morning, Brenda finished making coffee before Biggie got out of bed. She emptied the trash into the can outside the kitchen door. She noticed his boots and socks.

Brenda Stover wondered how they could have gotten soaked from politikin' on a rainless night.

Chapter 2

Charleston, W. Va., Thursday, October 2, 1975, 7:02 p.m.

"Don't do it, Jeep," Becker said.

James "Jeep" Delucci, Jr., kicked his wastebasket across his office. He wanted to kick a lot more than that.

"Did you hear what them two guys did to Vernie Skeens? Huh?"

"I heard the same thing you did at the same time," Becker said.

Jeep forced himself to breathe slowly and deeply. "They busted Vernie's nose and broke his arm with a baseball bat. He'll be off work for more than a month. Two of 'em on one broke-down miner who can't do nothin' these days but hand out cap lamps in the bathhouse. Vernie must be 60, 62, if he's a day."

"Vernie is also a local union president and one of your strongest supporters," Becker said as he stood to one side of Delucci's desk. He looked at the spilled mess from the wastebasket. He wished this Vernie Skeens muddle could be cleaned up as easily. He swirled the coffee in his Styrofoam cup. The usual end-of-the-day dregs. He chanced a swallow. Acidic.

Biggie Stover hadn't moved from his chair that faced his friend, Delucci. He cracked his knuckles. He looked out the window into the growing darkness.

"This story's gonna be all over the coalfields in a day or two," Delucci said. He closed his eyes and rubbed them. He felt a headache coming in for a hard landing.

Biggie shifted the toothpick in his mouth. He sniffed. "If this shit ain't stopped, our guys'll stay home on December 5th or vote for Joe Hunt."

Jeffrey Becker, campaign manager, shifted his eyes to the map of the United States that covered one wall of Delucci's modest office in his low-rent, campaign headquarters. Each of the 637 red dots represented one local in the American Coal Miner's Union. Green pins had been stuck in 483—a Delucci majority vote in the presidential nominating election that had ended on Monday, three days earlier.

Becker had expected about a 50-50 split in the local vote. Delucci and Stover had been hoping for 45 percent. Jeep Delucci had carried 57 percent of the local unions. No one was more surprised than these three that their thrown-together Miners for a Democratic Union (MDU) had won the first round so convincingly.

The Delucci campaign was the first challenge to a sitting ACMU president in 75 years. When the nominating results were announced on Tuesday morning, Delucci was giddy, Becker was stunned and Stover was wary. Becker had never won anything in politics. Delucci, at least, had been elected president of his local union and then president of ACMU District 17 in Charleston. Biggie Stover was not the sort who ever ran for anything, or from anything for that matter.

Becker put his cup on Delucci's desk and walked over to the window air-conditioner. It was inadequate for the modest room. Underpowered and overworked, it did its best to produce a small cloud of comfort in the heat steeping Charleston. Even in early evening, the August-like discomfort lay like a dead, decomposing snake in the rut of the Kanawha River Valley. Becker leaned close to the machine. He wanted that room to be cooler.

Biggie looked at Jeep. "It's like in the Delta. Deal with them like the VC deals with you."

Becker, the lawyer, winced. "This is West Virginia, not the Mekong Delta. It's 1975, not 1968."

"Well, you wouldn't know 'bout that, would you?" Biggie said.

Becker had been run around this circle before. "You're right, Biggie," he said in a bored singsong, "I was not born and raised in a West Virginia holler. That makes me a come-here. My father was not a coal miner. That makes me a non-Union outsider. I ducked Vietnam. That makes me a Commie coward. I went to college and law school. That makes me an intellectual snob. I work for the underdogs. That makes me a bleeding-heart sucker and…"

"…okay," Delucci said. "Okay!"

"…that makes me a fool. I eat yogurt. That makes me…"

"STOP IT!" Delucci said.

"…a hippie-dippie, do-goodin' elitist," Biggie laughed.

Becker caught his breath. "I'm tired of being baited by the guys who hired me. It doesn't get us anywhere. You understand?"

The 300-pound miner raised his muscled arms in surrender. "See, Jeep," Biggie said, "I knew Becker had fire in his gut. I told you he did."

"Asshole," Becker said. He felt better. Everyone did.

Biggie approached Becker and punched him gently in the bicep. Becker punched him back. Becker shook his head and rolled his eyes.

"I trust you, Beck," Delucci said, "and so does Baby Huey. He even told me so. Sometimes he just can't help himself."

Biggie's black beard covered some of his grin. "Sure. I even told Jeep to hahr you for campaign manager." He tapped his Lucky Strike in the ashtray on Delucci's desk.

"Then listen to me," Becker said. "Take this attack on Vernie Skeens to the county prosecutor in Logan. Give the story to the Gazette reporter up here. Charlie Frazier. He probably prefers Jeep to Joe Hunt. Let the law and the papers find out who those two guys are. Play the victim. Don't fight fire with fire. Fight fire with water."

9

Becker stopped. He heard himself lecturing in clichés.

"It'll look like we're runnin' to our big brother to take up for us," Biggie said.

"That's bullshit," Becker said to Delucci. "It'll look like we're law-abiding citizens who've done nothing but engage in union politics. And after we won the first round fair and square against all the odds, our supporters are attacked by thugs. Let the cops handle it. Anything else carries a very high risk to the campaign."

"That's not how my granddad built this Union. Jeep's neither. Sometimes they had to go leafin'. Ain't that right, Jeep?"

If Becker's ears could have squinted in bewilderment, they would have. Instead, he scrunched his face. Even after three years in West Virginia, he still didn't catch all of what was said or understand all of what he did snag. He cursed his college English and his Yankee ears.

Jeep sat down. He looked at Becker. "Sometimes they did, Beck, because sometimes they had to."

"Did what?" Becker asked, finally. He knew they knew that he didn't know what they were talking about. Bad lawyer, he thought, asking questions when you don't know the answer. Why, he asked himself, do I need to know more than I need to know?

"It was different back then," Jeep said. "The old-timers in the ACMU went through more than 30 years of strikin' and dyin' in the early 1900s for basic shit like a union contract, a few more pennies per loaded ton, a miner-chosen checkweighman to tally their coal, free speech in comp'ny towns, no more comp'ny police guards and no more required shopping at the comp'ny store. The mine owners on Cabin Creek and Paint Creek -- Sam Dixon, Charlie Cabell, Quinn Morton, Justus Collins -- were the worst of a bad bunch. They had armed guards evict strikers from comp'ny houses. They'd beat up guys, terrorized them to keep us down. They shuttled in immigrants off the boats in New York City and from down South. They'd run 'em up the two hollers in sealed trains and told 'em nothin' about a strike. This stuff went on until FDR's legislation in the mid-1930s. It was a war, on again, off again. We were losin'.

"When a strike was on, it was often a shootin' war. Our side would wait until the hardwoods leafed out in the spring. They'd take their rifles up in the hills where they had cover and then lay the lead to 'em. Comp'ny guards couldn't see where the shots was comin' from. That's just how things was back then. I'm not sayin' it was proper or even effective. It was, the men said, 'self-defense.' When you don't have no better choice, you do what you have to do."

"How did you find out about this history?" Becker asked.

"My Mom's parents were Rocco and Nellie Spinelli," Delucci said.

"Don't know them," Becker said.

"Didn't think that you would," Jeep said. "Rocco came from Calabria in 1905. Short, muscular guy. Had a big scar across his forehead and a dimple in his chin. Married Nellie Bowles, a local gal from Cabin Creek where he was a miner. He worked for Cabell who started Carbon Fuel and was the big stick in the Kanawha County Coal Operator's Association. When the strike started in the summer of 1912 -- the year they were married -- they went up and down Cabin Creek and Paint Creek pulling out the Italian miners. They helped hold the strike together. He told me about it when I was just a little kid just before he died. My Dad filled me in. Rocco said I had union in my blood."

Biggie brought them back. "Those two guys who roughed up Vernie were thugs with Pennsylvania plates on their Cadillac."

"But we don't know *whose* thugs exactly or why exactly," Becker said.

"Hell's fire, son," Biggie said. "It was Joe Hunt's boys. Who else gives a blessed shit about this election?"

"Beck's right, Biggie," Jeep said. "We ain't sure what's really goin' down."

"Here's what we do know," Becker said. "Vernie's wife, Alice, calls us 15 minutes ago. Dicey Shuck out front takes the call. Alice is crying and going bonkers. The Logan County rescue squad has just taken Vernie to the hospital. Dicey puts the call through to me, and then I get you two on the line. Alice says…here are my notes…two guys -- a big guy in a fedora hat and a little guy -- came to their door around supper time. About 5:30 p.m. Vernie answers. Alice sees and hears the little one offer Vernie $500 if he'll get his local to swing behind Joe Hunt in December. Waves five new $100 bills under his nose. Vernie says, 'No. They voted for Jeep. Let the men vote clean.' Then the big guy mashes Vernie's nose. And the little one whips out a sawed-off baseball bat and whacks his arm. They drive off in a new white Cadillac with Pennsylvania plates. Alice hears the big guy say, 'We'll be back.' That is what we know."

"These guys might be miners," Jeep said. "Joe Hunt's got support on those Pennsylvania strip jobs and in the old deep mines like Fricktown where he comes from."

"Coal miners? In a '74, '75 white Caddy?" Biggie asked.

"Shit," Jeep laughed. "Workin' miners these days can buy anythin' on enough time. Joe's '72 contract got us 50 bucks a day straight pay. And time-and-a-half for overtime. We ain't drop-dead poor no more."

"These boys ain't miners," Biggie said with deck-clearing certainty. "They sound like pros who are sendin' us a message. Look, man, they didn't make no mess. Didn't break up furniture. They mashed up Vernie just enough to make their point. If they was Joe Hunt's miners, hell, it'd be Vernie flyin' through a winder. Alice throwin' hot cornbread. Guns shootin', babies next door bawlin' and dogs crappin' on the living-room floor."

"I think you're right," Becker said. "They're pros, or, at least, semi-pros. And that's why it's even more important to let the law deal with them. We need to know who would send guys like that into Logan County. Who do they work for? Is there something going on here that we can't see yet?"

Biggie tapped out a Lucky from his pack and stretched in his chair. Delucci lit a Marlboro.

"First guess," Biggie said, "it's one of the big coal boys—USOCO, UNICOAL or AMSTEEL. They figure Jeep here will cost them money in the contract negotiations next year and maybe turn a blind eye toward wildcat strikes. So they want Joe to stay where he is. They sent them to scare off Jeep's support."

"Second guess," Jeep said, "it's Joe Hunt who figures that the only way he's going to win on December 5th and keep his fat ass in a big leather chair up in Washington is if my guys are scared to vote for me."

"Third guess," Biggie said, "is this: Joe Hunt figures that he got the best chance to win if Jeep's out of the way -- either voluntarily or involuntarily -- and he runs unopposed like always. Whuppin' up on Vernie may be sending you a message: 'Get out while you can.'"

Jeep sniggered: "Even with Joe runnin' against no one but his own sorry butt I'd guess he has at least a 50-50 shot at losin'."

"Fourth guess," Becker said, "is this: It's something we don't know."

"Like what?" Jeep asked.

"Like, I don't know what I don't know," Becker said.

"You got too much college, Beck," Biggie said.

"And we got too much of not enough," Jeep said.

"You're right," Becker said, "too much college."

Biggie stubbed out his cigarette. "Those two boys will be comin' over Lens Creek Mountain if they're headin' back home to Pee-A or just back here to Charleston."

Jeep dragged on his Marlboro and focused his thoughts.

James "Jeep" Delucci, 30, was a third-generation coal miner from Cinderella Hollow in Boone County, about 20 miles southeast of Charleston. Some who met him during the campaign called him "Jimmy," but he marketed himself as "Jeep."

His Dad, Jim, bought a Willys CJ-3B Universal Jeep in 1953, straight from the Toledo factory. He rigged it out with a Fisher snow plow so that he could make some cash in the winter if USOCO's Sunburst Mine was working short weeks. His eight-year-old, James, considered that Jeep to be the best vehicle in West Virginia, maybe the world. He'd sit in it after school and pretend to drive, growling to reflect gear changes. That year, the kids up Cinderella dubbed him Jeep.

The first thing Delucci did on returning from Vietnam in 1969 was to buy a red, four-wheel-drive Jeep CJ-5 with a V6 225 and a three-speed manual transmission. He stuck in a four-barrel Holley 390 carburetor for more power. He had no ambitions at that time beyond his CJ-5.

Jeep hired on at the Sunburst Mine a few weeks after being discharged. He hadn't thought very hard about other jobs in large part because there were no other jobs to think about. Following their Daddies into the mines was what most local boys did. Coal-mining wages and benefits were better than anything they could find on the surface, including the chemical plants in the Kanawha Valley. USOCO hired young veterans with the idea of blending them in gradually to replace the 50- and 60-year-olds who were the majority of the workforce.

Jeep wore his new-miner red hat with pride and a tiny swagger. Young backs like his started as General Inside Labor—shoveling spilled coal onto conveyor belts, laying in cement-block ventilation walls to channel air, humping materials where they were needed and doing whatever their section boss told them.

The '60s came late to West Virginia, but they did show up. Long hair. Marijuana. Rock. Clothes. Politics. Anti-authority anger. The coal industry's grip began to loosen here and there.

The War on Poverty's Economic Opportunity Act of 1964 startled the Appalachian courthouse politicians with its insistence on the "maximum feasible participation" of the poor in community-action programs as a condition for sending federal dollars. The poor wanted power, because power was the key to change. The locals who ran the coal counties didn't want to share. The poor and their advocates pointed to corruption; the authorities said the poor were just ragtails looking for a new handout. Coal companies were not the target of the War on Poverty, but they soon came under fire because they were the power behind the politicians.

The "helpers" who came to stir the poverty wars showed they had to be taken seriously. They were college-educated, middle-class, idealistic, suburban college kids who worked in low-paid private and federal anti-poverty programs. They were skeptical of The Authorities who dubbed them communists, subversives, outsiders, troublemakers, agitators, do-gooders, hippies, draft-dodgers, Yankees, dope-smokers, elitists, vegetarians, bearded long-hairs, city-people, atheists, liberals, socialists and moral degenerates. Some truth to those charges could be found among the hundreds of young people who came to Appalachia to change the odd and objectionable circumstances that trapped its poor.

Helpers brought certain skills—research, media, publicity, grant-writing, law, teaching, organizing and networking with groups beyond the coalfields. They quickly decided the poverty that lay beneath working-class miners was produced by the coal industry's economic and political domination—its low taxes on surface land, coal in the ground and production; its power over local politics wielded by the half-dozen largest landowners in each county who typically owned 75 percent of all the land; its hostility toward diversifying local economies; and its historic practice of pricing coal cheaply by not paying the costs of protecting workplace safety and the environment. The outsiders framed the Appalachian coalfields as an exploited resource colony run by absentee owners and left to rot amid the degradation of its people, land, water and air. The region was rich in natural resources—coal, oil, gas, water, timber and natural beauty. So why were so many of its people so poor? Why were local and state authorities able to provide only the most minimal services?

It did not take long for a few of the helpers to focus on the American Coal Miner's Union as the most logical agent to challenge the coal industry's power and, in the course of doing so, improve the lot of the non-miner poor. To recast the Union as the source of coalfield political and economic reconstruction, its membership first had to take control of the organization from Joe Hunt and then broaden the Union's agenda.

That was how Jeffrey Becker read the situation when he moved to Charleston to throw in with the small group of working and retired miners who had formed the Miners for a Democratic Union under Jeep Delucci in the early 1970s.

In the late '60s, a generation shift was taking place in West Virginia's coal mines as those who had entered in the '30s and '40s were being swapped out for their sons and grandsons. Black-lung disease became a front-page issue in 1969 when liberals in the West Virginia legislature and striking rank-and-file miners pushed through a modest black-lung-disability compensation bill. And then in November, 1969, Consolidation Coal's Farmington No. 9 mine blew up, entombing 78. Miners -- sons and fathers alike -- started asking questions about how to make mining safer, how to hold down the dust that caused black lung and why Joe Hunt wasn't doing a better job protecting their health and safety.

Jeep Delucci heard the music of the '60s, smoked its dope and let his black hair lap a couple of inches over his collar. He hadn't thought much about politics as a teenager, but he came home from the Mekong Delta with a clear belief that The Big Boys had trifled with him, Biggie and everyone like them. He didn't know who ran USOCO, America's third largest coal company and second biggest oil company, but he figured they were cut from the same cloth as the boys who ran the War. The System, he concluded, was rigged to use guys like him—use and use up. He got angry, and he wanted to change the way things were.

Delucci won a spot on his local union's mine-safety committee after only a year and was then elected local president in 1971. A year later, he was elected president of District 17's six counties south of Charleston. He felt the men moving under him and with him. His words were theirs.

Jeep grew into these responsibilities quickly. He was smart and charming. His dark eyes and good white teeth had gotten him most of what he wanted most of the time with the prettier holler honeys. His self-deprecating self-confidence worked with men of his father's generation, the kind of men he had known all his life, the kind who had earned the respect he extended. He felt he was more their representative and less their leader. Older miners liked what they saw and heard. Jeep had a sense about him that he was going somewhere with their help. His own generation felt he knew what they wanted. Both groups pushed him up the Union's ladder, not making him wait. Jeep found himself believing he was destined to do something more than work himself to death digging coal to keep the Nation's hair dryers blowing. He, Biggie and a handful of others formed the Miners for a Democratic Union in anticipation of running against Joe Hunt in 1975.

Joe Hunt recognized the threat to his position when Jeep won the District 17 presidency in a landslide. He offered Jeep the job of research director in the ACMU's Washington headquarters, because his friend and assistant, Larry "Skis" Sonoski, had said something to him about keeping enemies closer than friends. "Up here, he'll lose his base in a few years. Make him dependent on you. Then run him out," Sonoski advised. Jeep turned down that offer, because he had a target in his sights. It was Joe Hunt's job.

Joe Hunt wasn't like the older miners Jeep knew. They worked every day with their head, hands and backs. Joe, Jeep thought, had been sitting too long in a seat that was soft, warm and dry where the only thing he expected of himself was to sit in the same chair the next day and the next.

The job had changed Joe Hunt. He had lost touch with his members. Joe's constituents had become the coal operators with whom he negotiated contracts. He supported federal and state policies that subsidized coal production and promoted using more of it regardless of its human and environmental consequences. Joe had grown into a top-down leader, much like a coal-company president. He told ACMU members what to think, say and do. Those who objected were disciplined or bought off. Those who actively opposed him were squashed.

Jeep kept his distance from Joe Hunt but also kept him in his thoughts. Jeep read the phrase "union democracy" in a newspaper article. He started thinking about how that might work and how he could be the person who made it happen in the ACMU.

Joe and the other ACMU officers were in their late 60s, even older than Jeep's Dad. They'd barely survived The Great Depression and the layoffs of the '50s and '60s when mechanization cut the number of miners by 75 percent. Joe Hunt and his best friend, Skis, had been out of the mines for more than three decades. They didn't know about the clouds of coal dust the continuous-mining machines created or understand the black-lung epidemic the invisible particles caused. Jeep saw little difference between Joe Hunt's ACMU and how USOCO ran its Sunburst Mine. He realized he needed to do more than beat Joe Hunt in an election. He had to lead a movement to push democracy up through the Union and then, once the members were behind him, grab what he could in contract negotiations from the Bituminous Coal Companies Group (BCCG).

Jeep and Biggie began grumbling about the Union to each other soon after hiring on at Sunburst. Pay and benefits should have been better considering the difficulty and dangers of the work. To get those improvements, their conversations turned to "participatory democracy." More democracy, they believed, produced better working conditions and richer contracts. They knew ACMU members feared what Joe Hunt could do them—the power to have them blackballed from employment. Better leadership and less fear would follow from more union democracy—that was what they decided they wanted.

For this to happen, Jeep knew he needed Biggie Stover, his best friend since first grade.

Most miners in Boone and Kanawha Counties knew Frank Stover as "Biggie." He carried his weight -- now more than 300 pounds on his six-foot, six-inch frame -- mostly high on his chest. After Vietnam, Biggie let his black hair grow to his shoulders where it framed his black beard. His close-set eyes scanned his surroundings, looking for the unexpected, for the danger, for, as he put it, "the smilin', tail-waggin' dog that intended to bite me." Five years after returning from the War in 1969, Biggie Stover looked like how every Hell's Angel wanted to look. As a member of Jeep's campaign staff, Biggie made a small concession to respectability by wearing clean blue jeans, cowboy boots and a western-style shirt. Of the two, Jeep had taken to suits without a backward look. Biggie said he'd rather "run naked as a jaybird on Kanawha Boulevard from the Elk River to the Capitol's gold-leaf dome than wear a suit." Both figured that Biggie would deter physical attacks on Jeep in the campaign against Joe Hunt and, if necessary, stop them.

When he and Jeep returned to West Virginia, Biggie decided to become a professional wrestler as "The Coalfield Avenger." He enrolled in a school run by Cowboy Dick Crawford, a knobby, retired ring veteran in his 50s who trained and evaluated aspirants for Vince McMahon, Sr., founder of the World Wide Wrestling Federation. Cowboy Dick scratched out a living in his grungy gym-and-ring operation on MacCorkle Boulevard in Kanawha City next to the S&H Green Stamps store. He told his pupils: "If ya don't cut it in my ring, go redeem yourself next door."

Cowboy showed Biggie the difference between fighting and "worked-up wrestling"—how to throw a punch so that it didn't hurt; how to bleed his forehead; and how to kick, fall, stagger, leap, grimace, preen, taunt, gag, stomp, complain, gouge, spit, sneer, mock, chortle, flee, strut and eat the padding off the turnbuckles. The most important lesson Cowboy taught was how to create a character with a story line. Once Biggie had learned ring mechanics and dramatics, Cowboy cast him as the outraged, local "ethnic" baby face whose only desire was to rid West Virginia of the invading "Yankee heels," some of whom lived as much as 15 miles outside of Charleston. While learning the trade, Biggie picked up karate from the gym rats who took it seriously.

After two months, McMahon approved Biggie's debut in the Marmet Junior High School gym. He was to face "The Magnificent Mauler," a 274-pounder who taught science to fourth graders at the Garretts Bend School near Sod in Lincoln County. Biggie and the Mauler had rehearsed their upcoming Saturday night match the evening before. After 15 minutes, the referee told them to wind it up. Biggie climbed to the top ropes at the corner of the ring, shouted "Roof Fall!" and leaped spread-eagled onto the willingly prostrate Mauler who had thoughtfully positioned himself at a diagonal to the corner.

Jeep treated Biggie to a pizza and a beer later that night. Two high school girls recognized The Avenger and asked for his autograph as he bit into a slice. When they left, Jeep asked: "How much?"

"Thirty dollars," Biggie said. "For 15 minutes of dishonest labor."

"Not counting all the gym and rehearsal hours. You'd do better in the mines with me."

"Minin' is somethin' to fall back on," he laughed.

The Avenger used the Roof Fall to finish each match as he worked his way through the undercards against punched-out boxers, lard buckets and semi-retirees who needed every small paycheck they could obtain. After three months, Cowboy told McMahon that Biggie was sirloin, not hamburger, another Bruno Sammartino, the popular Pittsburgh nice guy. Biggie had size, speed, agility and a big personality. "He can sell his shit," Cowboy said.

Biggie Stover was on his way, and then he wasn't.

The Coalfield Avenger's career came to a dead stop when The Avenger's wife, Brenda, announced that the Lord had revealed to her that wrestling in fixed matches was a sin. The Reverend Ezra Powell, self-appointed preacher in the one-room Glorious Word Primitive Full Gospel Church that Brenda attended three nights a week, condemned Biggie for "debasin' athletics in a bathin' suit" before thousands of "misguided" fans, all of whom he would welcome as congregants. It was not enough, Ezra said, for Brenda to show the "baptism of the Spirit by speaking in tongues." Her salvation required that she reform her husband. Reverend

Powell encouraged her to get Biggie to attend his services, but he thought better of requiring it of her. Biggie had limited theological respect for Reverend Ezra whose Daddy had run a modest numbers racket in Boone County for years with his son's assistance before Ezra felt the call to preach. Ezra weighed his flock's financial needs against the potential loss of Biggie's $500 annual donation given through Brenda. Her contribution represented 20 percent of his church's annual budget. To his ministerial credit, he announced that Biggie would undoubtedly burn in Hell's fiery furnace if he continued his sinful ways much longer. Brenda began a no-holds-barred struggle to change her husband.

Biggie, who had seen in Vietnam more than his share of what he considered the Devil's work, doubted the Lord cared one way or another about nailing his insignificant soul to the side of His great barn. On the other hand, Biggie did not care to match wills with Brenda who since their high-school years had kept him in line with two submission holds—no cooking and no sex. Biggie negotiated. They finally agreed that he didn't have to go to Ezra's church in return for not making fun of "Reverend Pile." To stay in wrestling, Biggie offered Brenda a new persona: The Avenging Angel who forced the heels he beat to fall on their knees and shout "Hallelujah!"

"Nope," said Brenda.

Biggie caved.

He retired his costume. He signed on at USOCO's Sunburst Mine where Jeep had preceded him. He continued to visit Cowboy's gym two nights a week to improve his karate.

Biggie, unlike his peers, didn't have to go into the mines. He had known since childhood that he and his family were not in the same economic boat as the coal-miner kids he grew up with. The difference boiled down to land—3,200 acres on the Boone County side of Kayford Mountain that had come down to him in fee simple, surface and subsurface minerals together. Over several generations, Stovers had cut and sold timber, banking the cash they didn't need for a rainy day. More than $100,000 was now there for him. He kept the account in a Charleston bank rather than a local one so his neighbors would not find out the true amount of his difference.

A shrewd Swiss-German, Joerg Stover, had come to the newly independent United States with money from his father who owned a Bavarian workshop that made steins and mugs. Joerg's assignment was to buy "bounty land warrants" from Revolutionary War veterans who had been awarded land on the western frontier in lieu of pay. Promising "free" land to soldiers was a cheap way for Americans to finance the War. It also provided an incentive for Continental soldiers to both win and survive. If the Revolution failed, the colonial veterans would get nothing for their service. Land grants on the western frontier also had the effect of seeding military men as a buffer against the Natives whose land they had just been given and who had generally sided with the British.

Those veterans who needed cash more than property sold their wilderness acres cheap to men with gold. Joerg settled in Staunton, Virginia, where he traded land, cattle and slaves. On his death, his holdings south of the Kanawha River in far western Virginia went to his youngest son, Lewis. This land, considered to be his least valuable asset, was given to his least promising heir along with $1,000. Lewis Stover rode up the New River trail, then down the Kanawha to the tiny Charleston settlement in the spring of 1803. He hired a local guide to show him where his land lay.

They rode to the head of Cabin Creek and over what would be named Kayford Mountain. They spent a week riding the boundaries of the Stover claims, marking corners with iron rods set in rocks and wondering what in the world the thin dirt on these mountains might be good for. Lewis built a cabin and eventually married Becky Burdette who lived on the Big Coal River, about 10 miles west. Each of his three sons inherited an equal portion of land, a practice that subsequent generations often followed. The Stovers supported West Virginia's secession from Virginia in 1863. They didn't own slaves, and they cared even less for the slave-holding, plantation owners east of the Allegheny Mountains who saw western Virginia as nothing more than a source of taxes, land speculation and backwardness.

And then a few coal men came to Charleston from "The East" in the late 1860s. One was a lawyer who practiced politics, Willard F. Killington, who took over The Charleston Gazette. The other was a stiff and formal gentleman, Henry Hewitt, who, Lewis Stover's grandson, Asa, figured was "Big Money from Philadelphia."

Asa and his boys were comfortable mountain farmers, but not rich. His 3,200 acres provided woodland grazing for sheep, cattle and hogs. They cut timber when necessary and raised corn in the bottoms along the creeks. The Stovers were never hand-to-mouth mountain poor. They saved cash when it came in. Their money allowed them to say, No. And that is what Asa did when Killington and Hewitt offered him 50 cents an acre for his mineral rights. Asa figured the coal under his land would only get more valuable. No need, he reasoned, to sell a good thing for money he didn't need.

During the 100 years after Asa Stover had turned down Big Money from Philadelphia and subsequent offers, southern West Virginia was developed as one of America's top-producing coalfields. Thousands of mines, big and small, fed coal into a network of railroads that hauled it north to steel mills and in all directions for home heating. In the mid-20th

Century, coal's principal market had become electric-generating plants where it was burned to boil the water whose steam turned their turbines.

When the land passed to Biggie on the death of his parents in a head-on wreck with an overloaded coal truck in 1968, he figured the 3,200 acres of land with its two strippable and three deep-minable coal seams could be sold for no less than $3 million.

"That coal under us is money in somethin' better than a bank," his Dad -- Thurman -- had always said. Biggie agreed.

"It'll always be there; it'll always appreciate; it'll always be a quick sale," Biggie told Brenda on their wedding night in 1969. "But we'll do just fine on what I make one way or the other and the Stover Family Rainy Day fund."

By October, 1975, when Biggie Stover sat in the MDU campaign office with Jeep Delucci and Jeffrey Becker, the coal under his land had increased in value beyond his imagination. The OPEC embargo had lifted the price of coal as oil prices rose. Biggie figured that his mineral rights now had a lease value of $2 million or more with a minimum royalty payment of $1.50 a ton calculated against a recoverable reserve of about 35 million tons. Biggie knew he could collect enough in annual royalties to live as a wealthy man for the rest of his life. Maybe, he thought, he'd have "to go wealthy" when he got old, but for the time being he and Brenda had all they wanted on his miner's wages and hers as a teacher's aide at Whitesville Elementary.

The temptation to cash in had walked next to him since his inheritance. This made him an exception he did not flaunt. West Virginia was not a place where temptation of this type occurred very often, where great wealth was simply a matter of signing your name and moving to a big house somewhere else and living rich.

Biggie wanted to preserve his family's land -- Asa's Place, as he called it -- as it had been handed to him. He'd been raised on this dirt, and he knew firsthand how mining changed surface property even when underground methods were used. If he leased it, he knew the leaseholder would cut the top off his part of Kayford Mountain to get at the surface-minable seams. It was a new kind of strip mining called "mountaintop decapitation." Then the industry renamed it "mountaintop removal," which sounded less like an execution but wasn't. In a few years, it was renamed even more benignly, "valley fill." Asa's Place was an island of repose amid the turmoil of mining that surrounded it in Kanawha County to the north, Boone to the east and Raleigh to the south. It was a 3,200-acre hold out. Biggie was comfortable doing nothing with the coal under his land for a long time, maybe forever.

Asa's Place had given Biggie respite when he came home from the War. He hunted for squirrel, rabbit and deer without a rifle. He wanted to see how close he could get before they spooked. He valued knowing that generations of his family had hunted the same creatures in the same topographical nips and tucks. His people had crossed the same creeks in the same places. They had hunted the same natural openings that he did. He liked to rest on the little mossy flats near the ridge line. Under the pin oaks, the moss was soft and cool on hot afternoons. He'd eat a snack with his back against a chestnut oak near the crest of Kayford Mountain where Stover Branch began as a seep and ended in the Gulf of Mexico. One day, he thought, he might canoe the whole journey.

Biggie cut his winter firewood on cool Saturdays in September and October when he could sweat respectably but escape the August swelter. He'd pick a black locust or a red oak, preferring those that had died within the last year or two. He'd gas up his Homelite chainsaw, fill its receptacle with bar oil, unload wedges, sledge hammer, splitting maul and water jug. He'd fire up the saw, notch out a felling hinge, drop the monster pretty much were he wanted, cut the stem into 20-inch-long rounds, split them along the grain into sixths or eighths depending on the tree's diameter and load the sticks in an orderly manner into the bed of his shortbed pickup with its unfashionable blackwall tires. He always felt useful though not creative at the end of a firewood day. Biggie liked doing something tangible and beneficial—like killing a Vietcong who was trying to kill him.

After he loaded the truck, Biggie would sit in the driver's seat and smoke a dark Brazilian cheroot -- a Danneman Caballero -- as he listened to Asa's woods and savored the pleasant smell of chain oil, gasoline and split oak. He would consider where he was in life and why.

He planned the design and building of a cabin high up on the mountain for the kids Brenda had in mind. Well, it would be more than a cabin, but it would feel like one, he promised himself. He knew where he could salvage a 150-year-old log house that he would repurpose as a den. He had picked out a south-facing, natural bench with a long view into Raleigh County. He told himself a long view was best, but you also had to pay attention to the short one right in front of you. Asa's minerals would keep.

Biggie knew that people pigeon-holed him for his size and looks. He took advantage of that. He preferred being underestimated. So he affected a growl when it seemed useful, a buffoon quality when it suited and a mental slowness more often than not. But he knew -- and Jeep knew and Becker was learning -- that he was both highly intelligent and broadly read. Even as kids, Jeep understood that Biggie was not only smarter, but quicker and more insightful. Jeep allied with Biggie's talents and accepted them without envy. Biggie was the conceptualizer, the strategist, the plotter, the doer. Jeep was the front man, the wheeler-dealer, the charmer, the politician. Biggie was not jealous of his best friend. He preferred thinking to talking, doing to procrastinating. He liked working the backrooms and the back channels. He liked advising. He liked finishing a task. Jeep had the personality to be a television talk-show host. Biggie could have been a college professor or a thug...and was neither. He wasn't unhappy mining coal, but he didn't think it was his career.

Jeffrey Becker had come to know some of their stories during long politicking drives from mine to mine, shift change to shift change.

Becker had mothballed his bare-bones law practice six months earlier to run Delucci's MDU campaign. He had come to Charleston after graduating from Columbia University's law school. He had wanted to practice public-interest law in a state where, he said, "issues were clear but the air was not."

He spent nine months with Charleston Legal Aid and then rented a small office month-to-month in a cheap building down the block from the Holley Hotel, a once respectable establishment drifting into eccentricity and disrepair. He picked up a few worker-compensation cases, a disability claim and a discrimination suit against a Charleston bank—all on contingency fees. Two small unions hired him, and he quickly got a reputation as an effective advocate for grievants in arbitration cases. With a little cash coming in, he moved to a two-room office on Capitol Street across from the Kanawha County Library and above The Peanut Shoppe. Jeep threw him a couple of discharge arbitrations and liked the outcomes.

Jeep saw in Becker someone who could help him; Becker saw in Jeep someone who might do something special. They started going out after work for beer and pizza. They found that they liked each other and got along even when differences arose.

Becker respected both Jeep and Biggie but felt more comfortable with Delucci, because he was easier to read. Biggie, Becker thought, carried around qualities he concealed. Becker could not determine exactly what they were, but he suspected one was intellectual horsepower. He assumed Jeep knew what they were. Becker had seen both of them red-faced with anger. Biggie always seemed in control of his; not so with Jeep. Becker was not surprised to learn that Biggie had saved Jeep's life in a Vietcong ambush. He had seen them play basketball, coordinating moves without obvious communication. They worked that way in the campaign, leaving Becker feeling brain-slow when he had to ask one or the other to explain something he alone didn't understand.

Delucci's nominating victory had fired a warning shot across the bow of every top-down, out-of-touch American trade union, which was almost all of them in Becker's opinion. If Jeep beat Joe Hunt on Friday, December 5, 1975, reform-minded, rank-and-file insurgencies might erupt in many big unions. Coal miners might lead the way in uniting labor in all the energy sectors. One big energy union!—the old Wobbly concept resuscitated by OPEC, high energy prices and a West Virginia coal-miner's kid. With Delucci running the ACMU, labor might get an infusion of new blood and new life. With Nixon out, it was anybody's guess how the last half of the '70s might play out.

Just how well do I know these two? Becker asked himself. Becker slipped on his glasses and looked toward Jeep.

"The bigger problem we have than these thugs is money," Becker said. "The $200,000 that Biggie loaned the campaign is almost gone."

"What about contributions from miners who now see me as the winner?" Jeep asked.

"A couple of hundred dollars came in today," Becker said. "Maybe we'll get a couple of thousand over the next two or three weeks from individual miners. You'll probably get some money from liberal do-gooders who like your ideas."

"Great," Jeep said. "Joe Hunt will call every one of *those* dollars a contribution from Moscow. He'll give us shit about communists taking over the Union. He's already starting whispers about you."

"I'm an open book," Becker said.

"That's what he's sayin'," Biggie said with a grin.

Becker changed the subject with an obvious clunk. "You may be able to get some money from companies who want to do business with the Union -- convention hotels, travel agents, Washington restaurants, office supply stores up there, lawyers, accountants. They'll hedge with money to both you and Joe. I expect he'll get some money from other unions. And he'll wring money out of ACMU officers and staff. He'll embezzle from Union accounts. We have to assume he'll shake down every dollar he can."

"I beat him 57 to 43. You forgettin' that?"

"He barely campaigned," Becker replied, "and you had Biggie's $200,000. No one's ever beaten an incumbent ACMU president. No one thought you had a chance. Now you've stirred up the old lion. He'll fight for his waterhole."

"So what's in the account?" Jeep asked.

"As of this afternoon, about 20 grand," Becker said. "It'll keep you on the road for a couple of weeks, pay for the office and salaries. But you have no money for advertising, campaign mailings, literature, buttons, stickers or airlines. We still have some campaign do-dads here, but we gave out most of them. And we used about $125,000 of Biggie's money to buy support at the local level, as you know."

"Maybe Daddy can mortgage his house."

"How will *he* pay off the loan," Becker said, "particularly, if you don't win? I doubt that a local bank would give him more than 12 or 15. He doesn't get enough in pension and Social Security to carry a loan."

"We got two months to go until the vote," Jeep said. "What do you figure I need to be competitive?"

"Four hundred is the rock-bottom minimum. Five for a fair fight. Six to win."

"Jesus! Let me sleep on it," Jeep said.

"The campaign dies if we don't get at least as much as we got from Biggie, plus we have to pay him back. That's four."

"Payin' me back *was* the idea," Biggie said to Jeep.

"I know."

Biggie got up and stretched. "All right. I'm goin' home to a real warm Brenda welcome, I fear. Let's see what the mornin' brings. Brenda was expectin' me for supper. Brenda does not like to be disappointed in her expectations. For bein' late, I need to be ready to catch some Brenda shit in about an hour."

Jeep laughed. "Wear your hard hat." He had seen Brenda throw two books and a cantaloupe at Biggie on different occasions. Her temper was connected to a very short fuse. Biggie and Jeep liked to keep Brenda calm and friendly.

"I'll call her and lay it on you," he said to Jeep.

"Like always. I'll stay here for a while. I need to push some paper," Jeep said.

Biggie looked at Jeep who acknowledged the look.

"Archie?" Jeep asked, looking at Biggie.

Biggie thought for a moment: "Yeah, buddy."

"What's Archie? Who's Archie?" Becker asked.

Biggie said nothing.

"Oh, I was jes' askin' whether Biggie was goin' to stop off at McDonald's -- you know the Golden Arches -- for a snack on his way home. We just refer to it as 'Archie.'"

"I'll stop," Biggie said to Jeep. "You gonna stay over at the apartment on Quarrier?"

"Yeah," Jeep said. "No use drivin' so late to Dad's place."

"Okay. Later."

Becker heard Biggie stop by the front desk and call Brenda. He then had a short conversation with Dicey Shuck, the retired miner from Cabin Creek who had volunteered to work the office phones. Biggie walked back through headquarters to the belled rear door. Becker heard the door open and close. Biggie always parked his Chevy Blazer in the alley. Becker heard Dicey leave through the back door a few minutes later.

Becker walked over to get a fresh slug of air-conditioned air. "I'll make some fresh coffee," he said to Jeep. "Want some?"

"Sure. How 'bout we get some supper at Murad's in a bit?"

"Sure. How do you want your coffee this late?"

Jeep looked up. "Muddy'll do."

Chapter 3

Pittsburgh, October 3, 1975

The strands of morning, rush-hour traffic on I-279 wove into an ever-thickening braid that disappeared into the two northbound lanes of Pittsburgh's Fort Pitt Tunnel. Incoming commuters from plebian South Hills wove together with those from older, still-fancy Mt. Lebanon and the newer, more-fancy Upper St. Clair.

Allyson Pickering had come to hate the Tunnel's murky fumes but endorsed its enforced democracy. Everyone -- rich and poor, hourly and salary, mover and shaker, as well as those moved, shaken and even stirred -- traveled at the same pace and breathed the same lousy exhausts. She had dubbed the crawl-tube under Mount Washington, the Fun-nel of Zoom.

A daily commute through the Fun-nel was one of two credible reasons she could summon for not accepting Kennedy Brown's proposal and his grand house in far Upper St. Clair. His 12 acres even had a four-horse stable with two horses, a swimming pond with a dock and a fenced-in tennis court. The other credible reason was that she wasn't sure.

Allyson accelerated, braked, stopped; accelerated, braked, stopped. Make a decision! One way or the other! And now she found herself unable to concentrate on any subject other than the toxic gasses from the rear end of the vehicle in front of her.

Was Ken, she asked herself, worth this morning mess? On the plus side—he was nice-looking but not oppressively perfect, well-mannered, earnest, solicitous, without belly fat, dry-humored, funny without being nasty or gross, unburdened by notorious loonies in his family tree, blessed with inaudible intestines, not susceptible to hair-twirling or ball-scratching, lacking in snobbishness about junk food, reasonably athletic, likely to keep all of his hair into his 70s and very aware of having to tend her feelings and her feminism.

Evenings with him at his dressed-limestone Tudor in Trotwood Acres were filled -- but not to overflowing -- with informed conversation on current events and the local art scene. Ken had traveled before he settled in Pittsburgh; his porcelains were superb. He also owned quality Chinese cloisonné that his father bought before WWII while handling legal work for several American corporations in Shanghai. And he possessed a sneaky spin serve, which was reliable in mixed doubles. Time spent with Ken was pleasant. Weekends were relaxing. Sex was good. He drank a little more Scotch than she thought he should, but she'd never seen him college-kid drunk or even goofy. He was graceful and gracious. He was 31, just a year her senior. Money was not an issue and never would be. He managed wealth at Scraife National Bank where he was moving up. He wanted children, he said. He would be a good Dad, he said, and she agreed. He loved her, he said; he respected her, he said; he even liked her, he said. Kennedy Brown was more than suitable, more than a throw-in-the-towel choice, more than a good catch. He was, she admitted, a great catch!

Which made her SCREAM!

He had downsides, she thought. From prep school, he'd gone to Yale, like her father, Walton. He liked Yale, like her father. He would be successful, like her father. He would indulge her, like her father. He was rising at Scraife like a hawk in an updraft. He liked Upper St. Clair, but he said he would consider moving into the City -- Shadyside or Point Breeze -- if she insisted. He liked creamed onions. If he gave up creamed onions, she would have compelling evidence of an agreeableness so broad, so accommodating and so repressive that she knew it would drive her nuts. Scraife National Bank? Well, she kept *her* money at Scraife, which was the bank of her father's family. Creamed onions! Is that, she asked herself, how I make a marriage decision—on creamed fucking onions?

She honked too long at a jerk who changed lanes in the Fun-nel. Why was he hurrying to get nowhere faster than someone who was not? Why was she hurrying to get somewhere faster than someone else?

Allyson was always tense after spending a placid night at Ken's country retreat. It fit her too easily, and both were aware of it. The prospect of easy for the rest of her life left her unsettled. What would she accomplish in the world if she wasn't *in* the world? Were three kids and a Volvo wagon with a Christmas wreath on the grille her wombic destiny? As a down payment against the burbs she knew so well, she drove a '68 Volkswagen Beetle, which had no grille. So far, she had thwarted the inclination to celebrate Jesus's birthday on its snout.

Ken understood that Allyson needed her career. He knew she would fester were she to be locked down in the suburbs for 20 years, wiping noses, walking dogs and running bake sales. He would, he said, help her be the woman and the journalist she wanted to be. Money would plug their time-at-home gaps with nannies (not *au pairs*), maids, yard help, cooks, personal trainers, tutors and handypersons. Whatever she needed to make her life and career work the way she wanted, she would have. He supported her need to make a journalist's mark. Fine, sweetheart: Mark away! They could have, he said, a modern marriage, not like either set of parents. He wasn't stuck in that mud, he said. She believed that was true, largely.

They were going to the Pittsburgh Symphony that night. He was planning a formal proposal, he said. She was planning to give it the serious consideration it deserved, she said.

"I'll solve any problems you have with it," he said.

"I know you will," she said.

IDIOT! You don't love him, she scolded herself as she sat in traffic. IDIOT! You can make a life with him. IDIOT! Settling for convenience is giving up. She began to honk at the line of idle cars in front of her. I am, she thought, unable to see my way out of either tunnel.

When Allyson's puttering Beetle crawled onto the upper level of the Fort Pitt Bridge, downtown Pittsburgh spread before her. At night when traffic was moving, she'd blast through the Tunnel and onto the Bridge so that downtown buildings popped up all at once like a gang of jacks-in-the-box.

The Allegheny and Monongahela Rivers joined on her left at the Point, forming the Ohio. The reconstructed Fort Pitt Block House, a tiny pentagon that 220 years earlier had shaped a wilderness empire stretching to the Mississippi River and the Great Lakes, now commanded a sanctuary where men found friends in relative peace.

Whatever historic presence remained in the Fort's bricks was overwhelmed by what Allyson called, the "let's-see-who-has-the-tallest-prick" among downtown corporate skyscrapers. AMSTEEL's massive black shaft was the clear winner. But Allyson believed the most appealing erection was the 44-story, Art Deco Gulf Oil Building whose swollen tip -- a step pyramid modeled after the Mausoleum of Halicarnassus—a tomb for the Persian ruler, Mausolus, and his wife who was his sister -- glowed neon orange for fair weather and blue for precipitation. Each color pulsed when the temperature was falling.

In June, 1974, the Weather Underground, a splinter remnant from the defunct Students for a Democratic Society, claimed responsibility for detonating a dynamite bomb on the Building's 29th floor. It caused an estimated $1 million in damage, though no injuries. The bombing was a protest against Gulf's exploitation of the people and oil resources of Portuguese Angola, the group said. Gulf paid production royalties to colonial Portugal, not the Angolans.

Allyson was pleased the Weather Underground had not tried to blow up Gulf's flashing phallus, which, someday, might tell her which way the wind blew. Allyson had thought it was possible that Rooky Gondleman had participated in this bombing. He had dropped from sight in early 1970. Now, more than a year later, no arrests had been made. How, she wondered, could Rooky Gondleman, a chess nerd who was as dodgy as a manacled three-toed sloth, elude an FBI manhunt for more than five years? She'd met Gondleman in 1968 at Columbia University through Jeffrey Becker. She always fought an urge to retie Rooky's shoelaces and wipe his nose.

Allyson glanced to her right, east up the Monongahela River. On its north bank, she could see the Hill District where bears were once baited and later the City's poor were stuffed into tenements and shacks. In the

28

distance, she saw the hulking, black blast furnaces of the old Jones & Laughlin Steel works below Oakland. Ling-Temco-Vought bought a majority interest in J&L in 1968. She had heard the conglomerate might shutter the mill soon.

To her left, Allyson scowled at Three Rivers Stadium, a coiled pile sitting in the crook of the Allegheny and Ohio. An uglier and more fan-unfriendly ball field she'd never entered. The stadium's belly was draped with a cummerbund, "Go Pirates." Artificial plastic grass in the outfield! Artificial Christmas trees. What's next, she asked herself, artificial insemination for human babies?

And why there, of all places? Why on a field used for torture? Allyson knew Pittsburgh history.

After Braddock's defeat in 1755, the Delaware and Shawnee with hundreds of British scalps on their drying hoops, chose that spot to slowly roast a dozen surviving Redcoats while their women rammed fiery sticks into the victims' nostrils and ears. Allyson could never hear roars for the Pirates or Steelers without hearing British ghost cries.

Her tender heart spoiled many good times available to her in urban America. She understood that she had "inherited this disease" from her Quaker mother, Jane Andrews Pickering. Her father, Walton, interpreted his Quaker beliefs to exclude pacifism when a higher value called.

Allyson was too young to have seen Pittsburgh as Woody Guthrie's "smoky old town." By the time she was hired by The Pittsburgh Post-Gazette, most of the City's polluting mills and foundries had either closed or were closing. Pittsburgh's collar was changing from blue to white, with a lot of the newly collar-less left in place. Fern bars were replacing neighborhood taverns. The City's rich ethnicity was boiled down into pallid celebrations of tribal foods. Even so, Pittsburgh was a livelier place than Allyson's native Philadelphia where baked flounder at the Old Original Bookbinder's was considered haute cuisine.

As Allyson maneuvered into the right lane on the bridge, she fiddled with the radio tuner to get KDKA. She wanted to know the final ACMU results. She parked in the PG lot before the news break. She took the elevator to the fourth floor and walked into the newsroom.

"Delucci with 57 percent," Davey Bloom shouted from his office in her direction as she went to her desk. "Get me a feature for Sunday. At least 30 column inches. More is okay, hon. We can always cut."

Allyson walked over to her managing editor's office and leaned against the door jamb. His office was known as "The Wilderness." It was said that more than one reporter had disappeared in there after becoming disoriented by the clutter. Now, no one actually entered except Davey who paid no attention to the chaos of paper piles, book piles, clipping files and stacks of cardboard boxes labeled "Urgent Mail," two boxes for each year between 1949 and 1974. Reporters felt reasonably safe standing at his door.

Allyson took two steps inside, the bravest she'd ever been. She raised her eyebrows and waited for further instructions. She saw brightness in Bloom's eyes and energy in his face. The horseshoe of white hair that ringed his bald head bushed out, and the few hairs in his eyebrows shot up like permanent firecrackers. Some of the cleanest, clearest prose Allyson had ever read had come from this mess of a man who pulled orderly language out of self-inflicted anarchy. She loved the incongruity of it.

"Go to Charleston and interview Delucci. Give me a sense of who this guy is. What's driving him? Young reformers. Old incumbents. Miners. Hillbillies. The old ACMU in today's world. Energy crisis. Coal. OPEC oil. This is good shit. Maybe it's part of your ticket out of The Pitt."

Allyson smiled. Even Bloom knew she wanted to move to Washington and write for The Post. So much for confidential conversations with her colleagues.

"Why the sudden interest in the ACMU?" she asked. "I couldn't buy 10 inches from you for months. You were happy to rip the wires."

"It was predictable before. Who gave Delucci a chance? Not me! Where's the story in a couple of young guys bitching about the old guys who run the show? But now it's hot, hon. I can feel the heat. The young guy won the first round and might take the whole thing. That's a story."

Davey Bloom leaned back and kicked his feet up on a shedding pile of paper next to his 1931 Underwood manual. The knot of his tie -- Allyson had only seen him wear one tie in her five years on the paper -- was loose as it always was. His stomach rested contentedly between his suspenders. He held an unlit cigar, which he was no longer allowed to smoke. No doctor had yet told him that he was prohibited from waving one around for emphasis.

Bloom peered at her over his bifocals. "That's why I sit on this throne of the news business. The publisher thinks I'm good at feeling heat before something burns up or down. After more than 40 years of fire patrol, I'm better than Smokey the Fucking Bear. So, what do you know about it?"

"I've followed it locally, mostly in Pennsylvania," she said. "The hotbed of Delucci's campaign is in West Virginia, around Charleston. I have some sources on both sides up here, but nothing down there. I've met Delucci once, but I don't know who's running his campaign or where he's getting his money. I figure Hunt is squeezing campaign money out of the Union. Delucci's campaign money is, let's say, opaque."

"You gotta figure that Delucci needs at least three, four hundred grand or more for campaign shit—TV ads, mugs, bumper stickers, honest vote buying. Maybe he's borrowed it. Maybe he has a secret admirer."

"I can check into the campaign report he filed with the Labor Department," she said. "The most recent will be for the second quarter, which may or may not tell us something. The third quarter won't be available for another couple of months."

"And what's this 'union democracy, union reform' that Delucci's talking up?" Bloom asked. "I've watched labor 'statesmen' for more than 40 years. They hate democracy, though they preach it. Corporations aren't democracies; unions aren't democracies. Papers aren't democracies. Hell, democracies aren't democracies!"

"And there in one paragraph is Davey Bloom's philosophy of how the world is and always will be," she said.

"A guy I went to Peabody High School with once told me: 'I seen what I seen, which is why I see what I see.'"

"Peabody High School on North Highland Avenue," she said. "The fount of all wisdom."

"Better than Thomas Fuller for aphorisms, hon," Davey said.

"Who?"

"Fuller, Thomas. *Introductio ad prudentiam*. *Gnomologia*, 1732. Ben Franklin stole a ton of his Poor Richard shit from Fuller. 'Keep thy eyes wide open before marriage; and half shut afterward.'—Fuller. 'Keep your eyes wide open before marriage, half shut afterward.' <u>Poor Richard's Almanack</u>, 1738."

"How do you know something like that?" Allyson asked. She'd never heard of Thomas Fuller at either Bryn Mawr or Columbia's Journalism School.

"I checked stuff before I ran it," he said. "More checking is always better than less. I ain't <u>The New Yorker</u>, but I give it a shot. Now look. Hunt didn't take Delucci seriously before. That has changed. Joe will be scared but mostly totally pissed off. Watch what he does from here, how he does it and how the old guy is paying for it."

"Okay," she said, keeping her excitement to herself. "I'll need a couple of days down there. I'll file on Saturday as early as I can for Sunday. Davey, let's do this right. Let me stay on the story until December. Don't yank me off to do puff pieces on AMSTEEL's new paint job on a boiler at the Carnegie works."

Bloom had lived in the PG's newsroom his entire adult life. He was there in the days before air-conditioning when Pittsburgh's soot would waft through the half-closed blinds behind the open windows, sifting over his copy as he pecked it out with his index fingers. He remembered the rumbling of the big presses and the constant urgency they pounded into his heart and brain. He could still smell the hot lead from the old linotypes. He could smell the ink. He remembered ambition. He liked this girl a lot. He would have liked her more than a lot if he were 30 again. She could become a good one; maybe, even a star.

"The story's hot," he said. "That's why the publisher keeps me around. I'm a damn thermometer."

"I'll be calling it in close to deadline so hold the hole for me."

Bloom liked to describe his job as the daily feeding of a dragon with a 25,000-inch-long intestine. When reporters failed to fill the monster's belly, the publisher spat fire at his ME. If Davey gave Allyson time to dig out the ACMU story, he'd have to shake more words out of the other grunts. Reporters, in his experience, were prone to being both lazy and hostile to ambition greater than their own. He anticipated the whining he would hear. Charges of favoritism. He might be zinged with anonymous memos. Still, this ACMU election might be significant. What if a kid actually did overthrow a union boss? What if Delucci really believed in democratic unionism? What if Delucci actually delivered on his campaign promises? What if...hell, if Delucci did that, the local PG chapter of the Newspaper Guild would strike for a half-decent contract next time. Life is more complicated than shit, Davey thought. I, Davey Bloom, said that, not Thomas Fuller.

"Deal," Bloom said. "And don't forget to keep your head down, hon, when you're sticking your nose where it's not supposed to be stuck in West Virginia."

Bloom had covered steel strikes in Pittsburgh and Wheeling, Teamster strikes on Pittsburgh's North Side and the electrical workers' strike right after the War against Westinghouse that almost shut down the City. He knew about good unions and mobbed-up unions.

But none of those assignments had come close to what he'd seen at Fricktown, West Virginia, in the winter of 1932-1933. That, he feared deeply. Fricktown had unnerved him for more than 40 years.

"I'll keep my head down and my nose clean," she promised.

"I ain't kidding with you. Now git."

Allyson walked to her desk where she stood while phoning Delucci's Charleston headquarters. The man who answered said Jeep hadn't come in yet.

"How about Frank Stover? I think you call him Biggie."

"No ma'am, him neither. Would the campaign manager do?"

"Sure. I'm a reporter with The Pittsburgh Post-Gazette. I want to come down and do an in-depth story on Jeep and the election."

She heard a click, then silence, then a phone was picked up.

"Becker speaking."

Allyson caught her breath.

"This is Jeffrey Becker. May I help you?"

"This is Allyson, Jeffrey."

Chapter 4

Washington, D.C., Monday, October 6, 1975, 9: 15 a.m.

Joe Hunt gagged.

He looked again at the final tally sheet, and then he spit the tobacco wad into the old coal scuttle he kept beside his desk. Not only had he lost the local union vote 637 to 483 a week earlier, but he figured he would have lost the popular vote had one been taken.

"THOSE BUMS! They voted for a damn pup over me!"

"It's just the first round," Larry "Skis" Sonoski said as he considered alternative ways to patch the leaking vessel of Hunt's presidency. "We ain't out of it."

"I've given this fuckin' Union 42 years! When you and me started handloadin' in the '30s, we was paid for 2,000 pounds a car when the comp'ny cribbed up the sides to hold 2,400 pounds. Who got the men paid by the hour, not by the car? The Union! 1948. Who got 'em $2.50 an hour in 1950? The Union! Who got 'em $50 a day in '72? Me! And *who* got 'em free soap in the fuckin' bathhouse in '74?"

"You got 'em free soap in the fuckin' bathhouse," Skis echoed.

Joe heaved himself out of his deep leather chair. He knotted his big hands into fists.

"Aw shit," he sighed and kicked the scuttle against his oak credenza. Dark juice puddled on his deep carpet. "It'll stain. It always does."

Skis hustled over and retrieved the scuttle. He set it back in its place. He couldn't help but smile. Jeep Delucci had run his mouth against Joe for six months about free soap in the bathhouse. No good deed goes unpunished, Skis thought. Free soap saved the working miner about $10 a year, according to the Union's research department. Ten bucks was ten bucks even in 1975, Skis thought. That was 20 cups of coffee in Fricktown, 10 Bingo cards at The Moose.

"So what do my district presidents and board members have to say?" Joe asked. "Every one of 'em owes me. ME! I appointed almost all of 'em. I shipped 'em enough money to grease an elephant for this election. Hell, they had enough grease to screw the whole herd!"

Skis was calm. And he wanted Joe calm before the meeting. Joe needed a clear head for the coming discussion.

Skis spoke slowly and without emotion. "They say they bought the votes they could with the money you sent, but some guys took your money and voted for Delucci. People don't stay bought like they did when we was comin' up. Most of them said we didn't send enough money. The other thing was something Marv Shookoff calls 'rising expectations.'"

"I hate payin' Shookoff for those polls of his that tell us what we already know," Joe said as he stuffed a new chew into his cheek.

"Rising expectations means that all those good contracts you got in the past goosed up what they expected out of the '74 contract," Skis said. "They didn't think that another five dollars a day and free soap was good enough."

"So why'd they ratify it?" Joe asked.

"Because we turned the screws to get them to a yes," Skis said. "If they had rejected that contract, they'd have been on strike for a couple of months, which would have run through their savings. Some would have lost their vehicles, maybe even houses. They took the contract, because they didn't think strikin' would get them that much more. The cost, Shookoff says, was higher than the benefit they might gain. But votin' against you in the nominating round cost them nothing. They're sending you a message. We can use their unrest for leverage in the next negotiations. Lowerin' contract expectations would also help us."

"I ain't gonna lower shit," Joe said.

Skis skipped a direct reply. "Boyd Scaggs figures they got it out of their systems. He says it was kinda like a protest vote. He says his District 29 will come around in December. The other district presidents -- your guys -- say about the same. But they all are sayin' they need money to make sure."

Joe shook his head. "We sent out $25,000. That was more than any other election."

"Wasn't enough," Skis said. "Delucci sent out around $100,000."

"Where did a guy like him get that kind of money? Who's behind him?"

"Don't know yet," Skis said.

"It's all them damn hippies what came in the mines after shootin' up on marijuana in Vietnam. Booze wasn't good enough. That's the bunch with the big expectations. And Delucci leads 'em. They all came back crazy. Won't listen. Won't take orders from nobody—their Daddies, bosses, me. Just wanna wildcat strike over this and then say no over that. Ungrateful is what they are. They shoulda gone through what we been through."

Joe spit into the scuttle.

Larry Sonoski nodded. "The shit, it is a-changin'."

They both thought about that statement. It was the gorilla that filled Joe's executive office. They had heard the Bob Dylan song.

Joe Hunt blinked. "What the hell will we do if we get kicked out?"

"Retire with full pay," Skis laughed. "It's in the ACMU Constitution. You put it in there in '60. And on top of that we can get our pensions out all at once. Your pile is now about $250,000; mine is $100,000."

"But what'll I DO do?"

"Get a place in Florida. Fish. Eat. Die." Skis said this without humor.

"I don't want to fish, eat and die in Florida. I deserve somethin' else."

"Better?" Skis asked.

Joe Hunt thought about this. "Different. I want to win something. Anyway, it's too damn hot in Florida for a fat man. And what'll the men do without me up here?"

"It's gonna happen," Skis said, "one way or the other."

"Shit," Joe said. "You've been givin' me bad news since Fricktown."

"How about this?" Skis said, appraising their out-of-shape bodies. "We'll go back. We own houses there. We'll strap on knee pads and catch the first mantrip in on the day shift. Fricktown has to put us back to work at our last job at the current pay rate. You got that, too, for ACMU officers and staff."

"I haven't shoveled coal since 1942," Joe said. "That was my last job before I got elected to district office. I was good. I could ricochet them lumps off the roof and right into the cars."

"I'm sure handloadin' hasn't changed much in 33 years," Skis laughed. "But you were one of the last handloaders Fricktown had. And remember they don't undercut the face with picks no more. Haven't for years, not even in the crappy little dog-hole mines."

"I might last 30 minutes on a Number 4 shovel before I'd give out," Joe said.

"Thirty minutes? If it's high coal, maybe," Skis said. "Less in low coal, what with the water and muck. Maybe five minutes on an undercuttin' pick."

"*Depends* on how sharp the point is," Joe said. "Gussie Olin showed me how to lay up on my side and use one without the hangin' coal fallin' on my head. But then Fricktown brought in the undercuttin' machines after the '32 Strike and the old pick-minin' skill was forgot. I might have my old pick up at Fricktown. Wouldn't never pitch it. Daddy wouldn't never let me use his. Said I was careless."

"Did you keep it tooled up sharp?"

"Naw," Joe said. "It's as rusty as me. Just laid it down, dead and forgotten. Somewhere."

In the late spring of 1874, two agents of the newly formed American Steel Company -- AMSTEEL -- out of Pittsburgh slowly walked their rented horses up the bed of Black Creek, a lively stream that drained a branching network of hollers in northern West Virginia's Monongalia County. The landmen carried rolled-up maps in leather cylinders that were buckled to their saddles like rifle scabbards. The maps were roughly topographic showing estimated elevations. Known and inferred coal deposits were shaded in, and boundary lines were drawn for surface owners.

They were alert for outcrops of the Pittsburgh seam, a horizontal slab of coal, six-to-20-feet thick, which underlay thousands of square miles of southwestern Pennsylvania, southeastern Ohio and northern West Virginia. AMSTEEL geologists thought the Pittsburgh seam might contain as much as 10 billion tons of coal. Some of the Pittsburgh was capable of being processed into the coke that was necessary for making iron and steel. The West Virginia part of the Pittsburgh seam was good, but it wasn't quite the purity of the Connellsville metallurgical-coal deposit about 50 miles southeast of Pittsburgh. Connellsville set the standard for coking coal. It was the foundation of AMSTEEL's preeminent position in the fast-growing steel industry.

A coal outcrop on a hillside or road cut was like a layer of chocolate cake peeking through the icing. The men had pretty good hunches where the Monongalia County cake layers were, how thick and how rich. Millions of dollars lay under Black Creek alone. They stopped to admire an especially large outcrop where the stream exposed it. They actually knew very little about coal. They were hunters, not miners. They were looking for prey. They knew a lot about buying cheap.

Their patient horses walked up the wagon road, which shifted in and out of the creek depending on how much flat ground was available on either bank. Woods covered the hillsides above them on both sides. Every so often, they'd pass an acre or two of flat, open bottom ground recently planted in corn, kernel by kernel. They rode slowly, making sure that anyone observing them could see they were not looking for trouble. It didn't seem that they were in a rush, but they were.

Landmen scheduled these visits so they might "hello" a target cabin in the late afternoon. They'd look for smoke curling lazily from the sandstone chimney. A garden and some apple trees would be off to the side. They'd see a log barn and shy, curious kids hiding in its shadows. An older man would come out and onto the porch. They'd ride up to him, staying in their saddles. They'd "How do?" and the man would "How do?" back. The agents might say something about the farmer's stout split-rail, chestnut fences if the fences were stout, or the nice buck they'd flushed out of a laurel thicket if they couldn't praise the fence.

The farmer quickly registered they weren't carrying the new, lever-action Winchester '73 chambered for a .44-40 cartridge. The rifle cost $100 dollars, he'd heard. For him, it might as well have been a million. In fact, they carried no rifles at all. Of course, the farmer had a shotgun and his Pap's old flintlock rifle with the curly maple stock that was a straight shooter for 125 yards. The landmen knew he had an itch to try a repeating rifle like the Winchester '73; all of their targets did.

"Don't see many strangers up hyar," the farmer would say.

"First time for us," one would reply, "but we've been in the county for a while."

"Heard that," the farmer would say. "Y'er welcome to stay the night though hit's poor fare by your measure."

The agents smiled and thanked him, their bellies stirring. They knew the more their host belittled the coming meal, the better it was likely to be.

After supper, the three men would sit on the front porch and smoke their pipes. The agents would give the farmer a big can of good-quality pipe tobacco "for tomorrow," they'd say. The farmer's wife would "red up" the dishes and get the children settled in bed. They'd give the farmer a new coffee pot or bonnet for his wife and candy for his kids. The strangers would share news of the goings-on in Morgantown, Pittsburgh, Washington and maybe even Europe. Then they'd talk timber prices, hog cholera and corn borers. And after a second bowlful from a landman's pouch, after the farmer decided that his guests were not government whiskey men, he might break out a sippin' jug and finally get around to asking a question whose answer he thought he knew: "Now what jes' 'zactly brings fellers like you up hyar?"

Then the agents would lay down their pipes, look the mountaineer in his eye and one of the other would say, "Coal."

"Thought as much," the farmer would say, pleased with his perspicacity.

Coy Hunt had heard about landmen who'd been working Monongalia County. They had been buying coal rights all around Black Creek before they came to his place.

Later that night, he lay in the dark next to his wife, Lucinda, as the two agents slept in his barn loft on loose hay that still smelled a little fresh.

"Sounds like a purty good deal for us," he said in a low voice. "All they want is the min'ral rights. Don't want none of our pasture or the timber. Might take an acre or two in the bottom where hit's flat, and they said they might not ever even git around to usin' that, or even minin' at all. *Depends* on the market for steel and iron," Coy said, emphasizing "depends" just as it had been emphasized to him.

Lucinda didn't much care for her lot in life—seven living children and four buried on the hill above the cabin, the never-ending labor, the lack of female company. But she liked change she didn't know even less.

"'Purty good deal,' huh," she said in a way that she wanted him to understand she thought the opposite.

"Now, listen at me," Coy whispered. "They jes' want to buy the future right to mine the coal, which ain't a-doin' us a bit of good a-buried beneath us like it is. And our two grown boys can work in the mine if it ever does get up. It's work for cash money, which Lord knows they'll need. And they'll pay us a dollar a deeded acre for selling them the coal rights, maybe more. Jes' for the coal, not the land above. Two thousand acres is $2,000. Christa-mighty, it's like stealin' from 'em. That's more money for doin' nothin' than we'd see in 10 years of loggin' out our trees like slaves."

"Nothin' ain't free," Lucinda said.

"I could buy a team of work horses; no more contrary mules," Coy said. "Percherons. They'd make it easy for plowin' and cultivatin'. Bet I could drag out a 30-inch red oak log, 16-foot-long, with that pair. I know where I could get 'em, too. I could get me a WIN-chester '73. Lever-action .44. Only $100. Plenty be left."

"The mules do the work you ask of them. Your Daddy's flintlock always puts meat on our table."

"Times are movin' along. Better thangs cost money," he said. "The '73 has a *15-round* magazine."

"Are you plannin' to go to war, Coy? That Winchester you're a-pinin' for is a man-killer."

"You never know when a man has to defend himself."

"You need one shot, not 15, to kill a buck," Lucinda said. "Don't make no difference if that comes outa a flintlock or a repeater. Expensive thangs a-doin' the same thang ain't worth their price. It'll just get you in trouble."

"I'll be the judge of what gets me in trouble."

"I'm a-feared that's the truth," Lucinda said. "Coy, listen at me. I wouldn't care to see a coal mine in our bottom where the good dirt is. The noise and commotion would unsettle the cow. There'd be people up here, fer'ners, too. An' Coy, you ain't gonna do much plowing on a pile of coal. Not much huntin' neither."

"Stop bein' contrary," Coy said. "This is our chance."

"Thangs is good enough for me like we is," Lucinda said.

"Well, let me sleep on it," Coy said.

"Now, Coy Hunt, you jes' do that. You sleep on it."

Coy was taken with the idea of Big Money—cash, fast and easy. Others had signed AMSTEEL's dollar-an-acre mineral deeds, selling the coal and whatever else was under the surface. Big Money—in one pile and all at once; Coy Hunt had never had even Small Money in one pile and all at once. And since it was his land, his 2,000 acres by inheritance -- not hers -- by gift of the First Congress of the United States in payment for Revolutionary War service by his great granddad and subsequent purchases, it was his decision, not hers. I ain't no frownin' foot-dragger like Lucinda, he told himself.

Coy heard that a few farmers had refused to sell on the first visit. It was going around that a second offer might come in at up to $1.25 an acre, but he'd also heard that AMSTEEL might walk away after a rejection. If a second offer came, it was carried by the most important lawyer in Morgantown who rode all the way out to talk to each reluctant seller. In most cases, the agents returned to Pittsburgh with a signed letter of intent that bound the farmer to perform on a contract he'd never seen and often could not read. The transaction would be completed in the lawyer's office a week later and then recorded. The severance of the underground minerals from the surface by purchase was forever. Lucinda remembered the phrase, "in perpetuity."

"That's a long time," she'd said to her husband, "even longer than till death do us part."

Coy Hunt bid the two AMSTEEL agents on their way in the morning. He refused pay for the night's lodging, which wasn't much he knew, and the two meals, which were decent enough by any account. When Lucinda cleared the table, she found a new silver dollar under each of their plates. She stuck them in her beaded purse in expectation of a rainy day. Even the farmers who Coy had heard turned them down said the strangers had treated their women right. The agents rode up the holler toward the smaller holdings of Coy's relations, carrying his binding letter of intent. Coy's place was what they had needed. It was the best place to site a future mine.

Coy Hunt had negotiated $1.50 an acre for the sale of his coal, higher than anybody had gotten, higher than anyone had thought possible.

There was just one farmer -- a neighbor named Jacob Olin on Timber Ridge, which bordered Coy's land up the holler -- who turned the agents down and wouldn't even invite them in for a bite to eat. There was no need for a lack of hospitality, Coy thought. It reflected poorly on everyone, on all West Virginians. Olin, he'd heard, said he'd rather sell his blood for a nickel than his coal for a dollar.

Jacob Olin thought of himself as one of those mountaineers who clung to their fear and suspicion of outsiders as if they were keys to survival. He never sold his mineral rights to AMSTEEL or anyone else. He kept his 75 acres in fee-simple ownership. His hillside land and minerals were passed down intact to his son Arvil, and then to his son, Gus.

At the end of the week, George Chilton, dean of the Morgantown bar, handed Coy Hunt $3,000 in cash for his mineral rights and had him sign the deed that would be recorded in the Monongalia County Courthouse. The two landmen were not in Chilton's office that Friday, but Coy asked after them anyway.

And then for more than a decade after Coy and the other Hunts sold their minerals to AMSTEEL nothing changed in Black Creek Holler.

Every July 4th and election day, the Hunt men would get together, drink and laugh over their good fortune.

Andrew Carnegie, the Scottish immigrant who conceived and organized the American Steel Company -- AMSTEEL -- was also taken with Big Money.

Carnegie began buying the coal and iron-ore reserves needed to feed the vast mills he was planning years before he poured his first dram of molten steel, years before he would have to pay fair-market value for these minerals. Carnegie was confident that an industrializing America would buy what he was intending to make. Carnegie knew steel and iron ore, but his efforts to secure metallurgical-grade coal and coke-making facilities ran into his business equal, a coke man in Pittsburgh, Henry Clay Frick.

Frick was an Otterbein College dropout, the grandson of a prosperous whiskey distiller and the son of a failed father. He started in business at 21 with two cousins and a friend. They operated a single beehive oven that charred coking coal from Fayette and Washington Counties near Pittsburgh into almost pure carbon for making iron and steel. He sold some of his coke to Carnegie's AMSTEEL but not more than half his output. With loans from Andrew W. Mellon, a family friend, Frick soon bought out his partners, bought coal rights and built coke ovens in Connellsville under a new business name, H.C. Frick Coal and Coke Co.

Carnegie met Frick in New York City where Frick was honeymooning with his bride, Adelaide. Carnegie proposed a business marriage, and Frick accepted. Carnegie got coke at a discount, which generated higher profits on his steel. Frick got a guaranteed market for all of his coke at a guaranteed price.

Carnegie soon had Frick running AMSTEEL itself, with Frick Coal and Coke as one of its subsidiaries. Coal from the Pittsburgh seam fed Frick's beehive ovens, which fed coke to AMSTEEL's blast furnaces around Pittsburgh to make pig iron, which fed AMSTEEL's mills that made steel into rails, sheet, tube, plate, bar and girders for a country wanting all of those products, yesterday. AMSTEEL was America's first vertically integrated industrial business, a structure that allowed it to undersell its competitors and eventually drive most into bankruptcy.

By 1890, Frick's AMSTEEL had secured ownership, free and clear, to more than five billion tons of the world's best coal for less than one mil per ton. All of this resource was located in northern Appalachia, from Pittsburgh to south of Morgantown.

In the late 1880s, Frick started construction of another captive coal mine to feed his coke ovens. He sited it on Black Creek. His geologists were tickled with the coking qualities of this part of the Pittsburgh seam. The mining operation was projected to last at least 100 years.

Frick named the mine and the community.

Fricktown was laid out in Coy Hunt's bottom.

Frick's mining engineers drew up plans for the Fricktown shaft, about 300 feet down to the bottom of the seam. They designed a headframe for the winch that would operate the lift and the ventilation system that would course fresh air into the mine and push dusty, gassy air out. The eight-story-high breaker that sized the coal and the tipple that loaded it onto railroad gondolas dominated the town. The new double-track rail spur from the main B&0 line followed Black Creek up to Coy's land. The old horse-and-wagon road was almost abandoned, because it was easier to travel in and out by rail or walk the ties.

Equal in importance was the town itself. It was built to supply men to do the mining and services to support them. Apart from lumber, Fricktown had to import everything it needed and consumed. Every board and nail in Fricktown, every hour of paid labor, belonged to AMSTEEL.

Frick built Fricktown from scratch—800 houses, a large general merchandise and grocery store called "the commissary," churches, infirmary, baseball field, mine offices and a funeral parlor. Because AMSTEEL was planning a 100-year mine life, Frick instructed his superintendent and planners to do a good job, to build with that future in mind. They did—dressed stone for the superintendent's office, repair shops, churches and stables; two-foot-square chestnut beams, mortised and tenoned, for the breaker and tipple. The commissary with its accounting offices on the second floor was framed with chestnut and sided with milled red oak cut from Coy's land

Each of the identical four-room miner's houses was set above ground on stone piers—a front room, backroom/kitchen and two bedrooms. They were sided with green, rough-cut, board-and-batten pine. Each had a central chimney with a thimble hole for a cook stove and another for a parlor stove. Each had a roofed-over front porch and a privy at the back of the lot. In the beginning, AMSTEEL gave every working miner's house two tons of coal on November 1st and charged for only one.

AMSTEEL deducted rent from a miner's earnings. Other deductions were made for the camp doctor, infirmary, burial fund and sharpening tools at the smithy. The commissary extended credit to cover food, clothing, tobacco, supplies, blasting powder and carbide for the cap lamp. Anything that remained of earnings was paid in Fricktown scrip that was only good at the Fricktown commissary. Scrip could be cashed out at 80 cents on the dollar outside Fricktown. Profit from the captive town amounted to one-third of the Fricktown operation's total annual return on investment. Half-price house coal was ended in 1933 after the ACMU won representation rights for Fricktown's miners

The superintendent, office managers and supervisors lived on Bosses' Row, higher up Black Creek Holler than the Fricktown complex. This put them upwind of the miners and the mine's smoking pile of waste rock and smoldering coal fines. Teachers, storekeepers, preachers and saloonkeepers as well as the Fricktown sheriff and his deputies -- the salaried middle class -- lived on two streets that ran below Bosses' Row.

The first miners were assigned houses in a crescent of dwellings that ran along Black Creek opposite the mine. Near the tipple and gob pile were local white miners, like Coy Hunt's sons, in what everyone called "Dogtown." Irish and Welsh were housed near the stables; Poles below the repair shops; and Italians next to them. AMSTEEL built a school, infirmary, two churches (Presbyterian, Roman Catholic) a jail and four beer joints, one for each neighborhood.

When AMSTEEL sunk a second shaft in 1910, it erected bunkhouses for 200 miners who were recruited from Sicily, eastern Europe and the Black-Belt counties of the Deep South. When these men persuaded the superintendent to allow them to bring their families to Fricktown for "stability," houses were built for the whites on terraced benches cut into the hillside that had once been Coy Hunt's apple orchard and pasture. The black miners were set off on a site excavated out of the first gob pile. Both black and white miners called it "Black Bottom," which was the name of its saloon. Houses for black miners were the same as for white miners. But black miners were individually responsible for hauling dirt to cover the burned slate if they wanted a garden. Coal left in gob could smolder for years. Sometimes the ground in Black Bottom was warm enough to melt ice.

Coy Hunt rode into Morgantown on his favorite white Percheron to talk with George Chilton soon after Fricktown construction began. He tied Big Bob to the rail in front of the lawyer's new, three-story brick building. He stamped off the mud from his boots on the plank sidewalk before going in. Lawyer Chilton was known to not like mud from "farmer's boots" on his new Oriental rugs.

George Chilton told Coy to sit.

Coy asked his question: "How it is, Mr. Chilton, that AMSTEEL's a-layin' out a whole town in my bottom when I only deeded over the coal that's underground. It's every square foot they're a-takin', and even up the hillsides. The surveyors explained the ribbons and stakes to me."

"See it's like this, Coy," Chilton said, after asking his secretary to get the Hunt deed out of his filing cabinet. "It's this line on page 11. I'll read it. It gives the mineral owner -- that's AMSTEEL -- 'the collateral right to use all that surface estate of the Grantor' -- that's you -- 'deemed necessary in the Grantee's judgment to facilitate full expression of the Grantee's aforementioned rights above.'

"Coy, that means AMSTEEL can build a city as big as they need in your bottom and on the rest of your farm. They can dam your creek, cut down your trees and run a steam locomotive through your johnny house. That's why AMSTEEL gave you $1.50 an acre. Remember? It's clear language, right there to read in black and white. I wrote it."

"Clear as cowshit," Coy said and then spat on Lawyer Chilton's expensive new rug. He walked out, dazed. On the street, his humiliation and shame overwhelmed him. His breath was short. He cursed his greed. But he cursed his ignorance and illiteracy more.

He looked at Big Bob. A willin' horse, Coy thought. Ain't his fault.

As he mounted, George Chilton came through his building's door. "Still, a pretty good lookin' draft animal," he said.

"He weren't worth it," Coy said. "I see that now."

"No hard feelings from my end of things," Chilton said. "It's always easy to see things clearer when they're past. Coal is our future, Coy, because the coal is here. Where it is means that's where it'll be mined. You and I can't change geology and the needs of our industries. You and the boys should hook on as miners. Pay's good for around here. Maybe you know."

"I know now," Coy said.

Coy Hunt rode home on Big Bob. He brooded and berated himself. He was trapped in a closing circle without an exit. He felt like a ready-to-butcher hog cornered in his sty at the end of October.

He put up Big Bob next to Tom in the barn and gave each an extra flake of hay. He went inside.

He said nothing to Lucinda. She knew, had known all along.

"Frolic's over, ain't it," she said.

Coy took down the loaded Winchester '73 he had bought new 10 years earlier.

He went out to the barn, led both horses into the back pasture on the highest point on his land. He let them graze for a bit, rubbed their muzzles as they stood still, breathed into their nostrils so they'd remember him and reached high to scratch behind their ears.

"Ain't your fault," he told them.

He levered in a round, pointed the Winchester's octagonal muzzle at his heart and pushed the trigger backward with his thumb.

Big Bob and Tom bolted at the close gunshot and ran a few yards. They came back to nuzzle Coy Hunt as he lay in their pasture.

Coy's aim started straight, but ended a little off.

He hung on for a week.

Can't do nothin' right, Lucinda thought unwillingly.

She buried Coy in the Hunt family cemetery on the hill behind their cabin. The grave she had the boys dig had a panoramic view of Fricktown below.

The thought occurred to her as she walked home from the burial that her husband had planted himself years earlier. Fricktown had taken a while to close his grave.

In a few days, Lucinda learned the AMSTEEL money was gone. Coy had bought what he'd wanted and had worked little since the payment 10 years earlier. She'd suspected as much, but, when she asked, he told her it was his money, not hers, because it came from his land, not hers. Now, the 2,000 acres of surface rights were hers. At least, he had not mortgaged that.

Two weeks later, AMSTEEL informed her by letter that they would be using her land and timber for "necessary materials and mining needs." The Company said she could live undisturbed in her cabin for the rest of her days. Upon her passing, AMSTEEL said, Fricktown would build an auxiliary water tank where her house stood.

Her son, Coy, Jr., rented a place in Fricktown with the other new recruits and went to work in the mine.

Lucinda sold the Percherons to a logger from Preston County, West Virginia, for less than a quarter of what Coy had paid for them a decade earlier.

"Old plugs don't have much work left in them," the logger told her as he loaded his wagon with their two sets of double tack -- one for work, the other for show -- that he insisted be part of the deal.

"Then why do you want 'em?" she asked.

"Oh, I jes' like foolin' with the big fellers," he said. "I have a poor pasture that needs et down."

"Horses eat grass," she said. "They ain't partial to weeds and brush. Horses ain't goats."

"Horses are like us," he said. "They'll eat bad if that's their only choice." He tied the bridle leads to the wagon's seat, one on each side. He had figured the pair of 12-year-olds was good for woods-work for at least another six years. He'd paid Lucinda less for the two horses and their tack than what the tack alone was worth.

Lucinda knew the value of the horses and the tack, but she wanted "to be shut" of that part of her life.

The logger felt no guilt. A widder woman shouldn't expect to live off her husband's leavin's, he'd always told himself. A man, he'd always told himself, should use up his pile before he died. The kids could take care of their Momma.

Lucinda lived alone for the next three years, mostly off what her grim gardening produced and whatever Coy, Jr., brought up now and then from the Fricktown commissary. She died of pneumonia, alone, in late winter.

44

Her five children were not of one mind about burying her next to her husband, of whom they were more forgiving than she. Lucinda had not muzzled her opinions after Coy's suicide, or before for that matter. All of them had experienced her bitterness. But they could agree on no other place. "Sorry Momma," Coy, Jr., said. "It's the one spot on the farm that AMSTEEL won't build on."

Lucinda's handwritten will divided the land -- the surface of it -- equally among the five children. Coy, Jr., the oldest and the first son, got the 400 acres that joined Jacob Olin's 75 acres.

Coy, Jr., watched AMSTEEL over the years cut every tree at least four inches in diameter across the five Hunt tracts. Fricktown milled the hardwoods -- red oak, white oak, pin oak, black-jack oak, sugar maple, hickory, cherry, chestnut and black locust -- into mining props, entry headers, railroad ties, construction timbers, planks, construction lumber and board-and-batten siding. Lawyer Chilton in Morgantown showed Coy, Jr., the same deed he'd shown his father and pointed out the same sentence on page 11: "The Grantee holds the collateral right to use all that surface estate of the Grantor deemed necessary in the Grantee's judgment to facilitate full expression of the Grantee's aforementioned rights above."

"They're a-thievin' our timber," Coy, Jr., said.

"They're taking what's theirs, what they paid your Daddy for," Chilton said. "Perfectly legal."

"Ain't right," Coy, Jr., said.

Lawyer Chilton, an autodidact when it came to the ideas that lay behind his daily work, considered for a moment what was and what was not "right" when it came to land, minerals and ownership claims in the context of West Virginia.

"There's an old European anarchist who claims 'property is theft,'" Chilton said. "But that's just philosophy."

"Ph'los'phy, my ass," Coy, Jr., said.

From Lucinda's estate, Coy, Jr., was awarded his father's rapid-fire Winchester '73. He wiped it inside and out with gun oil and wrapped it in a worn-out pair of britches. He buried it at the bottom of his dresser drawer along with the never-used first box of ammunition his sentimental father had bought with the AMSTEEL money.

A few years after Lucinda died, Coy, Jr., and the other heirs sold the surface rights to AMSTEEL for $1,000. No one other than AMSTEEL would pay as much for land now so defiled by clearcutting, soil erosion, water pollution and coal dust. All of them remembered what Lucinda had said on her deathbed: "With land, you hold, not sell."

When Coy, Jr., died, the Winchester with its 24-inch-long barrel and the first box of .44-40 center-fire ammunition went to his first son, Joe, who left them where they were in his father's Fricktown house.

Joe Hunt knew his grandfather's story. He knew the rifle was a reminder to not be stupid about the ways of the world he did not know.

As AMSTEEL mined the coal it owned on Black Creek, not a penny in royalty was paid to Coy Hunt or any of his descendants. AMSTEEL had bought the coal outright rather than lease the right to mine it. Coy had never heard of getting paid a second time after selling something a first time. Lawyer Chilton who represented AMSTEEL had no fiduciary obligation to mention a leasing option. When Joe Hunt, as ACMU president, mentioned the absence of coal royalties on Coy's Fricktown land during a bathroom break in the 1964 contract negotiations, AMSTEEL president Ben Roberson laughed.

"We haven't screwed people like those old mineral deeds since the early '40s," Roberson said. "Anyone who owns the minerals now gets paid on the run-of-the-mine ton under a lease."

"AMSTEEL *bought* Coy's mineral rights, which split them from the surface. AMSTEEL paid AMSTEEL any production royalty," Joe said, as he accepted a towel from a men's-room attendant.

"Back then, fifty cents an acre for buying mineral rights alone wasn't that bad," Roberson said.

"Granddaddy got a buck and a half," Joe said.

"Big money, that," Roberson said.

"You took every tree on 2,000 acres for building Fricktown on our land."

"I'm sure it was all legal," Roberson said.

"You bet," Joe said. "Shootin' the landmen and the lawyer who snookered Grandaddy out of the minerals and surface resources to help with your minin', *that* would have been *illegal*."

"Indeed it would have been," Roberson said. "We're better now than we were back then."

"Only because my side has smartened up about your side," Joe said.

"Companies have to make a profit. If they don't, they disappear— along with the jobs they provide to your side."

Joe had expressed that very thought dozens of times in meetings with his membership. "Coal's a bitch, ain't it?"

"I'll make sure you start getting royalties from anything we mine from under your acres, even though we own that coal," Roberson said. "And I'll even have Accounting go back to 1940 and pick up any royalty you're owed."

"Thanks," Joe said.

"Since your land was all around our first shaft, it was probably mostly mined out before 1930," Roberson added.

"Mostly, but not all," Joe said.

Chapter 5

Fricktown, West Virginia: 1932-1933

The Great Depression began to settle over the coal industry in the 1920s and didn't leave until Pearl Harbor. In 1932, American coal operators produced only 359 million tons compared with 608 million in 1929. A ton in 1932 sold for less than half of what it had 10 years earlier.

Too much coal and too much competition drove down prices, which, in turn, forced mine operators to pay their labor as little as possible. Coal operators tried to stay in business by selling their coal more cheaply than their competitors. Prices fell, profits fell, wages fell and employment fell. Mine closures and bankruptcies rose.

The steel industry -- dependent on metallurgical-grade coal for its coke -- navigated the 1920s on growing demand and good prices, only to slide after the 1929 Crash into the same trough that coal operators were stumbling through. With the exception of the Empire State Building, construction of steel skyscrapers had almost come to a complete stop by 1931. Demand for rolled steel for autos was down; railroads were not buying new rails; demand for plate steel for defense and ships was almost nonexistent.

AMSTEEL found itself able to produce far more metallurgical coal than it needed or could sell. Having no choice, AMSTEEL and the others -- Bethlehem Steel, Republic, Jones & Laughlin, Inland and Armco -- cut their steel output to the bone, which meant cutting coal production into the bone. Layoffs and wage cuts followed. The coils of The Depression tightened.

Fricktown was AMSTEEL's largest coal mine, but, at age 40, not its most efficient. The coking-quality of its coal was not quite as good as that still coming from the Connellsville field. Fricktown's underground haulage lines were long, often several miles, which cut into daily production and increased the chance for mishaps. Bottlenecks appeared in moving coal from the mining face to the surface. AMSTEEL was slow to install the new undercutting and drilling machines, because its old haulage systems couldn't get the coal to the surface fast enough to keep up. The two hoists were subject to mechanical problems.

Fricktown management made plans to excavate a new portal that would eliminate the need for shafts and hoists, but that project was deferred until 1943. Short weeks were common in the 1920s, and became standard in 1930. Five days dropped to four, then three. Employment was cut from 1,200 miners to 500 in 1932.

In the spring of that grim year, Fricktown Superintendent Frank Gallagher announced that wages were to be cut again to $5 a day or $.38 per clean ton, whichever was less. When these rates were cut another 40 percent in August, the Fricktown dayshift dumped the water from their lunch buckets in front of the shaft elevator and refused to work until the old rates were restored.

"Wait a month, and they'll be back," Gallagher told AMSTEEL's president, Ben Roberson, Senior, at its Pittsburgh headquarters. "We've got plenty of coal stockpiled on the ground to wait 'em out. I can load gondolas with supervisors and salaried people. Fricktown miners don't understand that they aren't the top dogs in the Company. Just keep Connellsville working. Fricktown'll figure out its place in our line after a while."

Gallagher believed that miners on strike were not much different from half-drunk guys visiting a cheap whore: Everyone thought it was a fine idea when it was first proposed, and then no one quite understood why they had wanted to go after they had gone.

"They got nowhere to go, but here," he told Roberson. "No one's hiring miners at any wage. Eighty percent of the miners in Monongalia County have been laid off. They got no jobs, no food, no money and no ideas. Wait them out. Time will beat them."

A month later, the Fricktown miners were still on strike.

It was not easy for the men to be idle, penniless and hungry. It was even harder for them to watch their families shrink—to see their women in shapeless dresses sitting numbly on stained mattresses, trying to nurse crying babies from sucked out breasts; their kids in patches, coal grime crawling over their bare feet and up their legs like gangrene, so listless from hunger that they no longer even got underfoot. The men fled their Fricktown houses to squat together here and there, their frayed suspenders biting deeper into their shoulder bones. They passed information that wasn't news back and forth as if it was. They grumbled and cursed; resolved and promised; hoped and doubted; wavered and stuck. They wanted to work, but they wouldn't go back for $3 a day.

At the end of the fourth week, Gallagher asked the strikers to assemble in front of the commissary. He had something to tell them that came straight from Pittsburgh.

The miners gathered, hands deep in the pockets of their work britches, worrying lightly the stems of empty pipes. Women and children stood behind them.

Gallagher waited for the men to settle. "Boys, I'm for you. I hope you know that. I know every one of you and have for years. We've seen some good years and some bad. That's the coal business. This Depression is the worst you and me have ever seen. It's not just coal that's down. It's everywhere, every business, from top to bottom. It's strangling us; it's strangling America.

"Now I started by saying that I'm for you. So is Pittsburgh, from Ben Roberson, Senior, on down. We want you working. We want you making that $5 a day. We want you buying from the commissary. We want to make money on Fricktown coal and AMSTEEL metal.

"But, boys, it's like this. The Comp'ny hasn't made a profit since 1928. We lost more money in 1930 than in 1929, more in '31 than in '30. Projections for '32 are even worse; we'll lose more this year than in the last two years combined. Nobody's buying steel to speak of, and the prices they're willing to pay when they do buy a ton aren't enough to cover our expenses in making it. The Comp'ny is being squeezed by the Depression, and the only way to survive is to squeeze you. The only way you can survive is to squeeze down yourselves and wait for better times.

"Now I got more bad news. AMSTEEL operates nine coking-coal mines like Fricktown. That's down from 16 in 1929. We're the oldest and about fifth worst in productivity. We're the only shaft operation, which slows our production and raises our costs. The newer drift mines just run coal out from the face to the tipple, nice and level, either by mine rail or conveyor belt. Our coal is still good quality, but we cost about 20 percent more per ton to get ours into a gondola than the mine just above us in efficiency—and 30 percent more than the Comp'ny's most efficient mine.

"The other thing is we're still mining with old methods—undercutting with old machines or by hand, drilling the blast holes with old machines or by hand, loading by hand, hauling to the shaft with old locomotives and even a few mules, like ol' Smoke and ol' Ned. Pittsburgh sees our only chance to survive as a company is to put money into new machines—undercutters, drills, mechanical loaders and continuous belts. The old days -- when a lead miner worked his room to suit himself, produced as much as he wanted, had his boys load for him and was paid by the number of his cars -- are on the way out. And the faster we do that in Fricktown, the better the miners who are still working will be. Whatever happens with this strike, I promise you this: Handloaders are too expensive for us to carry. Mark my words: The future will be mobile mechanical loaders at the face and conveyors out to the surface. You men who've made your living handloading will either have to learn to run a machine or leave mining altogether.

"So, boys, what does that mean? It means you got no choice, because the Comp'ny got no choice. I got no choice. There are too many bobtail mines around that are paying their men $2 a day, producing too much coal and selling it too cheap—all of which is contributing to making Fricktown coal too expensive. We have to cut our cost per ton, which means we got to cut back on our per-ton cost of labor, one way or the other. We decided

50

to cut wages to $3 a day. We could keep it at $5 if we cut 300 jobs from the 500 who are still workin'. Hell of a choice, ain't it?

"It's okay with the Comp'ny for you to shut down Fricktown. We lose less money with Fricktown totally shut down than with you workin' it. Pittsburgh was thinking about doing just that anyway. If we stay up, Pittsburgh will be putting money into new machines, the kind that don't walk on two feet and carry a dinner bucket.

"Pittsburgh isn't ready to throw in the Fricktown towel for good. We want to keep you here, because we're hoping conditions improve. So, here's the deal. I can offer every miner who was working a month ago, three days a week at $3.25 a day. I can't do better than that. There's no negotiating. If you continue to strike, Pittsburgh will either find miners who will work for the new wage -- you know there are plenty of out-of-work men around these parts who will -- or just shut down the whole mine until the Depression eases up. If you leave your house in Fricktown, the Comp'ny will put a lien against any future income you earn to pay off your debt at the commissary. I know this is hard. I wish times were better. I wish I could stand up here and give you that $5 for 10 hours a day and six days of work. It just ain't in the cards. That's not the game we're in."

Gallagher had wanted to give the men 24 hours to think this out with their wives. He thought they'd argue themselves back, not because they had been licked, but because they were smart and would choose the least bad of their bad alternatives. They deserved the truth, and he had told his men the truth. Were he a working miner again, Gallagher thought he would come back and strike when AMSTEEL really needed Fricktown coal. You strike when it can hurt, not when it doesn't.

Had the miners been given a day to argue their choices among themselves, they would have returned to work as Gallagher had predicted. But Pittsburgh did not particularly care which path the Fricktown miners chose. So Pittsburgh instructed Gallagher to get an immediate work-or-strike answer. Ben Roberson wanted to put a stop to newspaper stories about the Fricktown strike. And, more than anything else, Pittsburgh wanted to send a message to all of its other employees: Take what we offer or bear the consequences, which will be worse.

Gallagher, a mining engineer by training and a retired captain in the U.S. Army, had his orders, so he said: "Yes or no, boys? I'll give you a minute or two, then I'll take a show of hands."

The miners stood silently, sneaking sidelong glances at each other. A few spat spit, not tobacco juice, because they no longer had tobacco. The women watched, saying nothing.

"Okay, boys, what'll she be?" Gallagher asked. "Those for working, for comin' back to work, raise…"

From the back of the crowd, a teenage handloader named Bryant in his first strike called out: "She be a bitch, Gallagher, so fuck her."

A few in the crowd laughed involuntarily. And then they stopped as if, as one, they'd just crashed into a stone wall.

Gallagher's face reddened. He understood their despair and anger, but insubordination was always a firing offense. He jumped off the commissary's porch and marched to his office, followed by his supervisors, followed by the Fricktown sheriff and his deputies.

The miners didn't move. The women turned toward their homes, knowing in their bones that something bad was coming next. The men stirred slowly. A few hitched up their trousers and plodded toward their houses. Most drifted toward the ball field for a meeting. Three older miners grabbed Bryant and assured him that the next time his tongue ran away from his brain he'd not have to worry about fucking any bitches again.

Gus Olin, a skilled miner in his early 30s, put his arms around young Joe Hunt and young Larry Sonoski, his two apprentice handloaders. Walking back to Dogtown, they heard its hungry mutts howl.

The next morning, a drizzly gray Saturday in October, Sheriff Clem "Buster" Nillis and his six deputies began the evictions in Dogtown. They started at the corner house on the street closest to the mine's hoist. The house was rented by John Sonoski, 47, who had spent his entire work life in Fricktown. He drove an underground locomotive that gathered coal cars from individual miners and trammed them to the shaft where they were winched to the surface. Miners had to trust John Sonoski to keep an honest count on their coal-filled cars, and they did.

The miners considered Buster to be a reasonable man on day-to-day matters like moonshine and Saturday-night behavior. Buster had been "raised up" in the next holler, and his brother, Dale, worked on the Fricktown tipple. He wasn't above sharing a pleasant evening smoke with the Dogtown Americans though he maintained a professional reserve. Gallagher told Buster, the mine's employee, early that morning that Fricktown had to be cleared quickly—orders from Pittsburgh. The choice between hiring strikebreakers and mothballing the operation would be made soon. Frank Gallagher handed Buster the legal papers for eviction.

Buster always tried to project authority above and beyond his average height and above-average roundness. His uniform was clean and pressed; his black-leather, knee boots polished; and his bone-handled .44 pistol with its custom-made, eight-inch-long barrel was well known for its ability to settle bad drunks. His sheriff's star shone. He wanted no trouble with this eviction business, which he didn't care for one bit. He was not looking forward to tossing his brother's furniture into the street. But, as he told himself, it's him or me.

Buster stood as tall as he could on his two-inch stack heels. He climbed on top of a discarded Dupont Explosives box that had once been packed with 50 pounds of red Gelex No. 1 in eight-inch sticks. AMSTEEL would sometimes give these dovetailed crates to miners who used them for shelves and bureaus, or kindling if they were a little better off. Fricktown was never short of dynamite. On average, every Fricktown employee used about 20 ounces of explosive every workday, or about one pound for every 3.2 tons produced. Buster wanted to project power. So what was better than to stand on a Gelex throne? Eviction wasn't a matter of discussion or negotiation. It was a simple matter of them doing what he told them to do, because it was going to happen one way or another.

Buster was positioned on the street side of John and Mary Sonoski's front gate, set into a picket fence. He held up the eviction order so he could read it exactly as it had been written by AMSTEEL's local lawyer, George Chilton, Jr., for county court the day before. Buster stumbled through the first wordy sentence when a rumble of protests and catcalls boiled out of the crowd standing in the front yard between the fence and the porch. Buster knew he had to read the whole order to make things legal, which he did, though no one could hear his words. John and Mary stood with their five children on the home side of their picket fence, embarrassed at their first-to-go fate. John was expressionless; Mary had fire in her eyes. They'd been evicted once before during an earlier strike.

Despite his vow to act big, Buster approached John and Mary with sympathy and resignation. He hoped they'd make this whole business easier on everyone.

"Now John," he said, opening the gate, "you know me and the deputies don't have no choice about this thang. And you don't neither. I'm jes' saying what's what. It'll be better if we all get through this business without a big fuss. When all the wash is up on the line, we both know we gotta live here with each other."

The crowd settled. John Sonoski had no idea why Buster wanted to start the evictions at his house. He wasn't a radical, and he wasn't a loudmouth.

"Buster, we can't make it on three days at $3.25. You know that."

"You can't make it even more on no days and no money," Buster said.

"Where'll we go?"

"Can't say, John, not for certain. Maybe you all can pitch tents up the holler back on Alvie Hunt's place like in 1920 when you boys dumped your water the last time. It's not really my look-out, ya know, once you leave Fricktown."

"This ain't right," Mary Sonoski said. Her thin face had grown thinner over the last month. Her dress did not cover her hunger. "Poor as this place is, it's where we've raised the family. You can't kick us out into the rain and winter."

"I'm sorry about this, Mary," Buster said. "I truly am. But you know I don't have no say about what's right and what ain't in this business.

Comp'ny will let you come back in when you're a-done with this strikin'. Like last time. Comp'ny knows John and your oldest, Larry, ain't Reds."

Buster had been through the 1920 evictions when he was just a deputy. He knew it was best for all concerned to do it fast. It was like killing a chicken, which squawked even after its head came off, because its voice box was in its chest, not in its neck. Same, he thought, with the evictions—there'd be squawking for a while after the deed was done.

Buster signaled his deputies. They came through the gate and formed a wedge to get through the crowd to the house. Their job was to put the Sonoski belongings on the dirt sidewalk. As the crowd jostled the deputies who were squeezing through, the gate came unhinged, its steel pegs torn from its mostly rotted post. Fricktown property became the first casualty of the evictions.

John Sonoski didn't move, and he didn't resist. But Mary moved directly in front of the deputies.

"No!" she whispered. "No. Stop!"

The miners, their women and kids, closed in behind her. The six deputies stalled. One took out his billy club, and the others followed. Somebody whacked John in the leg. Somebody threw a punch. More clubbing. More punching.

Skis, slight as he was, jumped the tall lead deputy and wrestled him onto the wet ground. The deputy rolled on top of the 15-year-old. Skis grabbed a handful of mud and pushed it into the man's eyes. The deputy, swearing and blinded, swung his club. It split Skis' forehead from the bridge of his nose to his hairline. Blood filled the boy's eyes. Skis lay still, stunned and unable to focus.

Buster assumed a fracas would happen. When it started, 30 county deputies and volunteers who had been hiding in a gondola on the main spur that ran in front of Dogtown clambered over its sides. They ran into the Sonoski yard with their pistols pulled and cocked. Buster fired twice into the air. The fighting stopped.

Snow came in December, but cold had wrapped around the Fricktown strikers before Thanksgiving. It burrowed into their bones and settled in. No one in the thrown-together camp could get warm enough. The short-wall canvas tents the ACMU provided, sagged and leaked. They were the same Army-surplus tents used in 1920 when the Union had won recognition as the bargaining representative for Fricktown miners after a two-month strike. The Union's strike tents had traveled a 12-year-long loop after their first stop at Fricktown—Mingo County in southern West Virginia, then Southeast Ohio, then West Virginia's Kanawha County, then southern Illinois and back to Fricktown. No one in camp expected much from these threadbare veterans. They were better than nothing, everyone agreed. Furniture that could not be squeezed into a family's 80-

square-foot shelter was discarded outside like broken toys. Rain swelled the joints on chairs and tables, peeled veneers and bled cheap floral patterns. By Christmas, 1932, most of the ruined furniture had been burned for heat. The dogs -- those that remained -- had given up gnawing the charred scraps.

Mary Sonoski tried her best to keep one step ahead of the disintegration that closed in. She feared it would find a way inside her family, and then they would be lost. So she imposed what order she could on the jumble of seven people in her tent. She straightened and cleaned, put back, put up, put under and threw out. She established routines and assigned responsibilities. She drew a line against the coming collapse and enforced it. She had John and Skis scrounge discarded wood boxes from the Fricktown dump, which they disassembled for floor slats and stove wood. In the tent's above-freezing "warmth," the mud beneath the slats softened and then oozed above the boards with each human step. Mary realized she could not defend against the mud under her feet.

Like the other tent families, John and Mary had nowhere to be by themselves, nowhere for private conversation, nowhere to bathe in privacy. The musty smell of mildew and mold filled their hours. They cringed when their skin touched the fuzzy growths on the underside of the always-damp canvas. Coughing became part of normal breathing. Noses stayed red and raw. The kids' sleeves were always wet with snot. Pneumonia picked through the camp, taking the youngest, the oldest and the weakest. The Sonoskis, like the others, grew short with each other over nothing and everything, then angry, then lethargic.

Mary stopped combing her hair in February, 1933, after her youngest died. That and the stench of herself and her family broke her. On Valentine's Day, she took to her rocking chair, the one in which she had nursed her children. The family listened to her singing softly to herself.

On March 4th, the miners listened in the big food tent to an ACMU-provided DELCO radio that was powered by a DELCO-LIGHT gasoline generator. The newly elected president, Franklin Delano Roosevelt, told them that "…a host of unemployed citizens face the grim problem of existence…." He blamed the "…practices of unscrupulous money changers.., the rulers of the exchange of mankind's goods…who have failed to match the plenty of American supply with the needs of its people."

"Who the hell is he talkin' about?" Skis asked his Dad in a whisper.

"Bosses, I 'spect." John said. "Bankers. Wall Street."

"Who's Wall Street?" Skis asked.

"Big bosses in New York."

"…the only thing we have to fear is fear itself—nameless, unreasoning, unjustified terror which paralyzes needed efforts to convert retreat into advance."

"What's he mean by that?" Skis asked.

"Maybe it's that you can't be scared to try somethin'. Like what we're a-doin' here," John said.

"You think the President knows that a mess of coal miners are starvin' and freezin' in Fricktown?" Skis asked.

"In a manner of speaking, son, I think maybe he has a notion. Maybe he's heard we're fightin' back."

They were cold in early March, but they had been colder. They were hungry, but that, too, was now normal. They had been through a long strike before, so the pattern, if not the precise outcome, was, at least, predictable. Each person put his or her head down like a work horse trudging toward a barn that never got any closer. They carried themselves past FDR's Inaugural speech on something more than his conviction they had nothing to fear. Not giving in had become a matter of dumb pride. Doing nothing was honorable work—the only work they had. Some were willing to die for pride; some already had.

March turned colder than February, every day was below 20. It seemed the winter refused to end. Even in the tight confines of the tents, the wood scraps didn't burn hot enough or hold a fire long enough to keep the cold from coming inside and wrapping around them. Without fuel and food, the strikers knew they would be done in a few weeks.

Gus Olin came up with a solution.

Jacob Olin never sold or leased the mineral rights on his 75 hillside acres that bordered Coy Hunt's land when the AMSTEEL agents came around. He liked his patch for the oak and chestnut trees that produced food for hogs and deer. It also contained a four-foot-thick outcrop of the Pittsburgh seam that AMSTEEL was working. Jacob punched a small opening into the outcrop for his own house coal and smithing. His son, Arvil, continued the digging each fall and brought his son, Gus, into the occasional work. In the mid-1920s, Gus asked Arvil to keep a wagon and a mule even though his father was bent over with arthritis from mining and no longer able to do any real farm work. The mule and rig could be used to haul coal even though Gus, now living in Fricktown, received two tons of AMSTEEL coal -- one free, one not -- for heating and cooking. When the Fricktown mine went through its more or less regular cycle of layoffs, young Gus worked a little coal out of his grandfather's tunnel.

By the late 1920s, three generations of Olins had excavated a single heading into the Pittsburgh seam about 300 feet. The further from the portal, the easier it was to stand as the seam thickened to about six feet. They excavated a narrow tunnel, no more than five- or six-feet wide, to allow the coal on either side to support the roof. Gus could blast down a ton or so at a time. With his dog, Red, pulling and Gus pushing, he could move 500 pounds to the portal in his homemade mine car. He used rails and wheels he had scavenged from Fricktown's discards with Superintendent Gallagher's permission.

To the best of Gus Olin's reckoning, his family had been mining Olin coal, not AMSTEEL coal. He guessed the property line was about 325 feet from his portal, but he couldn't be certain without a survey.

Gus was reasonably sure that Frank Gallagher suspected the Olins might be bootlegging a little Company coal for their own use or to give to the needy over the years. But AMSTEEL's president, Ben Roberson, Senior, told Gallagher to not bother with it. Roberson had always liked the Olins. He admired them for not selling their coal rights. Ben had developed a good relationship with Arvil and Gus over the years when it came to solving Fricktown matters. They approached problems as matters that could be analyzed and solved. So Ben, Senior, never made a point of fussing over a handful of tons that Arvil and Gus might be pulling off the Fricktown reserve during layoffs. Ben told his son, Ben, Junior, to leave well enough alone. When Gus took over mining the family drift, he cut a short T at the end of the main entry and left a buffer between him and where he thought AMSTEEL's coal started.

On March 1, 1933, Gus again took Skis and Joe into his mine to pull out a few hundred pounds to carry back to the tent camp. Gus Olin's coal kept the strikers just warm enough to keep the strike going.

"I hope this is AMSTEEL coal we're takin' back to the tents," Joe said as they loaded the feed bags they would carry home.

"Don't think so, Joey," Gus said. "But it's hard to say for dead certain where the boundary is underground. I don't have a map."

"It would only be right if it was," Joe said. "Then we would be takin' from the Comp'ny the winter coal that we always got."

"Each Fricktown house got two tons in October for *workin'* for AMSTEEL," Gus said, "not for strikin' against AMSTEEL."

"It would only be right if we was on them," Skis said.

"I don't think I'm bootleggin' Fricktown," Gus said. "Got plenty of coal on my side of the line. I'm too coal-rich to steal."

"If it was Comp'ny coal, it's be like compensation for our troubles in the tents," Skis said.

"Sure," Joe said. "Takin' AMSTEEL coal would be comp'sation."

"Ain't no comp'sation," Gus said, "for how far down we are. A tanker car and a teaspoon don't even up."

A week after Roosevelt's address, the ACMU's strike coordinator announced the Union was reluctantly leaving the Fricktown strikers on their own.

"We've backed you since October, but we don't have no more money for it," he said. "Strikes like this one have popped up all over the coalfields. Not near enough miners workin' to help all those that ain't. We gotta try to organize the unorganized, not the guys like you who are already in. We gotta cut our losses and concentrate our resources, is what they tell me. You boys can keep the tents until things wind up, but we gotta take the kitchen pots and pans with us to the next bunch."

The strikers understood the ACMU's position. The Union had supported them for five months. ACMU president, John L. Lewis, had concluded the Fricktown strikers were a lost campaign, because AMSTEEL didn't really care whether or not they came back. For the strikers and their families, the ACMU's decision meant: Go back or starve. If they continued, where would food come from? Milk for the babies, pinto beans, cornmeal, lard?

"Well," the coordinator said, "maybe some folks up in New York will help." He left that night and phoned a person he knew.

The steel barrels of cornmeal and beans emptied. The rasp of metal scoops on metal bottoms tolled through the camp.

Three days after the ACMU left, five Communists from New York City drove into Alvie Hunt's pasture with two trucks of food and an invitation to join the Party's union. A recent Vassar graduate from Darien, Connecticut, reorganized the camp kitchen, cleaned the pots reluctantly donated by her parents and some of their neighbors, posted schedules and made assignments. She also led nightly meetings on "theory and practice," which Gus was sometimes able to translate into words and ideas that a fair number of strikers more or less understood. But in their guts, the strikers knew the Vassar girl and the Party wanted something more than their attendance and attention at the "thee-ree meetin's."

A few cynics figured the Party wanted the Fricktown strikers to lose so that they, the proletariat, would become more revolutionary.

"In other words," Gus said, "worse for us now is better for us down the road. Hard to figure if we're all dead from starvin' and freezin'."

Gus thought to himself the Company wanted his back, and the Communists wanted his mind.

"What's she talkin' about?" Joe Hunt asked Gus. "She keeps talking about 'the point of the pick' is where it begins? What begins?"

"Communists think that coal in the ground has no value," Gus said. "They think it only gets value when you dig it from the face. When the Comp'ny pays you less than a fair wage for minin' it, that's value that they're stealin' from you and keepin' for themselves. So the moment your pick produces a chunk of coal, the Comp'ny is cheatin' you out of money. And it's this unfairness, this exploitation of you, which starts at the point of your undercuttin' pick, that will turn you and me toward Communism, which will fix everythin'. That's how they line it out."

58

"We always knowed that AMSTEEL was makin' money off our work when they paid us less than what it takes to live on," Joe said.

"That ain't news to me," Skis said.

"This Communism idea, boys, you gotta watch out," Gus said. "You can nip off a piece here and there that seems right. But when you follow that one piece back up to the whole thang, like suckin' in a real long strand of spaghetti to get to the pile on the plate, you find the whole shebang is a dictatorship like over in Russia."

"You a Communist, Gussie?" Joe asked.

"Not me," Gus laughed. "I'm a model worker. I pull the load as hard as I can for AMSTEEL every shift until I give out. But I think I got a little communist in me, because I'd like the workin' class of people to get a little more out of the capitalists."

"You think Communist Russian coal mines are better than here?" Joe asked.

"Probably worse. Bosses is bosses," Gus said. "Don't much matter if they're working under the Stars and Stripes or the Hammer and Sickle. Both bosses have to get out the coal, or else. I figure the Soviets care less about Ivan, the miner, than Ben Roberson cares about Joey, the miner, which ain't sayin' much for either of them. A miner's life is cheap here and there, but cheaper there."

"So why do you think American mines are better than the Russian mines?" Skis asked.

"'Cause the worse that can happen to our bosses if they don't meet production quotas is they get fired. In Russia, they get sent to a hard-labor prison camp. That's why I think their bosses come down harder on their miners."

"What do the Russians do with strikers like us?" Joe asked.

"They shoot guys like me," Gus said. "They don't like independence. Men, and ladies too, who don't follow orders get sent to Siberian camps to get rid of their 'capitalist tendencies.' Stalin calls it 'reeducation.' They're prisons workin' slave labor. I doubt many survive Professor Stalin's classrooms."

"For guys like us, is there an answer?" Skis asked.

"Answers are funny," Gus said. "They look good when they're all bright and shiny, and nobody's tried 'em out yet. Then they don't look so good after you fire them up and put 'em to work for a while."

"So why are we starvin' here if nothin' ain't gonna get better?" Joe asked. "Why do we work like mules for so little?"

"It's just how our world is, how things are," Gus said. "We work 'cause we're supposed to, I guess, and 'cause we have to eat and have a roof over us. When you're sitting at the poker table, it don't do no good to bitch over the cards you have in your hand. You play 'em the best you can. If you want an edge, you need to be a dealer."

As they carried their sacks of coal back to the tents that night, Joe thought about how he, Joe Hunt from Fricktown, West Virginia, might become a dealer some day, or, at least, get enough money together to buy a horse and wagon.

The Fricktown strikers talked it over and, within the week, invited the Communists to leave. It was a polite-but-strained parting. The Communists took their pots and pans but left the small amount of food that remained. They were headed for a strike in the anthracite field near Scranton.

Before she got into the Party's truck, the Vassar girl, Maude Andrews, gave her new friend, Edna Olin, Gus's young wife, a silk handkerchief.

"Just a keepsake," she told Edna.

In return, Edna gave Maude two mismatched buttons she had planned to sew onto her coat.

"Just a keepsake," she said.

The tents ran out of provisions a few days later. The men prowled the woods from light to dark, praying for a winter-thin doe to wander into their gun sights. None did, because none were left. Skis and the other teenagers fashioned snares. They hid them under the naked oaks and hickories for squirrels and deep in the blackberry thickets for rabbits. But the small game, even the smallest, had been hunted out on Alvie's land. The women pooled their knowledge of edible roots, hacking at the cold ground with rusty axes. Young girls made tea from sassafras bark.

On the third foodless day, Gus Olin led Skis and Joe out of camp after midnight. Each carried two burlap feed sacks. Joe, a big-framed 16-year-old, had a claw hammer stuck in his belt. They walked through the pasture's shallow snow pack under a black sky. They climbed over a low ridge and walked a deer trail toward Fricktown below. They descended behind the tipple and took cover in the shadows of the empty gondolas that lined the loading spurs along Black Creek. Most of the guards the company had hired after the strike started were sleeping in the community hall. The three strikers could see a light in that building where four were playing cards.

Drawing even with the commissary, they ducked under an empty gondola and ran one at a time to the loading dock. Gus slipped over to the building's near corner while Skis scurried to the far one, both posting as lookouts.

Joe pulled his Daddy's hammer and worked its claw under and along the double-hung window's casing. With that off, the window swung loosely on its cords. He climbed into the storeroom and filled the six burlap sacks with food from bins and barrels. He tied off the sacks, carried them to the window and handed them to Gus who began shuttling them behind the gondola. Joe climbed through the window and replaced its trim. Folding his neckerchief over the finishing nails, he gently tap-pushed them in. If their luck held, the commissary might never discover the missing supplies.

Joe and Gus were turning toward the gondolas on the main track with the last sack when a familiar voice cut through the darkness.

"Now a-hold it right there, fellers. I have a nervous double-barreled 12-gauge that says you best pay attention." Frank Gallagher chuckled with genuine cheer and self-congratulation. He'd had a hunch someone would try something like this as soon as his snitch in the camp told him they'd run out of food. Gallagher walked toward Gus and Joe while Skis, out of sight, hunched down behind his corner.

"I figured you all would be gettin' a bit hungry. Can't say as I blame you neither."

Gallagher closed to within 10 feet of them, then stopped to light his Dietz coal-oil lantern. It cast a yellow glow.

"Don't surprise me none, that you, Gus, are here. I heard about you and them Communists. But you should've left Coy Junior's boy at home. He's just a young'un. You, Joe Hunt. Come over this a-way. Now face the building. Both of you."

Gus and Joe turned toward the building, away from Gallagher who moved behind them, his shotgun leveled at their backs. He approached, holding the lantern in his left hand. He stopped two feet away and set the lantern on the ground while he adjusted his one-handed hold on the long gun.

"You boys will be fed now. Up at the Moundsville pen. Be warm, too. All courtesy of hard-working, tax-paying folks like me. Sure beats the shit out of camping up in Uncle Alvie's pasture. Now turn around real slow. Easy! Let's jes' walk over to the hall and let them do-little guards earn their pay."

Gus and Joe faced Frank Gallagher, their hands raised.

Gallagher reached down to pick up his lantern.

At that moment, Gus took three quick steps to his left, toward the shadows. As Gallagher swung his shotgun to bear on Gus, Joe pulled his hammer and smashed it against the superintendent's temple. Gallagher groaned and crumpled. Blood ran from his ear.

Joe stood over him, his knees about to buckle, his chest heaving. "My God! I think I done killed 'im!"

"Hope so," Gus whispered, as he snuffed the lantern's flame. "Didn't have a hell of a lot of choice. He was jes' doin' his job like the rest of us. Help me get him back in the storeroom."

"What for?" Joe asked. "What are we gonna do?"

"We're gonna burn the sunuvabitch."

Gus and Joe dragged the superintendent's body across the dock to the window. Gus undid the casing for a second time. They lifted the corpse inside. Gus climbed through and poured kerosene from a storage drum over the body and around the storeroom. Joe handed in Gallagher's shotgun, the lantern and his Daddy's bloody hammer. Gus wadded up brown butcher paper, lit the lantern and threw it next to Gallagher just before climbing back through the window. It took a few minutes for the coal-oil and kerosene flames to build and gather.

Skis joined Gus and Joe.

"I saw what happened," Skis said.

"Let's get out of here," Gus said.

They divided the six sacks and hurried, bent over, to the far side of the gondolas. They followed the cars along the main track for a bit, then cut straight up the sloping trail they had come down. Lugging the heavy, awkward sacks was hard on the slick hillside. They stopped in the scrub trees about 400 feet above the tracks. Orange-yellow flames were spreading through the commissary's storeroom. It would only be minutes before it burned through into the mine offices and shop space.

Someone in the community hall shouted "FIRE!"

Half-clad, half-awake mine guards tumbled out. They ran toward the commissary only to stand helplessly as the flames burst through at the eaves and licked at the metal roof. The payroll office on the second floor collapsed in a brilliant cascade of sparks that left the commissary's stone walls standing black against a golden inferno.

Mine guards and bosses who had gathered on the edge of the circle of light found themselves retreating from the intensifying heat. They pointed their pistols and shotguns at the flames. They wondered why Frank Gallagher was not there, standing with them. Finally, the assistant superintendent told them to get the pumper out of the firehouse and hose down the nearby buildings. The commissary, he knew, would be a total loss along with all of Fricktown's accounts, including who owed what.

The three strikers sneaked back over the ridge to their tents. They put the six sacks of food in the camp kitchen without being seen. Each took just a little for his own tent.

Skis told his father, John, about the raid, because he had no other way to explain the flour and lard he brought to the tent before daylight. He did not mention Gallagher.

When Coy asked his son that morning about the dried blood on his ragged overalls, Joe said: "Rabbit."

"Rabbit?"

"Rabbit," Joe said.

"Damn big rabbit for all that blood," Coy said.

"Yeah boy, Daddy. Damn big rabbit."

62

Coy didn't ask Joe why he hadn't brought home a damn big rabbit, not with a plate of hot, white-flour biscuits in his belly.

Gus Olin told Edna about the raid and Gallagher. He didn't say who had done what. Edna didn't ask.

Nothing of Gallagher was found when Fricktown supervisors and AMSTEEL officials poked through the commissary's still-smoking ruins days later. They opened the safe only to find that all the money and paper inside had burned. They did find shapeless lumps of melted metal in the ashes, but no one could distinguish the remnants of a shotgun from the remnants of a claw hammer from the remnants of a miner's pick.

Fricktown bosses and AMSTEEL headquarters knew Frank Gallagher had been murdered. But they had no body or evidence, no proof. They only had their firm belief that strikers had done it.

The newly appointed superintendent told the camp snitch to probe for leads. Who, he asked, had brought food to the kitchen that morning? That was the key, the superintendent said. The snitch tried. He produced two jugs of powerful moonshine that got several strikers "drunken up" enough for them to tell if they knew anything. But he ended with a handful of vomiting half-starved men who were united in their opinion that Frank Gallagher probably got what he deserved, whatever that might have been, even though, they conceded, he wasn't "that bad for a superintendent."

The Monongalia County sheriff sent two detectives to Fricktown to investigate the disappearance. They interviewed Fricktown bosses, mine guards and strikers. They sifted through the commissary's remains. They looked for clues on the ground. They questioned the strikers again about the "magical" appearance of food in the camp's kitchen.

"It was a gen-u-ine miracle," they were told. "Jes' like what Jesus done with them loaves of homemade light bread."

Coy Hunt, Jr., needed his claw hammer to reset his tent stakes a few days after the commissary fire. He couldn't find it. He asked Joe.

"Used it on the rabbit," Joe said.

Coy looked at his son as a man for the first time.

"I don't have no more hammers for you to go huntin' with," Coy said.

"Ain't no more rabbits out there anyway," Joe said. "I got the last one."

The fire and suspected murder brought reporters back to Fricktown and the strikers' camp.

Davey Bloom, a 25-year-old general-assignment writer for The Pittsburgh Post-Gazette, interviewed AMSTEEL's brass in Pittsburgh. He then talked with the Company's outside counsel on the 20th floor of the

City's Frick Building, which Henry Clay Frick erected in 1902 next to a building owned by Andrew Carnegie, his estranged and now-hated business partner. Bloom added a little color by reminding readers that Frick had insisted his building rise a few stories higher than Carnegie's so the latter's edifice would always be in his shadow. Bloom, the son of a turn-of-the-century immigrant and a Pittsburgh native, had been reporting Depression stories in the Pittsburgh area since Black Tuesday, October 29, 1929.

In the aftermath of the Fricktown fire, Bloom was told to drive to the idle mine and, for reasons of balanced reporting, visit the strikers camped in Alvie Hunt's field.

Spring mud swallowed Davey's city brogans. He sat in the strikers' rain-warped chairs and saw lice implanted on the heads of their kids. The tent camp was barely surviving on small food donations from Quaker meetings in Pennsylvania. He shared dinner with them at noon—water soup with dough balls, salt-risen wheat bread, lard. Some strikers he interviewed just shrugged when he asked why they were sticking it out. "Nothin' better to do," one said.

Davey quoted Gus Olin as saying "the Fricktown bosses and even AMSTEEL itself are just as much a victim of this economic system as us on strike. Like a bad marriage, we hate each other but also need each other, too." Davey ran Olin's quote in his second story from Fricktown— "The Strikers' Point of View." That afternoon, his managing editor told him to come home. His assignment after returning was the launch of the first "new" barge on Pittsburgh's three rivers since 1929. Davey agreed to his editor's suggestion that it wasn't necessary to include the fact the "new" barge was simply newly painted.

After newspapers rediscovered the Fricktown strikers, the ACMU was shamed into returning.

Local police quickly threatened the strike coordinator with charges of "concealing evidence" and "harboring a murderer."

"I wasn't here when the store burned," he said, "and no one's said anything to me about Gallagher's whereabouts. Wouldn't surprise me none if the Comp'ny hadn't staged this to gain sympathy. Frank Gallagher might be layin' up in Florida or even California for all I know."

The strike dragged on for another two weeks. In the third week of April, 1933, a compromise was reached—$3.25 a day in Fricktown credit or scrip and a promise to 500 miners of seven work shifts every two weeks. AMSTEEL quickly rebuilt the commissary.

It was no victory for the strikers, but neither was it a complete defeat. At least, they told themselves, Fricktown was still being operated, despite its age and inefficiencies. They could move out of the tents and return to rented houses. The commissary debts were reluctantly and officially forgiven as part of the new ACMU contract. AMSTEEL had no choice about that since the credit records had vanished in the fire. Fricktown began keeping a second set of ledgers once the commissary was operating. Duplicate pages were sent to Pittsburgh each Saturday.

It came be known as the "Strike of '32." Fricktown strikers became legends in the American Coal Miner's Union.

Mary and John Sonoski returned to their house with their four surviving children. It had stood empty for seven months. They were pleased the tarpaper roof had only one leak, which had raised the floor near the chimney in the front room. The house smelled musty. "Still, it was," John said, "more than a mite better than that tent, and we should be thankful." The kids started back to school. John and Skis went back to work for short pay on short weeks.

Mary spent most of her last decade in her rocker. She said little and asked nothing. The young Sonoski girls took up the cooking for the family, packing dinner buckets each work shift for their father and brother. Fricktown's doctor had no pill for Mary's sickness, and even the West Virginia University people in Morgantown had no medicine to fix her "malaise." The family learned to leave Mary to whatever ideas were in her mind. She was not much of a burden, and everyone understood. When Mary died in 1942, Skis's siblings fled Fricktown. The girls found jobs in defense plants, and his little brother, Jack, volunteered for the Navy. John stayed with mining until his retirement in 1949 when AMSTEEL brought in the first generation of continuous-miners, laid off most of its old handloaders and started retraining the younger ones to run the new generation of electric-powered machines.

Skis lived in John's house until 1943. He followed Joe Hunt out of the Fricktown mine when Joe won his first district office.

Skis had been surprised when Joe said that he was thinking of running for District 31 president. That was a big step up in ACMU politics from local union president, which was often all headache and no reward. More than once, Joe had swept out the union hall after a meeting, because he was president and no one else thought to do it. Cleaning up cigarette butts was not beneath him.

"Why do you want that job?" Skis had asked.

"Not sure, exactly," Joe said. "Maybe it's somethin' like I want us -- all of us -- to do better. I won't roll over for the comp'nies, you know that. I can do a good job and be pretty honest about it. I want to try my hand at dealin' the cards instead of bein' dealt."

"You ain't the smartest kid in the school," Skis laughed. "We both know that."

"That's why you need to come with me," Joe said.

AMSTEEL sold its Fricktown houses to their resident renters in the mid-1950s for $500 each. The price included the lot, the outhouse and whatever improvements the renters had made for themselves. After $100 down, each working miner could pay off the balance from paycheck deductions over the next four years. Unemployed miners had to come up with the full amount. About the same time, the Fricktown commissary converted itself to a cash-and-carry store that extended credit. Cars had ended the company-store system, because they allowed miners to drive to cheaper alternatives. Fricktown scrip was bought back at face value. A few miners saved some scrip coins as mementos. One granddaughter who worked for Bobby Kennedy in the spring of 1968 wore a Fricktown dollar around her neck, which Ivy League boys thought exotic and mildly aphrodisiacal. AMSTEEL continued to run the Fricktown waterworks for another dozen years until it was able to unload it on the newly incorporated town. In the 1960s, Lyndon Johnson's War on Poverty paid for a town sewerage system and a modern water-treatment plant. A regional utility was browbeaten into taking over the old coal-fired, 100 KW electric-generating plant.

AMSTEEL retained the mineral rights it had purchased over the decades and continued to mine coal. Its investment in new mining technology kept Fricktown viable after WWII. As the Connellsville field played out, the massive Fricktown reserve acquired strategic importance in the Company's supply stream. During the '50s and '60s, labor-cutting machines kept Fricktown profitable despite weak coal demand and soft prices. Ben, Junior, took over AMSTEEL in 1949 after promising his father he would do what was necessary to modernize the Company and maintain its leadership in coal and steel.

On the day in 1954 that his Dad had the deed to his Fricktown house recorded, Skis took a sledgehammer to its shabby picket fence. That, however, didn't erase his memory of being evicted in 1932. The scar running from his hairline to his nose had always been a sufficient reminder. But it did make him feel a little better. He took his mother's rocking chair with him to Washington. He stuck it in a spare upstairs bedroom where it would never be used or even seen very often. That it was there, was enough.

Neither Skis nor Joe Hunt ever married. They considered marriage too complicated to manage with their long workdays at Union headquarters. They found willing women through work—secretaries, bookkeepers and sisters of male staff. The ACMU filled their lives.

Both inherited the Fricktown houses of their parents. They rented them to unemployed miners as they moved up the ACMU hierarchy in

Washington. Neither liked being a Fricktown landlord, but neither could bring himself to sever his connection through a sale. The houses wore thin. Joe and Skis could not abandon the houses or dismantle them. Their acceptable alternative was to nurse them through a protracted illness.

Skis kept a small, jagged piece of dirty pine slat on his desk at ACMU's headquarters. It was no bigger than a dollar bill. He had no photograph of his mother, but this bit of tent floor on which she and his family had walked kept her in mind. Whenever it caught his eye, his memory flashed on the tents in Alvie Hunt's field, the mud, his mother rocking, the raid on the commissary and the moment that Joe Hunt killed Superintendent Frank Gallagher. He did not forget that the ACMU had helped the strikers, abandoned them and then came back. The Union was there at the end. No one else was. He did not forget that Joe Hunt and Gus Olin had fed his family and kept him out of jail.

Chapter 6

Washington, D.C., October 7, 1975

Joe Hunt had not forgotten Fricktown, but he didn't brood over it. He kept busy with ACMU affairs after escaping the AMSTEEL mine.

As a District 31 officer, he discovered he had a knack for politicking. He was good at understanding the wants and needs of his members, which were not necessarily the same in his opinion. He kept his own political interests in mind as he worked for his constituents. Miners liked his plain talk, his big body, his growly voice, his straight-forward style, his willingness to mix it up and not just talk. They found it easy to vote him up the Union's ladder. They believed his rise in their Union would align with their own advancement.

Joe built support in northern West Virginia locals in step with his success in representing their members in grievance hearings in front of professional arbitrators, most of whom were lawyers. He studied the ACMU Contract's 110 pages and schooled himself in arbitration rulings that interpreted those sections the parties had deliberately left vague during contract negotiations. Joe didn't try to come across as educated in a diploma sense. But he did teach himself to be smarter by listening and asking for help. Once an ACMU lawyer explained a legal principle to him, Joe could customize it orally and use it effectively in a hearing. He wasn't confident in finding information in books so he made his memory into his library. When a brief was required, he got the District 31 lawyer to write it rather than mangle it on his own. He took unwinnable grievances into arbitration if a visible fight would help him politically. "Losing a hopeless grievance ain't no skin off my nose, 'cause nobody expects me to win it," he told Skis, "and every once in a while I pull one out I didn't deserve." He won about 40 percent of his cases, with split decisions on another 25 percent—the best record in the Union. As he moved up, his positions in the Union gave him increasing authority to tell people with college skills they should do work he wanted done. Lawyers, consultants, Union staff, researchers and even doctors working for the miner's health fund—they all wanted to help his star rise.

John L. Lewis, ACMU president since 1920, liked Joe, and appointed him president of District 31 in northern West Virginia in 1953 after the incumbent died. Joe won election in his own right later that year. Before Lewis retired in 1960, he named Joe as his successor. The election was a formality; no one ran against him.

Like his loyal friend Larry Sonoski, Joe Hunt kept a reminder of Fricktown in his ACMU office. His family's coal scuttle proved to any rank-and-file miner sitting in front of him that Joe Hunt knew where he came from. He used it for spit.

The phone console on Joe's desk buzzed. It was Edie Morse, his secretary. Joe picked up the receiver and looked at Skis.

"Send him in."

A man of average height and unremarkable looks in his early 50s walked into Joe's office. He held himself tall with his head back and chin tilted up to project an aggressive presence, even importance. He wore a tailored black suit and a bone-white shirt with gold cufflinks. His salt-and-pepper hair was freshly barbered. A faint cloud of after-shave floated in with him, the kind that smells expensive. On appearance alone, he might have passed for a K Street lobbyist or corporate lawyer. He stood still for a minute, jaw up and out, like Mussolini. He carried a soft-leather briefcase with nothing in it.

Joe and Skis rose, extending their hands.

"Chickie," Thomas A. Siciliano said, shaking hands first with Joe and then Skis.

Joe nodded. "Joe Hunt. You know Skis."

Joe looked hard at Chickie's face. Tan. Smooth. Very closely shaved. He noticed that Chickie's eyes swept his office. Very dark eyes against a very white shirt.

Chickie noted the photos of Joe Hunt with every American president since 1960. He suspected -- correctly -- that Joe had retained the red-leather furniture John L. Lewis had used. He calculated the cost of the furnishings, a habit he learned watching his father buy produce in Pittsburgh's Strip District for their corner grocery. You made money, his father said, buying cheap wholesale, not selling high retail.

Chickie did a quick-but-thorough appraisal of the two former coal miners. He figured he could take Sonoski, but Hunt might still be a handful even though he'd gone to fat. He noted a faint scar running straight down the middle of Sonoski's forehead. Chickie was comfortable around guys with scars.

Hunt reminded him of an old walrus—all blubber, tusk and mustache bristle. You might push him, but you needed to be careful when you had him cornered. Neither was Italian, but Chickie had learned to deal with all types in Washington. Anyway, this was business, not Washington phony social shit. And his boss, Tony Bruno, had given him the assignment.

Skis feared this conversation. He saw that Joe was distracted, still impulsively angry over the nominating vote that had gone for Jeep Delucci.

Chickie stretched his forearms forward. "I'm Chickie. Can I call you, Joe?"

"Sure."

Chickie nodded. "How can I help you, Joe?"

Joe tried to focus on his task while looking both confident and non-committal. He knew he was both a buyer and a seller in this deal. He didn't want to look eager on either count. He also knew that Siciliano was the only guy willing to lend him the money to win the election. But this Chickie, Joe thought, was Italian like Delucci. That could be a problem. They could be cousins or from the same hometown in Italy. Joe had seen guys like him around—at the Union's conventions in Las Vegas and Miami Beach. They "comped" him women, rooms, food and booze. They were always friendly, always telling him who they knew that he knew, always looking for a way in. Joe knew some things about Tony Bruno, the Pittsburgh Mafia boss. Joe looked to Skis.

Skis sat up in his chair. "We need some help in Joe's campaign like I told you the other day. We can't take money out of Union funds, because that would be illegal. The feds are keeping an eye on that kind of stuff these days because of...well, you know, Hoffa and the Teamsters."

"The so-called Justice Department comes down on the Teamsters and never does nothin' about big oil," Chickie said. "The government's got a funny idea about which mob is runnin' the show."

"Right," Skis said, not wanting to pursue which mob was running which show. "See, we can't borrow from our bank—that wouldn't look right. And we don't have the cash ourselves to fund the campaign. That's why we're looking for an 'alternative lender.' So Joe had our lawyer, Foster Shives, get in touch with Mr. Bruno in Pittsburgh last week, and that's why I came to your office the other day. We can beat Delucci if we have the bucks to run a strong campaign. No question about it."

Chickie turned his smile down, but not off. "As I understand it, the vote of your locals was 637 to 483 against Joe, here. Yinz got stomped."

Both Joe and Skis recognized the Pittsburgh "yinz."

Chickie smiled. Joe and Skis would appreciate a tactically dropped "yinz," because he knew they came from Monongalia County on the Pennsylvania line. "Yinz" was regional glue for the area's working class. It was a way for the three to "bond," an idea Chickie had recently discovered on "The Phil Donahue Show." Chickie wanted his smile to project that the money to keep Joe Hunt in office was both chump change and of the highest value to Tony Bruno. He also wanted them to understand that he knew what was going on in the Union...and Bruno's money wouldn't come cheap. That was a lot of work assigned to a small smile.

Tony Bruno was already invested in the ACMU election with the loss of Little Louie and Bonk. "That job for Joe Hunt leaves me two down," he had told Chickie. "We need to level the playin' field in our favor."

70

Joe spat into his scuttle and tugged at his neck. "We got stomped," he repeated. "I know it; you know it." He didn't think bullshit would work with Chickie. "I didn't take the kid serious. Now I am."

Chickie was a smoker, not a spitter. Chewing tobacco was low-class in his way of thinking. "Mind?" he asked pulling out a silver cigarette case from his jacket pocket.

Joe shook his head. "Naw."

Chickie lit his Marlboro with a matching silver lighter that had his initials -- TAS -- engraved on both sides. Joe pushed an ACMU ash tray toward his visitor. Chickie placed his lighter with conscious drama on Joe's desk as if he were staking a claim.

Joe stared at the lighter, almost hypnotized.

"That's why we need the money," Skis said, "to even things up."

"Why'd yinz lose?" Chickie asked, dragging on his cigarette, then blowing smoke through his nose.

"It's the '74 contract," Joe said. "The membership don't think I got 'em enough. We do contracts every two years. Their expectations had rose up way high in '74 'cause of what all I got 'em in '72—$50 a shift. They figured I could get, maybe, $75 in '74. It wasn't possible, not when I had to get a higher tonnage royalty for the health and retirement fund. So they bitched at me about the contract. Here's the thang. They really wasn't votin' *for* Delucci. They was sendin' me a message that they were unhappy. Sometimes you need to jerk a kid in a knot to get his attention. That's what the voting did to me."

"Sometimes you do," Chickie said. "Sometimes you gotta straighten people out."

"Sure," Joe said.

"If your members wasn't votin' *for* Delucci, as you say," Chickie said, "their vote against you still comes out as a vote for him. It don't matter why a guy votes the way he votes. What matters is what his vote was. Why won't the same thing happen in your general election in December?"

"His support is a mile wide and an inch deep," Joe said.

"What do you think that means?" Chickie asked.

"Means his guys won't stick with him. My guys'll stick with me."

"So won't enough of the bums…ah, your members…still vote against you in December for him to win?"

Joe felt a little better. This guy talked regular. Bums were bums.

"Naw, they got this protest crapola outa their systems. And we plan to run lotsa shit over the dam before then, too."

"Lotsa shit costs lotsa money," Chickie said, pleased with the transition he had effected. He noticed that Skis was keeping his eye on the lighter as if that coiled snake might strike at any time.

"That's right," Skis said. "We need the money right now. We gotta firm up our base and add to it. Five hundred thousand."

"Where yinz been getting money so far?" Chickie asked.

"Me and Skis each kicked in $25,000. Got $5,000 apiece out of the presidents of the small districts; 10 grand each out of the big districts in Pee-A, West Virginia and Ohio. Got $2,000 each from the elected international board members, and some dribs and drabs from lower-down district officers. Put the arm on some companies that sell shit to the Union. As of last Friday, we had about $150,000 and spent about $125,000. Mostly in kickin' it back down to the districts to buy support."

"So tell me what fucked up?"

"Wasn't enough money to buy enough loyalty," Skis said. "The young guys today got an independent streak."

"And why do you think more money will swing these Delucci voters your way?"

"It's always worked that way for me," Joe said. "We'll be smarter about campaigning and puttin' the money to work. We are not stupid about how to do this even though Jeep got in the first lick. I've won a lot of elections, every one I've been in."

"Everyone learns from mistakes if it's not too late," Chickie said. "As you well know, Mr. Bruno sent two guys to Logan after you lost to deliver a message to Delucci's supporters on your behalf. They had a car wreck near Charleston. Both killed."

"Me an' Skis heard that," Joe said.

"Might not have been an accident," Chickie said.

"That stretch of Lens Creek Mountain is deadly, especially when it's foggy," Skis said, "and you can't see what's comin' at you in the dark."

"Do you think it was Delucci?" Joe asked Chickie.

"Not him, personal," Chickie said. "The kid ain't stupid. We don't know what happened. We're checking it out. I was told Louie's pistol was out, and he fired a couple of rounds through the rear window."

"Murder?" Joe wondered. ACMU elections had never been that rough. Murder was a big deal. You could try to hush it up, but Joe knew it never disappeared. Somebody always knew your secret. Joe Hunt blinked. "Murder!"

"Never saw that kind of meanness in Delucci," Skis said. "Of course, I was never at an occasion when I might have seen it."

"People do what they think they got to do," Chickie said. "Five hundred ain't a problem. If you need more, it'll be there."

"Well, jeez. Thanks, Chickie," Joe said.

"But you need to understand about our investment—your bank, the American Bank of Washington, the ABW," Chickie said.

"Sure," Joe said. "I told Foster to tell Mr. Bruno the Union would give him three seats out of nine on the board by November 15th."

Joe Hunt had negotiated six national contracts with the BCCG coal operators who everyone knew were the hardest asses and ballbusters around. Shit f'ar, Joe thought, this is a piece of cake.

Chickie Siciliano smiled, stubbed out his cigarette and rose from his seat. "Good to meet ya, Joe, Skis," he said, pocketing his lighter and turning toward the door. "Best of luck." He picked up his briefcase.

As a reflex, Joe stood and extended his hand. Chickie smiled. Joe wasn't sure what was happening.

Skis stood, too. As Chickie started walking toward the door, Skis asked: "What does Tony Bruno want?"

Chickie turned toward Skis. "Five seats, including the chairman no later than December 4th, the day before your vote. We will streamline the board to a total of five after the election. Our company will buy all of the Bank's stock at $22, which is a more than fair price. A lot more than fair. We will lend you personally whatever you need for the campaign, in cash. And we will provide other services as needed. As to the 500, if you lose, you figure a way to pay us back quick in one lump like a sugar cube. We're chargin' a little vig -- interest -- win or lose. Lose, and we get paid within two weeks after the election."

"How much is a little interest?" Skis asked.

"Tony hasn't said."

"If I lose, where would I get $500,000?" Joe asked.

"You got your own pension you can get at all at once. Same with money in your savings. You got a house here that you can borrow against. You got a house in Fricktown, free and clear, which ain't much I'll give you that. The Union can vote you some so-long money. Give the Union employees bonuses they donate back to you to pay off your debt. You got ways. Plenty of ways," Chickie answered. "And now you've got an extra incentive—if you win, you don't pay as much."

It was now clear to Joe and Skis that Tony Bruno wanted total ownership and control of the American Bank of Washington—the bank that John L. Lewis had the Union buy in the late '40s with the idea of making it accessible to coal miners. To Skis' knowledge, no coal miner had ever gotten a mortgage or a car loan from the Union's Bank in the ensuing 26 years. The ABW had branched into the Maryland and Virginia suburbs but never into the coalfields.

The American Bank of Washington's headquarters sat on the southeast corner of 14th and G Street, Northwest, on a lot that once stabled White House horses. The Neoclassical Revival design of the 1925 building projected unshakable solidness. Savers had forgotten its bankruptcy in the early '30s. Customers continued to be impressed with its Italian Renaissance banking area above street-level shops. They liked the hand-carved, Italian-walnut counters and the Florentine iron chandelier with 90 light bulbs.

ABW assets had increased as Washingtonians prospered and the federal government expanded during the New Deal, WWII and the post-War years. The ABW had paid low-but-not-unreasonable dividends to its stockholders since the late 1930s. It appeared to be respectable, even a little stodgy.

Skis, who Joe appointed to be the ACMU's liaison with the ABW, pieced together the story of good intentions never fulfilled.

John L. Lewis had always been a business-oriented wheeler-dealer imprisoned as a labor leader. The ABW -- the oldest bank in the District of Columbia and its second largest by assets -- gave him opportunities to build the ACMU institutionally and maintain political influence nationally.

To his relief, Skis discovered that Lewis had not used the Bank to enrich himself. Lewis bought his home -- the historic Lee-Fendall estate in Alexandria, Virginia -- in 1937, using savings and a small mortgage his salary easily covered. He lived there with his wife and daughter until his death in 1969. Lewis had not borrowed from the Bank to accumulate real estate or make shaky loans to friends. Skis understood Lewis's motives: Power, yes; ambition, yes; greed, no.

Lewis found himself in a trap in 1950. The ACMU-organized companies produced coal inefficiently with labor-intensive methods. They were struggling to hold their heating and steam markets against alternative energies -- oil, diesel, natural gas and electricity -- that were cleaner, easier to handle and sometimes cheaper. He decided to use the ABW's resources to buy and sell assets he thought would benefit his Union and the Unionized sector of the coal industry. Mechanization, he reasoned, would save the ACMU and the BCCG. But he knew the cost would be the loss of ACMU mining jobs. Lewis saw no choice other than making ACMU-organized companies more efficient and cost-competitive by substituting machines for labor and keeping wages and benefits low. Accordingly, he had the Bank lend to favored coal operators to buy the machines that threw his members out of work. No one raised an eyebrow when Lewis used ABW money to enable Cleveland industrialist Cyrus Eaton to buy control of non-Union coal companies, which then signed an ACMU contract. Skis knew that not a single ACMU member had any idea about what the Union was doing with the ABW's money.

Using the Bank in this fashion was part of Lewis's strategy to save the BCCG operators from adverse market conditions and keep them from repeating the self-destructive downward spiral of price competition from 20 years earlier. The choice he faced in his trap was simple: Let employers cut employment and wages destructively as they had done in the 1920s and early 1930s or help them manage, shape and offset those cuts to the limited extent he could.

74

Lewis negotiated a contract in 1950 with the ACMU-organized Bituminous Coal Companies Group that supported them through two decades of weak coal demand. In return for signatory companies supporting the Union's new fund for pensions and health care, Lewis encouraged their use of new underground and surface-mining techniques that cut the number of U.S. mineworkers by 75 percent between 1950 and 1970. Lewis understood that labor costs in ACMU mines had to be held down to preserve their markets. During the '50s, he never pushed for large wage increases, never sought reasonable increases in the tonnage royalty that financed ACMU health care and retirement and never challenged the companies when they collaborated in consensual consolidations in violation of federal antitrust laws. To keep BCCG companies competitive, Lewis signed sweetheart deals that allowed favored companies to ignore parts of the Union's contract or pay a reduced royalty to the health and retirement fund. He didn't press Washington for better safety regulations and enforcement. He did next to nothing to demand controls on the black-lung-causing dust that continuous-miners generated.

If Skis could have asked him, Lewis would have said he had walked the least harmful of the predictably damaging paths in front of him. Had he not done what he did with the 1950 contract and the ABW's money, the BCCG companies would have either gone out of business or quit the ACMU contract en masse. Any misuse of the ABW, Lewis would have argued, was forced on him by circumstances. Better a remnant Union, than no Union.

For their part, BCCG operators let Lewis control the pension and health fund that depended on their payment of a $1-per-ton royalty. At first, the ACMU's plan provided cradle-to-grave medical services to miners and their families. But as royalty income declined with falling BCCG production, services were reduced and benefits cut. A chain of ACMU-built, coalfield hospitals was sold. The pension fund was never adequately supported. ACMU retirees limped along on $75 a month for bituminous miners and $30 for those in the anthracite.

BCCG employers never complained about Lewis's personal control of the pension and health fund, which they knew was supposed to be jointly and honestly administered. They didn't care what he did as long as he contained their labor costs. Few people knew that Lewis and then Joe Hunt parked the miners' pension and health monies in non-interest-bearing ABW accounts. Had the tonnage royalty been prudently invested in stocks and bonds, both pensions and health-care benefits could have been raised. Neither Lewis nor Hunt was ever asked to explain this policy. No one -- coal operator, miner or prosecutor -- ever sought to stop their continuing and obvious violations of the Taft-Hartley Labor-Management Relations Act of 1947, which required joint administration of health and pension monies.

After Joe Hunt became president in 1960, Skis became convinced that ACMU members were getting little benefit from owning the Bank. He persuaded Joe to stop using the ABW to buy coal companies and financing job-cutting mining equipment. But they agreed the ACMU had to continue Lewis's practice of keeping wages and benefits low to help unionized companies stay competitive. They also decided to go along with the ABW board's practice of making unsecured loans to favored Washington business and political interests. "We're buyin' political protection," Skis told Joe. "We don't want this can of worms opened, ever."

Skis liked the idea of the ABW setting up coalfield banks for its members. Those branches could serve ACMU members and make money for the Union in doing so. Joe liked it, too. By the late 1960s, however, both men concluded it would be too hard to drive the Bank in a new direction. They feared that unwinding the old ways would end up with the Bank unraveling or, worse, going haywire. "The ABW is like nitroglycerin," Skis told Joe. "We have to handle it with kid gloves."

Skis knew that the conflict-riddled relationship between the ACMU and the Bank was ignored by Democrats and Republicans alike owing to ACMU cash given to politicians in both parties. Skis had hand-delivered contributions to key committee chairmen and coalfield legislators. He knew it stunk before he did it, while he was doing it and after he'd done it. The whole ABW thing—stink, stank, stunk, he thought.

Once Tony Bruno took over the ABW, Joe had a good idea what would follow. He and other Mob leaders would run dirty money from gambling and drugs through the Bank to scrub it clean. Loans would be made to Mafia fronts—hotels, casinos, swindles, scams and crooked outfits. The ABW's board would forgive selective bad loans, particularly to its own board members but not in sufficient amounts to trigger federal scrutiny. Payoffs to District politicians and those with Congressional and White House power would rise. But the Mob would be smart about how much it misused the Bank, which was much more valuable functioning than looted. It would, Joe thought, be quietly criminalized without giving notice or offense. The Bank might be made of marble with a guard at every door, he thought, but no one was guarding against what would be happening in the boardroom.

Joe Hunt had never been above using the ABW for what he had rationalized as "a little finaglin' for the benefit of the membership." But a sale to Siciliano and Bruno, Joe understood, was more than a little finagling. The Mafia would turn the Bank into a criminal enterprise. On the other hand, so what if the Mob corrupted the ABW after the Union sold it to them? The Union would be out of it with $222 million. It would not be his problem, Joe decided.

And then, as Joe looked at Chickie Siciliano standing in his office, it occurred to him that Bruno wanted both the Bank *and* the ACMU. The cash flow into the fund amounted to about $500 million annually. It held more than $75 million in income-generating investments. Joe figured Bruno would use the ACMU's fund to supplement or even replace the Teamsters Central States Pension Fund as the Mob's piggy bank. Who would care if coal miners got small pensions and few health services? No one would stop the fund from making investments that were never intended to be repaid. Other people's money, coal miners' money, would be free money—to be spent, lost and stolen.

Joe had heard John L. say more than once: "When you're an Anvil, hold you still; when you're a Hammer, strike your Fill."

Tobacco juice welled up in his mouth. The realization came to him: I'm the anvil, and Bruno's the hammer.

Skis looked at Joe. He eyes said that winning this last election isn't worth letting the Mafia inside the ACMU. Get in bed with these guys, and you have to expect they're going to want more than a good night's sleep. Skis wanted out. Stop the deal. He shook his head.

Joe figured he could do a lot for the members with $222 million from the ABW sale. He didn't care what Bruno did with the Bank. He would protect pensions and health care. He still gave a damn about the membership.

"So?" Chickie asked.

"You're makin' me an offer I can't refuse." Joe said the line without irony.

"That 'Godfather' stuff is just Hollywood make-believe from 30 years ago," Chickie said. "No one's gonna blow your brains out on your desk." He laughed.

Joe blinked. Skis cleared his throat. No one said anything.

"We're just business guys," Chickie said. "We're about makin' money for our investors. Like Exxon."

Joe looked at Skis. What choice do I have?

"You came to us," Chickie said. "We didn't come to you."

"Yeah," Joe said.

"It can stop here," Chickie offered, believing that it wouldn't and couldn't.

Joe swallowed, because he couldn't stop it here. "I need your money for the election."

"I guess you do," Chickie said.

"I'll sell the Bank."

"My people want no trouble," Chickie said. "You need to tell me that you understand how this goes down."

"No trouble. I understand. Deal." Joe walked around his desk and shook Chickie's hand.

Chickie smiled. "I'll have my lawyer bring over the paper tomorrow. It will be a sales contract. You'll have what you want for the campaign in the afternoon. In cash. Twenties and fifties. We deliver, just like a pizza joint."

"Cash? That'll be a pile," Skis said.

"Cash," Chickie said. "If the Labor Department or Justice ever asks you where you got $500,000, you say it was from personal savings that you and Skis always kept in your own homes, never in bank accounts. It was *always your own* money. You can spend your own shit however you want."

"So what do we say if they ask about the sale of the Bank to your corporation?" Skis asked.

"It's a clean buy. Straight up. More than fair price. Make sure not to use any of *that* money in your campaign. That's Union money. Keep it separate and clean. We'll get our money back slowly. Remember, our intention is to run the Bank, not skin it."

"I understand," Skis said.

"It's just business. Read the <u>Wall Street Journal</u>," Chickie laughed." And remember. There's no connection between the cash you're spending on your campaign, which is your own money, and your decision to sell the Bank for a fair price."

"No connection," Joe said.

"None whatever," Chickie said.

Jesus Christ, Skis thought.

Joe watched Chickie leave, holding the briefcase that he'd never opened. He wondered what might have been in it. A gun? Would he have blown my brains out? When the door closed, Joe barely had enough time to get to his scuttle and vomit.

He wiped his mouth with his cuff. "I begged."

"Yes, we did," Skis said.

"Haven't heaved like that since I was a kid and Gussie took us underground that first time." Joe wiped his mouth again.

"He's going to screw us bad," Skis said.

Joe wiped his mouth a third time. "Not as bad as Fricktown in '33."

"Different," Skis said.

"I felt his hands on my throat," Joe said.

"You should have," Skis said. "They run a fear game. They get what they want through threats, beatings, arsons and killings. They leech money out of the poor and make everybody pay more for stuff. The Mafia is all about makin' easy money dishonestly. They're straight up thieves. You…we…knew that when you sent Foster up to Bruno."

"They're the only money I can get in time," Joe said. "You know that."

"They want the fund, too." Skis said.

"I'll protect it," Joe said.

"You'll have to squeeze the 500 and interest out of Union money. He'll have that on you. He'll use it to get in our door."

"I'll draw a line," Joe said.

"They cross lines. That's what they do."

"I didn't back down in Fricktown."

Skis remembered. "Look, we could quit now with our heads high. Retire. Let Jeep run the place. If he fucks up, it's on him."

"If we lose or retire," Joe said, "we're out to pasture like a couple of no-count fleabags."

"If we win, we're in bed with the devil," Skis said. "We'd do better to stop here. No deal, retire and forget about it."

Joe thought about this path.

"You're right, but I can't leave," Joe said. "I'm afraid of what's out there."

"I'm afraid of what we let in here."

Chapter 7

Cinderella Holler, Comfort, W.Va., October 7, 1975

"Daddy," he whispered. "Daddy?"

The man stirred in his sleep. Each breath sucked in his thin cheeks. His pale skin stretched tightly over his skull, making his veins prominent like exposed plumbing. The arms that had once held his son, lifted mining timbers and built additions to this very house, spread flat on his bed, palms down. His barrel chest -- now just boney staves -- rose and fell in ragged, labored rhythm. A soft gurgle swam beside each breath. An oxygen tank and generator sat close to his head. His dresser top was crammed with plastic pill containers, tissues and aerosol inhalers. The bedroom was close and hot. It smelled of medicines and decay; the finish line was not far off.

Jim Delucci opened his eyes. He took a few seconds to focus and get oriented. His son sat next to him on the bed. Jeep took his hand.

"I beat 'im, Daddy," Jeep said. "Kicked ol' Joe's butt with almost 57 percent in the first round."

Jim coughed and tried to clear his chest and throat. He coughed again. "Sonofabitch deserves worse than 'at. What time it is?"

Jeep checked the clock on the bedside cabinet. "Tuesday mornin', 'bout nine."

"I shoulda been at work for an hour," Jim said.

"You been out for several years."

"At 58, I shoulda been at work, mechanicin' the damn equipment."

"That's right," Jeep said, "you shoulda been at work mechanicin' the damn equipment."

"Well, open the blinds and lemme see the damn day."

The one-story house was set in a bench cut at the mouth of Cinderella Holler in Comfort. Jeep pulled the curtains. The bedroom faced east into a high wall. Light without any October warmth seeped into the room. From his bed, Jim Delucci could not see his grapevines or his workshop.

"Too late to prune 'em now," Jim said.

"You'll get to 'em in March like always," Jeep said.

"Yeah, sure. They didn't bear much this year, which is what I'm bitchin' about. You gotta cut 'em back early to get a crop."

"I'm sorry, Daddy. I didn't have the time, what with the campaign and all."

"Your mother would have done 'em right if she could."

"She would have."

"Fine woman to have put up with me all these years."

"Fine mother. Fine wife."

"If it wouldn't be for her, I couldn't make it through a day."

"She's a blessin'," Jeep said.

"Now this other—Joe Hunt. I'da give anythin' to have seen his face when the count came in official. Now boy, I'll tell you. You best watch out. You wounded a big ol' boar bear. He's cornered. That's when he'll rear up so he can get both paws and his teeth workin'. Fetch me that Crisco spit can yonder."

Jeep lifted the can to the side of the bed, and his father tried to roll toward it. Jim jerked twice in that effort without success. Jeep gently pulled his father on his side. Jim coughed hard, then fell into a series of dry, breath-robbing hacks in an effort to both catch his breath and clear his throat. His eyes widened. Sweat popped out on his forehead. His hands flailed as if he were losing his grip on a ladder. Jeep reached quickly for the oxygen mask and placed it over his Dad's mouth and nose. He opened the valve. It took several minutes for Jim to settle. He dropped the mask off the side of his bed.

"Fuckin' black lung," Jim Delucci wheezed. "Can't even spit proper. Damn poor way to die."

Book Two

Chapter 8

New York, Early Spring, 1968

New York was cold that March, but Jeffrey Becker was not.

He was in his last semester at Columbia University. He'd been accepted at its Law School for the fall. His parents expected him to take that next step. But he was thinking of other things.

THE DRAFT!

Becker spent most of that spring in constant agitation, worrying and angry about what to do once he lost his student deferment. President Lyndon Johnson had ended that privileged haven in the summer of 1967 for most college graduates who wanted to continue their schooling. Becker had to make a decision. He knew that.

He wasn't a pacifist—so filing for conscientious-objector status was out. Faking pacifism was distasteful, because it was a lie. Alternative service was not granted to draft-eligible men who objected to a specific war. He understood the rationale for that policy; he even agreed with it. Any contrivance he used to get out of going meant that someone would be filling "his" boots.

Becker had studied American foreign policy under William T.R. Fox, Roger Hilsman, Jr., Warner Schilling and Zbigniew Brzezinski—all of whom supported America's War in Vietnam to one degree or another. Among the many things he didn't understand that spring was why these professors were still backing the War when the methods of analysis they taught should have led them to skepticism if not opposition. Maybe they, like President Johnson, still believed in the domino theory—the idea that any loss of territory to Communists anywhere would inevitably topple all territories everywhere one after another with Communists invading San Francisco and New York sooner or later. When Johnson ran as "the peace candidate" in 1964, he said nothing about escalating the War and his commitment to the domino theory. Those opinions surfaced after he was elected.

None of these professors -- the core of Columbia's foreign-policy expertise -- seemed to understand that the January, 1968, Tet Offensive was a sign that South Vietnamese insurgents, both nationalists and Communists, along with the North Vietnamese had given notice. They were, in John Kennedy's words, willing to "…pay any price, bear any burden, meet any hardship, support any friend, oppose any foe…" to assure their survival and reunite their country. If one Vietnam meant a Communist Vietnam, that would be to a large degree the choice of the Vietnamese themselves. Whichever side prevailed, Vietnamese on the losing side would suffer the dreadful consequences of their loyalties.

Becker did not understand why his professors did not use their embrace of *Realpolitik* to reach conclusions about the War that followed from seeing politics as conflicts of available power. The power the North Vietnamese had was superior to America's—it was their willingness to persist in their struggle for independence from foreign occupiers regardless of its human cost. America was not willing to match that power. Becker didn't see much difference between the aims and methods of the National Liberation Front and the American colonials who made victory too costly over time for the far more powerful British Empire. Had America been fighting in Vietnam 100 years in the past, his professors would have analyzed it as an unwinnable war with an unwinnable strategy for a questionable goal in a country that was not central to our national interest against a foe we did not comprehend on behalf of an undemocratic and not very popular regime being fought for reasons that were unpersuasive to more and more of America's citizens.

But it wasn't 1868, and Columbia's foreign-policy academics were too imprisoned by the Cold War to see beyond its bannered slogans. They found themselves crewing a doomed ship of war, a conclusion they would reach shortly before it sunk.

In April, 1968, 48,000 men were drafted, four times the number conscripted in that month a year earlier.

THE GYM

Columbia was planning to build a multi-story gym in City-owned Morningside Park, which separated Harlem from the University on Morningside Heights. The Park was a narrow, 30-acre strip that ran between West 110th St. on the south to West 123rd St. on the north. Frederick Law Olmstead and Calvert Vaux designed it in the late 19th Century. Much of it was occupied by a steep cliff on its western border. In Becker's first-hand observations, it was less a park and more a dangerous place that Harlem children were told to avoid. In decent weather, it attracted a share of the City's homeless. Paper-bag drinking and drug deals were common sights. Columbia students were told to stay out of the Park at all times. It was known for crime.

As a teaspoon-of-sugar concession to its black neighbors, Columbia belatedly offered to designate the bottom floor of the proposed gym, which opened at street level facing Harlem, solely for community use. Columbia students would use the top floors. The facility was cast by its critics as a "taking" of public land "from the black community." Columbia's proposed concession would result in building a functionally, physically and racially segregated facility, mostly for its students and partly for Harlem. The "gift to Harlem" was an afterthought, a late bribe to mute the opposition that had arisen. Had the Columbia administration been smarter and more attuned to community politics, it would have never chosen that site.

The Columbia chapter of the Students for a Democratic Society (SDS) played on white student guilt to stoke opposition to the gym. Black students, who had little to do with SDS and were dealing with their own questions of racial and community loyalty as well as their semi-marginal place on the Columbia campus, made stopping the gym *their* issue.

Becker guessed that Harlem kids would have loved to have had access to a first-rate, free gym despite Columbia students playing above them. But these likely beneficiaries were never asked to express their opinion. The University's administration never mobilized support for the gym -- in one form or another -- among West Harlem's leaders who, accordingly, gave it no political cover regardless of the gym's benefits. It was easy to see the gym as a white move into a black space, which it was. Opponents framed the gym as Columbia's latest occupation of local real estate—a practice that had evoked opposition in the crowded neighborhood for two decades.

Becker believed that both Columbia and West Harlem could use a new gym, but nothing about its operational segregation smelled right to him. He laughed when he thought that Columbia might even be pushed into building two gyms, side-by-side—physically separate and absolutely equal.

The gym's contractor had erected a chain-link fence around the construction site in early 1968 before beginning work.

It was a perfect political target.

THE INSTITUTE FOR DEFENSE ANALYSES (IDA)

In 1967, SDS member Bob Feldman discovered in Columbia's International Law Library that the University had secretly affiliated with and was institutionally sponsoring the IDA, the Pentagon's principal weapons-research organization and a central clearinghouse for university-based, defense-related research. Columbia was one of about a dozen universities that formed the IDA's umbrella consortium. After SDS revealed the IDA relationship, it came out that a handful of Columbia professors were secretly doing classified research. Some of this research was directly involved in developing electronic battlefield technology for use in Vietnam.

The University had a growing financial interest in expanding defense-related research. Almost 50 percent of the University's budget, about $60 million, came from the federal government in 1966-1967. This involved 770 contracts, of which the 18 classified projects accounted for almost $14 million. The IDA's financial connection to the University was not that large, but the institutional connections were meaningful. Columbia President Grayson Kirk served on the IDA's board. The University's administration had denied any IDA connection until Feldman found the proof. The Administration did not want to cut off either defense research or classified research. It appeared the University applied no ethical screens to faculty research projects, or, at least, no screens that would rule out "make-war" investigations as SDS might define them.

The IDA was largely a symbolic issue for most students that spring, as Becker saw it. The Columbia-IDA relationship bore the concentrated burden of the War, which a majority of students opposed though not stridently. The IDA was an immediate Columbia connection to the War, despite it being a modest link. Nonetheless, many Columbia and Barnard students saw "their" school supporting policies they either opposed or found troubling. SDS wanted the University to disaffiliate from the IDA.

Disaffiliation would not have materially diminished IDA's work, but it would have reduced the authority of administrators to manage University affairs as they saw fit. Columbia's management in 1968 -- staffed principally by white men in their 50s and 60s -- was not prepared to have faculty and students prescribe what it could and could not do. So a symbolic issue reflecting anti-War sentiment actually struck at the heart of who would run the University and the standards that would be followed. The University refused to consider modifying its ties with the IDA. Columbia, said Herbert A. Deane, vice-provost of the Graduate Faculties, was not a democratic institution and would not be governed democratically by votes of students and faculty.

Columbia SDS now had an issue that connected the widespread fear and hatred of the draft and the ever-more disturbing War to Columbia—its political-science administrators, its secrecy, its financial ties to big business, its policy and technology research for the Pentagon and its School of International Affairs, which fed 40 percent of its graduates into government service. SDS could do nothing about the War or the draft, but it might be able to make disaffiliation a surrogate, polarizing issue on campus.

Becker had gone to a couple of SDS meetings that winter, but he was discouraged and bored by the interminable and impenetrable debates over Marxist arcana. He was impatient with sifting all thought through mutually exclusive Marxist-Leninist sieves. No one outside these sects could understand the fevers motivating the debaters. Becker found himself thinking that this experience was what he might expect to witness in an ecumenical seminary where a dozen religions competed for student loyalty. He came to realize that the point at issue in these debates was often not the point at issue. He did not feel comfortable with the red-diaper contingent at the center of Columbia SDS or the various Marxisms that twisted them around each other like choking vines.

Becker saw himself as a small "d" democrat who thought bigness in and of itself -- whether capitalist bigness or socialist bigness, private bigness or government bigness -- was a driver of many social problems. Wherever institutions, governments, corporations and individuals got too big, outcomes were skewed toward their benefit. How big was too big— that was a question Becker could not answer.

Still, SDS for all its oddness was the principal student group that was protesting the War. Becker felt he was obliged to say and do something publicly to add his voice. He, like others of his generation, did not want to be a "good German" by going along, keeping quiet, not seeing what was to be seen and hoping things weren't as bad as they appeared. So he put his name on its membership list and got a phone call every couple of months from a Barnard student telling him that a general membership meeting was scheduled for the next evening.

Becker watched with wonder and amusement the rise of Robert "Rooky" Gondleman into the SDS leadership. Gondleman in his first year had roomed across the hall in Furnald. Becker, a junior, remembered him as a bookish loner, apolitical and timid with an odd fascination for baseball numbers. Gondleman installed his chess board and timer in the lounge where he would play anyone who could stand being humiliated. It was the only place Becker saw Gondleman show aggression. He seemed to need victory, crushing victory, which always ended with condescension toward the loser. Becker never played Gondleman, but he did talk to him as an older student to a younger one. Becker watched Gondleman glue himself to SDS politics at Columbia as tightly as he had once bonded with a chess board. In the substitution, however, Gondleman moved from love for a game to hatred for "The System" and its expression at Columbia. That hatred now defined him.

The gym and the IDA had become campus issues that provoked students to think about their relationship to timely questions of race, as manifested in the Gym, and war. Gondleman and SDS pushed a simple "No" to both. What distinguished SDS from others who felt the same way was its willingness to upset Columbia's business as usual, to force the administration either to change its policies or punish those demanding change. Punishment might lead to more dissent. Disruption made SDS points differently and more powerfully than petitions, referenda, letters to the editor and marches in circles around the campus. The right to disrupt became SDS's core issue.

86

Becker's issues were the War and the Draft. Mucking around with Columbia's connections to the IDA would do nothing to revise either one. Becker knew that both the gym and the IDA connection came out of the University's decision-making structure that vested almost all power in the office of its president. Reforming and democratizing that structure, Becker thought, would change the content of University decisions. Becker saw no hope that Columbia on its own would suddenly broaden its methods for making policy and big decisions.

While the Columbia lion looked formidable, it was vulnerable. Inflexibility was its weakness. It could not adapt to, or partially co-opt, the SDS message.

Gondleman, Becker thought, had a point when he said Columbia would change only when it was stopped in its tracks.

Chapter 9

New York, Columbia University, March-April, 1968

Allyson Pickering spent most Friday evenings in the winter of 1967-1968 putting her Quaker, anti-war principles into practice as a waitress at the FTA Coffee House near Fort Dix, New Jersey. She served sweet cider and highly glazed donuts to bewildered 18-year-old draftees from Georgia, Ohio and inner-city Detroit. Her customers were not quite sure what to make of the aging, cigarette-husky altos from Manhattan singing "I Ain't Marching Anymore." They knew if *they* refused, they'd be court-martialed and imprisoned. If the FTA could persuade some to lower their level of cooperation with an Army they did not want to be in, a step toward conscious, non-violent resistance would be effected.

Allyson was bait. She sat with conscripted privates, knee to knee, at the four-person tables talking about high school, girlfriends, younger brothers and, when she could work it in, in-service applications for conscientious-objector status. The problem these conscripts faced was that few, if any, were either religious or philosophical pacifists. They were not opposed to war in any form. She admitted to them that getting a CO while in the Army was even harder than getting one prior to being drafted. She also admitted that any applicant might be harassed as soon as his application was filed. So she and others from Bryn Mawr, Rutgers and Barnard found themselves doing very little anti-war proselytizing and a lot of just listening. She gently deflected their inelegant propositions, saying she had a boyfriend. And in a manner of speaking, she did—Winthrop "Trip" Pennington.

Allyson admitted she was amused, despite thinking the scene before her was even dumber than ordinary college-boy dopey. Trip had never struck her with a thunderbolt, but he did keep her entertained. He had an easy style that was familiar, one she'd known on the Main Line. He was smart and good-looking. He played sports, liked parties, majored in finance and grew up in Connecticut. He got along with his parents and displayed no interest in the existential doubts that were the medium of exchange within "meaningful relationships" on the Columbia University campus in the late winter of 1967-1968. The War in Vietnam was not personal; he had a "trick knee" that would keep him out. He did believe the War was not well-considered. Losses, in business and in war, should be cut, he said. Everyone deserved civil rights in America, including Negroes. Trip had solved the question, "Who am I?" It was a burden he'd never felt the need to carry. He was his father's son and as of his 18th birthday owned a two-acre lot on his parents' private road. He'd always been considered "a nice guy," according to the Darien girls Allyson consulted. He was not gross or out of control. He was courteous, kind, sociable, and he liked to have a good time. The word she'd heard was that he'd be a pretty faithful husband and a responsible father. He was, however, known to drink a little too much.

Trip was preparing to jump atop his fraternity's billiard table. It was Saturday night. The party had started a few hours earlier. The drinking had begun a few hours before that. On other Saturday nights, he'd done swan dives from the fireplace mantle onto a pile of mattresses and ridden a dining-hall tray down the main staircase. On this night, he was balancing a beer-filled mug on his head.

Allyson gave him her bemused smile as she sat a little primly on the cracked, green-leather couch that had been donated by an aging brother. House legend said he had once taken a reigning Miss Vermont on it in the waiting room of his father's Burlington law office. When the brother retired, he shipped his couch to the House on West 114th Street between Amsterdam and Broadway, with a note: "This couch works magic. Be inspired." Dates were told the story of Big Green on first entering.

The Rolling Stones pounded and pummeled. A strobe light pulsed through the dimness. Cigarette smoke mixed with marijuana, mixed with incense. Couples danced, even the mechanical engineers.

Allyson felt herself tipping from amusement to boredom. She had lost interest in her beer. She waved a "Let's get on with it." to Trip.

Jeffrey Becker watched her from the other side of the room. He, too, nursed a beer. He munched on M&Ms. He knew Allyson from a distance. Becker knew Trip from freshman year. Becker was an invited guest, not a fraternity brother. He caught her eye. She smiled with resignation. She always smiled when he saw her on campus up for the weekend. He'd heard that Allyson and Trip might be more than fun dates.

Trip was ready to launch. The crowd stopped dancing and began to gather around him and the table, clapping and chanting "Go! Go! Go!" He steadied the mug on his head. He took a deep breath, which nearly knocked him to the floor. He waved to Allyson who lifted her eyebrows and grimaced encouragement. With great deliberateness, he let loose a cleansing bellow of a burp. Applause followed. He gathered himself and visualized success. He jumped.

Trip was coordinated and athletic, but he was also more than a little bagged.

Both feet landed on the table's cushion, but the balance of his weight trailed. The mug tipped backward. Beer poured over his head and down his back. The mug shattered on the floor. He windmilled his arms. He teetered forward and then flipped back. He landed flat and spread-eagled. His nicely shaped head thumped against the parquet. A girl from Barnard gasped. A few fraternity brothers moved forward.

C. Chase Brooks, III, yelled, "Good show."

Trip lay still.

"Lucky he didn't land on the damn mug," Chase added. "It was a House heirloom from Nixon's first term."

Two pre-meds were rousted from the second-floor television room. They revived Trip with ammonia scavenged from the mop closet and carried him to his bed. They determined that he'd suffered a mild concussion, which he'd probably survive.

The party lost its energy. In twos, the crowd straggled and lurched toward the bedrooms.

"Leaving?" Becker asked Allyson as she got her things together.

"What does it look like? What do you suggest? Curl up at the foot of his bed for 24 hours?"

"No, I suggest leaving," he said. "In fact I suggest I walk you to wherever you're going. It's after 12."

She considered him for a moment. "Are you shit-faced?" she asked.

"No, ma'am," he said.

"Why not? Scared of it?"

"Just don't like the taste. Double Scotch on the rocks is my drink, hold the Scotch."

"Lame," she said, putting on her coat. "I can stay with a girlfriend on 106th and Riverside. We've done this before in similar circumstances. Okay, I accept your gallant offer." She smiled at him and threw in a self-mocking curtsy.

They walked without hurry in the unseasonably warm March night. The super-bright, crime-prevention street lights bathed them in a yellowy whiteness.

"Who are you?" she asked without any preliminaries.

"Jeff Becker. Jeffrey. Friend of Trip."

"I know that much," she said with impatience.

"Well, I'm a pre-law senior. Not sure I want to be a lawyer or go to law school. Have a couple of acceptance letters. Grew up in Pittsburgh. Not a fraternity brother, but sometimes I go to the parties. More interested in politics than that crowd. Against the War more than they are. Dad has a scrap yard. Mom is the bookkeeper and does volunteer work. Adult literacy. She's active in the community. Only child. Like books. Have a sense that the world is not fair and structured that way."

"You look semi-disheveled. SDS?" she asked.

"I've gone to some rallies at The Sundial. I'm on their call list. I don't have much patience for the internal debates."

90

"My mother joined the Left in the '30s when she was at Bryn Mawr. A lot of girls from good families felt guilty about The Depression. Some joined the Communist Party like my aunt Maude who insisted on Vassar, which, I suppose, explains her behavior. Some traipsed along beside. Good pearls and the noble oppressed—that is my mother, Jane Andrews Pickering. Her nickname is Boo."

"What about you?" he asked.

"Not sure," she said, stopping and looking directly in his eyes. "I'm a Quaker. Pacifist. I hate the War."

Becker fumbled. "I think Trip's not much of anything. More Rockefeller Republican than Lindsay Democrat I suppose."

"Like Bogart," she said, "he's a drunk, a global citizen when it comes to politics."

"I've only seen him drink on weekends. He's a good student. Makes good grades. He'll do well in finance. I think he'll go into the family business. He'll make money. Life will be pleasant. You'll be able to buy a new Volvo station wagon every year. Your future could be four doors, four speeds and four kids."

"That was mean," she said. "Random calamities can strike anyone. Not to mention things we do to harm ourselves. Do you have a type of law in mind?"

"Maybe, legal aid to get started. Public interest. Torts—personal injury cases. Fairness interests me. Civil liberties. Not sure after that."

"I see." What Allyson saw was a smart kid who hadn't yet set a career path or been consumed by the turbulence of their times. It was hard, she knew, to keep your eye on a career while Big Things were happening all around you. She, too, wrestled with the same foes.

"Well, you're bigger than you look from a distance," she said.

"You're prettier closer upper."

Allyson Pickering smiled. She looked at Becker again. She took his arm.

Becker stopped at an all-night fruit stand near the corner of 110th and Broadway. He bought a small bunch of green grapes.

"I hope you're not going to start tossing them in the air and catching them in your mouth."

"Who promised anything about catching them?" he laughed. "Actually, I was hoping you might feed them to me one at a time as I recline on your silk pillows."

"Moving right along are we? Think you're on a roll, do you?" She put her head on his shoulder for a second.

"If you don't ask, you don't get," he answered. He put his arm around her.

Allyson snorted, then a giggle came out. Allyson hadn't giggled like that since before her first women's liberation meeting more than six months earlier.

They walked down Broadway to 106th feeding grapes to each other. They turned toward Riverside Drive and stopped in front of a four-story walk-up on the north side of the street, one building away from Riverside Park.

"Carolyn's a receptionist at The New Yorker," Allyson said. "Her Dad knows the cartoon editor. Went to Sarah Lawrence. Spent a lot of time there with Jane Austen. Truly fucked her up what with, I'm paraphrasing, if a woman has the misfortune of knowing anything, she should conceal it as much as she can. Now she has a crush on William Hamilton."

"Great cartoonist," Becker said.

"He likes to poke his own kind," Allyson said. "Well..," she said, offering her hand, "thanks for the escort service."

Becker was surprised. "Some roll," he muttered.

"Let's not be greedy," she said.

"Why not?" he asked.

"It shreds our moral fiber," she said.

"I certainly understand why our moral fiber needs to be conserved."

"I'm not about a roll in the hay," she said without humor.

Becker felt slapped. And then he realized that a roll in the hay was what he'd had in mind.

"Sorry," he said. "Anyway, I can be called again for long-range patrol and escort duty."

She took the last grape and put it in his mouth. Then she buzzed for entrance, got the return and went inside.

"Ask again," she laughed.

He watched her. She smiled at him just before she vanished into the stairs.

Becker walked back to his apartment on West 110th, trying to puzzle out what had just happened and why he felt light.

The next weekend Allyson rode the train to New York to visit him. They had lunch on Saturday at a down-scale Hungarian restaurant at Amsterdam and West 111th. She went along with goulash though it was not a dish that had ever appeared on her mother's table.

"A movie tonight?" Becker asked. He poured a teaspoon of salt onto the slick table top next to his plate. He concentrated on the salt, swirling it around with his finger.

Allyson wondered if he were communicating in symbolic language. Was this an IQ test in linguistics? Was this some MENSA trick Columbia boys knew? If so, she didn't get it.

Becker made a little pile and then carefully propped the salt shaker upright at a tilt. Then he blew away the salt until the shaker was held in place by a single grain.

He looked up at her, grinning.

"Is this leaning phallus a metaphor for something? Are you warning me before we start that you're out of plumb?"

Becker gave a three-snort laugh. "Maybe both. Don't you think it's cool that this relatively huge thing can be balanced on one tiny cube of salt?"

"I'm bowled over," she said. "One person can carry a mountain if she's in the right position. Is this your way of wooing a Bryn Mawr senior? Do you think I haven't seen this before?"

"Have you?"

"No."

"Okay, then. If you want to look in a mirror, stick with Trip. Maybe you share ancestors."

"You have a mean streak. Look, I know who he is. I'm not stupid about boys. Most are bad around women."

"If you're a woman, then I'm a man," he said.

"Is that a joke?"

"Is feminism your way of taking your good looks off the table?" he asked.

"I'll age well. Good ankles. Good face bones. Firm convictions. I won't get fat, because I play with food more than eat it. I'm good enough to get by. But I'm not the 'toppest quality shit' on the shelf. My Jewish roommate, Shelly Eisenberg, says her Dad, who sells retail in Brooklyn, puts it that way."

"You'll do…for me," he said.

"Let's not get ahead of ourselves, Becker. Control your hormones."

"I want to sail into port under a true flag."

"Your flag is waving free at the top of your mast," she said. She pointed at the salt shaker. "So this miniature diorama is a signal after all."

Becker was off-balance. She was fast dancing, and he was doing a box step learned at Sunnyside Elementary and not upgraded since.

"I guess it's saying -- if it's saying anything, which I'm not claiming that it is, because I've never thought about it saying anything -- that there doesn't seem to be a straight up and down anymore in America. Balance is hard to find. Everything's crazy, wobbling on a narrow base."

Allyson looked at him. He didn't look demented. His sandy hair was long but not girlish or drawn in a ponytail. He had a mustache that did not need a mascara pencil to darken it. His blue eyes were bluer than she had thought they'd be. He was close to 6-3, she'd calculated this against her 5-10, reached in her above-the-calf, two-inch-heel boots. That would work, she thought. He probably played pick-up basketball but wasn't good enough to make a decent high-school team. He didn't twitch, scratch, smoke cigarettes or get stupid drunk. He didn't seem to be a pothead. He didn't look like he came from family money, but he had managed to get through Columbia so he couldn't be overly stupid. He hadn't tried to show off intellectually or put her down. He seemed normal enough. So why was she interested? She had run through several versions of normal and conventional. She had dated Trip in more iterations than she wanted to remember. There was something just a little off about Becker, off-intriguing, not off-putting. But she couldn't quite put her finger on it, or her dagger through it or her whole heart in it. Something.

"'Everything's crazy!'" she said. "Is that the best you can come up with after almost four years in the Department of Public Law and Government at Columbia University?"

"Pretty much," he said. "Political science, as it's being taught, does not explain what's going on in American politics right now. I'm not sure what does."

"'Yes, well, everybody in Casablanca has problems. Ours may work out,'" she said.

"Casablanca's an odd movie," Becker said. "Everyone lies in it. Ilsa lies to Rick in Paris by not telling him she's married. She lies again when she says she will join him on the last train to Marseille. She doesn't tell her husband, Victor, the truth about her relationship with Rick even when he asks her directly. She doesn't tell Victor that she loves Rick more than she loves him. Rick lies to himself that he doesn't care about anyone except himself. Then he reverses and helps Jan, the young Bulgarian, win at roulette to spare his wife having to sleep with Captain Renault. He lies to Renault about his plan to get Ilsa and Victor onto the Lisbon plane by boasting that he and she will be using the letters of transit. He lies to Victor at the end when he says that it's all over between him and Ilsa while he knows that he's sending her off with a husband she doesn't love. Renault lies at Rick's saloon when he announces that it is to be closed because gambling is taking place. Then he lies to the police when he covers for Rick after Rick shoots Major Strasser. Rick and Ilsa lie to themselves about how they feel to each other except in the scene in his office. And Victor lies to himself that his wife loves him. The ending is built on more lies, not fewer. Can truth emerge from this tangled mess?"

"I think you've been through this review before," she said. "It doesn't sound impromptu. Is this your idea of a line to get me in bed? Has it worked before?"

"I was just riffing on the movie," Becker insisted. "But nobody seems to see it the way I do."

"I will keep in mind that your instincts run counter to those held by the vast majority of Americans," Allyson said. "What you have to understand is that 'Casablanca' is a classic movie...for men. It feeds all of your goofball notions about war, sacrifice and the role of women. Ilsa is no more than a tug-of-war object between two older men. Rick cedes her honorably to her husband who will possess her physically without possessing her emotionally. Women would not -- could not -- have written this screenplay. Only men. The lying between men is typical. Women lying to men is self-protective. Men lying to women is what you do to get what you want."

Becker said nothing, just looked at her. "Maybe I should flee now before I get in over my head."

"Up to you."

"Take it or leave it, huh?"

"It's always like that," Allyson said, "no matter what is said."

Becker looked at her hard. He started to rise.

She hesitated, then put her hand on his arm. "I'm not this bad…all the time."

He stood up. "This doesn't feel right to me."

"I don't want to get hurt," she said. "With you, I can get hurt."

"Same here."

"It will never be as good as it is at the start," Allyson said. "I don't think you're my Prince Charming, but maybe you'll do."

"You can't start with the idea that it will fail," he said.

"I know you're right, but…"

"…but this could get serious."

"Yes," she said. "It could. The more serious, the more it will hurt."

Becker sat down. "Take it or leave it," he said.

"I don't like an ultimatum. I need to think this out," she said. "My women's group would, to a woman, walk."

"There's the door," he said, jerking his head toward the door behind him. "Don't stay if you don't want to. This isn't math. You can weigh this and that, but that's only part of the answer."

"Okay," Allyson said softly with her eyes on the salt shaker.

"It's not going to work if I'm arguing you into it," Becker said.

"Okay," Allyson repeated. "Maybe, I'm arguing you into it."

"You have a funny way of arguing," Becker said.

"There's one thing," she said. "I need space. And don't set this up as a choice between you and feminism."

"If you define men as the enemy, what else can I become?" he asked.

"We'll see," she said. "I don't know."

It occurred to Becker -- he would remember having this thought whenever he mulled over Allyson Pickering in the months and years that followed -- that he should leave, then and there. She was being pulled in too many directions to allow a full-faith-and-credit walk with him. He felt a pall of her feminism fall over them. He felt mostly innocent of what offended her, but, he conceded, maybe he wasn't.

So he waited for his goulash. If you don't play, you can't win, he told himself.

"Maybe, I *am* looking for Prince Charming," she offered.

"In that case, let's reexamine Trip," he said.

"You're right. No Prince is always charming. There is no magic kingdom and live happily ever after. I know. Still."

"Anyway," Becker said, changing the subject, "you're right about 'Casablanca.' I've never thought about it from a feminist perspective. Does its 'maleness' make it a bad movie?"

"I guess it's a good movie with a bad message between the lines," she said. Lecturing Becker on feminist film criticism was not exactly what she wanted to do at that moment. "It wouldn't work flipped around, two 'important' women tugging over a man who has nothing but looks."

They laughed, and that got them out of the hole they had dug.

"'You're all right,'" he said to her, quoting Eddie in 'To Have Have Not.' "'She can come, Harry. It's okay with me.'"

"I see you haven't totally wasted your college years," Allyson said.

"I've spent an increasing amount of time thinking about things other than classes," he said. "The draft is at the top of the list. Other things, too—civil rights, poverty…even women."

"I'm sure you've been thinking about women," she said. "Salt shakers, too. I see you're all worked up about a cube of salt. What's your point?"

"Things balance on something real. They can balance on a small truth but not big lies."

Allyson looked at Becker. "You may be smarter than you appear."

"I'm not taking that as a compliment," Becker said.

"Good. I'm hedging," she said. "But I should have said it differently, because I mean it differently."

"Okay. I'll understand it differently. I'm not sure I have a choice."

"You have a choice. We always have choices…until the end."

The waitress arrived with their goulash. Allyson stirred it around her bowl like a potentially explosive mixture. Becker sprinkled a tablespoon of paprika on it, then ate enthusiastically, wiping the inside of his bowl with bread.

"You have the table manners of a lumberjack," she said. "Didn't your mother tell you about no elbows on the table, no using bread as a clean-up sponge, no eating with your fork or spoon in your left hand?"

"She did," he said. "I even know how to set a place with three forks to the left of the charger plus the oyster fork to the right of the three spoons to the right of the charger, not to mention three knives and four glasses—water, champagne, red or white wine and sherry. Napkin on the charger, not under the knives."

"So?" she asked.

"It's not important to me, but I can do that if it's important to you."

96

"I'm not sure if it is," she said softly. "Maybe. Perhaps, I've misjudged you."

"No, you haven't," he said. "Mom learned it from an Emily Post book. It's not inherited. We are not money, old, new or otherwise. My Dad runs a junkyard. Maybe scrap sounds better to your ear. Mom handles the books."

Allyson blinked. "I'm not snotty or snobby," she said. "Eat however you like. I won't watch if it gets too much like a wolf feeding on a fresh moose carcass. I'm pretty sure it's not a deal-breaker."

"It might be," he said. "'Maybe not today, maybe not tomorrow, but soon and for the rest of your life.'"

"Stop, already," she said. "I'm not interested in derivatives. You're not Bogart, and I'm not Bergman."

"Here's stopping for you, kid."

She shook her head, a wince and a grin in spite of herself. "You're difficult, Becker" she said. "Let's start again, shall we? Do you have something in mind for this evening?"

"Movie-wise?" he asked.

"Otherwise."

"Yes, Pick, I do."

"Good," she said. "Let's move along, Magoo."

Allyson was a Quaker-diaper baby.

Her mother, Jane Andrews Pickering, and a small group of Philadelphia-area Friends, Unitarians, rogue Congregationalists and non-believers, had stubbornly reared their children in the 1950s to be question-askers, peace-seekers, social activists and individualists. Allyson had been given handmade Gandhi dolls instead of cuddly teddy bears. She was taught to be against capital punishment, segregation and the House Un-American Activities Committee. She was brought up to be for the shared humanity of mankind, peace, justice and tolerance. She was expected to compete for the common good and intellectual accomplishment. Jane Pickering was also concerned that Allyson's nurtured social conscience would be expressed in "good taste," as she wrote to Allyson in her freshman year.

Allyson tried hard to be her mother's daughter without being totally her mother's daughter. She didn't join any of the New Left groups at Bryn Mawr even though her mother, she figured, had traveled next to the Communist Party for a short time in the '30s when she had attended. Allyson met Kathy Boudin as a freshman in 1964 but found the senior's cant and her dogmatic, New York-Jewish-Left style jarring. Allyson was not surprised when Boudin descended into making bombs in 1970 as a way of persuading people that her ideas were correct.

Allyson felt misaligned with her fellow student peace-seekers in 1967 and early 1968, many of whom she saw as Johnny- and Janey-Come-Latelies to peace politics. She felt more comfortable with the policies and tactics of the American Friends Service Committee and SANE, the organization founded in 1957 to promote an end to the nuclear arms race and nuclear testing. To her, the red diapers and the first-generation radicals who filled the anti-War demonstrations were working out insecurities, guilt and issues with parents. She was appalled when 400 Columbia students followed Black Panther Eldridge Cleaver in chanting: "FUCK DONALD DUCK. FUCK RONALD REAGAN." It felt too much like a Nazi rally she'd seen in film clips. When she joined anti-War demonstrations, she refused to shout the slogans in unison. Allyson was not comfortable in any political pigeonhole in the early months of 1968. She hated the War, but she dismissed Columbia's anti-War warriors. The screaming SDS boys needed to get laid, she thought; same with the girls. She kept this opinion to herself. She tried to master the tangle of her instincts and opinions. She wanted to group and sort them neatly, understandably. She didn't like being unanchored. She made an uneasy peace with uncertainty. So she waitressed for peace at the FTA while socializing with Trip Pennington whose ways were known to her, and, for that reason, sheltering.

The handful of student radicals at Bryn Mawr were fighting among themselves to determine who was the most militant, the most in line with the rhetorical fashion of the moment, the most feminist and the most willing to take risks for her ideas. They considered Allyson a "closet debutante," which, she acknowledged, was more accurate than she would admit. Bryn Mawr feminists also labeled her a "closet heterosexual," which she also admitted; she liked sex with boys. She found refuge in uncomplicated and largely detached visits to Trip who had started mulling over the idea of something more after graduation.

Despite her reservations about Trip, Allyson found herself later that spring on the Columbia campus just before 1,000 New York City police ejected 700 students from five campus buildings. Trip had been with her earlier that night. He didn't like SDS students, but he disliked even more a hidebound Columbia administration that was unable to solve a political crisis without beating up its own students. Mainly, he thought, he should protect her. She resented having him protect her, but thought it might be helpful to go around with him. Allyson didn't blame the cops for being angry at privileged kids; she didn't blame the kids for being angry; and she didn't even blame the administration for reclaiming the campus. She chalked up the whole mess to "our broken times," as she put it in a letter to her mother. As the police began clearing the campus of everyone, Allyson found herself separated from Trip Pennington and on her own.

Allyson had felt the first stirrings of women's liberation at Bryn Mawr in conversations that started late at night and over meals. Books and pamphlets were circulating. Some students started speaking up in classes taught by male professors. They asked about the subject from a feminist perspective, which was new ground for almost everyone. What was the role of women in The Depression? What had women contributed to science and math that might be linked to their gender and their experiences as women? Why did American laws favor men? Why did white women earn less than black men in the same jobs? Why did women always earn a fraction of what men earned for the same work? Why did husbands get to work and their equally educated wives get to clean toilets? Why wasn't abortion legal? Why were most gynecologists men? Even the preppies had started to ask whether marrying a stockbroker with a Wharton degree wasn't selling themselves short. This was mind-opening stuff. It was oddly empowering for Allyson to think of herself -- a woman succeeding at an elite college -- as exploited and oppressed. Was second class the irremediable fate of most females in American society? The fight was no longer for someone else -- the disenfranchised, the poor -- or for a broad political cause like peace. To Allyson, feminism had brought a war home. It was personal. It was about her. It was a war that she hadn't even known she was in until she realized she had been taken prisoner.

Allyson had been sitting with Trip in the West End Bar on Broadway near West 114th St. when she heard that a Barnard sophomore, Linda LeClair, had circumvented her College's housing rules and was cohabiting with Peter Behr, a Columbia student. A New York Times feature described a "Susan" as reflecting changing campus mores. Barnard President, Martha Peterson, "freaked out," according to Trip, and tracked the identity clues back to Linda. The student-faculty judicial council found her guilty of violating rules and lying to housing officials. Her punishment: She was banned from eating at the college cafeteria! Linda, Trip said, argued that she had a right to live her personal life as she pleased and saw no reason why she should be prohibited from cohabiting with Peter Behr when Columbia did not prohibit him from cohabiting with her. "She had a right to Behr arms," Trip cracked.

President Peterson objected to the judicial council's faux punishment, and, provisionally, expelled her. A sit-in responded to Peterson's decision. Some 300 Barnard students signed a petition affirming that they, too, had broken the housing rules.

LeClair's position seemed reasonable to Allyson: LeClair, 18, was an adult, though barely; adults were supposed to take responsibility for their decisions, which she was doing; female students should not be treated differently than male students; and stupid rules should be replaced by less stupid rules.

"I can't imagine that this would be a battle either of us would want to fight, publicly or privately," Trip said. "Better to sneak."

"My mother would be appalled," Allyson said.

"Mine, too."

"But Linda's right," she said. "This is about power, not sex. It's about a college woman being allowed to make decisions."

"Behr is a little far out for me," Trip said, "a draft resister. But you're right about outdated rules. This is just the latest flap over the morals of the 'BarnYard' girls. Did you know that Columbia's president, Grayson Kirk, wrote a letter to Barnard's president, Millicent McIntosh, in 1960 insisting that Barnard students stop wearing slacks -- and worse, Bermuda shorts -- when they came on Columbia's campus? Kirk demanded that Barnard adopt a dress code. McIntosh caved, and she pushed the student council to adopt a rule prohibiting her students from wearing shorts that were higher than two inches above the knee at Barnard. When they crossed Broadway onto the Columbia campus, they were required to wear long coats over their shorts. Barnard girls did this, and some still comply."

"Men," Allyson said.

"Well, old men," Trip said.

"Men," Allyson said. "It's about exerting control over women."

"And just to keep the record straight," Trip laughed, "the Barnard Honeybears will soon be dressing as nymphs so they may once again cavort on Columbia's College Walk in their annual celebration of Pan. Barnard Honeybears. Columbia Lions. Such an enlightened university. Go Honeybears!"

"Columbia's granting degrees in mixed messages," she said.

"We live in a time of lagging indicators," Trip added.

Allyson felt aswirl in the small-but-rising current of campus feminism. She was thinking about the roles women defined for themselves and those that were defined for them—how to modify them, discard them and blend them. She was now giving thought -- a lot of thought, actually -- to her future career and a future family. But the questions feminism raised did not seem to have answers that would let her do everything as she pleased. She felt the emerging ideology was forcing her to be more self-centered, more career-oriented, more wary of family and more dismissive of men no matter how enlightened. Who did the cooking? Who went to work? Who changed the diapers? Whose career came first? Who was on top? It seemed to her that relationships, including marriage, were being reset into a zero-sum game where either the man or the woman had to win and the other had to lose. She looked for a way through this, but nothing had appeared out of the mists.

Women's liberation, from what she had seen, was still mostly talk when it came to getting males to change. The SDS girls who were with

SDS boys were shouted down, tolerated, dismissed or ignored…and then passed around to demonstrate the virtues of college communism. No one needed to point out to her that Bryn Mawr girls, Barnard girls and particularly Sara Lawrence and Bennington girls were slow-moving prey for every male teaching assistant with a convoluted-but-snappy line. And even her mother's Quakers and Unitarians were guilty. Their wives were expected to be "good women"—homemakers, mothers, cooks, cleaners, activists and CEOs of household details and organization. They were thought to depend on male conceptual guidance.

Were men -- as a class, a gender, a whatever -- her enemy? Could men change? Could women force men to change? Was she as much a victim of discrimination because of her sex as the Harlem slum-dwellers who were stacked next to Columbia's campus? Did males exploit her knowingly and unknowingly? Were there rules and structures that she couldn't see? Could a system of male domination that had been around so long ever be changed? And what was its replacement? And what would it cost? What would she lose? Sometimes, she was repelled by the women she heard demanding answers. Sometimes, their anger seemed juvenile and out of proportion to the grievance. Must every leaflet protesting the War now be typed by male fingers? Must all housework, all work for money, all child care, all parent care, all house maintenance and all everything be shared absolutely equally?

Allyson found herself thinking hard after each consciousness-raising women's meeting. She began to think of herself as an adult woman, a woman who should take responsibility for her life and do whatever she wanted, whatever that might be. The Saturday night Jeffrey Becker walked her to her friend's apartment, she carried The Feminine Mystique in her over-the-shoulder bag.

Becker became her first "meaningful relationship" as a feminist. How meaningful? That question dogged her. Could a feminist of her sort love a man? Must relationships stay in a non-danger zone of convenience and mutual benefit without the complicating mess of male-advantaged love? How might Becker fit into her career plans after graduating from Columbia's Journalism School where she was enrolled for the fall of 1968? Was she in love with Becker? The force of social change that was etching new lines in history seemed to be complicating something that only a few years earlier might have been no more than a college romance with possibilities. Now, it seemed swamped with political-personal implications and carried a load of unfamiliar cultural expectations.

Trip was trying to be a good sport after Allyson told him that she wanted to be with Becker more than she wanted to be with him. He focused on her eyes and paid no attention to the bar noise.

"When did this happen?" he asked.

"The Saturday night you did your header," she said. "He walked me down to Carolyn's place. I met him the next weekend. He's a different fit for me. I'm not sure it's as comfortable, but I need to find out what he has that I like."

"Becker's a decent guy," Trip said. "You could have done worse." Trip realized that he wasn't angry or even very much disappointed. Reshufflings were accepted. He had been on both ends of a dump more than a few times. "There are other fish to fry," he said.

"I'm sure there are," she said, pursing her mouth like a guppy. "You'll have another in the pan in no time."

"Oh, you know what I mean. I'm glad you stayed close to the House even through he's not a member."

"Yes. Well."

Allyson led Becker into and through her expanding feminist consciousness. He was a willing traveler. He agreed with what she was saying, but he also suspected the river she was navigating would inevitably divide with her in one channel and him in the other.

They worked hard on the vocabulary of themselves. She was not his "girlfriend." He was not her "boyfriend." That was too high school. She was certainly not his "chick." Or his "old lady." Or his "steady." She could not get him to drop "he" when using a pronoun to represent both genders. "He-she?" he asked. "She," she said. Becker said he'd try, if she accepted "heart throbs," which made her laugh. She countered with "buddies." They settled on "friends," but "friends" did not settle it.

He called her "Pick," and she, "Becker."

Chapter 10

Columbia University, April 23, 1968

I

April 23rd was a sunny day on the Columbia campus as the Vietnam War raged and ghettos smoldered. The civil-rights movement was dividing between non-violence and Black Power. Parents and their kids were dismissing each other's values as well as each other. The press called it "The Generation Gap."

Senators Eugene McCarthy and Robert Kennedy began slugging it out in Democratic primaries earlier that year to see who would lead the challenge to President Johnson's war policies. On March 31st, Johnson announced he would not seek a second term at the Democratic convention scheduled for Chicago that summer. He designated his vice-president, Hubert Humphrey, to succeed him. Humphrey entered the race on April 27th, too late to have his name appear on any primary ballot. So his campaign organized favorite-son write-ins wherever possible. Johnson insisted that Humphrey embrace the Administration's support-the-War policies. Becker had hoped that Johnson's resignation would lead to a quick settlement with the North Vietnamese. In that event, the draft might recede as the defining issue of his life. Despite mounting opposition in the country, neither Humphrey nor the Republican, Richard Nixon, seemed inclined to end the War with all deliberate speed or even at a snail's pace. No president wanted to be accused of losing South Vietnam.

April, 1968, felt different to Becker. Anger and division were alternating waves crashing into a beached country. Marijuana and rock music were everywhere. On April 4th, Martin Luther King, Jr., was assassinated in Memphis. Major riots followed in more than 10 cities. Black Panthers carried guns. Supporters of third-party candidate George Wallace had guns. Anti-War protests brought out police and Army troops with guns. The pressure cooker was building to a boil.

Much student energy had been drawn into the Kennedy and McCarthy campaigns in the first three months of the year. Even so, protests against the War and the status quo were breaking out everywhere.

In January, 500 demonstrators rioted in San Francisco to oppose a speaking engagement by Secretary of State Dean Rusk, a consistent voice in favor of the Vietnam War. This mirrored a similar riot against Rusk two months earlier in New York when 2,500 protesters struggled with police for two hours. In Poland, students at the University of Warsaw demanding rights fought with police in a series of marches. In Czechoslovakia,

Alexander Dubcek had been leading an effort since January to carve democracy out of the oppressive, Soviet-run Eastern bloc. It came to be called "The Prague Spring." Three black college students were killed and 28 injured by state police in Orangeburg, South Carolina, in a civil-rights protest over a segregated bowling alley. Ten thousand students in West Berlin conducted a sit-in against the U.S. role in Vietnam. In February, students at Harvard, Radcliffe and Boston University held a four-day hunger strike to protest the War. In March, Italian students closed the University of Rome for 12 days to protest the War. On the 6th of March, 500 New York University students demonstrated against Dow Chemical, a principal manufacturer of the napalm used by the U.S. military. Anti-War demonstrations took place in London, ending with 86 injuries and 200 arrests. Several hundred students and intellectuals occupied an administration building at Nanterre's Paris University in March to protest discrimination and educational policies. Led by Daniel Cohn-Bendit, they left of their own accord after a day. On April 11th, Rudi Dutschke, leader of the West German student movement, was shot in the head by an anti-Communist. Dutschke recovered, though he was permanently brain-damaged.

Becker read The New York Times every day. The number and escalating tactics of these uprisings caught his attention. He knew SDS was following the European protests. Gondleman's mantra -- Violence radicalizes. -- appeared to be true. The War was radicalizing the opposition, which was radicalizing the political middle. Becker had the feeling one night in April that things were coming apart, the Establishment was crumbling and no one could steer what would happen. It felt to him that the times might, in fact, might be changing.

And it was spring.

Becker finished his class at 11:50 a.m. and walked over to the Sundial on College Walk for a noon SDS rally. He hoped the speakers would focus on the War, but he wasn't sure what SDS was up to since he had skipped the planning meetings where the rally's issues and positions had been thrashed out.

Becker was not ready to burn his draft card, flee to Canadian exile, spend five years in jail for refusing induction or accept conscription and fight in a war he thought should not be fought. Given his attitudes, he figured he'd make a lousy soldier. He'd ask "Why?" too many times for his own good and probably end up in a military prison. His student deferment would end upon his graduation in two months. He had to make a decision.

Becker wore a sport coat that day, because he had a summer job interview in the afternoon. A jacket was a step up from his normal senior uniform of wrinkled shirt and blue jeans. He carried his books in a soft, draw-string Columbia bag that he slung over his shoulder. The bag was unusually heavy. He hadn't had a chance that morning to return four volumes on military air power to Butler Library.

Becker had increasingly mixed feelings about SDS that spring. The organization filled the anti-War hole. It was the campus group that was most dramatically against the War, which was why he supported it.

But the decision-making gears inside the organization were badly matched. They chewed each other up more than meshed together. Even its simplest positions were burdened with the scars of sectarian Marxist knife fights, some going back 100 years. With the rejection of both Cold War liberalism and democratic socialism, SDS students struggled to find an ideological footing in some communist text or action. They applied their frameworks to American workers, whom they didn't know, and Columbia University, which they did. SDS meetings were consumed with debates over theory and tactics where opposing interpretations of old Marxisms ground against opposing interpretations of new Marxisms. Becker found SDS meetings and debates boring, comical, obscure, unproductive, fascinating and unanchored in the life of ordinary people. Rarely did he find them persuasive.

The Action Faction, led by Rooky Gondleman and Mark Rudd, advocated upsetting University policies through disruption. It was dominated by angry, dogmatic freshmen and sophomores who Becker, as a senior, considered less manageable than a kicked-over nest of yellow jackets. Becker sensed younger students had a hard time remembering when Vietnam and the draft were not defining their lives. They were also much heavier into drugs. Cobb and Mace Sedgwick were the radical wing of Gondleman's radical core of about 25 students.

The Praxis Axis, led by Ted Gold and Stuey Fishbein, emphasized education and organizing. They considered Gondleman a "wild man" for always advocating disruptive "actions" over all other forms of education and protest.

A third group was the Progressive Labor Party. They believed workers, rather than students or blacks, were America's revolutionary force. They tended to ally with the Praxis Axis in advocating more conservative disruptive tactics.

Becker had little patience for ideological fencing. He saw each sect growing "purer" and more "correct" in their own eyes as they drew in their borders and grew increasingly distant from reality. At root, he saw their struggles with each other as a religious war to impose the one true faith.

Rooky Gondleman had propelled himself into his leadership position by consistently arguing for stopping Columbia's business as usual. He wanted to provoke the Administration into ham-handed responses that he hoped would radicalize students and escalate conflict. Disorder had become his political end.

Becker had never gotten much of an idea of what Gondleman wanted after disruption brought Columbia to a stop. Rooky did not want to improve policies or restructure the institution to make decisions differently. Gondleman wanted to break Columbia, clog it up, discredit it and shut it down. Cobb named the strategy the name "Bringing the War Home."

SDS was not representative of the University's student population, or even its Columbia undergraduates. In Becker's estimation, about half of the 40 or 50 SDS members came from the East-Coast Jewish Left, diapered in either red or pink. Their parents had once been members of the Communist Party, or the Trotskyite opposition, or the splinter sects, or socialists of one stripe or another, or sympathizers or unaffiliated left-of-center gadflies. Their children, he saw, were wired to oppose whatever "Authority" was running their lives, including their parents. Most of the others, like Rudd and Gondleman, came from non-political, aspiring, middle-class Jewish families from Eastern European backgrounds. For them, a child at Columbia was an achievement, a flag planted in American society not against it.

While no one ever discussed it openly, Becker sensed that part of the rising antagonism between SDS and Columbia's administrators derived from long-standing, suppressed social and cultural animosities between second- and third-generation-American Jewish students and the Establishment WASPs who led the University.

Gondleman, a junior from Passaic, New Jersey, was, indeed, the kind of Jew Columbia would have not admitted in 1955.

The University had been wrestling with its "Jewish problem" since the turn of the 20th Century. Assimilated German and Sephardic Jews -- preferably at least third-generation American and wealthy -- had been admitted in small numbers. But Eastern European Jews -- less assimilated, more ethnic, poorer, less refined and seemingly "less American" -- were to be avoided when possible. Exceptions were allowed for extremely bright or talented applicants. The 19th Century immigrants -- predominately from Germany -- tended to support reform Judaism, which deemphasized obedience and ritual, and sought integration into American life. It rejected the Eastern European *shtetl* culture of the poor Jews who washed up on Ellis Island in the late 19th and early 20th Centuries. The confining *shtetl* experience gave rise to three contradictory ideas—rigid religious orthodoxy that emphasized rote learning and rules, Zionism or radical left-wing, secular politics. Elite American universities wanted nothing to do with any part of that mix, especially the Marxist radicals.

In the early '20s, Columbia under President Nicholas Murray Butler followed Harvard and adopted a Jewish quota. Butler supported both fascist Italy and Germany until the outbreak of WWII. Columbia, like

106

other Ivy League schools, limited Jewish enrollment to about 10 percent until the late 1950s and early 1960s. Called *numerus clausus* policies, Jewish quotas were enforced through an application form asking for religious preference. Applicants were interviewed by alumni who applied their own ideas of appearance and suitability. Preference for legacy applicants had the effect of lowering admissions of better-qualified, non-legacy students. Neither Columbia's faculty nor its student body reflected the New York area's religious, racial, ethnic or gender demographics in 1968.

By the mid-1960s, Columbia, like other Ivies, was admitting Jewish students who were bright, conservative and career-oriented. It was also admitting Jewish students who were sympathetic to rebelling. The Vietnam War had the effect of mobilizing the latter group against their still conservative universities, which were the most convenient targets.

Institutionalized anti-Semitism had ended at Columbia by the 1960s, but the underlying and lingering disdain for people like Milt Gondleman probably skewed the admission chances of his son. Rooky was admitted owing to very high SATs, not because he was well-traveled, well-rounded, athletic, wealthy, connected, polished or culturally literate. He was an insular product of the Passaic Jewish experience. Admissions assumed he would find other alienated idealists like himself. He was the kind of kid who, they hoped, might find a cure for the common cold.

SDS Jews knew, or, at least, sensed, Columbia's history, but the War and the draft had stripped away their self-interested and fearful restraint. Gondleman understood that the marginal status of Jews as minority outsiders, both in pre-WWII Europe and the United States, produced a disproportionate number of individuals who sympathized with the idea of overthrowing the powers that were—be they Czars, Establishment WASPs like Grayson Kirk or Lyndon Johnson. That opinion was coupled with the never expressed feeling that Grayson Kirk came out of the same mold as Nicholas Murray Butler. To them, he represented their eternal *goyishe* oppressor, or, at least, its current ghost.

The other component that Becker saw in Columbia SDS -- and one very much in the minority -- were prep-school Protestants who almost without exception came from what they called "white, ruling-class families" of Old Money and Mayflower Republicans. For whatever reasons, they allied with one of the nightmares of their parents—the Gondleman-Rudd Jews spouting Marx, Lenin, Mao, Castro, Che Guevara, Regis Debray, Bob Dylan, LeRoi Jones and, perhaps most offensive of all, Lenny Bruce. Few Catholics joined SDS. Those who did had already rejected Church orthodoxy on birth control, ritual and faith. Campus opposition to SDS tended to be Christian, and drew heavily from fraternities and the University's sports teams.

Becker noticed that a freshman like Cobb -- who insisted on using one name -- embodied rage without discipline. What mattered to Cobb was smashing something, from a *piñata* to The State. Becker believed that Cobb's attraction to smashing came from his inability to execute that stroke despite extensive lessons from his club's tennis pro.

Becker learned that Cobb came from a New England family who had made a fortune speculating in southern real estate after the Civil War. It now ran the biggest independent investment bank in Connecticut and sent its sons to St. Paul's School in Concord, New Hampshire. It was there, Becker had been told, that Cobb grew to hate the pomp and hierarchy he first experienced in his family. Cobb -- tall, gangly and not very athletic -- fell short of the Paulie prototype. He retreated into a small group of liberal, intellectual, dope-smoking, mouthy outcasts who the conventional students avoided or bullied.

The handful of prep-school WASPs like Cobb and Mace Sedgwick in Columbia SDS were much more comfortable with physical violence and property destruction than almost all of the Jews in the Action Faction. While they came out of John Updike and J.D. Salinger rather than Emma Goldman and Philip Roth, Mace and Cobb saw themselves as carrying on the tradition of Samuel Adams and John Brown. To the extent that SDS engaged in fighting and destruction, Cobb was a Marxist. The rest of SDS theology and liturgy never interested him.

Only a few graduate students joined SDS. Most were put off by the antics of the undergraduates, particularly the youngest. They appreciated the risks to their future from fouling their own nest.

Rooky Gondleman's mother, Irene, was a homemaker, which was fine with her. His father, Milt, had taken over a small home-improvements business from his father, Nathan, a Russian immigrant. In 1897, Nathan started life in America peddling sundries and "female notions" door-to-door from two bags he carried from a shoulder yoke. In three years, he was able to buy a fifth-hand horse and a fourth-hand wagon, which allowed him to expand into pots, pans, brooms, pails and cloth. In 1933, he bought a third-hand 1927 Graham Brothers panel delivery truck he named Katrinka. He began picking up any usable cast-off item from his customers, which he hauled back to Passaic—"making a dime coming and going," as he put it. Nathan muddled through the Depression until WWII flushed a little cash through the hands of people like him.

When Milt was discharged from the Army in 1945, father and son jumped into what Milt said was the *farkakte* end of the housing boom—selling siding, roofing and storm windows door to door in New Jersey's less prosperous neighborhoods. A failing heart pushed Nathan into retirement. Milt, by that time, had learned to get through a housewife's door by pitching a cheap siding and then explaining why a higher-priced --

and higher-profit -- alternative was better and cost no more each month as long as "we are willing to extend the financing term from five to 10 years." The switch was sugared up by having the customer think she was getting a one-day-only, special low price. Milt's contract allowed him to place a lien on the customer's house for missed payments. This yielded one or two properties each year for him to sell. Milt once revealed to his 12-year-old son the truth of his business: "If I ain't lyin,' they ain't buyin'." Rooky was appalled.

In the early '50s, Milt opened a discount carpet store in the Newark ghetto where Rooky was indentured during his high-school summers. Slightly flawed carpeting was sold cheap with a high mark-up, since, as Milt said, "it's as good as the original if you know what I mean." Money was made on financing the sales. Milt had Rooky wait on carpet customers until he realized that his bright son "couldn't sell a one-dollar meal to a starving millionaire." For his part, Rooky hated selling anything to anyone. The traps his father routinely set for his customers disgusted him. When Rooky came home for Christmas break in his freshman year, he berated Milt for his business. Milt was hurt, and then said: "You should never forget that crap aluminum awnings and high-interest rates are paying for every one of your hours at Columbia. Your life will be better, because your mother and me do this work."

Milt Gondleman never had a choice about how to make a living. He and Irene had grown thankful for achieving a modest level of comfort in America, free of pogroms. Theirs was a life that was more than just a couple of steps away from peddling notions and sundries from a shoulder pack.

Rooky hated that his family's food, shelter and clothing -- and his education -- came from squeezing dimes out of the Newark ghetto. When Milt told him to lay a carpet there, Rooky always tried to throw in a runner for free or a remnant for a mat.

The Gondlemans were undistinguished in post-War America, except that their son, Robert, had done well at a competitive public high school, had near-perfect SAT scores and fives on four advanced math/science tests. As a youngster, Rooky had been in both Cub Scouts and Boy Scouts. For his Bar Mitzvah, he received a ham radio. He played chess in high school and was elected an officer in both the chemistry and math clubs. His only activity during his freshman year at Columbia was interscholastic chess matches. He liked castling where he moved both king and rook in an approximate exchange of positions. It was a defensive tactic that offered offensive possibilities. Hence, the name his teammates gave him, Rooky.

Milt and Irene were straight-ticket New Dealers in the 1930s and conditionally endorsed civil rights in the mid-'60s as long as "it wasn't against the Jews." Both had known a few radical students at their high schools in the '30s, but they were careful to avoid rocking the very boat they hoped would sail them to a better life. They'd been scared by the Rosenberg verdicts even though they confided to each other that they thought both were guilty, him more than her. And they trembled with the withdrawal of J. Robert Oppenheimer's security clearance and Congressional investigations into his loyalty. It was a dragnet "that came up with a hell of a lot more Jews than was good for Jews" in Milt's opinion. He joined the American Legion and the Veterans of Foreign Wars in 1950 to show that Jews were loyal Americans, not Soviet spies.

Rooky paid little attention to either news or politics until the War escalated in 1966, drawing in almost 400,000 American troops. As the War expanded and the draft came closer, he felt he needed to do something. So he joined SDS. He was surprised to discover that his brain worked with Marxist doctrines as it had with chess strategies. Both were about winning. Both endlessly debated long-term goals and immediate tactics. Both were complicated and obscure. Both attracted students who had brains, patience for endless discussion and faith in the ultimate triumph of their own reasoning. Both were addictive.

SDS became Rooky's fraternity. Its members were his brothers. He was elected chairman of Columbia SDS in the fall of 1967 by supporting the most extreme tactics within SDS debates. Advocates of less action-oriented positions were dubbed "deviants," or, when that failed, "chickens."

SDS was Gondleman's fraternity in a religious sense as well. Most members were Jewish and sociologically much like Gondleman—second- or third-generation Americans, middle-class, first- or second-generation college attendees, raised in nominally religious households and largely suburban or from the New York metropolitan area. He felt comfortable among those like himself.

Rooky had managed to grow a very small mustache that winter, which made him look at least 15. He had also acquired hipper eyeglasses and a black, thrift-store motorcycle jacket with lots of zippers and buckles that was too big for him through the shoulders. With this new "street" persona, Rooky discovered he was not shy about speaking in public without notes and without being giggled at. Cobb said that Rooky's jacket was his Dumbo feather—without it on, he would go mute.

Cobb wanted to spill blood like Ho Chi Minh; Rooky just wanted to shatter American institutions. The red-diaper Marxists saw Rooky as short on theory and long on pot-fueled, anarcho-recklessness, which they dubbed "infantile adventurism." They had come out of Old-Left homes and grew up arguing Marxism. Rooky had come out of Passaic Cub Scouts. His one tactic -- which came directly from tournament chess -- was to overwhelm his opponent by massing his pieces at a single point of attack.

Unlike Praxis Axis leader Stuey Fishbein whose parents had been minor Communist Party officials until 1956, Rooky never claimed to be grounded in Marxist theory and history. He succeeded on his boyish charisma that was enhanced by his ability to speak without running his listeners through a gauntlet of contradictory lesser and greater student Maoisms.

Gondleman's life had become SDS politics at Columbia, the activity that gave him an identity beyond "chess geek." Demonstrations that went beyond non-violent protest now defined him. He discovered that a hard line brought other benefits. The tougher he sounded in SDS meetings, the more Barnard sympathizers paid attention to him. His first experience came with the daughter of a Chattanooga rabbi who had informed her father over Christmas break that Jesus was a more likely historical person than Moses. From her, Rooky moved ecumenically into encounters with agnostic Episcopalians from good families with hard-drinking, remote fathers. He even found himself once with a rebellious debutante from a Richmond cigarette fortune who said self-mockingly that he was "as exotic as a kosher dill pickle." An older SDS woman who worked at the New York office slept with Rooky as part of her growing commitment to non-monogamy. Effortless sex, Gondleman thought, was pretty cool for a kid who never had a date in high school.

While Columbia's SDS males argued over whether workers, blacks, Third World peasants or students like themselves would lead the American Revolution, they were unanimous in thinking it was their opinions, not those of their girlfriends and female comrades, that really counted. A few years earlier, Black Power spokesman, Stokely Carmichael, had announced only half-jokingly that the "position of women" in the Student Non-Violent Coordinating Committee, his civil-rights organization working in the South, should be "prone." By 1968, most SDS males knew enough to not repeat that opinion publicly, but it wasn't exactly in the back of their minds. Had they dared express what they actually thought, the majority would have said the proper positions for women in student politics were phone calling, typing, stencil-making, publicity, cooking, affirmation of their boyfriend's opinions and uncomplicated sex.

In March, Rooky threw a lemon-meringue pie in the face of Colonel Paul Akst, the head of the Selective Service system in New York City, just as he began to speak in Earl Hall. A pie in the face violated the University's rule against indoor demonstrations. The University was unable to come up with any other rule violation.

Gondleman and five others were summarily placed on probation and warned against another indoor demonstration. Gondleman wrote in his defense to The Columbia Spectator that freedom of expression should not be any less protected inside a University building than "outside in the public square." Since Columbia had no rule against tossing pies at "war criminals," Gondleman saw no justification for the SDS Six to be punished. Akst did not press battery charges against Gondleman.

That February, Gondleman spent four weeks in Cuba with 22 SDS activists. He came back brimming. He was starting to believe that he, Rooky Gondleman, was on the same revolutionary path as Che, Ho and Fidel—and maybe, even Mao. All he had to do was continue to make demands and refuse to compromise.

By the spring of 1968, Rooky was as recognizable on Columbia's campus as the bronze statue of Athena, Alma Mater, in front of Low Memorial Library.

In his senior year, Jeffrey Becker rented a studio apartment -- 4F -- at 510 West 110th Street, about six blocks south of College Walk. A longtime resident told him George Gershwin composed "Rhapsody in Blue" during January, 1924, in 501. Becker hoped a little of that stardust might still be around. Rooky Gondleman lived two flights up.

In the second semester of the 1967-1968 academic year, they found themselves in a class on the causes of war taught by Warner Schilling. Gondleman would occasionally bait Schilling for his "dispassionate analysis" that wasn't, and his comment that humans practiced war because "it was useful, legal and fun." Becker estimated that 80 percent of Schilling's class of 30 agreed with Gondleman that the War in Vietnam was ill-conceived and probably unwinnable, but they had grown to detest Rooky's self-righteous stridency. Becker found himself walking with Gondleman to Schilling's nine o'clock class on Tuesdays and Thursdays.

"I was apolitical my first year," Gondleman said as they headed up Amsterdam Avenue in early April. "I played chess, got good grades and wondered whether I'd ever get laid."

"Typical freshman angst," Becker said.

"Then the War heated up. I felt trapped, like I was almost in checkmate."

"I lose my II-S when I graduate in June," Becker said. "I got into law school, but I'll have to deal with the draft over the summer."

"What are you going to do?"

"Not go," Becker said. "How is the question?"

"I found SDS last year," Gondleman said. "We were all in the same boat with the draft."

"You seem to have found a home, a club."

"Politics is larger than chess but follows similar rules of engagement. Changing situations force you to adapt fast."

"In a chess match, there's nothing at stake except your ego," Becker said. "Here you're playing for your future. You're on probation for pieing Akst. Keep it up and suspension and expulsion will follow."

112

"It was a pie, not a bullet," Rooky said. "Akst gets honored and defended for conscripting thousands of American kids to shoot and napalm peasants in Vietnam, and I get disciplined for blessing him with a pie that cost $1.75! This is asymmetrical accountability. By the way, I served him a quality baked good. The cheap-shit Progressive Labors wanted me to hit him with a Ding Dong. The Praxis Axis voted for a knish. Cobb argued for a scone with a rock in it. Half the membership didn't know what a scone was, including me."

"A pie-in-the-face is not considered reasoned, collegial discourse at Columbia," Becker said with a grin. "Kirk would like nothing better than to get you and about 30 others in SDS off campus, permanently."

"The best thing for us would be to take over a building and have the cops bust us. Bloody us up. That would ignite the campus. That won't happen if I compromise or negotiate."

"If you refuse to budge in the next demonstration, you're out of school. It's academic suicide."

"Not if we get Kirk to agree to amnesty," Rooky said.

Becker stopped in mid-stride and turned toward Gondleman. "Rooky, I know you know that Columbia has this 18th-Century rule that there's no due process and no appeal from a president's decision. You're not going to get Grayson to give you amnesty for what he considers to be your tantrums."

"Tantra, not tantrums," Gondleman insisted.

"It's tantrums. Tantrum isn't Latin. Tantra has something to do with Hindu texts."

"Yeah?"

"Sex tips," Becker baited him.

"I'll look into it. Anyway, you're right about Grayson. He won't give us amnesty. So we have to take it."

"It won't work that way," Becker said. "If he doesn't enforce the no-indoor-demonstration rule against you for the pie, he can't enforce any rule against anybody for anything. And you're not going to stop the War if you get Columbia to sever ties with the Institute for Defense Analyses."

"You're right. The IDA will work with another university if Columbia backs out. Then it's the responsibility of students there to do what we did. That kind of research doesn't belong in a university."

"It's the content of the research, not Columbia's sponsorship, that's your real issue," Becker said.

"Exactly. The IDA connects Columbia directly to the War. We found that IDA researched Agent Orange and carpet-bombing tactics in Vietnam. We've shown that half of Columbia's research money depends on defense contracts. We've found professors doing CIA research on Eastern Europe. The University plays a small part in the scheme of things. But if you subtract enough small things from one big thing, pretty soon you get to zero."

"Like in chess," Becker said.

"We can't get at the actual research, which will go on in any case, so we have to attack the pawn in front of us."

"I would not be comfortable having the Action Faction decide what research Columbia faculty should and shouldn't do, what material should and should not be taught," Becker said.

"There should be at least one place in America that provides research counter to the stuff that comes from mainstream academics and guys hustling federal money to advance their careers."

"You would have problems with that place, too."

"Maybe," Gondleman conceded.

"My other guess is that most Columbia students would love a new gym," Becker said.

"They are victims of false consciousness," Gondelman said. "It's a 10-story monstrosity with separate entrances for us and 'them.'"

"The community has gotten the University to change the original plans. Harlem gets an Olympic-sized pool and basketball courts."

"Basketball is a worse ghetto narcotic than heroin. Give those kids books, not hoops."

"A gym is a gym," Becker said. "Right now, there's nothing."

"It's a crumb thrown to pacify the hungry black underclass," Rooky said.

"A crumb they would not otherwise have. Crumbs for the hungry are better than no crumbs. Where would *you* put it?"

"That's not the point," Rooky said. "Urban universities everywhere -- Harvard, Yale, Hopkins, Penn -- they act like colonial powers, expropriating land from surrounding communities for their own purposes. They get whatever they want, and the residents have to move. Fishbein discovered that Columbia has bought about 100 SROs and buildings on Morningside Heights since WWII and evicted 7,000 renters over the last 10 years. These were poor people, living in cheap housing."

"Now it's off-campus housing for us and faculty offices," Becker said.

"It's urban imperialism," Gondleman said. "The rich taking from the poor. If we stop it here, others can too."

"So where would you put the gym?"

"I don't know. On land where Columbia wouldn't have to kick poor people out of their apartments."

"There are no places like that on Morningside Heights," Becker said.

"Not my problem. Let the community decide where it should go—students, faculty, neighborhood groups, renters, even administrators. Build on top of existing buildings or underneath them. I'm not an architect."

"Do you actually care about any of these 'issues'?"

"The issues are not *the* issue. The only real issue is destroying the American Empire through constant attacks. The Empire can't *really* reform the institutions that support it."

"I don't see any Soviet, Cuban or Chinese universities acting better than Columbia," Becker said. "They support their regimes. They do military research. If they need land, they take it. And they throw dissenting students into prison camps."

"They serve The People, not the exploiters," Gondleman said.

"Right," Becker said dismissively.

"My job is to tear America down," Rooky said, "not nitpik fellow communists. We can't bring a revolution to America by making its institutions a little more responsive. Reform just strengthens their grip. Reform makes oppression smarter. What comes next will be a struggle, probably armed. But I'll give you this: I hope it ends with a better form of communism than what the Bolsheviks and Stalin produced. Ick on that."

"'Ick on that.' Are you quoting Marx?" Becker laughed.

"Never got through him. I've picked up the general drift."

"Dictatorships are dictatorships," Becker said. "The form of government determines how it acts, Schilling said that. Marxism ends up in purges and dictatorships, not paradise and participatory democracy."

"Not every corned-beef sandwich can come from Katz's on Houston," Rooky said. "Some communisms are better than others. Some are historically incorrect. Our job, as my father would put it, is to peddle the most profitable item, which is not necessarily the best for the buyer but can be."

"Columbia SDS isn't capable of putting two batteries in a flashlight let alone constructing a new university or new society. What makes you think that you will be the ones rebuilding from the top shelf after the wreckage?"

"Because, Becker, we're smarter."

"If smarts alone made institutions work, why is Columbia so rigid and vulnerable?"

"Because capitalism hijacks smarts and turns them against the interests of The People," Rooky said.

"And communism doesn't?"

"Doesn't necessarily have to," Rooky said.

"But always seems to."

They turned into College Walk from Amsterdam Avenue and headed to their class in Fayerweather Hall.

"It's amnesty," Becker said. "You might be able to force Kirk to give in on both the IDA and the gym. But not amnesty."

"Yep. That's why amnesty is non-negotiable. You see where this goes?"

"I do. You're going to screw your followers to break Columbia's back."

"My neck is on the chopping block first, don't forget."

"No, you're already out. The paperwork just hasn't caught up to you. It will. So what do you think you'll be doing in 50 years?"

"Playing chess, probably. I could be dead. Or in jail."

"Do you think you will grow up eventually, get married, have a family and calm down?" Becker asked.

"I will get older. I don't know about 'growing up,' as you put it."

"It happens," Becker said.

"Here's a gloomy prediction. I wouldn't be surprised if I was teaching math at a university like, I'm sad to say, Columbia."

By noon on the 23rd, several hundred students on lunch break stood around the Sundial. Some were SDS members and sympathizers. Others were curious. A few were voyeurs hoping to watch a fracas. Speeches began promptly.

The Sundial itself was a shadow of its former self. It had begun as a 16-ton, seven-foot-in-diameter, dark-green granite sphere on a pedestal—a 1914 gift from the Columbia College Class of 1885. Cracks appeared in this gnomon over time that posed a hazard to both innocent walkers and boozy undergraduates who thought they needed to climb it at midnight. The sphere was removed in 1946 and shipped to Ann Arbor. Campus speakers now stood on its elevated base, facing several flights of steps up to Low Memorial Library, the University's administrative headquarters. There, President Kirk had an eight-room suite in the southwest corner of the second floor. The pedestal retained its inscription: *Horam Expecta Veniet—Await the hour, it will come.* But with its gnomon now disintegrating in the freeze-thaw cycles of the upper Midwest, the University's Sundial could no longer tell students the time of day.

Columbia and Barnard students were shaking off winter stiffness on that pleasant Tuesday.

SDS speakers were energized—the first stirrings of gym construction in Morningside Park could be heard from where they stood. The University's secret connection to the Institute for Defense Analyses had been revealed. Amnesty for Gondleman and the other five was at the top of their list of demands. Only four weeks had passed since President Johnson announced he would not run for reelection. Only three weeks had passed since the King assassination. It felt like something was going to happen— here, there, somewhere, even everywhere.

Thirty-minutes was the rule of thumb for rallies. After that, students drifted off to lunch or classes. At 12:30 p.m., Rooky Gondleman mounted the Sundial's pedestal with a battery-operated bullhorn. He took notice of about 100 anti-SDS students blocking Low Library's ground-level door at

116

its indented southeast corner. Gondleman realized the conservative opposition had acquired advance warning that SDS would be targeting Low for an indoor demonstration. Someone from their side had infiltrated SDS!

Showing the tactical flexibility he had learned in chess, Gondleman shouted into the bullhorn: "It's time to do something."

"Turn it on," the crowd shouted. "Flip the switch."

Gondleman grinned, shrugged into his leather jacket and laughed at himself.

"To the gym," shouted two Barnard students. "To the gym!"

"To the gym," Gondleman repeated through the activated bullhorn. "Let's go to the gym."

"No, go to Low!" Stuey Fishbein said. "That's what we voted to do."

"Fuck you, Fishbein," Cobb said, bumping the smaller student out of his way. "Fucking legalist!"

SDS factions had debated the night before what type of "action" would most likely radicalize the campus. The Action Faction led by Gondleman favored a sit-in at Low to challenge Kirk's ban on indoor demonstrations and the earlier probations. The Praxis Axis, led by Gold and Fishbein, thought an indoor demonstration was politically premature and suicidal. The Progressive Labors argued for more outreach to revolutionary white auto workers in Detroit. With the Action Faction in a slight majority, SDS had voted for a sit-in inside Low, blanket amnesty for past and current violations and a revocation of Kirk's ban on indoor demonstrations.

The small number of black undergraduates had never felt comfortable at white Columbia next to Harlem. Many were torn between getting an education that would allow them to advance in American society and maintaining roots in the community from which they came. Black students had organized the Student Afro-American Society (SAS) several years earlier with a modest, non-confrontational agenda. The siting, design and control of the gym was a clear example of Columbia's arrogant disregard for the community around it. SAS developed links to organizations in West Harlem that saw Morningside Park as Harlem's ground rather than Columbia's. After all, Harlem used it; Columbia avoided it. To SAS, the gym was both symbolic of white institutions "taking resources" from black communities and a genuine issue of who would decide what. At the time of the April 23rd rally, SAS was led by new, more confrontational leaders who focused on a single issue: stopping the gym. SAS was not interested in restructuring the University, severing ties with the IDA or amnesty for white pie-throwers, indoor or otherwise.

Becker was sufficiently curious and supportive to walk over to the construction gate with the crowd.

The gym issue did not stir him very much. He saw it as a blunder by out-of-touch, white administrators who never listened to anyone but their own culturally and racially limited selves.

In Kirk's mind, "the black community" had neither power nor money. It was a negative interest group that needed to be managed. It never occurred to him that *these* neighbors had a role in University decisions that affected them.

Gondleman led about 300 students -- of whom 60 or so were SAS members -- to a construction-site gate at West 114th and Morningside Drive. When they got there, he shouted into his bullhorn: "Tear it down!"

A handful of students began pulling at a 40-foot-long, 12-foot-high section of chain-link security fence. They bent the metal posts toward the ground until they could breach it. A melee erupted when 10 New York City police arrived. Becker found himself standing in the middle of a brawl, trying to keep from getting roughed up or losing his book bag.

Another 20 cops rolled up and blocked the entrance. Unable to move beyond this new police line, Gondleman quickly caucused with his supporters, then shouted: "Hamilton. Go to Hamilton."

"NO!" Cobb screamed. "Stay here and fight the pigs!"

"That's infantile militarism," Stuey Fishbein countered.

"Fuck you, Fishbein," Cobb said, as the crowd moved toward the campus.

The free-for-all at the fence seemed to energize something -- or some things -- in the crowd that was different than an hour earlier. Maybe, Becker thought later, it was the shared, frustrated anger about having little control over the big forces that drove their lives. Maybe it was the recognition that events had tossed American politics and society in the air like pick-up sticks—and no one knew how they would land or on whom. Maybe it was the allure of doing something other than talking about doing something. Maybe it was the same rush felt by Confederates firing the first cannon at Fort Sumter 104 years earlier. Maybe it was spring and being outside. Maybe it was just getting away with something.

The crowd stormed into Hamilton Hall where Columbia College had its administrative offices with classrooms on the upper floors.

Namesake Alexander Hamilton, Class of 1777, never graduated from Columbia's predecessor, King's College, because it was shuttered for eight years during the Revolution. Becker had learned that King's College was considered a Tory institution with a clear Church of England affiliation.

118

Undergraduate Hamilton was the chief, pro-American thorn in the flesh of Loyalist Myles Cooper, an Anglican priest and King's College president from 1763 to 1775.

A pro-American student mob formed in May, 1775, a few weeks after the Battles of Lexington and Concord with the intention of harming Cooper. Hamilton hated and distrusted mobs. He diverted his fellow students just long enough for Cooper to escape. Hamilton went on to serve as George Washington's aide during the Revolution. He saw his future coinciding with the American colonial elite rather than the near-impregnable British aristocracy.

Speeches sounded through Hamilton Hall's spacious lobby. Posters of Mao, Ho and Che went up. Gondleman announced that an "occupation was being held." Acting College Dean Henry Coleman entered the building voluntarily and walked through the undergraduates to his office, announcing that he would not negotiate anything in such conditions. Gondleman and SDS half-heartedly barricaded him in. Then, on his own initiative, Rooky announced that SDS would be holding a "hostage for at least 24 hours." He meant the building, but everyone interpreted it to mean Coleman.

"No one debated that," Fishbein shouted toward Gondleman. "Stalinism! Adventurism!"

"Fuck you, Fishbein," Cobb said as he and his friend, Mace Sedgwick, began stacking lounge chairs against Coleman's office door.

"Kidnappingism," Fishbein screamed. "Crazyism!"

"Go back to Flatbush and Erasmus Hall, Fishbein," Cobb said dismissively.

"I went to Bayside in Queens."

"A difference without a distinction," Cobb muttered to Sedgwick.

Gondleman and Becker knew Coleman to be a far better, more sensible and less doctrinaire official than University leaders Grayson Kirk, Vice-President David Truman and Vice-Provost Herbert Deane. Coleman knew Columbia College's undergraduates; the University's officials knew almost none. Coleman had worked hard to keep communications open with SDS, even playing chess with Gondleman before Christmas break. A Navy veteran and former captain of Columbia's crew, Coleman could, in Becker's opinion, have taken any two, or maybe three, SDS members had he wanted. Instead, Becker saw him calmly settling in and maintaining as much cordiality as possible. Later in the afternoon, Fishbein asked Coleman what he'd like for supper and then sent a Barnard student to get it. She rejected Coleman's offer to pay.

Dean-taking was an off step in a weird direction, Becker thought. It would build opposition not support. It seemed to have been a spur-of-the-moment mistake that did nothing to advance the core issues at the heart of the protest. Becker assumed Coleman thought that as long as he and two other College subalterns were in the building and feeling safe, the University would not send in New York cops to end the takeover. Had he wanted to, Coleman could have picked up his office phone at any time and called for police assistance. Everyone in Hamilton Hall knew that.

SAS leader Bill Sales made sure Cobb and Sedgwick did not bother Coleman who, he knew, was largely responsible for increased enrollment and financial aid for black undergraduates. Sales told Gondleman that SAS would not tolerate any destruction of University property or faculty research. Sales and Cicero Wilson wanted Hamilton's occupation to be orderly and clean—traits they found lacking in SDS.

By late afternoon, black SAS had decided that white SDS should leave Hamilton Hall and occupy its own building if its members were so inclined. SAS was only concerned about terminating the gym, which had become the impromptu, substitute target of the noon rally. That switch gave SAS leverage to tell SDS what to do. SAS had come to believe that SDS was a "bunch of privileged chaotics."

Becker had written a paper in Richard Hofstadter's history class on Alexander Hamilton a year earlier. He thought it appropriate that SAS wanted to make its stand in Hamilton Hall. As an adolescent, Hamilton had clerked for Beekman and Cruger, a prominent firm that traded goods and slaves on St. Croix. After 1780, he handled the buying and selling of slaves for the Schuylers, his wife's wealthy and politically prominent New York family. His grandson wrote that Hamilton himself owned slaves. While Hamilton favored voluntary manumission rather than state-ordered abolition, he was mainly interested in preserving the wealth of America's wealthy by protecting their property, including slaves. Hamilton would have opposed the rebellion SAS was conducting in his namesake. That was of no consequence to those who were sitting-in. The occupation, like Hamilton himself, was not simple to explain.

Becker hung around the Hamilton festivities during the early afternoon, went to his job interview and returned about 4:30. He wanted to see where Gondleman and SDS would take their occupation. He noticed the atmosphere in Hamilton's lobby had changed from a spring festival to a grade-school imitation of the defense of Stalingrad. Tables and chairs were piled in front of doors and windows. Clothes and blankets were scattered around. Empty food containers were spilling out of wastebaskets. The lobby, filled with sitting students, smelled of danger and bananas. Becker sensed that SDS was digging in. But tension was high between SAS and SDS over what to do next.

About 6 p.m., Sales and Wilson told Gondleman privately that SAS had decided "democratically" that SDS had to leave Hamilton. Rooky felt betrayed by the very constituency SDS was trying to support.

"Where to?" Gondleman asked.

"Your decision," they answered, "not ours."

A few minutes later, Rooky spoke quietly to the crowd of SDS supporters.

"SAS has voted that black students should hold Hamilton by themselves."

His members were stunned. They wanted to do this action black-and-white together.

"So it's back to the original plan. Collect your shit. Keep it down. Campus cops are outside."

In five minutes, SDS was ready. Gondleman mouthed the words, "To Low."

With those two words, Passaic's Rooky Gondleman was transformed into Columbia University's version of Che Guevara.

The Action Faction had been talking about staging a sit-in at Low for several months. It would directly challenge Grayson Kirk. It would provoke a forcible removal. It would be the riskiest thing anyone in SDS had ever done.

Occupying a campus building was an extension of the occupation of Sproul Plaza by the Free Speech Movement at Berkeley in 1964-1965. It echoed what French students did for a day in Nanterre a few weeks earlier. It traced back to the United Auto Workers' occupations of Michigan assembly plants during The Depression and the non-violent lunch-counter sit-ins of the early 1960s. Sophomore Steve Komm had urged a Low occupation in his "Spring Offensive Proposal." And graduate student Steve Halliwell had proposed taking over Grayson Kirk's office. But it was Rooky Gondleman who gave life to the idea at the moment when those around him were ready to do it.

Low Memorial Library had been built in 1895, using President Seth Low's own $1 million. He named it after his father, Abiel Abbot Low, a clipper-ship merchant who made a fortune in the mid-19th-Century China trade of silk, tea, spices, opium and smuggling. Later, he was a major investor in the Chesapeake and Ohio Railroad, which opened the southern West Virginia coalfields in the 1880s to western cities like Cincinnati, Chicago and Detroit, and the Virginia port of Hampton Roads.

The Library was a forbidding, neo-classical, gray-stone structure with a 106-foot-tall rotunda at its center. It overlooked the southern end of the University's campus. Low's architecture evoked Rome's Pantheon. Amid its interior marble walls, representations of ancient Roman and Greek gods and philosophers had been erected to inspire student readers. At its front, 10 Ionic columns faced south, overlooking a series of wide steps, College Walk and Butler Library on the south end of the campus. A network of underground tunnels connected it to circumjacent buildings.

Low's Greek-cross footprint had been laid over the ruins of the Bloomingdale Insane Asylum, a fact Gondleman pointed out in every speech. Waggish faculty quipped that Low Memorial Library had never been low and had stopped being a library 34 years earlier.

College Walk lay parallel to Low, separated by several tiers of broad steps. The Walk, once a public street, had been privatized and pedestrianized into a promenade connecting Broadway on the west with Amsterdam Avenue on the east. Dwight D. Eisenhower, Columbia's president from 1948 to 1953, had negotiated a swap with the City, trading low-value upstate land for this block-long section of West 116th Street. Building a Columbia gym in City-owned Morningside Park had ancestry.

Eisenhower was largely absent during his Columbia tenure owing to foreign-policy assignments. His most significant legacy was elevating Grayson Kirk to provost and then vice-president, positions from which Kirk acted as president in all but name. Eisenhower soon became disenchanted with Kirk's passivity and encouraged him to leave for the presidency of Rutgers. When Eisenhower left Morningside Heights in January, 1953, to begin his first term as president, Kirk was named his successor.

Low's ground floor resembled a bunker. Heavy steel bars fortified its few windows. At its southeast corner in its L-shaped indentation, one security door led inside. This was the door anti-SDS students had blocked during the noon rally, prompting Gondleman to target the gym's construction site.

In the fading daylight, about 75 students ran the 100 yards from Hamilton Hall to this ground-level door. Campus police, gathered at Hamilton, had left Low unguarded. Anti-SDS students had abandoned their blockade after SDS moved to the gym site. Becker trailed behind, still curious as to what Gondleman might do.

Gondleman found the door locked. His supporters skidded to a stop behind him.

As he walked toward Low, Becker noticed a lone figure standing behind a tree on College Walk. Becker recognized the distinguished profile of 64-year-old Grayson Kirk in a three-piece suit. He was leaving the campus for his eight-bedroom mansion on Morningside Drive, a block from his office. Kirk had stopped to watch the SDS crowd mass next to Low. He was smoking a pipe. No one in SDS had observed Kirk standing by himself, unprotected.

Gondleman stood at the doorway and began speaking to the group, which faced the building.

"We can stand in front of Hamilton to protect the SAS students," he said.

"No, they kicked us out," someone shouted.

"We can do dorm organizing."

"Bullshit!" Action Faction members cried.

"We can have a sit-in right here at Low."

"Bullshit!" Action Faction members cried.

"Educate and build the base," Progressive Labor students shouted.

"Organize and smash the state," countered the Action Faction.

As the dueling chants occupied SDS, Becker moved to the front to get Gondleman's attention. If Mace and Cobb saw Kirk, Becker knew they'd lead the group to surround him. He could be roughed up, or stripped of his clothes or taken to a hiding place and treated as a prisoner of war. Cobb and Mace saw Kirk as one of their own and, therefore, deserving of no mercy. Becker wanted Gondleman to do something before Kirk was discovered.

"We can..." Gondleman started.

"Bullshit," yelled Cobb.

Mace turned to see how many students had gathered. Becker saw him notice Kirk. He grabbed Cobb and said something.

"We can go into Low!" Rooky shouted.

"It's locked, Rooky," an observant Barnard student, Sarah Gildenstein, said impatiently.

Cobb and Mace began moving away from the door.

Becker knew what they were going to do. At that instant, he remembered Hofstadter recounting how Alexander Hamilton had saved Myles Cooper, the president he detested.

Becker took his loaded book bag and swung it around his head once and then as hard as he could into the door's window.

The sound of breaking glass froze the group. They were speechless. None of these communist revolutionaries had ever destroyed private property except for a fence 12 hours earlier.

Becker caught Gondleman's eye.

Into Low! Becker mouthed silently.

"INTO LOW!" Gondleman shouted as he reached through and opened the door.

The crowd took up the cry. Mace and Cobb hesitated and then followed into the building. They ran up the stairs and across the rotunda to Kirk's office.

"It's locked," Gondleman said.

Cobb picked up a free-standing, pedestal sign that announced "Office of the President" and rammed it through the door's glass pane.

"Not anymore," he announced.

The first thing Gondleman did as students explored Kirk's suite was to call Milt and Irene on the president's phone. While it rang, he doodled on Kirk's personal stationery and looked hesitantly through his desk drawers. Gondleman, the revolutionary, did not feel quite right rummaging through another person's belongings even those of An Enemy of the People. He berated himself for his squeamishness. Irene picked up as she was getting supper ready. Rooky thought it best to tell his parents what he had done instead of having them see it on television and then try to contact him. He didn't want his mother showing up at Low Memorial Library with cookies and a change of underwear.

"Hi Mom. We took over a building, the president's office," Rooky said.

"Are you *meshugeneh*?"

"I'm not crazy, Mom. This is politics."

"You took it, so now give it back," Milt responded on the bedroom extension.

"Breaking into a Columbia building and *skvating* in the president's office is crazy in my book," Irene said. "You were raised normal. You always had enough to eat. What am I going to say to people?"

"Tell them I'm a revolutionary. I'm an Americong."

"*Got in himmel*! Milton do something!"

"Aren't you taking rejection of your parents a little too far?" Milt said. "Can't you stop being angry at us for providing you with middle-class comforts?"

"This is not a rebellion against you," Rooky said. "I'm not throwing an adolescent fit. Grayson Kirk is not you."

"Are you sure?" Milt asked.

"He and his kind are the reason we're in the War. Vietnam is just the latest expression of Cold War capitalism's need to intervene in the American Empire -- like the Bay of Pigs -- to keep things under control."

Milt breathed deeply. "I don't think the Bay of Pigs is a good example of the Empire controlling anything."

"The Empire tried, but the People defeated it."

"Are you sure this isn't about the flooring and the siding. I'm...I'm sorry I made you work carpets in the summers."

"Please, Bobby," Irene said. "The pain you're giving me. A mother should not have to bear this from a son, except once."

"I'm not doing this to *you*, Mom," Rooky said. "This isn't about you. It's about American imperialism."

"Heartburn, you're giving me," Irene said. "I might have a stroke. I might have two strokes!"

"Calm down, Mom."

"Bobby, what about your education, your degree?" Milt said.

"This is the first shot in a revolution led by students," Rooky said. "'Up against the wall. This is a stick up!' Like LeRoi Jones said."

"I've known LeRoi since he was little," Milt responded. "His Dad, Colt, worked at the post office; his mother, Anna, was a social worker. Both, good people. I sold them wall-to-wall. LeRoi went to Barringer High. He's now some type of communist. He married a Jewish girl, Hettie Cohen. She's white. When she came in last year, I gave her a discount on the Evans-Black Creslan Crown Prince acrylic. She got the green. Twenty-two yards for their living room and dining room. I gave them half off on installation since it was for Colt's kids. The only thing LeRoi said…that's why I remember it: 'Milt, what's your mark-up on this?' I told him 25 percent for him and Hettie. 'Okay,' he said. 'That's fair enough.' I guess I now have something else to talk to Colt about. Both of us don't understand our kids."

"I'm a communist, too," Rooky said.

"*Oy vey ist mir*," Irene said. "Bad enough a revolutionary, but a communist on top!"

"They go together, Mom."

"The *goyim* will kill you like the Rosenbergs!" Irene said. "I knew a cousin of Ethel's. A Greenglass. She was second fastest in our shorthand class but had bad ankles like Ethel. All the Greenglass girls were real thick in their feet. I don't know why. Now she -- the cousin, I mean -- lives in Scarsdale. Her husband is in staplers. His father had a feather business. Women used to wear them in their hats. He had a plumassier where they made the hats for the carriage trade on West 23rd. But the Audubon ladies closed him down after the Great War. Staplers is a good business. You don't have to kill something to make a stapler."

"Okay," Rooky said.

"Bobby, listed to me!" Irene said. "Don't *schlep* secrets over to the Russians. Promise me!"

Rooky laughed. "I promise."

"What did the Russians ever do for you? I'd put *drek* in their borscht if I could."

"You'll be kicked out," Milt said. "You're throwing away a Columbia degree. Throwing away choices. You'll be damaged merchandise. You'll never get a job. I never had the chance to go to college. This crappy business was the only choice I had. Your grandfather -- the peddler -- would have been so proud of you and your accomplishments."

"I can't leave," Rooky said. "I'm the leader."

"This will be bad for the Jews," Irene said.

"You're acting the way they thought we would if they let us in," Milt said.

"This is about revolution, not *shtetl* Jews," Rooky said with exasperation.

"What do you know about anything?" Irene said. "You're 20 years old. I still do your laundry. How will you eat? Is there a cafeteria in this building where you are? Will take-out deliver? Are you getting enough bran?"

"I'm fine, Mom."

"Are you spitting out your one-a-days like when you were 10? It's the bacon that's doing this, isn't it?"

"Bacon has nothing to do with The Revolution, Mom."

"You didn't do this *mishegoss* when you were eating my food in my kitchen! *Traif* has started this in you!"

"This is not about food, Mom!"

"When will you have time to do your homework? Do you need money?"

"I'll study just like before," Rooky said. "I don't need money. Look, I got to go. I just wanted you to know what's going on and not get the TV version."

He heard his mother sigh, then sniffle. "Bobby, where are you going?"

"I'm going across the tundra, Mom."

"Take a hat, *boychik*."

Rooky hung up. He was embarrassed that his non-political, uneducated, bourgeois father who sold cheap siding, carpet seconds and trinkets to Newark's oppressed had figured out so much about him.

Becker had expected a rampage inside Kirk's suite, but what he saw was timidity. One freshman from Great Neck sat in Kirk's chair at his massive mahogany desk and put his feet up. A Barnard junior from the Upper East Side, Sally Partridge Hamlin, knocked his feet to the floor.

"Don't be an asshole," she said.

"Why not?"

"Because I said so," Sally said. "I know how to act."

Everyone admired Rembrandt's "Portrait of a Dutch Admiral," a bearded, rough-looking, self-confident figure with his hands defiantly on his hips. He resembled how SDS boys wanted to look. It had been donated to Columbia in 1958 by George Ludlum Hartford, heir to the A&P grocery fortune. It had recently been appraised for $450,000. Kirk kept it in his office.

Sedgwick passed out White Owl cigars to the males in the group. "Cheap American, machine-made shit," he announced. "If the clown had class, he would have smuggled in Cubans." A Barnard freshman, Beth Wolkan, demanded that she be given one anyway "as a matter of equal treatment under the Revolution." The boys suggested other uses for the

126

White Owl. She smoldered under their insults as she smoked it like a cigarette.

More than 100 students had squeezed into Kirk's office and began debating what to do next. Becker was complimented for his revolutionary act, but Cobb and Sedgwick knew he had smashed the door to protect Kirk. They filed this for future retribution.

Cobb wanted to leave the building after starting a fire but kept that proposal to himself. What was burning an American university office compared with the daily firestorms American bombers were inflicting on the Vietnamese? But Cobb knew that SDS was not ready to torch a Columbia building. The group had barely gotten past breaking a couple of windows.

"Leave the Ming vases alone," Fishbein warned. Kirk had a collection of 17th-Century porcelains on his shelves. Most used a mixture of kaolin and pottery stone to produce the characteristic intense whiteness along with cobalt for the decorative blue. Several were inlaid with gold.

"Fuck you Fishbein," Cobb said. "Put the knick-knacks on the window ledge so the cops won't shoot teargas at us."

They voted down Cobb's suggestion. They voted not to trash the offices. They voted to search the files for whatever incriminating information they could find. They voted to use ashtrays and keep Kirk's private bathroom as clean as they could. They voted to set up committees: food, defense, cleaning and leadership. The talk then drifted into the contentious area of what theory they thought they were following and where that theory told them to take their occupation.

"We need to barricade the door," Cobb said, "which is how Mao would do it. Desks, file cabinets, chairs—whatever's in here."

"No destruction," Fishbein said. "We want to gather support and not alienate the liberals."

"Menshevik deviant," Albie Green, a freshman from Levittown, charged.

"Mao, Mao, Mao Tse-tung. Dare to struggle, dare to win," the Action Faction chanted.

"Chicken," Cobb yelled at Fishbein.

The Action Faction picked up the chant. "Chicken! Chicken! Chicken!"

The Praxis Axis chanted back: "Educate and build the base!"

The Action Faction countered: "Organize and smash the state."

"Workers unite, make the Revolution," yelled PL members.

"Fucking crazies!" Fishbein's Praxis Axis shouted.

"Power to the workers!" yelled the PLs.

"Fucking chickens!" the Action Faction countered.

"Fuck you, Fishbein," Cobb shouted.

"Fuck you...fuck you twice over, Cobb," Fishbein responded. "Like a potato."

Even Cobb laughed at that.

Becker decided he had seen and heard enough of revolutionary communism in practice. He left as Cobb and others started working on the barricade. He dropped off the four incriminating air-war books at Butler Library on his way home.

II

As the occupation continued, student opponents formed the "Majority Coalition." Some in the Coalition might have agreed with SDS's opposition to Columbia's military and classified research. Most supported building a new gym near the campus. All were opposed to granting amnesty to SDS. They felt a small minority of Columbia's 20,000 undergraduates and graduates were depriving them of the education they had purchased and expected. The Coalition encircled Low to create a blockade that complicated getting food, supplies and supporters into the occupied office. The lines were drawn. SDS had stopped business as usual.

"Meet with them," Minas Barker urged, his hands jerking for emphasis as if he were playing a pair of maracas on important syllables.

Grayson Kirk -- president of Columbia University, political scientist, scholar, administrator, man of the world, director of this, member of that -- didn't respond or even blink. The Minas-Barker-type faculty was what Kirk detested about Columbia, along with a large number of its undergraduates and the endless fundraising that would pour his legacy into concrete. Minas was "the kind of fellow," Grayson once said to Dean Stuntz, "who would run away from the first bullet, whether it was fired at him or by the comrade next to him." Barker's liberalism, his vacillations, his neurotic need to compromise, dither, procrastinate, proclaim, judge, parse, quibble and talk everything to death—made Grayson Kirk want to vomit. Why the faculty elected Minas to represent them in this mess with Gondleman and his band of nihilistic extortionists was a mystery that perhaps, Grayson thought, historians might be able to explain. He couldn't.

Grayson puffed angrily on his pipe. The barbarians were in his office smoking his White Owls. They were special-order "Presidents," Cuban seed leaf grown in the Dominican Republic and machine-made in Dothan, Alabama. Kirk really wanted hand-rolled Cuban Cohibas, but he was afraid of being caught buying from a smuggler. And now, the SDS vulgarians had taped posters of Guevara and Castro on his office wall. Damn them!

Kirk eyed the men sitting with him in the Faculty House on Morningside Drive just north of West 116th Street. The club had been

128

turned into the University's ad hoc headquarters now that his own offices had been "liberated" in the parlance of the moment. Gondleman and his comrades had been there for five days. Kirk had sent a team of security guards to rescue the Rembrandt and the Ming vases. The students handed them over without complaint. Gondleman was quoted in The New York Times as saying that Grayson Kirk "cared more about bourgeois trifles than the University's own students."

Grayson understood that he had an A-Number-One, Big-C Crisis on his hands. Columbia was New York City's one world-class university, and he was its leader and steward. Through its board of directors, the University was connected to Wall Street, The New York Times, broadcast media where many alumni worked, major foundations, the shapers of thought and culture, government, foreign-policy and military communities, research institutions, old money, new money, corporate money and families of consequence. These were the men and organizations who moved things along from both the front and behind. They supported Columbia University financially. Who, he asked himself, would give big bucks to a school that paying students refused to attend? Gondleman had put the University's budget in play, its capital campaign and the very jobs of Grayson Kirk and his appointees. Gondleman had made this madness personal. Him or me, Grayson had decided.

Grayson Kirk was The Establishment's man at Columbia, part of its club by position and adoption, not birth. He came from a humble, central-Ohio, farm family and had not been processed through one of the Ivies. He landed a Columbia teaching job in political science when he was 37 and alternated climbing the faculty and State Department ladders. He acquired polish and affected gravitas as he rose. He took over the University presidency when Eisenhower left after grooming himself for the job. Grayson was a capable administrator—increasing faculty salaries, adding and strengthening the international components of the University's research and teaching, encouraging sponsored-research, constructing buildings and adding volumes to the libraries. In pursuing conventional goals, he was conventional. His one true initiative was to expand quickly and overwhelmingly the amount of federal research in both the physical and social sciences. With students, particularly undergraduates, Grayson was awkward, distant and uncomprehending. They, in turn, felt him to be cold, unyielding and patronizing. With black students and those who represented to one degree or another "the black community" bordering Columbia's campus, he was awkward, distant, uncomprehending and physically uncomfortable. He had come late to the rhetoric and practice of racial equality and had had few interactions with black people other than waiters, maintenance personnel and African diplomats. He went along with small increases in Negro enrollment.

129

Grayson Kirk was a man of the 1940s and 50s, not the spring of 1968. And he knew it. During those earlier decades, he'd supported McCarthy and said Communists were "unfit to teach." He rarely spoke to undergraduates. He particularly disliked having to manage SDS students who, because of their Marxist-Leninist rhetoric, hatred of authority, rigidity and rudeness, were, he thought, unfit to study at Columbia. They didn't negotiate; they issued "non-negotiable demands." Grayson believed he was dealing with little mutant Jewish Hitlers at a second Munich.

Yet, for all of his stiff whiteness and Establishment loyalty, Grayson had urged the United States "to extricate itself as quickly as possible from its current involvement in Vietnam…[by way of] an honorable and orderly disentanglement from this well-meant but essentially fruitless effort" on April 12th at the University of Virginia. Grayson's public opposition to the War was based on his analysis that it was creating enormous divisions in the country as significant as those in the Civil War. In contrast, the Gondleman-SDS opposition to the War was based on rooting for the North Vietnamese to win. Kirk favored a return to domestic tranquility; Gondleman favored as much institutional and social crackup as possible.

Grayson thought he understood undergraduate boisterousness. He had been Phi Kappa Tau at Ohio's Miami University. He understood alcohol-induced rowdiness, which, however, did not include, in his opinion, invading a Barnard dormitory to steal female underwear. The SDS fanatics had transformed traditional adolescent escapades into adolescent frenzies slathered with revolutionary ranting. After Gondleman threw the pie into Colonel Akst's face, Grayson decided that conciliation with SDS would only lead to more of the same. Were Columbia to fall to them, America's other great universities could be toppled in turn…like dominoes. Since Gondleman and his SDS followers mainly wanted to destroy Columbia, Grayson decided his mission was to strip them from the University. That meant no amnesty for the SDS leadership under any circumstances. And no amnesty meant no negotiations.

After five Columbia buildings had been seized that week by more than 1,000 students and others, Grayson heard from important people he considered friends of the University. They did not like breakdowns of great public institutions. They feared anarchy more than change, because anarchy would have to be repressed while change could be shaped. But mainly they were unsettled by not understanding the anger that had been brought to bear against Columbia by their sons and daughters. And Grayson knew the one thing his supporters said they wanted above all others was that whatever was going on at Broadway and West 116th Street, it needed to be ended.

In a career-defining crisis, Grayson knew that a great leader had to appear clear, firm and in control—and never publicly unreasonable. He saw the occupation as a hostage-taking, an extortion, a seizure of private property, a violation of his personal privacy, an infantile outburst orchestrated by several dozen teenagers who took refuge from reality in babbling at each other and everyone else. Aided and abetted by a few sons of genuine privilege and daughters of wealth, like Barnard student Josephine Duke, Grayson understood he was dealing with a volatile mob. In a way, he understood the Jews acting out—Gondleman, Fishbein, Rudd, Freudenberg, Jacobs, Stein, Aronovitz and the rest. Many came from left-wing backgrounds and a cultural history of exclusion and persecution. All Jews, he knew, were not as unpalatable as Gondleman and his SDS crowd.

But Gates Cobb, the son of his friend, Winston, did not belong with them. What were his reasons? And the Sedgwick boy? His was a Mayflower family that had contributed to the building of America in every generation—lawyers, bankers, business people, military leaders, donors. Cobb and Sedgwick had betrayed their families and themselves.

Grayson felt he was facing down a crazed mob from the French Revolution. They had managed to run amok by sitting immobile in his buildings. They had brought his University to a standstill. They refused to negotiate about anything, which was exactly the charge they leveled at him. At least, Grayson thought, the real Communists he had dealt with over the formation of the United Nations accepted a civil framework for unproductive discussions. No real Commie had ever called Grayson Kirk a "motherfucking dirtbag," as Gates Cobb had done.

Columbia sociologist, Daniel Bell, told Grayson the students were rebelling against their parents and their guilt at being privileged. They're acting in a world of their own imaginations, Bell said, even though it may not appear that way. "Yours may be an accurate analysis," Grayson told Bell, "but it doesn't help me get 1,000 brats out of five buildings where they believe they are destroying American imperialism by sleeping and, undoubtedly, fornicating at will."

Grayson's people -- those who counted in his world -- were watching how he resolved this challenge to normalcy. They wanted to see how long it took and what the deal would be. Grayson thought it might be possible to turn this pile of "horseshit," as he put it to himself, into an opportunity to demonstrate his ability to steer through a seemingly unmanageable situation. Skillful navigation might lead to a high position in the State Department or a foundation presidency, say Rockefeller or Ford. Fuck it up, he warned himself, and you're out on your ear with the phone silent for the rest of your life. Grayson, for all his sophistication and poise, knew he came from a hard-scrabble farm in Jeffersonville, Ohio, where his school shoes always carried cow shit.

Minas peered over his half glasses and ran his hand through his thin hair, which he allowed to run increasingly long and ratty at the back where he couldn't see it. His narrow, earnest face was drawn with fatigue.

Grayson looked strained but not rattled. He tried to not appear haggard. He told himself: You can't let them see you sweat.

Minas Barker loved Columbia University where he'd spent all 32 years of his academic career. He genuinely liked teaching anthropology, even to undergraduates. And he had always done enough research and writing to hold up his end of the bargain. Students, even those in SDS, valued Minas. With affection, they imitated his mannerisms and dubbed him Ichabod. They saw him working hard to make the University serve them. While the occupation was antithetical to everything Minas valued in academia, he strained to understand what the radical students were saying. He understood why they treated Grayson Kirk with obvious contempt. When Gondleman shouted at Kirk in a public forum "Up Against The Wall Motherfucker. This is a stick up." Minas recoiled from its brutal crudeness. Which was, he realized, their anthropological point. Even barbarians, as long as they were Columbia students, deserved to be talked to. And he supposed Grayson merited the same. Wasn't talking, and writing, and research, and opinions…wasn't all that what higher education was? SDS wasn't elegant. Their arguments made a kind of sense only within the disconnected world they inhabited. They were unappealing in their rejections, but they were, when more was said and done, students he wanted to teach, because that's who Minas Barker was—a teacher.

Minas stared at Grayson, a man ruling a school whose core values he doubted, staffed with a faculty he believed was quietly subversive of his authority, inhabited by students he ridiculed for their appearance and culture, in a city he feared for the blacks who seethed in its basement and the Jews who had hijacked many of its upper stories. If Grayson Kirk continued with his agenda, Minas believed Columbia would be turned into a trade school for the best and worst of American business, a preparer of managers, a research arm bought by whoever wanted its brains. Minas drew no comfort in knowing that great educational institutions were often headed by individuals who were uneasy with new knowledge and belittled the people who discovered it. Minas could see himself as Socrates setting up in the public square, discussing great ideas with his students and showing them how to argue positions through questions. Grayson Kirk might wear a toga, but Minas Barker knew him to be a Philistine.

Minas considered Grayson Kirk to be a scholar who had sold out. He was mainly an apparatchik for the University's donors who measured Columbia by the number of its bricks, square feet and endowed dollars. Neither Grayson's backers nor he himself cared much about what went on in classrooms or between faculty and students—as long as it wasn't openly sexual.

"They've been in our buildings for five days and four nights," Minas said, stating the obvious, his voice neutral through great effort. "We are

132

teachers, Grayson. The three of us -- elected faculty representatives -- are here to help resolve this situation. What lessons are we teaching by refusing to talk to them directly and genuinely? What are they learning from this tactic? Discursive exchange is what we do, after all. Isn't it?"

"I'll talk directly and genuinely when SDS indicates that it is willing to talk directly and genuinely," Grayson said.

"We should isolate the SDS radicals from the more reasonable idiots in the buildings," Lair Smallwood said. "Marginalize the loonies and then take them out. The body stops when the head is severed. First principle I learned."

Smallwood didn't have to explain where he learned his first principle of dealing with insurgencies. An expert on Asian Communism, Lair had been asked to head the University's East Asian Institute after a career in the Office of Strategic Services and Central Intelligence Agency. A gruff, pipe-smoking man who looked as if he was more comfortable with a five-foot-long Stillson wrench than a fountain pen, Smallwood had been organizing faculty and student support for Grayson Kirk.

"We should negotiate," Minas said. "We are adults. That's what adults do. We should see what they say in private without the television cameras turning Gondleman and the others into instant superstars. We are members of a community of scholars. Reasoned discussion, critical analysis, peer review, peaceful resolution of differences—these are the methods of a university, including ours."

"Quite," said Downing Goolsby, the University's most distinguished poet. "Concede this, Grayson. They have drawn our attention to issues which, in all honesty, none of us would have come to on our own."

"They're not genuine issues," Smallwood sneered. "They're stalking horses. They're excuses to give them cover for being bandits and hooligans. SDS has made SDS's actions the only 'issue.' Their official issues are a phony pretext for action just like the Gulf of Tonkin attack that never happened the way we had to say it did. It was a fake excuse to do what Johnson wanted to do—get in there and kick ass. The SDS 'issues' are no more than rallying cries."

"Yes, well," Downing sniffed. Downing rearranged his New England body, his merganser's nose that sniffed as much as it breathed and his old-Boston sense of civic probity. Luck had given Downing Goolsby a way with language as it had Hawthorne, Melville, Thoreau and Frost. He considered himself fortunate to have been born in the 20th Century, a time when a not-too-bad, mainstream poet from the right background could land a sinecure at a first-rate university that would lend stature to anything he might publish. Downing, who opposed the student occupation, was, nonetheless, enthralled with its Joycean complexities and resistance to being comprehensible. A wonderful tonic for the blahs, he had opined to his third wife, Benedicta, over the egg she had soft-boiled that morning in the French manner. He liked his yolks soft and runny but not watery.

Walter Stuntz, dean of instruction, brought them back from the jungles of recent history. "They are holding a great university hostage to their pathologies. It's their way or nothing."

"When powerless people negotiate from their powerlessness, they never get anything," Minas said. "They only get something when they contrive a way to get a little power. I believe the economists call it, 'leverage.' Of course, high finance is not my field."

"They are students, not 'powerless people,'" Dean Stuntz said. "They are not the wretched of the earth. Well, maybe they are. They are adolescents acting out. We cannot accept *ultimata* given to us by a minority of students."

"*Ultimatums*," Downing corrected, "is now the preferred standard, to our detriment."

Dean Stuntz seethed but did not respond beyond, "Well."

"Quite," Downing offered as a peace-seeking apology. "But they *are* in our buildings regardless of how we feel about their toilet training and, perhaps, the background of a majority of them."

"Once they leave the buildings," Lair Smallwood said, "we can talk with them. But not with a gun at our heads. Never."

"Never," Dean Stuntz repeated.

"I agree," Grayson said. "Negotiating while they are willfully breaking the law of trespass violates the letter of the law, the spirit of scholars and our investment in value-free inquiry. These, these…what do they call themselves, 'geeks..?'"

"'Freaks,' Grayson, not 'geeks,'" Minas said.

"'Freaks,' exactly," Grayson repeated. "Yes, these freaks in the Action Faction are not students. They're Nazis wearing a different insignia. I've seen their kind before."

"'Freaks,' as I understand their usage of the term, refers to the hippie element, not the SDS stalwarts," Downing offered. "I don't think 'freaks' are occupying our buildings."

"A comforting point of information," Grayson said. "Thank you, Downing."

"If you won't talk with them," Minas asked, "what do you propose as an alternative?"

"I'd give them fair warning and then remove the whole kit and caboodle who remain," Dean Stuntz said. "It's a valid use of force, of police power."

"Goddamn right," Lair Smallwood seconded.

"And then?" asked Downing.

"And then the playing field is level once again, and we can talk all we want with them," Dean Stuntz explained, "subject, of course, to disciplinary measures."

"And then," Downing followed up, "you will have a thousand bloodied martyrs to a cause you detest, which will not go away as long as the Vietnam War drags on. I do not support their occupation of the University. But I think the way we act in resolving this will ultimately be more important than the details of the resolution itself."

"I agree," Minas said.

"Better a thousand martyrs than a single successful terrorist," Lair snorted.

Downing Goolsby took note. He was slightly impressed. He had always thought Lair Smallwood had the linguistic agility of a Prussian cabbage.

"Don't people," Minas said, nodding at Lair Smallwood without looking at him directly, "in the military ask of each mission a mantra that goes Purpose, Methods, End State before they start shooting and bombing? Downing's point is that you will achieve an End State through forcible reoccupation that is not in the long-term interest of both this Administration and the University."

"And what would you people," here Lair indicated both Minas, chairman of the Anthropology Department and the poet Downing, "know of military strategy? Really."

"We both served," Minas said matter-of-factly. "I was in the Signal Corps. Four invasions—North Africa, Sicily, Anzio and southern France. I was in the second wave, establishing shore-to-ship communications. With my radioman, I was the target of every German who saw me. Downing drove a tank for Patton. He was second or third into Bastogne in December, 1944."

"Quite," Downing said. "A good bit of excitement except when the Krauts were shooting at me with their King Tigers or the 88s on their *Jagdpanthers*. Their medium tanks were bad enough. Good thing the weather cleared for our planes. Then, they ran out of fuel in the Ardennes. Arthur Rimbaud was born in Charleville on the Meuse River, incidentally. 1854. The poet. Charleville is in France. Bastogne is in Belgium."

"Well, I didn't say what I said the way it might have sounded to you both," Lair backtracked.

"I think we both understood what you meant," Downing observed.

"Lair's point is simple," Dean Stuntz said. "This situation cannot be allowed to go on. Each hour they sit in Grayson's office, Architecture, Fayerweather, Mathematics and Hamilton is an hour of legitimacy credited to them and stolen -- hear me, please -- STOLEN from us and from every student on campus. Students have paid us for our services. We are not holding up our end of the transaction. We would be derelict to allow this farce to continue."

"Some on their steering committee have requested a neutral mediator and negotiations," Minas said. "Fayerweather seems more mature and the most reasonable. Fewer undergraduates there."

"Publicity stunt," Lair scoffed. "Just trying to extend their time in the buildings."

"We have to realize that SDS and those inside are not a majority on campus," Dean Stuntz said. "Most of our students want to go here to get a wonderful education, to get ahead in life. A majority opposes the disruption of classes. The Majority Coalition now surrounds Low. We should support students who support us."

"Supportive faculty are standing with them," Downing added. "Nonetheless, I think it less than wise to act precipitously and drive the independents and undecideds into Mr. Gondleman's arms. We don't want that, do we?"

"If we don't act, they win," Dean Stuntz said.

"I believe that a sizable portion of the student body supports at least some of the SDS demands—canceling the gym in its proposed form and disaffiliating with the IDA," Minas said. "Surely, this protest has shown us that both of these University directions are dubious, certainly in the present context of urban volatility and the War."

"These are University decisions that I am paid to decide," Grayson said. "These are not decisions for undergraduates sitting in my office with their sneakers on my desk...or, for that matter, faculty."

Minas persisted. "Of the 1,500 who agree with at least some SDS demands, only a fraction -- perhaps 30 -- belong to Mr. Gondleman's Action Faction. The other SDS factions, sects, if you will -- Progressive Labor, which is a kind of Maoist grouping and the Praxis Axis, which is more University oriented and more comparatively speaking, mature and reasonable -- together, have maybe another 75 adherents. The most militant are concentrated in Low and Mathematics. An older fellow, Lynn Marcus, some kind of communist who runs the Labor Committee, has influence over Tony Papert, a PL in Low. All of us have heard that Mr. Gondleman opposes negotiations. He was pressured into half-heartedly proposing them. The University would be best served by talking with them if only to isolate the Action Faction for being intransigent and for, I fear, wanting to precipitate a forcible retaking of the buildings. Mr. Gondleman wants us to stain the campus with blood. We should use negotiations to build a bridge to those who share our hope for a peaceful resolution, at least, as peaceable as possible."

"Don't build a bridge unless you're prepared to walk across the damn thing," Lair said. "There's nothing to negotiate until they get their asses out. But I do agree with Minas on one thing. We can beat these bastards by dividing them."

"That is NOT what I meant," Minas snapped.

"But that IS what you said," Lair countered.

Minas persisted, knowing that as a solitary voice in this meeting he had no hope of winning the argument. "We need to encourage the reasonable elements within the buildings by being responsive. That is not manipulation. Our motive should be to do the right thing for the University over the long run, not pick a tactic that might resolve the immediate crisis in our favor. We may still be able to turn this…this episode into a positive. Negotiations will let them air their views to us in private. We should respond reasonably to what we believe are reasonable requests for change. Let Mr. Gondleman be seen as intransigent, not us, not the faculty and Administration of our beloved University. Not us, the adults in the room."

Grayson Kirk relit his pipe and blew out smoke through his nose.

"Gentlemen," he said. "We are being asked to negotiate with those who reject American civilization and our University. They demand amnesty from the very authorities whose legitimacy they deny. They demand we abrogate lawful research for our own government, research to protect America. They support our enemies abroad, enemies who are at this very minute killing our fellow Americans. They demand that we not provide our students with adequate gymnasium facilities.

"They talk about 'democratizing' the University. Would you, Professor Barker or you Professor Goolsby, care to define that term for me? What is this 'participatory democracy' about which they speak? Which model of democracy are they advocating? That of Athens? Of Jefferson, the slaveholder? A New England town meeting? No, not these. It is the democracy of mob mayhem. It is the democratic centralism of Marxist-Leninism in some form or other. Perhaps it's the civil liberties of Uncle Joe or Uncle Ho. These SDS are communists, not democrats. Let us not be innocents. If they say they are revolutionary Communists, the least we can do is believe them. Practically speaking, I doubt that we can resolve this situation through negotiations. I think we're faced with a question of how big and how bloody a reassertion of legal authority will be. I would like all of us at this table to face this reality."

"They are acting out," Minas responded, "because we provided no channels for them to communicate with us."

Lair Smallwood exploded: "Right! The 'SYSTEM' is to blame. Law creates criminals. Wealth creates poverty. Hospitals make you sick. Schools make you dumb. This is nonsense, fashionable nonsense. Straight out of The New York Review of Books."

"One should not blame a mirror," Minas countered, "for the reflection."

"Bullshit," Lair spat.

"They have channels," Grayson said to Minas. "The students have an observer at the faculty senate. My door has not been closed to them. I've had discussions with Gondleman's group twice this academic year. I walk to my office every day. We have deans at every level of instruction. Coleman knows them. We have always been prepared to listen to them in the normal course of University business. But we are not -- and cannot ever be -- prepared to suspend our procedures in the face of blackmail, or to stop acting legally or to forsake judgment and reason. I was available for talking with them at any moment until they seized my buildings. I remained ready even after I saw them break a window at Low. I am not going to capitulate."

Minas looked to Downing Goolsby who, though he opposed the occupation, was his one possible ally. The poet had no more to say.

The men sat uncomfortably with each other in silence.

"This University," Lair Smallwood said, "is like any organism. It has a right to protect itself against cancer, to fight it off, to kill it. We will be best served by viewing Gondleman and the SDS as a spreading tumor. And the best way to deal with a malignancy is to cut deeply and get all of it out as fast as possible."

"Surgical wounds heal," Dean Stuntz added.

"They are wounds of the flesh," Downing inserted.

"But those of the spirit…" Minas began.

Lair Smallwood rolled his eyes and mocked playing a violin.

"Amnesty implies that we tolerate what they have done," Dean Stuntz said. "If we were to give them amnesty, we would face an occupation every spring, followed by a demand for amnesty."

"If you gave them amnesty and offered to negotiate," Downing said, "my, my, I think they would have no further grounds for continuing their occupation."

"You, Grayson, have the power to lift the probation of the six," Minas added. "Bring no charges against the thousand in the buildings…and, maybe, we can slip out of this trap."

"Remember," Downing said, "George Washington granted amnesty to participants in the Whiskey Rebellion. Andrew Johnson granted amnesty to all the Confederates who committed treason against our country."

"The first example, I believe," Minas said, "was in Athens in 403 B.C. It ended a civil war."

"Amnesty implies that we, the adults, are willing to discuss our shared problems in good faith absent vindictiveness," Downing said.

"I cannot absolve the guilty," Grayson said. "I cannot negotiate with trespassers and kidnappers."

"They're our students," Minas said.

"They're criminals," Dean Stuntz said.

"Talk with them," Minas pleaded.

138

"No," Grayson said. "If we give in to Gondleman, we will never regain our moral authority."

"What moral authority do we have left?" Minas asked.

The question stayed among them like an uninvited guest who no one wanted to confront.

III

The late night on April 30th was pleasant. A soft breeze from the west swept over the University, laying Hudson River's breath over the campus. The new sodium lamps, which Grayson Kirk had installed the previous fall, made Columbia's grounds glare like a prison yard. Almost 900 students were barricaded in five University buildings, awaiting removal by 1,200 New York police and plainclothes officers.

Jeffrey Becker was standing on the brick sidewalk with about 75 students in front of Low's southeast security door. The window he had shattered with his book bag eight days earlier had been repaired. Students opposed to removing the occupiers by force had wedged themselves in front of the door. They sat or stood, arms linked, facing about 200 policemen who were lined up silently in full battle dress five feet away. Technicians adjusted spotlights to improve visibility for the police.

Becker linked his arms through students on either side. This was not going to work, he thought. This was going to be a massacre.

As rumors of the impending police action -- The Bust -- grew, Becker and several hundred others began patrolling the campus each night to place themselves between the police and those inside. This unnamed, unorganized, unaffiliated group opposed using police even though they did not support one or more aspects of the takeover or Gondleman's refusal to negotiate.

Becker squinted into the bright lights that were focused in his face. He could only see police silhouettes and their nightsticks, but not who looked scared and who eager.

John O'Malley, assistant police commissioner, stepped forward in full uniform and unfolded a legal-sized document. He began reading the injunction through a bullhorn. It authorized the police to reestablish full "ingress and egress" for the benefit of Columbia University. The students loudly sang "We Shall Overcome," deliberately drowning out O'Malley's words, which a first-year law student optimistically announced would make them immune from the injunction's penalties. Between the end of "We Shall Overcome" and the beginning of "We Shall Not Be Moved," O'Malley shouted that anyone blocking the doorway had 10 minutes to leave or suffer the consequences.

Becker tried to think through one last time how he had ended up "protecting" Rooky Gondleman and the Action Factionistas after withdrawing from Fayerweather Hall because of him and them.

He could identify three reasons. He likened two of them to weak grips on a greasy trapeze bar.

The first was sort of stupid, he conceded. It was a fuzzy abstraction that you either embraced or rejected. Becker believed that History gave most people a chance to take a small turn pushing its wheel only once or twice. When it came around, you took your place and leaned into it. As screwed up as the occupation was, as manipulative as the occupiers were, these eight days would be considered History. So he would take his place pushing the wheel that was presented to him.

Reason Two was simple. Becker believed that police intervention in a University dispute would have miserable consequences for all sides apart from the resulting injuries. He could see a way through the stand off without falling into Rooky's trap, but it required what political scientists called "give and take."

Reason Three was easier to explain but harder to live with. Becker saw Gondleman for all of his insufferable posturing as not much more than an inexperienced 20-year-old. The press in its desperation to "explain" the Columbia rebellion by plastering a face and a personal history on it had anointed him the Malcolm X of the white New Left. Rooky was not a victim who elicited sympathy. Becker knew he was in no sense blameless for America's impression of him as a loud-mouthed, anarcho-Maoist nut.

Becker had seen Gondleman saddled and now ridden with notoriety and symbolism even he didn't deserve. Publicity had launched him as a new product to America's parents and their children. The three television networks, each competitively desperate for the inside quote from the "leader," interviewed him daily. Time and Newsweek ran his picture. The New York Times carried a personality profile, which mentioned to his mortification the red vinyl dinette set in Irene's kitchen and her decorative plastic fruit. Irene was quoted as saying: "I raised a Boy Scout, not a communist." Milt said: "We don't know why he's doing these things." Several stories dwelt on the recollections of classmates at his Bar Mitzvah party. Time devoted three-quarters of a page to a description of Milton's siding and carpet business. Four reporters searched in vain for evidence that he was a ghetto slumlord.

Reporters groped for ways to explain the unprecedented. They retreated into quoting sociologists and social psychologists. The photograph of plastic fruit showed New York Times readers that Rooky Gondleman was just a lower-middle-class Jew from the white, refugee enclave of Passaic who, for that reason, could not really be expected to understand how the world worked. A sociologist said that Gondleman was "rebelling against the angst of upward mobility."

140

The way reporters magnified Gondleman was to frame the crisis as a personality clash between representatives of two generations: Kirk, the unyielding, aged guardian of the East Coast, WASP Establishment's interest in business as usual versus Gondleman, the firebrand who spoke for alienated youth.

The magnifying glass of press attention turned Gondleman from a self-righteous, dismissible ideologue into the closest thing America had to a revolutionary Lenin. Reporters broadcast his words through their megaphones. This doused him with the flash notoriety that added weight to his every opinion, leaving him defenseless against his own ignorance. Intransigence sold. Confrontation succeeded. Disruption worked.

Gondleman understood that he was ensnared in the odd sycophancy of reporters encouraging him to "say something radical." The more he disdained "Establishment" reporters, the more hostility he displayed toward them and their work, the more they unfurled his origins for late-night snickering. They anointed the Columbia demonstration in their between-the-lines smugness as an Oedipal conflict—a primal, teenage surge against America's paternalistic, middle-class myths by America's most middle-class children. They let readers draw their own conclusions about SDS's advocacy on behalf of people who mostly wanted to get some of what Gondleman rejected, people who Gondleman didn't know and likely feared or dismissed. So the louder Rooky roared in anger and frustration, the bigger the crowd of reporters grew around the cage that he and they had constructed.

It was obvious to Becker that Rooky had started something that was now leading him more than he was leading it. But it was also clear to Becker that Rooky had become addicted to the attention he received. He was a pawn who had crowned himself and, in turn, been crowned a King with little idea of how to rule. He had no experience managing a complicated crisis. Those of Becker's professors who did -- with the exception of Alan Westin -- had shown themselves to be as clumsy and rigid as their student opponents. Rooky's only way of handling something that was over his head was to reiterate the SDS demands without flexibility. He had no interest in making Columbia better or different. SDS had a single line—stop classes, research and functioning.

Becker walked out of Fayerweather Hall after five days, disgusted with Gondleman and SDS tactics. The Action Faction feared Grayson Kirk might actually act like the political scientist he was and negotiate a compromise acceptable to most on both sides. A negotiated settlement would undercut the Action Faction's analysis of Kirk as no more than a puppet for America's ruling class. A negotiated settlement under which they left the buildings voluntarily, the Action Faction agreed in private caucus, would be a loss, not a win. Gondleman wanted the police to evict them in a manner that would polarize the campus, radicalize the liberals, force the independents to choose a side and discredit the Administration. To scotch negotiations, Gondleman demanded as a precondition for discussion that the University grant amnesty to all students even though a likely majority of occupying students favored negotiations without any precondition. Gondleman, who chaired the strike's steering committee's meetings, made sure negotiations never took place. Amnesty was Gondleman's worst fear.

"So what can I do about the press distorting us?" Rooky had asked Becker a day earlier following a steering committee's meeting. "Shut up?"

"It couldn't hurt," Becker said, as they sat on the floor of Grayson Kirk's office sharing a lukewarm pizza.

"How about if I appoint Cobb to be our spokesman?" Gondleman joked.

"If Grayson thinks you're impossible to deal with, let him live with Cobb for a while. Or Godzilla."

"Cobb's father still plays squash with Grayson at the New York Athletic Club. Cobb admitted he played doubles with Grayson a couple of times when he was in high school," Gondleman said. "Grayson pretends he doesn't know Cobb. To protect his Dad, I guess."

"Cobb's a semi-psychopath who's infatuated with violence," Becker said. "Still, he might be able to work things out over drinks with Grayson, sweaty knee to sweaty knee in the locker room."

"Maybe Episcopalians make their deals when they're toweling off or comparing squash rackets," Gondleman giggled. "Jews like me do it over brisket and salt sticks."

"Cobb has America's magic, except he's gone crazy," Becker said, "temporarily, anyway. I think he'll grow out of it."

"Maybe it's the kind of crazy that made revolutionaries in 1776."

"I think it's the kind of crazy that can kill a large number of people in the name of a greater good, like Stalin," Becker said. "Anyway, whatever the magic is, I don't have it and neither do you. But even you, even now that you've become mythic, even you Gondleman can be anything you want in America."

"No one can take a college education away from me," Gondleman laughed. "Except me, of course."

"Well, you haven't gotten one yet," Becker said, "and at this rate you won't get a Columbia degree."

"The Revolution will be my career credential."

"You're an idiot," Becker said.

"I can always finish at some rinky-dink school. Peehead State."

"You are forfeiting a lot, maybe everything. You'll end up in jail."

"It's where revolutions simmer before they boil."

"Jail is where your ass will be fried," Becker said.

"A prison record," Gondleman laughed, "is always something I can fall back on."

"Your odds are certainly better for wearing stripes than commanding America's military."

"But I am moving up in the world. My mother sees me on TV. She says, 'Why is Bobby doing this to me?'"

They laughed at that. And then stopped.

"Are you sure you have to quit?" Gondleman asked.

"This demonstration changed," Becker said. "You changed it. You could get something reasonable out of this, a win. My guess is they're ready to give up the gym now and the IDA down the road. That's a victory. But that's not what you want. It's dishonest to use people this way."

"I started it."

"That doesn't make it yours to decide for everyone. You're playing God with the lives and careers of hundreds of students. You're using them. You're sacrificing them"

"No one's forcing them to support us."

"Most, like me, want to negotiate, to get something out of this. You know they won't concede on amnesty. You want a police bust."

"No one's keeping them in the buildings," Gondleman said. "If they don't accept SDS's leadership, they can leave."

"Which is exactly what I'm doing. And you're the reason."

"Bullshit! You just don't want to be here when the shit comes down."

"The real shit has already come down. That's why I'm leaving. I don't have the stomach for what you're doing."

"So go hide in the stacks with the other liberal intellectuals," Gondleman said and then bit into the last slice of pizza.

Becker stood up. "Who's the real enemy?"

Gondleman looked up from the floor. "You."

Becker nodded. The gap was unbridgeable.

Gondleman said: "C'mon Beck. I won't put you up against a wall."

"I'm not sure I can say the same," Becker said. "I hope I wouldn't. You're killing what's moving in the right direction."

"We'll see," Gondleman said. "Don't miss the Rooker's end game."

"Queens into pawns," Becker said sadly.

"Pawns into Queens. Grayson will do it for us."

As the spotlights made him squint, Becker thought to himself, I am an idiot. The students stopped singing. The police tensed. Becker saw that people were going to get hurt; possibly killed. He felt angry and foolish for trying to "protect" Gondleman and the others in Kirk's office. But he would feel worse if he didn't try. It occurred to him at that moment that

143

adult life in modern America was likely to be a series of unavoidable choices between not-too-bads on one hand and not-too-goods on the other. Congratulations, he said silently, you've just received your degree.

"We're going to get creamed," Becker said to the kid standing next to him.

"You'll remember it fondly 30 years from now. You can tell your grandkids."

The police spread their lines sideways to contain the students within the corner of Low Library.

"A rock and a hard place," Becker said.

"In between-ness is no longer an existential abstraction, is it?"

Assistant Police Commissioner O'Malley pointed to the center of the first line of students, standing three deep in front of the door. A wedge of police formed and stepped forward.

"POLICE OFF CAMPUS! NO COPS!"

O'Malley, a career officer in his mid-50s, pointed to a captain who tugged his ear for the benefit of Sgt. Jack McCracken who stood at the point of the police wedge. McCracken leveled his arm at the students. The wedge flew into them like a team charging in a game of Red Rover.

Becker saw the two student lines in front of him recoil under the attack. The first line broke as the police pulled apart linked arms. When students couldn't be separated, the police dragged them in pairs over the sidewalk. Frustration led to nightsticks being used, first on arms and shoulders, then on heads. The night filled with odd sounds—the thunk of wood hitting flesh and bone, the grunts of policemen, the cries of fear, anger and pain. Some students on their backs kicked like overturned crabs. Others wrapped their legs around each other to stifle the police. Shouts of "HOLD ON!" turned into a chorus. Then "HOLD THAT LINE!" Becker thought of Peabody football games.

Even the strongest cops began to bog down amid the mass of unwilling, struggling, resisting students. Becker saw they had lost control even though the resistance was mostly passive. Each cop was working in his own manner to disentangle students. Anything went, and everything did. One by one, students were eventually pitched into the middle of the wedge where advancing ranks pummeled them. A few girls were dragged off by their heels and manhandled before being abandoned. No one was arrested.

The police had been idling on the Columbia campus for a week. They were tired of watching kids of privilege thumb their noses at authority. Many were itching to even up the class score even as SDS proclaimed its solidarity with The Workers.

144

The student line closest to the door sat down. A sweating cop stood over Becker. "MOVE! GODDAMN IT!"

Becker looked up. He saw the shiny black nightstick rise. He tucked his knees against his chest, covered his head with his arms and hands and rolled onto his side. The nightstick landed on the flat of his left shoulder blade, leaving a line of pain. He spun and crawled out of his protective curl. He scooted on his knees between two cops who were working on other students. As he stood, a short man in a dark windbreaker swung wildly at his head. Becker, who was taller than his attacker, leaned back. The pull of the missed punch swiveled the plainclothes cop into a tailor's seat. Becker looked down at him, puzzled. "Why did you do that?" Becker asked. The cop shrugged and gave him an embarrassed grin. Becker smelled alcohol. He wasn't sure whether the cop felt funny about throwing a wild punch or about having missed.

After about 15 minutes, the entrance was cleared of students. A double line of police formed and marched into Low Library through the security door. Becker rubbed his shoulder as he watched. It didn't feel like a broken bone, but it hurt. He turned to walk to the west side of Low Library where Gondleman and about 150 others had barricaded themselves in Grayson's office.

As each of the five buildings was cleared, several hundred students like Becker and a few sympathetic faculty milled around College Walk, between busses filled with captured students and a row of tall hedges bordering the grassy South Field. Many prisoners had been knocked around. Their mood was as much shock and disbelief as anger.

Becker noticed President Kirk and Dean Stuntz standing with O'Malley who was speaking into a walkie-talkie. A half-dozen uniformed police stood protectively behind them.

Becker stepped in front of the three men. "Is this what Columbia is now?" he asked.

Grayson Kirk stared blankly across the lighted South Field toward Butler Library, beloved for its cubbyholes and open stacks. Grayson wanted nothing more at that moment than to be sitting in his special room on Butler's third floor, a fresh legal pad on his desk, thumbing through recent books on political behavior. Instead, he watched City buses on College Walk, grille to exhaust pipe, from Broadway to Amsterdam, being filled with hundreds of chanting, screaming, bloodied students in handcuffs. "JOIN US! JOIN US!" Those who resisted were tossed roughly and headfirst into a paddy wagon, not a bus.

"Whoever you are," Dean Stuntz said, "I suggest that you leave the campus immediately. This is not a time for debate. You people had your chance. Now it's adult time."

"I want him to answer, not you," Becker said.

"Ya don't belong here, kid. Now SCRAM," O'Malley brayed in a Bay Ridge voice that had once cheered the Dodgers in Ebbets Field.

Becker ignored him.

"Wait," Kirk said. "You're the one who broke my window."

"I'm the one who saved your ass...for this!"

"THROW DA KID OUTA HERE," O'Malley shouted to the uniforms standing behind him.

They moved quickly, twisting Becker's arms into hammerlocks. They flung him down the steps onto College Walk.

"My men are through their fortifications," O'Malley reported to Grayson Kirk. "They piled up desks and chairs. It took 15 minutes to clear a way through. McCracken reported that a lot of students resisted. They soaped the floors and steps to injure us. Jeez! What kind of kids are these? I heard them over the walkie-talkie calling my men, 'PIGS!' This ain't going to go down well with my police. There will be some injuries."

"Whose?" Dean Stuntz asked.

"Theirs, mostly," O'Malley said.

"Theirs" meant ours, Grayson thought. "Theirs" meant his. Grayson knew Gondleman had won. Kirk had made Gondleman's point.

"SHAME!"

Minas Barker stood shaking before Kirk and Stuntz as blood ran down his cheek and neck from an open slash across his forehead. His gray hair was matted with sweat and blood.

"This is your doing," Minas said, pointing his wobbling finger at Grayson's chest. "SHAME!"

"Minas, you're hurt. Let me get you an ambulance. My God...I didn't.... Minas, what happened to you?"

"I volunteered to be a faculty observer. To restrain by our presence these Nazis of yours," he said, looking at O'Malley and the cops behind him. He pointed to a strip of white adhesive tape wrapped around the upper arm of his sports jacket. "They beat us in front of Mathematics. We were just standing in front, not resisting. Then again in front of Architecture. Sam Meeker, from public law and government, your own department, was clubbed to the ground. And Irv Odleman, the Dante man, was carried off on a stretcher."

"I was assured that.... Wait. Minas. Walter will help you to the hospital or home," Grayson said, glancing toward Dean Stuntz.

"I'm not going home. I need to bear witness to this...this holocaust."

Minas Barker, respected chair of the Anthropology Department, stumbled toward the crowd on College Walk. He pressed his folded hanky against his head wound, hoping to stop the bleeding before he went back to his apartment on Riverside Drive. He did not look forward to explaining to his wife, Phoebe, what a 55-year-old academic whose specialty was Mongolian taboos was doing fighting with New York City policemen.

146

Grayson watched him go. He started mumbling about an article he had written years ago when he was still an instructor. "This is like MacArthur ordering 500 infantry with fixed bayonets, 500 cavalry and six French battle tanks under George S. Patton against the Bonus Army veterans camped out on the Anacostia Flats in July, 1932." He was speaking out loud but only to himself. "They killed two, teargassed them, injured four or five dozen, arrested more than 100. The Bonus Army was evicted. Herbert Hoover ordered the eviction. He lost his reelection. I'm Hoover, and this will be my deepest scratch on history. I've written my obituary."

Amid his self-pity, Grayson Kirk knew that blood had not stopped flowing on his campus.

"The five buildings are now free of students," O'Malley said, with the walkie-talkie held to his ear. "We have about 800 arrests. We have Gondleman. He offered no resistance. All the blacks left Hamilton Hall without a fight. None of them suffered a scratch. No firearms were found. At least seven of my men have sustained injuries. One seems to have a broken back from a kid jumping on him from a second-floor window. We should clear and secure the campus."

"Clear?" Grayson asked.

"Otherwise, those who are left will retake your buildings. You filed the trespass charge. We're enforcing the court order."

It occurred to Grayson that Assistant Police Commissioner O'Malley was not asking for his permission.

"This is to be done without brutality," Grayson said. "The minimum amount of force. The absolute minimum."

"Of course. But my men are under orders to protect themselves at all times in hostile confrontations. Your students threw books on my men from the third-floor windows at Mathematics. I have three down with backs from slipping on soaped stairways. And one heart attack."

"I want to see my office." Grayson wandered up the steps into Low Library and then into his suite. The wreckage and chaos stunned him. His beautiful inner door -- a nine-foot walnut masterpiece with a hand-carved University seal -- had been smashed by a battering ram and torn from its top hinge. Miss Thorner's file cabinets were overturned, their contents on the floor. The suite of offices was littered with paper, ripped clothing, tennis shoes, books, comics and coffee cups. It smelled of sweat, fried chicken, corned beef and peanut butter. "CHE LIVES!" was spray-painted in red on his office wall, facing his desk in letters the size of cheerleaders.

He leaned against his office doorway. His desk lay upside down against one wall, hacked and scarred by police fire axes used to break through the furniture barricade. SDS had piled his four handmade Windsor guest chairs against the door. They lay sprawled like Civil War casualties. He noticed the slogans on his walls: "End war research at Columbia,"

"Stop the War," "No gym," "Kill pigs" and "Pigs eat shit." (Later, Grayson learned that plainclothes officers had contributed the pig references after his office had been cleared of students.) He retrieved his empty humidor and put it under his arm. He heard a sound like a small sail luffing in a light breeze. The change of underwear he kept in his bathroom dresser hung on a cord in a shattered window.

"How could civilized people do such things?" he asked to no one in particular.

Dean Stuntz said: "Now we know exactly what we're dealing with. They have forfeited any claim to be our students."

"And I have forfeited any claim to this office."

As Grayson was examining the shambles of his career, O'Malley was ordering his men to form three long parallel lines in front of Low Library, overlooking the crowd on College Walk. The police faced Butler Library. Minas Barker and a handful of other faculty walked among the bedraggled, angry students trying to calm them and get them to leave the campus. "It's the nature of the beast," Minas said repeatedly, referring to police behavior. The last bus and paddy wagon drove off College Walk and turned left onto Broadway as the prisoners sung and stamped their feet.

Becker saw her by the Sundial. He went over.

"What are you doing here?" he asked.

Allyson Pickering turned toward him. Her right eye was swollen shut and purple in the high-intensity light. Blood seeped from her nose.

"Jesus!" he said.

"Four of us drove up late this afternoon. We thought it was time to put our Quaker principles into practice. I called, but no one answered."

"Let me take you to St. Luke's Emergency Room. It's just a couple of blocks away."

"Some cop hit me in front of Fayerweather. They were going crazy. Hitting everybody. No reason. Out of control."

"A doc better take a look at your eye. You might need stitches. Is your nose broken?"

"It feels sore, not broken. I don't want to leave. I want to see how this ends," she said.

Without warning, the three lines of police charged down the steps toward College Walk. They barreled in with nightsticks and rubber truncheons. The crowd fell back and piled up against the thick hedges. People tried to push through the bushes to South Field but were stopped by a slatted snow fence. Those who lost their footing were clubbed and trampled.

Becker and Allyson retreated down the wide sidewalk that connected the Sundial to Butler Library. They ran past Butler's main entrance to a tall, ornamental iron gate on West 114th Street. It was locked with a steel chain.

"CLIMB IT," he shouted.

They were straddling the top pikes of the 12-foot-high gate when dozens of terrified students appeared below them just ahead of the police line. The boys boosted the girls up onto the iron framework. Some fled into the basement of Ferris Booth Hall, an adjacent student center. The police closed, hitting the climbers with their sticks. Other policemen ran into Ferris Booth in hot pursuit.

On the other side and on the ground, Becker looked toward Broadway. A line of police had assembled across that end of West 114th Street. They were preparing to move down the block toward Amsterdam Avenue, driving and clearing students from a public street.

"Shit," he said, "they're coming this way."

He looked toward Amsterdam Avenue. A line of six mounted police were slowly walking their horses toward them.

"Open your doors! Let us in," Becker shouted to the boys watching from the windows of fraternity row.

"Fuck you. Die pukes! Go cops!"

"There's Trip's house," Allyson said.

Beer bottles splattered on the street.

"They're throwing bottles at me," Allyson said in disbelief, repeating the obvious.

Becker's eye fell on the trash cans in front of the fraternity houses.

"They'll kill us here in the middle of the block," he said. "If you don't want to run through the horses, hide under a car. Maybe they won't see you. If you're going with me, grab beer bottles from the trash. Get as close to the horses as you can, then break the bottles right in front of them as you run past. Stay low and move fast. It's our only chance."

Becker, Allyson and a handful of others scooped up bottles and ran toward the horses.

"Now!" someone shouted.

Bottles shattered, popping like firecrackers. The riders stopped their horses, not wanting them to step on the broken glass. The horses milled, opening narrow escape lanes. The riders were slow to realize they should dismount. Becker heard them swearing. As the Broadway police line closed toward the middle of the block, they looked under cars and yanked hiders into the open where they were clubbed for no reason.

Where 114th met Amsterdam Avenue, Becker turned back toward Allyson to get her to St. Luke's. She wasn't there.

He looked down the block.

She was backed against Butler Library, a pretty girl with a purple shiner and a bloody nose, hemmed in by angry cops under the unforgiving brightness of Manhattan street lights.

Some moments hang in the mind's permanent gallery. Although time would fade details -- names, faces, exact words -- Becker would never forget the image of Allyson Pickering, her eye closed like a beaten boxer, her nose dripping blood, her hands open with palms up, walking toward the closing circle of cops, saying calmly "I am a pacifist. I will not hurt you."

Becker heard footsteps and heavy breathing behind him. He jumped away from the sound. The swishing arc of a nightstick whizzed past his ear. A cop grabbed his shirt. Fear pumped adrenalin. Becker broke free and ran down Amsterdam Avenue toward his building.

Becker sat in his small living room in apartment 4F at 3:35 a.m., stunned, exhausted and trying to make sense of what had happened. He was glad to have escaped. He hoped Allyson had been lucky. He berated himself for not saving her, for not even trying. Instinct, not thought, had made him flee. It was cowardice, he thought, as he sat sheltered.

I love her, and I ran away when she was in trouble.

Why did Gondleman play this game like a dummy? Becker asked himself. Everyone should have just walked out when the cops started massing. Victory could have been declared as everyone left just like Johnson should do in Vietnam. No arrests, no injuries, no penalties—yet the point of the protest would have been stuck in just as deeply. What revolutionary hero sets himself up for arrest, or worse? Not Che, not Ho, not Mao. Who indeed but Rooky Gondleman, Gates Cobb, Stuey Fishbein, Mark Rudd, John Jacobs, Mace Sedgwick, Stu Gedal, Tony Papert, Ted Gold and Dave Gilbert?

To Becker, the truth was that SDS could not make a decision to leave with a victory. Its internal dynamics permitted no decision other than what it did. It had no plan for what Columbia might be.

IV

Those hours in April, 1968, changed Grayson Kirk and Rooky Gondleman, and everyone else who went through them.

The University's troubles did not end with the retaking of the campus. Many students went on strike to protest the police action. A few weeks after The Bust, SDS organized another building occupation that produced more arrests. Classes were canceled. Professors stopped teaching in classrooms and switched to blankets spread on the four grassy acres between Butler Library and College Walk. Grades were waived in favor of pass-fail.

The police action had deflated the University like a pricked soufflé just as Gondleman and SDS had hoped. Its offices functioned, its phones rang and were answered, but it was educating its students by its behavior. Gondleman and some 30 others were expelled that summer. They no longer cared. Rooky and a dozen from Columbia looked forward to making a revolution.

Columbia University changed, mostly for the better after the spring of 1968, but it was a long, hard journey. Alumni donations slacked. Grayson Kirk left. Vice-President David Truman left. University administrators became more student-friendly. The faculty took on a more prominent role in University governance. Minas Barker was elected president of the new faculty senate with a seat on the University's Board of Trustees. Institutional ties with the IDA ended. The gym was not built in Morningside Park; it was built at the north end of the campus. The student body became more diverse. Applications fell. The campus calmed; no one wanted to go through another 1968. It took years for the trauma to wear off. Anyone who was there did not forget.

By the end of 1969, SDS national membership had dwindled to a few hundred after its leaders took them through a series of bizarre "actions" to toughen themselves and radicalize white, working-class youth. To promote a communist revolution, they picked fights with working-class guys they called "the grease." Some 70 SDS women ran through Pittsburgh's South Hills High School in September, exposing their breasts, yelling "Jail Break" and chanting slogans for women's liberation and victory for the Vietnamese National Liberation Front. The high-schoolers stared in wonder. Twenty-six women were arrested. More than 250 arrests followed in October during the "Days of Rage," a series of street fights in Chicago between SDS and police. SDS leaders had predicted thousands would show up—only 500 did. This failure led the Gondleman faction to move toward guerrilla war rather than more mass organizing. By the end of the 1960s, SDS could no longer function. It was divided into factions with each promoting a cultish ideology to increasingly fewer adherents. Where it had claimed 100,000 members and 300 chapters in 1968, SDS had whittled itself down to about 50 individuals who were willing to go underground.

The Gondleman faction -- headed by him, Paulette Rotz, Bernadine Dohrn, Jeff Jones, John "JJ" Jacobs, Dave Gilbert, Howard Machtinger, Karen Ashley, Bill Ayers, Mark Rudd, Ted Gold, Terry Robbins and Kathy Boudin -- led itself into a hole of its own digging in early 1970. They called themselves Weathermen—because, they said, you didn't need any ideology other than theirs to know the correct path to communist utopia. They believed in four Maoist ideas: 1) the end justifies the means; 2) violence is the way to acquire and keep political power; 3) nothing would change unless leaders controlled what everyone thought; and 4) top-down leadership and follower obedience was the only way to win.

The approach of the Weathermen -- later the Weather Underground -- in the 1970s was to make war on America by Americans against Americans from within America. This strategy was carried out by hidden cells operating secretly. They were following the *foco* theory of Regis Debray, a French philosophy professor and Guevara friend. Debray argued that small, nimble guerrilla groups could activate a broad, working-class rebellion through violent attacks.

The Weather Underground initiated a decade-long campaign to dismantle American capitalism and its governing system through more than 30 bombings that targeted police facilities, corporations and federal institutions. The communism they sought borrowed heavily from Mao and Castro. Unlike Mao's revolution, the Underground's version shied away from killing, kidnapping or maiming people. It never fought gun battles. It was mild in comparison with what it might have been and with its American precedents.

Rooky found himself both notorious and celebrated for his role in Columbia's miseries. In 1968 and 1969, he was feted by some in New York City's Old Left who wanted to rub against the now-trendy chevrons of student revolt. Others from the Old Left considered him to be undisciplined and juvenile.

As a revolutionary leader, SDS women were available to Rooky, along with pot, LSD and other drugs. Sex within the group was now a compulsory part of the share-and-share-alike communism they believed would bind them into a revolutionary fighting force. Couples were discouraged. With random sex, came body lice, gonorrhea and various genital infections, the most common of which they called "Weather crud." Even so, this, Rooky understood, was better than sliding through life as a chess-nerd King whose closest female companion was his inanimate Queen.

Paulette Rotz was the fountainhead of SDS in the late '60s and then of the Weather Underground. She was a bright and serious woman who had edited her suburban Detroit high-school newspaper and had been accepted into the National Honor Society. She entered Denison University where Beta Beta Beta blackballed her for being half-Jewish. She transferred to the University of Pennsylvania at the end of her freshman year and went on to earn a law degree.

Unlike most SDS/Weather women, Paulette was genuinely sensuous. She had the mesmerizing looks of the high-school cheerleader and dancer she had once been. She had learned how to use her intoxicating mix of hardness, intelligence, outrageous opinions and sexual availability to control the men around her. She played up her striking face and figure for media photographers and her followers. Favoring mini-skirts, high leather boots and low-cut tops, she often pinned a button on her tight sweaters: "Cunnilingus is Cool; Fellatio is Fun." She created a Weather style. During street riots, she kept an eye-liner pencil in her pocket. When arrested, she managed to look put together. SDS men lusted after her; SDS women wanted to be her. She welcomed Rooky into her bed as a reward for his Columbia accomplishments. She paved his way into the older leadership group within SDS's make-war faction. Mark Rudd, one of Rooky's classmates from Columbia, observed that "Power [in SDS-Weatherman] doesn't flow out of the barrel of a gun; power flows out of Paulette's cunt." Paulette urged the group to fight the enemy in "Wargasms." Rooky later conceded: "It was sort of like Wendy and the Lost Boys, except Wendy liked to put out. That was how she ran things."

Paulette's approach to leading the boys was to out-macho them. She was always first among Weatherman's equals.

In the early days of Columbia SDS, Barnard women had been relegated to support activities. Their political insights and advice were barely tolerated. By 1969, SDS feminism was anchored in Paulette's street-fighting chic.

Rooky found that his claim to leadership in this revolutionary cadre depended on advocating the most violence-provoking position on whatever issue was being debated while maintaining a working relationship with Paulette. He told her that he was like Herman Melville's Captain Ahab—monomaniacal "about killing the whale of American imperialism." When they were alone, she teased him by calling him "Captain." From street fighting with cops and working-class kids, to Molotov cocktails, arson, robberies and bombings—Rooky found himself in ever more extreme actions to maintain his identity and position. He realized in the very early 1970s that in following Paulette, he had given up independent judgment. To himself, he called her "The Spell Lady." He felt addicted.

Gondleman stayed with Weatherman as it went underground in early 1970, because he believed America could not reform itself. He was confident that History would justify him and the Weather Underground as it had Lenin, Mao and Castro.

The Weather Underground believed that bombings would mobilize workers and lead to the collapse of American capitalism. Their initial strategy in early 1970 was to kill police and military officers. They wanted to support the Black Liberation Army and the Black Panthers who they saw as leading The Revolution. A Berkeley police-station bombing in February, 1970, killed one officer and badly wounded another. The Weathermen never claimed responsibility for that attack, but police gathered two eyewitness statements from Weathermen that Dohrn led the planning and Howard Machtinger was the likely bombmaker. It appears that prosecutors did not bring murder charges, because they feared that the immunity they would have to grant to their informants would be used to take responsibility for the crime, which would get the other plotters off the hook along with themselves. The police never had corroborating evidence to convict Dohrn and Machtinger.

A month later, three Weathermen died in a Greenwich Village townhouse explosion. Two of the three -- Terry Robbins and Diana Oughton -- were fabricating anti-personnel bombs from dynamite and roofing nails they intended to explode at a noncommissioned officers' dance at Ft. Dix and, possibly, a Columbia University library. Robbins, presumably, crossed a wire and triggered the blast. Ted Gold was killed as he entered the townhouse. Kathy Boudin and Cathy Wilkerson escaped. In the rubble of the four-story structure, police found 57 sticks of dynamite, four 12-inch-long pipe bombs packed with dynamite, 30 blasting caps, alarm clocks and one 37-mm anti-tank shell from 1916. They also found a map of the tunnel network beneath Columbia University.

After this disaster, Ron Fliegelman, a doctor's son who was a hands-on mechanic, took over all bomb construction. No more accidents occurred. The townhouse fiasco led the Underground to focus on brick-and-mortar targets instead of people. They began phoning in advance warnings. In the early 1970s, some 2,500 bombings were logged. The Weathermen were not alone. When they took responsibility for a bombing, they issued a statement explaining their target choice and what they wanted to accomplish.

Gondleman spent five years in hiding and on the run after he was indicted on multiple charges of riot, conspiracy and related crimes for the Chicago "Days of Rage" in October, 1969. He helped on several bombings in the early 70s but began to have doubts. He had played chess with Ted Gold and never quite got over his death. He hesitated to express his reservations, because he knew they would have little support. He feared being isolated or cut from the group.

 Gondleman moved every six months, or sooner when he felt he might be discovered. He occasionally stayed with friends, relatives of friends and closet supporters, but, as a rule, he lived alone. He picked up day-labor jobs so he would not be dependent on Weather handouts to survive. He changed his appearance by growing a beard. He dyed both his beard and his hair. Every so often, the group would gather to plan what they might do next while hiding as FBI-wanted fugitives. Rooky went to these gatherings for several years, but he could not shake the growing feeling that the Underground had become more of an out-of-fashion and irrelevant death cult than a revolutionary force. He realized he was not free despite not being caught. More and more, he thought his underground life was pointless.

154

Still, Rooky felt his dreary existence had, at least, a little value. It showed that the FBI was unable to capture two dozen middle-class 25-year-olds. So far, the Underground had escaped prosecution for the bombings they claimed—that, too, was something, Rooky thought. Accordingly, he bent to his grunt work for which installing carpet had prepared him. He watched television, especially "All in the Family," which he thought was brilliant. He stayed away from politics and demonstrations. He tried to keep his spirits up. He tried to not feel totally alone, out of touch, politically discarded and remorseful for his past decisions. He spent his free time playing chess against himself and fiddling with baseball statistics.

Hiding took its toll. Rooky's face became thinner. His beard grew scraggly. His hair thinned. He rarely smiled, joked or laughed. He had to watch what he said to those who helped him. He never forgot that anyone could turn him in for the $25,000 FBI reward.

He tried to think of places that no one would expect him to go, where he had never left a footprint. He tried to think of people who might let him rest for a week, or give him money or pass him along to another friend willing to do the same. He thought of old friends from high school, none of whom were political. He thought of former chess opponents. He learned that surprise visits afforded him the best chance for being sheltered for a few days or a little longer. He appeared unannounced around 9 p.m. and asked for a place to sleep. His mother got cash to him through intermediaries without telling Milt. He saw neither parent for more than five years. He felt regret and guilt over what his mother said to him before he went underground: "Through the washer ringer and iron mangle, both, you're putting me."

Weather leaders decided Rooky had become increasingly dysfunctional, weak and untrustworthy. His value was his reputation from Columbia, admittedly faded over time. They feared what he might say if he decided to turn himself in. Rooky had progressed from a revolutionary star to a liability. At a meeting in 1973, they assigned Weez Draney to be his caretaker. She was to manage his life, make sure he wasn't caught, keep him underground and prevent him from cutting a deal with the police. Weez accepted this job as necessary revolutionary work, but she objected to "babysitting a burden." Weez considered it "shit work" below her abilities and status. "Give it to one of the men," she said. He's not into guys, she was told, so that won't work. In other circumstances, revolutionary comrades would have shot him. In Rooky's circumstances, he got Weez Draney.

Weez got together with Rooky in Los Angeles in March, 1973. Having known each other since 1969, neither was enthusiastic about the arrangement—ideologically, personally, sexually and politically. She was moving into a hostile feminism that had increasingly less use for political foundlings and the male gender. Nonetheless, both accepted direction from the leadership. Weez took them to Seattle for several months, then Minneapolis, then Denver. In late November, 1975, she decided they needed to move to Baltimore.

Weez structured his life with attention to detail. They avoided making friends. They stayed away from any activity or conversation that would draw scrutiny. They obeyed all laws, even refusing to walk on grass where it was *not* prohibited. They avoided coffee houses, campuses, concerts, post offices, traffic stops and bookstores. They always returned library books before they were due. She, being the less recognizable, rented their apartments in white working-class neighborhoods. Rooky tried construction, landscaping and temporary factory work. They both cleaned offices at night with Mexican crews. They concealed their educational backgrounds, dropped Marxist rhetoric and provided false information when needed. Each had several sets of identification papers. They lived modestly, wore disguises, changed their routines and avoided phoning their families.

Underground survival was largely an exercise in managing boredom and marginal involvement in life. But the boredom was cut with flashes of alertness and laser panics. They often felt like bears constantly sniffing for hunters. They worked hard on their cover stories and were determined to never make a mistake. The price of being careless was the loss of their freedom, such as it was. This was not the guerrilla war against the Empire that Rooky had anticipated. It was not making a Revolution. It was not a combat patrol into the heart of darkness. It was simply living with so little effect that it became unfathomable for someone with a remnant ego. By 1975, Gondleman realized he'd made a grievous mistake, that a revolution wasn't going to happen, that his ideas were inapplicable and and he was living the life of a fool. He said nothing to Weez Draney, because he was afraid of what she might do—like killing him.

Weez bought a used car -- a no-frills, eight-year-old Chevy Biscayne sedan -- from a fellow who advertised it on a supermarket message board. She dickered him down to $750 cash, and he signed over the title to Mary Little. She also bought two additional pistols from separate classifieds in weekly community bulletins. The sellers wanted cash; she wanted no questions. It worked for both sides. Rooky admired her negotiating skills; his father would have liked that quality in her. Each of them now traveled with two Colt 1911 pistols and two 10-gauge shotguns. They found themselves firmly supporting the Second Amendment.

If he were cornered, Rooky hoped he would go down fighting. He did not want to rot in prison. And then he asked, What am I going down for— some minor charges from 1968? In 1975, who cared? The draft had ended. The Vietnam War had ended. Nixon had resigned. Even though only a few

156

years had passed, events had made him, his rhetoric, his revolutionary violence and his life passé. He, too, no longer cared.

As they drove out of Denver on their way to Baltimore, Weez asked if he had any idea where to put up.

"Maybe," Rooky said. He remembered that Jeffrey Becker lived near Charleston, West Virginia.

Chapter 11

New York, End of May, 1968

They sat on a bench on Riverside Drive in the early evening before Jeffrey Becker's graduation. They had scheduled what they called A **Serious** Talk.

It was easy to see the Park below, the Henry Hudson Parkway, the Hudson River and New Jersey. Families were walking dogs and little kids in about a five-to-one ratio. Allyson wore a cotton polo shirt with jeans and sandals. Becker wore jeans and a button-down, blue dress shirt that could no longer pass as dressy owing to an irremediable-but-small mustard stain between its third and fourth buttons. They sat turned to each other, cupping drinks. Their agreed agenda: What next?

"Are your parents coming in?" she asked.

"I told them to stay home," he answered. "I'm not planning to participate in the ceremonies."

"They earned a glimpse of you walking off with a sheepskin, don't you think?"

Becker scoffed.

"They did pay for it after all."

"You're right. I'm a lout. I graduated the night of The Bust. About half of the undergraduates will walk out to an alternative ceremony. My parents want to see me marching to Elgar's 'Pomp and Circumstance,' not picnicing with incense, 'pot' luck and girls running free of bosom support."

"Bryn Mawr will not bend to the times, either," Allyson said. "Our upper lips are stiff. Our slips will not show."

"Thank God, one institution is still pushing women into the world knowing that someday they, too, will be happy wearing old-lady oxfords." He paused. "I'm stalling. "Have you decided for sure on journalism school in September?"

"I'm leaning toward Columbia Journalism."

"Leaning a little or a lot?"

"Closer to a lot," she said. "And you? What about law school?"

"I'm tired of books and papers," he said. "Political science and higher education are disappointments. But the draft has a hot breath. I'm in Columbia Law. The II-S no longer covers me. I'll get scooped up like cat shit in a litter box."

"So where does that leave you?"

"I guess I'll start here at the law school if I'm not drafted. I've sent in the forms and the money. But I get bad vibes walking across campus. I remember cops running after screaming girls, busses filled with chanting students. Your scar looks better."

"Thanks," she said, running her hand along her nose. "My father was outraged that a public servant would club *his* daughter. Apparently, the cop didn't know who Daddy is. He was ready to sue the NYPD."

"My parents were pleased that I didn't get expelled for breaking a window."

"Go to law school here," Allyson said. "I'll get an apartment with you. I'll be Linda LeClair; you be Peter Behr."

"Graduate students are free to live with whomever," Becker said. "We won't even be breaking any rules. How much fun can that be?"

"Maybe a little, still."

"I don't know, Pick. I need to get out of New York for a while. Will you come with me to Mandy's farm this summer?"

"To do what?"

"They're remodeling an old farmhouse and need a little help."

"They would certainly get very little from us. Bryn Mawr did not offer a class in hippie homesteading. How many barges have you toted lately, not to mention bales lifted?"

"They know," Becker said. "They come off the same shelf in the same bookcase."

"Becker, listen to me—the voice of reason," she said. "The knowledge we, together, have about remodeling homes consists of being able to either dial the super's telephone number or ask Daddy to send over a plumber."

"I worked in my Dad's scrap yard in the summers. I can cut and weld. I can run a crane. I'm not an idiot about tools. We can learn new skills. We'll broaden ourselves."

"We'll smash our fingers and skin our shins," she said. "You have to be smart to work with hand tools, don't you? What do I know about a crowbar, except it probably doesn't have much to do with either a bird or a Martini."

"So our mistakes will teach us. It's a good way to learn. It would be useful work, not another term paper."

"Becker, you're an idealist—a stupid, dopey, fucking dreamer."

"So?"

"And what is the other shoe that is about to drop?" she asked.

"They're getting together a collective, or something," he said. "They want to start an elementary school and other stuff not far from Greenfield."

"I dated some guys from Amherst. Very horny."

"Amherst is about an hour's drive east. So let's cross dating spare Amherst boys off our to-do list before we get there."

"They weren't that spare," she said.

"Allyson! What would your mother say?"

"She'd say: 'Really, dear. Must you.'" Allyson paused. "Playing the ingénue after two children works for her, because she sells it earnestly, not because it's true. Anyway your plan is to have you and me labor 10 hours a day in concrete and sawdust?"

"You make it sound like work," he said.

"You make it sound like not work," she said.

"There's no pressure. It'll be fun."

"Just whistle while we work," she sang, imitating Dopey, the Disney Dwarf. "All right, maybe. So where will we live while we're indentured to The Project?"

"On their farm," he said.

"In a barn?" she wrinkled her nose at the thought of nights in a hayloft ducking bats.

"A tepee," he said.

Allyson stopped in mid-wrinkle. "A tepee?"

Two days after the Serious Talk, Mr. and Mrs. Walton Pickering arrived at Bryn Mawr College on the morning of Allyson's graduation. It had been a short drive from their home in Upper Providence. Both were worried.

Walton had never quite made peace with Allyson's decision to attend Bryn Mawr. He preferred Vassar—his mother and grandmother's alma mater. But Jane Andrews "Boo" Pickering, Class of 1937, had insisted that Allyson be permitted to go to the college of her choice—as long as it was Bryn Mawr. Boo's sister, Maude, had gone to Vassar to be near a Yale boy. The Andrews had never quite recovered. Walton's preference was not of great concern to Jane. Walton muttered when Allyson announced her decision, but accepted defeat with the grace that comes from having been defeated on other matters of this sort. "Vassar's not quite the school it once was," he said after Allyson notified Bryn Mawr of her acceptance. Still, he did hope that Margie, his second daughter, might consider 'Poopkeepsme,' as his mother fondly mangled Poughkeepsie. Pickering women, he believed, were more Vassar than Bryn Mawr, though he admitted to himself the differences were not as large as he once imagined. He liked the idea of sending another generation of Pickering women to Vassar. Of course, he admitted, Jane's people had a similar tradition with Bryn Mawr.

After the graduation ceremony, the Pickerings drove to Mario's in Haverford, Walton's favorite Italian restaurant, where he always ordered chicken parmigiana. Jane deferred to Walton's enthusiasm for what he knew. Mario's menu bored Allyson. She had discovered Mexican heat in New York City. But Italian would sedate and comfort Boo and Walton. She wanted her parents at ease—actually as much ease as possible. She was about to inform them of a change in her summer plans. This, she knew, would go down like a hairball.

160

On finishing lunch, Jane, Walton and Margie planned to drive to their retreat at the foot of the White Mountains in Wonalancet, New Hampshire. Allyson had been "written in" for at least six weeks in July and the first two weeks of August when the blueberries on the ledges were ripe and the Wonalancet River was warm enough for brave skinny-dippers.

The Pickering place was a rambling, two-story cottage set in the woods, about a half-mile north of the tiny post office on Ferncroft Road, which ran toward Mt. Whiteface. Walton's great grandfather built the original farmhouse in the 1820s, using local lumber and rounded river rocks left by a retreating glacier. The hand-split, white-cedar shakes had been replaced three times since. A fourth round was needed, but this Walton was reluctant to do. He doted on a certain level of wrap-around disrepair. He found virtue in the algae on the cedar, which benefited the moss, which fed on the cedar, which, taken together, created a charm that could only be achieved by six or seven decades of slowly gathering decrepitude. Various Pickerings had added bedrooms, or bathrooms, or a breakfast room, or garage (née stable) or a barn as the need was perceived. Each addition had subsequently survived two or more remodelings. Indoor plumbing arrived after WWII along with electricity—two "upgrades" about which Walton still fretted. Walton's family always spent their summer in Wonalancet where they hiked, read, played board games and swatted No-See-Ums, black flies and mosquitoes. Walton fished for trout with flies he had tied all winter. He puttered and drank. Boo cooked, gardened and sewed. Allyson and Margie ran barefoot, mostly free of adults.

Among all of the reasons Walton loved Wonalancet, none was higher than it provided an excuse for him to come to the cottage alone every fall and hunt Canada geese and ducks. He had learned to shoot from his father and found that he loved the sport.

Walton hunted with his father's 12-gauge, side-by-side shotgun crafted by James Purdey and Sons of London. It was a bespoke heirloom—as valuable as a quality house, handmade, custom-fitted and perfect. It had a sidelock, hammerless ejector action, two 30-inch-long Sir Joseph Whitworth steel barrels and a carved Turkish-walnut stock. The actions had been engraved by Ken Hunt with scenes of pheasants, partridges and mallards. When Walton inherited the Purdey after WWII, he flew to London to have the stock and mechanicals refitted to his arm, shoulder and hand. He spent a day taking instruction on English shooting etiquette and a long morning the next day devoted to the proper use and care of this gun, which, he was informed, would be delivered to him "no sooner than six months from today." That, Walton thought, was a reasonable wait in light of the 18 months spent on crafting it from scratch in 1927. He enjoyed the stuffy fussing and fiddling that Purdey practiced, because he knew their guns were art, as perfect an object as a human hand could make.

Preparation was necessary for Purdey to entrust its guns to owners who were not likely to meet the craftman's standards. The Purdey fitter understood why Walton did not want any bluing restoration. His father's honest use had taken off perhaps 25 percent over two decades. Diligent oiling had kept it rust free, a practice Walton would follow scrupulously.

Walton also looked forward to asking permission to hunt from the tall, beautiful blonde who lived on nearby Birches Intervale Farm where Rt. 113-A made a 90-degree turn. At the back of her place, generations of beaver had created a wetland where migrating fowl stopped. He liked talking to the young woman who was Allyson's age. She had a quirky sense of humor and a solid New Hampshire grounding. He didn't think he was flirting with her when he asked for permission to hunt, but maybe he might be a little. She was, after all, a knockout. She never failed to admire his Purdey shotgun, which Boo and her Quaker rigidity wanted to banish to their attic under the eaves. Although Walton hunted waterfowl on the Delaware in season, he preferred the cozy backwater of Helen Read's place.

For different reasons, each Pickering loved the cottage and its traditional activities. The family was good with each other there. Allyson wanted to spend several weeks in Wonalancet before starting journalism school, but she was not sure how she was going to work Jeffrey Becker into the Pickering scene, or not work him in for reasons she didn't want to explain to him.

Even as she sat at Mario's cloth-covered table, her straight-forward intentions exceeded her uncertain plans. The first step, she knew, was to announce that she would not be coming to Wonalancet for six weeks, because…well, she thought, because the reason was concrete but a little fuzzy. Actually, a lot more than a little.

She decided then and there to get it all out just after they ordered. Two or three short, declarative sentences. Overwhelm them with details.

"LIVING IN A WHAT?" Jane Andrews Pickering said as forcefully as an always self-controlled matron of her station could whisper. Boo felt an involuntary froth of incredulousness rising.

"A tepee, Mother. It's near Greenfield, Massachusetts, a fine old state that adjoins both Vermont and New Hampshire," Allyson said brightly. "We have family connections in Boston as you know. I have friends who own a farm near Greenfield, which is almost New Hampshire, though not as good, of course."

Allyson did not insert the small qualification that she had never met these "friends."

"And they want us to help remodel their farmhouse this summer. Learning through labor. Very Quakery."

Jane took several deep breaths, which she thought might be related to yoga, which she did not practice. "You could go on a Friends work group to help Southern Negroes if you want to spend the summer as a carpenter's maid."

"This is similar."

"Are your friends Negroes?"

"Not visibly," she said, "but all mankind -- humankind -- did spring from a common African ancestor. They are as Negro as we are."

"Well, in a manner of speaking, to be sure," Boo said. "And are we to understand that you will be living in a tepee?"

"Yes, Mother. Twenty-four feet in diameter. Genuine lodgepole pine for the supports. Just like the Plains Indians. Tepee comes from the Sioux word for dwelling. It's very authentic. Very whole earthy."

"A tepee," Walton Pickering repeated. "I lived in one at Boy Scout camp in 1927. For a week. I was in with Scooter Smith. Of course, Scooter was not his given name. It was Percy. And Hugh Breakstone. And Alton Forbes. We called him, Snoopy. Or maybe it was, Loopy. Or Sloopy. Anyway, some derivative of 'oopy,' and…."

"A tepee," Jane Pickering repeated. "Really."

"Jeffrey says it's quite comfortable. 'A lot of headroom toward the middle.'"

"Yes, there is," said Walton. "Droopy or Goopy, or whatever, got poison ivy on his…well, I can't say what he got it on, and then Scooter…"

"Jeffrey says there's excellent ventilation through the flap."

"'Through the flap,'" Jane Pickering repeated.

"No, Soupy had a zipper, not a flap. Even boys as young as we had zippers back then. Flaps were for toddlers. That is where he got it, the poison ivy. How in the world? we wondered."

"No closets but wonderful storage around the sides, I'm told," Allyson said. "And the canvas is specially treated to shed water. Jeffrey says a lot of people in California are thinking about tepees as alternatives."

These were brave words, and Allyson said them bravely with confidence and enthusiasm, neither of which she felt. Only two days earlier as she sat with Becker on Riverside Drive had she herself said: "IN A WHAT?"

"Alternative to what, dear?" Walton asked.

"Oh, you know, Daddy," she said in her perky get-Daddy-to-do-something voice. "Alternative to…uh…uh…ticky-tacky boxes like the ones they're building out beyond the Main Line."

"There's no craft left in the trades," Walton admitted, "no individuality anymore. These tract houses sprout along newly paved culs-de-sac like spring dandelions. Pre-cut. Pre-fabbed. Preee-ty bad. The firm has handled a number of these developments. Without my enthusiasm, I should add."

"You find a wigwam preferable to Wonalancet, do you?" Boo asked.

"It's a comparison between apples and oranges, Mother," Allyson said.

"Apples and lemons," Boo said, and then regretted her sharpness.

"A wigwam is a hut by the way," Allyson said."

"Perhaps I should refer to it as a fabric-clad mobile home," Boo said.

"Is this summer plan the Becker boy's idea?" Walton asked.

"It is *our* idea," Allyson said, a lie so large that she thought her eyeballs would ring up like lemons in a slot machine.

Walton chewed his chicken with great thoroughness. He was nimble with numbers and clever with legal reasoning, but he was not quick in repartee the way litigators are. So he plotted out his sarcasm, which he hoped would back his daughter into a corner.

"Do you think Mr. Becker is an Indian of full blood or only fractional?" Walton asked, pleased with his opening.

"I never asked."

"Was he born to the deerskin?" Walton asked.

"It's possible," Allyson answered. "He likes to whoop it up after he counts coup."

Jane sniffed a sexual innuendo as it blew by.

Walton, smelling nothing, persisted. "Does Mr. Becker wear war paint and a feather in his headdress?"

"Only at anti-War demonstrations, Daddy," Allyson replied. "His tribe is very vocal but nonviolent. They've beaten their bows into backscratchers and their arrows into chopsticks for Chinese takeout."

"Amusing," Walton allowed. "I did see some students on television with peace signs painted on their foreheads."

"He's doesn't wear war paint, Daddy."

"You know, Allyson, that Indian men did not treat Indian women, their squaws, very well," Walton said. "Indian men would not have met with your approval as a modern woman."

"I'm not asking you to walk in my moccasins, Daddy," she said. Allyson had anticipated that she would be cross-examined on these matters. She understood the helplessness of being who you were. Her parents were who they were, and she was who she was. So be that.

Boo was uncomfortable with this controlled unpleasantness, but Allyson was the only source of answers about Allyson. Walton was entitled to say what he thought. She had long ago made peace with her understanding that he couldn't be different than the upright man he was. Now that she'd let Walton have his moment, she'd try her hand.

"The Becker boy, Jeffrey...." Jane said as neutrally as possible. "Jefferey? Geoffrey? Jefferee?"

"Conventional spelling, Jeffrey."

"And he's from…?"

"Pittsburgh."

"And his people?" Boo asked.

"They're from Pittsburgh, too."

"*Originally*, I mean," Boo said.

"'*Originally*' from Africa, I suppose, along with all the other walking hominids who fled north to get out of the heat."

"We evolved large brains so that we could use them," Boo said.

"I don't know about 'originally,' as you mean it," she answered truthfully.

"And what kind of people are they?" Boo asked.

"The two-legged kind," Allyson said. "Just like us."

"This is a step forward," Walton said. "Your mother and I have a lot in common with them."

"And what happened to Trip?" Boo asked. "Too, might I say, too suitable?"

"He was very suitable," Allyson said.

Jane Andrews Pickering suspected as much. "So Jeffrey. What may I ask is he up from?"

"I haven't asked; I don't know; I don't care."

Which means, Boo thought, what she suspected was true.

"I haven't met his parents," Allyson said. "His father owns a scrap business if that's what you're asking."

"Scraps?" Boo asked.

"Scrap," Walton corrected her.

"Scrap," Allyson repeated.

"Junk?" Walton asked.

"Like rags?" Boo asked.

"Scrap," Allyson replied. "He buys and sells old materials for new uses, like metals, glass bottles, paper. Very good for the scenery. Like The Nature Conservancy projects you contribute to."

"Scraps," Boo repeated with finality. "Well."

"His mother keeps the books. That's all I know."

"Admirable," Boo said. "Up by their own bootstraps."

"I'm not sure how 'up' they've lifted themselves," Allyson said. "And there is something else. His grandfather on his mother's side -- he died a year before Jeffrey was born, a nice man from what he's been told -- he was a peddler. Went to the little coal camps and steel towns around Pittsburgh. Took orders from women for dresses that they paid off over a year or more, something like 10 cents a week and interest. He'd do collections on Friday. From what Jeffrey knows, he wasn't very good at collecting."

"'Collecting,'" Boo repeated. "I recall peddlers coming to our back door during The Depression. My mother always tried to buy a little something from those who still looked presentable."

"It's not relevant to me," Allyson said

"I suppose that means it should not be relevant to us," Boo said indicating her and Walton.

"Jeffrey and I are friends, mother. If it goes beyond that, you can express your objections. I am not eloping to a reservation if that's your concern."

"I have friends in the Pittsburgh Bar," Walton said. "I know John-Cee Smithers in coal and the Block boys at the paper. But I'm afraid I don't know anyone out there in scrap. Or here either, I should add."

"I'm sure we…you…have more money than his parents have," Allyson said.

"ALLYSON!" Boo whispered as loudly as she dared in a public space.

"Would it be worse if they had more than you or better?" Allyson asked.

"ENOUGH!" Boo whispered. "Wealth is not our concern. You are."

Allyson felt advantage swing to her. "Jeffrey graduated from Columbia, and he's admitted to the law school. He's smart and nice. An only child."

"I imagine he's the first in his family to go to college," Walton observed.

"True, as far as I know," Allyson said. "I haven't asked about his pedigree. He's not a St. Bernard. I've checked his hips, not his papers."

"I like St. Bernards," Walton said. "You can't use them for birds, of course."

Boo cleared her throat. "We're just curious about your friend who you will be, let's say, keeping company with this summer."

"More than that," Allyson said neutrally.

Her mother ignored that comment.

"Dear, you come from American families that were here at the beginning," Boo said. "My people, as you know, go back to William and Mary Brewster on the Mayflower. Your father is descended from Timothy Pickering who served in George Washington's Cabinet and as vice-president under Thomas Jefferson.

"Yes," Allyson said, "the troops under his command arrived too late to fight at Lexington and Concord."

"He served capably as the Army's Quartermaster General, beginning in 1780," Walton inserted.

"Then he moved to Pennsylvania after business failures in Massachusetts and made his fortune as a land speculator in the western part of the state," Allyson said.

"Land investments," Boo corrected.

166

"Then he negotiated a treaty with the Iroquois that gave them calico cloth for their land."

"They needed trade goods more than wilderness" Walton said.

"And after Jefferson came into office, Timmy Pickering, an Anglophile Federalist to his bone, opposed the Louisiana Purchase and tried to organize the secession of New England."

"Secession against the War of 1812 was quite fashionable," Walton said. "Madison's War led to the bankruptcy of our country and brought a halt to all commerce in New England. Timothy Pickering was not alone at the Hartford Convention, which, I should add, wanted to do away with the three-fifths rule for counting Negroes."

"He wasn't that opposed to slavery," Allyson said. "He and the Federalists were against the South counting slaves as anything at all, let alone three-fifths of a person."

"Well, George Cabot and others of that stripe believed as he did," Walton said. "You can't apply 1968 opinions to 1815 issues."

"Agreed," Allyson said. "Let's not get on too high a horse about what Jeffrey Becker's lineage is in light of our own mixed record. And just to get everything on the table, I will be having sex of various kinds and in assorted positions with Jeffrey Becker this summer in a tepee and maybe other places."

Jane's eyes widened.

Walton shook his head, trying to clear it. Who was this child? he asked himself.

Boo couldn't steady her hand, which rattled her teacup in its saucer. She took a deep breath. She knew that composure was required. "We're trying to understand, dear, but the idea of living in a tepee for two months is simply outside our first-hand experience."

"Not exactly," Walton piped up. "Whoopy, or whatever his name was, and Hugh and Scooter and I, we did it for a week. I *do* have first-hand experience. It was leaky."

"I'm sure manufacturers have improved their tepees during the last 40 years," Allyson said. "It will be like the Friends' summer camp, Mother. We did a lot of overnights in tents. I've even slept under the stars. Camp White Tail had tepees and canoes. The boys even put out the campfire Indian style."

"ALLYSON. THAT is plenty," Walton said. "Your mother is sitting here."

Heads turned. Jane reddened.

"I see her, Daddy."

"Camp White Tail did not include living with a man named Becker," Boo said, "or in a canoe."

Allyson thought better of recounting several nights spent in the White Tail boathouse the summer before she entered Bryn Mawr. Two Bucks had discovered two Does in the canoes. "Athwart the thwarts" was a phrase that carried physical memories. It still brought a chuckle when the participating Bucks and Does recalled the experience.

"We're very careful, mother. I've read all the books."

A long strand of mozzarella cheese dangled and swayed from Walton's fork, which had stopped dead with a silent screech in mid journey.

"Walton," Boo said.

"What?"

His wife hesitated. "Uh, close your mouth, dear."

Walton closed his mouth and placed his fork on his plate with great restraint. "Jane," he said beseechingly.

There was a part of Allyson that enjoyed her parents' discomfort. Sex, money and bathrooms were never discussed. Neither Boo nor Walton had ever talked to their daughters about sex, except the time Boo had spoken approvingly of a neighbor who had "saved herself for marriage." Fortunately or not, several seniors at the girls-only Baldwin School on Montgomery Avenue in Bryn Mawr had shared themselves with a couple of freshmen from Penn. Their empirical knowledge quickly spread horizontally and vertically. Allyson was friends with these pioneers from field hockey.

Jane Pickering recognized a losing fight when she was in one. Her daughter's resistance to abandoning -- even modifying -- the Tepee Summer would increase in step with maternal pressure to do so. Boo straightened her back, which was already dead plumb. Then she straightened her dress, which was as smooth as a dress can be on a sitting body. Then she patted her hair, which was in place. She glanced at Walton with control if not calm. The more she and he fussed, the more uncomfortable they would be with a decision that had already been made. Their wishes were known and had been dismissed. Boo had a hunch that Allyson was not quite as convinced about the Tepee Summer as she sounded. Lines of communication, Boo now believed, needed to remain functioning. She hoped Allyson would have the good taste to keep her revelations on such matters from her 13-year-old sister.

"Your father and I know you will handle this situation with maturity," she said. "We have great confidence in you. Perhaps, you'll still be able to spend some time with us at Wonalancet. It's not but a paddle and a portage or two from where you'll be."

Bravo, Mother, Allyson thought. You've just kept the door open and the porch light on. If Chief Scrappy and his interim squaw, Bra Burner, have a falling out, refuge at Fort Wonalancet with the white folks awaits without judgment. At least, she thought, Boo would refrain from expressing her thoughts until Allyson was back in the family nest.

"Thank you, Mother. Of course, a visit would be fun."

168

Walton was pleased that his oldest daughter had the good sense to avoid specifying whether it would be she or they who might be dropping by. Perhaps, he thought, Becker carried his lodging with him like the nomadic Mongolians. Could Becker be part Mongolian? Becker didn't sound like an Asian name. A father in scrap! Heavens! Now wait, Walton thought. Mongolians used yurts, not tepees. Still, they were of the same Oriental stock, one branch having stayed put as the other wandered across the Bering land bridge in search of mammoths and lobster bisque. Well, Walton reasoned, if the Becker boy really were a Native that might be all right. Can't beat a line into the real first families. Scrap, when he thought about it, wasn't so bad, maybe. Somebody had to do the cleanup.

And then he remembered Poopy. It was Poopy. Walton heard that he had gone into the Army Air Corps after Dartmouth—and then nothing until the end of 1944. Alton "Poopy" Forbes died over Germany piloting a B-17 when a Focke-Wulf Fw 190 attacked head on, raking his cockpit with machine-gun fire. Scooter Smith kept in touch—Christmas cards from his wife, mostly. Every three or four years, a phone call came to Walton late when Scooter was drunk and sad about his journey through life's ups and downs. Hugh Breakstone had died at Anzio. Scrap! An image appeared in Walton's mind of his daughter presenting him with a papoose swaddled in junkyard rags and old newspapers scavenged from a bale. His grandson. A bastard at worst; legitimate at next worst. He shook his head to chase away the papoose.

"Did you have a camp nickname, Daddy?" Allyson asked.

"Plugger," Walton replied.

"Plugger?" Boo said with surprise.

"I was a good shot with a .22 on the rifle range."

"Let's keep that in the family circle," Boo said.

"So when do we pow-wow with the Chief?" Walton asked, despite the sharp disapproval he caught full-face from his wife.

"Are you planning to smoke a peace pipe with him, Daddy?"

"Your father doesn't smoke," Boo said.

For all of Walton's peculiarities, Allyson knew that he had been raised to protect women. The joking was a smokescreen, not a smoke signal. If Becker hurt his daughter, Walton would make him pay. Daddy had connections.

"Maybe, we'll do a meet and greet," Allyson said. "But I'm not ready for a formal presentation. And neither is anyone else."

Walton took a deep breath. "Allyson, I want to talk to you about another matter."

Allyson smoothed her hair. Maybe he was giving her a graduation present.

"I guess there's no easy way to say this," he stumbled, "you have a trust fund."

169

"Okay," she said. "Which means what?"

"Which means about $2 million," he said. "It's in stocks, bonds, a little real estate. It's yours on your 21st birthday."

"That's in September," she said.

"Excellent memory," her father said.

"What am I supposed to do with it?"

"Anything you want," Walton said. "We can talk about it when you come to Wonalancet. I'll manage it until you want me to stop or make other arrangements. If you need money, it's there. Jane, we need to be moving along to the cottage."

God that was hard, Walton thought.

Boo and Walton finished eating. They picked up Margie who had not felt well that morning and drove straight through to New Hampshire.

Allyson drove her VW Bug to New York where she picked up The Chief for their drive to Massachusetts.

"My father wants to know whether you will be wearing your loincloth if you visit Wonalancet?"

"Can't," he answered. "It's on loin."

"My father likes puns. My mother thinks they are a debased form of language used only by certain juvenile adults who can't resist unleashing them."

"I'll charm her," he said.

"*That* is unlikely," Allyson said.

"I'll be myself," he said.

"We're doomed," she said.

"Are you ashamed to introduce me to your parents?" he asked.

"Not ashamed," she said. "But uneasy. They're liberal Quakers on certain things and set in their ways on others. They're comfortable with people like themselves. So are you, and so am I. They don't like their noses rubbed in it."

"Rubbed in what?"

"Their own failings, limitations," she said. "Let's just see how the summer works for us and leave them out of the picture for now."

"You'll scare my parents," he said.

"Let's put that off, too."

"Agreed," he said.

"My father said he lived in a tepee with some Boy Scout friends in 1927. It brought back memories."

"I'm sure we'll make some of our own," Becker said.

"Our living together was too much for them to discuss," she said.

"Did you frame it as a feminist 'rite of passage'?"

"No. I framed it as wanton sex."

170

"Very tactful. Did you consider euphemisms?"

"No. It's best to get all the bad news out to them in one indigestible clod. One big retch is better than five or six small ones."

"I didn't say anything about you to my folks," Becker said.

"If my parents believed in sin, this would be one," she said. "It's a slap in their face. They don't like to feel illiberal. Not to mention the poor example I'm setting for Margie."

"It's a bigger deal for you than I thought," Becker said.

"Yes, Becker," she said, "it's a bigger deal than you thought."

Chapter 12

Near Greenfield, Mass., Summer, 1968

From I-91's Greenfield Exit, they drove along a narrow blacktop road that curled west and then south away from town. The headlights on Allyson's VW captured the thick trunks of giant sugar maples that lined the road. They could see an occasional hole from a late winter tap. Bugs flew without purpose in their moving light. It smelled wet and clean. The pleasant June night snuggled into countryside quiet.

Allyson drove as Becker read directions to her. They turned left onto Hawk's Road, a modest gravel lane that ran parallel to the Deerfield River with unseen fields and woods in between. Curious Holsteins nosed up to barbed-wire fences while producing the next hundredweight of milk.

"There," Becker said. "Turn right at the rainbow mailbox. We're late. It's almost 11."

"Rainbows! I better unpack my 'groovys.'"

Becker did not bite. "Can't miss a rainbow even in the dark," he said neutrally as he suppressed his own cringe. He hoped he and Allyson were not about to be sucked into the vortex of drop-out hippie land. That's not how he had billed the summer to her. He was still unable to say "Groovy" with a straight face. He had similar issues with "Far out!"

Allyson turned into the driveway and drove forward with uncharacteristic timidity. Light flooded from the downstairs windows of a three-story farmhouse that was connected to a line of gabled buildings, the last of which was a large livestock barn. Parked in front of the house were a red-and-white VW microbus with a peace symbol painted on the back and a green, 1953 Ford pickup truck with a "STOP THE WAR!" sticker on its bumper. The driveway looped in front of the buildings. A tepee rose inside it like a giant white vegetable. Allyson was startled by its height.

Allyson stopped in front of the tepee and cut the VW's engine. They got out, stretched and peered into the clear, fresh night. A light mounted above two sliding barn doors provided dim illumination. Allyson thought that Massachusetts didn't smell like the conifers around Wonalancet. Jeffrey thought it smelled like manure. It did not smell like Manhattan, they could agree on that.

"Listen to the peepers," Allyson said.

"I thought peepers looked in silence," Becker said.

"Becker, stop."

Two Yellow Labs barreled up—barking, wagging, licking and jumping on them and then each other. Mandy and Rick followed with flashlights. Introductions were made since Becker didn't know Mandy, and Allyson knew neither Mandy nor Rick. They hugged: Mandy and

Allyson, Mandy and Jeffrey, Rick and Allyson, Rick and Jeffrey; then, laughing at themselves, Mandy and Rick, Becker and Allyson. The frantic dogs wove among the fast-changing couples. What began as hugs ended as people holding onto each other for balance.

Inside, Mandy set out cheese, crackers, whole-wheat bread that she'd made that afternoon, fruit, hard salami from Zabar's, beer and soft drinks. Allyson sized up her hosts as they assessed her.

Mandy Klein, a 1966 honors Barnard graduate in sociology, was a petite, trim strawberry blonde who wore slightly shaded Granny glasses. She spoke with authority in a crisp alto bordering on tenor. She moved quickly and surely in a faded blue workshirt and jeans with embroidered rainbows on the back pockets. She had coxed Barnard's eight-woman shell through two winning seasons. She was comfortable telling much larger people what to do, when to do it and how to do it.

Rick Matthews was broad and muscular, though only a few inches taller than Mandy. He had wrestled at 160 pounds in his first two years at Columbia. As a junior, he lost his competitive drive to marijuana. A full black beard concealed his square, stumpy chin. He had begun as a pre-med major but switched to history when he quit wrestling. He wore a ragged pair of blue Columbia gym shorts and a gray T-shirt. When everyone including the dogs were inside, he lit several candles on the dining-room table and rolled three joints. Mandy brought out a package of Oreos and a quart of hand-packed vanilla ice cream.

"Nice place," Allyson said, looking around the large dining room and kitchen.

"My Dad bought it from a broke dairy farmer two years ago," Mandy said. "He thought 160 acres with a house would be a good investment for the $25,000 he paid. He's a stockbroker on Long Island. He's smart about money."

"My Dad is, too," Allyson said. "My mother, sister and I bear it as best we can."

"My Dad isn't," Becker said.

"My Dad isn't either but has still made a fair amount," Rick said before inhaling deeply.

"We lease the 90 acres of pasture to the neighbor next door for his dairy cows," Mandy went on. "The rest is woods—beech, birch, sugar maple, some oak, a little spruce and pine. The Deerfield River lies about 300 meters -- sorry, not quite 330 yards; it's a hangover from rowing 2,000-meter races -- behind the house. Nice little swimming hole there. You have to cross the railroad tracks."

"So what do you guys know about farming?" Allyson asked. She heard her mother -- and a bit of her father -- in her voice and question.

"I rode a horse in high school," Mandy said. "English."

"And I fed a class hamster in third grade," Rick added.

"Did it graduate with your class?" Becker asked.

"A long summer awaits us," Allyson said.

Mandy had prepared an answer to the question she had anticipated, one that she had asked herself.

"I guess we're getting out of the urban trip more than being into farming, which we're not actually doing," she said. "The whole New York City scene bummed us out. After graduation, we spent the last year driving around the country. Rick's bum shoulder got him out of the draft. We wanted to see where people were at. We spent some time with an SDS community-organizing project in Chicago and the Panthers in the Bay Area. But they weren't for us. We concluded that we can't win a gunfight with the State. So there's no sense in joining Gondleman and Cobb at their impending Alamo.

"My Dad asked us whether we wanted to do some work on this place. He thinks we will come to our senses, go to graduate school and join the burbs. We drove here in April. Snow was still on the ground, but we could see it was ready to get green. We liked the smells and bells. A bunch of people like us are around doing a land trip. So we're going to liberate our own little piece of America. If there are enough of us, we can take over."

"Take over?" Becker asked.

"You know. Vote ourselves into office, eventually. Restructure the system," Rick said, followed by a deep drag on the joint. "Vermont is the real target. But we could do it right here in Franklin County."

Allyson coughed when it was passed to her, both before she inhaled and after.

"You're supposed to hold it in," Mandy said as non-correctively as she could.

"Involuntary actions are involuntary by definition," Allyson said stiffly. Allyson had never liked bossy girls, especially little know-it-alls. "Like orgasms."

"Right on," Rick said.

"Blessed be their name," Becker added.

"Don't you think 'taking over' is sort of imperialistic, sort of using your money and educations to subjugate the locals?" Allyson said. She figured it was best to get a big fight out of the way quickly. I am my mother's daughter, she confessed to herself.

"Some people could see it that way," Mandy said. "But that's exactly what you learn at Columbia and Barnard—how to turn the thesis into the antithesis with clever words."

"I went to Bryn Mawr," Allyson said.

"I'm sure you were similarly processed," Mandy said, not backing down.

"We see ourselves as low-impact people," Rick said. "Our first principle is to do no harm. We want to be in harmony with the land, our

174

neighbors and each other. That's our revolution. Along with this." He lit a second joint.

"Heavy," Allyson said. Becker caught her sarcasm. So did Mandy and Rick.

"But you're right," Mandy said to Allyson. She didn't want a girl-fight all summer; she wanted sisterly solidarity. "It does amount to big-city money coming in and buying out locals who really don't have a choice other than to sell at their inflated prices to guys like my Dad. The locals would be fools not to sell for more than their farms are worth. It's capitalism."

"I don't come to this discussion with clean hands…or maybe they've always been too clean," Allyson said. "My family owns an old farm in New Hampshire that's now our vacation place. We've turned various 'locals' into indulged and treasured servants."

"Don't romanticize them," Mandy said, passing the joint to Becker. "They're mainly looking for a way to unload these can't-pay-for-themselves dumps to people they hate. Then, they move to the very burbs from whence we've fled. And they're not agrarian populists or oppressed southern tenant farmers struggling to organize a union. Most are Goldwater-Nixon Republicans."

"Well, then, they hate the State," Allyson said.

"More like they hate government and love the country for which it stands, albeit rottenly," Rick said.

"You'll see what I mean," Mandy said to Allyson, "the first time you get hassled by redneck guys in Greenfield. All hippie girls are considered prey. They think we'll drop our bib overalls for anything male, especially the likes of them."

"The idea of taking over Vermont is not much different from creating 'liberated zones' at Columbia two months ago," Rick said. "That was taking property to make a political point and do something different with it. Something better. We're into that, too."

"I remember what a good job SDS did there," Allyson said.

"I remember the debate about bathrooms," Becker said. "Fayerweather was the most rational of the buildings. Mostly graduate students with a handful of unaffiliated undergrads like me. Anyway, our Stalinists wanted two bathrooms divided by sex, but no more than two."

"The Maoists wanted 100 bathrooms to bloom," Allyson said.

"The Anarchists wanted everyone in one bathroom at the same time," Becker said.

"And the hippies wanted no bathrooms at all."

"You're kidding," Mandy said, hopefully.

"Not by much," Becker said. "It was a trip."

"Has the take-over crowd resolved the bathroom question yet?" Allyson asked.

"Outhouses, all around," Mandy said. "And speaking of bathrooms."

"Is that one of the projects you're planning out here on the Gilligan's Island of the lifestyle revolution?" Allyson asked.

"Take another hit, sister," Mandy said. "You'll settle down in a couple of days. I'll wait."

"Yes," Rick said. "There's a bathroom project. We're also thinking hard about setting up an alternative school a year from this September. More and more of us are having kids. And I'm going to learn how to build post-and-beam houses and barns. I could make a living at it. A lot of folks are congregating around Amherst. They have money and are into handmade shelters."

"Do you know anything about carpentry?" Jeffrey asked.

"I got an A in high-school geometry," Rick said. "I can figure the volume of a cone."

"Handy that," Allyson said.

"I like the idea of working with my hands. I'll learn as we redo this place. Always make your learning mistakes on a nickel not your own."

"I've always made mistakes on my own nickel," Becker said, though he wasn't sure why he had made that contribution to the night's conversation. It must be the joint, he said to himself.

"I am not a mistake," Allyson said with no fight in it.

"Too soon to say," Mandy laughed, passing Allyson the last Oreo on the plate. Allyson took it as a peace offering.

They finished the third joint, ate their fill of munchies and drank enough beer to get sleepy.

Rick showed them to their tepee and left a Coleman lantern after explaining its operation.

They unrolled pads and spread one down sleeping bag on the bottom and covered themselves with another.

"What do you think?" Becker whispered into her ear.

"We're gettin' into harmony with the land, ya know."

"There's a rock under my harmony," he said. "Move over a little."

"You smell like marijuana," Allyson said. "Did your brush your teeth?"

"I have in the past, though not within the last few minutes."

Allyson did not make it into an issue. "Are you going to go full-out, back-to-the-land hippie on me, Becker?"

"Not with the draft breathing down my neck. I need a way out. I have an idea."

"So what would you do if you were free?"

"Don't know. Never been. The draft's been there since I turned 18. I have heard that five-grain bread full of gluten clogs the brain cells and makes you dopey enough to contra dance. That might get me out."

"I like to contra dance," Allyson said with finality.

"Not with me, you wouldn't."

"We'll see," she said.

"Maybe they're actually on to something," he said.

"Who knows anymore?"

"'Harmony seems to be the slogan of the day,'" he said.

"Move over, Becker. Give me some cover."

"Are you going to stay?" he asked.

"Oh yeah. 'Far fuckin' out,'" she said snidely. "I need to know the zeitgeist of my generation. I'm a participant-observer. Maybe I'll learn something."

"'Tomorrow's another day,'" he said.

"'Rhett! Rhett!'"

"Yes, Scarlett, you manipulative bitch."

"Manipulative sister in the struggle," Allyson said.

"It's all very confusing," Becker said and then kissed her. And she kissed him back.

They began the next day. After breakfast, they settled themselves on the kitchen porch and spent the morning reading do-it-yourself and how-to books on home construction and remodeling. Rick and Jeffrey were only slightly more familiar with tools and carpentry concepts than Mandy and Allyson, but each male had used a hammer and handsaw at least once during mandatory woodshop class in the eighth grade. No one laughed when Mandy insisted that "joist" was a misprint for "joint," with which, Becker said, she "was more familiar than moist." Allyson bestowed a world-class eye roll in his direction, which he took to mean: Lay off the puns and don't tease the girls. Good advice, he thought, better take it.

They broke for lunch and drove into Greenfield with a shopping list. Three hours later, they returned with more than $3,000 worth of tools and supplies charged to Mandy's father. The heavy building materials arrived the next day. They began in the back bedroom and worked until dark. Crowbars, hammers and nail-pullers were passed around, the boys getting the bigger ones of each species. By the end of the first day, they had taken a wall off, a ceiling down, a window out and a floor up in part of one room. They discovered that fully dimensioned, rough-cut oak studs and joists were impossible to nail into. One-hundred-year-old red oak also clung to nails like the terminally ill to life itself.

"You would have thought the wood would want to spit them out like the invasions they are," Allyson said.

"Familiarity breeds familiarity," Mandy said.

"The French -- many of them, anyway -- made peace with their increasingly familiar Nazi invaders," Rick said.

"It's one thing to accept what you can't do anything about," Allyson said, "and it's another to embrace it. My Quaker mother refers to refusing to embrace what you can't do anything about as her 'struggle.'"

"Far out," Mandy said.

Not that far, Allyson thought.

Day Two: Sick Call. Seven blistered fingers, five scraped knuckles, two deep splinters requiring tweezers, two broken fingernails (Mandy), one blood blister (Rick), one smashed index fingernail (Becker), one something in one eye (Allyson), one cut requiring two adhesive bandages, two cuts requiring mercurochrome, one gouged forehead from crowbar kickback (Becker) and general muscle soreness treated with aspirin and pot in breakfast waffles. They slunk into Day Two's labors.

At the end of the month, they had gotten down to the studs, joists and rafters in nine of the 13 rooms. It had been hot, dusty, sometimes even dangerous grunt work—the first of its kind for each of them. Plaster, drywall, old linoleum and rotted boards had to be carried outside, loaded into Melvin -- the 1953 pickup Mr. Klein was depreciating as a farm-business vehicle -- and ferried to the county dump. By the end of the month, they'd lost count of the number of runs Melvin had made, usually in mixed-gender pairs of mixed couples inasmuch as they were trying not to be exclusive with each other up to a point. To facilitate the renovation, Rick and Mandy managed to consolidate their growing stash of antiques into one bedroom, one living-dining room, one bathroom and one kitchen.

Next to a bedroom fireplace in between the wall studs, they uncovered a front page from The Boston Globe of November 14, 1889. It reported that Nellie Bly had begun her around-the-world trip she hoped to complete in fewer than 80 days.

"Who's Nellie Bly?" Allyson asked. "Isn't she a song?"

"A reporter," Becker said without gloating. "She wrote Ten Days in a Mad-House after feigning being crazy so she would be committed to Blackwell's Island Insane Asylum in New York City. She started investigative journalism."

"And just how did you come to know a feminist fact?" Allyson asked.

"I did a report on her in my high-school journalism class," he said. "She published the series in Pulitzer's paper, The New York World."

"Well," Allyson said, "my guy is full of surprises."

"She was very pretty," Becker added, giving Allyson a cue.

"That explains it," she observed, knowing that Becker was a self-acknowledged sucker for pretty girls, especially blondes like her.

178

The four took off a couple of "play days" and then began bone grafts on the framing that time, water, insects and rot had weakened. Once they began laying plywood subfloors and drywalling ceilings and walls, they discovered that no surface was level, no corner square and no wall plumb. Every new stick and sheet had to be fitted individually to the eccentricities of the settled framing or adapted to the mistakes committed more than a century earlier by who knew whom.

Allyson came to feel that the process of uncovering the covered was like reporting a secret. Fitting new -- all of which, she said, was true -- to old -- all of which was false -- was like "plowing through a novel that might be called <u>Oblique House</u>." She admitted that she actually liked the digging and picking work of a house dentist.

Becker pointed out that the modern 2x4s they were installing were only 1 $^5/_8$ x 3 $^5/_8$, and, to add injury to insult, they were going down to 1 ½ x 3 ½ in a couple of years.

"What!" Allyson exclaimed. "The nerve of those cheats."

"How did you know that?" Rick asked.

"At my Dad's yard. I heard customers bitching when I worked on Saturday mornings and over the summer. The old lumber he had couldn't be used with the new stuff. You had to use one or the other. The length was the same, but not the width and thickness."

"My Dad sells short stocks," Mandy said. "Or he shorts stocks. Or he stocks shorts…something like that."

"They're not exactly the same activities," Becker said with meek helpfulness.

"I actually do understand stocks," she admitted. "He says I have a head for them."

"Those new studs—that's like buying a pound of cheese and only getting 10 ounces," Allyson said.

"Nine point six ounces," Becker said before he could stop himself. Allyson glared.

"The lumber guys argue the consumer is only paying for what he's getting," Becker said. "A full 2x4 would cost more than the chintzy ones."

"A ton of lead is 2,000 pounds," Allyson insisted, "not 1,200."

"Money sometimes changes the content of descriptive language," Becker said. "Companies charge the same price, or more, for a bar of something, a bag, a can or a stud that's less than it used to be. At Columbia, we were sold a three-credit course with 200 enrolled for the same price as one with 15. We didn't get the same value. The more big courses they forced us to take, the cheaper it was to educate us, and the less we got."

"That's deeper than shit," Mandy said.

"You never know with Becker," Allyson smiled. "He can surprise you."

The refitting went slowly and wasn't fun. Progress slowed, and the four grew short with each other. Sides developed during the plywood subfloor. The boys -- who were called guys not men -- were faster but less careful. They would zip along, make a mistake, zip backward to correct it, zip ahead, make another mistake, zip back, zip ahead, back, ahead and finish. The women -- who were never called girls and preferred guys or women but tolerated ladies -- did carpentry as they had been taught to sew—slowly, tranquilly, double-checking all the way. Dressmaking had given them something of an architect's eye, so they found themselves better able to anticipate mistakes. But they lacked Becker and Rick's intuitive sense of when dumb strength would achieve an objective that could not be gained simply through good planning. Prybar work made the boys seem better than they were; adding new clothes to the house's old bones evened the sides.

They experimented with different work-team combinations, and then settled into a gender-based division with political resignation. They handled their backwardness lightly. The women dubbed themselves "The Hammerin' Honeybears" while the boys came up with "The Banzai Nail-Bangers." Allyson asked Becker whether the nails he was so "banzaied about banging were made of steel or your own keratin?"

Work rooms divided by gender were usually completed at about the same time. Shared ignorance created a simple democracy. With the rough carpentry completed by the end of July, they began laying finish flooring and then wall paneling and drywall. This work was easier but no less tedious. With more confidence and experience, they sometimes agreed to work in mixed doubles. They became more amiable with each other as they grew stronger, faster and better.

Jeffrey and Allyson found themselves pulling closer within the claustrophobia of group cooking, group smoking, group living and group working. She said they all had a "bad case of group." But she, more than he, found that group became important. She even took on the occasional role of "serving as the group-process lady." Later, she came to feel that "group" was holding her back from her life's real mission as a journalist.

She and Becker exchanged their share of sharp words during work and in the tepee when one or both were frustrated and tired. But they also learned to clear the air and prevent small annoyances from becoming larger. After work, they would skinny-dip in the Deerfield River. They took running dives into a deep pool next to a clump of white birch. The water moved slowly in this bend. They floated on their backs and didn't drift with the current. They treaded water together and joked that they "left the river well-trod." They lollygagged. They enjoyed the late-afternoon wetness and the feeling of refreshed cleanliness it brought. About three weeks into the project, Mandy discovered biodegradable soap in a newly opened "organic" store in Greenfield. They kept the plastic bottle at the River. Allyson and Becker soaped each other, massaging their slick, foamy fingers into the other's knotted muscles. After a rinse, they'd lie on their backs, watching the sun descend between their feet. They liked being quiet with each other.

It surprised them that the numbing drudgery of their work increased their energy for sex. They saw a lot of each other's bodies during the day, most of the time without the kind of clothing that either conceals flaws or highlights virtues. Becker watched Allyson's freckles emerge as tiny, earth-colored blooms in a field of milky cocoa. Her blue eyes brightened in contrast. Her hair thickened and curled. The muscles in her arms, thighs and stomach tightened. Her hands roughened even under work gloves but retained their slimness. She saw him hardening in the same way. The bone-lines in his face sharpened. A big vein ran vertically along each bicep and networked on the back of his forearms. His hands became a collage of nicks and callouses. He let his hair grow and tied it back with a red bandana. Their bodies seemed to fit together better as they became toned and strong.

One afternoon in late July when Rick and Mandy had gone to Greenfield for groceries and spackle, Becker found himself in the hallway staring at Allyson's back as she stood on a stepladder. She was stretching to knock in a sheetrock nail above her head. He watched her legs lengthen as she stood on her tiptoes. She wore a red T-shirt and faded, cut-off Levis. A patch of sweat darkened her shirt between her shoulder blades and under her arms. The intenseness of her absorption -- and the vulnerability it produced -- caught him.

He walked over to her silently from behind. After she flushed the nail, he put his hands on her hips. She jerked slightly and then relaxed. She held both hands over her head pinning the hammer between them. She spread her legs to the edges of the step. He drew his hands slowly down the outside of her legs, across her calves and then up, along the inside of her knees. She closed her eyes. He gently ran his tongue over the same route on each leg. He tasted her mild sweat-salt. She laughed softly and rotated her hips. He dropped his hands to the insides of her ankles and ran them lightly up and down her legs. He tickled her skin with his tongue and hair. He slipped his hand along the front of her belly and into her shorts, pressing her back toward him. Her head dropped to her chest. He played with her, gently stroking, touching, rubbing. He found her. Allyson inhaled. He massaged. She breathed more and more deeply. He felt her grow tense. She strained, pushing down, moving against his hand. She shuddered once, and then again. She cried out. He kept his hand inside her, quiet now. He hugged her and snuggled against her legs.

"Rascal," she purred.

"Damsel, no longer distressed."

That evening in their tepee by candlelight, Allyson began to kiss his neck and shoulders, his sides, the back of his legs, the soft inside of his elbows. He began to reciprocate, but she pushed him flat. "Relax, Becker. Well, not all of you."

She kissed his chest, his neck, cheeks and eyelids. She ran her tongue around the inside of his ear. She knelt between his legs and teased him with her tongue, tickled him with her hair, blew on his skin. She kissed him and licked him when he rose and took him inside her. She brought him over onto her and drew him in. Slowly, patiently, they joined, not deeply at first, but then more. He reached her and tightened his buttocks as she held him. They began moving together. He held, waiting for her. She clutched him and shouted. Her body tightened and then his. They stayed locked together for many minutes, whispering and smiling. Then they were quiet and good.

They had never said they loved each other, never freed the words from their hidden caches. They never knew whether they did or did not, could or could not. Whatever it was they had, it was deep, deeper than each had ever been.

They avoided talking about fall plans, about themselves, about how they might navigate whatever came next.

Becker and Rick were kicking around the idea of starting Roaring Lion Construction Company after they finished rehabbing Mandy's farmhouse. This depended on Becker getting a medical deferment at his draft physical, scheduled for late August.

Allyson listened to those discussions, but said nothing for or against. She liked this summer with Becker, but she knew that the drop-out life of a yeoman hippie was too small and self-indulgent for her. She dreaded being cast into a pre-defined gender role, be it hippie farm wife or chainsaw lady with leg hair. Becker understood her thinking. He felt her edging away as July turned into August. Say something, he told himself, but he said nothing. When their conversations drifted into the chop of what they felt about each other, one or the other would grab the tiller and steer them away. He considered moving back to Manhattan and going to law school. But he recognized that he wasn't ready to "settle down and be normal," as his Dad put it. Sometimes, he imagined them living together on a farm in Greenfield, raising children, being married. But he knew that even if that worked for him, it would not work for her unless she was fully committed. He accepted that summer that he lacked the power to set his future.

The notice to report for his pre-induction physical had come in late June. Becker contacted the allergist who had treated him as a kid. He responded: "Latent asthma might work." If that failed, Becker would fake the color-blindness test. If he still passed, he was, at best, undecided. He doubted the Selective Service System would accept his confession of fighting in Spain before he was born.

Allyson drew into herself as the end of August approached. She didn't show him the official Columbia Journalism School letter or her reply. She didn't take him over to Wonalancet to skirmish with her parents. She wrestled with knowns, unknowns, probabilities, likelihoods, improbables, uncertainties and worst for her, feelings.

And so their future was decided on the third Sunday of August, 1968, during a volleyball game. At least in some ways.

Becker was still as he lay next to her that morning. Both were one-third asleep, one-third awake and one-third sliding back and forth between the two. She lay with her back toward him. He had his arm around her. They breathed softly. They thought these moments were stolen from the thief of time passing.

It was getting light. The air around their noses was chilly, and it carried the stale, damp pungency of a dead fire and marijuana butts. The tepee's canvas skin started to catch the morning light. She moved first, breaking their seal.

He slipped away from their sleeping bags. They hated leaving their comfort each morning. They liked to drift on their youth while knowing that getting from Point A to Point B was a decision that awaited them.

Allyson turned toward Becker. He snuggled against her neck. "I love you, Pick," he whispered.

"I know."

She buried this with other things that might turn out to be treasures. She wondered if she should make a map so she could find them again.

Becker was playing next to her as usual. Allyson was the setter, and he was in the left, outside-hitter position. The serve came to the back row and was bumped to her in the middle. She tried to set him for a spike, but her high-arching ball drifted to the other side of the net where it was pounded back.

"Don't worry, Pick, we'll get 'em next time," he said.

The next serve was bumped badly to her. She set awkwardly over her head with her back to the net. She flubbed it out of his reach and out of bounds.

Then she set the next one too far from the net for Becker to hit it hard and down. But he was able to dink it over for a winner. They rotated.

Allyson hated Sunday afternoon volleyball at Mandy's farm. It wasn't her sport. Field hockey -- women with sticks -- that was what she liked.

She was also impatient with the sociology of the players. They were, too, too, too hippie, she had concluded. Yet, all of them took these meaningless games seriously. She never understood why volleyball was the last bastion of competitiveness for hippie males. And the game was rigged against women, because they could not spike over an eight-foot-high net. She hated being relegated to setter, especially when she was in a spiking position. She didn't like being forced into playing the "girl's position." She hated the "two-minimum-women" rule for what it assumed.

Volleyball was a peculiar exception to what Mandy and Rick, along with their friends, were "now about," as they put it. They insisted that they were purging themselves of bourgeois values and American militarism, getting back to the land (with the financial assistance of their bourgeois parents) and learning new roles for men and women. An "alternative" was what they invoked. No more materialistic competition. "Lifestyle"—was their word. So they set up their stereos, their food coops, their throwing wheels, their underground papers, their sound systems, their windmills, their tepees and, occasionally, their menagés of two, three and many. And they put down their bourgeois origins, their sexual baggage and their neighbors—"the locals." They were "into" things that got them back to, but they were not into things that were immediately behind them or of them. No one had trouble with the contradiction. They named their male dogs Tulip and Wonton; their children, Sunbeam and Sanskrit. Some of the women took to steel-toed boots and long dresses; the men wore pony tails or shoulder-length hair as they practiced expressing themselves. Women learned to cut firewood with a chainsaw. Men ran day-care centers. Animals ran loose, and children ran amok. And for all of that, Sunday volleyball remained the Gulag of the Old Order, a prison they couldn't escape.

It was hard to figure, Allyson thought. She understood and agreed with their critique of society, parents, roles and politics, but their embraced "alternative" was not hers. She had ambition—career ambition. This crowd had its hands full getting out of bed in the morning.

Allyson hit the ball with no more confidence or skill as the games continued. The four teams were never remixed once the lose-and-sit marathon started. She always played next to Becker. She was messing up more sets than she got right.

Becker praised her good sets and said nothing about the flubs. She knew he was grimacing and wincing when she screwed up, but not so that she could see. Still, she knew. Becker had been through this with her on other Sundays. He suggested that she stop playing in the Sunday games, which would have parked her in the shade with the Earth Mothers, talking miso recipes.

Becker began playing closer to her center position so he could do some of the setting to their other outside spiker. After a while, he was taking bumps that were clearly hers to set. She knew he was compensating for her play, which she resented as much as the public knowledge of her ineptitude. He was stealing her humanity, she thought, though that was really an over-the-top way of putting it. Her teammates began hitting the ball away from her, and the guys on the other side targeted her for their hard overhand serves. She felt her concentration slipping. She felt anger building.

Allyson was miserable—hot, cranky, dusty, sore, tired, sweaty and pissed off. She could not quit because that would unbalance the sides and even invoke a forfeit, though no one actually knew whether a forfeit rule governed these games. She was not a quitter, no matter how badly she played. She felt like the single cube on which Becker had once rested the giant saltshaker.

By mid-afternoon, the two surviving teams were tied in their rubber game. Winning would decide who went swimming in the Deerfield first, and who cleaned up the dishes and tables. They continued to wisecrack and claim "Treesies" or "Dogsies" whenever one or the other interfered, but now, Allyson noticed, that players -- the women, too -- had begun diving for the ball and arguing over whether someone had touched the net.

She tried to concentrate more intensely, to "look" the ball onto her fingers, anticipate where spikes would go, position herself to get bumps for easier sets and avoid mental mistakes. The more she concentrated, the higher her anxiety. Becker was playing above his ability, which he had to do for them to win. They were down nine to seven and then tied at 12. Allyson hadn't botched anything for the last eight points. She had even dug out a vicious spike for which she was cheered and even acknowledged by the other side. Becker had slapped her ass after that one like football players do, not like boyfriends do. They tied again at 13, then at 14. The game was 15, win by two.

Allyson was once again in the center-front setter position with Becker on her left. A hard, line-drive serve flew over her head to the back line. The bump to her wobbled and drifted between her and Becker. She scuttled toward it for the set. But he went for the spike without waiting for Allyson's set. It was her ball not his, but he leaped toward the net, his right arm cocked, his eyes focused. Allyson was locked onto the ball. She positioned herself under it and crouched, waiting for it to drop. The sun suddenly blinded her. She blinked and lost her bearings. She stumbled. Becker landed clumsily against her shoulder and side. Their legs gave way. They fell into each other on the dusty ground.

Her mind blurred. She was disoriented. Players hurried over asking whether they were hurt. She lay with her eyes closed, trying to get all the crockery back in her cupboard. Jeffrey disentangled himself and then knelt next to her.

"Pick, you okay? Pick? I'm sorry. It was your ball."

She opened her eyes. "I hate volleyball, and I don't like you a whole lot right now. Let's finish it."

They lost the next point and the game. Nobody whooped or made the usual comments about the losers' ancestors. The winners deferred swimming to help with cleanup.

Allyson walked toward the tepee instead of the River. Becker followed.

"Do you want to talk this one out?" he asked.

"Not right now. Go for a swim."

Allyson sat cross-legged in the tepee thinking about newsrooms and Becker. If she tried to do everything, she would, she thought, do nothing well. Dropping out, however, did not suit her at all. She'd had enough of Mandy's farm. She had to find out what she could do in the world. She had to be bigger. That's what it came down to.

And there was the other thing that she had just learned that she didn't want to discuss. She had to decide what to do without the confusion that Becker would bring.

She doodled aimlessly on the dirt floor with a charred stick from the fire pit. She found herself crying against her will. She began packing. She left a note on a scrap of shopping bag. "You're not Prince Charming, but I like you anyway. I've decided to go into journalism. You know why. I can't marry you now. Maybe never. I'm sorry that it didn't work better. Maybe in other circumstances. Maybe I love you. I don't know. Allyson."

After a few tortured phone calls during her first semester at Columbia's Journalism School, they stopped bleeding on each other. She hadn't heard from him or about him for seven years. Once, on a depressing Sunday evening, she phoned the last number she had for him in Greenfield only to be informed that "this line has been disconnected and is no longer in service."

"Yes, I guess that's right," she said. "No longer in service."

She carried with her the good memory of holding him in the tepee on pleasant mornings, the bad memories, the mixed memories, the uncategorized memories and the sense of not fitting in with this alternative group. She stuffed all of it in her back closet. She wasn't a broody hen, her mother had always said. Allyson didn't sit on the past hoping it would hatch something different than it had.

186

When Allyson Pickering called Jeep Delucci's campaign office in Charleston, she was not thinking of Jeffrey Becker. She was thinking about where this union-democracy story might take her. She was thinking about becoming more important.

And then he answered.

They thought of the tepee on Mandy's farm—and all that was contained within.

Book Three

Chapter 13

Pittsburgh, October 9, 1975

Johnson C. "John-Cee" Smithers, president and chief executive officer of UNICOAL, America's largest coal producer, was, he admitted to himself, bored with it all. So he straightened his silverware, then his plate. He was even losing interest in getting older, because it was a problem without a working solution. A matter like that angered a mining engineer.

UNICOAL ran smoothly. Departments were structured to analyze what needed to be done, what capital had to be invested, what risks might arise and what money might be made. It was now more efficient and more professional than the company he'd taken over 20 years earlier. Public relations and lobbying were an ever-bigger part of what he worked on as distasteful as they were. John-Cee and his fellow operators had to implement the 1969 Federal Coal Mine Health and Safety Act, which regulated respirable dust to limit future black-lung cases and imposed many safety practices. And shortly thereafter, the Nixon Administration passed the Environmental Protection Act, which began to impose limits on air, water and land pollution that coal production and combustion caused. Compliance with these complex regulations was all work and no fun from his perspective. It made no money. It provided no satisfaction. It burned time. Increasingly, John-Cee saw himself not as the leader of the largest coal producer but as simply the required signature on work done by others for others. Even the strictly business decisions gave him little satisfaction, because they were not much different than those he had made a decade earlier. The equipment was better and more productive, but the calculation of cost, risk and profit was the same. He needed something to keep his head in the game. He wanted to lead again, to cut through the mess to a goal, to make something happen.

Maybe, he thought, he'd order dessert. That would be wild.

"The usual, Ernie," he said to the waiter at the Duquesne Club in downtown Pittsburgh.

The gray-haired waiter nodded.

"Same for me, Ernie. Better hold the sour cream," Ben Roberson, Junior, president of AMSTEEL, said. AMSTEEL was the country's largest domestic steel producer by tonnage and its fifth largest coal operator. Ben and John-Cee had been friends for decades. AMSTEEL operated captive coal mines that fed the company's coke ovens, which fed its steel mills. UNICOAL mainly produced thermal coal that electric utilities burned to

188

generate steam. AMSTEEL's metallurgical coal had different characteristics. Ben and John-Cee were not competitors except occasionally.

Ernie agreed with "the same." He had been holding Ben Roberson's sour cream on his baked potato for six years ever since his bypass surgery.

"Your boy going to start this year?" Ben asked.

"Yes sir," Ernie replied. "He's up to 260 after working with the weights."

"Thatsa boy," Ben said. "Pitt needs some beef on the defensive line. Maybe, he'll go pro. Then you could retire in comfort." He blew cigarette smoke onto his plate through the Princeton nose that a Yale tackle had broken in 1935. Forty years later, his knees hurt, and he missed playing on Saturday afternoons. He smoked against his doctor's orders but only a couple a day that he counted. He tried not to inhale too much. These restrictions were like living with black lung, he thought.

"No plans to retire," Ernie said. "I like my job a lot."

"I wish I liked mine as much," John-Cee muttered.

"Mr. Maggard?" Ernie asked.

"Son, fix me up one of your Bugs Bunnies. Hold anything that tastes good. Shit. Well, I won't pick off some bacon if the cook happened by mistake to lay three or four strips on top. BY MISTAKE. Along with some of that blue cheese, also BY MISTAKE."

Burton "Buzzy" Maggard had grown up poor during The Depression in East Kentucky, which was about as poor as poor got. His Dad was a miner who was never able to work a single five-day week between 1929 and 1940. Nine Maggards living on $10 a week made a lasting impression. The University of Kentucky let him in, because it was desperate for males on campus, even those, like him, who were blind in one eye. He scraped through on what he earned packing munitions on the night shift at the newly built Blue Grass Ordnance facility south of Lexington.

Using $300 of his War-time savings, Buzzy returned to his native Pike County in early 1946 driving a War-surplus, Deuce-and-a-Half dump truck. The long-wheelbase of this GMC CCKW -- "Jimmy" -- was rated to carry about 5,500 pounds on the road. With the sides built higher, Buzzy could run double that weight. He'd buy coal at a mine for less than $3.50 a ton and sell it at a tipple for $4.25 or more. Three runs a day, 30 tons, at least $.75 a ton profit, almost $25 a day. As long as the Jimmy held up without a need for major repairs or tires, $25 a day was pretty good money for a kid. It was more than the $15 his Dad was making for 10 hours underground.

Buzzy had worked for a year after graduating in 1940 from Pikeville High for Oshel and Hassel Cornett who owned a dog-hole mine near Jonancy. The Cornetts worked one crew of 12 men, using beat-to-death equipment from the 1920s and sweat. They tunneled horizontally into a 40-inch-high seam with hand-powered breast augers, undercutting picks and blasting powder. Electrical equipment was uneconomical for the Cornetts to use when desperate labor was so plentiful and cheap. So their crew muscled loaded cars out to the drift mouth over narrow-gauge rails and dumped their coal into an open chute above a waiting truck. To save time and money, the Cornetts would sometimes shoot coal off the solid rather than undercut it. Buzzy lost his eye to flying coal shrapnel in one such blast. Exempt from conscription, he drifted into the University where he met his wife-to-be, Betty, who saw something in him that he didn't know was there.

Buzzy winced at the thought of yet another salad. His notion of an edible leaf was greens boiled in fatback. Betty had made him change, at least when she sat at the same table.

"Cholesterol! Damn heart doctor says no eatin' nothin' worth swallerin'. Can't smoke Luckies. Can't drink whiskey. Can't fuck. Can't even pee off the back porch. Glad you still smoke, Ben. I sure am livin' it up off you. Blow some over here."

"Maybe your doctor will next cut out your current exercise regimen—splitting stocks," Smithers said. "He'd do Ben and me a big favor if he'd retire you and your low-paid, no-benefits miners out of the coal business. We've been trying to get rid of you for years."

Buzzy scratched his forearms. "John-Cee, you and the steel boys like Ben and the oil companies what bought coal, like USOCO—not this year you ain't buyin' me out. By God, them A-Rabs are makin' me rich. You, too. I can sell anythang that's hard and black for as much as $25 a ton, more than double my cost."

John-Cee and Ben understood. They, too, were making more money in the coal business than ever before.

"One year of fat for years of lean," John-Cee said.

"I do okay in them leans," Buzzy said.

Buzzy snugged up against the linen tablecloth. He stuck his drop-leaf face over his plate. "Boys," he whispered, "we oughta send them O-Peckers a solid gold camel every month. Their high-priced oil is a pure comfort in my old age. Best thang that's happened to the coal business since the Japs bombed us in '41. Now that's a fact that we need to keep here at this table."

Ernie, the waiter, listened while he filled their water glasses carefully and slowly.

Buzzy grabbed a warm roll and ripped it in half. He speared a pat of iced butter on his salad fork. He rammed it into the bread and bit off half with his molars.

Smithers and Roberson chuckled. They appreciated Buzzy Maggard who liked to show off his "lackin's," as he called his absence of polish, as the foundations on which he built his success. If you pointed at your own weaknesses, he had discovered, nobody else bothered to point at them. He confessed to having an undergraduate degree from UK to those who might be impressed with that accomplishment. He never mentioned he was a big donor to the University's endowment. He loved to wear his up-from-hillbilly-poverty medals on his chest, particularly with friends like these in a place like the white-linen Duquesne Club. John-Cee and Ben knew that Buzzy Maggard was, hands down, the shrewdest CEO in their industry.

After the War, Buzzy hauled coal for the Cornetts and every other dog-hole mine he could hustle. But coal demand slacked in the post-War recession. The big coal haulers were squeezed out of business when orders fell. They could not cut costs fast enough while generating the cash to pay off their truck notes. Using a life-insurance payment that had come to Betty, Buzzy started buying their used equipment. His first trucks were bought from desperate competitors who wanted to get a few thousand dollars in hand for their escape to Detroit. In two years, Buzzy was running 13 trucks, which were, occasionally, legal to drive if weight limits were ignored.

Buzzy's big break came in 1947. Oshel and Hassel Cornett along with three employees drowned when they drove their working face into an abandoned, unmapped, water-filled tunnel in front of them. During the Depression, out-of-work miners stole coal out of these tiny "bootleg" mines. In time, their excavations filled with explosive methane or water. Had Oshel and Hassel been drilling test holes in advance of mining? the Kentucky mine inspector asked.

"Sure they was," Buzzy said, even though he'd never seen the Cornetts drill a single test hole.

"Victims were using an inaccurate map," the inspector wrote in his report. "Illegal mine was not mapped. Fatalities were caused by unforeseeable accident."

Test holes cost money and took time, Buzzy knew. That's why the Cornetts never drilled them. The Cornett heirs escaped liability.

In light of his helpful testimony, Buzzy was able to buy the mine from the Cornett widows on the promise that he would pay out the purchase price from production earnings over the next 15 years. His plan was to buy used mining equipment and hire the best mechanic from the hundreds of unemployed he saw stuck in the dying coal camps. No more handloading coal. No more pushing cars to the portal. Bring in a used transformer, hook up electricity and pick a crew who knew how to keep cheap junk running. *Mechanize* pounded through his brain. "*Mechanize as cheap as possible.*"

His first machines were snatched from bankruptcy sales. He'd buy three loading machines for $500 each. He'd keep two working off the cannibalized parts of the third. If he had a still-working piece of near-dead junk, he'd sell it to someone lower on the list of bottom-feeders trying to copy his success. He paid the Cornett widows in three years.

Buzzy followed his plan again and again over the next 15 years, buying used equipment and picking up mining properties for pennies on the dollar. Unemployed coal miners would work for as little as $10 a day when the alternative was no work and no dollars a day.

The hills of East Kentucky were desperate for a homegrown hero during the economic despair of the 1950s and 1960s when three out of every four American coal miners lost their jobs owing to stagnant demand and mechanization. Maggard circled the coal auctions "like a damn buzzard," the flat-bust sellers grumbled to themselves. They dubbed him "Buzzy." The name stuck, because he liked it. The combination of wringing the last ounce of production from used equipment, paying his labor no more than $1.25 an hour with no benefits and obtaining long-term supply contracts with the Tennessee Valley Authority made him and Betty rich. He began to sell his least productive mines, which he called, "dumpin' the trash and uppin' the cash." He bought better coal properties with the money he put together from these sales. Bigger reserves. Thicker seams. Higher quality. Safer roof conditions. More rail spurs and fewer truck hauls.

A decade after the Cornetts died, folks would drive slowly in their rusted-out cars past Buzzy's hammered iron gates that protected his black-stone mansion with a back porch to pee off of. They wanted a glimpse of the gun turrets they'd heard he built on the corners. They wanted to gloat in the wealth of one of their own. Buzzy was invited to give talks to Kentucky business and civic groups on the "secret of his success." He condemned "Warshington welfare" without mentioning the TVA's small-business, set-aside contracts that were the foundation of his own wealth. He pointed a finger at the "Happy Pappy make-work program" as ruining individual initiative by paying the unemployed to clean up roadside trash, fill potholes and paint the schools their kids attended. The patched-coat children of Harlan, Bell, Letcher, Pike and Martin Counties in East Kentucky were told to see Buzzy Maggard as no less an inspiration than Daniel Boone. Buzzy saw himself as singled out by good fortune to be in the worst place at the right time with a wife who had some cash.

John-Cee Smithers, a Yale-trained engineer with an MBA from the Wharton School in accounting, doubted he could have matched Buzzy's success had he started on Pike County's Muddy Creek rather than Persimmon Road in Sewickley, east of Pittsburgh. He doubted he would be running UNICOAL had his father not run UNICOAL before him. Coal was the family business. He had hopes his son, Hanky, would follow in their footsteps though it was his daughter who had the smarts. It was

192

starting to occur to him in 1975 that he should bring Carol Ann into the coal business.

"Our problem, Buzzy," John-Cee said, "is that our friends in the ACMU have big eyes. They now see themselves as middle-class, above blue-collar labor. They want wage rates that match the autoworkers, which we can't sustain. Toyota and Datsun can produce the same car as GM for half the money, because their labor cost is one-half ours. If we go to autoworker's wages, foreign coal will come in from South America, Canada and even Australia. Our problem is that we're making too much money right now. They can subtract cost per ton from price per ton as well as we can. But we know this sunshine is temporary. Jeep Delucci thinks it's permanent. He's scoring points with that line about the 1972 ACMU contract being 'two tons short a nickel.' That contract fit the money we were making three years ago. The '74 contract—well we finessed an extension of '72 with a small raise and a few upgrades. And if we settle the new contract high next year, our labor costs will drag up yours and the other non-Union operations. Everyone will lose."

"Won't argue with anythin' you said. "But do you fellers know somethin' I don't? Sounds like you've given up on ol' Joe Hunt workin' with you."

"Old Joe got his old ass kicked," Ben said, looking over his half-glasses at Buzzy.

"If Hunt wins, we're going to have to give him a better contract in '76," John-Cee said. "If Delucci wins, the same thing. We'll probably end up giving less to Joe than to Delucci, but I'm not sure that we net out with a plus with Joe. Not at his age. He might beat Delucci this time, but that's the last we'll see of him. If Hunt settles for some small improvements next year, we'll be fighting wildcat strikes, absenteeism, work-to-rule and sabotage for the next two years or more. It'll be ugly. Our interest right now is running as much coal as we can. The extra pennies for wages are small potatoes in light of the groaning board before us."

Ernie, the waiter, replenished their bread basket, butter dish and water glasses. Slowly.

"But thar's no guarantee that a fat contract with Delucci won't end you up in the same mess with the ordinary miner," Buzzy said. "You know that revolutions build on risin' expectations, not them that are fallin' through the floor. And bigger paychecks lead to bigger expectations. The more you give 'em per day, the fewer days they'll figure they need to work to make it. That's how I'd figure it. I've always been partial to playin' this game as cheap as I can. I can't save or spend money that I've given to employees, bless their hearts."

Ernie, the waiter, brought lunch. He placed a filet mignon, medium rare, in front of John-Cee with a baked potato and sour cream. He placed the same in front of Ben, without the sour cream. He placed a large salad in front of Buzzy Maggard with a thimble of mostly vinegar dressing. Buzzy scowled at the lack of bacon.

"Mrs. Maggard gave me strict instructions," Ernie explained.

Buzzy growled unintelligibly and buttered another roll.

"Two's the limit," Ernie warned.

"So whacha gonna do if I go out of here and eat the biggest damned triple bacon cheeseburger I can find, maybe two of 'em?"

"I'm not going to do anything, sir, but Mrs. Maggard will know, won't she?"

"You're damn right she'll know. The girl's a hawk. Got sharp eyes and a sharper beak. Don't miss nothin'. Got informers everywhere, includin' you. Best damn thang I ever did was marry her."

Ben picked up the thread of their conversation. "We face the danger that a generous contract in 1976 with OPEC-inflated coal prices will stretch us out over a time when oil prices fall. If oil price regresses to its norm, so will coal price. And that's when we'll get caught if we let our labor costs exceed what we can justify with productivity increases."

Ernie brought Buzzy Maggard a thimble-size service of Roquefort dressing to mix with his mostly vinegar. He slipped it on the table with the back of his hand as he looked off in the distance.

"That's worth a $5 tip," Ben laughed.

"Ten!" Buzzy said.

Ernie busied himself mixing the Roquefort with the initial serving in a clean bowl. Slowly.

"Regulations are killin' me on productivity," Buzzy said. "I have to hire all kinds of extra people -- environmental people, compliance people, lawyer people, technician people, water people, dust people, paper people -- to deal with the new pollution and safety regulations that Richard 'Millstone' Nixon put on us before he got his ass caught in Watergate."

"We're all in the same boat. The extra people lower our productivity and cut straight into our net," Ben said.

"The upside is that big companies like ours can carry these costs and pass them through," John-Cee said. "Higher regulatory costs help us in the long run, because they kill the little guys who can't afford to comply."

"Do you have anything on this Delucci kid?" Buzzy asked.

John-Cee put down his fork. "I had our people in that area of West Virginia send me a report. They've been working with him as district president for a couple of years. We got his FBI file, which doesn't give us anything. He seems to be bright enough. Not ideological. He doesn't seem to be the guy who 'sees' the deal or the guy who puts it together, but he's the one who'll close it."

"Nothing we can sink our teeth into so far," Ben said.

194

"It's this Becker fellow, Jeffrey Becker, a lawyer and his campaign manager, who is a cause for concern," John-Cee said. "He's a do-gooder who was in that mess at Columbia University in 1968. He was even against building a new gym for the student body! Got his FBI file. He was in that Students for a Democratic Society but dropped out before they started blowing things up, including themselves. He's likely to give us fits at the negotiating table. Becker's not a politician. Delucci, on the other hand, seems to be someone who will learn to work with us. We can teach *him* the ropes."

"Give Delucci enough rope, and he might just hang hisself," Buzzy said. "Now if that Becker boy's a pinko, you can paint him fire-engine red quick enough. Jes' get you a dab of color and a very big, very wet brush. Then stick a red light on his head and a sireeen in his mouth."

"Slow down, Buzzy," Ben said. "If the miners find out we're partial to Joe Hunt, they'll swing behind Delucci. And vice versa." He pushed his plate away, with most of the potato uneaten.

"Let's get Joe to do Becker," John-Cee said.

"You boys might do better with Delucci over time," Buzzy said. "Show him the truth: If his boys want jobs, you boys gotta make your bucks."

"Joe Hunt is an empty lunch bucket if you ask me," Ben Roberson said, "and I've known him since Fricktown. I think we're better off bringing Delucci in now than to run Joe through the wringer one more time. Sure, we can get more out of Joe -- or put it another way, he can get less out of us -- but we'll pay for it in wildcat strikes and slowdowns. We want a strong ACMU that can control its members. We want a contract the Union lives up to, imposes and enforces."

"You ain't gonna get that with no basket-case Humpty Dumpty like Joe," Buzzy said.

"Reluctantly, our guy is Delucci," John-Cee said.

"Agreed," Ben said.

Ernie busied himself near their table, folding napkins.

"Suppose some enterprising reporter discovered something that makes it appear that we're trying to help Delucci," John-Cee said. "And then that something turns out to be false so that Delucci looks like he stood up to us."

"Clever," Ben Roberson said.

"That's slicker than a greasy eel," Buzzy said. "But what you boys gonna do about Becker?"

John-Cee looked at Ben. "We could tell the truth, couldn't we?"

Ernie, the waiter, brought dessert.

"No harm in that," Ben replied. "Joe's using Marv Shookoff as his campaign consultant. Let Shookoff take Becker down in Joe's name."

"One of my guys can get Shookoff started with some clippings," John-Cee said. "There's one more item. Ben has a little something on Joe Hunt that was never proved. He was never charged. But it's certainly possible that he was involved. And the best that he can say is no he wasn't."

"Ben, whadda you got on Joe?" Buzzy asked.

"It was during the strike in the winter of 1932-1933 at our Fricktown mine. Our superintendent, Frank Gallagher, disappeared. Probably murdered by one or more of the strikers. His body was never found. Probably burned up in the commissary fire that happened the night he was last seen. Joe Hunt and Larry Sonoski were strikers. No evidence was turned up about what happened. But we have a letter from one of our people at the time speculating that Gus Olin and Joe Hunt, who was one of his loaders, were probably involved. Joe Hunt, our snitch said, probably brought supplies to the camp's kitchen, but we couldn't prove it. We could leak this information and suggest it be looked into. I'm not sure that it matters whether it's true or not at this point. A murder question would be a big cloud hanging over Joe's head. Maybe a reporter could actually dig out what happened to Gallagher. That cloud might rain on us if we poke it."

"You scamps," Buzzy said. "Some ACMU miners will think old Joe's a damn hero for killin' a superintendent in that strike."

"Some will," John-Cee said. "But we wouldn't need to convince every miner that electing a murderer is unseemly. Just enough to swing the election behind Delucci."

"The reporter," Ben said, "will have to be someone who is not seen as being in our pocket."

"I'd go with the double cross and the Commie stuff," Buzzy said. "Don't see how you win with Joe. Delucci's your boy."

"We need a reporter to work this stuff," Ben said.

"I think I know our man, who, I might add, is not," John-Cee said.

Ben Roberson ate his usual lime sherbet for dessert. John-Cee had a Manhattan instead of the fruit cup in front of him: "It's a digestive," he explained. Buzzy was given a serving of chocolate mousse that amounted to three level teaspoons, three "runts-of-the-litter" teaspoons in his opinion.

Ernie, the waiter, bussed their plates and wondered, what, if anything, he should do with the information he had overheard.

Chapter 14

McDowell County, W.Va., October 11, 1975

Willie Rutherford was feeling good.

Susie's garden was still producing—potatoes, cabbage and second-planting lettuce and spinach. The kids over their summer vacation let him get some sleep during the day, because Susie had shooed them out after breakfast. Now that they were back in high school, he felt rested on top of rested.

Susie had gone into the cellar and brought up a half-gallon Ball jar of Sun Haven peaches she'd canned in August. She always tucked in a stick of cinnamon, because Willie liked his peaches that way. As a matter of fact, she liked them that way, too. Then she baked a double-crust pie. He saw her slip two big pieces into his lunch bucket before she went to bed. That gave Willie a lot to look forward to at 4 a.m.

Willie Rutherford liked going to work with a positive attitude. It made everything easier. The shift went faster if he wasn't looking at his watch every five minutes. "A smile goes a mile," he said to himself, "helps everyone get along." Good attitude made him feel light on his feet, shifty like a halfback juking out the big clumsy tackles of life. He had wanted to run the ball, but the coach said he wasn't big enough. So he learned to kick. You made your kicks with attitude more than your leg. His section crew always worked more efficiently when Willie, the man on the continuous-miner, had his "'tude." Then everyone slipped into a groove. When Willie was running coal and all the support jobs were in sync, everyone was dancing to the good beat of old rock 'n' roll. Mining coal wasn't fun, but a man could get with it when his crew and conditions were right.

Willie settled in behind the wheel of his 1969 F150 pickup. He owned it free and clear after finishing the three-year note. He'd bought it new from a dealer in Beckley. He liked the long bed, which was good for hauling plywood and drywall in case he needed to haul either, which so far he hadn't. Its eight-cylinder, 360 engine was big enough to carry a load of house coal. He liked its four-speed manual shift on the floor, next to the four-wheel-drive transfer case. The Ford's gas mileage was low, but gas had been cheap in 1969 and stayed that way until the OPEC oil embargo in the fall of 1973. With just 23,000 miles on it, Willie could see the Ford starting to rust. Another '69 F150 on dayshift had needed a new engine at 36,000 miles. Cheap metal, shoddy welds, sloppy tolerances. He never understood why Detroit didn't build vehicles that got 75,000 miles before they started falling apart. He'd heard someone say, "planned obsolescence." Willie felt *that* was cheating. Well, that wasn't something he could do anything about. Just like OPEC and the price of gasoline. And like that factory paint he bought—Lunar Green. What kind of funky-shit color was Lunar Green? He knew what kind of color it was—it was the kind that Susie wanted. Lunar blessed Green, he thought, I'm a spaceman. Next truck will be fireball red!

Willie liked working the hoot-owl shift. If the night shift left the machinery in good shape, his crew could run coal between 12:25 a.m. when they got to the face after their 12 a.m. start to about 7:35 that morning. And if maintenance had to be done, the mine was quiet and the dust was down. Either way, Willie was okay with it. Some guys called the third shift "graveyard," not hoot-owl. Those were the guys who didn't get their sleep during the day. It was rotating shifts -- not straight shifts -- that Willie hated. After three weeks on one shift, the whole mine had to change—day shift to night, night to hoot owl, hoot to day. And then three weeks later, everyone moved again. A man had trouble adjusting. Willie was glad that UNICOAL worked straight shifts. John-Cee Smithers had been honest with his men when he promised them no rotating shifts in the '74 negotiations.

At 45, Willie felt he was still in decent shape even after 20 years underground and even though his belly pushed tight against his shirt, which kept crawling toward the steering wheel a little bit every year. When he'd first gone underground, he'd been six-feet tall and 155 pounds. He was still six feet but was now carrying about 200 pounds. Most shifts, he'd just sit in the continuous-miner and work the controls. There'd be some twisting around and checking behind, but it wasn't like when his Daddy was handloading on his knees and pushing loaded cars out to the main haulage track. Things were better. Rumor was that the federal MESA boys were thinking about requiring permanent lighting at the face and safety canopies on all mobile equipment like his miner. That would be good, he thought.

Willie Rutherford was satisfied with his job and his life, with the comforts he'd earned and the blessings of being alive. He was planning to retire after he'd logged 30 years. He and the family could get by on Social Security and his puny ACMU pension, along with whatever off-the-books cash he could scrape up from odds and ends, including his regular poker game. A positive attitude helped a lot with life, and Susie's peach pie created a lot of positive in his way of lining things out. There were days when Willie knew he could still make the kick. This day in mid-October, 1975, felt like one of them.

Willie drove out of Anawalt Holler on schedule. He got to UNICOAL's American Eagle Mine Complex at the mouth of Bloomingrose Creek at 11:30 p.m. He parked in the lot covered with "gravels," as the miners put it. He clocked in and picked up his recharged cap light in the lamproom. Cubby, the lampman, had been crushed between a scoop and a timber prop. So for the last five years, he'd hobbled about attaching battery lamps to the wall-hung charger station and handing out charged lights to the miners going in. Cubby had another two years before he could retire. Willie liked to get his cap lamp before he got dressed for work. It was one of those routines that had brought him luck. He flipped his brass tag on the board, showing that he was underground.

Willie walked into the changing room that everyone called "the bathhouse." Men came and went between the benches in various stages of being dressed for the mine, dressed for going home and undressed in transition to one or the other. The air was moist from steam drifting out of the showers.

Willie had heard that a woman had begun mining coal in 1973, and now more were being hired because the companies needed miners. How that gonna work in a bathhouse? he asked himself. Comp'ny ain't gonna be happy about buildin' a separate place for the ladies. An' what they gonna do underground when they have to go? They gonna go in the returns like the men? On the other hand, he'd heard stories about women working in the mines as recently as 75 years ago, some dressed as men, some working with their husbands. And families working together in the mines, he'd read, had been the common practice in Scotland, England, Wales and Belgium 175 years earlier. White folks were near slaves back then, he shook his head. He'd also heard that slave women were sent underground in Virginia and Alabama before the Civil War. Well, when all was said and done, he thought, this bathhouse shit with the ladies ain't my shit. It's UNICOAL's job to figure it out.

His crew was dressing for work in their corner next to the showers. He counted heads as he worked his ceiling pulley that lowered his clothing cage and his stiff-dry work clothes. Willie was pleased that all eight had come in. That made the work easier and safer for everyone. He felt confident and reassured when everyone was together. There were no red-cap trainees on his crew. Everyone knew what he was supposed to do and how to do it safely. He slipped into his coveralls, which were still a little clammy in the armpits from his last shift. The crew was loose, talking and joking as they readied themselves to get on the mantrip for the ride into the mine. Toilets flushed. Somebody was taking a shower before shifting in. On the other side of the room, Bugs Baker had snatched Lurty Crisco's hairpiece once again and was running it up and down his chain pulley. Every time it got to the ceiling, Bugs saluted. A couple of young miners not long out of high school were playing grab-ass. Conway Twitty and Tina Turner were both singing about love but on different stations.

Willie finished lacing up his vulcanized boots with the steel safety toes and lighted a Tiparillo. He liked to taste it while he was running his miner in one of seven producing sections that American Eagle operated in separate parts of the mine. Willie was known for his skill with the ponderous machine whose bit-studded cutting drum clawed coal from the face and fed it into a rubber-tired haulage buggy snugged up behind. Each section crew typically had one continuous-miner, two shuttle buggies, roof-bolting machine and scoop.

A section's spirit and efficiency were an expression of its continuous-miner operator, not the section boss. Everyone took cues from how the miner was run, foreman included. A crew could be no better than the man who ran the miner, and Willie Rutherford ran the most productive miner at American Eagle. Willie inhaled the cheap smoke, for which he was also known. Some called him "White Tip Willie," which was okay, because he knew no offense was intended. My White Tips are better than those funky Swisher Sweets that some of these other boys like, Willie thought. Rather be known as White Tip than Swisher Sweets.

Willie sat on the bench, taking it all in. He heard Mike Decker telling Billy Burdette about the elk-hunting trip he planned for Colorado over Thanksgiving. Down the bench, Ghostman had his nose stuck in his pocket-size, hard-cover Bible. Willie dabbed a bit of shaving cologne on his neck, a good-luck ritual that had kept him safe for two decades. He sucked on the plastic tip when the lit-end was close. The smoke was harsh and probably, he admitted, not worth the effort. But Willie didn't like to waste a cigar, even a cheap one. Willie knew that top-quality, hand-rolled Churchills got smoother and tastier the closer they got to being finished. He'd smoked a couple of $2 cigars on vacation just to see. A Davidoff was $5, and he couldn't see spending that much for one cigar. Cigars, he told himself, are just another one of those things in life. If you got the coin, you smoke good; if you don't, you enjoy what you got. Like a lot of things.

Artie "Pins" Smith sat down next to him.

Willie had helped his younger neighbor break in at American Eagle where Pins spent his first six months wearing a red hat. "A mine is like a woman," Willie said, "you gotta listen for what she sayin', what she ain't sayin', what she meanin', what she feelin' and what she hidin'."

Pins worked his first three years underground as "general inside labor"—carrying materials, rockdusting tunnels with inert pulverized limestone to suppress explosive coal dust and shoveling loose coal onto conveyors. In their first six months, Red Hats did whatever grunt work needed to be done. Pins learned how to lay in concrete block walls -- called "stoppings" -- in the tunnels to channel fresh air from surface fans up to the coal face and lead dusty air from the face outside through a return tunnel. He'd also "hung rags," canvas curtains used for temporary, air-channeling walls. GI was hard, dull, numbing work. Much of it involved lifting, carrying, pulling and dragging mine timbers, roof bolts, cement blocks and 40-pound bags of rockdust. Pins was young and liked things quick and easy. He hated donkey work; he hated being at the bottom of the ladder. But Pins knew you didn't get higher-paying jobs without getting through GI. He had to prove himself willing and competent.

On their 30-minute dinner break at mid-shift, Willie showed Pins how to operate the continuous-miner, roof-bolter, shuttle buggy and scoop. On his breaks, Pins practiced.

When the roof-bolter's job opened, Pins put in his bid and was able to show Lee Roy Stump, their section boss, that he knew how to drill the roof and insert the steel rods.

"I'll do a good job for you," Pins said. "Safe, too."

"You're young to be boltin', Artie," Lee Roy replied.

"And damn good-lookin' in the bargain."

Lee Roy laughed and nodded. "Okay. You need a new handle. Can't be calling you 'General Inside Shithead' anymore. How about 'Pins'? Yeah, Pins," he said. "And be careful, you'll always be stickin' them bolts up into unsupported roof."

Pins knew the risks of running the bolter. It was easy work compared with GI and paid better. But it was also far more dangerous since the bolter operator was the man in each section most exposed to roof falls. Willie had showed Pins a federal mine-safety report that found bolter operators had the highest fatality and injury rates of all coal-job classifications. Pins understood he had to tamp down his pedal-to-the-metal instinct. Mine is like a woman, he repeated every day before he activated his bolter. I gotta pay attention. No Speedy Gonzales. Gotta be a slow hand or I be a dead man.

Artie Smith proved himself over the next two years to have a knack for safely drilling and inserting steel rods into sandstone and shale. He made Willie proud, and both were proud that American Eagle's most productive section had a black man running the miner and a black man pinning top.

"You hear, Willie?" Pins asked. "Our Local," he said, lowering his voice and nodding slightly toward the main part of the bathhouse, "went for Joe Hunt. Only five locals outa 14 in all of McDowell County went for Hunt."

"Lota folks likes the horse they on 'cause they know he can carry them. Don't know that about the young one kickin' his stall back at the barn. Maybe, he jes' want more grain in his bucket."

"If you talkin' horses, man, Joe Hunt—he a nag."

Willie chuckled deep in his chest. Then he pulled on his Tiparillo. Sometimes Pins, all 25 years of him, still caught him with a line like a late-night TV comedian. Maybe, he thought, it was just the irreverence of being young. Willie rubbed his head where he once had hair.

"Hunt, he okay," Willie said. "Done us some good. Everyone gotta remember that Joe been workin' low cotton the last 10, 15 years. Non-Union strip mines closin' down our deep mines. Lot more productive than we are. Them big western operations in Wyoming takin' customers from eastern coal where the ACMU is strong. Non-Union mines, even around here, are almost payin' our scale, but they're not carryin' retirement or the health care we got. That means ACMU coal is the high-price spread. That just bidness. None of that is Hunt's fault."

"Sheee-it. Hunt—he a chump for the comp'nies," Pin's said in a voice that was very quiet but explosive. "He get us a couple of bucks more every couple of years. My own sorry black ass could get us a couple of bucks more every few years."

"I'll keep that in mind," Willie laughed. "But what we do if this Delucci boy turn out to be a dud squib?"

The two friends giggled between themselves with muffled snorts and snickers. They didn't want the other miners in the bathhouse to notice they had something going on.

"What Delucci ever done in District 17 that you like so much?" Willie asked.

"I hear he did a good job in arbitrations," Pins said. "But the real thing is, the boy, he hungry. Like me. He'll go for bread. I knowed a couple of dudes like him in Nam. Bidness heads on 'em. Sold dink AR-15s to white-boy newbies comin' off the plane. They'd pick 'em up in the field or buy 'em cut rate from 'friendlies' around our base. Made a bunch. Those kind of guys had a feelin', like an instinct, for gettin' somethin' better than the shit they in."

"He do fo' himself, sure," Willie said. "What about the men?"

"He do for us, then we do for him," Pins said. "That Delucci boy ready to rock 'n' roll."

"You think we need James Brown runnin' the Union?"

"No man. 'Rock 'n' roll' mean your M-16 on full automatic. Mean you ready to take care of shit."

"Good thing you think he ready," Willie said, "'cause when that boy start doin' a man's job runnin' this Union, he make a whole lota shit to take care of."

"How much Hunt give you?"

"That $50 ain't my reason," Willie said. "My reason is I feel better goin' with what I know 'stead of what I don't know."

"Willie, man, you gettin' ol' head on you. You used to be feisty."

"Ol' head keep me safe. Keep my money safe. Ol' head ain't so bad if it ain't too ol'. An' what about Walter Bishop?"

"Yeah, all the white dudes know that story same as us."

"Hard for me to vote for Delucci with Walter Bishop hangin' on his belt."

"Ain't sayin' Delucci's as perfect as me or you," Pins laughed. "Hey, you bid on that 'lectrician job?"

"I did, but I dunno," Willie said. "I like runnin' the miner. I like playin' quarterback."

"How you like eatin' the dust up there, Mr. Terry Super-Bowl-Nine Bradshaw?"

Willie drew on the last of his Tiparillo. "It's a col', har' fac'," he admitted. "Dust is gettin' to me. I started coughin' up black shit in the mornin'. Breath is a little shorter walkin' up steep stairs. An' Lee Roy still ain't got all them water sprays workin' right on the miner."

"See."

"I'll tell you somethin' else," Willie said. "All that rattlin' around, gettin' shook this way and that when the miner's cuttin' in—it's wearin' out my bones."

"You be 'lectrician, man, then you workin' in good splits of air almost always," Pins said. "Do your work in intake air. None of this dusty shit at the face all shift. An' no more bein' bounced around like a popcorn in a pot."

"Yeah," Willie said. "We eatin' the dust that feed our family."

"Heard someone say that miners be diggin' their own graves," Pins said.

"You right smart for a dumb ass," Willie grinned.

"But you ain't gonna get it, that 'lectrician."

"I'm most senior," Willie said. "I got papers. I can do the work."

"You got two things against you. First, you is most blackest. American Eagle ain't never had no black 'lectrician. And second, you the best miner operator they got. Why they take you off the miner when you so good?"

Willie nodded in agreement. "Well, son, we'll see. Delmer and Lee Roy know I done a good job for 'em for a long time."

"That my point, fool," Pins whispered. "That why they want you to stay right where you are—on the miner. You might have the most seniority, but it's up to the comp'ny to say who *most* qualified to do the job. That's how they gonna knock you out. You ain't never gonna be **MOST** qualified for 'lectrician even if you be Ready Kilowatt."

"Delmer always been right with me," Willie said. "None of that shaky race shit."

"Runnin' the miner different than makin' splices on cables," Pins said. "Miner—he the man. Eee-lectrician—he jes' a prince with a cush job."

"Ain't so easy if he sticks them cables together wrong," Willie said. "If I do that, I be burnt sausage. Anyway, we'll see. Folks said the same thing when I bid on the miner. First black on the miner. Everybody got cool with it after a little bit."

"Miner is one thing, 'lectrician is another," Pins said, not quite willing to let it rest. "You can count the number of black 'lectricians at American Eagle on a hand with no fingers."

"None of us ever bid on that job before," Willie said. "We'll see."

"And while you're doin' all this 'seein',' why don't you see ol' Lee Roy 'bout the top. That roof ain't feelin' right to me. Feel loose, like sometimes I'm torquing my bolts into a bag of marbles. Not sure the expansion joints at the end of the pins are grippin'. Not sure the pressure plates on the bottom cover enough area. Could be shaly shit hidin' above the sandstone."

Willie frowned. He trusted Pin's judgment. The whole crew did.

"I'm trying to pin together a beam in the roof, laminate the layers out of whatever's up there," Pins said. "Can't anchor into top made of ball bearings."

"Maybe I'll jes' take a little cut three or four feet up into the roof first thing," Willie said. "See what the top's like going forward."

"Yeah, boy," Pins said. "See, I was puttin' four-foot bolts in on three-foot centers all last shift. And maybe I should be goin' to five- even six-foot bolts. Maybe eight-footers!"

"Three-foot centers! You supposed to be spacin' 'em out four feet between each bolt on a grid. That's the roof plan."

"I'm usin' my bes' judgment," Pins said. "Top don't feel right. Scared me. Hey, man, fuck 'em. If Lee Roy think I'm wastin' too many UNICOAL bolts, he can hold the top up with his head. He give me shit about the centers or how long them bolts are, I'll get the safety committee to give me an 'imminent danger' and shut the whole damn section down 'til they scope the roof out."

"If you pull the section right now, be hell to pay," Willie said. "No slowin' up now. Did Lee Roy tell you to stick with the four-foot bolts?"

Leaning back, Pins smiled. "Naw. He said, 'Pins, you do it however you think makes it safe. Don't want no roof falls on my watch; they cut production.'"

"Can't fault the man for workin' both sides of the street," Willie laughed.

"'Deed, I can't. Then he say, 'Pins, you got my confidence, and I got your back on this. Delmer ain't gonna come down on you about the cost of longer bolts and the tighter spacin'.'"

"The roof ain't really the real thing," Willie said. "It's the speed-up. They're pushin' us for every blessed pound we can get as fast as we can get it."

"Don't blame 'em," Pins said. "With coal prices so high, they got to be clearin' 10, 12 bucks a ton profit."

"You can only speed up so much," Willie said, "before somethin' goes wrong…machine breaks down, man does somethin' stupid cuttin' a corner."

"We can slow it back down to normal," Pins said. "We know how to jam Lee Roy. He can push all he want, but we the ones in the machines."

Willie considered the prospect of this declaration of hostilities. "Let's see how thangs work this shift. Then maybe we talk it over with our crew an' a couple of others."

Pins took Willie's concession as a victory. "Okay, we see how it goes."

"An' this'll stoke you some more," Willie said. "If you hang on 'til dinner break, Susie packed you a piece of her peach pie. Not that a youngster like you deserve it. 'Course a fool like me could be persuaded to eat both pieces to make sure that Pins, ol' Mr. Hound himself, keep in tippy-top shape for chasing the foxy Miss Wanda."

"You a damn lucky dude to have Susie," Pins laughed. "Wanda always slip me them sorry little white girls for dinner, them Little Debbies."

"Yes sir," Willie said. "I'm a lucky man. And I know it."

Willie and Pins slid elastic bands around their pant cuffs so loose clothing wouldn't catch in machinery. Each buckled on a wide leather belt that supported a battery pack for their cap light and a self-rescuer for getting a miner through a 30-minute, carbon-monoxide episode. After that, they had would have to make do with whatever air the mine offered after an explosion. Willie tossed his pack of Tiparillos and lighter into his basket, raised it to the ceiling and secured it. Some guys, he knew, sneaked cigarettes underground and smoked them in old entries near outtake air. Some guys, Willie knew, were just stupid. No one on Willie's crew sneaked smokes; he wouldn't have it. He tossed his dead cigar into a sand bucket for Cubby to clean out. His crew tapped their hard hats into place and met the night shift as they unlimbered themselves from the mantrip trolley that had brought them to the surface.

"Hey Jasper," Willie called over to a coal-blackened bolter operator. "How that top in Two North?"

"Same as yesterday, White Tip. I done what Pins done. Bolted up the whole mess on threes," Jasper said. "Goose okayed me using six-foot bolts about midway through. No bitchin', no moanin.' Wonder why the top changed?"

"Somethin' stirred around how the sand and dirt was laid in back in the dinosaur days," Willie said.

"Saw this fossil in the roof rock," Jasper said. "Looked like a big lizard."

"Could be a small dinosaur," Willie said. "It's good luck to rub it. Did you take the time to scope the roof, to figure out what in the blue blazes is up there?"

"No, we didn't have no chance. We were told to bolt up tighter and keep runnin' coal. Goose didn't want to lose production on his shift."

"Later, man." Willie tapped Jasper's metal lunch bucket with his own for luck—both ways.

The crews rode from the mine's portal straight into the tunnels excavated in the six-foot-high Pocahontas 2 seam. Willie and Pins sat next to each other in silence as the electric trolley clattered and rattled its way through the rock-dusted tunnels. Inert limestone dust had been wet-sprayed onto surfaces to prevent coal-dust explosions. Bloomingrose Holler was above them.

American Eagle was laid out in a grid like Manhattan. Its Park Avenue and Broadway -- called "main entries" or just "mains" -- were intersected every 40 feet by crosscut tunnels. The mains were 20-foot-wide avenues, running north to south. Electric-power cables hung close to their ceilings where roof met wall. Electric lights brightened some of the mains. The electric trolley ran down one main. Conveyor belts in return tunnels carried coal from a take-out point near each section to the surface.

The 12-foot-wide crosscuts ran east to west. In the squares and rectangles formed by the intersecting mains and crosscuts, big blocks of unmined coal were left in place to support the roof. The working end of a tunnel was a "room" and the coal blocks, "pillars"—thus the name, room-and-pillar mining. The room-and-pillar method went back to Roman excavations.

After a working area -- called a "section" -- had been advanced as far as the boundary line of the Company's coal, American Eagle miners would start "retreat mining." They would remove the pillars of roof-supporting coal one by one as they proceeded backward toward a main. The combination of advancing tunnels, crosscutting and then "pulling the pillars" could usually extract about 85 percent of the coal that was accessible. Good crews under good top could get most of the pillar coal without roof falls injuring or killing anyone.

The trolley that carried Willie's shift into the mine stopped every so often to let off crews near their working sections. His crew was the last stop. They stashed their lunch buckets in a crosscut close to the face and next to the main that carried fresh intake air. This was their "dinner hole." Each man went to his machine or assignment.

Willie found his 60-ton, Joy12CM continuous-miner parked about 20 feet back from the working face in the section called Two North Entry. The fire boss had just come though checking for methane and told Willie it was "good to go."

Willie's crew was advancing four faces into the coal seam from this section. Once Willie's continuous-miner had advanced his entry into the face about 16 feet forward, he would back out and tram the miner to the next face. Pins would take Willie's place and bolt up the just-mined, unsupported roof between the pillars. In this fashion each of the four faces in Willie's section were advanced and bolted in turn. The Joy could cut 20 tons a minute when everything was right.

Willie circled his Joy. He checked the cutting drum to make sure that its carbide tips were sharp. If they were dull, they'd have to be changed out. He examined the two lobster-like gathering arms on a metal pan that caught the dropped coal as the cutting drum tore it from the face. He took a grease gun and lubed some fittings. One of the water sprays was still bunged up. He flashed his light on the conveyor that ran through the machine, looking for problems in the chain and sprockets. As he walked, he checked the bulldozer treads for wear and looseness. At the rear, he looked at the take-up reel that automatically let out and spooled up the thick insulated cable that carried 440 volts to the miner. All the hydraulic hoses looked good—no leaks. The splices in the power cable were tight.

He saw no cracks in the welds that formed a canopy over his seat in the miner. UNICOAL had recently ordered American Eagle's shop to fabricate a canopy out of steel plate and four lengths of tube steel that was welded to the miner's frame. The Mining Enforcement Safety Administration had let the industry know that it was about to issue a regulation requiring cabs or canopies on all underground mobile equipment. Everyone felt better about the MESA rule. Without a canopy, nothing would protect Willie in a roof fall.

Willie eased into the cramped metal seat and made sure his sight lines were as clear as they could be. He scooted around adjusting the raggedy pad beneath him, searching for maximum thickness over maximum area. He'd admitted years ago that old pillows provided mostly psychological protection against the bumps and jostling. He could never understand why a $400,000 machine couldn't be outfitted with a decent seat—and when that one wore out, why it wasn't replaced. Mining would go better and faster with $10 worth of two-inch-thick foam under him and behind his back. Maybe, I'll just buy some cushion with my own money, he thought. But then he'd either have to leave it underground or take it in and out with him on the mantrip each shift. If he left it, someone would steal it. If he carried it around like a briefcase, he'd start up a round of hemorrhoid jokes. Maybe UNICOAL would go for pads now that they put in canopies. It was possible. They could experiment—see if a comfortable seat in their mobile equipment got them more coal each shift. He was glad he'd remembered to pop two aspirin before he left the bathhouse. They took a bite out of the discomfort he'd feel in his back about dinner break.

He activated the machine. Lights came on. Gauges moved. He raised and lowered the cutting drum, worked the gathering arms and the conveyor and made sure the machine tracked backward and forward, left and right.

Willie trammed up to the face where he stopped under roof that Jasper had bolted an hour earlier. He checked the pattern—three-foot centers, not fours. He thought about waiting for a buggy to mate in behind him to accept the roof rock he was going to remove, but he was anxious to see what the roof's consistency was before he started pulling coal out from beneath unsupported top. He wouldn't need a buggy for the little cut he planned to make. He raised the miner's boom, which was 15 feet in front of where he sat. He delicately eased its rotating drum into the angle where coal met roof rock. Then instead of going forward into the coal to make a normal cut, he slowly raised the boom into the sandstone. The sprays cut the rock dust a little, but soon he was two feet into the roof and cutting mostly by touch.

It didn't feel right. He could sense the roof loosening in pieces. He backed out and cut the power under bolted roof. He wanted to hear what the roof was saying, what it had on its mind. He sat still in the quiet.

Willie Rutherford heard the roof come down in a thunder crack. It fell so fast that he saw it only as a flash in the beam of his cap lamp. It sounded like a flood of boulders. At 12:48 a.m. on a peaceful Saturday morning, Willie Rutherford was buried alive as he sat listening to ancient geology in his Joy mining machine.

Willie didn't try to move after the roof swallowed him in its fallen chaos. The cave-in's concussive force had taken his breath. He coughed in the silence. He concentrated on breathing. He tasted the dust from the rocks covering his machine. He listened hard for more movement above him. It was dead quiet. He touched the canopy's new steel supports and was thankful that they'd held. He felt the steel plate above his head. It wasn't bent downward. He had no idea whether a one-foot-thick layer of roof had fallen on him or 30 feet. He figured it was rubbly, not solid, but he couldn't see into the hole above him. He rubbed the steel plate—for more luck.

Willie knew he'd been given a pass. The roof fall could have collapsed his canopy and crushed him. He'd carried out miners with backs, arms and legs broken in roof falls. He'd seen one dead from a collapse, eyes popped out of his face. Then it came to him: he'd forgotten to rub the fossil in the roof.

"Damn," he said aloud. "Okay, let's see what I got to work with." He licked the Tiparillo taste on his dry teeth—that was good. He had no water or food on board—that was bad. He swallowed. Could be a long time before I have any water, he thought. He moved his head slowly anticipating pain but felt none. He wiggled his hands, arms, back, left leg—all good.

Right leg was wedged in by a sandstone slab. The leg didn't seem crushed, but it was mostly immobile. Wiggled his right-foot toes, they worked. He made his mind drag along his right leg, beginning at his toes. He moved up—foot good, ankle good, knee. KNEE! Pain exploded when he moved his knee. He lost his breath and sweat beaded on his forehead.

He felt chilled and slightly nauseous. He flashed his cap light on his right knee. He saw no blood on his pants leg or bone sticking out. Probably broke, he thought; maybe the knee cap's crushed or dislocated. Don't want to go into shock. He felt himself sweating.

"Okay! Okay, knee," Willie said to his right leg. "We do a deal. I don't move you, and you don't hurt me."

Willie reached for the rock hammer that was strapped to the miner's chassis on his left. He would tap on the canopy's steel supports to signal that he was alive. He toggled the miner's switch. Nothing—falling rock had cut the power cable. His light showed chunks of rock in front and on both sides. He twisted his head to look behind. The miner was rocked in.

He turned off his cap lamp. Pitch black had never scared him. He held out his hand. He couldn't see it. White hand be the same, he thought and laughed. "Life is just a bed of roses," he said to the roof fall, "but sometimes you find yourself layin' on more thorns than petals." He wiggled around on his pad, careful not to disturb his right leg. "Shoulda bought me that foam," he said, "'stead of jes' runnin' my mouth." He thought of Susie. He thought of her peach pie. He thought of his kids, Mikey and Connie.

It's goin' to be a long night, he thought. I need to be tough, whatever comes. Probably enough air in the rubble. Can go two or three days without water. He laughed as he thought: Comp'ny'll have to pay me for the time I spend underground. Time-and-a-half for Saturday shifts and double time if I loaf it out into Sunday. Susie won't have enough money to get by. She'll miss me. She'll be angry. But we done okay, considerin' we started with weddin' cash of $12.50. Hope she remarries. A man'd be lucky to get her. She knows this is the way thangs are in McDowell County. You takes your chances in the mines. 'Course you also takes your chances walkin' across the street or jes' gettin' outa bed in the morning. Sure don't want her goin' into the mines to work. Hope she can get by with the ACMU accidental-death benefit and a pension. Maybe UNICOAL will give her somethin'.

Willie settled in as best he could, careful not to disturb the armistice he'd negotiated with his knee. He knew there was nothing he could do to get himself out of this coffin. He just had to wait and see what came next.

Was never much for church, Willie conceded. But I tried to do right. Even Korea never pushed me through them church doors. Don't see the point now. Prayin' can't hurt, but if anybody's gonna get me outa this damn hole, it's gonna be miners like me. "I ain't the best soul in the world," he said aloud, "but I ain't the worst neither. Cut me a break if you got the time and the inclination. Much appreciated and best wishes. Willie Rutherford. Amen."

Willie Rutherford sat in his dead Joy several thousand feet from the portal of UNICOAL's American Eagle mine. Broken sandstone filled the entry tunnel behind him. He was imprisoned in the dead vegetation of a salt-water swamp that had died 150 million years before and the rocks that had formed above it.

Something had messed up the sandstone back then, he thought, that prevented the granules from binding together in a solid layer. There's a damn Joker in every deck.

His powerful machine lay as quiet as a sunken ship. Willie listened to the stillness. He heard water softly trickling through the rocks. Might be able to catch some on a rag, he thought. Coldness wrapped its damp shawl around him. He shivered. He closed his eyes; he opened them—no difference.

He knew they would come for him as he had come for others. It would take a while to get authorized and organized. They'd calculate roughly how many linear feet lay between Willie's miner and the last stable, supported top where they could start the rescue. They'd have to guess about why the roof fell despite being bolted. They'd have to feel their way through the rubble, removing what they could, bolting, cribbing and propping with timber. They couldn't be sure about what was above them. They'd have to be slow and careful when clearing fallen debris from the tunnel, because the roof above the fall had no support. Willie knew how they'd go about it. They'd tram a miner up to the fall to dig out the loose material. A couple of brave ones would take long steel bars and pry down loose rock from the top if they could reach it. They'd learn more as they advanced, confronting the problems the jagged hole in the roof posed.

The roof could get worse or better the closer toward Willie they got. They might have to crib up with six-foot-long, 8x8 beams, stacked in Lincoln-log fashion from floor to ceiling. The rescue tunnel would be higher than the normal six-foot height of the seam. The rock fall might have pulled down five or even ten feet of garbage rock above that. They might have to build up the floor to get a roof-bolter in position to pin the jagged top. Cribs would provide better support than vertical posts with wedge caps, but they took much longer to install. The more cribs, the more time. The higher the cribs, the more time. The fall might have taken so much roof that they could neither crib it nor bolt it. In that event, they'd just have to risk it. If the roof had dropped in large chunks, they might have to winch them out to make a rescue opening. If they couldn't clear the entry, they might hand-dig a crawl space through the fall. They might have to blast the rock chunks into manageable pieces at the risk of shaking down more roof. They might cut out some of the sandstone with a continuous-miner, which would be bad, dusty work. He knew they couldn't be sure of exactly where he was and whether he was hurt or how badly. They didn't know if Willie Rutherford was alive or dead.

Willie knew his crew knew they were running against his clock—his air clock and his thirst clock. They were in a race against how much rock had come down, how bad the broken roof was, how fast they could find him and how long he could hold out, assuming he wasn't dead. It would take time no matter how hard they worked.

Willie was on the clock. He estimated he had hours of air, maybe a day or two with luck. He switched on his cap lamp for a second. He saw dust suspended and unmoving in front of him. He felt no air cooling the sweat on his forehead. That meant the roof fall had blocked the tunnel behind him. The mine's ventilation fan on the surface was not pushing fresh air into his space. He had to count on whatever air there was between the rocks in the fall.

Might be a choice between dying of thirst and suffocatin', he thought. It was like being trapped in a plastic bag, sucking air until there wasn't any left. He felt for his Daddy's old Buck knife in his overalls—two blades, stainless steel. He kept them sharp. If it came to that, he'd open his wrists.

The brave ones, like Pins, would take their chances and come for him, because they knew that Willie would take his chances and come for them. They had to count on each other. Sit tight, he told himself. 'Course ain't much other way to sit. Nothin' to do but sit and think.

Willie flicked off his cap light to save the battery. He felt the silence and total blackness. Neither bothered him after his years in a coal mine. He'd never felt claustrophobic underground, but now the closeness of the fallen rock and the tightness of his survival hole spooked him. He strained to hear machine sounds or feel vibrations, but he knew it was way too early for that.

Can't have been more than 10, 15 minutes. Maybe other guys got trapped, he thought. He searched again for sounds. Don't panic!

Somebody might be listening for his signal, he thought. No, too early, too soon for that. Still, he took the hammer and tapped it hard against a canopy post—two beats, rest, one beat. The feel of it in his hand settled him. It was something he could do to help himself. He checked his wristwatch. Okay. Set up a schedule. Every 30 minutes, tap for a minute. He scratched out the time on the underside of the canopy's roof with his knife. He'd watched his Daddy use it for a hundred different things—peeling apples, skinning rabbits, whittling geegaws out of cedar blanks once he left the mine. What would Daddy say? he asked himself. He'd say, "Long as you livin', you ain't dead." Willie laughed. Daddy tough. Daddy'd get through this. Minin' was a lot harder, lot more dangerous in his day. I can do this. Jes' have to sit and wait.

Then it came to him. I'm walkin' in the shadow of death, Well, I ain't exactly walkin', more like sitting' in it. I don't fear no evil, but I do fear dyin' of thirst or suffocation. Well, we'll see if anybody with me. Wonder what it mean to get comfort from His rod and His staff?

211

Suddenly, Willie Rutherford laughed hard. Pins'll eat both pieces of Susie's pie. Now her peach pie *is* somethin' to live for. He felt better.

Chapter 15

American Eagle Mine, October 12, 1975

Charlie Frazier wiggled his skinny butt against yesterday's newspapers in an unsuccessful search for either warmth or comfort on the stone steps of UNICOAL's American Eagle office. It was too damn early, he thought, for the most prominent reporter on <u>The Charleston Gazette</u> to be sitting outside, waiting. His shoulders and hips ached in the chill. Fifty-seven-years-old, he thought. Need to boldface the **old**, maybe italicize it, too— *old*. He shivered and squirmed deeper into his windbreaker, which, it occurred to him, had never broken wind in its life. I am cold, and I am tired—two separate but related thoughts in one compound sentence. Sleeplessness had settled in his lap like a homeless cat who liked his smell. Disasters no longer interested him; he'd covered too many. Charlie stretched his thinly muscled body and yawned involuntarily. The night had deepened the lines in his face. He kneaded his forehead. He ran his hand over his thick hair. He picked at his nose, flicking discards. His watch said 7:42 a.m. It was Sunday. This is my day off. I should be asleep. It's not even time for coffee and the Sunday edition.

American Eagle was overrun with cars, pickups, ambulances, fire trucks, award-winning mine-rescue squads, police vehicles, mobile media buses for television, UNICOAL supervisors and managers, miners, women, children, ACMU staff, federal and state mining officials, inspectors, in-state reporters, out-of-state reporters, clergy, medical personnel, politicians and gawkers. The Governor had helicoptered in late Saturday for two hours. The Fourth District Congressman was expected that afternoon. Willie Rutherford's entrapment and fate were high drama.

Meetings were almost constant. They occupied UNICOAL managers from section bosses on up, mine-safety officials from MESA and ACMU officials, including Joe Hunt, who'd come from Washington. Sub-meetings took place as needed and ran parallel to the main one in the mine's headquarters on whose steps Charlie sat, waiting to be fed news.

The sun was dragging its feet, allowing the overnight chill to hang on. Charlie hoped it would be a nice day weather-wise once it got to 11. But nothing nice had limped in yet. He figured it would be a really bad day in all other ways.

Warm fall days, Charlie remembered, were once used for killing—the harvest was in, hardwood leaves were in color, travel was dry and easy. Indian summer -- 200 years earlier in what was now McDowell County -- was still free of colonial settlers, two-man cross-cut saws, axes, railroads and coal mines. It was a country the Cherokee claimed but did not settle. Its narrow valleys and steep slopes were inhospitable for growing their corn, beans and squash. It was even hard to travel through.

The British Crown claimed western lands as did the Virginia colony by the same principle—it belongs to me because I say so. George III in his Royal Proclamation of 1763 had drawn a line along the crest of the Allegheny Mountains, reserving everything west to the Mississippi River for the Natives. Wealthy colonial speculators who wanted these former French lands felt the King had double-crossed them after the Americans and the British had won the French and Indian War in 1763. Speculators, landless immigrants and land-hungry frontier farmers ignored the Proclamation. They drifted into Kentucky and northern West Virginia in search of open, flat, fertile land along rivers. The Shawnee and their allies fought the settlers—raiding, killing, scalping, kidnapping and burning out those who were clearing tiny farms and small settlements in their hunting grounds. The whites fought back, using the same tactics in the same ways. In northern Appalachia, a series of treaties, raids, skirmishes, militia actions, occupations and rogue seizures effected the transfer of what was claimed as "private property" before 1775.

Most of southern West Virginia, including all of McDowell County, escaped these battles, because its mountains were hardly worth fighting over. McDowell County was too remote and topographically unyielding to be considered a destination for farming. The few whites who drifted in were subsistence homesteaders, happy to be fairly free of government. They hunted, ran a little livestock and raised patches of corn and family gardens. They made do with a largely cashless economy.

The American government granted tracts of southern West Virginia to Revolutionary War veterans and well-connected speculators. Investors bought most of these grants from veterans for cash, very small amounts of cash. Few settled in what became McDowell County until the early 1800s and then not very many. The area was skirted for better ground and easier transportation in Ohio and Kentucky.

The future McDowell County was controlled in 1795 by Wilson Cary Nicholas and Jacob Kenney. They sold it to Robert Morris, the Philadelphia financier who had funded much of the Revolutionary War. Morris, America's largest land jobber in the 1790s, became over-leveraged and landed in Philadelphia's Prune Street debtor's prison. A few years before that, he acquired a huge portion of southern West Virginia for a few pennies per acre but couldn't flip it or keep squatters from occupying it. By the 1830s, much of the future county had reverted to the Commonwealth of Virginia through tax forfeitures. In 1860, Virginia owned two-thirds of the County that had come into existence two years earlier.

Only a handful of hardscrabble mountain farmers wanted land in McDowell County after the Civil War. Then coal was discovered. Then the Norfolk & Western Railroad drove tracks into southern West Virginia. The N&W took over the County's biggest landowner, the Philadelphia-based Flat-Top Coal Land Association with about 400,000 acres. It reorganized Flat-Top into the Pocahontas Coal and Coke Company. Other coal interests, including Pittsburgh-based UNICOAL, bought tracts from the State and private owners. Mining got underway in the late 1880s with the N&W shipping coal to Norfolk, Virginia, for export along the Atlantic Coast. By 1900, most of the land in McDowell County was owned by northern corporate and financial interests that were associated with coal, railroads and steel. Coal companies built towns to service their mines. These were located along the N&W line and its spurs. Political control followed those who owned the land and its resources.

A small breeze came through Bloomingrose Holler. Charlie Frazier shivered. It's an ill wind, he thought, that blows no one any good. Maybe, he hoped, this was a breath of fresh air. Clichés, he admitted. He had avoided hundreds over the years. His hopes did not rise for Willie Rutherford, but there was always a chance that luck would turn the cosmic tables. Hope springs eternal—another cliché.

The American Eagle compound still sparkled like a birthday cake even after being up all night. Officials had spent the darkness in the conference room—planning, coordinating, acquiring information, evaluating ideas and getting feedback from the rescue crew trying to dig through the roof fall. The preparation plant had shut down as had all the working sections. When the conveyor brought rock rubble to the surface from Two North, a front-end loader trammed it over to the slag pile. There wasn't enough coal mixed in to run the material through the preparation plant where coal would normally be separated, crushed, sized, washed and loaded into rail cars. Normal operation had stopped. Hundreds of people were focused on Willie Rutherford.

The parking lot was full. Overflow vehicles had been settled along the mine's entrance road and around the shops and other buildings. Two emergency-rescue lanes were kept clear; they ran directly to the portal. Helicopters would arrive now and then, bringing persons of importance in and taking them out. The Red Cross had set up a free canteen in a food truck next to its tent that shielded tables and chairs. All three shifts were standing around, talking with each other. Volunteers had scrounged up trash barrels, which they had to empty about every two hours. Women gathered. Some brought food; most brought kids and cigarettes. Dust and exhaled smoke mingled at eye level.

Susie Rutherford was camped in one corner of the Red Cross tent surrounded by women from her church, the wives of Willie's crew, classmates, her kids and family. Her pastor from the Mt. Zion AME Church in Eckman sat in her corner.

Four reporters had banded together on the office steps after interviewing Susie again earlier that morning. Newly arrived reporters made the rounds—Susie, mine officials, safety officials and bystanders. Susie said the same thing to each reporter: "We're praying for Willie and the others trying to get to him. That's as much as we can do—and wait."

The Charleston Gazette's Charlie Frazier hated coal-mine disasters. Just flat-out hated the sons-of-bitches. Hated the things themselves and hated covering them.

In his experience -- this was his eighth -- they rarely turned out well for reporters, regardless of what happened to the miners. Mostly, it was wait while wives begged for a miracle. Then talk to other reporters. Then a teaspoon of information that was impossible to verify and equally impossible to resist was dropped into their raised and open mouths. Wait. And wait. Another teaspoon. A lot of waiting for very few spoons. He hated waiting with women who were waiting to see whether they were widows. Interviewing them was distasteful to both sides. Some were angry, some resigned, some said that whatever was God's will was how it would turn out, some hoped for deliverance, preferably from God, but any respite would do. Charlie had visited parts of "these UUUU-nited States," as he pronounced it exaggerating his West Virginia accent, that never had a coal-mine disaster. Not one. Not ever. No vigils for life or death. No coal, no mines, no disasters. People in those places died like normal people—heart attacks, cancer, strokes, auto accidents. Not blasted to pieces or buried alive.

"Hate these fuckers," Charlie muttered to himself. "Ain't no miracles in West Virginia. Never saw a one. Ghouls are what we are," he mumbled to Owen Paige who had just arrived with coffee for his friend and a paper plate of sugar doughnuts.

Born to school teachers in Salt Rock near Huntington, Charlie Frazier was a homegrown reporter who almost won a Pulitzer Prize for The Charleston Gazette in 1964. He still had enthusiasm back then. He still believed in journalism and making things right. That was 11 years ago. The Gazette, West Virginia's largest and most influential daily despite its liberal editorials, was a comfortable perch for a populist.

Charlie's three articles described how agents for John F. Kennedy's campaign purchased the support of West Virginia's county bosses in the 1960 Democratic presidential primary. A month earlier, Kennedy had won 56 percent of the primary vote in heavily Catholic Wisconsin against his

216

principal rival, Minnesota Senator Hubert Humphrey, a Protestant. Despite this victory, Kennedy's campaign believed he had to win in predominately Protestant West Virginia to show he could win a predominately Protestant American electorate. Charlie Frazier found himself covering a national political campaign that had landed on his typewriter like a winning number blown in through an open window. His daily reporting was picked up by the AP's A wire. National reporters covering the campaign checked their opinions with him.

Charlie knew West Virginia politics was a "shit hole," in words from himself to himself. Votes were openly bought for a sawbuck each. Free whiskey was expected in certain precincts. How people voted was known. Helpers went into voting booths to assist those who agreed to be assisted; in Logan County, Life magazine labeled these assistants "lever brothers."

At the heart of corrupt politics lay the practice of candidates buying onto a candidate "slate" assembled by a county boss who ran a faction in the Democratic Party. The kingpin used the candidate's "slate money" for buying votes directly, indirectly, publicly, secretly, legally, criminally and by any other means he could imagine. A portion of the money stayed with the faction boss and the workers in his machine. Where one party ruled a county, the boss was the source of employment in an unemployment-rich economy. Every county employee, teacher and state road worker was boss-approved. And each public employee knew he was expected to support the boss's slate and make sure his family and friends did the same. If a candidate refused to pay to be slated, he would lose. The system perpetuated itself, because candidates were afraid to buck the bosses, and voters were afraid of retribution. Faction bosses grew increasingly rich and ever-more entrenched from these fears. It was, Charlie thought, like the Mafia had been scripted into local politics.

Charlie thought of himself in those days as a Jeffersonian Democrat—a little guy, a farmer of sentences in whom civic virtues, the property rights of yeomen citizens and the freedoms for which Americans fought, had gathered in a righteous-but-silent simmer. Crooked elections based on money and slating were despicable, but they were, he always said, "*sui generis* to West Virginia, like ramps." And then he saw the Kennedy campaign come through and throw money at the faction bosses "like it was free confetti on New Year's Eve."

In Logan County, Charlie later wrote, local boss Raymond "Cathead" Chafin accepted $2,500 from the Humphrey campaign to be slated. When Kennedy's agents asked Cathead how much he would need to double-cross Humphrey, he said, "about 35," meaning $3,500. Kennedy assistants delivered two suitcases filled with $35,000. Chafin, honest in his corruption, phoned Kennedy headquarters and reported the error. He was told to put the cash to good use. A rival faction leader in Logan County, Claude "Big Daddy" Ellis, received $50,000 from Kennedy's campaign, a part of which he doled out at $10 a vote and in half-pints of moonshine. In Logan County and others, Bobby Kennedy, campaign manager, paid to have his brother slated by every faction that would take him.

Charlie had never seen so much election-day cash dropped into so many willing hands in a state boasting that mountaineers are always free. The faction leaders passed out cash to drivers, poll workers, men who could deliver their family and the miscellaneous category of "election-day worker." Charlie interviewed dozens of West Virginians who'd been handed a $10 bill to vote a slate with Kennedy's name at the top. "Nobody got hurt by it," they told him.

Charlie thought at the time that Kennedy could have beaten Humphrey with the two spending even up just on the basis of his charm, looks and youth. Kennedy also had his PT-l09 narrative working for him with the strong veteran-preference among West Virginians. Humphrey, in contrast, was twice rejected for WWII service owing to a hernia. But Humphrey had Senator Robert C. Byrd's endorsement, which carried weight in the state, even though Byrd, too, had no military service during WWII. Humphrey's record on issues important to West Virginia was stronger than Kennedy's, but West Virginians were drawn emotionally to the never-had-to-work-a-day-in-his-life candidate. Kennedy looked like and came across as a Hollywood star; Humphrey looked like and came across as a glad-handing, small-town pharmacist, which he had been in the 1930s. The good-looking guy always gets the pretty girl, Charlie thought, just like in high school. After losing West Virginia 61 to 39 percent, Humphrey dropped out of the race for the Democratic nomination.

The ACMU backed Humphrey in the West Virginia primary and supported Kennedy against Nixon in the general election, reluctantly. Joe Hunt in his first year as ACMU president objected to Bobby Kennedy's investigations into unions: "The little runt oughta look at the comp'nies if he wants to do somethin' about real rackets. I'd like to see Buzzy Maggard grilled on television like he done Hoffa who ain't no angel in my book." Privately, Joe told Skis that "Hoffa was crookeder than a pup's hind leg."

After the election when Charlie had time to investigate, he learned most of the Kennedy-campaign money that paid the faction bosses came directly from Joseph P. Kennedy, the candidate's father. The Kennedy spending estimate that Charlie cobbled together was about $10 million for a primary election where $1 million would have been an unusual high end.

Then Charlie got wind of at least another $2 million that had been slipped into West Virginia from Sam Giancana, head of the Chicago Mafia, who had leaned on his Mob connections for contributions. This money went to bribes, vote-buying and union-related, get-out-the-vote efforts. Charlie found Mafia cash turning up in the Kanawha Valley's chemical plants and the Northern Panhandle's steelworker and Teamster locals.

Charlie pondered this information. It didn't make sense in light of how much Mafia bosses hated Bobby Kennedy for his pursuit of their associate, Teamster president Jimmy Hoffa, when Bobby was chief counsel to the U.S. Senate Select Committee on Improper Activities in Labor and Management from 1957 through 1959. Bobby and his investigators had exposed Mafia ties to several unions, most pointedly the Teamsters. The Committee required testimony from Sam Giancana; Carlos Marcello, New Orleans boss; and Vito Genovese, New York boss, among other Mafia leaders.

Charlie reported that Giancana expected his Kennedy contribution to buy a low-level of prosecutorial interest and limits on deportations under a Kennedy Justice Department. The handful of Mob prosecutions under Eisenhower was acceptable. Giancana made his wishes known to Joe Kennedy, not directly to either of his sons.

Joe Kennedy had come to know the Mafia during Prohibition when he obtained legal permits to import medicinal alcohol. A few weeks before Prohibition's repeal, Joe secured exclusive U.S. rights to distribute Haig & Haig Scotch, Dewar's Scotch and Gordon's Dry Gin. He had also lined up distribution networks and bonded warehouses. His partner in Somerset Importers was James Roosevelt, II, son of the just-elected president, who helped obtain franchises from the distillers. Joe named his company, Somerset, after the exclusive club in Boston that refused to accept Roman Catholic members. He later sold Somerset Importers to bootlegger Joe Reinfeld and Abner "Longy" Zwillman who had been involved in New Jersey bootlegging, prostitution, illegal gambling and labor rackets since the 1920s.

Charlie heard that Joe Kennedy had worked through Frank Costello during Prohibition to sneak in off-shore liquor the Costello organization then watered and distributed, but he never found hard evidence that Kennedy had been a bootlegger.

Both Kennedy and Zwillman moved into Hollywood, financing pictures and dating stars—Kennedy with Gloria Swanson, Zwillman with Jean Harlow. Joe Kennedy bought the Chicago Merchandise Mart in 1945, then the second largest building in the world after the Pentagon. The Mart opened connections into Illinois Democratic politics that Joe Kennedy used in 1960 to help his son.

Joe Kennedy believed Giancana, who was rejected for WWII service by his draft board in 1944 for being a psychopath, and his associates could influence both the 1960 West Virginia primary and the Illinois general election. The Mafia made their deal with Joe who then informed his sons of the expected *quid pro quo*. When Bobby Kennedy, as Attorney General, increased the number of Mob prosecutions and targeted Giancana, among others, the Mafia bosses felt they had been swindled. And they had.

For reasons known only to himself, Joe Kennedy was not confident that his own money and Jack's charm would win the West Virginia primary. He wanted the Mafia's help to close the deal in Wheeling, Weirton, Morgantown, Fairmont, Charleston and Clarksburg.

Charlie Frazier had developed sources over the years in law enforcement and on the street who knew about Mafia activities in West Virginia. The Mob ran loansharking, brothels and illegal gambling. The West Virginians also provided hit men for other families. The term they used for these assassins was "housepainters," because "they paint houses [with blood]." The West Virginia mobsters were tied to the Licavoli family in Cleveland and the Luparelli family in Pittsburgh. The most powerful West Virginia Mafia family was in Clarksburg where a large Italian community had gathered around jobs in heavy industry and coal mining early in the 20th Century. The Clarksburg Mob was directly linked to the Luparellis and, through them, to the Costello family in New York.

While some of Giancana's $2 million campaign contribution to Kennedy came from other Mafia bosses, the bulk of it was drawn from Teamster funds with Hoffa's approval. Hoffa wanted a Kennedy Administration to lay off. Sam Giancana's contributions would, he hoped, make this happen. West Virginia was the model of cooperation between Giancana and the Kennedy campaign. It was then applied in the general election to win Illinois against Nixon, which helped elect Jack Kennedy. Charlie concluded that had Giancana and the Mafia not assisted Kennedy in West Virginia and later in Illinois along with Chicago Mayor Richard Daley's machine, Richard Nixon would have probably been elected president in 1960.

The first of Charlie's articles focused on election fraud. This was familiar territory covering how the two candidates paid county bosses to be slated. He reported finding direct vote-buying, moonshine voting and paying "campaign workers" for standing around at the polls. No one had ever put this general knowledge in print as explicitly as Charlie did. He provided no wink and nod between the lines. He was disgusted with it; that came through. What was really different in the 1960 primary was not the amount of money that was doled out to each voter, but how much the county bosses could keep for themselves and still deliver a convincing majority.

Charlie's second article showed the amounts of money the two candidates, but principally Kennedy, had stuffed into West Virginia Democrats. Charlie wrote that most of Kennedy's out-of-state money came from Joe Kennedy. He offered his best estimate of what each county Democratic boss received for slating Kennedy or Humphrey.

His third article focused on the cash that came through Giancana to the Mafia's contacts in the state. He reported that Joe Kennedy had met with Giancana and had promised his sons would go easy on the Mob in return for help in the primary and general election. With that assurance, Giancana got many Mob bosses to chip in. Carlos Marcello was the most prominent holdout. Mafia money, Charlie wrote, helped buy Kennedy's victory.

Part of the Mob's money, Charlie reported, was funneled to the county bosses through Paul "Skinny" D'Amato, the dapper tuxedoed owner of Atlantic City's 500 Club on South Missouri Avenue, open daily from 5 p.m. to 10 a.m. Before 1976 when gambling was legalized in Atlantic City, paid-off police protected illegal gambling. The games Skinny ran in his club's backroom were the City's major draw. "The Five," as it was known, was the "in" place where politicians like Jack Kennedy, Hollywood celebrities and Mobsters socialized. What happened at Skinny's stayed at Skinny's. Skinny's wouldn't have been Skinny's without the presence of Mob-friendly entertainers—Frank Sinatra, Sammy Davis, Jr., Dean Martin and Jerry Lewis. Skinny's motto was: "No matter what you do in life, don't be a stool pigeon."

The Five was America's premier gambling club in the '50s and early '60s. While Charlie Frazier never determined whether Skinny was a made man in the Mafia, he did learn that Skinny knew everyone in the Mob he needed to know, or, at least, he knew the right person who knew the person he needed to know.

Skinny had connections to the illegal gambling clubs in White Sulphur Springs, West Virginia, that county sheriffs frequented when they visited the Greenbrier Resort. Skinny handed out more than $50,000 of Mafia money to cooperating West Virginia sheriffs to keep things orderly and going in the right direction on primary day.

Charlie called the Kennedy cash to the county machines an "engine of economic development running down the wrong track" in an accompanying editorial he wrote on the third day. "And what did Mr. Giancana of Chicago expect for his contribution to Senator Kennedy's efforts in West Virginia? Good government in the Mountain State? Free and fair elections here? An electorate educated to the great civic issues of the day? All of the above, we're sure. He may have also held a small interest in less federal scrutiny in his affairs with JFK in the White House."

Charlie Frazier didn't win the Pulitzer Prize in 1964 that his investigative reporting deserved. He wasn't even named a finalist. The national media was too traumatized by Kennedy's 1963 assassination to honor Charlie's important work. The big national dailies and the three television networks refused to pick up his stories. The 1960 Democratic primary in West Virginia was old news in early 1964, Charlie was told more than once. Jack would have won West Virginia even without the money from the Mob. Charlie agreed with that opinion, which made him wonder even more about why Joe Kennedy involved the Mob and jeopardized his son's campaign and presidency. One UPI reporter in

Washington, D.C. put it to Charlie bluntly: "Who gives a shit about 1960 West Virginia? Let dead dogs lie in their fleas."

The shunning he received from his media colleagues surprised Charlie less than the mercenary attitude of West Virginians who sold their vote. Charlie, like most West Virginians, knew about candidates buying slate support with money that then went to buy individual votes, but even he was shocked at the enormity of the corruption. It violated his Jeffersonian sympathies. Even Estil Chumley, his ninth-grade, social-studies teacher who had Charlie's class memorize the Bill of Rights, pocketed a $10 bill from his precinct captain. "I was going to vote for Kennedy in any case," he told Charlie. "It's not like the 10 changed my vote."

Charlie, at first, came to blame what he called "the cultural fiber of my own kind" for participating in the corruption of their politics. At root, it was a semi-feudal system in which state and local employees in each county owed their employment to the local "lord" who demanded their service and political loyalty. But when Charlie considered it with more dispassion, he concluded it was more the lack of cultural fiber in the faction bosses and the candidates who paid to play than the people in general who were caught in its trap.

After 1964, Charlie never wrote another syllable about political corruption in West Virginia. He cared too much to be ignored a second time. And he never wrote a comma more than what was required to keep himself employed. As he got older, Charlie belabored his West Virginia speech, particularly around "outsiders" and newcomers. It was his way of declaring both pride and embarrassment in who he was. Whenever he thought about his good-civics series from 1964, he felt nothing but sadness and shame. Why was West Virginia like this? he asked himself.

"This Rutherford is news, Charlie," Owen said in the soft swells of his native Richmond. "Live miners aren't news; dead miners aren't news; but a miner who might be one or th'other, now, son, that's news. Purgatory's news. Hermaphrodites, they're news. Miscegenation, that's news. And a miscegenatin', purgatory-bound hermaphrodite, now that's front page! Hope you have at least one of them stashed up one of these hollers to liven up a slow news day."

Charlie laughed in spite of himself. He sometimes had a short fuse with Owen Paige's thoughts on race, always humorously put. The Richmond News Leader, Owen's first employer, had led the public clamor for "massive resistance" to the 1954 Brown v. Board of Education Supreme Court ruling that outlawed racial segregation. Its editorial page clamored to close public schools rather than integrate them. Even 20 years later, the segregation-forever views of James J. Kilpatrick, its then editor, stuck in Charlie's craw.

White West Virginia wasn't all that enthusiastic about desegregating, but it followed the Warren Court without mayhem. Charlie thought West Virginia had a little easier time desegregating, because it had been a break-away border state during the Civil War. The remote mountains of western Virginia never had much of the Deep-South, plantation-slave economy and self-delusional culture that dominated eastern Virginia.

The irony to Charlie was that John W. Davis -- Clarksburg native, two-term West Virginia Congressman and unsuccessful Democratic presidential candidate in 1924 -- argued the no-integration, separate-but-equal position for South Carolina before the Court in 1954. This was the same Davis who had defended black voting rights in the South as Woodrow Wilson's Solicitor General and denounced the Ku Klux Klan in the 1920s. Davis, Charlie knew, had a streak of populism—he had been one of the authors of the Clayton Antitrust Act that substantially strengthened and expanded federal anticompetitive measures and exempted trade unions from its purview. But Davis also opposed women's suffrage, federal child-labor regulation, anti-lynching legislation and poll-tax elimination. While he once opposed concentrations of corporate power, Davis spent the last 30 years of his long legal career arguing against New Deal regulations and defending corporations in the Supreme Court. He rode for the brand, Charlie thought. You paid John W. Davis, and he would do your work. Charlie thought Davis was much like his home state—better to be here and there on race than to be outright segregationists like Virginia and the Richmond News Leader. Best, of course, was to be not mixed about it at all. That dream still smoldered in Charlie's pipe.

"Charlie, Charlie," Owen whispered *sotto voce*, "we must bend to our reportorial tasks and find peace within to be bent in turn." He put the coffee and doughnuts down and unlimbered a cigar with a Connecticut Maduro wrapper.

"We are broken, not bent, on Life's great torture wheel," Charlie offered.

Owen used a gold cutter to clip off the cigar's end. He fired up with a mother-of-pearl lighter.

"Charlie, you are *noir* these days."

"Look around you, Owen. This ain't normal America."

"About that, you are correct."

"Well, maybe, it is normal. Maybe, the crap here is just more visible," Charlie said.

"This place, this state lies in a different existential zone," Owen said. "One unknown to Camus and those French boys, except, perhaps, under the Nazi occupation."

Charlie clapped his forehead. "You amaze me," he said to his friend. "After 20 hours into this, your shoes are still shined, your shirt don't stink, your tie ain't even loose and you're as insufferable and as pompous as that other insufferable and pompous Richmond dandy, Tom Wolfe. And you're huffing a cigar before 9 o'clock!"

"You, Charlie, are embarrassingly jealous, because Tom tapped into the zeitgeist while you excavated nothing but self-righteous indignation," Owen smiled. "Which do you think brings success in this world?"

"That don't explain your shoes, your shirt and tie," Charlie said, regrouping as best he could. "You Owen, you are, you are morally disheveled on the inside. You're the Immaculate Deception."

Owen smiled and touched his hand to his ear in a casual salute. "I do find satisfaction in upholding standards of personal appearance." He paused. "Mainly, though, I can't help it. Breeding rules."

"Inbreeding, you mean."

"Indeed," Owen said. "Same thing. Not to mention that tobacco in all of its poisonous forms is the mother's milk of the great Commonwealth of Virginia. Insult me at will but spare the Devil's leaf."

Owen Paige, a déclassé Virginian and fifth-generation Richmonder, had quickly accommodated himself to the anonymity and modest pay of being the lone feature writer in West Virginia for the Associated Press. He told Charlie that he left the <u>Richmond News Leader</u> for Charleston as a "spiritual lark, a chance launch into the vast Unknown, a thing I was not brought up to do. It was time that one of us Paiges did something different." He had confided to Charlie after a year in the Charleston office that he'd learned to appreciate life's ironies: "Mine being, to be imprisoned in America's largest Third World colony—and a mostly white one at that. My employer expects me to narrate in the softest tones how the big ones here eat the little ones—and then spit out their bones. I try not to empathize. Identification with the poor and pitiful can redirect high-flying careers into the dirt."

Charlie shook his head with a doughnut in hand: "Why is it that your kind of people always need someone below you to kick? Black folks in Richmond; poor whites here?"

"Well, first my friend, it's arguable that we don't *need* to have someone to kick as much as it is that we always have had some around who just naturally lend themselves for that purpose. It's the wisest order of things, the pecking order, the alphas and the zetas. God created the poor for a reason, don't you think? And keeps them that way for a reason, don't you know? They are the necessary foundation for those above on whom they depend for the little they are allowed to possess. There would be no top were there no bottom to support them. Blessed be their unknown names and their persistence in bearing selectively useful children."

"I'm not arguing that in all societies there won't always be some rich, some penniless and everyone else in between," Charlie said. "I'm saying that you people *need* to kick 'em, humiliate 'em, give 'em your worn-out clothes and think you've done 'em right."

"Charlie—your unprofessional sympathies are ruling your roost," Owen said. "We kick them, because it keeps them in line. It's also true that we know better than anyone else *how* to kick them—this is not something that any Tom, Dick or Harry off the street knows how to do. There are ways to kick them so that they stay in place. And then there are ways that stir them up. And, finally, kicking is good exercise. Not like drinking. Kicking those we oppress makes us feel better about ourselves. And spares our dogs. And don't forget, my friend, these West Virginians are ethnically and racially close to the Richmond gentry. We kick your kind of whites just as much as the colored. You should praise us for equal treatment."

Julie Cogswell had had enough of Owen Paige. "We natives are tired of being kicked by the likes of you."

"And you have every right endowed by your Creator to be tired of it," Owen replied, offering her coffee. "Were I poor and oppressed and ignorant and stupid to boot, I, too, would be tired of being poor, oppressed, ignorant and stupid to boot. I'm not saying it's right, exactly. I'm saying it is what it is—and always has been. It's who you people are. Your culture. If you want to get up off the floor, madam, get up!"

"Easy to say, hard to do," Julie said, "when you got a ton of dead weight on top of you and no ladders. The difference between what you see around here and other rural places with better politics is ownership. Most of our land is owned by coal companies, timber companies, railroads and outside investment organizations. They won't sell it to individuals. Land that is worked to produce something of value builds wealth for individuals over time and keeps politics reasonably balanced and clean. The parts of West Virginia that are small farms with no coal don't have the corruption that we see here, because people there own the land and its resources. Put lack of land ownership together with an extractive industry like coal mining that takes what we have and hauls it off, and you have a weight that keeps us pinned down. Coal is not a ladder for us. It's a flotation device…until it pops."

"That doesn't explain the culture—the backwardness, suspicion, ingrownness and lack of ambition to change," Owen said.

"Same could be said of your beloved Richmond," Julie said, "backward, suspicious of outsiders, ingrown, lack of ambition to change. You can explain every poor community by pointing to the poor. And true enough, people adapt to the circumstances forced upon them. Those adaptations are often dysfunctional and help keep the poor poor. But behind that is a system that profits from keeping a community poor and corrupted. Look behind the curtain."

"Fine with me, darlin'. Kickees Unite! Storm the Palace of Versailles. Liberate the Bastille. Right On, Sister Julie. Send the capitalist swine to the rice paddies for weed patrol. You people *should* fix guys like me. But know this: Ain't nothin' gonna change. When the poor and piteous win, it'll just be different folks doing the kicking, and different ones being kicked. I think it's called the dictatorship of the proletariat."

"The problem is, Owen," Julie said, "that the poor and the piteous around here don't have the luxury of avoiding your boots. We have to survive with what's available, which isn't much. If you're at or near the top, at least you can escape, use your money to build walls and put up gates."

"The impressive young lady has a point," Owen said, "and genuine indignation honestly earned becomes her."

Julie took a small bite of the doughnut she had brought from the Red Cross. She crinkled her nose. "Lemon again," she said, eating the rest of it. She preferred the raspberry.

Julie Cogswell had eaten at least a dozen Red Cross doughnuts across West Virginia since taking over her father's weekly, the Mountain Sentinel, three years earlier. Tom Cogswell had begun his independent voice in Boone County in 1936, composing on a very used linotype machine and printing on a small, cranky press that he set up in his parents' basement. He was -- and his paper was -- one of those West Virginia anomalies, a fiercely independent individual who managed to ignite a subsistence income from rubbing two stones together. Tom did not duck the journalistic task of taking on The Authorities in his own backyard.

"I've set a bad example for you," he told Julie when a weakening heart forced his retirement. "But it's your duty as a West Virginian and my daughter to take up a losing and obviously hopeless cause."

"Thanks, Daddy," she said without gratitude.

Julie had known from the day Tom had first set her name in hot lead as a six-year-old that the Sentinel would be hers. For years, she tried to put it off, because the Sentinel's curse was to shout truth to people with their hands clamped tightly over their ears.

She fled West Virginia to go to Ohio's Oberlin College where she discovered she was the only West Virginian in her class of 445 and one of two in the entire student body. (The other was the son of a physics professor at West Virginia University.) Some faculty assumed her presence was the result of a new and unannounced affirmative-action admissions policy to recruit culturally deprived Appalachian whites who were expected to be poor as well. Her freshman English professor spoke slowly and more crisply than normal when he talked with her during office hours. Her advisor wondered how poor she really was when he asked her how much financial assistance she had received. Her political science professor joked with her after class about "wearing shoes." He also wondered whether one leg was shorter than another, an evolutionary adaptation in his mind for walking on West Virginia's hillsides.

"My people keep your ass warm," she'd said.

"Huh?"

"The Oberlin College heating plant burns coal that's mined in my county."

The college boys she dated liked to mimic her accent, which she refused to drop or even soften. They usually came from New York or other northern cities. They had read a lot of books and knew how to do almost nothing. They were pointed toward being college professors and lawyers.

Urban liberals, she discovered, hated and feared those they called "hillbillies" and "rednecks"—white people from beyond the suburbs in the "great yonder to the south," as she put it. For a while, liberal prejudice amused her. She had fun for a few months exposing the fears from which it arose. She told her classmates who called her Daisy Mae about the 40-foot-long rattlesnakes that were constantly underfoot "back home," the 30-point buck she claimed was mounted in her family's outhouse and the number of McCoys she'd shot before leaving Boone County for Oberlin. But Julie eventually grew tired of defending, interpreting, correcting, disabusing, explaining and mocking.

At 20, Julie had had enough of northern white liberals with guilt wrapped around them like swaddling clothes. She gave up her original idea of moving to New York as a first step in a literary life. She had come to feel that the America of their books and letters would never see her as anything other than a semi-trainable primate. She transferred to West Virginia University in her junior year and came to an armistice with the self-hatred she found in the low expectations shared by its students and faculty alike.

Gradually, she gathered some pride in her people from the snatches of their history she found in obscure academic articles and oral accounts in the Appalachian Collection on the third floor of Wise Library. She started learning about the efforts of rural people who grubbed a living from small, marginal farms to adapt to being industrialized in coal mines and mills after the Civil War. This was not the history of increasing powerlessness and exploitation or the alternative of heroic struggle in the name of The Revolutionary People. This history was all over the place--sometimes heartbreaking and outrageous, sometimes wistful and nostalgic, sometimes stirring, sometimes disappointing, sometimes baffling, sometimes discouraging, sometimes violent and sometimes hopeful. She learned that it had never been linear or one dimensional. Even in her native Boone County, she found everything mixed together at particular points in time as well as across generations.

After graduating, Julie kicked around Europe until her feet grew tired from standing in front of gothic churches and stone Virgins. She returned to Boston during the late 1960s. But she never felt that she fit in with the increasingly enraged student left or the highly educated women who gathered to talk among themselves and share their grievances. She taught English in a New Hampshire high school for a year, worked as a reporter for the Littleton paper the next year and then accepted that her life needed to be played out in West Virginia. She took a job doing public relations and writing grants for West Virginia public broadcasting in Charleston, about 30 miles from her parents' home in Madison.

She took pride in her father's compulsive opposition to the metastasized corruption in West Virginia politics, but the burden seemed so endless, so futile and so solitary that taking it up as her own seemed nothing short of masochism. Nonetheless, when, at last, he said he needed her, she moved into a small house about 10 miles from his and took over the Sentinel. That was three years ago. Now she was 31 and fully committed to living alone and writing for people who read her work but were afraid to go where it pointed.

Julie passed her plate of doughnuts to Allyson Pickering. "Stick your finger in 'em first, honey," she said, "so you'll know what you'll be a-swallerin'."

Allyson looked at Julie Cogswell. Was she a ventriloquist? How did that accent come out of that woman? Julie Cogswell didn't look like the miner's wives, daughters and sisters she saw huddling in clutches, seeking comfort in numbers. Julie seemed a lot like her.

"Excellent advice to a reporter from the big city covering the Mountain State for the first time," Owen added.

Charlie grimaced and thought he might do a feature story on Red Cross doughnuts—who made them, who financed them, who ate them and who detested them.

Allyson smiled coldly. As the designated virgin on a West Virginia mine-disaster watch, she knew her life would be easier if she made herself one of the boys, as despicable a prospect as that was. Nothing she'd heard that morning made her want to pal around with the jaded likes of Charlie and Owen. And this Julie—she was like the Black Panthers Allyson met in the late '60s who spent most of their time disparaging the whites who were working with them. Any minute, she figured, Julie would tell her why Earl Scruggs was more musical than Beethoven.

"Allyson, please exercise patience with us," Owen said. "It will be rewarded, I promise. And remember stories like this one always end."

"It's not the waiting that bugs me," Charlie said. "It's those television and radio crews, stickin' a damn mike in front of the Rutherford woman and askin': 'How do you feel, honey?'"

"Well, what would you ask?" Allyson asked. "What other question is there?"

"At this point, you're right," Julie said. Allyson had stood up to Charlie, which indicated some spunk and pluck. Like her Dad, Julie gravitated toward spunk and pluck.

"The questions of who did what, who fucked up, who bears responsibility, why did it happen, what could have and should have been done differently—those questions are coming soon," Charlie offered as a peace gesture to Allyson. She wasn't a total idiot, he thought. The Pittsburgh Post-Gazette was a good daily paper—good newsroom, good people. Davey Bloom wouldn't have hired a total idiot, he figured. At least, not a gin-u-ine **total** idiot.

"They're reporters like us," Allyson said. "Doing their jobs, reporting as best they can with what they have at the moment." She wiped her hands on a paper napkin and resolved to skip lunch. "TV and radio report feelings. What do you expect?"

"Nooooo, buddy," Charlie said to her. "Miss Rutherford's feelin's ain't news. Her thoughts, now they're news and fair game. What she does, that's news. But the privacy of her feelin's, they ain't news for 15 seconds on News at Six."

"How lucid, Charles. How kind. And even before lunch!"

"It's *dinner* here, Owen," Charlie said. "In West Virginia, it's fuckin' dinner, not fuckin' lunch. You're simply impervious to local wisdom."

"It's one of my few admirable qualities," Owen said. "Our broadcast colleagues do turn my stomach, which doesn't turn at much anymore."

"We're not much better to be honest about it," Allyson said.

"Indeed, we do intrude with our questions," Owen said. "We get to pick at the carcass after the meat has been tossed into the soup."

"Intrudin's the least of my criminal activities," Charlie said. "The Gazette pays me $350 a week to break and enter. We are pickpockets, petty criminals. Questions are what we use to jimmy the safe."

Low, circumspect laughter reflected shared discomfort. None of the reporters wanted to appear callous.

"Did you ever back off from asking a question that you should have asked?" Julie asked Charlie and Owen.

"Of course, darlin'," Owen said. "All the time. I'd be unemployed if I asked questions that I should ask and reported the answers."

"Once," Charlie replied. "Only once."

"It was after the Buffalo Creek disaster in Logan County, three years ago in the fall of '72," Charlie began. "Owen was still with the News Leader in Richmond, covering whatever he covered for that piece of shit."

"My derrière, mostly," Owen inserted. "Lifestyle, features, the poohbahs and their good works. Three tasteful cheers for the prosperous."

"Julie hadn't taken over The Sentinel yet. Your Daddy was there. I was at Buffalo Creek for The Gazette. There was the AP guy and the UPI girl.

"I was probably the first pencil-and-notebook guy up that holler, or what was left of it after the dam broke on February 26th. Flew in with the toad who ran the State's Department of Mining on Governor Arch Moore's helicopter. The Governor ordered the State Police to block all road access into the holler."

"What kind of dam?" Owen asked.

"Gob dam," Charlie said. "It was like this. Buffalo Mining is a subsidiary of the Pittston Corporation—they have coal mines and Brinks. Buffalo Mining had three gob dams at the head of Buffalo Creek, that is, all the way at the back end, at the top where the holler narrows. Gob is the shit that's left after the preparation plant extracts the coal. It's rock, ash, junk, dust, sand, dirt, slate—loose material, like tons of pennies. There's weight but not much stick-um. They dump this stuff across the holler and then dam up water behind the pile. Usually, they pump the waste-water slurry from the coal washing in behind these dams. The slurry's fines -- the gunk -- settle out over time, eventually filling in behind the dams. They can take the clean water from the top of the impoundment and run it back through the prep plant to wash coal.

"Buffalo Mining just slung the gob across the holler to block up their wastewater. Number 3 dam was farthest up. It had been inspected four days earlier and given an okay. It rained hard the night before. People who lived below the dams had worried for years. The men who worked at the mine lived in the little towns strung out 17 miles downstream from the dams. They knew these impoundments were not engineered. They had no spillways or outlet pipes. They knew full ones could be breached or collapse. Buffalo Mining had been dumping 1,000 tons a day of mine refuse up there. That hard rain kept people up all night.

"Rain kept falling heavy into the early morning. But Buffalo Mining never stopped pumping black water into Number 3 impoundment. The coal fines buried in the dam itself had been smoldering and smoking for years. So when the water finally saturated the dam that morning, it hit the burning core and a steam explosion blew the whole thing to hell. All of that happened about 6 a.m.

"A 20-foot-high wall of black water and whatever else swept down Buffalo Creek after blowing through the two lower dams. Doing 60 miles per hour, they estimated. One-hundred-and-thirty-million gallons ran over 16 little coal-camp towns. Five hundred homes totally wiped out. Four thousand left homeless. I saw train rails twisted like vines around trees and bridge piers. Houses, trailers, vehicles and people washed up miles from where they'd started. One-hundred-and-twenty-five killed, more than 1,100 injured. Seven missing. Woooosh! No more Saunders, West

Virginia. No more Pardee, Lorado, Craneco, Lundale, Stowe, Crites, Latrobe, Robinette, Amherstdale, Becco, Braeholm, Accoville, Crown, Kistler and Man. The National Guard was digging bodies out of the muck for a week. Everyone was traumatized. Little kids, adults, too. Three years later, they still freak out when it rains no matter where they are.

"Big lawsuits were filed against Pittston. Its lawyers said it was an 'Act of God,' which meant it wasn't the Company's fault. Sue The Lord, folks. Some 600 survivors sued Pittston and settled for $13,000 each after legal costs. About 350 child survivors settled for $4.8 million, a little bit less per head after the lawyers were paid. Governor Arch Moore filed a $100 million suit against Pittston for the state's costs of relief and clean-up. Then he and his lawyer, Stanley Preiser, settled with Pittston for a flat $1 million and no further liability three days before his gubernatorial term ends. When all was said and done, West Virginia -- not Pittston -- had to pay the Corps of Engineers more than $9 million for its clean-up costs.

"And get this. Good ol' Buster Skaggs, who led a Democratic faction in Logan County that had backed Republican Moore in '72, was the one who built the unlicensed dam when he owned Buffalo Mining, which he sold to Pittston. Moore was protecting ol' Buster and Pittston—his real constituents. Arch Moore had no shame. And get this. Nobody was indicted for any blessed thing. All of Pittston management from top to bottom got off. Oval Damron, the prosecutor in Logan County, showed no defensiveness about the absence of prosecutions. The dams never had a state license, but ol' Oval says that's just a misdemeanor and don't count anyhow since there's a one-year statute of limitations. And after all, Oval says with regard to homicide, 'there's no way to put a corporation in jail.' Made me want to puke."

"The question you didn't ask, Charlie?" Julie said.

"Gettin' there, darlin'. My train starts slowly but gathers speed when it's goin' downhill in a righteous cause. Now there was this guy. Mr. Browning. A real big guy, maybe six-six or seven, about 60 or so. Heavy set. Wearing bib overalls. Working in low coal would have been hard for him. Crewcut. Normal guy. Had a hawkish nose, but a fleshy face. Well, Mr. Browning had lost his wife, one of his kids, several grandkids, neighbors. You could see him wrestling with his grief and the terror of his own inexplicable survival.

"Governor Moore holds a press conference in the lunch room of the grade school at Accoville, near the mouth of Buffalo Creek. The West Virginia National Guard had worked all night shoveling the muck out of the lunchroom and wiping down the tables, chairs and walls to make it look half-normal. But you could still see the brown scum line that showed how high the water had gotten inside the room. And there was this gritty, black powder on the linoleum tiles, the ones that hadn't come up after being drowned. They set up a generator outside so the lights would come on. Provided drinking water out of plastic barrels and coptered in portable johns special for the Governor and his entourage. Had some cheese-and-baloney sandwiches on white bread set out at one table. Had fresh jars of mayonnaise and mustard, too. Who said there ain't no free lunch?

"Everyone's sitting on these brown metal folding chairs a size too small. Governor Moore is standing behind the lectern with the TV lights on. He's up on the stage, 'cause the lunchroom doubled as the auditorium. Mr. Browning is in the back just in front of the milk machine and the candy dispensers. He's trying to fit into one of the elementary-school chairs. He's bent over at the waist, holding his head in these huge, gnarled hands. His palms are in his eyes. He doesn't want to see what's in front of him, or behind, or ahead. He's just shaking his head in his own blackness.

"Well, ol' Arch stands up and, nice as you please, he drops the busted dam in the lap of the Lord. Says nothing about Buster Skaggs and Pittston never engineering those gob dams or failing to get a state permit. Not a word about the absence of overflow pipes or emergency spillways. Says nothing about his own dip-shit inspection agency that knew the dangers of these dams and dozens of others just like them in the coalfields. Regulation without eyes on the ground and enforcement amounts to not much. Says nothing about how Pittston never warned the people below the dams that the water was close to the top. Says, instead, it was an 'Act of God.' Gave Pittston its courtroom defense against liability suits and criminal prosecution. He had to have worked this out with Pittston and the lawyers before he got to that sorry lunchroom in Accoville.

"Soon as Arch shifts liability onto the Lord and lifts Pittston and his own complicit administration out of the negligence briar patch, you can see those silky Pittston lawyers down from Connecticut -- they're all lined up along one side of the lunchroom under the finger paintings that didn't get drowned -- they all stop sweating. They get to relaxing so much that they lean up against the cinder-block wall and walk around for the rest of the day with flood scum on the back of their suits.

"Mr. Browning was a born-again Christian and all that. Probably got saved in his teens and filled with the Holy Ghost in his 20s. Worked in the mines his whole life. Never took a step out of line or over a line. Paid his taxes. Didn't bitch about payin' ACMU dues. Probably a WWII vet. Voted Democrat, but never gave a shit about politics. And you could just see the ponderous trouble he had asking why his Lord would do such a thing to him and his. It was like Jesus had just up and pissed on his good Christian head for no reason. I expect Jews in the Nazi concentration camps pondered the same.

"So Mr. Browning stands up after the Governor finishes. He keeps his hands straight down at his sides. He has tears rolling down his face, and he starts testifying:

232

Mr. Gov'nor. My name is Tolbert Browning. I done lived my whole life -- 60 yars -- in this holler, workin' for Buffalo and the Piss-ton Comp'ny, too. I never got no education hyar, 'cept what I l'arned under the mountain. Coal minin's in my blood, and coal dust is in my lungs. I never ate ahead of my paycheck, and many's the time back in the '50s and '60s when we was laid-off, I had nothin' but a speck of gov-mint cheese and a dab of peanut butter to eat—and mighty glad to have 'em too.

Four days ago, I had me a wife, two daughters, one son, an' three grandkids. Four days ago, I had me a house in Amherstdale, a garden patch and a Ford truck. Now I got almost nothin'. Almost nothin'. Lost my wife, a daughter and two grands. I want to say their names right h'yar so they'll be remembered and not just warshed away like so much dirt in a laundry tub: Alice Browning, my wife; Jessie Lyn Blankenship, my daughter; her kids, Boyce and Bonnie.

Comp'ny done mashed up my Daddy under a runaway mine car in nineteen-and-twenty-seven, because they was still usin' wood sprags to brake the wheels. Comp'ny done took my oldest boy, six y'ars ago. Gas 'splosion. Done took two brothers. Lungs was filled full of the dust. Comp'ny done took my wife, my girl and the babies, even. My house, my car. They done took it all. I wish'd to God the Comp'ny took me 'stead of mine.

Mr. Gov'nor, Mr. Moore. You say hit was an Act of God. T'weren't no such thang! T'was an act of man. T'was an act of the Piss-ton Coal Comp'ny.

T'was an act of that man, a-standin' right thar, plain as day— Steve Dasovich, Buffalo Mine superintendent. And Buster Skaggs—he's a sittin' up on that stage. Buster, he built them gob dams. Then sold them to Piss-ton. Buster started 'em. And Steve Dasovich, he run all that black water in behind 'em from the warsh plant. He done run that water right up to when the dam broke. Steve Dasovich was a-feared to shut down production. Everyone up this holler knowed what Buffalo Minin' was a-doin'. They wasn't hidin' nothin', 'cause they couldn't hide it from those of us hyar who was a-doin' their labor. But there wasn't nothin' that anyone like me could say. Who in Piss-ton would listen to me? An' Piss-ton knowed nothin' was ever to goin' to happen to them for a-breakin' your rules. So they had no reason to hide nothin' from nobody.

Those men from Piss-ton a-standin' along that wall over thar are a-listenin' to me now only because they have to. They ain't hearin' nothin' for the future. They're just figurin' out what to say back to make me disappear. They jes' want to get out of this as

233

cheap as they can. They jes' want to warsh me away like they done my family, 'cept they want to do me with paper and words, not warsh-plant water from up Buffalo Holler.

Comp'ny done it, Mr. Gov'nor. Comp'ny done it.

Not God. Not Jesus.

Comp'ny done it, and you, too.

"Mr. Browning just stands in front of his seat. No one says a word. He just keeps standing there, waiting. I heard feet shufflin' and noses snifflin'. But nobody says a blessed word against the truth.

"The Pittston lawyers have not twitched muscle one, but I could see that they were frantic to figure out how to get the Governor off the hook and how to move the coming trials o-u-t of Logan County, say to the North Slope of Siberia. Ol' Arch is still standing still as stone at the podium, lookin' like he's just been told his fly zipper's open, but he's too ashamed to go down and pull it up. The silence is so powerful, so overwhelming, that even I was rooting for somebody to get things moving again.

"Finally -- it must have been three or four minutes of silence -- the head Pittston lawyer slides up next to Arch. He clears his $100-an-hour throat and starts blah-blahing about legal this and legal that. Says Mr. Browning's 'heartfelt statement' is not legally admissible in a court of law. That, at this point, it's hearsay, though he doesn't doubt Mr. Browning's loss. He gave everyone in that room a chance to breathe. Bullshit probably saved the lives of a dozen or so folks who would have otherwise self-suffocated. The Governor, and I'll give him this, at least he had the decency to keep lookin' at his brightly polished cordovan shoes. The corrupt bastard couldn't look an honest man like Mr. Browning in the eye.

"But Mr. Browning is still standing. All six-six, six-seven of him. Just looking at the Governor. He doesn't know what else to do. He didn't know he was supposed to ask a question, not make a statement. He doesn't know it's time for him to move out. He's waiting for someone in Authority to explain things to him. The lawyer is filling air time. Mr. Browning wants the powerful to talk to him, man to man. Maybe apologize. After another five minutes or so, he finally feels that his time has come and gone. There is no answer to his testimony, except confessions by Pittston and Arch Moore, which ain't gonna happen. It's now kind of embarrassing. He doesn't sit. Other people have started to ask questions. All of us sophisticated types from Charleston and beyond, we know that after you say your lines, you're supposed to get your ass off the stage.

"We ask Arch some reporter-type questions. I watch Mr. Browning wander out of the school. No one talks to him, comforts him. Ain't nothing to say. Ain't no comfort. Then a tiny little woman he knows, about his age, comes up to him. She hugs him the best she can. Comes up to a little over his belt. Doesn't say a word. Just wraps her arms as far around him as she can get. He's crying. She's crying. Finally, her husband comes over, says something to Tolbert, and takes her away.

"I follow him. I don't give a shit about what Arch Moore is saying. Mr. Browning is walking through the devastation toward what was his place in Amherstdale, a couple of miles. There's a kind of path that's been bulldozed through the wreckage. I trail behind. I want to talk to him. I want his story. I want people to know.

"He just keeps walkin' up the holler in a daze. I'm almost stalking him. And then I slow down. Then I stop altogether next to the spilled guts of somebody's trailer. I'm standing on little-girl dresses in the mud. I look down, and then I see him still walking. I turn and go back to the school."

The four reporters -- Charlie Frazier, Owen Paige, Julie Cogswell and Allyson Pickering -- sat silently for a moment.

"Only time, I didn't ask a question. Simple human decency won," Charlie said. "I was proud of myself as if anyone gives a shit."

"I think I would have asked him," Allyson said softly. "People need to hear it."

"I knew one of his nephews," Julie said. "He was at West Virginia University when I was there. He told me the end of the story.

"Tolbert Browning was living in a government emergency trailer in a bulldozed spot cleared out for people where Amherstdale used to be.

"Six months after the flood, Tolbert drives his truck up to the Buffalo Mining entrance, takes out a pound of rotten baloney, sticks the point of his pen knife in it so that it stands like a flag pole, takes out his .38 and blows his brains out all over the KEEP OUT sign."

No one said anything.

Finally Charlie added: "The Gazette ran his obit without…your details."

Julie Cogswell looked over the American Eagle Complex. "I had to go up to Buffalo Mining a couple of months ago on another story. I could still see the stain of Tolbert's blood on the chip-and-tar pavement. They put up a new sign. There's no blood on it."

"Can't beat decency," Owen Paige said, shaking his head.

Chapter 16

Bloomingrose Holler, October 12, 1975

UNICOAL's American Eagle Mine Complex spread along Bloomingrose Holler, up Bloomingrose Mountain and down Bloomingrose Creek. Two communities lived there. Whites lived on the Creek, strung out for about two miles below the mine. Blacks lived in Anawalt Holler, a narrow-cut valley that joined the Creek where white housing ended. Once out of Bloomingrose Holler, the closest settlement was Cucumber, then Pie, then War Eagle. Cucumber had a one-room post office next to a two-room general store. Pie had a gas station. War Eagle had a six-stool café.

American Eagle was a multi-million-dollar operation, the biggest underground mine in McDowell County. It employed about 250 miners on three shifts. It lay close to the Virginia line, and some employees drove as much as 75 minutes each way to work there.

UNICOAL was a good employer as long as you did what was wanted. Management did not value independent thinking or even suggestions. It offered steady employment supported by long-term contracts with reliable customers. In return, it demanded loyalty and compliance.

UNICOAL led the Bituminous Coal Companies Group (BCCG), an organization of 22 coal operators that bargained for a single contract with Joe Hunt's ACMU every two years.

American Eagle's scattered facilities were tied together by electric lines, conveyor belts, water pipes, dirty waterways, roads and railroad tracks. Nicked into the hillside above the Complex were benches for the mine's ventilation fans and electrical transformers. Old machines were parked on a distant bench with an ever-decreasing possibility they might still be cannibalized. On normal days, people moved routinely from portal to preparation plant, mine office to equipment-repair shops, underground to surface and parking lot to bathhouse. On this day, people were moving from huddle to huddle, from mine office to television interviews.

Above the buildings and equipment stood the coal-preparation plant, which filled the narrow valley from hillside to hillside. A conveyor belt carried whatever came out of the mine to the prep plant where coal was separated from waste. Every non-coal material went to the gob pile— incombustible rock, chunks of wood, busted lunch pails, trash, dead rats and an occasional smudged centerfold. On a typical day, the plant crushed coal to a uniform size, washed it and loaded it into at least 50 rail cars of 115 tons each. This high-Btu, low-sulfur fuel was burned for steam in electric-power plants in the Ohio River Valley and the Southeast. A painted sign covered most of the plant's three-story front wall in flaming orange-red letters:

236

UNICOAL FUELS YOUR ELECTRICITY

Normally, the prep plant's digestion rumbled in the background. But on this Sunday morning, it was silent. Coal was not being mined, processed or loaded. American Eagle was hushed.

UNICOAL miners in their work clothes stood together in groups of three or four, smoking, chewing, sipping and talking in low tones. Someone would look toward headquarters every so often, then to the portal, then to the women, then to others standing around. Reporters had tired of wandering from group to group, taking notes. Radio people had lowered their tape recorders. Television people rested behind cameras they'd set up for an impending announcement at the top of the office steps.

The Gang of Four, as Charlie called them, had drifted off to ask the same questions they had asked yesterday—of different people if they could and the same people if they couldn't. They left paper swatches on the steps: "Reserved for the press."

Susie Rutherford sat in her corner of the Red Cross tent. Friends stayed with her. Strangers came by to say a word or two and offer their prayers. She folded her hands on the Red Cross table. Hands on either side touched hers.

Biggie Stover eased his black Chevy Blazer up the American Eagle entrance road. Vehicles were parked on both sides. The parking lot was jammed. He found an opening to his right that was only wide enough to drive through. He backed in at a right angle to the road so he could leave quickly.

Jeep Delucci stirred in the passenger seat. Jeffrey Becker jerked awake in the back. Becker blinked in the frosty sunshine. It was his first time in McDowell County. He'd slept from Beckley to the UNICOAL Complex, about three hours. They'd left Charleston at 4 a.m. It was Becker's first mine disaster.

Jeep pulled down the mirror on the sunshade. He smoothed his hair and then rubbed the sleep from his eyes. He tightened his tie and straightened his campaign button.

Biggie burped.

"How many friends we got here?" Jeep asked Becker.

"Some. But this local -- 4355 -- are 60-40 for Hunt. The officers are older guys. The young guys -- our guys -- are only about 20 percent of the 250 in the bargaining unit. Freddie Pruitt is our contact. He's on the safety committee. I talked to him yesterday afternoon. The old guys are suspicious of you, he says, because they think you'll bargain for higher wages at the expense of getting a higher pension, which they will need in a few years. Only working miners vote in Union elections as you know. So they think you'll short the non-voting pensioners. Also, they know Joe Hunt. Same generation. Some came out of The Depression, and most came through the War."

"Was Willie Rutherford one of ours?" Jeep asked.

"Don't know," Biggie said. "The brothers lean our way, but most of 'em don't care to wear one of your cap stickers. They don't want to make this a black-white thing."

"Can't blame them," Becker said. "We have one black guy on our ticket, Byron James, for one of the auditor jobs."

"That's better than Hunt," Biggie said. "He ain't got none runnin' for nothin'."

"We're a model of progressive race relations by comparison," Becker sniped.

"Okay, enough," Jeep said. "The Union is color-blind. Always has been. We've had black officers in the past. You were at my nominating convention, Beck, when we drew up the ticket. None of the brothers we liked could bring any strength with them. We'll appoint some when we get in. You know that."

"Hunt's got him a black doorman up at Washington headquarters," Biggie added. "John L. hired him back in the '30s."

Becker signaled that he was ready to drop the subject.

They got out of the Blazer and walked toward the center of the Complex. Jeep was quickly recognized. He stopped to shake hands with supporters, nodded with a smile toward those who nodded toward him and nodded with no smile to those who turned away or found something important to observe on the ground. Jeep turned to Biggie.

"Why don't you scare up Freddie and anyone else with my button. Get a group together and see what's goin' on. We might need to lay some fire under this griddle."

"I counted a dozen Hunt bumper stickers to five of ours," Becker said."

"'Bout what I expected," Jeep replied. "Might get a little tense. Heard Joe was around."

Biggie shifted his shoulders and stretched his arms. "Griddle might warm our cakes too."

What the hell are they talking about? Becker wondered but asked nothing. He knew Jeep and Biggie had a private communication system.

238

He wasn't supposed to know some things, which he accepted, usually with unspoken appreciation.

Biggie wandered toward the Red Cross tent. Jeep walked over to a group of long-haired miners and extended his hand. Then he knocked out a Marlboro, lit it with his Zippo and started asking questions. Becker tagged along, watching, listening, wanting to be inconspicuous.

Jeep noticed Becker, standing off to the side. "Hey, Beck, why don't you work the press? See what's up?"

Becker headed for the office-looking building. He assumed reporters would be hanging around there. He estimated 500 to 600 people were waiting.

Becker dropped a dollar in the "Donations-Accepted" can filled with quarters at the Red Cross tent and carried his coffee over to the steps where he greeted the four he knew: Allyson with stiff cordiality; Charlie Frazier with the respect due a good writer; Julie Cogswell with disguised curiosity; and Owen Paige with more formality than Becker had mustered in a long time. He liked Charlie, because Becker understood the roots of his cynicism. He found Owen to be a willing accomplice in his place and time. He thought Julie Cogswell was a pistol with possibilities. And he had no idea what to think or feel about Allyson Pickering, about whom he had thought and felt a lot.

"Jeep just got here," Becker said. "What have you heard?"

"Rutherford's still inside," Charlie said. "Haven't found him yet. Slow going through the crap rock that's between him and the crew trying to dig through it. Been inside for more than 30 hours."

Julie sized Becker up like she was judging bread-and-butter pickles at the Boone County fair. When they'd met for the first time at a Delucci campaign stop, Becker reminded her of guys she dated at Oberlin. Do-gooder lawyer, come to save the sorry hillbillies from themselves, she'd thought. Some version of left-wing politics. Might be a year or two older. Might be interesting. Might be not for her. Might be more than she expected, even different.

Julie Cogswell always tried to be helpful to those who were more or less on her side, so she added: "We were told late last night that parts of the roof keep collapsing as they dig out the rubble."

"Have they let any of you go in?" Becker asked.

"Dumb question, Mr. Beckah," Owen Paige sniffed.

Becker laughed, a small laugh. No question was dumb, he thought, if you wanted to know the answer.

"Dumb question, indeed, Mr. Paige. How about this? Are they really trying to get Rutherford out or are they just going through the motions after all this time?"

"Hey buddy," Charlie said, "we mushrooms are always the last to know. We sit here and hope the next warm load lands on our heads so we don't have to work hard to get it."

"Just like at the White House with the press corps," Julie said.

"Now what would a disadvantaged hillbilly like me know about how they nourish the Big Mushrooms?" Charlie asked in a tone of exaggerated effrontery.

"It is similar," Owen Paige said, "except that our eminent colleagues in the District of Columbia believe themselves to be thorn-bearing, blue-ribbon roses, not mushrooms."

"I thought they saw themselves as Venus flytraps," Becker said.

The four accepted the truce he offered.

Charlie turned serious. "I think UNICOAL wants this thing buttoned up one way or the other pretty soon. John-Cee Smithers, his very own V-I-P self, is supposed to say something more than nothing in the next few minutes. And Jeffrey, it's going to be a joint session with your favorite cham-peen of the o-pressed coal miner and still reigning monarch, Joe Hunt."

"The leaders united can always be divided," Becker said.

"Yes, well," Owen said. "A play on the Allende slogan in Chile if I'm recalling Leftist cant accurately."

"The People united will never be defeated," Allyson said.

"Right," Julie said with undisguised-but-muted sarcasm. "The P-P-P People for P-P-P Peace was another."

"I'm sure differences between Jeep and Joe Hunt will come out on this and most other things," Becker said to Charlie. "We hope you report them."

"Everyone wants to rescue the guy alive and unhurt," Charlie added. "No disagreement there. We report what we can."

Allyson felt reassured: Becker still had the ability to put off friends. Law school, apparently, had not rounded his edges. This trait had never won her heart, but she had come to understand that it was deep in his wiring. Had it been willful, it would have been a deal-killer. Maybe it had something to do with his parents who, he had told her, rubbed each other the wrong way, mostly out of habit. They had not felt comfortable with Allyson for reasons they never made clear to their son. It didn't matter that Ed and Lillian had never met her. Of course, her folks never cared for Chief Becker either. They had no problem making their feelings known while obscuring their reasons. Their discomfort, she knew, had been a small part of his attraction. She still wasn't sure who he was. At least, he now had a trade and a job—that was two steps up from Mandy's farm. Maybe he was still the gadfly-populist that he was back in the late '60s.

Maybe he could still get to her. She wasn't surprised that she wanted to find out.

"Jeffrey," she said, "you still have a way with people, don't you?"

"A scrappy charm," Becker responded, "but not princely."

"'A scrappy charm,'" she affirmed.

Julie realized from their conversation that Becker and Allyson had history. She expected she'd get the details from one or the other.

Becker might be acceptable, she thought. She wasn't sure where he was from, how long he'd been stirring the West Virginia pot, or why. But he wasn't self-important or overly manipulative. He was less a missionary than others she'd known. No one denied that he'd done an impressive job with Delucci's campaign. That was a big positive to be weighed against his negatives, which were more than several but possibly smaller than she had first assumed. The net tally, she thought, was TBD.

Julie Cogswell liked guys who actually accomplished something. She'd heard that Becker worked hard for his clients and did a good job, even with the hopeless cases. He was earnest, probably too earnest. But she noted a sense of humor, even irony, when he wasn't talking about "issues." Becker could be worth exploring. He was interesting in an odd way, less intellectual than she expected and more practical. He might know which end of a claw hammer you hit with and which you pried with. It dawned on her that she might be willing to be pried but not pounded.

Julie was more certain about Allyson Pickering. Don't like that girl, she thought. Too composed. Too put together. Too pretty. Too powerful, maybe. Julie kept coming back to fifth grade: Allyson Pickering was "stuck up" but without being obvious about it. Stuck up in a very toned down and covered up way. Julie sensed that Allyson had money behind her even if not in a current account. She suggested comfort and a good education. Definitely East Coast. Confident, muted but not in-your-face snooty, which made it harder to handle. Maybe, Julie, thought, the word about Allyson was "destined."

Julie sensed that Allyson might be trying to ride the ACMU story into a bigger corral. Well, most young reporters had that going on. Woodward and Bernstein wannabes. It wasn't that way with Charlie Frazier who Julie liked almost as much as she had loved her Dad. Charlie didn't want to go anywhere. Owen didn't want to be anywhere. Julie didn't want to move anywhere.

"So, Mr. Beckah, what does Mr. Delucci have to say about the current plight of Mr. Rutherford?" Owen asked.

"Mr. Paige," Becker replied with his own formalities, "Jeep is right over there. Ask him."

241

"Now, Jeffrey," Charlie said, "your boy is campaigning on mine safety. Said Joe Hunt hadn't done enough to get the 1969 Federal safety and health act passed. Hadn't fought very hard for black-lung benefits and a tough dust limit. Delucci said Joe had given MESA under Nixon a pass on enforcement. I expect you yourself wrote some of the statements to which I refer. Jeep's here for a reason, ain't he?"

"Jeep's here because an ACMU member has been buried in a rock fall for more than a day. Joe's here for the same reason. Maybe their presence can help. At least they can show their concern for the people involved."

"I'm taking notes," Charlie said.

"It's funny," Becker said, "how papers get indignantly interested in mine safety only after a big explosion kills a bunch of miners or some human drama like this happens. One out of every ten miners had a lost-time injury last year, but no one did a single story about that."

That's my boy, Allyson thought. Piss off the best reporter in the state, the one who likes your candidate.

"Are you suggesting a cabal of capitalist publishers in cahoots with their brothers, the coal barons, to censor the news?" Owen asked, arching his eyebrow, something he'd practiced in front of his mirror during college. Owen didn't figure Becker was either *that* dumb or *that much* a captive of leftist fashion.

"Or are you suggesting lazy reporters?" Julie asked, looking at Owen.

I'm suggesting a little of everything, Becker thought, but avoided a confrontation with those Jeep needed. He hoped Allyson would notice the improvement.

"No. I don't think there's a conspiracy of capital. I don't think half a dozen people run the world. I don't even think capitalism is all bad. It does hurt those who can't make it work for them. And it does shift costs onto the public and taxpayers. I think we all have class biases as well as other kinds. And biases skew what we believe news is and isn't." Becker cursed himself for being preachy.

"An example, sir?" Owen asked.

"A friend of mine showed me this," Becker said. "Daily newspapers always run business and financial news whether they have a liberal or a conservative editorial policy. Readers see at a glance the price of every stock. That's useful. Is there a page in a coalfield paper where a miner can find monthly employment and unemployment numbers, the number of workers injured and killed year-to-date at each mine, average wages and benefits for union and non-union workers, average health-insurance costs for ACMU and non-ACMU miners and average life expectancy by the collar of your profession?"

"My, my," Owen said. "We are derelict. I will report this to my editors this very afternoon."

"I see your point," Charlie said. "But we need hooks for stories. A guy sprainin' his back liftin' a Moon Pie out of his lunch bucket ain't a hook."

"That's what I'm saying," Becker said. "You shouldn't need a hook for basic information for blue-collar workers. The 'news' I just mentioned is the equivalent for a coal miner of financial and business information for white-collar folks. Stories are one thing—you do need hooks for them. I understand that. I'm talking about routine data for hourly people. News for stockholders is fine. Run the accident records of every mine in West Virginia once a quarter—that's news for coal miners."

"Arise ye workers from your slumbers *etcetera*, *etcetera*," Owen sniffed.

Julie rolled her eyes at both of them, but said: "Arise ye editors. That'd be nice." She looked at Becker. "Owen, I heard a year ago that you were a fellow traveler with the Party when you were at the University of Virginia in the late '40s. That you were the campus contact for the Wallace campaign in '48. Is that how you come to know *The Internationale*?"

"I happened to be broadly literate, Miss Cogswell, and I'm willing to converse with those with whom I disagree. It is one of my few admirable qualities if you must know. The other one I will identify at this moment is a willingness to suffer great disappointment in my earlier beliefs in light of certain unfortunate practicalities. I trust the five of us share this interest in shelter, food and drink." He paused: "It was a long time ago, Julie."

"Owen decided the great arc of history did not bend toward justice as much as it pointed like a dowser's forked stick toward money," Charlie said.

Owen ignored that comment. "Now, friends, I might note amongst ourselves that Mr. Delucci may be bearing a minor blemish or two himself. Case in point: two gentlemen from the lesser Pittsburgh area. They seem to have had a successful launch from Lens Creek Mountain several weeks ago, but, lamentably, an unsuccessful landing. Charles and I have been informed the State Police matched bumper chrome on their vehicle with Mr. Delucci's own Jeep, which served as a booster rocket."

"Old news, Owen," Becker said. "Jeep phoned in the car's theft to the Charleston police early that morning."

"Yes, indeed," Owen said.

"...and witnesses place Jeep either in our Washington Street headquarters or in Murad's Grill down the street until around midnight when he discovered the car missing.'

"So we've been told by the authorities," Owen said.

"Even if you doubt the witnesses, do you really think Jeep would have those two killed with his own vehicle?" Becker asked.

"Not hardly, normally speaking," Charlie said, "but maybe things ain't as hardly normal as we might suppose."

"One starts with motive, Mr. Beckah," Owen said, drawing with great elaboration on his cigar. "Always motive."

Allyson caught Becker's eye. Murder was not the Becker she knew. Covering up murder? Well, she wasn't sure about that. Criminal defense lawyers represented guilty clients most of the time. Maybe he'd changed since 1968. She felt doubts rising.

Julie Cogswell had grown up in Boone County, a coal county. She knew that ACMU people had done illegal things in years past to protect themselves. She'd known Jeep and Biggie since high school, though they were two years older. She knew they had heard the stories she had heard. Shootouts with hired thugs. Tipples torched and dynamited during organizing campaigns. Threats. Fights. But that stuff was in the past—in the early 20th Century, The Depression and the '50s when John L. Lewis was trying to organize companies that refused to sign the master BCCG contract. She shook her head. Jeep and Biggie were not stupid enough to have killed those two guys, not after Delucci won the first round. No one would be that stupid. On the other hand, she didn't know anything for a fact. She had taken a course in epistemology at Oberlin. She knew how easy it was to not know the truth about what you said you knew.

"Now, I'm not saying these ruffians -- Yankees, I might add -- didn't deserve punishment for mistreating Mr. Vernie Skeens, as I recall his name, a supporter of your current employer," Owen said to Jeffrey. "Left to themselves these scoundrels might have intimidated many of your supporters. So Mr. Delucci had motive and means. Opportunity has, of course, yet to be established."

"As well as commission," Becker said. "Opportunity doesn't mean guilt of a criminal act. And a number of individuals had motive, means and opportunity. Let's start with Joe Hunt. It's possible he could have set this up."

"A frame job! How delicious!" Owen said.

"Anybody could have stolen the Jeep to confuse things or put the blame on Jeep."

"Of course," Owen added with a delicate twist, "we've not established that Mr. Delucci's vehicle was *actually* stolen. I doubt that Vernie's friends could have driven to Charleston, found Mr. Delucci's vehicle and then driven to Lens Creek Mountain before the two baboons got there. Why would Vernie's friends have stolen Delucci's Jeep? But I must admit that laying these two murders on Mr. Hunt imputes to him a level of imagination I've never observed heretofore."

The five of them shared a laugh.

Owen and Charlie were smart, experienced reporters, They doubted Jeep Delucci's alibi, but neither cared enough to spend the time and take

244

the risks needed to test its truthfulness. Investigative journalism was a young reporter's game. They had decided several hundred thousand column inches before this meeting that they were better at reporting news than making it.

Julie Cogswell was troubled. Jeep and Biggie—with them, who knew what they might do? But Becker was a different story. She knew his type. She'd dated Beckers, even slept with several. His type could shave the truth. His type could manipulate the truth. His type could use people with ends justifying means. But his type, she doubted, could apologize for murder with a straight face. So why, she asked herself, was the word "squirm" howling through her brain?

Allyson Pickering was intrigued. She knew she didn't have a good read on Delucci. He'd winked at her at a press conference a few months back, which hadn't offended her as much as she wanted. He was handsome in a country way. She liked his talk about bringing "union democracy" to the ACMU, about "unions from the bottom up." She liked the name of his campaign, Miners for a Democratic Union. She liked hearing him say that "unions needed to reinvent themselves, that it was time for new leaders who were willin' to do new things on behalf of their members." She knew she wanted Jeep Delucci to beat Joe Hunt. She wasn't neutral, though her reporting would be. But she couldn't shake her doubts about the murder of these two Pittsburgh goons. She decided that doubts deserved to be followed, wherever. It was her job.

Becker drained his coffee. Reporters would do whatever reporters decided to do. He expected further digging. Fair enough. He didn't know what he didn't know. And maybe there was nothing more to it than what Jeep had told him. Maybe it was a frame up; anything was possible, wasn't it? It was obvious that the two sluggers had been sent from Pittsburgh to send the Delucci campaign and ACMU members a message. Three facts. Somebody had sent them. Somebody had killed them. And a message had been delivered and returned.

"Hell, I don't know," Becker said. "I'm just a dumb-as-a-post, outside-agitator, hippie lawyer."

"You got that right, Jack," Charlie laughed. "But you have potential. Purty soon, you'll figure out the difference between bulldog gravy and a bulldog first. At that moment, son, you will be close to stealin' West Virginia's sacred fire."

"My fondest dream," Becker said.

I was your fondest dream at one time, Allyson thought. And I'm a lot better than either gravy or your first bulldog.

Becker nodded to the group and headed for the Red Cross tent where Susie Rutherford was keeping her vigil. He wasn't sure what to make of Allyson in her current version. Julie Cogswell was a native exotic. She was worth keeping in mind.

"Man in the middle," Charlie observed after he left.

"Where a man gets squeezed," Owen said.

Chapter 17

Two North, October 12, 1975

Ten black-faced men stood around a grimy picnic table just inside the Number 11 Crosscut where it intersected Two North Entry. Bloomingrose Holler lay some 500 feet above them. It was Sunday, just before noon. Willie Rutherford's crew had returned after taking a sleep break. A rescue crew from Westmoreland Coal had relieved them around midnight. Willie's crew, back at 8 a.m., wanted to be the one that pulled him out either way.

Ventilation fans on the surface were pushing hundreds of cubic feet of fresh air at the rubble plug every minute. Some, they hoped, was getting through to Willie. The moving air chilled the sweat on their faces and made their long johns clammy. Given a choice, they preferred to be warm and sweating rather than cold and sweating.

The roof fall lay in front of them. They could only guess how far they were from where Willie was buried.

They had stopped clearing rock for a quick dinner. As they rested in the crosscut, someone dragged his beam along the two rattlesnake-thick electrical cables that led to their own continuous-miner and Willie's. Their cable was live; his, wasn't. They checked both for bad splices and deep cuts out of habit.

They opened their lunch pails on the picnic table they had carried in the day before the roof collapsed. They spread out thick sandwiches of ham or baloney with mayonnaise and tomato, cold fried chicken, potato chips, cans of Libby's Vienna sausage, store-bought cakes, cookies, brownies, hard candy, chocolate bars, sodas and thermoses of black coffee. Wives of other miners had insisted they take something of theirs with them. They had returned packing three times their normal amount of food and drink. They ate standing, swapping and sharing silently. They pointed their heads at odd angles so as not to shine cap lights into each other's eyes. They threw most of the leftovers back into their pails. A telephone, linking them to the mine office, sat on the table. They had turned off the two, 400-watt, explosion-proof portable lights that had been illuminating their efforts to remove the roof fall from the main entry. They preferred eating in the semi-darkness of their own lights. Their beams occasionally skittered along the ribs of the dinner hole, a place that felt safe. A few bits of food were thrown down the crosscut for the rats even though they had failed miserably in warning Willie.

Artie "Pins" Smith gobbled two chocolate bars in three bites each. He bit into a sandwich disregarding the dark prints his fingers left on the Wonder Bread. Artie had seen his grandparents, and occasionally his Dad, eat small chunks of coal, so he figured that running a little black grit through his guts couldn't do too much harm. I wonder, he said silently to the bread in his hand, can you help us out with a little WONDER here? Like RIGHT NOW. Willie's lunch pail sat in the middle of their table where Willie had left it. Pins was saving both pieces of Susie's peach pie for a celebration. He chewed hard and swallowed fast, eating and drinking for quick energy. He had been running the roof bolter for four hours without a break, trying to bind the roof together and anchor it securely.

In 10 minutes, everyone was finished. No one said anything about UNICOAL supervisors sharing their table, which was uncommon but not unknown. Everyone was in this Willie-rescue together.

"This ain't workin'," Pins muttered. "I can't get the top to hold my bolts."

Section Boss Lee Roy Stump agreed, reluctantly and silently. He'd seen Pins drilling into the friable sandstone with eight-foot-long bolts reaching for solid rock to tie into. He'd seen some of the roof fall just after it had been pinned and the bolts torqued snug.

Lee Roy knew the roof above the Pocahontas 2 seam as intimately as any miner on his crew. Pokey 2 always had had "good top" under Bloomingrose Holler—at least, in the 23 years he'd spent beneath it. Lee Roy knew it as fairly dense sandstone that held roof bolts tight and stayed in place. For more than two decades, the standard roof-control practice in Pokey 2 had been "four on four"—driving four-foot-long bolts into the roof and spacing each bolt four feet from the others in a grid. The bolts laminated a beam from the various rock strata that bridged the open space over a tunnel. Lee Roy couldn't remember when the roof had dropped in one awful mess like this. Lee Roy and all American Eagle miners considered themselves lucky to work in the high Pokey 2 seam where a miner could stand straight and not worry about bad top.

Lee Roy had faith in Pokey 2's roof. It had been remarkably free of clay veins, fractures, irregularities, folds and deadly "kettlebottoms"—the vertical stubs of fossilized trees that could drop out of their sandstone sleeves without warning. He thought of this roof as a good woman—stable, predictable, consistent, unsurprising and cooperative. When the roof collapsed on Willie Rutherford, Lee Roy's first thought was White Tip had done something to cause the fall. Then he saw the rogue, disaggregated shale above the sandstone, and he understood why the roof bolts wouldn't hold. "Hope" was where Lee Roy had been. Now, he felt betrayed. He had trusted the roof. Its time-tested virtues had lured him into complacency. The outlaw shale had given way twice as the rescue work went forward. Those falls had slowed the clearing. Lee Roy was watching every bolt go in, cursing each one to hold. He had given up on praying they would stick. Lee Roy had phoned Delmer Estep, superintendent at American Eagle, a little after nine: "This roof, she's just gone wild. Not

248

like anything I've ever seen. You better come down." Pins had every right to bad mouth this top. They'd been able to clear only 40 feet or so in 30 hours. That was pitiful.

"This roof is jes' bein' hateful," Lee Roy said to Pins.

"The bitch has a mind of her own," Pins said. "That's who we dealin' with."

Superintendent Delmer Estep had spent his life working for UNICOAL, mostly at the American Eagle Complex. At 57, he had five years left before full retirement.

Delmer saw himself as an "envelope-pusher" in the coal industry. He was devoted to bringing modern technology and progressive personnel management to his mine. He was proud of his workforce. They were as productive as they could be with the continuous-mining machines they were using. UNICOAL liked Delmer's aggressiveness, so they tolerated his suggestions, recommendations, proposals and requests.

Once Delmer completed installing the new long-wall mining system he had finally been authorized to order, its movable continuous roof-supports would make mining safer than roof bolts while running several times more coal per shift with fewer miners. "A win-win," he'd boasted to John-Cee Smithers who signed off on the $5 million investment. Delmer's employees just had to get used to 1,000 feet of unsupported roof falling in the mined-out area behind the advancing hydraulic roof supports—just feet away from where they stood under the protective steel canopy. They had to overcome their first instinct, which was to run like crazy. And they had to accept the reductions in force the long-wall system would produce, which Delmer hoped to minimize through retirements.

Long walls were the next generation of safer, more productive underground-mining equipment. In his lifetime, Delmer had seen mining go from hand tools to mobile machines. The long wall was the next step toward producing coal more safely at a lower total cost. In five years, American Eagle's need for continuous-miners would be cut from eight per shift to three, and the survivors would only be needed to drive the tunnels on each side of the long wall's block of coal. American Eagle miners would need to be retrained for jobs related to "the wall." He anticipated resistance. No one liked to change. The older guys would drag their feet. But Delmer was certain he could sell the wall after this cave-in on Willie Rutherford. Every cloud has a silver lining, he thought. Of course, this roof fall was more like a thunder storm than a cloud, he admitted.

Delmer took deep satisfaction in the plain-as-your-nose fact that modern mining methods made the miner's work easier and safer. Miners were reasonably well paid in 1975, he acknowledged. They weren't poor anymore. They didn't live in shacks. They weren't forced to buy food and clothing at a company store. They were no longer paid in scrip, which federal and state laws had banned by the late 1950s. Miners had joined America. Delmer Estep believed he had done his part to make this happen for "his" people.

And now this thing with Willie Rutherford made Delmer feel as if he had lost 20 years of purchase on his campaign for modern mining. He hoped this tragic mess would end soon, one way or the other.

"I can't quarrel with you, Pins," Delmer said. "I've never seen Pokey 2 top act so contrary. Never saw shale like this above our sandstone."

"My bolts ain't anchorin' tight," Pins said. "Willie, he runnin' outa time, 'specially if he mashed bad."

Lee Roy and Delmer said nothing by way of agreement.

"I figure we're about 45 foot short of Willie," Pins said. "We not far from the outby side of Number 12 Crosscut. So we got to clear that intersection and the rest of the entry to get to where Willie be. Top came down a few minutes after he started cuttin' into the roof to check it out."

Delmer stopped: "Willie wasn't runnin' coal when the roof came down?"

"Naw, he was cuttin' into the top because I asked him to 'cause the bolts weren't holdin' right for the last two shifts. Willie wanted to know what was up where we couldn't see. We needed to know whether we needed longer bolts, or glue bolts, or something else."

"I didn't know nothin' 'bout this," Lee Roy, the section boss, said to Delmer.

"Look, man, you can fire my ass after we get Willie out," Pins said.

"Nobody's gonna fire you," Delmer said. "You and Willie made the right call. I know you guys know what you're doin'."

John Stefanik, the MESA mine-rescue coordinator, had an idea. "Maybe, we could try pinning with super-long roof bolts and use the resin grout with them. Twelve footers, maybe." He looked hopeful.

"Don't have no 12-foot bolts," Pins said. "Might have a couple dozen eights left after what I already used. Sixes after that."

"It'd take at least three hours to get 12s from Beckley or Bluefield," Delmer said, "assuming I could find them on a Sunday. Don't know anybody in southern West Virginia ever used 12s."

The group shifted around.

Pins sighed in frustration. "Man, I could be pinnin' with 50-footers and that shaley-shit wouldn't hold. It's like tryin' to bolt into an upside-down bucket of basketballs. Now here's a col' har' fac'. We ain't gonna get to Willie in time drivin' through this fall the way we is."

Nobody said anything.

Delmer finally said in a low voice. "I agree."

Willie's crew heard their superintendent's tone of resignation. Delmer wasn't giving up on trying, but he didn't have to say that he thought Willie was not going to make it out alive.

"Well, we've done this rescue by the book," John Stefanik said defensively. "We've done everything the right way."

"Maybe so, but it comin' out wrong 'cause Willie ain't comin' out," Pins said.

"What else can we do? How else can we get to him?" Stefanik asked.

No one said anything.

"Okay. Try this," Pins said tentatively. "How about no more clearin' the fall in Two North like we been doin'. Instead, we drive up the next 45 feet right next to, you know, par'llel, with the fall. *In the coal, not through the rock fall in the entry.* We clear 12 Crosscut then we move down 12 a little and turn back into the coal. We mine up beside Two North where the rubble is and leave some coal in between. Then we cut back into Two North where we think Willie be. We can get there in jes' two hours, maybe less."

"Too risky," Stefanik said. "Too much unsupported roof. Too wide a span under these conditions. You're talking about ribs supporting the width of two tunnels, maybe 24 feet. Too dangerous."

"Top's too unstable," Lee Roy said. "Rock strata ain't settled yet. You can hear it workin' right now. The weight of the bad roof might ride over onto the parallel entry where you'd be takin' out the coal."

Delmer Estep understood the clever simplicity -- as well as the palpable dangers -- of Artie Smith's plan. "If you don't catch Willie on the first cut that damn top might not give you another try. You have one shot. Same with the parallel entry. Too much roof, and not enough coal holding it up on one side. On the Two North side, you're only talkin' about a three- or four-foot-wide sliver of coal."

"You right, Delmer," Pins said, "but you gotta figure there's rock all the way up and back, side to side, packin' Two North, top to bottom. So all that fall stuffin' up the entry could support the par'llel tunnel in the coal."

"But not bottom to top," Delmer said. "There would be space where the roof was. Maybe, it could work like you want. Might could for a short period of time."

John Stefanik liked nothing about this proposal. It hadn't been engineered. It wasn't textbook. It hadn't been tried before. No one at MESA would like it. It wasn't safe, and it wasn't approved. Early in his career, he had learned the First Commandment of mine rescue: "Avert risk to rescuers as much as possible." During his 16 years of federal service, first in the Bureau of Mines and then after 1969 with the federal Mining Enforcement and Safety Administration, he had seen that rule serve well all parties—rescue crews, mine managers and federal civil servants.

"You're still talking another eight, 10 hours, maybe more, if you drive in a new, parallel entry and bolt up," he said.

"We go faster with no boltin'," Pins said.

Petey Jones, a black miner who was older and more experienced than Pins, snorted, "What you plan to prop up the roof with, son? Yo' prayers? Yo' life without sin?"

"Timber," Pins said, "like in the old days."

"Ooooooeee, this nigger crazy," Petey said about his distant cousin.

All of the blackened miners laughed, the whites a little softer than the blacks.

"We timber up behind the miner along the sides," Pins said. "Props and cap wedges. Use headers and cribs only when we don't have no choice. Put in just enough timber to keep the roof up temporarily and hang enough rag to keep us in half-decent air. We will be eatin' dust. Wouldn't need no long cut over, either. We be drivin' the par'llel entry right up beside Two North. Let the damn rubble over there take some of the roof weight. We'll have one good rib of coal, and one rib of fall plus the coal sliver. I say we'd cut through only a couple of feet of coal, not more than five."

Pins paused. Speeches were not what he was used to making, particularly to Delmer Estep. "Willie be dead if we don't try, and y'all know it."

Willie's crew, volunteers to a man, hitched at their heavy work belts and dug their steel-toed, rubber boots into the floor. Beams of light from their cap lamps fenced with each other as they shifted their faces toward the fallen roof in Two North and then back to each other.

"I'd have to get permission from someone at the top to change the rescue plan like that," Delmer said, jerking his head toward the surface to indicate UNICOAL upper management. "If someone else gets hurt on this kind of thing, it's going to blow up in the Comp'ny's face."

"Might as well jes' forget it then," Pins said. "Comp'ny ain't gon stick its neck out fo' no...for Willie."

Delmer blinked. The almost-articulated accusation had caught him on his blind side. I am UNICOAL, he thought, and I think I've always tried to treat everyone the same.

"If you mine through the seam, somebody up top is gonna see coal comin' out the conveyor," Lee Roy said.

"Forget the belt," Pins said. "We can run the loaded buggies into 10 Crosscut and dump there. We clean up later."

Delmer Estep had never felt claustrophobic in his mine until that moment.

"You'd have to leave the continuous-miner all the way in there, in the parallel cut," Lee Roy said. "Get Willie out. Get your asses out. Come back later for the miner. The cribs and props could be in the way of backing the miner out. Might lose the miner altogether."

"Yes," Pins said. "You right. You might."

"Hold on, now, Pins," Delmer said. "You're talkin' that you want me to kick this plan of yours into gear without getting an okay from upstairs? An unauthorized rescue plan?"

"They wouldn't never give you no green light, Delmer," Pins said softly. "Too risky to us. I know that. And there'd be umpity-teen bosses from here to Pittsburgh that would have to sign on. Hell, I can't even get Wanda to agree with me on anything half the time, and I only have that one boss."

The joke broke the tension. Everyone -- black and white -- knew that Wanda Smith had a mind of her own with a tongue to match. They also knew she loved Pins hard and true.

John Stefanik said: "There are good reasons to stick with what we've always done. We're maximizing the probability of getting to Willie while keeping all of you safe as we can."

"You're asking me to gamble the lives of the rescue crew -- these men here, Willie's crew -- against Willie's life," Delmer said. "Assumin' that Willie's still alive."

Delmer was on the spot, and he didn't like it. Until then, he believed decision-making was the easiest part of being a successful mine manager. Choosing the best option, or the least bad option, was the last step, just a mechanical formality, in a long process of gathering information and penciling out the costs and benefits of each alternative. Numbers drove decisions. Delmer was fond of saying that "decisions really decided themselves once the numbers were in the can." He stared at his hands. If he could put numbers to what Pins was saying, it would come out against doing it. But there were no numbers to work with, just feelings and hunches and intuitions and experience and loyalty.

"That top already come down on us twice," Pins said. "We in shaky shit now. New tunnel through the coal ain't gon' stink no more 'n what we already in."

"I can't order you men to do this, to take that risk," Delmer said. "I can't even ask you to consider it."

Pins wanted the crew to decide Willie's fate. That was Willie's chance. If the new plan worked, Delmer could take the credit and be praised for his boldness. If it failed, Pins knew he would bear the responsibility and blame.

The crew examined the idea. Each felt that a piece of himself lay next to Willie. Each knew he would be risking death or injury.

Pins said: "I'll take the load. I'll hump the props, set 'em, an' hang the rags. But I need a man to run the miner an' someone to run the buggy in and out. I can't do it all myself. Three of us could do it."

"Three assholes workin' like sumbitches," Billy Burdette said. He spit into a puddle.

No one said anything.

"I do the buggy for you, Pins," Byron Lewis said softly. "Willie, he be my second cousin, man."

No one said anything.

"I'll run the miner."

Cap lamps swung toward the smudged-black face of a slender white man who mostly kept to himself, Darrell V. Dorsey.

Pins was surprised. After Byron had volunteered, he'd been expecting Timmy Buchanan or Petey Jones, the other blacks on Willie's crew, to step up. Darrell Dorsey! The Ghostman! Pins didn't think Darrell and Willie had ever done much more than blink cap lights as they trammed their machines past each other.

Darrell had worked underground for eight years, the last three at American Eagle. He had run a continuous-miner before he came to UNICOAL. Darrell Vee spent his free time over at what Pins said to Wanda was "a holy-roller church, gobblin' in tongues, washin' shit off each other's feet and who knew what else white folks did when they thought they had been got with the Holy Ghost."

"You think he crazier than Sophia Ethelene Moore and her bunch with their fallin' down and foamin' at the mouth?" Wanda asked.

"No," Pins admitted. "When it comes to whoopin' and wailin', I'd say we are every bit as equal as any white folks."

"Praise God," Wanda laughed. "The race has arrived."

No one on Willie's crew ever said a word to Darrell about his church. He worked hard, always helped out and never gave offense. He was the only man on hoot owl who always read the Bible during dinner break. That's why they called him "The Ghostman," which he accepted as a friendly compliment.

"You sure, Darrell Vee?" Pins asked, deliberately not using his nickname. "Ain't no one pushin' this on you, man. Ain't no one 'specting you."

"I'm sure. 'Spect it of myself, Pins."

"Well, shit. I'll run the other buggy for you," Billy Burdette, a white miner, said. "Go twice as fast with two of us haulin' out."

"You four boys are volunteerin'," Delmer Estep said, stating the obvious. "I'll let you try this on your own, but the Company can't be liable if anything happens. I'll stand for the equipment, but I need to hear a 'Yes.' from each of you."

"Yeah," said Pins.

"Yeah," said Byron Lewis.

"Yeah, boy," said Billy Burdette.

"Yes," said The Ghostman, Darrell V. Dorsey.

254

No one said anything.

"I he'p you hump them timbers, Pins," Petey Jones said quietly.

"Me, too," added Timmy Buchanan.

"I'll set posts and hang rags with you, Pins," said Mike Decker, a big, tough white miner in his early 50s who had served time for putting two guys in the hospital in a beer-joint fight.

All seven members of Willie's crew were in.

"All right," Delmer said. "Me and Lee Roy will bring up timbers and curtains in the scoops."

"I'll help outby," John Stefanik said, indicating the roof-supported area in the Number 12 Crosscut.

"Darrell Vee, you be careful as you can," Lee Roy said. "You'll be minin' under unsupported roof all the way in. The dust won't have no place to go. You won't be able to see shit."

"I know."

"Okay, let's do it," Pins said.

The crew started talking and walking forward. Then they heard The Ghostman's quiet voice speaking softly…

Yea, though I walk through the valley of death.
I shall fear no evil.
For thou art with me.

The men -- some church-goers, some not -- stopped. One by one they came over to The Ghostman, gathering like a football huddle, their heads bowed, believer and non-believer alike. They touched each other, shoulder to shoulder.

"Do it from the beginning," Pins said.

The Ghostman started. They joined in, mumbling the words they knew. They were holding hands at the end.

As they walked toward the coal, Pins came over to Delmer and Lee Roy.

Pins touched Delmer's arm. "Thanks for stickin' with him."

"I've known Willie since he was a Red Hat," Delmer said. "I hired him. I'm gonna be the one to kick his ass out to pasture. I'm in."

Lee Roy Stump eased over to Delmer Estep as the group separated.

"I dunno 'bout this, Delmer," the section boss said to his superintendent.

"Nothing's certain about anything we're trying," Delmer said.

"This idea ain't approved by anybody—not Comp'ny, not MESA," Lee Roy said. "What if somethin' happens?"

"Then I'm fired. I'll cover your butt, LeRoy. They'll only need to sacrifice one of us. I'm close to retirement. Doris wouldn't mind too much havin' me at home. I could clean out the garage once a week."

"Not what I mean," LeRoy said. "What if somebody gets hurt doin' this?"

"No one forced anybody to do anything," Delmer said.

"Somebody gets hurt, somebody gets a lawyer, somebody sues UNICOAL. Negligence. Failure to follow approved rescue plan. Willful disobedience. Failure to supervise."

"You're right," Delmer said. "You can leave. Wash your hands of it. I'm not forcing you to have any part in this. Go up the main if you want. I won't think less of you."

Lee Roy felt like he was standing on the lip of a chasm. He had a family with three kids. He had more to risk on the job and at home than Delmer. No one acted without authorization from above. Section bosses took orders and relayed them; they weren't supposed to be creative. He saw himself sitting in a courtroom saying, "Well, see, Pins suggested we try this other idea." He shook his head to clear the image. UNICOAL managers and superintendents did not follow suggestions from a kid like Artie Smith.

"You want me to tell you to leave?" Delmer asked. "I will. Leave."

Lee Roy hesitated. Loyalty to his crew, his superintendent—that was the issue. If this idea worked and Lee Roy wasn't part of it, he'd have a hard time managing miners again. If it didn't work out, he might not have to worry about managing miners again.

"No," Lee Roy said. "I'm in."

Once in the miner, Darrell Vee cleaned up the scattered rocks in Number 12 Crosscut. The main blockage was directly in front of him, in Two North leading to the face. He swung the miner into the Crosscut, then after a few feet, turned 90-degrees into the coal on his left. Byron snugged his shuttle buggy behind Darrell Vee's miner to receive the newly cut coal. Lee Roy and Delmer trammed their scoops back to the supply dump with Petey and Timmy. They loaded six-foot-long oak props, ventilation curtains, crossbeams and cribbing timber, wedges and cap blocks. Delmer assumed they had a couple of hours before someone came down to see what was going on. If this rogue rescue ended badly, Delmer knew he could retire comfortably, assuming he didn't go to jail. A bad ending would be harder on Lee Roy who was only 46 and aiming toward superintendent when Delmer left.

John Stefanik did not know what to do. He hadn't volunteered to help. He hadn't volunteered to keep quiet. And he certainly hadn't volunteered to come to Bloomingrose Holler. His years of federal employment told him to call the surface and have the higher-ups stop this too-risky rescue effort. On the other hand, he agreed that the new plan was Willie Rutherford's best hope, maybe his only hope. He stood in 12 Crosscut and watched the miners and supervisors working.

Darrell Dorsey's miner cut easily into the coal, digging out a six-foot-high tunnel. He made it 15-feet-wide to give the guys behind him room to slip up on either side with their roof props. Byron and Billy alternated their buggies behind Darrell's miner. Lee Roy and Delmer drove into the 12 Crosscut with their loaded scoops. They, along with Timmy and Petey, unloaded and carried supplies forward. Pins and Mike Decker were setting props next to the ribs, often close to Darrell's miner. This was a too-tight space, very dangerous and never done in normal circumstances. John Stefanik could not see them from where he stood; too much dust.

They started tacking up ventilation curtains from post to post along the right rib when Delmer decided he'd rather keep as many of them out of Darrell's tunnel as possible. That meant little good air would get to Darrell Vee and no dust would be removed. It would be harder on The Ghostman but safer for the others.

Darrell understood and kept driving steadily into the ancient vegetation that hadn't seen the sun for 150 million years. He drove as straight as he could using nothing but dead reckoning. He tried to keep at least a four-foot thickness of coal between the rescue tunnel and the rubble in Two North to support the roof. The Ghostman hunched his shoulders and swallowed dust as it rolled back from the face. He knew the deadly risks of working under unsupported roof when the top rock was solid; this roof had proven itself to be the opposite. He hoped his cutting bits wouldn't ignite a methane pocket. He felt his Bible tucked into the vest pocket of his coveralls. "For thou art with me," he repeated. "For thou art with me."

Darrell cut the ignition after Billy Burdette backed out his loaded buggy. He walked toward the others. He handed the end of a steel tape to Pins in the center of 12 Crosscut and returned to the back end of his miner. Then he added 20 feet, which represented the length of the machine. He didn't know where Willie was in Two North. But if Willie had been scratching around in the roof as Pins thought, he should be sitting about 40 to 45 feet in from where Pins was standing.

"What you think?" Pins asked Darrell.

"I think if we angle in right here, we'll come on to his miner but maybe not right at his seat. We'll jes' have to see."

"We got one shot," Pins said. "If you start pulling out this coal between the two tunnels more than once or twice, the whole thing will come down. Gotta hit it right the first time."

"We can only do our best," Darrell said.

"Yeah, our best better be good enough," Pins said. "We've timbered up to the back of your miner. You need to do this fast Darrell Vee and as gentle as you can. This sandstone top is holdin' up a slop jar. Them green posts we set are poppin' under the weight. Never saw such."

"Fast. I'm with you," Darrell said. "Hard to see. Only have to cut out a few feet between the entries."

"This timberin' has got me whipped," Petey Jones said.

"Me, too," Billy Burdette added.

"We all is," Pins said.

"Give me your hammer, Timmy," Pins said.

Pins tapped five times on a heavy metal prybar that he rested against the left coal rib.

They listened.

Each of them heard five taps.

They cheered. It could only be Willie.

The Ghostman clamored into the miner and swung its cutting head into the rib. Rattling and yowling, the drum bit into the coal. Darrell stared straight into the cramped airless hole, searching for the first sign of a punch-through. He didn't want to run the cutting head into Willie's miner, which might create a spark that would trigger an explosion. And he didn't want to bite into Willie himself. This fast work had to be done slowly, inching the 60-ton machine forward. A million specks of coal dust swirled slowly in the lights of his machine. The Ghostman thought they looked like sparkly black snow at Christmas.

Darrell stopped. He took his hard hat and tapped it on the miner. Willie responded with five taps. Less than a foot, Darrell guessed by the sound.

Timmy and Petey brought up water, chocolate, blankets, the big first-aid kit and a stretcher.

Darrell took out the next inch, cut the miner and listened. He started again, took out the next inch. He was feeling his way through his machine to the cutting drum that was 15 feet in front of where he sat. It's like doing brain surgery with a blindfold, he thought.

He started the miner and moved it forward, less than an inch. Suddenly, the face collapsed. Darrell cut the ignition. He could see Willie's miner, some orange steel plate. He backed out of his cut so they could crawl toward Willie. He walked up to the breakthrough with Delmer and Lee Roy who were carrying posts and two bow saws.

Mike Decker and Pins scooted next to Willie's miner, clearing coal behind them. They found themselves at the back right, a couple of feet from Willie. Bits of roof fell lightly on their hardhats.

"Hey White Tip?" Decker called. "You hear us?"

"Ain't nothin' wrong with my ears," Willie said.

"You okay, Willie?" Pins asked.

"I can't turn my head much. My right leg's broke or mashed. Knee hurts. Thirsty. What took you so long, man? You been readin' <u>Playboy</u> in the dinner hole again?"

Mike and Pins started passing coal chunks back to the others, working toward Willie as fast as they could. They used pry bars to enlarge the opening.

"Ya don't *read* <u>Playboy,</u> fool, you look at that shit," Pins said, as he stabbed his bar into the rubble, freeing pieces he could pass back.

"So I'm right," Willie said. "You was tryin' to read it, which was why it took you so long."

"Hey, man," Pins said. "Why I wan' be down in this hole, messin' with some no-count bullshitter like you. I should be up top, sippin' coffee and tellin' everyone what a fine fellow you once was."

"Is. Still is."

"Ghostman ran the miner that punched through," Pins said.

"Glad I took that boy on," Willie said. "Figured you'd mine up through the fall, not come in through the side."

"Top wouldn't hold," Pins said.

"Pins figured out how to get to you," Mike said. "Ghostman and Pins, they're your guys."

Pins called for posts cut into 24-inch lengths. Billy Burdette and Petey Jones grabbed the bow saws and started cutting.

Delmer and Lee Roy squeezed forward to have a look. "Jackass work from here on," Delmer said. They joined in the chain handing coal and rock away from Willie's miner.

"Willie, you sit tight," Mike Decker said. "We're no more than a foot away."

Decker worked his way on his belly and knees along the side of Willie's miner. He shoved rock and coal back with his feet. Pins handed the material back to Lee Roy in the chain. Pins propped in the two-foot wood stubs every eight inches of progress. He used cap wedges to fill in where a prop was short. The men breathed in short hard bursts.

"I see your light bouncing off my control panel," Willie said, as he switched on his own.

"I got you," Mike said, touching Willie's shoulder.

"Nice," Willie said. "Glad you made it. I wouldn't turn down some water if you have any handy."

The chain passed forward a thermos of water and another of coffee.

Pins wiggled up between Willie and Mike. "Hey, here yo' Susie peach pie," he said taking a smashed lump of aluminum foil out of his overalls and flipping it into Willie's lap. "Room service."

Tears came to Willie's eyes.

"Well," Pins said, as he and Mike cleared space next to Willie's miner, "you ain't no better lookin' than I remember."

"I been doin' the best I could to catch up on my beauty sleep."

"Shit, Willie," Decker laughed, "don't say that. Lee Roy will dock you for sleepin' on the job."

"Damn right," Lee Roy yelled in.

"Man, you stink, too," Pins said, as he worked to free his friend.

"Roof water been drippin' on me."

"That ain't no roof water. That piss."

"Well, there ain't no bathroom down here."

"You jes' too lazy to pee in a potty like a Class One human being," Pins charged.

"Gimme your hat, an' I'll piss in that."

Pins flicked his cap lamp toward the slab of rock that pinned Willie's right leg. "Mike, we'll have to use the big pry bar and chocks to lever this up. You be the donkey, and I be the mule," Pins said to Decker, the much bigger and stronger man.

Decker positioned two chocks next to the slab and jammed the heavy bar under the rock.

"I think I can give you enough to drag him out," Decker said. "But you gotta move quick. I won't be able to hold for very long."

Mike got on his knees and prepared to push down on the high end of the bar. Pins crawled next to Willie and got his arms under Willie's armpits.

"Might sting a little," Pins said, "when I yank on you."

"Now!" Willie said.

Mike leaned down with his arms and weight. The slab lifted slowly. Two inches. Pins, lying on his back, pulled, using his legs for leverage against the machine. Willie grunted, then screamed. Pins had him moving. "Two more seconds, Mike," he breathed. "Give me two more!"

Pins dragged Willie partly out of the miner's cab and free of the slab.

Mike eased the rock down. He stopped to catch his breath. Then he and Pins worked Willie back through the opening. Next to Darrell Vee's miner, they had blankets, food and a stretcher.

"Should we take him out on the scoop?" Lee Roy asked Delmer.

"Let's walk him out on the stretcher," Delmer said, "it'll be easier on his leg."

"But slower," Pins said.

Petey peeled the wrapper off a chocolate bar and fed it to Willie. Billy pulled a couple of blankets over him.

Delmer got a hand under Willie's arm and Byron Lewis gripped the other side of his overalls. They pulled Willie over to one side while others slid the stretcher under him.

Pins and Mike stood next to Darrell's miner in the rescue tunnel. They were winded. Mike trembled from the strain of lifting the slab.

Timmy Buchanan, who had emergency-medical training in the Army, cut off Willie's pants leg. "Bring your cap lights down so I can see what's what," he said.

"Wiggle your toes."

"Hurts," Willie said.

"Expect it does," Timmy said, as he ran his fingers lightly over Willie's swollen lower leg and knee. "Feels like you done broke it at least once. Can't tell how bad the soft stuff around the knee is tore up. I'll splint you up under good roof."

"Let's get the hell out of this hole," Delmer said.

Pins, Darrel, Mike and Petey lifted the stretcher and started walking as quickly and as gently as they could down Darrell's tunnel toward safety. Lee Roy and Billy were in front. Delmer, Byron and Timmy trailed the stretcher.

Willie winced as the stretcher bobbed. He looked in amazement at the temporary timbering and the absence of roof bolts. His leg throbbed. His urine-soaked clothes chilled him.

"Reporters waitin' for you, Willie," Billy Burdette said. "You gonna be a TV star. A hero. Tri-Cities TV, Charleston, Roanoke and everywhar."

"Some hero, me," Willie grunted. "You boys. You the heroes. Sayin' thanks ain't enough for what you done for me. I see how you drove in. How you timbered up."

"Delmer was the one," Pins said. "He gave us the go ahead."

"The idea came from Pins," Delmer said.

"Darrell Vee, he run the miner all the way in," Timmy said.

"Big Mike, old shit that he is, moved that rock off your leg," Pins said.

"I saw Mike doin' the hard work while you was workin' on your tan."

"I tol' these boys we should leave you where you was," Pins said. "If Susie had packed you a whole pie, none of us would have ever left the dinner hole."

"You saved me," Willie said to Mike Decker.

"All of us," Mike said.

"Fac' is," Pins said, "them TV gals gonna regret you being saved when they get a sniff of you."

Willie, on his back and looking up, was the only one who glimpsed the long crack splitting the middle of the roof. The fissure seemed to take its time opening and then it thunderclapped.

Willie yelled, "TOP'S CAV...." And then roof rock rained down in pieces large and small. Willie raised his arms over his face. The others had no time to make sense of the primal bone-cracking sound. Rock fell on their heads, shoulders, backs and legs.

John Stefanik, standing outby the rescue tunnel, heard the roof come down. A bellow of air knocked him backward. He scrambled toward the phone. "SEND DOWN TWO CREWS AND MEDICS. ANOTHER COLLAPSE. HURRY."

Then he got up and ran toward the new fall. He heard moaning. He tore at the broken rock.

Chapter 18

American Eagle Mine Complex, October 13, 1975

Johnson C. Smithers knew when he assumed the job of running UNICOAL that he would have to do things he didn't like. This was one of them.

John-Cee waited on a landing at the top of the three, 20-foot wide steps that led to American Eagle's office. He would have preferred to stand behind a lectern, but none was available. A dozen microphones pointed like a Hydra at his mouth. Others were taped to a stand with lines leading to cassette recorders. He waited for the television crews to adjust their cameras and their audio. He put both hands in his trousers' pockets but decided he would appear too casual in that stance. So he let them hang naturally, which didn't feel quite right either. He wore a dark blue suit and a white dress shirt with a paisley tie. The rising sun had burned off the night chill. It was now more hot than comfortable. John-Cee wanted to loosen his tie and take off his jacket. He was starting to sweat in the before-noon sunshine under his combed hair. His wire-rimmed glasses made him look more like an engineering professor than a CEO. People commented that he reminded them of Robert S. McNamara.

He scanned the crowd, which he estimated at about 600. He took note of a CBS crew from Washington, D.C., with satellite dishes and antennae on their bus-truck. Reporters were in front of him. Joe Hunt was directly behind.

John-Cee had grown up in a wealthy Pittsburgh suburb, the son of Holland Smithers who had taken over UNICOAL from his father and built it into America's largest coal company. John-Cee had been around coal and miners his entire life. For his sixth birthday in 1921, Holland had given him a one-of-a-kind, scaled-down Holt 60 bulldozer, a special order from the factory in Stockton, California, along with one acre of the family's 25 to do what he wanted with his present.

John-Cee was groomed to take over UNICOAL. Holland introduced him to miners. When he was a Yale student, he drank beer with them during his summer jobs. As president, he wanted to take care of his people. He built ball fields for them, stayed with the ACMU contract, paid decent wages and gave two of their promising kids college scholarships each year. He'd even married one of their daughters, Delores Liptrap. UNICOAL people, he felt, were his personal responsibility.

John-Cee nodded toward Fletcher Waddington, UNICOAL's director of public affairs, who was buttoning his suit jacket. Just before they had walked out of the office, Fletcher said to him: "Don't try anything fancy with reporters in front of *this* crowd. Straight answers on matters of fact. What we know at this time; what we don't know. Don't offer opinions. Don't speculate. Kick as much as possible into the future—'We'll find out what happened.'"

Fletcher moved easily behind the microphones as John-Cee stepped aside. The media crews were ready. "Mr. Smithers, president and CEO of UNICOAL, has a short statement about what we know at this time. I'm Fletch Waddington. Media folks can contact me for updates. Mr. Smithers will take a few questions following his remarks…from reporters. All of us are terribly saddened by this event. I hope the media respects the privacy of Mrs. Rutherford and her family. Everyone in this Company is praying that Willie Rutherford walks out of Two North unhurt."

Fletcher Waddington looked out of place at a coal mine. A Princeton graduate, he'd fallen into public relations in the early '60s, because it was easier than law or engineering. He had a knack for writing, though not enough of a knack to be a writer. Now in his late 30s, he still dressed like an Ivy Leaguer. He bought his suits at Brooks Brothers across from Pittsburgh's Scraife Square. He preferred blue, oxford-cloth, button-down shirts and black-leather, cap-toe shoes. In his own office, he slipped into tan bucks with red soles. It was his statement about something to someone. Fletcher Waddington looked as inoffensively corporate as possible, but inside he was a libertarian who believed that an individual should be allowed to do what an individual wanted to do.

John-Cee moved to the microphones.

"UNICOAL is continuing our efforts to rescue Mr. Willie Rutherford who was trapped in a roof fall at the beginning of his shift, some 38 hours ago," he said, reading from the statement that Fletcher had typed for him.

"The hazardous work of clearing the collapse has gone very slowly due to extremely unstable roof conditions.

"In the 43 years that UNICOAL has worked the Pocahontas 2 seam at American Eagle, management has never, NEVER, encountered roof conditions as friable as these.

"UNICOAL, with the cooperation of MESA, fully intends to recover Mr. Rutherford.

"We pray that he is alive. Our prayers are with Mrs. Rutherford and her family, and the magnificent UNICOAL employees who are trying to save her husband. We are grateful to the rescue squads from other mines and local law enforcement for standing by. The Westmoreland crew pulled a shift last night. Thanks is inadequate.

"Superintendent Delmer Estep and Section Foreman Lee Roy Stump are supervising our rescue operation. MESA's John Stefanik is also underground at this time."

264

John-Cee looked up and nodded toward the reporters.

"Mr. Smithers, Charlie Frazier, <u>Charleston Gazette</u>. What do you think caused the cave-in?"

"I can't give you a definitive answer at this time, Charlie. We're doing the best we can to get Mr. Rutherford out. We'll follow with a thorough investigation.

"It appears from what I've been told that he encountered a geological freak of nature in the roof strata."

John-Cee paused, because he wanted to make his words easily understandable.

"Mr. Rutherford appears to have encountered a layer of friable rock -- shale -- within the mine's sandstone roof. Think of it as a gravel layer in a lasagna. This is material that never cemented to itself under heat and pressure over time. It never tied in to the material above or below it. No one had any idea it was there. It's a tiny anomaly in an otherwise near-perfect roof. Unfortunately, Two North was driven directly under it. That's why the rescue crews have experienced such delay getting to Mr. Rutherford. The top keeps coming down.

"I'm told Mr. Rutherford's crew was installing roof bolts in a pattern that was even more protective than what we are required to do under our MESA-approved, roof-control plan. His crew started pinning four-foot-long roof bolts on a grid of three-foot centers instead of four-foot centers. The tighter bolting pattern should have provided an extra margin of safety in typical conditions. But no one could anticipate or detect the hidden freak of nature above them. We have never run into this before. Never. Not at American Eagle in the Pocahontas 2 seam."

"Geological 'freak of nature,'" Charlie Frazier muttered as he underlined the phrase in his notebook. "Can 'Act of God' be far behind?'" He glanced toward Owen Paige, but the AP reporter was concentrating on taking notes. Allyson Pickering looked skeptical. A tight smile crossed Julie Cogswell's face and then disappeared into her memories.

Freddie Pruitt, chairman of the ACMU safety committee, crossed his arms over his chest and spoke out. "They was a-boltin' on threes 'stead of fours 'cause they knew the top was bad. Should not have been in under that roof no ways. They was being pushed for production. No time to figure it out. Just bolt and go."

A crescent of grim-faced miners rumbled agreement.

"What about that Mr. Smithers?" Charlie asked.

John-Cee tried to smile, to loosen the tension. "Folks," he said in a calm, sincere and authoritative voice, "UNICOAL is a law-abiding, responsible coal operator. We run our mines by the book. Safety is our first priority. We don't compromise on safety. The short-cut days are over—and good riddance. If we know miners are doing unsafe work, UNICOAL stops it. Period! If we find our employees in a situation of 'imminent danger,' we get them out. If I were to find a supervisor engaging in unsafe practices, I'd boot the son...the man out on his...a...ear."

The crowd laughed. Fletch smiled.

"Folks, this is not a promise. This is how we do things. We reap what we sow. We do everything we can to provide a safe and healthy workplace. Our injury and fatality rates are among the lowest in the industry for the mining systems we use. Year after year. And when our people do experience an injury, we report it honestly to MESA. We don't have our injured bench-warming in the bathhouse to keep our non-fatal rate artificially low. You miners know some other operators play that game; UNICOAL doesn't.

"Delmer Estep and his people had this crew doing more than what was required for extra safety. They had had problems with the roof during the last couple of shifts. If a glue bolt every six inches would have done the trick, UNICOAL would have either done that or pulled out of that entry altogether. One or the other.

"The Union's safety committee was informed of the tighter bolting pattern. If the safety committee or any individual miner thought the roof in Two North presented an 'imminent danger,' the men would have been pulled out or pulled themselves out. Any individual miner can refuse to work in an 'imminent danger,' and nothing will happen to him. Not at my Company! It's the law. I would have supported that decision 100 percent as I have in other situations. We do not want to endanger our people! I can't say it any plainer than that.

"Coal mining is risky in the best of circumstances. You can't mine out a six-foot-high space under 500 feet of rock without accepting that. We all know it. It's not like an assembly line where employees perform the same task over and over in a static environment. Underground mining changes the workplace every minute. Miners must constantly adapt to new conditions.

"That's what the tighter bolting pattern was—adapting.

"A mine's 'shop floor,' if you will, is the geological strata that were put in place millions of years ago. Layers of rock are never perfectly uniform, consistent or standardized. Making rock is a messy process. It's saltwater, mud, rotting plants, chemical reactions, hardening, softening, heat and pressure over more time than you can imagine. That's what makes coal and the rock above it.

"This coal seam and this mine are known for good roof conditions. Every American Eagle miner knows that. But it's technically and humanly impossible to detect every hidden flaw in a mine roof. We can prevent almost all accidents if we follow safety procedures. But accidents will still happen. Sometimes no one is to blame for an accident. Sometimes it's human error—a coal miner not doing his job in a safe manner. Sometimes it's our fault. Or, it can be a combination.

"This came from being dealt the joker in the geological deck—the bad card that comes out of nowhere. You reporters who have covered coal know what I'm saying is the truth. Some accidents are caused by Nature's quirks. No one's to blame."

Several rank-and-file miners in the crowd mumbled agreement: "He's right. That's true."

Fletcher Waddington scored it, Home run! He kept his face grim and impassive.

"I just want to say one more thing," John-Cee said. "I promise, you have *my* word that we will find out what happened, what we could have done better and that I, personally, will tell you the whole truth and make this right."

Joe Hunt moved to John-Cee's side and indicated he wanted to speak.

"I'm Joe Hunt, president of the American Coal Miner's Union. We represent Local 4355 and have since the '30s. Willie Rutherford is one of us, one of my Union brothers. We will do all we can to get to him and bring him home.

"Now lemme say this. UNICOAL is prob'ly the best company to work for in the coal industry when it comes to safety. They play straight. They cooperate. It's not like in the old days when I was comin' up and a damn mine mule was valued more than a miner. I'm jes' tellin' it like it was. Some other comp'nies ain't like UNICOAL. I don't have to mention no names to this crowd. John-Cee is right. Anybody who's been underground for a time knows that thangs happen sometimes, thangs you can't prevent."

Charlie Frazier scribbled: "'Thangs happen sometimes.'"

"I, myself, was buried in a rock fall up at Fricktown and…"

"…and we're gonna bury you again come December," Biggie Stover shouted out.

Delucci's supporters hooted. Hunt's followers who were the majority glared at Stover.

"Zip it, Mack," a big, towheaded miner in a camouflage shirt hollered in Biggie's direction.

"Grow up, sonny boy," muttered another.

Fletch Waddington felt the press conference sliding toward the far edge of the known world. This was UNICOAL's moment to get in front of a story whose ending was in doubt. John-Cee had captured the crowd with his blunt sincerity. Fletch did not want his boss in the middle of a fracas between Hunt and Delucci. Fletch knew John-Cee was uncomfortable in unscripted public appearances. And Delucci might be using this incident for his own political gain. Fletch tried to catch Joe Hunt's eye to warn him off, but Joe was completely focused on Biggie Stover. Fletch started to move toward the microphones to get John-Cee out of whatever might be brewing.

Joe Hunt was embarrassed. Coal operators with a Union contract expected the ACMU president to control his members. Union presidents expected no less of themselves. Joe Hunt needed that credibility with the CEOs to negotiate contracts. Joe's standing with them depended on the willingness of his members to follow his lead. Mine operators could live with Joe Hunt being slow, but they could not long tolerate a fool who would be challenged, or worse, rejected.

Joe gathered himself and spoke calmly. "Come on, boys. We're all members of the same Union. Let's not play politics with Brother Rutherford. Let's do all we can to get him out alive. That means Comp'ny and Union working together."

Most of the crowd clapped, loudly.

"Suits me," Delucci shouted when the applause ended. "But an ACMU president shouldn't be takin' up for UNICOAL until we find out this Comp'ny ain't to blame."

Fletch had almost reached the microphones when a young section boss burst out of the office and ran toward John-Cee, bumping Waddington out of the way. This was his first year in management, his first crisis. He stumbled to a stop, just short of knocking John-Cee down the steps and into the reporters. He haltingly raised his hand to tap Smithers on the shoulder when John-Cee turned around. The "cherry boss" froze, his pointing finger level with John-Cee's chin.

"What?" John-Cee asked, both surprised and angry at finding a pointing finger in his face.

Fletch Waddington knew something bad had been communicated. John-Cee's face sagged. He put his hand in front of his eyes. Fletch silently cursed whoever allowed this kid to break into his press conference. Now John-Cee would be tied to a rocket of bad news, whatever it was. Fletch began composing an opening sentence to end the press conference.

John-Cee turned to the crowd. "I have bad news," he said, "terrible news. A tragedy has occurred."

The crowd gasped, then grew still with tension. Reporters steadied their pens and notebooks. Television crews checked their dials.

"Ten men, including two supervisors, were caught in a massive roof fall about 10 minutes ago. Three fatalities have occurred. There may be others."

Low sounds of anger came from the miners. Several women cried out. Everyone moved forward, closer to the information.

"They found Mr. Rutherford safe but with a badly broken leg. They were carrying him out when a second roof fall happened. Delmer Estep, our superintendent, and Lee Roy Stump, the section supervisor, were involved. A relief crew is trying to get to them at this moment. I can't say...I can't tell you how sorry we are that this...."

Susie Rutherford, a woman in her mid-40s, moaned deeply and began to sob. Women tightened their circle around her.

"We will get to the bottom of this," John-Cee said, wiping his forehead with his hand. "UNICOAL's good name, the safety of our employees, are on the line. I will get you the status of the men as soon as possible."

Fletch Waddington stepped in front of John-Cee. "Mr. Smithers will issue a full statement once we get the facts. Reporters should work through me."

Fletch turned with John-Cee and began moving toward the office where, he hoped, the roof might still be overhead. This ordeal is just starting, he thought. He cursed for only bringing one change of clothes. The nearest marginally acceptable men's store would be in Beckley, a three-hour drive one way. Maybe the UNICOAL chopper could fly clean ones down from Pittsburgh.

Joe Hunt was confused. He considered following Smithers, but that would look bad. Instead, he started down the steps toward Larry Sonoski who was moving toward him.

"Mr. Hunt. JOE!" Charlie Frazier barked. "What's the Union intend to do about this?"

"I'm not sure yet." Joe hesitated, because he wasn't sure about anything at that instant. He stood in place, groping for direction.

Reaching Joe's side, Skis said to Charlie: "Jerry Crowley, the Union's safety director, will investigate. MESA will investigate. UNICOAL will investigate. That won't bring none of 'em back, but it's the first step in..."

"Sure as shit won't," someone said.

"...those are the first steps the Union'll take. Make sure the truth comes out."

"Why doesn't President Lard-Ass talk for himself?" Biggie Stover shouted as he started moving toward the steps. Stover was more than a head taller than anyone in the crowd. Several were as heavy, but not as muscled. No one got in his way.

Joe Hunt clenched his fists and started moving toward Stover. He stopped when he came to the tangle of reporters, cameras and wires.

"PRESS! PRESS!" reporters cried as miners started bunching them together like asparagus. Skis grabbed Joe.

Biggie was pushing through the scrum. Jeep and a dozen supporters were right behind him.

A woman's voice cut through the growing turbulence. Joe stopped.

"Mr. Hunt! How will this tragedy affect your reelection campaign?" Allyson Pickering shouted.

Joe searched for his questioner. When his eyes landed on Allyson, she gave him a little smile and a nod. She mouthed "Me."

"Safety ain't negotiable, young…Miss. This ain't Union politics. We're all brothers underground. Black or white, we're all black at the end of a shift. We all got coal tattoos. Whether you're for me or Jeep over thar, it don't matter on safety. None of us should politick over this disaster, this tragedy. The campaign for Union president stops at the mine portal."

Allyson finished scribbling these words and glanced at Becker who rolled his eyes.

"That's about half right, Joe," Jeep said, his voice strong and clear as he stood next to Biggie at the bottom step. "Safety is politics with the operators. Safety is a negotiated part of the contract jes' like wages and pensions. When the Union gets some safety thang that costs money, it means we had to go short on somethin' else that costs money. But the '74 contract was short on safety AND short on everythin' else, too. All the men got was comp'ny soap in the damn bathhouse."

Mean laughter rolled up from the long-haired miners behind Jeep and Biggie. Even some Hunt supporters nodded. While Hunt had actually raised wages and benefits modestly, critics latched on to "free soap" as a shorthand dismissal of the entire contract.

Biggie turned to Jeep and whispered. "If we're gonna make a stand, we better get on the high ground and fast."

"Feels like I'm fuckin' General Custer," Jeep whispered back.

"You may be," Biggie said, "in both senses."

Biggie pushed up the steps and shouldered Joe to one side, though not aggressively. Jeep was beside him. Delucci's supporters followed and filled in behind Jeep and Biggie, facing the crowd.

Joe's supporters formed up in front of the bottom step. Joe and Skis joined them and then turned to face Jeep and Biggie. Joe's people were in their 40s, 50s and early 60s, men with 20 to 30 years underground. The oldest were WWII and Korea vets. The two sides were members of the same ACMU local. They bowled together, hunted together, married each other's sisters and went to church and bars side by side. But the generational divide that split the country in the late '60s had now turned up, bright and shining, on a Sunday morning at American Eagle in 1975.

Jeep was warmed up and getting hotter. "And then you talk about the Union's safety department. You got one old rummy up thar a hidin' behind his desk calendar. Crowley ain't stuck his butt underground for 10 years. He thinks a 'buggy' is what his woman used to push his babies in."

Delucci's miners laughed loudly, and even some of Hunt's boys sniggered in agreement. Jerry Crowley filled a chair. This was no secret.

Jeep puffed out his chest. He felt support welling up behind him. He shouted: "I'll tell you, Joe Hunt, and UNICOAL, both: **Coal should be mined safely or not at all!**"

Becker felt an electric current zap the crowd. A wildcat strike over safety—that wasn't just campaign talk. Strikes affected everyone. Jeep Delucci had thrown down a challenge to Joe Hunt, coal operators and every ACMU member.

Fletch Waddington thought it was as brilliant a campaign slogan as he'd ever heard. That Jeep Delucci appeared to have thought it up extemporaneously amazed him. He now assumed the BCCG companies would be dealing with Delucci after December. So what might 'or not at all' actually mean day to day?

Joe Hunt knew Jeep had bested him. The kid was quick.

"I don't think we should wash our laundry in front of the press," he shot back. "If you got a beef with Crowley bring it to the Executive Board. You've been District 17 president for two years, and you never said word one about safety to him or me."

Skis wanted this to stop. Joe was an action guy, not a speechmaker and certainly not a debater. But Skis couldn't think of any way to rescue Joe without appearing to be rescuing Joe from himself.

"Now Joe, you say what a good job UNICOAL done," Jeep continued. "Well, hell's fire, if UNICOAL's doin' such a *good* job on safety at American Eagle, what kind of damn job are you lettin' the bad comp'nies get away with?"

Joe Hunt was stung. Delucci knew UNICOAL was the most safety-conscious company in the industry. The Union's research department had compared company fatality and injury rates. Delucci had been in the meeting when Joe presented that report to the Executive Board and all the District presidents. Hell, Joe thought, every miner at American Eagle, every miner in the damn Union knew UNICOAL walked safety.

And then a small smile crossed Joe Hunt's face.

"Ya know, Jeep," he said, "you remind me of a dumb little Beagle pup I had yars ago. That pup had a real bad habit—it wouldn't suck tit. Now I did everythin' I could to show him his mistake, but that pup wouldn't suck tit. Thought he knew all thar was to know about the world. He was jes' too knot-headed to listen to a guy like me—a guy who knew where thangs was and how they was a-laid out. Poor little feller died after a few days…suckin' tail."

Even Delucci's friends broke up. Jeep flushed, then he grinned tightly and threw a half salute toward Joe. Hunt had surprised him. Skis was no less startled. He'd known Joe Hunt for 60 years and had never heard him tell that story. He knew it would get around. Delucci would have a hard time shaking the image of a tail-sucking pup who refused to listen to sound advice. It had been a flash of the young Joe Hunt, the Joe from the 1932 Strike, from a time before Joe was "a widely acknowledged elder statesman in the pantheon of the American labor movement."

"Now I got one last thang to say," Joe said as he stood with his back to Jeep and Biggie. "We are gonna find out about these brothers. We're gonna mourn for the dead. And we're gonna celebrate the ones who lived through this. And if UNICOAL's been negligent, the Union'll take 'em to the mat. Take 'em to court. Whatever needs to be done, the Union'll do it. I'll do it."

Joe walked along the edge of the crowd and stopped in front of Susie Rutherford.

"Ma'am," he said softly so that bystanders had a hard time hearing his words, "I'm terrible sorry 'bout what happened to Willie. Sounds like his buddies just about got 'im out and then all of 'em got caught. But he still may come out okay. I didn't know him personal, or any of 'em. But they are good men. Good husbands and fathers. Good Union men. If any of 'em don't make it, I'll person'lly make sure the widder's pensions and bereavement benefit starts right away. No waitin'. And I'll have one of the Union lawyers see about suing the Comp'ny over negligence."

Susie Rutherford faced the man whose picture stared at her each month from the back cover of the ACMU Advocate as she walked it from her mailbox into her kitchen. He looked older in person. His large fleshy face hung loosely. His cheeks and jowls drooped like a bloodhound's. He sounded sincere and looked concerned. Still, Susie Rutherford had never cared to be close to large, sweating white men.

"Thank you, Mr. Hunt. I hope you can do somethin' for the miners like Willie. To make their work a little better and safer."

"I'm tryin', ma'am. I pray your man and the rest pull through. Here's my card. You call me, personal, any time."

Joe turned toward the office and walked toward Jeep. Sweat dripped from his chin. He wiped at it with his sleeve. His damp collar chafed. He felt tired. His big body sagged, his thighs and arms felt heavy. He felt his belly straining against his belt. Sweat stains were spreading from his armpits. Joe wanted to get out of the sun and into the air-conditioning. His temper had shortened as the temperature rose. He wanted a cold pop with ice chips he could chew. He wanted to sort this out with Skis.

Jeep positioned himself between Joe and his path up the steps to the office. Jeep looked down on Joe's bare head, glistening in the sun. Jeep, too, was hot, but he was not cranky or impulsive. West Virginia heat had never seemed that bad after spending the better part of a year in the Mekong Delta where he and Biggie had survived by channeling discomfort into focused, controlled aggression. Jeep didn't move when Joe indicated he wanted to walk up the steps.

Joe squinted with his face upturned. The sun was almost in his eyes. "Let's lay the politics down, Jeep, until this thang is over," he said mildly. "Reporters an' all. Come on. Grow up."

Jeep spoke loudly with confidence. "As President of District 17, I'm askin' you to call a National Day of Mourning for our brothers who've been killed today in this mine. It says you can do that in the Contract and our Constitution. No work on that day."

A couple of miners moved in behind Joe Hunt, then several more, then about two dozen. Behind Jeep and Biggie, a handful of younger guys stood together.

Becker saw the sides take shape as he stood between Allyson and Julie. It's like high school, he thought. Images came back to him from a decade earlier. Black kids welling up against white kids at the Peabody flagpole at 3 p.m. Over what? Nothing and everything.

"What are they doing?" Allyson whispered.

Julie Cogswell didn't laugh. But it amused her that smart, "liberated women" of her generation never understood why the toilet wasn't working and what men were going to do next.

"They're fixin' to extend their discussion by other means, cupcake," Julie said to Allyson.

Allyson bristled. People did not treat her with condescension, particularly women.

"I think it's time for me to stop being a campaign manager," Becker said, handing his eyeglasses to Allyson.

"What should I do with them?" Allyson asked.

"For starters, hold them."

"Jeffrey…this is tribal," Allyson said, watching battle lines being drawn. "You're not a participant anthropologist! You're a lawyer!"

"They disbar lawyers for stealing from their clients, not for getting into a fistfight."

"That's not what I meant," Allyson said.

"I know," he said.

Julie Cogswell put her hand on Becker's shoulder. "Dad always told me to duck the first punch and come up swinging. It worked for me in third grade."

Becker edged behind the group that was behind Delucci. He had been careful not to trip while walking up the steps, which had been a little blurry without his glasses.

Julie strolled over to the Red Cross food trailer. She asked for a bottle of water and some clean paper towels.

Allyson had never seen a high-school fistfight, let alone a brawl. She would, however, admit to engaging in a little justifiable stick-slashing for The Baldwin School's field-hockey team. She was comfortable with her pacifist's mother's simple-no-exception rule: Human beings should not knowingly do physical harm to other human beings under any circumstances.

"It's the exceptions, dear, that lead us into predicaments," Boo warned her.

The impending violence made Allyson nauseous, but she couldn't take her eyes from the scene. What should I do to stop this? she asked herself. The memory of being beaten by New York City cops at Columbia in 1968 flashed back. She considered curling into a civil-rights-worker fetal ball between the two sides. "You put the load right on me" went through her mind. But she did nothing, hypnotized by forces she did not feel.

Charlie Frazier and Owen Paige, without a word or look between them, hurried over to the bathhouse, out of the way and in the shade but with a clear line of vision.

Julie Cogswell watched from the Red Cross tent. Unlike Allyson, she had seen her share of fights and was not a pacifist.

Joe Hunt was hot, frustrated, tired and angrier than a bucking bull being ridden into the dirt. But he didn't want a fight. Not in front of television cameras.

"Come on, Jeep. I'll work with you as soon as I find out what happened underground."

"That's not good enough, Joe. Not no more. We gotta show the comp'nies the Union'll stick up for safety. We gotta slow down the speed-up. We done stuck our butts in the air long enough."

That pissed off Joe Hunt, the old Joe Hunt.

"You listen here, you little stink-nose pup. I'm runnin' this Union until the membership says different. An' I say we'll settle this later, in private, you an' me. Now get the hell out of my way!"

"I may be a tail-suckin' pup," Delucci said, "but everyone knows you been suckin' the comp'ny tit for years."

Comp'ny suck. That did it for Joe Hunt. The accusation lifted the years. His mind cleared. He had a plan.

Joe started up the steps with Skis on his right. His supporters packed in, moving them forward and up. Joe had his big right hand clenched. It wasn't the rock-hard fist of a handloader from the 1930s, but it was still big and heavy, and, under the manicure, it was still a coal-miner's fist.

Jeep Delucci didn't move.

Joe had had enough talk. He threw his right toward Delucci's heart. But the punch snagged on Skis and landed on Jeep's arm. Off-balance, Joe lurched forward.

Jeep calmly kicked Joe Hunt in the pillow of his belly. Joe doubled over, his breath leaving in a rush. Jeep banged once on Joe's head with his fist as if he was pounding a podium. Joe fell flat on the ground.

Skis tried to pull Joe backward, but the Hunt crowd blocked the way. They wanted to get at Jeep. Kicking the president of 125,000 coal miners in his gut was an insult, a low-class, honky-tonk play. Skis dove on top of Joe to protect him.

Biggie Stover spread his legs into the basic karate stance, left leg forward and bent, right leg straight back. He squared his hips, bounced and drew his right hand back while he pushed his left fist forward. The Hunt guys in front of him stopped. They were ready for a bar fight, but not a 6-6 "Billy Jack," a movie they all loved. The guys in front lurched toward him, pushed from behind. Biggie moved faster than anyone expected, throwing karate punches into their chests and noses. Three miners dropped, blocking the way up the steps.

"WATCH OUT! HE KNOWS THAT JAP SHIT," someone shouted.

Jeep brought the sides of his fists down on the back of Skis' neck. Skis and Joe were out of the fight.

The melee spread. Hunt's miners gave Biggie room, keeping him focused while trying to stay out of range.

"TACKLE THE SUMBITCH!"

A miner who'd played linebacker at Montcalm High School came toward him low. Biggie brought his knee up and knocked him cold with a blow to his forehead. That gave the others a chance to come in closer. Biggie started putting them down with uppercuts to the chin and kicks to the knee. Those who were left standing decided to find some Delucci supporters who weren't instant disability. Biggie laughed.

The fight spread up and down the steps. Biggie stuck close to Jeep who had picked up a little karate and judo in the infantry and later from Biggie. As long as Biggie was on his feet, they were confident.

Jeep's side was outnumbered, but Biggie had put eight out of the fight at the start and discouraged a similar number from doing much of anything except sniping a punch around the edges. Jeep's supporters had circled up like musk ox under attack and held their own. Joe's guys could not break their unity.

Jeep took a few punches but stayed in it.

A middle-aged miner targeted Becker who was standing near the office door. He looped a wild roundhouse punch at Becker who ducked. The man leaned forward. Becker, who had seen Jeep hit Skis, chopped him to the ground with the side of his closed fist. Where'd that come from? he asked himself. As he was questioning himself, a second miner ran Becker into the side of the building. Becker grabbed the guy and wrestled him to the ground where they rolled around for a while without anyone getting hurt. Then a third miner kicked Becker in the ear with a heavy boot. He went starry, then black. He remembered someone yanking him up and pushing him out of the fight. He sat next to the building in the shade, trying to regain his senses.

At that point, police separated the sides, which were more than willing to have an excuse to stop. Three or four dozen coal miners stood trying to catch their breath while at the same time trying to look ready to start again, which none were.

"LET 'IM UP. GIVE 'IM SOME AIR."

Skis heard the words. Maybe he was shouting them; maybe not. He was pulled off Joe who was helped to his feet. Blood ran from a scrape on Joe's forehead, a wound that bled a lot but wasn't serious.

UNICOAL supervisors boiled out of the office. They helped separate and settle the miners with little resistance.

Becker got to his feet. He was dazed. He couldn't see clearly. Concussion, he thought. Brain's scrambled. He kept shaking his head, which made things worse.

"Here, hold this against your ear."

Julie was standing in front of him, holding wet paper towels. She put a pad over his ear and then lifted his hand to hold it in place.

"Our hero," she laughed.

"What happened?"

"Well, honey, you were doin' just fine until that little squirt over there kicked you upside yo' head, as the brothers say, when you were exchanging pleasantries on the ground with that other little squirt. Looked like you were making out with him to tell the truth."

"My head hurts."

"Imagine it does," she said. "Swaller these," she said, giving him the water bottle and three aspirins from her purse.

"Who got me out of it?" he asked her.

She cocked her head toward Biggie. "Looked like he was having a ball."

"Who won?"

"You lost, but I'd say Jeep's side came out better than Joe's," she said. "Come on. I'll walk you over to the First-Aid. Good thing you got into a fight at a mine disaster. Top quality emergency medical care's available for the asking. The EMTs and docs have been looking for somebody to work on. And here you are. Along with two dozen other walkin' wounded. Damn good fight if you ask me."

Allyson came over. Her faced was contorted. "You're bleeding. Jeffrey, you're bleeding. What can I do?"

"I need to get to a doc. And sit down. Maybe lie down. Have a headache."

"X-rays. You need them. I know a neurologist in Pittsburgh. He works with the Steelers."

Julie took Becker's arm and walked him through the crowd to where the medical people were set up. Allyson did not follow.

Joe Hunt knew he had not landed a single punch. And now his head was throbbing. He was standing, gasping and humiliated. He wanted to lay one clean lick on Delucci, just one. He started toward him.

"JOE. JOE!" John-Cee shouted his name above the crowd noise. "We need you. We'll get you cleaned up in here. Forget it."

Joe looked at Jeep and then at John-Cee.

"This ain't settled, Delucci," he spat and staggered into the office with John-Cee on one side and Skis stumbling along on the other.

"That's right, asshole!" Jeep shouted. "Time to go in. You Goddamn comp'ny suck!"

Owen Paige was delighted. "This one will make the A-wire," he said to Charlie Frazier. "One half of the ol' proletariat trying to kill the other half. My lagging career may have a new trajectory—boxing columnist. Someone might buy me lunch or a mixed drink."

Allyson Pickering felt as if she had been knocked down, which she hadn't been, and scraped up, which was a total self-delusion, and bounced around in the backwash, which, indeed, had been the case. Pummeled, she thought, I feel pummeled by this ridiculous violence that served no end and accomplished nothing. I am offended. Charlie and Owen helped to settle her in their shade.

"Not trying to be a sexist pig or anything," Charlie said, "but you look rattled by the squabble in the brotherhood."

"I've never seen anything like that," she said.

"Well, damn, neither have I," Charlie said. "Did you see that big guy next to Delucci? Stover. He was like Charlie Chan."

"I believe you mean, Jackie," Owen said, with a little gloat. *Jackie* Chan."

"Some en-*chan*-ted morning if you ask me," Charlie countered.

Allyson asked for coffee. Charlie headed for the Red Cross where he thought he might celebrate an easy feature with a couple of boiled hot dogs.

"I feel violated," she said.

"It wasn't about you, darlin'," Owen said.

"It was like blood-sport gladiators in the Colosseum."

"You have to look at all sides of these people," Owen said to Allyson. "Not just what they do that you like."

He started writing in his notebook. "Have to get to a phone quick. Charlie will be back in a minute."

"Sure." Allyson took out her own notebook and tried to write a lead sentence. In the space of 30 minutes, she had experienced at least three fatalities and a rumble in some Godforsaken West Virginia valley where Hatfields might still be gunning for McCoys for all she knew. Culture shock, she said to herself, I'm in culture shock.

Then she started: "Three deaths were reported around noon at…."

Becker and Julie walked out of the first-aid station.

"You'll live," she said. "It's a great head bandage. Want me to take a picture for my next edition? Or your grandkids?"

"Please, no. Thanks for getting my glasses from Allyson," he said.

"She was, um, processin' a sepulchral mood," Julie laughed.

"Everything is personal with her," he said.

Julie waited.

"I knew her. We spent a spring and summer together. 1968."

"Bad year. I thought something was back there."

"She bailed out."

"Perfectly understandable."

"She wanted a career on the national stage. She wanted to follow her feminist star."

"An actress! I should have guessed. And what did you want?" Julie asked.

"Purpose. Do no harm. Keep clear of money. Be useful. Do good."

"Did you love her?"

"Maybe," he said.

"Uh oh. One of those."

"One of what?" he asked.

"Too much college. Too much rational analysis. Too much pooh-poohing the other side of your brain. Too much fear."

"Yes," he conceded, "I guess I did."

"Better answer," she said. "Do still?"

"Hey. My head hurts. Let's give me a break."

"It's easier to survive a break than a bend. A break can heal good as new. A bend stretches you out. You might never snap back. Which is it with her?"

"Why are you asking?"

"I'm a reporter. Just trying to get the story straight."

"It's sort of none of your business," he said.

"Maybe."

"Maybe?"

"Maybe."

"Are you the girl in a flatbed Ford slowin' down to take a look at me?"

"Ah, boys and their fantasies. I ain't no rattletrap Ford flatbed, champ. I'm a heavy Chevy."

Becker looked carefully at Julie Cogswell. She returned his look. Eye to eye. Neither blinked.

"Maybe I should duck," he said.

"Always a good first move. Then what?"

"I have a lot going on right now."

278

"I'd say, based on what you haven't said, you two were a bend."

"I dunno," Becker said.

"Is that right? Well, it's something to think about," she said, ending whatever was going on for the time being.

"My head hurts," he said. "My ear is ringing."

"School bells or tinkerbells?"

"Cow bells."

"Cow bells—you'll live. You're a hero. Take your new ding-dongs over there to Jeep and Biggie. They'll tell you how proud of you they are. It'll make you feel better."

"How do you know so much?"

"I know guys like you, Becker. I know guys like Jeep. I grew up with them. It's not hard to fill in the blanks."

This girl is too fast, or too something, for me, Becker thought despite always liking smart girls, women.

"Next time I'm in Charleston," she said, "I'd like to set up an interview with Jeep."

"Sure."

"Maybe we can have dinner," she said.

"Sure. I'll arrange it."

"Not with him, dummy," she said. "With you."

"Oh."

"I'm cutting you some slack given your injury."

"I don't think Charleston can match Bloomingrose Holler for entertainment," he said.

"My expectations of our future visit are modest. Let's say, 'realistic.' I'll call."

Julie Cogswell walked toward the mine office and went through the door.

The police arrested no one. Nobody wanted to press charges against anyone. Those who needed tending were sitting together in first-aid or standing in line. No one left the area.

The families of Willie Rutherford's crew were standing near the portal from which answers would be coming.

Charlie and Owen called in their stories. They stood together, smoking, away from the families.

"That might have been the Pickett's charge, the high-water mark of the Delucci rebellion," Charlie said. "'Tail-suckin' pup' will get around."

"This wasn't Gettysburg," Owen said, shaking his head. "This, my provincial friend, was guerrilla theater. And we were part of the intended audience. The most honest thing we could do is report it as a contrivance, a stunt."

"All those who are gonna ruin the moment kindly raise your ink-stained hand," Charlie laughed.

"Come now, we waiters," Owen said, "not to announce the menu but to stir the soup."

Biggie Stover drew on the cigar he had purchased earlier that day when they had stopped for gas in Beckley.

Biggie felt good. He didn't mind getting into fights.

Delucci did. He had a cut lip.

Becker's head throbbed.

They were watching the portal from folding chairs under the Red Cross tent.

"Yes sir," Biggie boasted, "we did just fine. D'ya see our lawyer, Jeep? Chopped some guy like he knew what he was a-doin'."

"I'm just a tomcat," Becker mumbled just before swallowing two aspirin with a pint of milk. "Wildcat, not tomcat."

"I think we sent a message," Jeep said. "Who was standin' up for the men; who was kissin' ass."

"And then there was who was suckin' tail," Biggie mentioned with a grin.

"I was the one standin' at the end. Joe Hunt was at my feet with Sonoski layin' on top of 'im. That's the picture I hope those reporters run."

"I'll check it out," Becker said. "Photo of reform-minded challenger bloody but on his feet."

"Hell of a line, I come up with: 'Coal should be mined safely or not at all.' Damn good!"

"What's it mean?" Becker asked.

"It means I'll get the operators and the bureaucrats to do a better job. That's what it means."

"Sounded like you were calling for a strike over safety," Becker said. "A stop-the-speed-up strike."

"A strike *would* send a message," Biggie said. "Doesn't have to be long. It does have to be long enough to make the point."

"Well, Beck, it could mean a strike, and it could mean a lot of thangs between doin' nothin' and a strike," Jeep added. "We'll find its meaning as we go forward."

"If you call a strike over safety, the non-Union companies will sell the coal that ACMU operations aren't producing," Becker said.

"You're ever helpful," Jeep said.

"It's a great slogan," Becker said. "It tells the guys where your heart is, and what you're going to focus on. But you may get asked for specifics. We need to think this through."

"I agree," Jeep said.

280

"I don't want the campaign to promise changes that we aren't going to do or can't make happen," Becker said. "If you raise expectations and don't meet them, people will say you were just another politician out campaigning."

"I won't succeed at everything. I'll make mistakes. But you know I want what's best for the men."

"Women, too," Becker said. "A few were hired this year."

"I dunno about that," Biggie said. "They'll take a job away from a man."

"They have a right to a job just like anyone else," Becker said. "Moms have kids to support just like Dads."

"I know a few girls who'd make it," Jeep said. "They'd have it rough, though. From our guys."

"What'll you say if you're questioned about it?" Becker asked.

"I'll say the comp'nies do the hiring, not the Union. Anyone who's hired under our Contract is a brother or a sister. Simple."

"I'm against it," Biggie said, "but there ain't no percentage in fightin' a losing battle."

"Okay," Becker said. "One other thing. Did you two plan this fight?"

"Becker," Biggie said, "could two ig'nrant hillbillies like us who are too inbred to butter our own bread plan anythin' as complicated as a free-for-all?"

"I take that as a Yes."

"Sure, we could've planned somethin'," Biggie said. "That ain't sayin' we did."

"Biggie's playin' with your head," Jeep said. "We won the nominatin' round one way. We outsmarted Joe. Caught him sleepin'. Now we gotta adapt to new circumstances."

"Words are words," Biggie said, taking a deep draw. He blew a perfect smoke ring with back spin.

Becker shook his head, partly in genuine amazement, partly in anger. Wrong move—shaking made his head hurt.

"Beck, you need to know some, not all," Biggie said.

"Some thangs aren't *planned* planned," Jeep said. "Then again some thangs aren't not planned either. Some thangs happen, just because."

'Because' is not a reason or an answer, Becker thought. How many times had his father said that to him as a kid? They didn't trust him. They never would. He wasn't from their tribe. They were right—he didn't need to know everything. But he did need to know the things that could come back to bite him. Or maybe it was better not to know those things.

Becker considered asking about the two guys on Lens Creek Mountain, and then he didn't. But he couldn't free himself of the question: What kind of guy was he working for?

"We nimble," Biggie said.

"Yeah," Becker said, "we nimble."

Allyson Pickering sat on a chair in the American Eagle office, waiting for Davey Bloom to pick up. She was still trembling. She found her sweaty legs and back sticking to "the hide of the wild Nauga," as her college roommates put it. College was a long time ago.

She was glad to be in air-conditioning and away from what she had seen men do to each other. Fists smashing faces kept playing in her mind. She noticed the wall plaques that celebrated American Eagle's good works—United Way, Welch Lions Club, Ruritans, sponsor of ball teams, patron of the hospital. Some reporter, she thought, she still didn't know whether Rutherford was alive or dead. She held the receiver in the crook of her neck as the transcriber read her story back to her.

Allyson was angry—at herself for being her mother's daughter; at Becker for acting like a hooligan, like one of those miners; at herself for letting Julie Cogswell make a move while she was counting posies; at these men who had offended her with their violence; at the coal industry for accepting this behavior as normal. Joe Hunt, Jeep Delucci, Johnson C. Smithers, Willie Rutherford, Biggie Stover, Julie Cogswell, Owen Paige, Charlie Frazier—inmates all in one asylum, in her opinion. She felt herself getting stuck in this crazy goo like Uncle Remus's Tar-Baby.

Jeffrey Becker. Becker…was the best guy she'd dated. Which could say a lot for him or not much for her, she thought. He was still in her head and had never drifted very far. Had she loved him? Maybe. More than maybe, but maybe not all out.

It could have been stagecraft. Delucci could have set it up, picked a fight with the old fart and not let him back out. Or it could have just happened spontaneously.

Davey Bloom came on. "I'm reading as we're talking."

"Three confirmed deaths," she summarized. "I'll update as soon as they make the announcements. I haven't seen anybody or any bodies come out of the mine as yet."

"Big fight, huh?"

"My first. I'm not counting the time I pulled my sister's hair and was sent to my room."

"Recently, huh?"

"Little bitch deserved worse."

Davey laughed.

"I was, as you know, also at Columbia when students and cops expressed their affection for each other. I got knocked around in that melee."

"You hurt?"

"No. Rattled, yes."

"I'm pulling wire photos. Hey. Here's one off a TV feed with Delucci standing over Joe Hunt who's on the ground and being covered up by some guy."

"The guy is Larry Sonoski. He works at headquarters, I was told. Joe's childhood friend."

"I'll run it. Yeah, I remember both of 'em," Davey said. "Hunt was a big kid who looked a little dangerous. Sonoski had some subtlety. Forty-three years back."

"You've told me. The fight goes to Delucci. I quoted Hunt's good line about the pup, and what Delucci said about 'Coal should be mined safely or not at all.'"

"What's it mean?"

"Delucci wants a National Day of Mourning to be declared. It's a one-day stoppage. He might have staged this fight. Deliberately."

"You'll never get confirmation. Don't waste your time. Did you pick up anything on the two Pittsburghers who got whacked?"

"Nothing. But I think Delucci did it, or was behind it, or knew about it in advance, at least. Or gave a wink and a nod. Or maybe he was intentionally kept out of the loop."

"JESUS! Is any of that more than speculation? Or a hunch? Or woman's intuition? Is it something you can support with more than your pretty face?"

"Hunch, at this point. I have a source, an old boyfriend who is the MDU campaign manager. Jeffrey Becker."

"He told you this?"

"No. I think he doesn't know either, and it's troubling him. He has flaws, but he's a lawyer, not a murderer. He's not a cover-up kind of guy."

Bloom dragged on his Chesterfield. "'Old boyfriend,' huh? How old? Did he dump you? I don't like this 'old-boyfriend' shit. He'll ask you for a favor, sooner or later. Don't like this shit."

"I left him. Summer of '68. Nothing's there."

"Is he single?"

"Yes."

"Are you sleeping with him?"

"No."

"Might that happen?"

"I don't think so. Unlikely. I'm not stupid."

"Smart doesn't count for much in matters of the lower regions. You got history, hon. You got hormones. You got means and opportunity. You got his shit in your head."

"That's one way of putting it," she laughed. "My mother would express the same sentiment differently."

"The answer is NO. NO. NO. This is bad, bad, bad. Either he'll compromise you or you will compromise him. Or both. Don't use him as a primary source on anything. I'd say don't use him at all. It's way too chancy. For you."

"Agreed."

"And what kind of guy would rat out his employer to a reporter?"

"A scared guy? One who doesn't want to go to jail for conspiracy or perjury. Becker signed up to make history, not excuse crimes."

"Maybe I should take you off this story, hon."

"No. I am not a rookie," she said.

"Stick your hand in a cesspool like a union election, and it won't come out smellin' like a rose," Bloom said.

"I picked up another angle," Allyson said, "a Fricktown man, Gus Olin. Maybe you remember him?"

"I do," Bloom said. "Smartest cookie in that sorry jar."

"There was a fire during a strike. In the department store. The mine's superintendent was probably inside and killed."

"Commissary. It's where the company kept stuff to sell. So?"

"Maybe Gus Olin knows something."

"Where'd you get this?"

"Can't tell you quite yet."

"JESUS!" Davey swore.

"Say the Lord's name some more, and we'll need to arrange a conversion."

"Fricktown! All right. Get the disaster story. Number of killed, injured, excuses and so on. Then stop at Fricktown on the way home if you must. Gus Olin is not going to give you a scoop on who killed Frank Gallagher or how it was done. But you can pan the sluice and see if anything's there when the mud clears. Just keep your head down, honey."

"That advice now has more relevance to me than the last time you gave it."

Davey Bloom considered Fricktown an industrial tar pit: Stick a toe in it, and you were stuck forever. He stubbed out his cigarette and thought of his reporter.

The men sat around a long, rectangular table in the conference room as if they were in contract negotiations: management on one side with John-Cee Smithers in the center and Fletcher Waddington next to him, and Joe Hunt, on the other, facing him. No one sat at either end. Skis sat on one side of Joe; Foster Shives, Union counsel from Washington, on the other.

John Stefanik was still in his coal-blackened overalls and miner's boots. His hardhat rested on the table. He had yet to wash his face or hands.

"They were heroes. Each and every one of them. Management and labor alike. Volunteers. Against my advice. Genuine heroes. I told them not to do it. They were almost out, almost clear of the bad top. Wasn't but another few yards to safety. They were carrying Willie on a stretcher. I started moving toward them. To help. They were almost into 12 Crosscut and good, bolted roof. Almost. Just another couple of feet. I never saw anything like that. I'm always sent in after the accident."

He choked up. The other men caught their breath. All could see the scene. Handkerchiefs came out. Noses were blown.

"Of the 10," Stefanik said, reading from a paper scrap, "we have seven fatalities—Delmer Estep, Lee Roy Stump, Arthur Smith -- they call him, 'Pins' -- Petey Jones, Darrell Dorsey, Timmy Buchanan and Billy Burdette. Willie Rutherford, Byron Lewis and Mike Decker survived. Willie has a bad leg and knee from the original fall. He also had some ribs broke in the second fall. Byron and Mike—different things. Byron—some internal injuries the docs underground weren't sure about. Decker probably has a concussion and real serious injuries. They were so close to being safe."

"We'll take care of the widows," John-Cee said. "That's of no concern at this table."

"It looked like the roof came down from 12 Crosscut where I was to where Darrell Dorsey's miner cut in to Rutherford's miner. Must have been 40 feet or more. All at once."

"What do you mean 'cut in'?" John-Cee asked.

John Stefanik had dreaded this moment. "Like this. They decided to dig a parallel entry through the coal next to Two North, because its roof kept coming down as they went forward. Dorsey cut in where he thought Rutherford was trapped. Punched through three or four feet of coal. Bullseye breakthrough. Pulled Rutherford free. They were walking him out on a stretcher. That's when the roof in the rescue tunnel came down."

John-Cee Smithers was processing information as fast as he could. "There was no parallel tunnel in the rescue plan," he said.

"Right. They changed the plan on their own initiative," John said. "I advised against it. They didn't call in for approval up here."

John-Cee had known Delmer Estep from his superintendent's first year at American Eagle. He wondered how Delmer could have done something so blatantly contrary to UNICOAL policy, so unauthorized by federal authorities, so counter to his own experience. Such an act might now make UNICOAL negligent, reckless, capricious and whatever other damn charge a plaintiff's lawyer would throw against the Company. Delmer and Lee Roy were official agents of UNICOAL, so UNICOAL was the wallet that would pay. There would have been no parallel entry had Delmer not approved.

"Why didn't he call me for a yes or no? He knew I was here."

"I can't say for sure. I think he thought it was the best chance of getting to Rutherford before his time ran out. The clock was ticking fast on him."

"Shit," Joe Hunt said. "Ya mean they was runnin' a wildcat kind of rescue?"

"They were off the approved plan," Stefanik said. "They all volunteered to go up parallel...without bolting. Just some timber props."

No one said anything. This news was so unexpected, so startling, so radical, that it left everyone without even the handiest expletives.

"No bolting?" John-Cee asked. "Can that be possible?"

"I told them not to do it. To stick with the plan."

"Who authorized the parallel tunnel and no bolting?" John-Cee asked.

"Well, it was sort of a group decision," Stefanik said haltingly.

"This Company does not make 'group decisions' like that," John-Cee roared. "Hourly employees are not part of planning and decisions."

John Stefanik figured that MESA would either bury him in a broom closet or transfer him to Attu Island, the closest America came to Siberia. Maybe he would be fired and made the scapegoat. Maybe he would serve time.

"It was Pins," John said. "That Artie Smith, he suggested the idea. The miners volunteered. Then Delmer and Lee Roy threw in with them. All the miners agreed the Company wouldn't be liable for anything that happened to them. Lee Roy said he would stand for any damage to equipment. They didn't bolt, because the bolts weren't holding. They figured the timbers against the sandstone would give them enough time to cut the tunnel, get to Rutherford and get out. Dorsey cut the entry and the others propped up. Decker lifted a rock that was pinning Rutherford. He and Smith got him out. Delmer and Lee Roy were with them when they were carrying Rutherford out on the stretcher. They had been hauling supplies in the scoops. If they'd stayed where I was in 12 Crosscut, they would not have been killed."

The men looked at John Stefanik.

"You stayed in 12?" Joe Hunt asked.

"Yes."

"Tragic," Fletch Waddington mumbled.

"Tragic," Foster Shives agreed.

"I don't know what to say," John-Cee said. "This might have been avoided. We might have lost one man, Rutherford, but not seven. Lawyers will eat me alive."

Fletch Waddington imagined picking clean a turkey carcass. UNICOAL could be made to look heroic, he supposed, but not blameless and not without full liability. Delmer Estep ignored and violated the approved rescue plan without authorization. The Company could not fund enough contributions to the Pittsburgh Symphony and free hat days at Three Rivers Stadium to offset this error, he thought. Stefanik would testify truthfully. It would be best to cut the loss as soon as possible. Settle with the widows quickly.

286

"The Union may be liable, too," John-Cee said to Foster Shives who was doodling interlocking cubes on his yellow legal pad. "Delmer's widow and Lee Roy's might sue you for the actions of your members. What a fine fucking mess! Why in the hell didn't you stop it?"

"I spoke against it," Stefanik said.

"You 'spoke against it.' The awesome power of the federal government."

"They wanted to do it," Stefanik said.

"Tell me again," Joe said. "The miners -- all of 'em -- volunteered?"

"…and they all agreed the Company wasn't liable if anything bad happened."

"Did they put this on paper and sign it?" Fletcher Waddington asked.

John Stefanik looked at Waddington as if he were hanging snot. "No, they didn't put it on paper and sign it. They also didn't have their non-existent signatures notarized."

"Careful," Fletcher said. "I didn't fuck up. You did."

"And the supervisors didn't go in with 'em?" Joe asked.

"In and out. They were in when Willie was on the stretcher."

Joe felt whipped. Another bad thing had piled on top of many other bad things.

"Ya know, John-Cee," Joe said, "I've been in coal with you guys for a long time. On the Union side. An' it's always our people who get themselves smashed and killed. What I said to them reporters is true. UNICOAL is the best of your bunch on safety. But I'm just tired of going to Union funerals. I been doin' it all my damn life. Ever since I was a kid in Fricktown."

John-Cee spoke softly. "I appreciate what you said out there to the reporters and your members. I appreciate what you just said right here. It takes guts to say the unpopular truth about UNICOAL. We are the biggest, the most important operator. We're an easy target. We…I won't forget it. We'll work with you on this. Make it right as we can, all the way around. I promise this to you."

He paused.

"It's a hard business we're in, both of us. It's just a damn hard way to make a buck."

The men at the table felt the sorrow that had come from the depths of Bloomingrose Holler was now something different, something more. No one could be sure what it was or might become.

Chapter 19

Washington, D.C., October 14, 1975

Foster Shives had always benefited from being typical, ordinary, presentable and carefully trimmed. He wasn't quite six-feet tall with an unremarkable nose above decent teeth. He was thin without being skinny. He liked to walk in the mornings in his Bethesda neighborhood, greeting others. At 57, his graying hair was still thick. The fleshiness he saw creeping into his cheeks and the loosening he saw around his mouth were, he accepted, semaphores of the lifelong self-doubts he had tried to conceal. He had the odd habit of tilting his head like a puzzled turtle when he was lost in thought. If an observer noticed anything unusual about Foster Shives, it was his inability to smile without opening his mouth. For that reasons, his grade-school classmates called him "Fishy."

Foster grew up outside of Newton, Iowa, on 160 down-at-the-heels acres his father inherited in 1928. His parents were humbled children of failed farmers.

His father, Edmund, finished breakfast on a dreary morning in December, 1932. The auction notice lay next to his bowl of oatmeal—no sugar, no milk.

Saturday, 10 a.m. sharp.
For failure to satisfy a mortgage lien held by
First and Citizens Bank of Newton

Edmund had run out of ideas, pleas and wiggles. Begging had not worked; it never did. Prices for corn and hogs had fallen steadily in the '20s as American farmers produced more and more of both. Abundance drove down prices. Edmund's family could squeak by on the food they raised, but he needed cash to pay property taxes and meet the payment on the $3,000 mortgage he had taken in 1929 just before The Crash.

In August of 1932, Edmund said to his wife, Jean: "It's over. I can't make it on eight-cent-a-bushel corn, gettin' 35 bushels an acre on the 50 of ours that's tillable. That ain't even $150 for this whole year's labor. And that ain't countin' expenses for seed and the rest. Might as well go on welfare and see our names in the newspaper. I can't make the mortgage."

"What sin did we do to deserve this?" Jean asked.

"We farm for a livin'. That's our sin."

"Farmin' ain't sinnin'," she said.

repeated each day as the DOW slid lower slowly. He felt the way his father felt in 1932.

The partners suspected Foster was having financial troubles, but none were interested in lending either money or a sympathetic ear. They tolerated his limited practice even though it barely covered his salary and yearly bonus. He had, after all, arranged favorable mortgages for them with the ABW. Several had borrowed to buy and renovate run-down, 19th-Century rowhouses on about-to-be gentrified streets east of Dupont Circle. Foster didn't blame them for dismissing him. He was not generating new business. Their disappointment reflected his own. He felt slightly backward and held in place by the limitations of his Iowa youth. "If you come from nothing," he'd say to himself in his darkest, private moments, "you end up with nothing. It's the Iron Law of Ancestry."

Foster had never believed he could be a first-rank lawyer who belonged in the thick of Washington's wheeling and dealing. While no partner ever mentioned it, he was aware that he alone had graduated from a state law school. It was a mark against him, a scarlet "I" for Iowa. Among themselves, the partners referred to Foster as "Shorty"—because they knew he was never quite able to get his ends to meet. When he overheard the name, he was thankful they had never heard him called "Fishy."

By the time of the 1975 ACMU election, Foster was totally beholden to Joe Hunt for his livelihood and equally resentful of his dependency. He blamed Hunt for his stagnancy, for being captive.

Foster Shives unlatched the Rococo wrought-iron gate that was set into the distressed-brick wall. He could not miss the large S that was entwined in the middle of the metalwork's fuss and fancy. A cobble-stone courtyard separated the four-story building from 19th Street, near the corner of Q Street in Northwest Washington. A security camera was pointed at the gate. Another was aimed at the locked building entrance. The building carried no nameplates.

Foster pressed the buzzer. An all-business female voice requested his name and the person he wished to see. After he answered, a uniformed guard appeared and escorted him into a private elevator that took them to a security lock on the top floor. Foster looked at the arm patch on the guard's uniform, "Ultimate Protection, Inc." He'd never heard of the company. A secretary activated the sliding glass door and indicated Foster should sit on a sofa in the corner. He noticed a security camera pointed at his seat. The pictures on the wall were nondescript. The reading material laid out in neat, overlapping, publication-specific rows was conventional—Reader's Digest, Business Week, The Wall Street Journal. He sat on the sofa, looking around without turning his head.

After more minutes than were necessary, the secretary motioned toward a door, "Go in."

Foster went in.

A man stood facing a window that looked out on 19th Street. "Have a seat. In the chair."

Foster sat in the office's one chair, which was positioned in front of a highly polished walnut desk that was clear of all paper.

"We haven't met before," Thomas A. "Chickie" Siciliano said as he turned and walked to his side of his desk. He sat. He did not offer his hand.

"Right," Foster said as he settled into his chair, the comfort of his briefcase by his side.

"But I know of you by reputation," Chickie said.

"Something positive, I hope," Foster said.

Chickie stared at Foster without saying anything. The silence made Foster uneasy. "My associates and me are looking for a lawyer."

"I have a narrowly focused practice," Foster said. "I represent the American Coal Miner's Union and the American Bank of Washington."

"I understand. Are you open to another client?"

"Certainly, assuming I can help. This tragedy at the American Eagle mine might be taking a lot of my time."

"I understand," Chickie said. "The assistance we need won't take much of your time. It's about a few things related to the Union and the Bank. We are buying 100 percent of the ABW's stock for more than full market value."

"Yes," Foster said, though this was the first he'd heard of this deal. Why, he asked himself, had Joe not brought him in for advice?

"Joe Hunt has signed our purchase agreement. It will need to be approved by the Union's board of directors and the Bank's."

"That shouldn't be a hurdle. Those votes are *pro forma* when Joe wants something done."

"I want your help goin' forward," Chickie said.

"I have to be careful of conflict of interest," Foster said.

"No conflict of interest with me," Chickie said. "We want you to be our Bank lawyer after the sale. You'll be working closely with one or two of my lawyers. I want you in my corner before then to make the transition go smooth."

"Much appreciated."

"We want you…on the side," Chickie said.

"'On the side'?"

"I'll pay you directly without going through your firm," Chickie said.

"Why not go through Puddy, White on an hourly basis?"

"In cash," Chickie said. "For you. That's just how we work."

Foster said nothing. His brain was not completing the jigsaw puzzle, because he couldn't see the pieces clearly. Why cash? Why not through the firm?

"What legal services, what issues, do you see me handling?"

292

Got him! Chickie thought.

"Protectin' our interests," Chickie said.

"Well, of course, that," Foster said. "That's my responsibility to my client."

"That's it. Details will come up. Like this election."

"Yes. Quite a surprise, Joe losing the nomination round."

"You know Delucci?"

"I worked with him on a couple of arbitration cases. He's a District president. Late 20s, maybe 30. Dad's a miner with black lung. Did a tour in Vietnam with his friend, Stover. Has some kind of left-winger running his campaign. A lawyer. Jeffrey Becker. Don't think he ever had much of a private practice. Jeep's not married. I've seen him drink but never drunk. He's probably smoked marijuana."

"Really!" Chickie said.

"He's bright enough," Foster said. "You don't find many like him in the mines. Has ambition. He'll probably win the presidency some day."

"This December?"

"I wouldn't bet on it. Next time, after Joe retires."

"What does Delucci want?" Chickie asked. "Money?"

"I'm sure that's part of it," Foster said. "Sixty-thousand a year and big benefits as president is a lot more than the 20 he gets in District 17. He says he wants to improve things for the membership."

"Well, politicians have to promise some kind of shit to get elected, and then they have to do some shit to get reelected," Chickie said, dropping into his more natural speech. "The system don't work if politicians do nothin' but steal. Stealin' has to come second. Is he a Jesuit?"

"I don't think so," Foster said.

"A missionary type? A crusader?"

"He's Catholic. I don't think he's religious."

"Can he be bought?" Chickie asked.

Foster rolled his answer around, looking for a grip. "Most people, all people, I suppose, well, all politicians, probably have a price," he said. "No one's tried to buy him as far as I know."

"Does he need money?"

"Everyone needs money," Foster said.

"How's he fundin' his campaign—the office, staff, campaigning? That costs money."

"I don't know. He'll have to file reports with the Department of Labor. I'm assuming big contributions will be cash and not reported. Same with Joe—again I'm just assuming. Delucci's friend Stover owns a valuable coal property. I know some rank-and-filers have grumbled about that. But it's not cash. It's land he inherited. The coal rights have never been sold. He could take a loan against his land."

"Anything more about Delucci?"

"He has an apartment in Charleston. Walks the six or seven blocks to the District office. His mother and dad still live in Boone County. I've heard her described as a typical West Virginia wife, whatever that might mean. I don't know what it means, personally. I haven't heard anything scandalous."

"That's a start," Chickie said. "I want you to dig into him as part of your work for me. Here's the main thing. I don't want no *confusion* around the Bank's sale. It don't need to be a campaign issue. We've scheduled the closing for just after the election. I want no complications."

"Makes sense."

"I'd like you to set up a meeting with Delucci. You can be there as a neutral facilitator. That's the word, ain't it?"

"Sure. What's the meeting about?"

"Introductions. Friendly. Just a what's what."

"He might be a little suspicious of me, but I can do that."

Chickie pulled an envelope from his desk drawer. He slid it across his polished desk. Foster had to lean forward to take it.

"Twenty-five grand," Chickie said. "Retainer, isn't that what lawyers call it? I'm retainin' you."

Foster looked. One-hundred-dollar bills, 250 of them, he guessed. Used. The wad was an inch thick and wrapped in a rubber band.

"For what?"

"For you. I don't need no receipt. Don't want one."

Twenty-five-thousand dollars was one half of Foster's annual after-tax, take-home pay. He didn't have to turn the money over to the firm; his client would not like it if he did. Same with disclosing this new income on his 1040. He could start paying down the brokers who were hounding him. He'd be smart and pay them in a series of cash deliveries, a few thousand at a time. No suspicions would be raised. He would escape the debt that doomed his father.

"What kind of business are you in, Mr. Siciliano?" Foster asked.

"Investments," Chickie said. "We also run a small security firm called Ultimate Protection. I know it sounds like a cheap rubber."

Foster knew enough to laugh.

"Ultimate also does a little consulting, special assignments. Problem-solvin', you might say."

Foster hesitated, then chanced it: "Above board?"

"This Bank deal is straight-up business. That's all you need to know. We want you to help make sure it goes down like both sides want. No one wants no bumps in the road."

"Why did Joe sell?" Foster asked.

"Because we paid more than anyone else would pay."

"Why didn't you shy him down?" Foster asked.

294

"Didn't want no problems, no biddin' war. The ABW will be a good investment over the years," Chickie said. "You don't need to know nothin' more."

Foster was not stupid or naive. He knew Chickie Siciliano had, what were called in the white-glove firms that represented him, "connections." He had also heard that Chickie's associates owned legitimate Washington-area businesses—high-end steak houses, downtown parking lots, office buildings, a trucking company and real estate. Big-shot litigators represented Siciliano when needed, which wasn't often. His lawyers never got in trouble. If Joe had sold the Bank, it was not Foster's business to second guess him. A deal done is a done deal except in those instances when his client said it wasn't. That's how Foster Shives looked at it.

"I need to think about this," Foster said with a coyness that came across as phony as it was. He started to put the envelope back on the desk.

"No thinkin' needed," Chickie said. "You're either in now or you're out now. Simple, see."

It occurred to Foster that "out" could have several meanings. Foster realized that "out" was not an option.

"I suggest 'in,'" Chickie said.

Foster hesitated for a few seconds, his hand holding the envelope in the air. Then he tucked it into his suit jacket. "In."

"I'm a cash guy," Chickie said. "You need to be, too. Don't deposit this money in an account. No trails. It's just for you. Are you followin' what I said?"

"Yes."

"No trails. No payin' off your stockbroker in one dump. No squeezin' juice out of my orange. You'll be fine with this deal as long as you don't get no sticky fingers."

"Yes."

"Now let me ask you about Delucci a little more. You heard about those two from Pittsburgh who wound up dead."

"Yes."

"What do you know about it?"

"I don't *know* anything, really," Foster said. "It would be logical to suspect those two were Joe's supporters or they were hired by Joe to send a message to Delucci's people. But I've heard nothing like that. No one at the Union seems to know who they were. It's possible that Delucci set this whole thing up."

"Is he that smart?" Chickie asked. "Or ruthless?"

"You know these hillbillies can be rough customers."

"'Rough customers,'" Chickie said, grinning. "Haven't heard that in a long time. The West Virginia state cops are investigatin'."

"I understand that Delucci's Jeep was involved," Foster said, "but that may be just hearsay."

"I've heard some 'hearsay,' too. Heard the cops think there's a paint match or a metal match from his Jeep with a scrape on the car that went over the hill."

"I can't see Delucci being dumb enough to kill these fellows with his own car," Foster said.

"You sure these two guys were not Joe's boys?" Chickie asked.

"The Union checked. They weren't miners or retirees. I haven't seen any connection to Joe. Maybe it's a coal operator behind them."

"Maybe," Chickie said. He now knew that Foster Shives was not involved in Hunt's campaign and didn't know very much about what was going on. "When the bank sale gets nailed, you get another 75. Same way."

Foster tried not to look nonplussed or greedy. That kind of money would give him options. He could get out of the market forever. He could move and take up being a country lawyer. A fresh start. Maybe he'd look up that girl he dated in law school, the one whose husband died two years ago. She might still be in Des Moines. He should have stayed in Iowa. You didn't have Chickies in Iowa, except the clucking kind.

Right, Chickie thought, 75. Fat chance.

"You run all the legal work for the sale through your law firm," Chickie said. "Like normal, no slick shit. You represent both sides of the deal. Bill honest, both sides. No paddin' hours. Keep everything kosher, like a salami. I want you to help Joe get approval from both the ABW board and the ACMU board. I don't want no trouble and don't expect none. Your job is to make sure that trouble don't come up. The Bank may expand its business after the sale. Coordinate with Shermy Coverall on the second floor. He's my investment adviser. Shermy will relay directions, and you get them done. You need to get smart about Joe's campaign. That will get you 15 grand a month, on the side, steady Eddie. U and A?"

"U and A?"

"Understand and Accept," Chickie said impatiently.

"Yes, U and A."

"Good," Chickie said. He rose, came around his desk, put his hand on Foster's shoulder where it joined his neck and gave a squeeze that was a little harder than necessary. "Good."

"Yes," Foster said. "I understand and accept."

Foster picked up his briefcase and walked out.

Jesus Christ, Chickie thought, the idiots I have to work with.

Foster figured he'd have to pay the brokers back slowly, very slowly.

Chapter 20

Fricktown, W.Va., October 14, 1975

Allyson Pickering stopped her 1968 VW Beetle at Shorty's Gulf on Main Street where an old iron bridge crossed Black Creek. She needed direction.

On this Tuesday morning, Allyson had driven north on the new I-79 from Charleston to the Osage exit, west of Morgantown. She then picked up Rt. 7 through Monongalia County—Cassville, Core, Pentress, Blacksville, Bula, Wana, Klondike and Fricktown. It was after 1 p.m., and she had eaten nothing except coffee earlier that morning. She considered using the restroom and then thought it might be wise to skip a visit to Shorty's facilities.

She'd driven into Fricktown cautiously, passing the sign:

Ⱶome of Joe Ⱶunt, President American Coal Ɱiner's Union

She looked for a roadside marker that mentioned the 1932-1933 strike, but the State did not think it was worth remembering.

Before pulling in to Shorty's, Allyson had eased her way along Main Street toward the AMSTEEL mine. She noted two stop signs and little traffic. She scrutinized the lonely strip of stores facing the double railroad tracks that ran through the middle of town, with Main Street on one side and Black Creek on the other. Farmers and Miners' Bank was in the middle of the three-block-long business district. She passed an IGA, the four-unit Black Gold Motel, Post Office, Doris Jean's Family Café (offering the "world's best mac&cheese"), Barney's Laundromat, Katz Brothers' Hardware, The Dinner Hole Bar, a concrete-block honky-tonk called Hunt's Paradise and a scruffy soft-ice cream place named Dare Ye Delite. She counted a half-dozen empty stores. Several old men in overalls or new polyester pants with flared bottoms sunned themselves on the bench in front of Town Hall. Each wore a soft gimme cap. One man was missing a leg. A couple of older teenage boys lounged next to their cars at the Dare Ye, hoping to see either a set of lifters on a pickup or a girl a year or two younger without a baby. Fricktown was functioning, but whatever thriving it might have done was in its past.

Mountains rose on either side of the town. From the narrow valley floor, Allyson noted terraced rows of houses running parallel to Main

Street. The core of every wood-frame house was the same, but over the years, each had been modified differently with room additions, garages, carports, porches and decks. Roofs and sidings varied in color and materials. Several houses still made do with asphalt roll roofing, the cheapest choice. Most owners had covered up the original boards and battens with asbestos shingles or aluminum siding. She saw pickup trucks in driveways, along with the occasional trailered bass boat or camper.

Allyson wore the stone-washed, denim dress she had on at American Eagle on Sunday. Indian summer's heat made her uncomfortable. She had refused to buy an air-conditioned car as an act of solidarity with those who couldn't afford one. It had not been clear to her at the time how her refusal helped the poor keep cool, but she felt better by making herself share their discomfort. The dealer had tried to sell her a new VW when she brought her '68 in for repairs, but she told him that she'd rather "drive a Bug than a Rabbit that looks like a squashed pig."

She waited next to the two gas pumps. A small man in his late 40s, Allyson supposed he was Shorty, walked out of the station. She released the front lid so he could access the gas cap in the luggage compartment. As the tank filled with regular, he checked her oil, brake fluid, clutch fluid, windshield fluid, hoses, wires, connectors, plugs and tires. He was paying more attention to her Beetle than she had in the seven years since she'd bought it.

Shorty was not a subtle man. His scoping of a stranger was as sly as an ooga horn. Pennsylvania license plates were common enough in a border county like Monongalia, and a '68 VW Beetle was not completely unfamiliar. Other small foreign cars had begun appearing as the OPEC embargo and high gasoline prices forced Americans to seek better mileage. A nurse who worked at West Virginia University Hospital drove a Datsun B210 that Shorty believed had cost him fill-ups he thought were rightfully his. Her Datsun was Fricktown's most exotic vehicle. Its ethnicity came in for local criticism as WWII vets recalled fighting Nissan-built planes and vehicles in the Pacific. The nurse said that she would never buy another American gas-guzzler—a statement that drew a number of silent endorsements in the community and several loud condemnations. Shorty knew this Beetle was worth checking out on its own merits apart from those of the driver. Having the engine in the back made sense to him for traction but not for a head-on crash.

After 10 minutes, Allyson considered asking Shorty to check her cervix while he was rooting around under there. But she knew he would be embarrassed. She didn't feel the need to use the line once she thought of it. She also needed Shorty's help.

"Gotta be careful, Miss, that you don't rear end no one with your gas tank up front like it is. Engine's in the back, not like Americans."

"Thanks," she said.

"From around here, Miss?" Shorty asked finally, as she handed him her credit card. He looked at the name. "Can't recall any Pickerings in Fricktown, Miss."

"Pittsburgh," she said casually.

"Oh, you're from Piksburg. How 'bout them Bucs! Stargell and Parker kept them in the race. Won the National League East, but couldn't beat them Reds. Stargell played hurt. Still had 90 RBIs and 22 homers."

"Willie Stargell's real name is Wilver," she said. "Wilver Dornell Stargell."

"Stargell ain't a Willie?"

Allyson laughed. "Nope. He's a Wilver. But he goes along with Willie. They also call him Pops."

Shorty wasn't sure what to do with this lady who seemed dead certain that Willie wasn't a Willie. "Well," he said finally, "we got end-zone seasons for the Stillers. Franco Harris, he come down for the annual sports dinner over at The Moose. Franco!"

Shorty stood by the driver's door, staring at Allyson's legs. She smelled motor oil, which was not unpleasant.

"I know him," she said, without giving the statement the thought it deserved.

"You know FRAN-CO! Number Thirty-Two!"

"He plays racket ball downtown. We're members of the same club. He drinks V-8 juice after a workout."

"Franco does? V-8?"

"He's a nice guy," she said.

"You know Franco Harris?" Shorty said, looking again at her credit card in hope of finding a clue to such privilege.

"I went out with him a couple of times," Allyson said, and then decided that she'd stretched the lie beyond its usefulness.

"You went out with Franco?" Shorty shifted his feet and closed one eye in thought. He looked at Allyson's fair skin and hair. Then he shrugged. "He don't fumble much, that Franco."

Allyson smiled and signed the receipt. She accepted her card. "Maybe you could help me," she said. "I'm looking for an older man. Gus Olin. Does he still live in Fricktown?"

Shorty was trying hard to figure out why a pretty girl in an old VW Bug who dated Franco Harris in Pittsburgh would be looking for Gus Olin in Fricktown, West Virginia. Gus read a lot of books, Shorty knew that. Maybe this girl had something to do with books. But maybe something else was going on with this stranger in a short skirt made out of what looked to Shorty like old blue jeans ready to be parted out for knee patches.

"Oh, I see. You're lookin' for Gus Olin. You kin, Miss?"

"No," she said.

"Oh." He didn't feel right asking her business straight out. Maybe Gus wasn't interested in seeing this outsider.

Allyson sensed that Shorty was being careful.

"Gus Olin," Shorty mused.

"I'm a reporter. For the <u>Post-Gazette</u>. In Pittsburgh. I want to ask him a question or two. History questions. About the coal industry in the old days."

"Now that's Gus for you. Always talkin' about them days. Has a whole room of books an' papers and maps and thangs. Drives Edna crazy with it. Sure. Gus lives up there in the blue house, third row up the hill." Shorty pointed to the house.

"Thanks," she said.

"Everything checked out good," Shorty said. "Don't have no water-cooled radiator in these, so I couldn't check your water."

"Right," she said.

"I've heard brakes ain't that good on VWs. Not like American brakes."

"I'll drive slowly. It's hard to drive fast in a Bug."

"Heard one other thing, Miss. You put that heater handle somewhere between Heat and Defrost, you'll be gettin' carbon monoxide from the engine in with you. That's a bad gas, Miss. Fricktown knows about CO. It'll kill you."

Allyson thanked Shorty again and drove toward Gus Olin's place, passing the AMSTEEL mine buildings and the new preparation plant that straddled the railroad tracks. Allyson turned off her radio, which was having a hard time bringing in a clear signal. She noticed new metal buildings in the AMSTEEL compound. Then her eye fell on a row of older stone houses behind big, beautiful sugar maples in full orange-red foliage. As she drove, those of the Fricktown community who were on Main Street swiveled their heads in unashamed synchronization with her progress. The boys at the Dare Ye smirked, and the old men warming on the benches thought themselves frisky and vaguely protective. Women either ignored her as they looked or didn't like what they saw.

Allyson wound her way up toward the 12 houses on the third terrace. She found it easy to keep the one blue structure in sight. Rooftops below her were even with the road she was driving. The layout reminded her of Greek villages she had visited. She pulled into the three-car parking area next to an early 1960s International pickup. A chain-link fence encircled the Olins' small, steep lot. A grape arbor ran along one side. Concrete steps led up to a freshly painted, one-story house with red window boxes. She noticed "GO" scratched neatly into the first step. She gathered her purse and the shoulder bag that held her note pad and tape recorder. She opened the latched gate and walked up.

As she stepped into the porch shade, the screen door opened. A man in his late 70s or early 80s, slightly bent, his hair white and thin, stood in the doorway. He wore faded overalls and a white T-shirt. He mopped his face with a red neckerchief. He didn't smile.

"You're from Pittsburgh," Gus Olin said. "Someone named, Allyson Pickering. A reporter from the Post-Gazette. Shorty down at the Gulf called in case I didn't have no use for you."

Allyson felt as if she had been knocked backward.

"What do you want?" he asked.

Allyson liked nothing about Gus Olin, not his sharp eyes, not his thin lips, not his fitness, not his tone of voice, not the deep blue-black lines on his cheeks, not his unspoken male authority.

"Who is it, Gussie?" a woman called.

"Ain't sure yet," Gus said.

Gus sized up what was standing in front of him. The lady -- taller than most and a little skinny -- didn't look like the tall, skinny girls around Fricktown. Her bones hung different, he thought, and she didn't seem uneasy about her height. She didn't slouch or round her shoulders. He didn't care much for the sunglasses she wore propped on her head like Jackie Kennedy. He had never seen a dress made out of dungarees, but he was worldly enough to know it was not purchased for lack of money. Even by the standards of teenagers, her dress stopped short from where he thought it should have. Gus didn't think she had simply forgotten to fasten her two top buttons. Gus also guessed her jangling bracelet hadn't been bought on time at Cohen's E-Z Credit Jewelry in Morgantown. She smelled rich to Gus Olin. He hadn't smelled much rich over the years, but he had a nose for it just the same.

"Mr. Olin, I cover labor for the paper. Unions. Management. Health and safety. The ACMU election. I'd like to talk to you."

"What for? I left the mines years back. What do I know?"

"I understand you're retired," Allyson said, "but my editor, Davey Bloom, thought you might remember him. From the '30s. The strike."

"'Course I remember him. Nearly got the young feller canned for writin' the truth. Truth don't get you far enough in this world, Miss."

"I hope it will," Allyson replied.

Gus Olin knew exactly why this strange woman was standing on his porch.

"Did Davey send you here?"

"No, but I told him I was coming."

"Where'd you get my name?"

"From an AMSTEEL executive in Pittsburgh. He said you could background me on Joe Hunt when he was a young man working underground. My father knows the AMSTEEL man."

"Your Daddy in the coal business, Miss?"

"No. He's a lawyer in Philadelphia. He did some work for AMSTEEL once. On export regulations, I think. They sell metallurgical coal to the Japanese."

"They do. I 'spect AMSTEEL has a file on me somewhere. 'Personnel files,' they call 'em."

"I don't know anything about that," Allyson said. "Davey told me you would tell me the truth."

"There's truth, Miss, as you might think about it, and then there's understandin'. They ain't always wired up together."

"Maybe, you'll tell me both," she said with a smile that she hoped was winning.

"You're after a story, Miss. I could talk to you for an hour or two. Then you'd boil all that down to a sentence or two. Them two sentences might be what I said, but they wouldn't be all that I said or meant."

"I try to be fair and accurate."

"You work for a dollar, don't you?"

"Pardon? Well, I suppose, I guess, but...."

"When you take a man's money, whether it's a coal comp'ny, a still mill or a newspaper publisher, you are a-sellin' yourself for the dollar. Don't matter none whether he's a-buyin' your back or your brain. He bought; you sold. When you sell your back, your mind can be free. Not necessarily is, but can be. But when you sell your brain, Miss, you can't never be free for the time on his dime."

Allyson didn't know what to make of this old, hostile, unschooled coal miner who troubled her more than any of her Bryn Mawr professors. 'Time on his dime.' Where did he come up with that? she wondered.

"I don't think much any more about 'free,'" she said. "I left that in college philosophy class."

"That ain't where 'free' is," Gus said. "Free ain't in a book. It's how you work it into your life."

"Mr. Olin. I'm just a reporter who's writing..."

"Nobody ain't just what they do," he said.

"Sure. I understand, but..."

"It's like this. Back in the '20s and '30s, the weigh boss docked me if I loaded too much rock in my mine cars or if there was too much fines -- dust and such -- and not enough lumps. Dust couldn't be sold; lumps could. Your boss does the same. He looks at your words real careful. He wants a story that's a clean ton, all good-burnin' lumps, not one loaded up with filler. Lumps keep folks warm. If stories don't keep folks comfortable or interested, then everyone gets upset. See, if you load out a ton the

302

comp'ny can't sell, well, you'll be a-lookin' for work sooner'n you can blink. He's payin' for lump coal, so you gotta load him out lumps. When you write for the dollar, Miss Pickering, you can't write the whole truth even if you was to larn it. You gotta write the lumps that your paper can sell."

"Mr. Olin, I'm a member of the Newspaper Guild, the reporters' union. I've been a member from the first day I worked for a paper. I'm proud of my union card. I believe in unions for working people."

"Union is unions," Olin said. "Sometimes they do right by the laborin' class of people, and sometimes they don't. I seen it both ways. Tell me, why do you want to know the truth?"

Allyson sorted through the answers she had on hand—the public's right to know, the miner's right to know about his candidates, her ambition. Maybe it was just curiosity.

"I personally don't need to know. But miners have a right to know about who leads them."

"And there's the question of timin' and truth," he said, not bothering much with her answer. "You see, truth at one minute in history counts different than truth at some other minute down the line. Truth has a way of scootin' this way and that way over the years."

"I understand what you're saying. The politics of a particular time can define what we think is true."

"The problem we got here is that you want one little bit of yes-or-no truth. What I'm a-sayin' is that you need a whole lifetime of understandin' to make sense of that little yes-or-no truth. If you were back there, back then, you might could understand. But, Miss, you don't shape up to me like a lady who woulda been here even if you was as old as me. Well, now hold on, old Gus. We did have us a nice Vassar girl, runnin' the kitchen for a spell. Sort of looked like you, even. But you wasn't raised in no coal camp, Miss. Yer Daddy didn't breathe no dust 10 hours a day. He didn't feel the hunger. Yer family never lived in no tent during the winter. And your Momma didn't bury no starved-dead babies."

Allyson felt her face flush. Gus Olin had caught her drift a lot better than she had caught his.

"I grew up in Philadelphia. My parents are Quakers. Liberals. They support civil rights, unions. They're pacifists."

"Pacifists. That's nice," Gus said. "Them folks won't last long in the mines."

"Mr. Olin. Did Joe Hunt kill Frank Gallagher, the superintendent at this mine during the strike in 1932 and '33?"

Gus Olin looked her in the eye.

"Have you ever kill't someone, Miss?"

"No. Of course not."

"Not yet."

"Tell me the truth, Mr. Olin."

"I just did," he said, as he closed the screen door and walked back inside.

Allyson stopped at the Dare Ye Delite to use the bathroom and the pay phone.

"Well?" Bloom asked at his end of the line.

"He's a funny guy," she said. "I'd say he confirmed."

"Did you get it on tape?"

"No. It wasn't a sit-down interview. He talked to me on his front porch. We were standing the whole time."

"What exactly did he say?" Bloom asked.

"I asked him: 'Did Joe Hunt kill Gallagher, the superintendent, during the strike?' He said, 'Yes.'"

Davey Bloom hadn't seen or spoken to Gus Olin since 1933, but a flat-out yes to that question didn't sound like the Gus Olin he had known.

"You're sure he said Yes?" Bloom asked.

"Well, he might have said Yeah."

"I better call him to double-check."

"You don't need to do that," she said. "I'll get confirmation from other sources."

Davey now knew what he had suspected. "What else did he say?"

"It was a strained conversation. He didn't invite me in. Talked a lot about what 'Truth' is, and the difference between truth and understanding. I wrote my notes after I left. He talked about how awful the strike was, the tents, dead babies from starvation. He said no one could imagine those circumstances today. I have specific stuff, quotes, details."

"And you're absolutely sure he said Joe Hunt killed Gallagher?"

"Absolutely," she said.

"That's funny, hon. I remember Gus as a guy who talked in simple metaphors and similes. Homespun philosopher. Elliptical. Kind of a coalfield Socrates. Should have been a teacher. You're certain he said Yes?"

"Yes."

"I dunno, hon. You don't have it on tape or in his hand. Well, let's see what you get from Sonoski and Hunt. Nobody was ever charged. Never found Gallagher's body. Never found a murder weapon. Never had a snitch give up a name. Why would Gus Olin finger Joe Hunt now?"

"Maybe he favors Delucci. Maybe Joe's been a disappointment."

"Maybe. But those boys -- Larry and Joe -- were Gus's blood even though they weren't family. If you went through that strike, you were blood for life."

"Gus Olin's a special man," Allyson said. "I don't think he'd tell a lie."

"Yeah. That's him," Davey said. "We need confirmation. I'm not running that without two confirms, preferably on tape."

"I'm sure of this," Allyson said.

"Well, hon, there's sure and then there's indisputable proof. We're in the proof business."

"I know that."

"And I know you know. This thing may be coming to a boil. Keep your head down."

They rang off.

Davey Bloom had managed ambitious reporters before Allyson Pickering. He hoped she would straighten out on her own.

Chapter 21

Charleston, W.Va., October 16, 1975

Jeep Delucci sat at his desk in his Charleston campaign headquarters nursing his first morning coffee. He and Biggie Stover were scheduled to drive to Fairmont to campaign. They were planning to be back in Charleston by eight or nine that night. He jerked his tie loose.

Dicey Shuck rang from the switchboard.

"Dicey?" Jeep said.

"You got a call from headquarters. I'll put it through."

"Jeep? This is Foster Shives. How are you?"

"What can I do for you, Foster?" Jeep asked in a neutral voice.

"I'd like to meet with you late tonight in Charleston."

"Union business?" Jeep asked. "I'd rather do it first thang tomorrow morning."

"Not Union business," Shives said. "Election business."

"What kind of election business, Foster?"

"Give me 30 minutes. It's important. I'm bringing a friend, a business associate, a client. This is a private meeting. Just you and Biggie. Keep Becker out of it. After 10 or 11."

"Is this a bribe from Joe to drop out of the race?"

"No."

"Foster, what the fuck are you up to?"

"Thirty minutes," Foster replied.

"Oh, all right. Make it 10 at my headquarters. You know where I'm at?"

"I do."

That night as Biggie sat with Jeep in his office, they heard knocking at the front door. They walked through the hallway. Foster was in a sport coat and carried no briefcase. The other man was carrying an aluminum suitcase. Jeep unlocked the door and opened it.

Jeep and Biggie shook hands with Foster perfunctorily.

"This is my friend," Foster Shives said, "Tom Siciliano."

"Chickie," Siciliano said.

Jeep didn't know the name, but he had a hunch. He and Biggie shook hands with Chickie. Jeep led them back to the campaign's utility room where they seated themselves around a work table the campaign had scavenged from Goodwill.

"So what's this about?" Jeep asked.

"As you know, I've had one client for years," Foster said. "Now I have a second, Mr. Siciliano. He asked me to arrange this meeting."

"Here we are," Jeep said.

"Friends call me Chickie."

"Jeep," Jeep said, "This is Biggie."

"I've made a deal with Joe Hunt," Chickie said, as he put his suitcase in the middle of the table, "to buy the American Bank of Washington. The money that the Union will get is more than generous."

"First I've heard," Jeep said. "That's our biggest asset."

"No one knows at this point except the people in this room, Joe Hunt and Larry Sonoski," Foster said. "It's coming up at the next board meeting for Union approval and at the same time for the Bank's directors."

"Tell me—who are you?" Jeep asked. "What's your business?"

"My people are investors. We have an office in Washington. Foster's been there. We buy and operate businesses. Real estate, finance and security work. That type of thing."

Jeep sized up Chickie Siciliano, one Italian to another. He was reasonably sure Chickie represented "additional interests." Jeep cut his eyes toward Biggie. Danger!

Chickie continued. "We don't want our investment to become a campaign issue and get fucked up."

Okay, Jeep thought, the white, silk-lined, kidskin gloves are off.

"Are you Mafia?" Jeep asked.

"I'm always asked that," Chickie said with a tolerant smile, "because of the name. Siciliano must be from Sicily. If you're from Sicily, you must be a Black Hand. Not every Italian is a gangster. Take you, for instance. You'd be insulted if I asked you what you asked me. Right?"

"The Mafia is a big business," Jeep said. "It's not Hollywood make-believe. Every Italian in this country knows what it is."

"I'm a business guy," Chickie said.

Jeep dropped the attack. If Siciliano was connected, he couldn't do anything about it. "We was thinkin' about openin' up branches of the Bank in the coalfields to help our members," Jeep said."

"If there's a buck to be made, my group could do that, too," Chickie said. "We could extend good rates and credit without a lot of bullshit. A steady mining job is good security in my book."

"So what's the money?" Biggie asked.

"Twenty-two a share," Chickie said, "for all ten million shares, 100 percent ownership. That's $222 million. Cash."

"Jesus Christ," Jeep swore, "what would the Union do with all that money?"

"The Bank's appreciated in value since Lewis bought it almost 30 years ago. That money can do a lot of good for your miners," Chickie said.

"It's a windfall," Foster said. "Almost like found money on the street."

"So what's the catch?" Biggie asked.

"Ain't no catch," Chickie said. "Clean deal. Cash. More than fair price."

"What's in it for you?" Biggie asked. "Investors buy value; they buy at a discount. They buy distress. They don't pay fair-market price unless they have to."

"We don't want nobody second-guessin' this deal. It has to look right and smell right from the start," Chickie said.

"Who the hell *are* you?" Biggie asked.

Jeep gave his friend a warning look.

"I told you," Chickie answered, his voice rising.

"You're with Bruno, Tony Bruno," Jeep said without emotion.

"Tony is a guy I know. We've done business."

"Luparellis," Jeep said to Biggie. "Pittsburgh. Part of Frank Fagano's New York outfit. That's the money."

"We got all kinds of money," Chickie said without hostility. "We got Italians. We got Jews. We got Greeks. We got Americans. We're businessmen from Washington."

"My Daddy hates the Mafia," Delucci said. "You screwed Italians to get your start. Now you screw everyone."

"Business is business," Chickie said, calmly. "I'm in business like everybody else. This ain't 'Godfather' shit. We don't send dead fishes in newspapers to our competitors."

"This is a clean sale," Foster Shives said to Jeep. "More than fair price. What happens to the Bank under new leadership is not your responsibility. It's like a house. Once you sell it, you're out of it. It's not your fault if the new owners play rock music too loudly or paint it purple. As president, just think what you can do with $222 million."

"Anyway, the deal is done," Chickie said. "Foster did up the paper. Joe Hunt has the authority to make the deal on his own. The two boards— that's just goin' through the motions as you know. But I don't want no publicity or a political fight. Papers are signed. Understand what I'm saying?"

Very carefully, Jeep said: "I understand your position."

"I hear you're financing your campaign yourselves," Chickie said. "Biggie took out a loan usin' his land as security. How you gonna pay it back? Two hundred on his note, right? No interest for six months."

Jeep was stunned. How would Siciliano know the details of Biggie's loan? The lien was recorded, but there was no notice in any paper. No public connection had been made between Biggie's borrowing and Delucci's campaign.

"Now you need more," Chickie said. "To close the deal."

"Maybe," Jeep said without conviction.

"My guess is Biggie's money is pretty much gone," Chickie said. "You'll need cash to cover the last seven weeks of the campaign and the transition if you win, which I expect you will if you get the money. I'm told Hunt has come up with at least $400,000."

"Maybe more," Foster added. "He's hired a top-notch campaign consultant who worked for Humphrey in '68 and McGovern in '72. Marvin Shookoff. Also works for the Teamsters."

"Must be a real sharp guy seein' how good Humphrey and McGovern did," Delucci said.

"Maybe Shookoff knows what happened to Hoffa," Biggie said. "Seems ol' Jimmy just up and disappeared in July into thin air."

Delucci cut his eyes toward Biggie.

"Both Humphrey and McGovern were damaged goods when they entered the general election," Foster said. "Neither had a chance. Shookoff is making Joe into a saleable candidate. By December, you won't recognize him. He'll be blue-collar Joe with coal dust under his finger nails and fire in his belly."

"It'll be a big fahr in that belly," Biggie cracked.

"I beat Joe 57 to 43," Jeep said.

"Joe didn't take you seriously," Foster said. "Now he is, and he has the money to beat you. He's bought television time. As far as I know, you haven't bought any. He plans mailings, phones. He's going to work through retirees as much as he can, because their generational loyalty to him runs deep. They'll lean on their sons to vote for Daddy's union pension and health benefits."

Delucci knew he had no television lined up, because he had no money to make commercials.

"Joe's going to attack Biggie's money," Foster said. "Shookoff will say it's coal money that's paying for your campaign."

"Biggie Stover, stooge for the comp'nies. I love it," Jeep laughed. "That dog ain't gonna hunt. Everybody we growed up with knows that Biggie owns that land, which he got when his Daddy died. Ain't no secret it's got a pile of coal under it and a pile of timber on top."

"Don't matter whether flyin' shit is true," Chickie said. "What matters is when enough fools think it is, some always sticks. And if it doesn't stick, the smell hangs around for a long time. That's why people throw it."

"Sticks on the thrower, too," Biggie said, looking at Chickie.

"There's another matter," Foster said. "Becker."

"What's the matter with him?" Jeep asked. "He's done a great job for me. What'd he do—smoke a joint in college? Piss on a Columbia lawn?"

"It doesn't matter what he did or didn't do. What matters is how long and how loudly Shookoff has Joe's campaign saying he did something," Foster said.

"He's a lawyer for Chrissakes," Jeep said. "The morals committee of the State bar said he was clean enough to practice in West Virginia."

"Well, that speaks for itself, doesn't it?" Foster sniffed. "Shookoff will Red-bait you through him. Becker was against the War."

"Hell, Biggie an' me was in that hole for a year. We was a lot more against that War than Becker ever was. I was crawlin' through rice paddies gettin' shot at when Becker was feelin' up sophomores in his dorm room. Those chucks were tryin' to kill my hillbilly ass. Like Muhammad Ali said, no Viet Cong ever called me a white-trash redneck."

"Becker was an SDS member when they took over Columbia University in 1968," Foster said. "SDS was the outfit that started fighting with police. They blew up the townhouse in Greenwich Village where they were making bombs they were going to plant at a Fort Dix dance. They bombed our Nation's Capitol. They say they are revolutionary communists. They went underground, and most of them still are."

"Becker wasn't into that," Biggie said.

"No, not as far as Shookoff can tell," Foster said. "Becker left when his comrades went off the deep end at Columbia. But it doesn't matter what Becker did or didn't do. It matters what Shookoff and Hunt say he did, might have done, might have thought about doing and might have been around when something was done by somebody else. You'll spend half your time denying Becker's a revolutionary communist who has a bomb in one hand and a marijuana cigarette in the other."

"He doesn't smoke," Jeep said. "I asked before I hired him. Every guy under 30 in the mines has smoked marijuana. Half of them smoke before they go to work. I'm more radical than Becker, an' Biggie's crazier than me."

"Miners are patriots," Foster said. "They'll say, 'Where there's smoke, there's fire.' If you say something loud enough and long enough, people'll believe at least some of it."

"We trust him," Biggie said.

"Dump him," Foster said. "The kid'll cost you the election. The worst Joe can then say is that you *used* to employ a revolutionary communist with a bomb in one hand and a joint in the other."

"No," Jeep said.

"Why not?" asked Chickie.

"Well, for one thang, he holds the campaign together. He's smart. He's loyal. He wants the Union to do better for the membership."

"And?" Chickie asked.

"He knows too much. He knows about Biggie's loan and what we did with it. Other stuff. He has a couple of reporter friends. A girl in Pittsburgh who works for The Post Gazette, Allyson Pickering. Couple of others, Charlie Frazier at The Gazette. Maybe he'd talk to them if I fired him; maybe not. Too risky to chance it."

"What does Becker want?" Chickie asked.

310

"Sure as hell ain't money," Jeep said. "Campaign's been paying him $100 a week for the last four months."

"See that proves he's up to somethin'," Chickie said. "Where's he gettin' his dough to live on? Why's he workin' for peanuts? Who's payin' him to work for you if it ain't you?"

"He lives cheap in a little rental farmhouse on Middle Ridge out Davis Creek," Jeep said. "It's country. He probably has some money saved from being a lawyer. His parents ain't rich. He can get by for another couple of months. After that, it's either work for me at headquarters if I win or go back to his law practice."

"Maybe he's a plant for those SDS Weathervanes," Chickie said. "You know, he keeps his true intentions hidden until the time's right. That's how communists do it. They infiltrate, then they take over. I understand how that goes. I would've made a good communist or FBI agent."

"I'm sure," Jeep said.

"He probably wants to use a Union position to foment labor unrest," Foster Shives said. "I'm sure Becker favors a right to strike for each local. That would mean chaos in coal, which might spill over to other industries. Communists pull down legitimate political leaders through provocations and disruptions."

"You mean legitimate political leaders like Nixon who resigned last year," Jeep asked without asking.

"Nixon *was* a crook," Chickie said, "a really dumb crook. Smart guy, but a dumb crook. I've seen a hundred like that. They don't understand that good crime is a business, and you have to run it like one. Real criminals strip risk out of their investments. You...they get good people to work for them and pay them good. And they make sure their workers do what they're supposed to do. No skimmin'; no shortin' the boss. Dumb crooks get caught; smart crooks get good seats and nice people coming to their funerals."

"You asked why Becker is in the MDU campaign," Jeep said. "He believes in our ideas. He wants a better deal for coal miners just like me. He thinks I'll do a better job than Joe Hunt. It's that simple."

"So," Chickie asked, "are you in this for your pocketbook and your ego or are you a half-ass idealist like Garibaldi?"

"I got in the race for the membership. The Union needs new leadership, young leadership. Let's say it's gotten more complicated within the last 15 minutes."

"Yeah," Chickie said, "life's a bitch, ain't it?"

"Are you planning to bring Becker to ACMU headquarters if you win?" Foster asked.

"Probably. Sure. Why not? He's earned a job. He was with me when it was just me and Biggie. He'd be a big help. Maybe general counsel, Foster."

"Fuck Becker," Chickie said. "He can't be trusted."

"Well, if Joe comes after Becker maybe I know something about ol' Joe Hunt that could turn this election on a dime."

"Like what?" Chickie asked.

"Like I ain't sayin'. He pulls that Becker shit on me, I could double him down and double him over."

Chickie weighed this information. He didn't think Delucci was bluffing. Chickie decided he preferred Delucci to Hunt. More promising for the long term. Delucci was his horse.

Foster was puzzled by Delucci's claim to have secret information on Joe Hunt. He hadn't heard anything. He didn't like what Delucci said about Becker coming in as general counsel. At his age, Foster knew he had to stay where he was for as long as he could. If he was out of the ACMU and the Bank, he was out of everything, including Chickie's "side" cash, which would free him of debt.

"Foster, why are you here?" Jeep asked. "Who are you for?"

"I'm for me," Foster said. "I want to keep serving the Union, the men."

"So if I win, I keep you around. That's your proposition?"

"That's my reward -- my fee -- for being the middle man in this deal that will make sure you win."

"I'm in good shape," Delucci said. "I have rank-and-file campaign workers in almost every local. They produced during the first round."

"You beat Joe, because he wasn't campaigning," Foster said. "Now he is, and he has the cash and the people to beat you."

"Where'd his money come from all of a sudden?"

"Who do you think wants him in office for another six years?" Foster asked.

"Coal boys," Delucci said. "UNICOAL, USOCO, AMSTEEL. The big guys."

Foster said nothing.

"So what's your proposition?" Delucci asked Chickie.

"This suitcase has $500,000 in 50s and 100s. It's your own money. Your savings and Stover's. If you're asked, it's saved money that you kept at home in a glass jar buried in your garden or under your beds. You're giving the money to yourself. This will keep things even. More can be had if you need it."

"Five hundred," Biggie said, then whistled for effect.

Chickie popped the catches and opened the suitcase.

Jeep stared at the money. Biggie stared at Chickie.

"But you need to dump Becker," Chickie said. "Lawyers are a dime a dozen, and sometimes you can get 'em for a nickel off."

"What do you want in return?" Delucci asked.

"Don't make the Bank sale a campaign issue," Chickie said. "We don't want no front-page stories in The Washington Post like they done to

312

Nixon and Hoffa. Publicity is bad for a quiet business like ours. I don't want to be no celebrity. We don't like spotlights on us. We're just trying to make money like everyone else. "

"The price you're payin' is more than fair," Delucci said. "After it's sold, what you do with it is your business, not mine and not the Union's. So why do I feel I should walk away from this generous offer?"

"Because it's money from me," Chickie said. "You come from a family that has prejudices against certain other Italians."

"Yeah, it's money from you," Jeep said.

"We're not trying to muscle in to make the ACMU a junior partner. You won't be frontin' for us. You're out of the Bank free and clear. No strings."

Jeep doubted money like that -- more than double the ABW's true value -- came without strings.

"With cash from the sale, you'll have $222 million to pay off your $200,000 loan to Biggie," Siciliano said. "You'll have a dozen ways to slide that money out without causing a stink."

They sat silently, Jeep and Chickie looking at each other.

"No!" Jeep said finally. "I'm not taking it."

Jeep rose from his seat and shut the briefcase. He forced it into Foster's hands. "No deal."

Chickie got up. Foster followed, shaking his head.

Biggie stood in sync with Jeep, ready for whatever was going to happen. He could get to the pistol in his shoulder holster quickly.

Chickie and Foster walked to the front door and left. Foster Shives tried hard to not look bewildered. Chickie Siciliano wore a tight, hard smile. He liked the kid, sort of.

Jeep and Biggie heard the front door open and close. Jeep looked at Biggie.

"I didn't take it," Jeep said.

"You didn't take it."

"It would have paid for the rest of the campaign," Jeep said. "It must have weighed 25 pounds."

"We ain't worse off than when them two walked in here," Biggie said.

"Yeah, we are. Now we know that Joe got at least $400,000 from that dirt bag. And we got zip."

"When the Mob gets in, they'll corrupt the Bank," Biggie said. "Maybe you could stop the sale."

"He said it was done," Jeep said.

"Maybe it doesn't have to be," Biggie said.

"Nobody's going to pay $22 for ABW stock," Jeep said. "I've not heard $15. Ten is more likely, and I think we'd take eight in a heartbeat. I could do a lot of good with $222 million."

"If Siciliano is fundin' Joe Hunt to grease this sale, where are we goin' to get $500,000 to stay in the race and pay off my loan?" Biggie asked. "That's seven, total."

They heard the front door open.

"JEEP?"

"It's Becker," Jeep said.

"JEEP?"

"In the back."

Becker came in. "You're here late. I was going home and stopped to get that press release for tomorrow morning. What was Foster Shives doing here? I saw him walking out with some guy."

"He was staying in town tonight on his way back to Dee Cee. Wanted to talk about the UNICOAL disaster. Says Joe wants to keep it out of the campaign."

"He's here late at night to talk about that?" Becker asked.

"Some other ideas, too," Jeep said.

"Is he switching over to us?" Becker asked.

"I wouldn't say Foster is switchin' as much as he's straddlin'," Jeep said.

"He wants to keep his job when you win," Becker said.

"Sure he does," Biggie said.

"Who else but Joe Hunt would have kept Foster around all these years?" Becker said.

"Foster says he can find us cash to float the campaign through the end. He says he knows some investors who'll be good for it."

"A loan?" Becker asked.

"More like a contribution."

"For what in return?" Becker asked.

"Not clear. Maybe they're idealists who want the reformers to win. Maybe they want ACMU business. And something else. Foster says I should kick you out of the campaign and not bring you up to headquarters if I win."

"That I can understand."

"Foster says Joe is planning to say you're an SDS communist with the Weathermen, and I'm a stooge."

"You're also a hippie pothead," Biggie noted.

Becker pulled a legal pad from his briefcase. He scribbled a sentence on it, tore it off and handed it to Jeep.

"Please accept my resignation from the Miners for a Democratic Union campaign, effective October 16, 1975. Jeffrey Becker," Jeep read aloud.

"I told you what I did, and what I think," Becker said, "before you hired me. Joe will play on fear of outsiders taking over the Union. Denial

314

is not much of a defense. You'll take a hit. Say something loud enough and long enough, and people will assume there's truth in it."

"That's exactly how Foster sees it," Jeep said. "Joe now has $400,000 or more in hand. He's hired Marvin Shookoff to help his campaign. Shookoff is the one who is piling up the dirt on you."

"I've heard the name," Becker said. "He's a Washington consultant who works for Democrats and unions. Heavy duty. Where'd Joe get the cash to hire him?"

"From an investment group, according to Foster."

"'Investment group.' What do they want from the Union in return for their investment? Anything more you want to tell me?"

"No," Jeep said.

"What was in the suitcase that Foster was carrying?"

"Change of clothes, I reckon. I didn't ask to see his pajamas."

"One suitcase between the two of them? Odd. Well, you can accept my resignation at any time. I don't want to be the reason your campaign loses. Who was the guy with Foster?"

"Uh, Ray somebody. I didn't catch it," Jeep said. "He said he was a partner in Foster's firm. He's the connection to the investors."

"Didn't look like a lawyer," Becker said.

"Most of the time neither do you," Biggie laughed.

"I mean he looked rough. Like he spent time trying to round off his edges," Becker said.

"Blue-collar guys go to law school and pass the bar," Jeep said.

"Okay. I'm an elitist snob. I'll see you in the morning unless you tell me otherwise," Becker said.

"Biggie an' me need to give this some thought," Jeep said. "There's no point in us runnin' to lose."

"I agree," Becker said. "Maybe you'll do better without me from here on."

"Do you want to quit?" Jeep asked.

"No."

"Okay. Let's leave it right there for now."

The next morning, Becker checked Martindale & Hubbell. Puddy, White had no Ray anything listed as a lawyer. And when Becker called and asked for Ray, the secretary said no Ray worked there.

"Maybe in the past?" Becker asked.

"I've been five years on the front desk," she said. "No Ray during that time. Sorry."

Becker showed up at campaign headquarters where Jeep said nothing to him about the night before.

Chapter 22

Charleston, October 17, 1975

John Corelli didn't feel a need to talk in darkness. He liked sitting in it, listening to the quiet, interpreting it, working with it. The streetlights on Quarrier Street were more illumination than he wanted.

He kept his eye on the three-story apartment building. He scanned the block—up and down, side to side.

He glanced at the two men in the other car. They were talking. Cigarette smoke drifted from both windows.

John Corelli had timed it well. He'd only been waiting three hours.

The red Jeep pulled into the parking space that Corelli had kept unoccupied. Delucci got out, locked the door and approached his building.

It was Friday, a little before 11:30 p.m. The wind had picked up, blowing from west to east.

When Corelli had driven along Kanawha Boulevard late that afternoon, he passed West Virginia's Capitol. Five feet higher than the U.S. Capitol's dome, it was gilded in 23 ½ karat gold leaf. Who are they trying to fool? he wondered. Must be the people who live here.

Corelli eased out of his car. No overhead light came on; he had removed the bulb. He came from behind while Delucci was getting his keys out of his pocket.

Corelli placed the blunt tip of his left index finger against the back of Delucci's neck.

"You're not going to get hurt. Don't move," Corelli said in a calm, almost gentle voice that carried the menace he intended.

Delucci didn't startle. His mind raced. Street robbery? "I'll give you my money."

"Not interested, Jeep," Corelli said. "I have a .38 snubbie pointed at the small of your back. Want to feel it?"

Jeep knew he was not being robbed. Maybe he was about to be killed.

"I don't think I need to."

"Are you carrying?" Corelli asked.

"I will from now on."

"I'm going to pat you dahn. Don't take it personal."

Delucci grew curious despite his fear. The guy with a gun was not a mugger or a thief. Was this something Joe Hunt had cooked up? First Vernie Skeens. Then Chickie Siciliano. Now this.

"Spread your legs. Clasp your hands behind your back just below your shoulders."

Corelli searched for weapons with his left hand—under each arm, small of the back and pockets. He used his foot to search between

Delucci's legs and around his ankles. He didn't think Delucci would be hiding a pistol at the front of his waist, so he skipped a pat there. He knew if he reached around from behind, he would be vulnerable to a fast elbow to the head.

"You don't want money. What do you want?"

"A friend wants to talk with you. Don't worry, Jeep, it's just talk. They want you alive. Dead would have been easier on everyone. Move back to the street. They're in that Buick Electra on the other side."

"Big ride," Delucci said.

"Yeah. Big trunk, too," Corelli said. "Get in behind the driver."

Delucci opened the back door and slipped in. Corelli slid into the seat behind the passenger. He held his pistol next to his heart, aimed at Delucci.

"Thanks for stopping by," Foster Shives said from the driver's seat.

"Out for a drive, Foster?"

"In a manner of speaking," Foster said.

"The sluggo with the gun," Jeep said to Chickie, "is he part of your security business?"

"Independent contractor. Helps resolve problems."

"So...I guess I'm about to be propositioned in the back seat. Wish I had this Electra in high school. My propositions might have been more successful." Jeep did not feel as chipper as he sounded.

A car drove slowly along Quarrier toward The Capitol three blocks away.

"Like here are your three choices," Chickie said. "You can say 'Fuck you!' I respect a man of principle. Of course, that ends you up dead. But you'll have my respect.

"Second is you get outa this car after sayin' yes to my proposition. Then you call the FBI or the federal prosecutor. They come after me. I deny everything. They got squat for a case, and you, Mr. Stand-Up Citizen, spend the rest of your very short life in the witness protection program, hoping my friend never finds you. That ain't a winning gamble. If you do that, you don't get the chance to do all the good things you want to do. And you probably won't get a chance to testify."

"Or three?" Jeep asked.

"Take the money, win the election and help the miners."

"What if I take the money and lose?"

"That's my loss as well as yours," Chickie said. "Nothin' never works perfect. Losses is a part of my business just like gains. I'm bettin' you'll win."

"I should drop out of the race," Jeep said.

"That ain't one of your choices," Chickie said.

Jeep Delucci did not want to spend the rest of his life either in federal witness protection or dead. That left one choice—take the money and win.

"I need to pay Biggie back 200 that I've used for the campaign."

"I have 500 with me," Chickie said. "That's for the campaign. You pay your friend back out of Union money after you win. Now what do I get for 500?"

"What you asked for. The Bank sale goes through like you want."

"More," Chickie said.

"What more do I have to give?"

"Let's see if I can think of something," Chickie said. "How about I bring you a few investments for the pension fund and the Union's treasury that now has a bunch of my money from the sale of the Bank? Clean loans. Totally legit. No bow-wows."

"Like the Teamsters? Vegas casinos?"

"No. Better, much better. We're cashing them out. I'm talkin' real estate. Apartment buildings. Offices. Motels. Restaurants. Malls. Justice and Labor won't give you no grief over them. We learned a few things with Hoffa and the Teamsters. Good loans."

"You say 'good' like my Uncle Dominic who peddled vegetable and fruit seconds in Charleston door to door years ago," Jeep said. "Every apple was 'good,' every peach."

"He was an honest businessman, tryin' to support his family," Chickie said. "If he sold his customers rotten fruit, they wouldn't buy from him no more."

"He ran numbers for your local organization," Jeep said. "Small-time guy, small-time outfit down here. The fruit truck was a moving front. Cops never caught on."

"I know about your uncle. And one other thing," Chickie said. "You pay back all the money I'm givin' you in small bills with 10 percent interest when you win. I'm cuttin' you a deal on the vig, which I would be embarrassed for my associates to hear."

"Ten a year, I can live with that."

"Every six months," Chickie said.

"Six months!"

"You want it a week like normal?"

"Jesus."

"On the original 500 until you get it paid off," Chickie added for clarification.

"Jesus Christ!"

"He would have done better if he'd joined the moneylenders," Chickie laughed. "He wouldn't have ended up like he did."

"Where am I goin' to get that kind of money?"

Chickie looked at Delucci as if he had a brick between his ears. "From the $222 million that's comin' into the Union from the sale of the American Bank of Washington, dumbshit."

318

Jeep now saw what the light at the end of this tunnel illuminated. I'll have to embezzle a million or more to pay back this hood who can make or break my election, he thought. Great way to start as a union reformer.

Chickie continued. "I don't want paid back all at once, in one lump. You spread it out over a year or two so as not to be noticed. You can say this money is for research expenses, consultants, bonuses and raises to you and your staff. There are a dozen ways to milk a cow without her knowin' about it."

"You're not gonna let me get out of this car without my hand on that suitcase, are you?"

"Your first two choices are not in your best interest," Chickie said.

"Looks that way," Jeep said.

"And don't say anything to Becker about this arrangement," Foster warned. "He doesn't understand politics."

"With him," Chickie said, "the best thing to do is keep him where he is right now. Don't shitcan him yet. It'll look wrong. Reporters will stick their noses into your business. Tell Becker that Stover borrowed more against his land. If he found out, Becker might be dumb enough to turn you in. You don't want his mouth zipped, do you? You understand what I'm sayin'?"

"I do."

"Dump him after you win. Tell him to go into the mines if he wants a Union job," Foster said.

Delucci said: "Under these circumstances, deal."

He took the suitcase, got out of the Electra and walked to his door.

John Corelli laughed silently. Would it be, he thought, too obvious to conclude that the fix was in? Tony Bruno would be pleased. Chickie had gotten the job done. Tony had always told John the key to making money was to strip risk out of risk.

Corelli got in his car and started the five-hour drive back to Pittsburgh. He always liked long drives at night by himself. No radio. Just driving in the quiet.

Chapter 23

Middle Ridge, November 1, 1975, 7:47 a.m.

"Who the hell is Jackpot Ginsberg?" Jeffrey Becker asked into his bedroom phone. He scrunched his eyes while he held the receiver away from his ear. He guessed he probably wanted to know less not more.

"Sounds like I got you up," Mort Blatnik said without sympathy. "I thought big-time Communists like you rose at dawn to urge the proletariat to work harder."

"It's Saturday. I give all 'woikers' a day off from making the revolution. Jackpot Ginsberg? What are you talking about?"

"You are in an interesting situation," Mort laughed. "Sit back and listen. Jackpot owns Metropolitan Refuse, the Washington area's largest trash hauler. The others are mostly gypsy outfits—black guys with rattletrap pickups, scratching out a living off the misfortunes of their neighborhoods. Jackpot has a lock on most of the big private and federal contracts. He doesn't care about the penny-ante hustlers in Anacostia and Brightwood."

Becker felt an ache crawling into his head. He stumbled out of bed and dragged into the kitchen where he switched to the phone with the extra-long extension cord. He started the coffee maker. He swallowed an aspirin.

Mort Blatnik was the one labor representative on the board of the American Bank of Washington. He had directed the United Auto Workers' Washington office since the mid-'50s. He was a Depression-era socialist who had willingly transformed into a liberal Democrat with a trade-union agenda. Mort joined the UAW staff as a City College of New York grad and non-paid, go-fer economist during the 1936 Flint sit-down strike at General Motors. He moved up the UAW staff hierarchy as that Union grew in numbers, importance and wealth.

When Delucci won the nominating round, Mort called Becker with encouragement and congratulations—"Unofficially and on the Q.T., of course, President Woodcock feels the same. We think union democracy helps us in collective bargaining. We are, however, and as you know, in the closet on this matter in the multi-roomed house of labor."

"Why do I care about Jackpot Ginsberg?" Becker asked.

"Patience my young friend," Mort said. "I'm getting there in my own non-methodical way. Jackpot and I go to the same synagogue. He likes to be a big *macher*. He drops a lot of money on the rabbi. Let me not mince words. He's basically a hoodlum who has the Italians do his heavy adding and subtracting. Jackpot gives Jews a bad name if you ask me."

"What do you know about him?" Becker asked.

"A lot, unfortunately," Blatnik said. "Jackpot plays poker with my wife's cousin, Sy Rapkin—the highly esteemed cosmetic dentist in Georgetown. They grew up together in the District around F Street. Jackpot's football teammates at the old Central High had been calling him Jumbo, which he hated. He passed 300 pounds in his senior year, the biggest kid in the school. His parents came over just before WWI from Lithuania. His Dad was a butcher who died when Jackpot -- Sidney is his given name -- was nine. They were so poor they couldn't even go once a month to Posin's Deli up on Georgia Avenue.

"A month after his graduation in 1940, Ginsberg was playing poker on Friday night in the back office of Big Arnie Chodock's Garage near the corner of 7th and H. He cleaned out Morry Feldman who had just thrown in his nearly worthless 1927 Ford Model T pickup to see Ginsberg's hand and call. Morry's two jacks didn't beat Ginsberg's two queens, so Jackpot won some cash, the truck and a little black guy named Floyd who picked up the garbage. Morry gave him the name Jackpot, which Ginsberg liked a lot more than Jumbo.

"Having no other plan for his future, Jackpot bought two pairs of overalls from Sears on Saturday and took over Feldman's trash route on Monday. Floyd taught him the business. About three-quarters of his small stable of small customers were kosher butcher shops, corner groceries and delis in Jewish neighborhoods. He and Floyd scooted open barrels of rotting food scraps to the truck, lifted in unison and dumped each load in a ravine just beyond the District line. Jackpot grew to hate the smell of garbage. It made him gag and retch. In July and August, the putrid glop made him vomit into the barrels. I guess Floyd was used to it, or maybe he made the best of limited life options.

"Jackpot is not bright, but if he learns one winning trick he'll use it over and over. He stuck with garbage through the War, which his 360 pounds allowed him to skip. He met Rose Ziskind just after the Doolittle Raid in 1942. She was doing books for her Dad's pickle business at Eastern Market up on Capitol Hill. She had already noted the absence of eligible men. Rose was looking for any pig's ear she might turn into something that might pass as a silk purse, or just a purse. Jackpot was her ear. She saw he was willing to work hard and stick with it. Rose believed Washington would grow beyond anyone's imagination with the War and even after. Growth meant garbage. Garbage meant money. Garbage meant Jackpot.

"They married. Rose kept his books. It was she who suggested Jackpot move more into trash and less into food wastes, because, she said, 'it's classier, cleaner, easier and more profitable.' Her real motive, she later said, was that she detested washing his encrusted overalls in their bathtub every other evening.

"With Rose's agreement, Jackpot bought several used trucks on time and fell into a fortune hauling solid waste during the War. Construction and demolition residue, waste paper and food garbage—those were his big three. He never gave up the food waste, because he no longer had to work the truck with Floyd. He greased his first couple of contracts with a box of cigars and a case of good liquor. He soon learned that cash in a blank envelope worked even better.

"Jackpot filled the ravine and covered it with free dirt from the Pentagon's construction. Then he worked a deal with his brother-in-law, Max Ziskind, a Silver Spring lawyer who was slapping paint on slums for the new federal workers. Max set up a chain of a half-dozen sham corporations to own a 150-acre, worn-out farm in Charles County near a spot called Burnt Store. They built a landfill, which was just called a dump back then. Charles County was a farm wilderness after the War—mostly tobacco, no Beltway, just two-lane roads, no suburbs yet. You remember the Bob Dylan song, 'The Lonesome Death of Hattie Carroll'? Well, the drunk, 24-year-old, tobacco-gentleman, Billy Zantzinger, who killed her was from that part of Charles County.

"Anyway, the County said nothing about their dump, because there were no ordinances or zoning at the time. Jackpot and Max paid their property tax promptly. Their only neighbors were some poor-as-dirt country Negroes who they hired to unload the garbage and cover it up. When the County passed some ordinances in the late '60s, I've heard Max purchased permits without inspections after slipping 10 times the fee under the table. When neighbors complained about the smell and the taste of their well water, they were either bought out or persuaded to shut up.

"As the metropolitan area grew after the War, Jackpot's business grew in step. He cut a sweetheart contract with Vince DeFazio, business agent for the Teamsters' local, to keep down his costs for drivers and helpers. Vince got a house in Great Falls out of Jackpot's bribes. I've heard Rose labeled them in her books, 'fees to transportation efficiency consultant.'

"To his credit, Jackpot defended Floyd who DeFazio wanted to ditch. DeFazio said his local would not object to keeping Floyd as a helper on a trash truck 'but not a union driver, because a lot of white vets need work.'

"'Fuck 'em,' Jackpot said. 'Floyd was good enough for me so he's good enough for them. Fuck with him, and you fuck with me.' DeFazio saw Jackpot's logic after Rose agreed to add a den onto his house. Floyd drove a truck for Jackpot until a few years ago when he had a heart attack pushing the compactor button on his new garbage truck."

"So what's all this have to do with Delucci's campaign?" Becker said.

"Patience, my friend," Mort said. "You've heard of the pending sale of the American Bank of Washington?"

"In a round-about way," Becker lied.

"Chickie Siciliano is the buyer. $222 million!"

"You're joking!"

"That's what I've been told. Siciliano is the Mafia's front-guy in Washington. Chickie hides Mob money behind legitimate and semi-legitimate businesses. He reports to Tony Bruno, the Pittsburgh boss who goes upstairs to Frank Fagano. That's what a Labor Department investigator told me. The ABW is a prize for a dirty hand."

"So Jackpot Ginsberg is...who...what?" Becker asked.

"The Bank sent me my dismissal letter yesterday, along with two other board members. Siciliano has named two replacements, plus himself, and cut the board to five. Jackpot is one of the new directors. I expect the two remaining incumbents will get the heave-ho pretty soon. That will give him all five. So here's Jackpot's connection to Chickie.

"After the war Chickie partners up with Wyndham Clippinger, an old WASP money guy. Clip was buying land downtown near main boulevards like Massachusetts Avenue and Connecticut. Chickie's demolition outfit took down the crap buildings—most of which would now be considered historically significant. Chickie's asphalt company paves it over for a parking lot. Then he and Clippinger wait for the feds to show up with a need for a new office building, which they build and lease out. The asphalt is cheap surface and lot jockeys are paid next to nothing. Parking revenues cover their costs until the feds come along. And every building they erect has one of their underground parking garages. At last count, they had about 45 parking lots and 30 office buildings. Clip and Chickie are 50-50 partners in the land deals, parking lots, construction and leasing.

"Jackpot -- see I've come around to him -- got the refuse contract for every building that Chickie and Clip took down and replaced since the early 1950s. I've heard he pays them a 15-percent cash sweetener on the face value of every multi-year contract—the cost of which is then folded in to the rent, which our tax dollars pay.

"Chickie and Jackpot liked each other and found their rough edges fit together. They were both handshake guys who preferred to interpret contracts with baseball bats.

"Their relationship matured and evolved. When Jackpot needed 'some mechanics to work on' the dumpsters of a start-up competitor, Chickie sent them. Chickie also made sure that DeFazio's contract with Jackpot stayed comfortably below the union scale that was applied to his competition. And I've heard there were times when Chickie asked Jackpot to send Floyd out for a 'special pick-up' that was trucked directly to Jackpot's incinerator.

"Jackpot had something big on Chickie, but Rose told him he couldn't use it without getting killed in return. 'Chickie doesn't recognize the idea of immunity from revenge,' she said. And I've heard that her husband said, 'Don't want to use it Rose, I just like having it.' 'And he has just as much on us,' she said, ending that conversation forever.

"When The Post wrote a snide, up-by-his-own-smelly bootstraps feature on Jackpot in 1966, the cutline under his full-figured photo was: 'I'm in the business of solid-waste-removal systems, not garbage haulin'.' The story's hook was Jackpot's new, glass-and-brick, clean-as-a-whistle headquarters for Metropolitan Refuse on the site of Big Arnie Chodock's garage. Chickie built Jackpot's five-story building and became a 50-50 partner in Metropolitan Refuse, which meant he no longer had to ask for favors. 'Fifty percent of a safe, big something,' Rose said, 'is a lot better than 100 percent of a small, risky nothing.' The Ginsbergs grew rich as partners with Chickie Siciliano.

"Rose did her best to clean up her family's presence in the community—charities, contributions, sponsorships, synagogue, scholarships for poor black kids. But she always knew the score. I heard she confessed to her rabbi: 'Wipe a clean wet rag over a dirt-black window, you schmear it up. But a schmear is better than no schmear.'"

"Sounds like Jackpot's one vote for Chickie," Becker said.

"Here's number two," Mort said, "Chris Chaconis. Another American success story. He owns the Greek Isles restaurants, each of which is named after a Greek mythological character.

"Chris was a cook in the Army. When he got out in 1945, his Dad gave him $1,000 to open a stand-at-the-counter, hot-dog joint near McPherson Square. He and his wife, Annette, struggled for two years. They worked 15-hour days, six days a week, over a plate-steel gas grill, because that's all they could afford. One day they fried up bacon for breakfast and forgot to clean off the grease before putting on the lunch-time dogs. Customers liked the taste. So they started advertising bacon dogs, then bacon dogs with Swiss cheese, then bacon dogs with chili, then bacon dogs with whatever they could think of. Bacon lifted them.

"Early in the 1950s, Annette took a pencil and wrote a sign that she propped on the counter:

SPECIAL TODAY! MOUSSAKA.
Pronounce it right, and it's free.
Only $.25 a square with a hot dog.
Only $.50 by itself.

"Annette didn't know what else to do with the huge pan of untouched moussaka she had left after her parents' Plymouth DeLuxe broke down again on their Sunday drive from Baltimore to her place in Rockville. Annette's father kept insisting that each collapse was a 'freak accident, because everyone knows Chrysler cars are mechanically better than Fords and GMs.' Annette did not want to toss the moussaka.

"Moussaka in a hot-dog stand? Well, the worst that could happen would be that she would dump the whole pan into Jackpot's garbage.

"Her customers were construction workers and secretaries, none of whom were Greek. She knew them by name. They trusted her American cooking. But she had doubts when one regular thought moussaka was, maybe, Japanese—'Mouse Saki,' he said, before he declined a square. Another thought it was 'Arab like 'sheep kablobs.' By 12:30, Annette was desperate. She offered a free square to the first three diners who volunteered. She had one taker, who, after a forkful, proclaimed, 'It's real good, but different.'

"That broke the ice. Annette and Chris sold 17 squares that day of the 20 in the pan and figured they made a 50 percent profit. 'Heck of a lot better than dogs,' she said to Chris as he drove them home. She made spanakopita for the next Monday's 'Greek Special.' In a couple of weeks, she was getting new customers who wanted to try the foreign food.

"It took only two months for Annette and Chris to realize plain-vanilla Greek cooking served to non-Greek Americans was their gastronomical ladder out of hot-dog prison. They opened a Greek restaurant about a year after 'Moussaka Monday,' as they came to call the first try. By the late 1950s, they had four restaurants.

"Chickie started having lunch at Minerva on Pennsylvania Avenue, close to his office. It wasn't the Italian food of his childhood, but he knew he was in a village of not-too-distant cousins.

"When Chickie built his next office building, he worked out a 50-50 partnership with Chris to operate a restaurant on the ground floor. Jackpot got the trash contract. When Chickie suggested every so often that Greek Isles buy some seafood at a cut-rate price that he had 'brokered through some special connections,' Chris realized he was serving hot fish off a hijacked reefer truck. Meat, fruit, liquor, beer and cheese came in the same way.

"It was better, Chris and Annette thought, to go along than to stop and suffer the consequences. Chris figured Chickie would torch his free-standing restaurant and break the leases for the three in the office buildings. 'I expect,' Annette said, 'that would be our *best* outcome if we told him, no more.'" Chickie, soon, became half-owner in the Greek Isles chain.

Becker kneaded his eyes. "How do you know all this?"

"I was around when Chickie, Jackpot and Chris were coming up," Mort replied. "Washington, the business side, is a very small town. Some unions were tied into these guys, which, of course, we would never admit. Walter Reuther tried to do something about Hoffa and the Mob in the '50s and '60s. He had me look into them, to confirm or deny the rumors. Some rank-and-file Teamsters talked to me off the record, way off. Through some UAW guys, I made a connection to Floyd's brother. He and my wife's cousin, Sy, told me about Jackpot. The UAW's Washington lawyer filled me in on Clippinger and Chickie. I'm friendly with a couple of good guys in the Department of Labor, the ones who went after Hoffa. It's just a matter of asking around for a long enough time. When Reuther approached other unions about Hoffa, no one was willing to take Jimmy on. It was common knowledge that DeFazio was working sweetheart deals with Jackpot and Chickie. Everyone was scared of retaliation. They feared Chickie would target their locals for takeover just like DeFazio's.

"So far, the cops have been live and let live with Chickie. He's tied in to too many politicians at all levels. You open him up, you get hookers, backroom gambling, gifts and secret campaign contributions. It's our local version of what came out this year in the Church committee about the CIA's 'family jewels'—how the CIA used Sam Giancana, Johnny Roselli and Santo Trafficante as 'arrangers' to kill Castro with exploding sea shells, poisoned cigars and poison pills. 'Operation Mongoose' is what they called it. It would surprise me if Chickie wasn't the connection between the CIA and the Mob. Giancana, Roselli and Hoffa were murdered before they could testify in front of the Church committee.

"Chickie Siciliano may be a hood, but he's too useful and too knowledgeable about too many powerful people in Washington to be questioned, let alone prosecuted. He keeps his profile as low as a snake, which keeps him palatable to the pols. He's bipartisan. Every regime, every American administration -- no matter how virtuous -- needs its thugs."

"Is there more?" Becker asked.

"I'm afraid so," Mort said. "Jackpot and Chaconis are the first two of Chickie's picks for the ABW's board," Mort said. "Clippinger might be number four. There's also Moe Kazin who runs Mammoth Groceries. Five prominent, respectable businessmen.

"Siciliano wants to keep the ABW functioning, not loot it. He's not putting Mob meatballs on the board, except for himself. He's using businessmen who have been compromised, guys who have played ball for years. The Mob will go to the ABW through other parties for real-estate deals and takeovers of clean businesses. I'm also guessing he will bring in dirty money from off-shore and clean it through the ABW. He'll deposit cash in Grand Cayman, then transfer it to an ABW account. I wouldn't be surprised if the purchase money for the Bank isn't coming from an off-shore corporation through an off-shore bank."

"I don't know what Jeep can do," Becker said.

"They're closing the ABW sale before your election, I've heard. Maybe publicity…exposure?"

"Exposure?"

"Maybe a newspaper story would stop it," Mort said.

"An investigation like that would take months. You'd be accusing Siciliano of being a mobster, and Ginsberg, Chaconis, Clippinger and Kazin of being willing partners. You'd also be accusing them of doing something with the ABW they hadn't done yet—namely, corrupt it. It'd be a hard sell to any reporter. We have your stories, but no documents. No inside source. No money trail."

"That's true," Mort said. "The Bank's done nothing wrong in advance of the sale. Then, there's the other thing to consider."

"What 'other thing to consider'?" Becker asked, not wanting to consider any other thing at that moment.

Mort took a breath that Becker heard.

"Shit," Becker said.

"It's just a guess, Jeff, just a guess," Mort said quietly. "But my guess is that Chickie is trying to make sure -- or has already made sure -- that he'll get what he wants out of the ABW *no matter who wins the ACMU election.*

"Here's the second shoe dropping. Whoever wins the ACMU election doesn't matter, because Chickie will be coming after the Union's new wad of $222 million *and* its health and retirement money. It'll be like the Teamsters' Central States Pension Fund, which gave the Mob $250 million to finance their Las Vegas casinos. They skimmed profits and kickbacked $1,500 a month to Hoffa and others in the leadership. Chicago, New York and Cleveland bosses were behind that. Siciliano has ties to New York, but he's under Bruno."

Becker did not reply. Suddenly, his life had become much more complicated and dangerous. A long-shot election about union reform had morphed into a shadowy struggle to protect the Union's money and the health-care benefits and pensions for 125,000 working miners and 95,000 retirees.

"But the health and retirement fund isn't connected to the Bank," Becker pleaded.

"The fund has a board just like the Bank," Mort said. "Gain control of the board, and it's in your pocket. The fund processes lots of cash. It invests pension money. It's supposed to be a 50-50, industry-union board, but the coal operators always let the Union do whatever it wants. If Chickie has hooks into the winner of your election, he has to be looking at the fund."

Becker closed his eyes again, searching for escape, not sleep. He rubbed his forehead. Now he was facing two probable murders involving Jeep Delucci's signature vehicle and a Mafia plot to loot the ACMU health and pension plans. But what most disturbed him was Mort's warning that Siciliano would try to compromise Jeep. Threats? Warnings? Blackmail? Campaign contributions?

"Shit," Becker said.

"Shit is right," Mort said.

"What am I supposed to do?" he asked.

"Keep your eyes open and watch your own back."

Becker took a deep swallow of black coffee. "What can Jeep do? The bank sale will be approved by both the Union and the Bank's board. The price is more than the Union could have ever hoped for."

"What makes you think $222 million is going to stick with the Union?" Mort asked.

"If Joe wins," Becker said, "I suppose some bucks will leak into his personal pocket. But how much can one amateur crook steal? And I guess he'll use it to pay for the avalanche of advertising and bribes we've seen in the last couple of weeks. He can't steal more than a million or so out of 222. That's not so bad."

"And what if Jeep wins?" Mort asked.

"What do you mean? Jeep wouldn't steal from the Union."

"Not directly. Not into his pocket. But just consider how much of the $222 million Chickie might be able to claw back from Joe…or Jeep? I ask that reluctantly."

Becker shook his head, trying to banish Mort's thought to Siberia, or farther.

Mort Blatnik liked Jeep Delucci. The UAW had given Jeep its back-door approving nod. Blatnik liked the idea of democratic unions. He wanted young guys to step into leadership positions. He wanted labor's house to be cleaned up from the inside, not by the Department of Justice and Senate investigations.

"What are you saying?" Becker asked.

"I'm not saying; I'm asking."

"You mean Siciliano would get most of his $222 million back out of the ACMU? How?" Becker asked.

"Unsecured loans to his front businesses. Loans that never get repaid, or paid pennies on a dollar. Investment capital put into front businesses. Consulting fees. Salaries for no-shows. My guess is he's figured how to buy the American Bank of Washington for pretty much nothing over time."

"Jesus! Maybe this is paranoia," Becker said without much hope.

"Maybe. I don't know enough to know what I know or what I don't know."

Becker flinched. And then he flashed on the quicksilver image of two men leaving Jeep's headquarters at night—Foster Shives and the other one, "Ray," his "law partner," who wasn't.

"Do you have any reason to think Siciliano got to Jeep?"

"I bet he's been approached," Mort said. "Maybe threatened and told to keep his nose out of the sale."

328

"The ABW horse is out of the barn," Becker said. "Jeep can't do anything about that now. But I doubt he'd go along with corrupting the Union or the fund. He's not wired that way…I don't think."

The conversation stopped. Then Mort asked: "Where's Jeep getting his recent money? From my perspective as a total outside observer, it looks like your campaign's been matching Joe Hunt dollar for dollar over the last couple of weeks."

Becker felt his unease rise with his uncertainty. "I don't handle the campaign's money. Biggie Stover does. I know Stover borrowed against a big piece of land he owns to get us through the nominating round. I was told he had borrowed more against this property."

"How is Delucci going to pay him back if he loses?"

"I don't know. Maybe he'll take over the payments," Becker said. "I was never part of that discussion. Money has always been just between Jeep and Biggie."

"And how is Delucci going to pay Stover back if he wins?"

"I don't know. I never asked. It's between them, not between the campaign and Stover. The borrowed money went straight into the campaign accounts. That much I do know."

"How much came in the door after your win in the first round?"

"Four hundred, maybe five, from Stover's additional borrowing, I guess," Becker said. "I just spend it. We were pinched, out of money after the nominating round ended. Then we got one big infusion."

"You're sure the big money came from Stover?" Mort persisted.

"That's what I was told," Becker said defensively. "Am I sure in any absolute sense? In an epistemological sense? No."

Mort laughed. "The epistemology of campaign contributions. How do we know what we think we know? Well, it's something to put an eye on. An eye on, not a nose in, is my suggestion."

"Right," Becker said, not knowing how much he wanted to know or not know. "So Chickie reports to Pittsburgh's Tony Bruno?"

"Yes and no," Mort replied. "If you ask me, a move this big, involving this much money, so soon after Hoffa's disappearance and the Church Hearings has to come from Frank Fagano, head of the Commission. More speculation, of course."

Becker grimaced, his eyes closed, his head pounded.

Mort Blatnik heard the silence. "It's hard to know what to do."

Becker was trying to think. "Would the Mafia kill Delucci if he refused to take their money and refused to let them in to the Union?"

"Maybe. But I doubt it," Mort said. "If they killed him, then they don't get what they want from him. They could certainly threaten to kill him. That might work. From what I've seen, they generally prefer extorting or blackmailing prominent people. Killing their patsy is an admission of failure. They could threaten to kill someone in his family or Stover. They might be able to get something on Jeep, something they could leverage. They like to give their targets one-choice choices. Then squeeze them slowly, so they don't feel it all at once. The target soon realizes he can't escape additional 'cooperation.' I saw this with Hoffa and the Teamsters. This is what Siciliano did with Jackpot and Chaconis."

"Take this to The Post, not me," Becker said. "Give it to Woodward and Bernstein. It's small potatoes after Nixon, but it's their kind of carbs."

"Very good," Mort laughed. "I had the same thought. So I went through the Post's clips. I couldn't find a single investigative story on organized crime in the District in the last 15 years. They report Congressional investigations, but they don't do local tie-ins. They stick with the little, easy stories, not the big, hard ones.

"They'll run pieces on prostitution rackets in Prince Georges County when arrests are made. They like hooker-and-pol stories. They did a piece on a bookmaking operation in Laurel. They identified the bookie but ran nothing about the organization behind him. That's it. The stories that mention Siciliano, Clippinger, Ginsberg, Kazin and Chaconis were frosted flakes.

"Maybe the paper doesn't want trouble with DeFazio—you know, Teamster drivers calling in sick or delivery trucks suffering 'break downs' that magically fix themselves after a field mechanic is sent out for a road call. Drivers and mechanics could mess up deliveries in a dozen ways. The Post is going through a bad pressmen's strike. Local 6. Katharine Graham wants to back them out. She trained non-union pressmen and keeps the paper running through the strike. Don't let her pearls fool you. She's a hard-ass. She doesn't see a future for high-cost and redundant pressmen. Neither do I. She needs to automate the presses as much as possible and cut labor. The pressmen want to protect their jobs. They're not going to succeed. Taken altogether, I don't think The Post wants to target another union right now."

"Don't Justice and Labor look into this kind of mess?" Becker asked.

"The UAW's experience with both federal agencies is that something has to attract their attention, something outrageous like a newspaper series, a murder, flagrant acts—something that can't be ignored. Then they look into it. Siciliano and Clippinger are big contributors to both parties. They also give to Senators and Congressmen on committees that might scrutinize their activities. Jackpot gives to whoever is mayor or likely to be mayor. The politicians might move if it became too hot for them to refuse to do so. On his own, Gerry Ford won't take them on."

"So what reporter would be dumb enough to take up this thankless, dangerous task?" Becker asked.

"I have the minutes of the ABW's board meetings, which would help that person," Mort said. "The two other ABW directors who were just canned might talk off the record, as would I."

330

"Let me think about it," Becker said. "Thanks for calling, I guess."

Mort sighed audibly. "Life is full of hard choices, Jeff. It's easy to duck them. I've done that and usually regretted it. Avoiding the right choice usually ends me up facing a new set of worse alternatives. You're not the first person in the world to be asked unfairly to make a risky decision for the common good."

"Yeah," Becker said. "Maybe, I'll get my nobility badge."

"Maybe you can do something, maybe not. It would be worth a try if there's a chance to stop the steamroller. If we could only find someone to write it," Mort said. "We owe it to the miners."

"Yeah, 'someone,'" Becker said. "Okay."

"I'll let you know if I hear anything more."

"Sure," Becker said. "Thanks for the call."

Becker hung up. He thought of Allyson, a reporter in need of a big story. And then he thought better of that.

As Saturday passed, Becker kept telling himself to stay away from it. And the more he thought about staying away, the angrier he got.

Chapter 24

Bloomingrose Holler, November 3, 1975

The picket line appeared at American Eagle's front gate in Bloomingrose Holler at 10:30 p.m. Everyone was on time. Miners coming to work the hoot-owl shift that would begin at midnight were the target. Five vehicles were parked on the State's easement across from the entrance. High-intensity security lights lit the double gates.

Ten women stood in the cadaverous whiteness. They were dressed for warmth—winter coats, scarves, boots and gloves. This early November night was cold and getting colder.

They walked in a circle, holding homemade signs. One read:

American Eagle Widows Say
STOP THE SPEED UP
NOW!!!!!

At 11 p.m., the first pickups approached the entrance bringing miners to work. They pulled off the highway and stopped, engines idling, heaters on, lights ablaze and radios tuned to either WHQX country in Gary or WHKX country in Bluefield. Seven trucks stacked up quickly. Then 15 more. Men got out, looked at the women and then at each other. Each woman had a black mourning ribbon pinned to her coat.

"Evenin' Miz Smith, Miz Decker, Miz Estep, Miz Rutherford," Freddie Pruitt, head of Local 4355's elected safety committee, said. "What do you all have in mind here?" He checked his watch. It was about 10 past 11. More vehicles stopped behind the others.

"We're a-protestin', Freddie," Wanda Smith said to him and the men gathered behind him. She pointed to her sign:

Remember the American Eagle Seven

She pointed to another sign:

Coal will be mined safely or not at all!

"Nice penmanship," Freddie observed.

"That's Miz Estep's doin's," Wanda said. "The teacher."

"I know who Miz Estep is," Freddie said. "She taught most of the people in both hollers, includin' a rockhead like me."

Freddie nodded to Doris Estep, the superintendent's widow, and Linda Faye Decker, Mike's wife. Mike and Freddie had bowled together. Freddie noted that Susie Rutherford was in the group, along with the wives of all the others who had been caught in the roof fall three weeks earlier. He gave a second look at Doris Estep and Lee Roy Stump's widow, Alma Rae. Management wives on a wildcat-strike line! Women picketing out a shift of coal miners was unheard of, but bosses' wives joining them! Now that, Freddie thought, had to be both a first and a Guinness World Record.

"It's a mir'cle that Willie an' Byron and Mike got out," Freddie said. "Everyone is hurtin' over this. Union's supposed to be lookin' at it, along with the feds and the state."

"We want the men to honor this picket line," Doris Estep said.

"Miz Estep," Freddie said, "you and Miz Stump, good evenin'. You all sure you want to be doin' this?"

"We talked it over, Freddie," Doris said to her former pupil. "Alma Rae and I, we lost our husbands, the fathers of our kids. Just like five of these other women and their families. We're no different in death. And we know what we know. UNICOAL can't do anything against us. Not now."

"Safety committee has been on UNICOAL 'bout the speed-up," Freddie said. "You know a lot of this has to do with them damn A-Rabs. Excuse me. Them OPECers. That oil boycott lets UNICOAL sell anything that's black an' hard an' burns for three times more than what they had been a-gettin'. They're goin' to put in that long-wall machine next year. Produce a lot more coal with it. But now they got us movin' as fast as we can to sell into a hot market. Other operators doin' the same."

"We know," Doris said. "Delmer talked about it at home with me. Lee Roy, too. The order came from Pittsburgh, from Mr. Smithers."

"If they hadn't been a-runnin' that fast," Susie Rutherford said, "they could have pulled out of that bad roof. They could have checked it out better. Wasn't safe for Willie to go cuttin' into it blind like he did."

"You ladies are right," Freddie said. "Got no quarrel with anythin' you've said. Maybe Willie would have tested the roof different if he hadn't been under pressure to run coal that shift. Maybe we should have just backed out of the bad top and stayed out. Maybe I shoulda pulled the men away from an 'imminent danger.' I'd heard it was bad top."

"We want you men to honor our picket line," Wanda said. "We got us a committee—American Eagle Widows and Wives for Safety Now. It's too late for some of our men and for some of us, but it ain't too late for you all."

"Ladies, I know you know when miners see a picket line, we don't cross it," he said.

The women nodded. They knew. That's why they were standing there at night, in the cold, feeling uncomfortable in their role but determined.

Freddie Pruitt knew each woman, most by their first names, even Mrs. Estep who went to his Methodist Church. She had taught him math and English in the sixth grade and coached his grade-school basketball team. The white women lived along the creek in Bloomingrose Holler where Freddie had been raised and now owned a double-wide mobile home on a permanent foundation. All the black women lived up Anawalt Holler. Kids from both hollers had their rivalries and snowball battles, but once in the County's consolidated high school, they tended to stick up for each other since all were considered to be "American Eagles." Freddie knew each of their men as did most of the miners reporting for their shift.

Freddie understood wildcat strikes. You honored picket lines from fellow miners. That rule had been cold hammered into ACMU miners in the 1930s. A picket line was leverage. It was a negotiating instrument. It sent a message. It got immediate attention.

But a picket line from the widows of miners? From the widow of a superintendent and the widow of a section boss? Freddie didn't know about that.

This decision came down to how many shifts were he and the others willing to lose, how much income were they willing to forgo, how much were they willing to risk fines and jail to support these ladies in their protesting? And, by the way, he thought to himself, what exactly are the strike's demands?

"Speed-up killed them," Sharon Lewis said.

"I heard Delmer talk about it," Doris said, looking Freddie straight on just like she'd done when she called him to the blackboard to do long division.

"So how's Willie doin'?" Freddie asked Susie.

"He mendin'," Susie said. "They took his leg. It's in his mind more than anythin'. I'm glad he still with me. Don't care 'bout one leg shorter than the other."

Freddie nodded. "Yeah, we heard."

"I care about his heart."

Wanda Smith wanted Freddie to focus. "Onliest way we get anythin' down here is to stop the coal from goin' up there. Sometimes, you gots to deal from the shoulder. You mens knows that."

Words the men had said themselves had just returned with topspin.

"No one here disagrees with you," Freddie said. "But you're askin' us to give up this shift and who knows how many more? That's $50 each, straight time. If we're out for a couple of weeks, then all of us will be hard up to make our bills. Wildcat strikes are easy to start but not easy to stop."

"We stop when the comp'nies take their feet off the gas pedal," Wanda said. "Go back to regular minin.' Safe minin'. Safer, anyways."

"No one thinks you're wrong 'bout that," Freddie said. "You all prepared to see this through?"

"We're as ready as we can be," LeeAnn Dorsey said, holding The Ghostman's Bible against her breast. "We've got people to watch our kids if…when…they arrest us."

Freddie Pruitt turned to the miners standing behind him. They had heard the women. All agreed with what both the widows and Freddie had said. Although he was not the local union president, Freddie was respected for his leadership. His shift, at least, would do what he recommended.

"You boys know what this will cost you," Freddie said, addressing the group of about 80. "On a wildcat, no one gets strike pay from the Union. Joe Hunt will have to tell us to go back to work; otherwise, they'll put his ass in jail. Excuse me, ladies. We'll be on our own—each of us with whatever we have to get by. They'll hit us with a temporary restraining order, a T-R-O, to keep us from picketing our mine and pullin' guys out at others. If we violate the TRO and don't go back to work, they'll hit us with fines. Maybe I'll end up in jail for disobeyin' a federal court order. We been down this road a time or two, but we've never led anythin'."

"They'll hit us women with a T-R-O," Doris said. "They'll scare us with legal, legal, legal."

"Well, ladies, jail *is* scary," Freddie said.

"I been once," Wanda said. "I ain't afraid of boredom and bad food again."

"No one wants to go to jail," Doris said. "And I'm sure that UNICOAL will not put seven UNICOAL widows in jail."

"Depends on how much coal you're stopping," Freddie said.

"We womens are ready," Wanda said.

"If'n we do this," Freddie said quietly, "we got to have you women on board. Shoulder to shoulder. Side by each. If you stick, the men won't go back no matter how bad it gets. They'd be ashamed to."

"Us ladies have talked this over," Susie said. "We ready."

"They're gonna paper us with injunctions and you women, too," Freddie said. "We don't have the local right to strike in the '74 Contract. We got no legal cover for a wildcat."

"We're ready," Doris said.

Freddie shook his head. "Ladies. If they break you, this end-the-speed-up strike will stop like it hit a brick wall. They'll threaten you with cuttin' off your widows' benefits, life insurance, medical coverage, comp'sation. They'll fight you on getting black-lung benefits. You'll need to get some lawyers workin' for you. The comp'nies will pressure Joe Hunt to shut you down. An' they'll work through the management wives on you, Miz Estep an' Miz Stump. And then they'll try to buy you off with money.

UNICOAL won't play nice, no matter what John-Cee said when he was down here."

"This ain't about money," Alma Rae Stump said.

"I ain't for sale," Wanda said. "Least wise not for less'n a million." Everyone snickered at the outrageous sum.

"Miz Estep, Miz Stump. You ladies prepared to go to jail?" Freddy asked. "For us?"

"For us, too," Doris said. "We want to make something good come out of all this bad."

Alma Rae nodded: "We want to make it count. Not just go on like nothin' happened here."

"We have made arrangements," Susie said.

"Toothbrushes are packed," Wanda added.

"By God," Freddie grinned. "I do believe we got us some home-grown, right *dis-ruptive* elements here on Bloomingrose."

"These women done lost their men, Freddie," Linda Faye Decker said. "Everything after don't matter much. The rest is just inconvenience."

"I know," he said. The men behind him agreed.

"You all know what you're askin' us to do, and we know that you're ready to see this through," he said.

The women nodded.

Freddie faced his shift. "I ain't local president. An' we don't have no strike committee set up to make this kind of call. Boys, it's up to you, right here, right now."

Freddie had grown up with many of these men, gone to school with them, knew the rest from work. One had been his Little League coach. The older men had worked with his father and his older brother. All of them carried coalfield history. They'd heard the stories about organizing drives in the '30s. They were Pruitts, Rutherfords, Smiths, Adkins, Ramellas, Wills, Nelsons, Sweets, Bells, McGraws, Barnellis, Deckers, Buchanans, Stumps, Guerrants, Millers, Guskys and Andersons. Second- and third-generation UNICOAL workers. Blacks, whites, locals, Italians and mixes. They had their differences, their quarrels, their prejudices. Delucci supporters and Hunt loyalists were at odds though they might be hunting companions or even kin. The whites on Bloomingrose didn't socialize with the blacks up Anawalt, not counting the interracial sex that trafficked both ways now and then. But all of them worked together, played ball together and believed the only chance they had to improve their lives was to stand together.

"If it ain't unanimous, I say we don't do it," Freddie said. "This strike is for stoppin' the speed-up. Give me a show. For?"

Hands went up.

"Against?"

No hands went up. About 20 percent of the crowd didn't vote.

"You boys that didn't vote either way, you willin' to stick it out? If not, now's the time to have at it."

"Got bills comin' up," one said. "Don't have no savin's."

"Same," another said. "I can go two weeks, maybe, then it's damn tight. Sell somethin'. Maybe I can borrow from my folks."

"I was puttin' aside for a Christmas elk hunt to Colorado, not no strike," said a third.

"I think it'll go like this," Freddie said. "If we can pull all of southern West Virginia, southwest Virginia and maybe some up north real quick, like within a week, they'll settle with the ladies and slow down the pace. If all the comp'nies stop the speed-up together, no one gets an advantage. But if the strike stays local, we lose. If us and the ladies can't spread this thang, then we should go back to work in a week. We'll know right quick if it's cookin'."

Freddie Pruitt felt their assent to his one-week test. Each agreed in silence, and he looked into their eyes to make sure it was meant.

They would lose pay. That was certain. A week for sure, maybe a lot more than that.

But the real risk -- The Big Hammer -- was being fired for wildcat striking, which the '74 Contract prohibited. Any miner with a reputation for leading a wildcat would be blacklisted. If a miner wasn't allowed to work at mining in West Virginia, Kentucky or Virginia, he faced a simple choice: Leave the mountains or starve.

Freddie walked to his truck and took out his lunch pail. He held the chubby aluminum cylinder and took out the top pan that held his food. The lower two-thirds contained enough water for a day, or even two, as a precaution against being trapped underground. He spilled his drinking water on the ground. Those who weren't carrying their dinner buckets with them returned to their vehicles and dumped their water, too.

The light from American Eagle's security lamps shimmered brightly in their road puddles.

"Awright, boys, we ain't a-goin' back till we get us some safety and stop the speed-up," Freddie said. "We're a backin' this Widders Committee down the line. That's the deal. But listen up. No nailjacks on the roads. Don't want no blown tires. No bad publicity. Now let's divide up and picket out the morning shifts as far as we can go. You know what to do. Get them boys to jump it to the next mine, and them, the next."

The women smiled little smiles, tight little smiles. The men straightened their backs.

"Anyone who knows someone on midnight shift at another mine, get on your CB right quick and see if we can't pull them before they go in. Tell 'em, we'll get someone over there to picket them out official as soon as we can. We gotta move fast and hard. I want some of you Hunt people -- you, Windell Wayne -- to get up with the District 29 people in Beckley

337

and let 'em know what we're doin' and why. Let's try to hold Joe Hunt in place for as long as we can, just doin' nothin'. He'll come out publicly to go back. I'm talkin' about what he can do within the Union against us. I don't want to be kicked out of the ACMU for backin' these ladies. I'll call Delucci up in Charleston. Let's keep this strike for the women -- and for us -- out of Union politics.

"Awright, boys, let's roll out this ol' dance rug. Ain't a-gonna be no fire in the hole tonight."

Linda Faye Decker sat with Wanda Smith, Doris Estep, Alma Rae Stump, Susie Rutherford, LeeAnn Dorsey, Jeannie Lou Burdette, Sharon Lewis, Daisy Jones and Juanita Buchanan. The founders of the American Eagle Widows and Wives for Safety Now arranged themselves in the living room of the Deckers' brick rambler that Mike built in the mid-1950s. Smithers Elementary was across the road. She heard kids arriving.

Linda Faye served coffee and Oreos, which she'd bought the day before so they'd be fresh. She'd lived with "nerves" before the cave-in, but they were twice as bad since. So she ate cookies for comfort and calmness. She'd also gotten some sugar-free biscuits for the diabetics among them. She promised herself that she'd get back to Weight Watchers once Mike healed. She hated being so round—particularly since she was not yet into her 50s. She hadn't baked anything, which she knew Susie or Doris would have done.

It was still early. The sun was rising out of the clouds that clung to the ridge east of Bloomingrose. Kids filing into school were buzzing and not from lack of sleep. The Widders Committee, as the miners immediately dubbed them, had started something that had never been done before. The kids knew something was up when they didn't see the hoot-owl shift leave the mine and the day shift go in.

The women had neatly stacked their picket signs in the front hall under the nine-point buck that wore Mike Decker's ball caps. He was asleep in the bedroom with casts on both legs, dreaming on pain killers. His doctors were not optimistic.

Linda Faye poured coffee and put a quart of half and half on the dining-room table, along with spoons, paper napkins, sugar and Sweet'NLow packets.

None of these women had ever done anything like what they had just done. It was too soon to brag. Their first step was no more than one step. But each felt a power she had never known before.

Linda Faye bit off half a double-stuff. Damn, she thought, what *did we* just do!

Doris Estep adjusted the eyeglasses that hung from a ribbon around her neck. She'd taken a leave of absence from her sixth-grade class after Delmer's funeral. She'd taught American Eagle kids for 24 years—math, English and science. She'd taught Billy Burdette, Darrell Dorsey, Freddie Pruitt, her own two kids and Lee Roy Stump's two. She'd taught the kids of Timmy and Juanita Buchanan, Sharon and Byron Lewis and Daisy and Petey Jones after the old school "for the collard up Anawalt" was closed, and everyone jammed in to Smithers Elementary and Middle School.

Doris, Superintendent Estep's wife, was an important woman in the American Eagle community, perhaps the most important. But apart from that, Doris had a presence she'd developed lion-taming "jumpity" children who were getting their hormones ever earlier. She'd faced down out-of-control, 14-year-old loser boys in her class more than once. She didn't scare before she'd lost Delmer, and she certainly wasn't about to scare after. She'd always been glad she'd been raised as an up-lift kind of Methodist. The women in Linda Faye's living room trusted her. She was now Delmer's widow more than a superintendent's wife. She was ready for the pressure UNICOAL would put on her—a manager's wife leading a wildcat strike against his employer. If Martin Luther King could sit in the Birmingham jail for civil rights, Doris Estep was willing to be locked up for the kind of mine safety that would have saved her husband. No brainer, she thought. Maybe she'd write a "Letter from the Welch jail." Maybe she'd be fired from Smithers Elementary. It was hard to say what UNICOAL would do with her.

Wanda Smith felt an unfamiliar power flowing through her. At twenty-three, she was in no mood to be nice as pie. The southern civil rights movement in the 1960s had mostly missed southern West Virginia. But she'd heard stories and seen television clips of Freedom Riders, Birmingham, Freedom Summer, SCLC and SNCC. Although some locals believed as a matter of faith that wild panthers still roamed Appalachia's backcountry, Wanda had never met a Black one. And, in all honesty, she knew by 1975 those times were gone. She'd been too young for the 1960s. She had also seen that life up Anawalt Holler was changing a little for the better each year.

Wanda married Artie Smith at 18 immediately after graduation. She'd done some secretarial work at the Community Action Agency in Welch. She found those folks tired and cynical after eight years of trying to mobilize the poor and keep them fighting once the retributions started. She'd heard about women's liberation. At first, she thought it might be more of a white-girl's gripe than hers. But marriage and television had opened her eyes about women. With men, she'd had her eyes opened as a 14-year-old. She and Pins had had their fights. Neither knew much at first about working things out. But they both understood their fights came from their intense feelings for each other, a sense they were two against the world. They both knew she was smarter. If she'd been born somewhere else, she would have gone to a good college and become a focused professional, maybe one who joined a group of hell-raisers of one sort or another. A college like that didn't happen for smart girls from Anawalt Holler unless, Wanda would say, "they played football good enough for a scholarship." Wanda Jackson Smith was now a widow of a dead coal miner and impatient with life in Anawalt Holler.

"Now befo' we get to thinkin' we can walk on water," Wanda said, "we gots to understand that the mens was easy. It'll be the womens who gives us a fit. They want them paychecks rollin' in every two weeks."

"Can't blame 'em none," Linda Faye observed. "I want that paycheck too. We're still payin' a mortgage and truck note. We're all in the same boat. All of us live on that UNICOAL paycheck."

"I think, maybe, the womens are the key to this lock," Susie Rutherford said.

"Me, too," said Alma Rae. "The men'll take care of the workin' miners. They'll either dump their water or not when a picket shows up. I think we'll do best by goin' around and talkin' to the ladies. Go to the stores, even door to door like Avon or Jehovah's Witnesses. Each one, reach one. Explain the speed-up, and how we don't want them to lose their men like we did."

Alma Rae had surprised Doris Estep. Doris always understood that she, herself, was different from the ideal, UNICOAL management wife. She'd grown up in Arlington, Virginia, the daughter of a mid-level, federal civil servant and a high-school English teacher. She'd gotten her undergraduate degree at Ohio's Denison University and then met Delmer -- his first name still sounded a little hicky to her even after everything -- when she was getting her masters at the University of Virginia. He was there in engineering. She'd never been to West Virginia before he took her home to Beckley over Christmas, 1945, after he'd returned from the South Pacific.

Alma Rae, on the other hand, was a coal-camp girl from Slab Fork on the Slab Fork of the Guyandotte River in Raleigh County. W. Gaston Caperton and his brother, George Henry, opened Slab Fork Coal Co., in 1907, the first mine in West Virginia's Winding Gulf coalfield. They built a big camp and recruited local whites along with blacks from Louisiana. To keep the new pot of labor stirred and unmelted, they also recruited Italians and Poles. Alma Rae's great grandparents, Homer and Lottie Lester, moved into their rough-sawn, coal-camp house in the mine's first year. They saw it as a step up from the poor mountain farms they'd been born to in Letcher County, Kentucky. Cash wages, even if they were paid in Slab Fork scrip, were irresistible. Alma Rae was a WWII baby and spent her entire life in Slab Fork until she left for Beckley to waitress at the King Tut Drive-In on Eisenhower Drive. Lee Roy had stopped in for a burger and fries on his way to American Eagle for his first job. He courted her every weekend for a year. She thought marrying a section boss in training was a better deal than marrying one of the men he would be bossing.

"You right, Miz Stump," Susie Rutherford said to the younger woman. "We the ones to spread this strike."

"Maybe this strike'll make it easier for us widders to get our husband's black-lung check," Daisy Jones said. "Petey only had five years in but he was startin' to cough up the dust."

"He just 25 or 26," Wanda said. "Ain't been underground long 'nuff to get disabled on the X-ray."

"My Mom got on even though Dad was workin' when he died," LeeAnn Dorsey said. "But it was hard to prove he was totally disabled from minin' when he was still workin' full time."

"My Dad, too," Jeannie Lou Burdette said. "He worked while being disabled, because he had to. The family needed his paycheck. Ain't no mystery why used-up miners are workin' every day. You work and eat, or you don't and don't."

"Government sometimes approves widows even though their men were workin' when they was killed," Linda Faye said. "But the dead man has to be pretty old with a lot of years in. Their widows are way old, too. Shoot, ain't none of us a day over 40."

"Speak for yourself," Doris grinned.

"I am, truly," Linda Faye laughed, brushing back her bottle-blond hair. "Ain't seen 40 for a spell, a long spell. Ain't 50 yet."

"Government ain't gonna give no black-lung comp'sation to any of us, 'cept maybe Mike Decker if he can't go back in," Wanda said. "Mister Delmer and Mr. Lee Roy, they has the years employed, but not the day-to-day underground like Mr. Decker. And the res' of the mens, most of 'em wasn't old enough with enough years. Didn't have no terrible x-rays. We can't prove nothin'. Willie might have a shot. I knows he has the dust."

"Mr. Hunt, he give me his card and his personal phone number," Susie said. "Maybe Miz Estep would call him for help."

"That's your ticket, not mine," Doris said. "You can call Mr. Hunt anytime. He'll either push your applications through or he won't. If he doesn't, you're no worse off than you were before. What I'll do is send copies of our applications to our Congressman and Senators. Maybe they'll call over and see if we can't get approved before they turn us down."

The women laughed. They knew that most black-lung applications were rejected the first time. Then followed an expensive and multiyear appeal process.

"May be time for some of us girls just to haul ass outa Bloomingrose Holler," Linda Faye said. "Ain't no jobs for widder women here. We'll just be a reminder of a bad time. An embarrassment to the living."

"That or marry another minin' man," Juanita Buchanan said. "Timmy an' me, we talk about that. He said it wasn't no never mind to him after he gone."

"You really want to go through this shit again, darlin'?" Linda Faye asked.

"Timmy, he was a good man," Juanita said shyly with conviction.

"They all were," Linda Faye said.

"Well, Artie, he wasn't no saint," Wanda said. "But he tried, leas'-wise most of the time. More tryin' lately." She stifled a giggle. "Didn't run around on me that I know of. He knew I wouldn't put up with I'm-married-but-I'm-still-datin' shit."

"Well, it wouldn't have got him nowheres with a good-lookin' gal like me," Linda Faye said "I'm retired."

"They was all good 'nuff," Susie Rutherford said. "Not a one deserved to be roof-falled into the ground like that. Wouldn't none of us do that to a dyin' skunk. I…I can't say what I feel for you ladies whose men got killed. They was savin' my Willie when…."

"Hush, honey," Linda Faye said. "They was doin' for Willie what Willie woulda done for any of them. Weren't no collard an' white underground, Susie. Not that much anyways. Mike's said a thousand times. 'We're all black at the end of the shift.' He believes that, and so do I. That's the way we should do this committee. I'm black as a spade, an' you Wanda, you Daisy, you Sharon, you Juanita, you Susie, you white as snow."

"Well," Sharon Lewis said, "maybe we should all just settle for one shade of tan."

"Artie, he say, that UNICOAL treated all the hourlies as niggers," Wanda said."

Doris sat up. "UNICOAL" meant Delmer and Lee Roy, among others.

No one wanted to go down Wanda's path or even acknowledge they'd come to a fork.

"Delmer was far from perfect," Doris said, spacing her words. "His attitudes about race were not mine. He was a man of his generation, time and place. He grew up in segregation, which was what we all had right here until 10 years ago. He was an employee who had to get coal mined and on railroad cars if he wanted to keep his job. But he tried, I hope, to treat each man as an individual as well as everyone alike."

Wanda thought better of responding with, Like I said.

342

"When it counted," Susie said, "Mr. Estep and Mr. Stump threw in with the workin' miners fo' Willie. White and black, everyone threw in jes' the same. I think that's what we got to keep in our minds."

"Yes," Daisy said. "Roof come down on Mr. Estep and Mr. Stump just like on Petey and them others. Rock fall don't pick and choose between black and white. Kills everybody like there was never no difference between 'em."

Jeannie Lou who'd never felt comfortable around the "Anawalt collards," which they knew, said: "Us, women, too. Everyone together. Like the men." She felt proud of herself for pretty much believing something as radical as what she'd just said.

They stopped to catch their breath after leaping so fast over such wide chasms.

"Me an' Timmy got us two kids and a trailer," Juanita said. "Doctor told me a couple months back that I got the sugar. At my age! You tell me, how I'm gonna make it without a regular paycheck?"

"We'll do what we can to tighten up and stretch what we have," Linda Faye said. "Sooner or later the widders will get some money outa this shit. Excuse me."

"And we'll help each other through this," Doris said. "I have some savings. I'll help when you need it. You pay me back when you can."

"I'm sure we can stick it out for four or five weeks," Sharon Lewis said. She felt guilty in this group, because Byron had lived. She didn't think he was special or more deserving. "It won't last more than that."

"They'll try to split us up," Linda Faye said. "The operators will put the law on the men like they did the last time. They'll throw a few in jail to scare the rest. Then they'll tell 'em their jobs are on the line. They'll try to work a deal with us ladies that's less than what we might could get if we're solid together. Stores won't extend credit. Repo man will show his ugly face. Comp'ny secretaries will start rumors about whose husband is a-sleepin' with one of us, or more than one or us."

"Maybe all of us," Jeannie Lou said.

"At the same time?" LeeAnn Dorsey exclaimed. How would that work?

"I'm flattered," Doris laughed.

"Well, maybe not you, Miz Estep, bein' a teacher what everyone knows," Jeannie Lou said.

"My feelings are hurt," Doris laughed. She took a breath. "Wanda, you're the one they'll come after."

"Me?"

Doris hesitated. "Wanda, honey, I'm just an old, uptight, white-lady schoolmarm who married without any experience to speak of. They'll come at you with the past, the boys."

Wanda knew. "There was three in high school. Artie was one. The other two--one white; one black. I ain't run on Artie since we was married. What that old shit have to do with anything?"

"Well, the women in other coal camps, they don't know," Doris said. "UNICOAL will put the word out that you're runnin' around with a picket sign looking for a new man."

"Union'll do it, too. Mr. Hunt's mens," Juanita Buchanan said. "Mister Hunt, he don't want no wildcat strike. Make him look bad during his campaign."

Alma Rae took a deep breath. She primped her hair and sat up straight on the edge of her chair. "They'll say, you lookin' for white," she said directly to Wanda, "now that you might get some widow's comp'sation." It was the first time Alma Rae had ever uttered words about race and sex with someone who wasn't white. "That's what I might say if I didn't know you."

Alma Rae's honesty gathered them up like a pulled drawstring.

Doris and Alma Rae had talked this over with Linda Faye, Jeannie Lou Burdette and LeeAnn Dorsey the day before they picketed out the hoot-owl shift. The five white women -- two of them management -- had agreed that Wanda Smith was both their weakest link and their strongest. None looked forward to this discussion with her or the other black women.

Wanda was so pissed off that she thought her eyes would cross. "Those mothafuckas drop that mothafuckin' shit on me, I'll sue their sorry asses from here to Juvember! Girls with white skin don't have that shit said about them forever."

"Well, there *was* the two *other* boys...one white," Alma Rae said timidly and with obvious reluctance.

"Now, you listen at me, Alma Rae. I married my own. I loved that white boy, still do in a memory kind of way. But you all need to know that I ain't lookin' for no man, no more. If somethin' comes along, I'll see then. I got my eye in the mirror, not out no window."

Alma Rae was now party to a second topic of conversation that she'd never visited before. LeeAnn Dorsey and Jeannie Lou Burdette were squirming while trying not to. Sharon Lewis, Daisy Jones and Juanita Buchanan had grown up with Wanda. Her history was old news, and her reaction was what they would have predicted. But they understood the point the white women were making.

"That's what Doris means," Susie said to Wanda. "They'll try to pick us off. You be the easiest...for...whatnot. So you...we...gotta be prepared for it when it comes down on you."

"Can't change what I can't change," Wanda said. "I know it'll be hard for some of you to walk next to me. I ain't never been no model lady."

No one knew how to respond.

344

The women knew a favorite tactic in their community was to tarnish by association and rumor, to maintain divisions and create new ones.

Finally, LeeAnn Dorsey said: "What Peter said to Jesus in *Mark 14:29*: 'Even if all others fall away—not I.' I will walk next to you, Wanda Smith if'n it suits you."

"Thank you," Wanda said to LeeAnn. She thought it was the first two words she had ever spoken to LeeAnn directly.

Doris spoke. "Wanda, it's like this. You start throwing around 'motherfucking honky shit,' then this wildcat strike would do best to end right now in Linda Faye's living room."

The women were dumbfounded. No one had ever heard Doris Estep say more than "Golly Ned."

"Golly Ned!" LeeAnn Dorsey breathed. It was the strongest expletive she allowed herself, and she only said it once or twice a year. At that moment, she believed The Lord would understand her situation and forgive the thoughts running around her mind like mice in a cat-panic.

Doris said to herself: In for a dime, girl, now cough up the dollar. "Wanda, honey, if you come across as a foul-mouthed, race-baiting black...well, let me just say it straight out, black bitch, the white newspapers and TV will focus on you and your temper and your cussing and your Black Power. The speed-up, the safety, the point of what this strike is about, will get lost and overwhelmed. You can't win a fight against mean and evil talk. Don't give them any more ammunition than what they have. All of us need you to keep yourself in control, whatever you really think or want to say. Just like Jackie Robinson. You have to pick a path here. You can blow up or you can lock it down so that we might win this strike for everyone's benefit."

Wanda eyed Doris Estep with whom she'd never said more than a semi-formal, perfunctory "Mornin', Evenin' or Nice weather, today" as they passed on the street. Both Artie and Wanda had just missed having Miz Estep for sixth-grade math and science when the McDowell County School Board moved the Anawalt kids into Bloomingrose's school. But Wanda had heard the talk among the younger black children, "Miz Estep...she cold."

The women, white and black, looked to Wanda.

"You right, Miz Estep."

"Doris," Doris said.

"Doris. You right. I understand. From here on out: no mothafuckin' this or honky that."

"Well, bless your heart," Linda Faye snickered. "I better walk the same line. I promise I won't come out with no hillbilly-redneck shit either! 'Cept if I'm talkin' about my family."

That lightened the mood.

"Miz Estep, Doris, why don't you be the talker for our committee," Juanita Buchanan said. "You the best. Folks aroun' here always pays attention to what Miz Estep says in class."

Doris laughed. "That, I hadn't noticed."

"I think Juanita right," Wanda said.

"I think we should have co-chairs," Doris said. "I'll do it if Susie Rutherford joins me."

Their eyes turned toward Susie. The idea of standing in front of people, of white people, of educated people, of people from cities and The North, of reporters and TV cameras made her nervous beyond words. She felt her throat constrict and her hands tremble.

"Yes, ma'am," she said to Doris, "I do it with you."

"Good," said Alma Rae.

"If Wanda can keep her mouth shut, which I know is hard, I probably can open mine, I guess," Susie said.

"Good Lord, we now have us a stand-up comedienne," Linda Faye laughed.

"It's for Willie and all of 'em," Susie said, embarrassed by the self-confidence she'd expressed.

"Maybe, jes' maybe, we started something that'll do some good," Alma Rae said. "If the miners pull mines all up and down, from Pittsburgh to Alabama, and out to Illinois, then maybe they'll stop the speed-up. Our men will rest easier, and the mines will be a little safer. That would be somethin' to be proud of."

"I ready," Susie said.

"I'm ready," Doris said.

"If those fools dumb enough to throw Doris and Susie in jail, that's the best thing that could happen for us," Wanda said. "We win if they do that. If they throw me in jail, they win nothin'."

"Ladies," Doris said, imitating Sonny Corleone, "I think it's time we go to the cars."

As they walked out, Doris pulled Susie aside.

"I'm glad you agreed to work with me," Doris said.

"I'm scared to death. But I'll try," Susie said.

Doris paused. "There was always something I wanted to ask you or Willie. There was a famous scientist, Lord Ernest Rutherford, who was the first to split the atom. He won a Nobel Prize. Have you heard of him?"

Susie smiled, but just a little. "Willie has two of his books on radioactivity and one called The New Alchemy. Willie worked his way through all three. He figures that's why he can do big multiplications in his head. They're kin, way back in Essex, England, he's tol' me. Says Lord Rutherford figured out how atoms worked. 'Course Willie's people came here from South Carolina. The Rutherfords owned the plantation his people worked. There was some mixin' around over the years befo' the War durin' slave times. Willie knows he part Mr. Ernest Rutherford."

"Amazing. Tell him I'm honored to work with him."

"I'll do that Miz Estep."

"Doris," she laughed.

"Doris."

Chapter 25

Washington, D.C., November 9, 1975

As he sat in the taxi, Jeep Delucci closed his eyes. He felt Biggie next to him and was glad for it. This was his fourth time in Washington, D.C. He'd given the address to the driver. He knew how to get to ACMU headquarters downtown, a Georgetown bar and a hotel.

Is it worth it? he wondered as they drove through traffic. Is winning worth it? He felt himself in an enemy's sights.

"You know my Daddy gave some thought to askin' the Mafia for help once," Jeep said in a low voice to Biggie.
"What about?"

Jeep's thoughts wandered back to a day 20 years earlier when he was nine. It was a Saturday afternoon in 1955, early June.

Jeep and his Dad had stopped for soft ice cream at the Dairy Queen in Marmet after his Little League game. As they sat at the picnic table, Clyde Moore, general superintendent of USOCO's Sunburst mine where Jim Delucci worked, pulled up in a showroom-new, Chevy Apache 3100 pickup. It was turquoise, a color Jeep thought he might have seen in a big crayon box but never on a Boone County vehicle. The Apache's steel rims were fire-engine red. Its tires were fat white sidewalls. Clyde walked over to their table.

"Thought that was you, Jimbo," Clyde said. "Mind if I join you men."
"Have a seat," Jim said, as Clyde slipped in next to Jeep.
"Nice truck, Mr. Moore," Jeep said.
"Picked it up today, son, over at Joe Holland's in South Charleston," Clyde said. "Three-speed manual on the column. A 235 with a six-cylinder engine. Short bed. Nice radio. Even had them stick in AC. Probably the only truck around with AC."
"Good luck with it," Jim said.
Jeep noticed his Dad stiffen a little. Jeep shifted his attention back to stirring the soft chocolate ice cream in his root-beer float. He wanted the ice cream to lose its identity and the soda to thicken. The afternoon was a little colder than it should have been. He saw rain clouds drifting eastward up the Kanawha Valley. Sitting in his still-sweaty baseball uniform, Jeep felt chilled, which didn't stop him from drinking his cold float. He had considered asking for a hot-fudge sundae to fight off the cold but stuck with the float even though he knew he would shiver. Dairy Queen was a big-city treat. It was not to be squandered on a sundae he hoped might keep him warm.

Jeep had heard his Dad and other miners talk about Clyde Moore. They feared his power, so they avoided confrontations as much as possible. Occasionally, they would belittle his penny-pinching and his efforts to run "their" mine ever more productively. "Any fool can buy a machine and put 10 minin' men out of work," his Dad had said about Moore's ordering three continuous-mining machines that Joy Manufacturing had delivered a week earlier. Still, every Sunburst miner knew Clyde Moore had the power to lay off any of his 230 employees. The ACMU could take a discharge to arbitration, but layoffs were not grievable. In Boone County in the spring of 1955 with two of every five miners out of work owing to slack demand and mechanization, Clyde Moore's power was, if not life and death, at least, the power to determine whether you ate regularly from foods of your choosing or lined up for surplus commodities—lard, flour, pinto beans, peanut butter and powdered milk—that were begrudged and belittled.

"Howdja do in the game, Jeep?" Clyde asked, looking sideways at the dark-haired boy sitting next to him with his treasured glove in his lap.

"Kanawha City beat us, 4 to 3, but I got two hits, one a double."

"That's good, son," Clyde said. USOCO sponsored Jeep's team, the USOCO Stars.

Jim Delucci finished his small vanilla cone. He wanted to go. Instead, he tapped a Camel from the pack in his shirt pocket. He took a long, deep first drag.

"Your Daddy was a pretty fair third baseman in his day. Did ya know that, son?"

"Yes, sir. I seen his pictures. His mitt's at home. I keep it oiled."

"I was the pitcher on your Daddy's team. Didya know that?"

"No, sir, I surely didn't. Daddy never did say."

"I was big for my age. We won the league championship one year," Clyde said.

"Was a long time ago, Clyde," Jim said, with a small smile.

"That it was."

"We was jes' kids then. About Jeep's age, I reckon," Clyde said. "Your Daddy pulled my chestnuts out of many a fire with his glove and his bat. He was a line-drive hitter. Had some power, but mostly singles and doubles."

"Me, too," Jeep said.

"Don't recall ever seeing him strike out."

"I'm sure I did," Jim said.

"Maybe," Clyde said, "but not in the clutch, not when the team needed a hit."

"Long time ago, Clyde."

"Yeah, it was. But Jimbo, ya know, we're still on the same team."

A frown flashed for an instant across Jim Delucci's face. Jeep saw it, but wasn't sure what it meant, if anything.

"Oh, I know you're hourly and ACMU and I'm management, but we work with each other every day. You need the mine, and I need my miners. You don't get no bread for your table, less'n USOCO's bread is buttered first. Jes' a fact. We need each other, plain as day."

"I need *my* job," Jim said, "now that's a fact." He didn't know where this conversation was going, but he was a little afraid. Clyde Moore was not a superintendent who had heart-to-heart talks with his hourlies for no reason at all.

"It's sort of *our* job," Clyde said. "We pay you to do it, because you're good at it. But it's a job that was there before you were given the work, and it'll be there after you retire for someone else."

Jim Delucci didn't like this turn. It felt like he was being boxed in.

Jim had worked at the Sunburst deep mine since 1938, the year he graduated Sherman High. He took off three years for Army service and came back from Europe without a nick. He married his classmate, Juanita Pauley, in 1944 and welcomed his son, James, Jr., the next year. In 1955, he had 17 years of credited service, 14 underground. He needed 20 to get an ACMU pension. He planned on working at Sunburst as long as he could. You didn't find a $9.45-a-day job in West Virginia that year except in an ACMU mine, and sometimes not even there. In Boone County, an unemployed miner would work for $3 a day and count himself fortunate. Jim Delucci had watched unemployment gnaw the flesh off his next-door neighbor, a brother-in-law and his Dad.

"You fixin' to lay off some more soon?" Jim asked, his voice barely steady.

"Not jes' yet. But them three new Joys will let me cut back on general labor, the last few handloaders and the shot firers sooner than later. You all know that as well as I do. I want young guys trainin' on the miners and the bolters. I want young guys learnin' mechanics and electrician. Nothin's in the works for Monday, but that's the shape of things. We gotta keep mechanizing to keep our costs down. Labor costs kills us in competing for sales with them non-ACMU mines out of East Kentucky and Southwest Virginia. They sell our kind of coal for a buck or more a ton cheaper. On five-dollar-a-ton, that's a bunch of cost advantage. USOCO's raggin' my butt about it all the time. I gotta hit quarterly production numbers and quarterly costs. Ain't easy. They squeeze me. I squeeze you. Jes' how it is."

Jim considered Clyde's predicament. He repeated what he'd heard: "Them non-Union operators are a-payin' their men not but $3 a day, with

350

no health or retirement. They have to put in 10, sometimes 12 hours a shift. No time-and-a-half for overtime. We hear the stories from our laid-off guys tryin' it out when they're desperate. That Appalcoal outfit in East Kentucky is settin' the standard—low. Maggard, Buzzy Maggard, is the owner. He pays as low as he can with his men 'cause he knows there's a dozen or more waitin' in line for each job. Jes' a-sweatin' his dollars out of his people."

"You're right," Clyde said. "Them operators are undercuttin' us Union comp'nies on costs and price. They use beat-to-Hell equipment and pay their men as little as possible. Their accidents rates are three times ours, because they don't mine safe. But desperate people will work for next to nothin' if nothin' is their only other choice. I'd do the same. The only thing USOCO can do with an ACMU contract weighin' on us is to buy machines, which'll let us survive. Wouldn't nobody -- you, me, nobody -- have a job if we don't bite the bullet and buy them new miners."

Jim Delucci didn't respond. He knew the Company's story and didn't disagree with it. He also knew he was lucky to have been born with "good hands." USOCO had picked him to be trained to "mechanic" the new electric-powered equipment -- continuous-miners, haulage buggies, roof-bolters and scoops -- when USOCO started shifting away from blasting and loading in 1949. Had he not been talented, Jim Delucci knew he would be whittling nonesuch on his front porch in 1955 instead of buying his son a $.25 root-beer float at the Dairy Queen.

Clyde continued: "I know you need your job, and that's what I want to talk to you about."

Jim stiffened. He felt adrenaline moving through him. He tried not to look scared. Fear was no friend of his. But he and every underground miner knew how to stuff it down to get through each shift. Clyde's words spooked him, sending a liquid jolt through his veins. He did not want to join the permanently jobless in Boone County. He knew what that meant.

"Now what I'm aimin' at, Jimbo, is this. Ol' Lee Ray's gonna retire here 'round the first of the year. Has 35 years in. He's havin' trouble with his breath, which you know. Too many cigarettes, I guess. Anyway, we're lookin' for a man to take over bossin' his section, your section. You have your state papers. The men will run coal for you. We think you'd do a fine job."

Jeep looked at his Dad. Theirs was the world of West Virginia coal camps where sides divided for life between "comp'ny" and "Union." Clyde Moore was a local boy, but he was the son of a superintendent. He had gotten a mining degree from Virginia Tech and then signed up with Sunburst where his Dad worked. Clyde Moore didn't exactly count as rising from the ranks. A bridge always connected coal management and miners, but Jim Delucci knew if he crossed he could never go back. It would never be the same with his friends.

Jim Delucci once had ambitions. When he returned from the War, he tried to open a service station in Racine at the intersection of Rt. 3 and Rt. 94, the road to Marmet and Charleston. The lot was $900. He had that -- and more -- saved from his stateside $50-a-month buck private's pay and the additions he got as he rose to corporal. His experience maintaining military vehicles qualified him to work on almost any car or truck that might pull in for repairs. He'd located several thousand used concrete blocks for the garage's shell. He could mix the concrete for the floor by hand and dig a grease pit so he could work under vehicles in the shop and out of the weather. He needed to find two 20-foot-tall garage doors, some used metal-working tools and a tire changer. With the cash he had, he could get a bank loan for what he lacked.

But Jim could not line up a supplier. Esso wouldn't work with him, and neither would Gulf. He didn't understand why. His option on the lot ran out. And then an Esso station appeared within nine months, owned by the son of Boone County Sheriff, Okie Shreve. Jim concluded his reach had been about right, but he hadn't counted on the unseen grasp that had yanked him back to stay where he was. His stymied ambition went cold.

He hired back at USOCO and bought a surplus 1944 Willys MB Jeep with a "Go-Devil" four-cylinder engine that was optimistically rated at 60 horsepower. He scrounged a used canvas top that provided some protection in the winter. It wasn't a practical car for a family, but it got him to work on time. He and Juanita bought a small house in Cinderella Holler in Comfort. It had clapboard siding and a basement, a two-step-up improvement over the prevailing board-and-batten, Jenny-Lind houses set on cinder-block piers. He built a 20' x 30' shop where he kept his tools, worked on cars and nursed his one big grudge.

Jim Delucci quickly settled into the routine. As long as he worked efficiently, caused no trouble and kept up his "mechanicin" skills on new machines, he'd have a mining job. The idea of walking over the bridge to boss his own crew was disorienting and fraught with risks. Clyde understood the issues that Jim faced.

Jim picked through the words that were in his mind. "Don't know about that, Clyde. 'Preciate your thinkin' of me. Never did think about bossin'. Jes' happy to be workin' as a mechanic in these times. You have your pick for Lee Ray's replacement, seein' as half the men in the bathhouse has got their bossin' papers."

"I understand your position," Clyde said. "But we think it would work for you *and* the men, because you have their respect. Mine too."

"That's nice of you to say in front of the boy."

"I mean it Jimbo. I know you do things right. You don't cut corners. I 'spect the boy here has learned from you. The man who cuts corners ends up short on the suit."

Jim laughed. "Can't he'p myself."

"You'll make twice the money on salary in your first year. An' that's not countin' production bonus or Christmas bonus. The men'll work for you. You're easy on them, but you'll run coal."

"I s'pose," Jim said.

"Benefits are better than the Union's."

"I need three more years for an ACMU pension," Jim said.

"Well, them boys might work that out with us," Clyde said. "USOCO won't jack you around. You come over, we're not gonna cut you out down the road. I know the situation. If you want to go back to hourly after two years, I'll do it for you."

"Men would be worked up if I started bossin'," Jim said. "Ain't no one in my family ever done that. We never were lined out that way."

"Here's your chance," Clyde said. "Look. I've known you since we were kids. I know who you are. I've known Juanita almost as long as you. I know you got gypped out of that gas station after the War. I'm givin' you a shot to move up. This'll roll 'round just once. Let me know at the end of your shift on Monday. Nice seein' you, son. You keep up that ball. Maybe you can get a scholarship. Comp'ny helps out on that, too, 'specially if you're management."

"Yes sir," Jeep said as Clyde walked to his new truck.

"Whatja gonna do, Dad?" Jeep asked as Clyde drove into traffic.

"What do you think I should do?"

"Mom always says we could use more money. She wants to fix up the house. Get a TV for your bedroom. A new couch for the living room. Electric dryer."

"You're right about that. She wants them thangs."

"You could buy them for her if you make more money."

"Reckon so."

"An' for yourself, too. Metal lathe for the shed. An' how 'bout that Remington 749 Woodmaster .30-06 you've been wantin' for deer season? With cut checkering on a walnut stock, it's $139.95."

"And how do you know that?" Jim asked with a smile.

Jeep was embarrassed. Talk was cheap, his Dad always said. "Well, me and Mom thought we might try to get you one for Christmas," Jeep admitted. "But it's more than we can come up with."

"That was a nice thought," Jim said. "Thanks. I could get you some thangs too."

"So are you goin' to take it?" Jeep asked, with his hoped-for "Yes!" hanging in front of his face like a blinking neon sign.

"I'll talk it over with your mother," Jim said.

Jeep heard the doubt in his Dad's noncommittal tone.

"I'd do it," Jeep announced.

"Ambition is good to have, Jeepie. But sometimes it's like bein' in a mud hole. The faster you turn your wheels, the deeper you sink."

Jeep didn't understand.

"You ain't gonna do it, are you?"

"Prob'ly not," Jim said. "Jeep, son, I've learned one thang in the mines. When you eat the comp'ny's corn, sooner or later you'll be chokin' on the comp'ny's cob. I want you to remember that."

"Yes sir. I'll remember."

"Why do you think Mr. Moore asked you?" Jeep asked.

Jim thought a moment. "I guess he figures I'm the one who can make the next round of layoffs slide down our throats easiest for him."

"But you could do it, Daddy. You'd do a good job."

"S'pose that's true," Jim agreed. "S'pose that's true."

Jim Delucci spent the next dozen years maintaining and repairing the machines that continued to eliminate the jobs of his friends. Then his lungs got too bad—coughing, spitting up black gunk, labored breathing, shortness of breath, inability to work. He felt like he was suffocating half his waking hours. He knew black lung had gotten him. The radiologist told him he had a "good X-ray," which meant the fibroid growth of pneumoconiosis was so obvious and severe that his claim would not be denied. He retired in 1972 with 34 years of service, more than enough for an ACMU pension but too young for early Social Security retirement. He began receiving $250 a month in federal black-lung compensation in 1973. He considered himself lucky he didn't have to drag through three or four years living on almost nothing while he sweated out an appeal of the initial denial of his claim. He did easy putters around the house as long as he was able, but within a year of leaving the mine, he was bound to the house and mainly to his recliner. Juanita cared for him, drove him to his medical appointments in Charleston, paid the bills, kept up the house and tried to make his life easier. Jeep helped when he could, but his job as district president and then his campaign centered him in his Charleston apartment more than his old bedroom in Cinderella Holler.

Jim never passed that two-bay Esso station at Racine without feeling he'd been robbed of what should have been his. He could have handed it over to Jeep. Had he opened the station, he and Jeep would have been free of the mines. He never stopped there even though it was convenient. It was a reminder that rising was not there for the doing. He tried to explain to his son how he had dragged ambition stillborn into his future.

His oxygen tank appeared in 1974. And then it was all he could do to walk into the living room, sit in his chair and watch television until he fell into a fitful sleep.

In the taxi, Jeep looked at Biggie, his best friend. "Remember that gas station Daddy wanted to build in Racine after the War. The one the Sheriff put his boy onto instead. After Daddy realized what was going on, he thought about gettin' some Italians out of Clarksburg to even things up."

"Your Daddy knew Mafia guys?"

"All Italians, even hillbilly Italians, know them. Daddy went through his Uncle Dominic, a fruit-truck peddler who ran numbers, to contact them. Word came back it would be a $2,000 job, because it was the Sheriff. And Daddy would owe them a favor, maybe, down the line. They promised he'd get the garage. No problems with supplies, equipment and collections."

"So what happened?"

"Daddy said he could've come up with the money. He certainly wanted that station. He was pissed, because the idea and the garage were bein' stolen from him. But he never said yes to the Mafia."

"How come?"

"The one time he talked to me about it, maybe I was 16. We was workin' on his car in the shed. He said his hang up was the Mafia always fucked their own, meaning other Italians. That's how they started. If they did two for you, you better be prepared to do 10 for them. An' once they did for you, you could never escape. They always had to be fed. He figured he'd have to kick in so much every month to keep them away, which they wouldn't never be. So he spent his life workin' in the mines for a paycheck and black lung. Justice woulda cost too much. The best choice of the bad ones in front of him was to forget about escape."

"Like a slave stayin' on his master's plantation," Biggie said.

"Wasn't that bad, but he knew the place where he was supposed to stay in."

From National Airport, they crossed the Potomac River, passed Dupont Circle and headed north on Connecticut. The driver wanted to chat, but he got no response from his passengers. He soon stopped trying. The November Sunday was sunny but chilly. Noon traffic was light. Past the Hilton Hotel, they turned left onto Kalorama Road. It narrowed and ducked down along Rock Creek Park. The cab turned into a driveway that led to an enclosed plaza in front of an older, Federal-style house. A covey of clean, expensive, new cars were parked.

"Low-mileage folks," Biggie muttered, nodding at the cars.

Delucci and Stover got out. As Jeep was reaching for his wallet, Biggie leaned in with a $50 bill and told the driver to keep the meter and the motor running. "Point to the street; don't be blocked. I'll make you good for whatever it'll be."

Biggie looked directly at the driver's face-card identification so that he understood his name was being remembered. Biggie put his hand on the driver's shoulder. "No leaving." The driver nodded in agreement and rubbed his shoulder.

They walked to the front door. A large man in a loose, dark suit opened it before either could knock.

"He ain't no British butler, Jeep," Biggie said under his breath. They were escorted to the library where leather-bound books were shelved according to height and color.

Chickie Sciliano, wearing a blue blazer and gray-flannel slacks, greeted them. He motioned to the man in the suit. "Sorry Jeep, but I don't believe 100 percent in the Fourth Amendment's right to privacy."

The man gestured with his arms for Jeep and Biggie to raise theirs and then turn around. He found Biggie's pistol and said nothing as he lifted it from its holster and placed it in his jacket pocket. "You'll get it when you leave. Don't need no heat here," he said. "No recorder either."

"We found," Chickie said to lighten the search, "that tape recordings are the way our enemies mess up our plans. I'm sure you understand."

Chickie asked what they liked to drink. Then he introduced them to Jackpot Ginsberg, Wyn Clippinger, Vince DeFazio, Chris Chaconis and Moe Kazin.

"These gentlemen are the new directors of the American Bank of Washington," Chickie said to Jeep. "Vince runs the Teamsters in the District and around. Moe peddles fruit and vegetables. Wyn hops cars in a local lot. Chris slings hash, and the big guy over by the dictionary stand is Jackpot. He takes out the trash in the Nation's Capital."

Everyone, grinning at the descriptions, shook hands with the two coal miners. Jackpot who prided himself on being the largest human in whatever room he was in didn't like looking up to a hippie-wildman-redneck wrestler from West Virginia. Chickie had briefed the five on Delucci and Stover.

Delucci checked out his brother unionist, DeFazio, with particular scrutiny—mid-40s, big watch, flashy ring, paunched out. Jeep understood unions were a favorite Mob target, because they offered many ways to obtain cash illegally.

Delucci had no illusions about this meeting.

Biggie kept an eye on the beef brothers standing as inconspicuously as they could by the floor-to-ceiling volumes near the windows that looked into a formal garden.

"Please," Siciliano said to the group, "sit and make yourselves comfortable. I want to thank our guests, Jeep Delucci and Frank 'Biggie' Stover, for flying in to meet us. We appreciate their good faith."

Jeep looked at Biggie. What choice did we have?

A bartender placed each man's drink order on a sterling silver coaster that was embossed with the initials "TAS."

"I wanted to personally introduce you, Jeep and Biggie, to my friends and associates for 25 years or more. We helped to make the District into a safe and profitable place for business. Clip and I have invested in dozens of office buildings and apartments. Chris has restaurants in many of our facilities. Vince DeFazio runs the Teamsters in the District, Maryland up to Baltimore and northern Virginia. He works with all of us. Jackpot built his trash business off one old pickup truck through hard work and a smart wife. Moe runs a chain of supermarkets. We're business people, friends, allies and, in a sense, brothers. We help each other prosper. We are what America's about."

He left out what he himself does, Jeep thought.

"I wanted to introduce you personally to four friends who contributed $125,000 each to your campaign. Vince wanted to help, too, but I thought these guys had you covered. Clip's agreed to be the ABW's board chariman."

"These contributions came officially from you to yourself. You list those dollars as your own on your Labor Department contributor's list. It's money that you and your Dad saved, that you kept in your father's house for a rainy day. And if anyone asks, you kept it at home 'cause you don't trust banks."

Chickie laughed along with the new directors of the American Bank of Washington.

Jeep shook hands with and thanked each donor. He returned to his seat and swallowed a long drink.

"With your help, our campaign to bring democracy to the Union and clean it...and bring reform for the rank and file has a real good shot," Jeep said. "I won't forget your generosity."

He looked at Biggie who was looking at his boots.

"Jeep," Chickie said, "we've started a long-term relationship with you. We want the Bank to keep working with your Union. We want the Bank to continue to handle the Union's checking, savings, borrowing and investments. Exclusively."

"No problem," Jeep said.

"We want the Bank to manage investments for your health and retirement fund," Chickie said. "We'll put top-quality guys in place at the Bank to do this work for you at very reasonable fees."

Teamsters' Central States Pension Fund, Jeep thought. Here we go.

"The Union has about 220,000 miners, working and retired, plus wives and kids who depend on our health fund," Jeep said. "We have 95,000 on pensions in that number. The pensions are not much by anybody's standards, but they're better than no pensions. You can scrape by on it, along with Social Security and black-lung benefits. The health fund and

357

the pension fund are run separately, but both come out of the same pot, so we call them one fund. The coal operators put the money in, and we run it. It's supposed to be joint management, but you guys know the score on that. I can't agree to anything that cuts the membership's health and retirement. I have to have these funds managed honestly."

"No problem," Chickie said quickly. "Nobody ain't sayin' different, are we?"

Jeep looked at Vince DeFazio who met his gaze. "My Daddy and Mom need that pension check and health card. Daddy ain't no different than any other worked-out, ol' miner with a wife he's about to leave with whatever the Union can do for her."

"We understand your position," Wyndham Clippinger added.

You, Delucci, need to understand *your* fuckin' position, Chickie thought. Once you are bought, you were supposed to stay bought. You don't get bought twice over like some baked potato. Jeep seemed to be backing out of the place where he had agreed to be a few days earlier in Charleston. I don't like independence in my suppliers. Maybe, Delucci needs a third visit. Maybe John Corelli needs to get more involved. Or, maybe, Chickie thought, Delucci was just trying to look like a man more honest than he was in front of Stover.

"We expect all partners to live up to their word," Chickie said. "That's what a business relationship is. We do that with each other. We've given you friendship and assistance. We gave it fast and clean. You ain't going to have no problem with the Department of Labor. We've learned how to do things different after the government's persecution of the Teamsters."

Jeep felt himself astride and strapped to some large, slow-moving, unstoppable horse that was walking him into blackness. He was in the saddle but not in control.

Jeep shook his head. "My Daddy once told me if you eat the comp'ny's corn, you eventually end up chokin' on the comp'ny's cob."

Biggie was trying to make sense of this conversation. He knew nothing about a deal involving the ACMU's health and pension fund. He told Jeep he had "no beef" with the Union's sale of the ABW to what he called "them unjailed criminals." The Bank wasn't doing much for coal miners, he said, so why not cash it out? But turning the ACMU fund into a loan racket for the Mob wasn't part of that deal. He stirred in his seat, trying to catch Jeep's eye. These slicker-'n-snot crooks weren't going to run a Teamster ripoff on ACMU pensions and health care if he could do something to prevent it.

Biggie moved forward on his seat. He figured he could do something with the two gunners if things came to that.

Chickie didn't like this turn. The kid needed to be straightened out.

"You understood this, Jeep," Chickie said. "You remember the other night in Charleston. In my car. You said, 'Deal.' Deal means deal. It don't mean somethin' else. That's why you're sitting here and not layin' somewhere else."

Biggie sat straight. This was new information.

Jeep understood Chickie's deal. He saw no way out. "Guys like me don't drink expensive whiskey with guys like you in a house like this. Guys like me, we mine coal. We fix your pipes, dig your ditches, haul off your shit, grow your food and fight your wars. We done okay in this country; I ain't complainin'. What we don't get is a fair shake, a clear shot at better unless someone helps, and we're lucky.

"I made the deal, and I'll stick with it. I understand you'll expect money out of the Union to repay your 'investment' in my campaign. You'll get your money. But you'll bring down the feds if you loot the health and retirement fund."

"We're about business," Win Clippinger said. "We want to stroke the goose that lays golden eggs, not kill it."

Jeep persisted. "The feds will be lookin' for hanky-panky."

"We understand the situation," Clippinger said.

Jeep capitulated. "I will work it out. I understand how you fellas operate."

Jeep was ashamed of himself. He had fallen short of his Daddy.

Chickie's side of the room breathed easy.

"What deal?" Biggie asked to everyone and Jeep in particular.

"About what I jes' said," Jeep replied under his breath.

Biggie was thinking quickly. Siciliano had to have threatened Jeep's life to get him to agree. Or maybe his family. Or maybe Biggie's life. Or maybe all of them together. Once they gave him campaign money, they would control him as Union president. Biggie knew he had to be careful.

"It ain't jes' Jeep, you know," he began. "The Executive Board, the district presidents and the Convention that's a-comin' up next year—all of them will be lookin' at Jeep under a microscope. Them lawyers in Justice and Labor will be goin' over our campaign contributions and expenditures. They're gonna be lookin' for monkey business. Nobody's gonna believe Jim Delucci saved $500,000 out of his wages and pension. If you push this real hard, you boys'll end up like Hoffa."

Jeep knew "you boys" included him.

Vince DeFazio bristled but said nothing. He understood he was window dressing.

Chickie ignored Biggie. "Now, there's one other detail," he said.

Jeep looked at the door.

"This Becker," Chickie said. "He has to go."

"What's Becker got to do with anything?" Jeep asked.

"We -- you -- can't trust him," Clippinger put in. "I had him checked out. Lawyer. Liberal idealist or something. He's not in the same position that Jeep is with us. I doubt we can get him on board."

"What do you want?" Biggie asked.

"Get rid of him," Chickie said.

"Now?" Jeep asked.

"No," Clippinger said. "Dump him after you win. Don't name him to any position at the Union. Thank him profusely. Tell him he was a big part of your victory. Big strokes. And then say something like, you want the Union to be staffed as much as possible with coal miners, not outsiders. Cut him out, but throw him a few chips. Legal work; nothing important. Be nice about it. Continue with Foster Shives as your general counsel. We'll find a suitable replacement very soon. Foster will help make the transition. Maybe give Foster a small bonus for a job well done."

"This ain't right," Biggie said. "Becker was there from the git-go. Jeep wouldn't have won the first round without him. He got us organized. Did the press. Managed the campaign."

"You owe him nothing," Chickie said.

"Yeah, I do," Jeep said.

"You don't understand," Chickie said. "Becker is out, one way or another."

"He knows stuff," Jeep said quietly. "Like I said the other night."

"'Becker knows stuff,'" Chickie repeated.

Clippinger looked at Siciliano. "Let's put Becker on the back burner until after the election," he said.

"Nothin' happens to Becker," Biggie said. "No accident shit. No...whatever."

"Okay," Chickie said. "Becker's off the table for now."

Chickie adjourned everyone to his dining room where a buffet awaited. His partners chatted easily among themselves. They worked at pulling Jeep into their conversations. Biggie said little and ate less. Jackpot was very interested in Biggie's wrestling career and kept asking how he faked body slams. Clippinger made a point of watching Biggie.

After an hour, Jeep and Biggie left, got into the waiting taxi and were driven to National Airport for a 5:16 p.m. flight to Charleston.

"What deal?" Biggie whispered when they were sitting in the cab.

"You figured it out in there," Jeep said. "They put a gun to my head the other night and said, 'Do what we want or you're dead.' What would you have done?"

"Where?"

"Near my apartment, on the street. Some gun thug snuck up on me. Big guy. Looked Italian. Pro, I'd guess."

360

"Who leaned on you?"

"Siciliano, the gun thug and Shives."

"What did they make you take?" Biggie asked.

"A suitcase with 500 in it."

Biggie said nothing.

Jeep continued: "The deal is they will get their purchase money for the Bank out of the Bank and out of the Union, one way or another. Never enough to bring down the heat. A slow bleeding. I got the feelin' Siciliano is frontin' for big Mob guys. The ABW could do the laundry for a lot of crooks, not just the Pittsburgh outfit."

"Probably did the same deal with Joe Hunt," Biggie said.

"That must be where Joe got his campaign money after we won in September."

"What about the health and pension fund?" Biggie asked.

Jeep stalled. "I hope we can keep it free and clean. The wise guys don't want what came down on the Teamsters. I don't know, man."

"Why didn't you tell me?" Biggie asked.

"What could you do except get yourself killed?"

"You want to go to the feds?" Biggie asked.

"That would be the end of my life. Witness protection, hiding from every stranger. They'll find me."

"I could go."

"That'll be the end of your life. And you have Brenda."

"Maybe she'll understand."

"Not likely," Jeep said.

"You never know with that girl. You could drop out of the race. 'Personal reasons.'"

"Then Joe does what they want!"

"Which is a hell of a lot better than you and me doin' what they want. We didn't start this campaign to screw miners. An' that's exactly what we'll be doin.'"

"I dunno," Jeep said.

"Maybe we could leak this mess to a reporter like that girl in Pittsburgh or Charlie Frazier," Biggie said.

"Maybe," Jeep said. "Maybe if it came out that way, it'd stop 'em. It would have to be after the election. The Mafia kills witnesses it don't trust. Like Sam Giancana. A story would lead to a federal investigation and trial. Siciliano would come after me. If ya want someone killed, it's not that hard."

"Witness protection," Biggie said.

"Maybe I can keep their hands off the health and pensions."

Biggie looked at his friend.

Jeep shrugged. "Let's sleep on it for a day or two. Keep Becker out of this. For his own good."

"He'd say, 'Get your ass to the feds,'" Biggie said.

"Yeah. That's what Becker would say."

As Chickie showed his friends to the door, Wyndham Clippinger made sure he was the last to leave. He came close to Chickie's face: "Stover."

Chickie replied with a nod: "Becker, too. I'll talk to Tony."

Chapter 26

Washington, D.C., November 10, 1975

"Thank you for seeing me, Mr. Sonoski," Allyson Pickering said as she slipped into a green-leather chair positioned in front of his desk. She placed her purse next to her feet after taking out a tape recorder and note pad.

As she settled in, she noted the framed photos hanging on two walls. She tallied a grip-and-grin handshake with Lyndon Johnson and another with Richard Nixon. Coal-state Senators -- Jennings Randolph and Robert Byrd from West Virginia; Charles Percy from Illinois; John Sherman Cooper from Kentucky; Harry F. Byrd from Virginia; Howard Baker from Tennessee; Hugh Scott and Richard Schweiker from Pennsylvania and even Gale McGee from Wyoming -- smiled beside lesser coalfield Republicans and Democrats.

Wyoming, Allyson had just learned, was projected to become the top coal-producing state within a decade owing to its 100-foot-thick seams of low-sulfur coal mined from low-cost surface pits. Western non-Union coal might supplant ACMU-mined coal even east of the Mississippi River owing to cheaper delivered cost and fewer air-pollution issues. The ACMU, she thought, might become a remnant organization whose past was far more important than its future.

Around the politician photos, she saw others of Sonoski at ACMU conventions with delegates. He had framed awards from the American Cancer Society and the United Way that thanked him for raising money from ACMU staff. She also saw a photo of Joe Hunt and Lyndon Johnson squatting on their heels on the front porch of Elzie Nicewander, an unemployed coal miner in Black Diamond, Kentucky, on the day in 1964 before Johnson announced Appalachia was to be one of the battlefields in his War on Poverty. Allyson noted Larry Sonoski had no picture of West Virginia Congressman Ken Hechler who had been the coalfield politician who fought hardest to pass the 1969 Coal Mine Health and Safety Act, which established higher safety standards, promulgated a compliance level for dust and created a black-lung compensation program. Hechler didn't think Joe Hunt's ACMU worked very hard for passage. Allyson was unable to find anything in Larry Sonoski's office that would show a visitor he'd once handloaded coal in Fricktown, West Virginia.

As Allyson readied her notebook, she noticed a fragment of wood on Sonoski's desk. An odd paperweight, she thought.

"I have questions I hope you can answer," she said.

Skis avoided reporters whenever possible, particularly those with questions. He was not a PR guy, and he didn't want to be an inside source.

He did, however, seek out a couple of reporters when Joe had something he wanted in the papers that wasn't official union policy. He was in those instances "an unidentified source within the Union." But this situation was different. He'd taken the call from Gus Olin within minutes of Allyson Pickering driving away. Better to tell her nothing than to refuse to talk to her, Gus said.

"No tape. No notes. No quotin' me. You like bein' a reporter, Miss?" he asked.

"Please, Mr. Sonoski, call me Allyson. It's what I went to school for. I'm a good writer. It's the only job I've ever had."

"I dropped out of high school to go underground," Skis said.

"I know a little bit about you," she said. "Born in Fricktown. Worked at the AMSTEEL mine for a while. Came to Washington when Joe Hunt won. Anything else I can include?"

"My Dad was a miner for 33 years. Mother was a mom. I went in the mine when I was 14. Handloader. Laid track. Built stoppin's."

"'Stoppens?'" she asked.

"Stop-pings. Walls made outa concrete blocks to channel good air to the face and take bad air from the face outside. Stoppin's are built to control air flows. Brattishas are..."

"I'm sorry. Radishes?"

"BRA-TIS-ES—brat-tice curtains. They're heavy cloth, canvas material. Ventilation curtains. Miners call them 'rags.' You tack them up to direct temporary ventilation in and out. You need good air to stay alive. Once good air -- intake air -- passes a working face, it's loaded with mine dust and possibly methane. You gotta get the bad air out to the surface through return tunnels in a way that no one has to breathe too much of it. Brattishas temporarily channel air where you want it to go, and where you don't want it to go."

"I see," she said, wondering when she would. "And your title?"

"Special Assistant to the President of the American Coal Miner's Union."

"I'd like to ask you about something I heard. It goes back to Fricktown in the 1930s. There was a strike there in 1932 and 1933. You and Joe Hunt were part of it."

"Joe and me were teenage handloaders. Our Daddies worked for AMSTEEL. We shoveled coal into mine cars. We worked under a veteran miner who undercut the coal by hand, a-layin' on his side. Then'd he drill the face by hand, fill the hole with powder and blow it into nice lumps for us to load.

"When the strike was called, me an' Joe went out with everybody else in Fricktown. No choice about that back then. A lot of life is about not having great choices in front of you and never being able to forget regretted decisions behind you."

"Very good," she said. "I guess conditions during the strike were pretty bad."

"Most of the folks in the winter camp survived; some didn't. My mother lost a baby."

"I'm sorry," she said. "Do you want to fill me in?"

"Not really. It's like underground minin'," Skis said, "you have to have been there."

"I visited poor black churches in Mississippi with a Quaker work group when I was a senior in high school," she said. "We built a picnic shelter."

"Not exactly the same thang," he said, "but I'm sure you learned a lot."

"Okay," she said, ignoring his put-down, "do you remember a man named Gus Olin?"

"Of course."

"He's still alive," she said.

"Glad to hear it."

"I interviewed him. In Fricktown. He still lives there. Retired. I was on his front porch."

"You interviewed Gussie on his front porch? How come he didn't invite you in for a coffee or a pop?"

"I can't answer that."

"I'm surprised Edna let you stand there. They're hospitable people."

"Right. Well, I asked him about the Fricktown Strike. All three of you were involved in the strike, right?"

"Yes. Miss. We lived in Fricktown when we was workin'. When we was strikin', we lived in tents on Alvie Hunt's farm way up the holler. Joe's uncle, Alvie. Took in almost 2,000 folks. This Union gave us tents and food. If you was strikin', you was 'involved' in the strike whether you wanted to be or not. You didn't have no choice 'bout it."

"You were on strike and living in a tent," she repeated.

"I was 14. Joe was 15, maybe 16. I'd jes' started handloadin' for Gussie 'cause my family needed the money. He and Edna never had no kids. So Gus took us under his wing. When AMSTEEL cut our wages, we went out. We couldn't make it on what they wanted to pay. Hell, we couldn't make it on what they was payin' before the cut."

"You dropped out of high school?" she asked.

"Hardly started. The Depression was rough. Don't believe them Hollywood movies from the '30s with people paradin' around in tuxedos and top hats, talkin' and dancin' with silver spoons up their trashcans. A lot of folks was plain starvin'. Shirley Temple never made no tap-dancin' movie in a coal camp."

"Fourteen?"

"Had my 14th just after the strike began. I guess I was 13 when I went in. Had one whale of a good time with all the cake and presents."

She heard the sarcasm.

"My Dad come up with a one-pint cannin' jar of moonshine," Skis laughed. "My first drink. My first hangover was a doozy."

"The strikers moved into tents. I read the old clips my editor, Davey Bloom, wrote."

"I remember him. More than 40 years ago. Nice young feller. Wrote good stories. Someone in Pittsburgh sent them down to us in the tents. Lot of water over the dam since."

"Why did you leave the houses you lived in for tents?" she asked, hoping she could get him to relax with cluelessness.

Skis took off his glasses and rubbed his eyes. "We was e-victed. Kicked out. See, we were jes' a-rentin' from paycheck to paycheck. AMSTEEL deducted rent from our pay. If you was on strike, you couldn't pay rent. If you can't pay rent, you get kicked out."

"That must have been dreadful," Allyson said.

"You askin' or makin' a statement?"

"I read that your superintendent disappeared the night the mine's grocery store burned."

"Commissary. It was a store for all kinds of thangs folks needed— food, clothing, mining supplies. Had some offices upstairs. Bookkeepin' and payroll, as I recall."

"Yes. His body was never found. No one was ever charged with murder if that is what happened, which I'm not saying it did. Did you know Mr. Gallagher?"

"Sure. I worked for him like every other miner in Fricktown. I knew him the way we Catholics know our archbishops. Orders come down from the boss…that's how I knew him. I heard he wasn't that bad from the older guys. I was too young to have an opinion either way on Frank Gallagher. He evicted us, that's true, but he was jes' followin' orders from Pittsburgh headquarters. Mr. Roberson, Ben's Daddy, Ben, Senior. That's who ran Fricktown. Everybody knew Gallagher was followin' what Ben, Senior, said. AMSTEEL probably had to do it. How would it look if they let strikin' miners live in Comp'ny houses for free?"

Allyson breathed a little deeper than she wanted to show: "Do you know who killed Frank Gallagher?"

Skis shook his head: "No ma'am. First off, I don't know he was killed. You're assumin' somethin' that was never proved. The police never even brought charges against anyone. An' his body was never found. But maybe you know more about those times than me."

"You're right," she said, "about his body. And you're right that no one was ever charged. Still, it's obvious Gallagher was murdered that night when the commissary was burned."

"Not obvious to me. Guessin' ain't facts, ain't evidence, ain't proof, Miss. Guesses ain't 'obvious.' Miss, you don't *know* Gallagher was murdered. The commissary fire may have been set, but no one was ever charged. Could have been set by a Comp'ny guard who was angry over poor pay. Gallagher might have set it himself to give us strikers a bad name. Maybe he was in his own store stealin' supplies and set a fire by accident."

"I think you know who killed him," Allyson said.

"You're welcome to think whatever you like. That's what your Daddy fought for in WWII. But what you think ain't necessarily a fact. It ain't necessarily what happened, or how, or why. It's just an idea. The world is flat is also an idea. You know you can't write your speculations in a paper? You do know that, don't you?"

"Yes, Mr. Sonoski, I know what I'm allowed to write, and what I'm not allowed to write."

"America, and Fricktown, too, is considerable different today than in 19 and 32. That was the deepest bottom of The Depression. It's hard to imagine today one out of three workers with no job. People was a-hurtin' bad on both sides, labor and management. We knew coal comp'nies was goin' out of business. People didn't have no money to buy coal. Nobody wanted steel. The operators had to squeeze labor to stay in business. In '31 more than 1,000 miners was killed on the job. Think about the last time you was in a room with 1,000 reporters and at the end of the year, they're all dead from their jobs. But you can only squeeze your people so much. AMSTEEL squeezed too hard. That's why we stopped work. Wasn't much different workin' for next to nothin' and strikin' on nothin'. But when all is said and done, I don't really 'spect you to understand back then a-settin' here in my office."

"I might understand more than you think," she said.

"Anythin's possible, Miss," he said.

"What do *you* think happened to Frank Gallagher?"

Larry Sonoski looked at Allyson straight on and said in a level tone: "At this point, I don't give a damn."

"I see. Do you know who killed Frank Gallagher, Mr. Sonoski?"

"The times killed him," he said.

"Well, how about this? Did Joe Hunt kill him?"

"That kind of question don't deserve an answer. You should be ashamed of yourself."

"A question is a question," she said.

"It's time for you to go," Skis said, rising from his seat.

She sat still, making no effort to turn off her tape recorder. "Gus Olin said Joe Hunt killed Frank Gallagher in the commissary."

Skis laughed, a big genuine laugh that seemed too large for his slight frame. "Gussie Olin never said that to you or anyone else, and you, you little…, you know it."

"He confirmed it," she insisted.

"You're a liar!"

"Gussie Olin is a truthful human being," she said.

"That he is. And you ain't."

"Who killed Gallagher?"

"'Who killed Gallagher?'" Skis repeated. "Hunger killed the sonofabitch. Economics killed him. Poverty. Geology. Capitalism. Working conditions. Wage cuts. The Depression. Ben Senior. Every miner and his family in those tents killed Gallagher. Every stockholder in AMSTEEL. Every bank that wanted its money from AMSTEEL. Every director on its board and every man in AMSTEEL's management. Everyone done it. An all of us died some ourselves a-doin' it. You see that piece of stinkin' brown wood on my desk? That come from the floor of my tent. That slat done it as much as anybody."

"Joe Hunt killed Gallagher, didn't he?"

Skis came around his desk, stood her up and pushed her out of his office. He threw her bag and recorder after her. "Get the hell out of my office and this buildin'. You're stinkin' it up."

Allyson gathered her notebook, her tape recorder, her purse and all the other things that had been scattered including her rattled dignity. She left ACMU headquarters, composed herself and stepped into the public phone booth on the corner. She scribbled hurriedly in her notebook. She dialed. Davey Bloom came on.

"He confirmed," she said. "Sonoski confirmed."

"Whoa now. You're saying Sonoski 'confirmed' Joe Hunt killed Gallagher. Are you absolutely sure?"

"He confirmed Gallagher was killed."

"Directly?" Davey asked. "Like, 'Yes, Gallagher was killed, and Joe Hunt did it.'"

"Yes."

"Did you tape it?"

"No, he wouldn't let me. He said, 'No tape. No notes.' Those were the ground rules. And no direct attribution."

"So what did you do?" Davey asked. He felt as if he was walking in football cleats over a floor covered with thin-shelled eggs.

"I reconstructed his words as soon as I left the ACMU building. Wrote it in my notebook."

"Did you ask if you could attribute to an unnamed source?"

"Of course," she lied.

"An unnamed ACMU source?"

368

"Yes," she lied.

"An unnamed ACMU headquarters source?"

"That was implied in our conversation," she said.

"I dunno. People get sued over implications. What did he say exactly?"

"He started -- I'm reading from my notes -- 'Hunger, poverty, wage cuts, working conditions, capitalism, The Depression—all of that killed Gallagher.' Gus Olin, he said 'would say it was the profit motive and capitalism that killed him. Everyone was responsible—bankers, miners, management, people in the tents, AMSTEEL.'"

"Aw shit, he's talking philosophy and crap like that. A few of these old miners think they're fuckin' Platos after they realize reality is not limited to the holes they dug in the blackness. Anyway he's way short of confirming anything."

"Hold on," she said. "I'm getting there. He said: 'The police never charged anyone with murder, but everyone knew Gallagher died the night the commissary burned.'"

"Nothing there yet, hon. Gossip and hearsay. You can write that as his opinion, but it doesn't prove Gallagher was murdered."

"That's context. Then I asked: 'Did Joe Hunt kill Gallagher?' He said: 'Everyone killed Gallagher.' Everyone includes Hunt. He answered yes without having to name Hunt directly."

"He's also saying that he killed Gallagher, Gussie Olin killed him as well as the other 2,000 souls who were toughing it out in the tents. Not good enough, hon."

"But put it together with what Gus Olin said," Allyson pleaded, "which amounted to the same thing."

"Nope. You're not there."

"And then he said, 'I wouldn't be surprised to hear it's going around that Joe killed Gallagher. I figure it's Delucci tryin' to smear Joe. Joe Hunt won't lose a single vote even if it was true that he killed Fricktown's superintendent during that strike.'"

"Hypothetical," Davey said. "Was any of this on the record?"

"He never asked specifically that all of it be *off* the record," Allyson answered. "I can go with an unnamed ACMU source. And then I asked him: 'Yes or no, did Joe Hunt kill Gallagher?' Then he threw me out of his office. That lack of denial was a confirmation. It can't be taken as anything else."

Davey Bloom took a deep breath. "Take a deep breath, Allyson," he said. "Why would Larry Sonoski, Joe Hunt's best friend since childhood, suggest Joe killed a guy 40 years ago when they're in the middle of the hardest election campaign Hunt's ever been in? There's no statute of limitations on murder. He could still be prosecuted."

"Maybe, it's his conscience speaking. Maybe he couldn't tell me a lie directly to my face. Maybe he thinks Joe's time is past. I don't know the why, Davey. I just know what he said, and what he implied."

"And maybe you're being set up?"

"By whom?"

"Who got your nose open on this?"

"Someone from AMSTEEL told my Dad who had done some of their legal work a while back. He said the Company had a private investigator look into Gallagher's disappearance. He'd seen the report years ago, but didn't have a copy to give my Dad. He said the investigator wrote he had reason to believe Gus Olin was involved and probably behind it. The amount of food that appeared the next day in the camp could not have been carried by one person. The investigator said three or four would have been needed. He believed Olin had taken his two crew members, Hunt and Sonoski, on the raid. A snitch said he saw Joe Hunt the next day with what looked like blood on his pants. Hunt said he caught a rabbit in a snare the night before and skinned it. The snitch never saw those pants on Hunt again. He believed Hunt, not Olin, had a hand in killing Gallagher. But the investigator could not put together any evidence to justify an indictment. AMSTEEL figured it was an impossible case to win. The local prosecutor said he had no grounds for bringing charges against anyone. A couple of local detectives poked around and even questioned Olin and Hunt who, as you might expect, denied they knew anything about either a murder or about the food that appeared in camp that night."

"If there was nothing then, why is there something now?" Davey asked.

"Because they're not denying it."

"But you don't have it on tape. It's your word against theirs as to what exactly you asked and what exactly Gus and Sonoski answered."

"All right," Allyson said, "call it reporter's intuition."

"Not enough," Davey said. "And why would AMSTEEL want to leak a report about Joe Hunt to you? Sounds to me like the coal boys might be figuring that Delucci is the best of their two bad choices. Maybe they're thinking they can't ride Joe any longer, and it's time to switch horses."

"So what? A story is a story is a story. How it benefits or penalizes someone is not my concern."

"Yeah," Bloom said. "I'm sure you learned that at Columbia's Journalism School. And what if the leak is a fake? What if there is no investigator report from 1933? What if Joe Hunt is actually behind it so he can shoot it down and look like he's a victim of a coal-operator media smear?"

"Joe Hunt isn't that smart," she said.

"You don't have to be smart in politics, hon," Bloom said, "just wiley. So here's what you do. Keep on it. Write what you have. Let me see it in black and white for background. Don't stretch. You hear me, Allyson. Don't stretch! I'll be looking for stretch."

"Okay," Allyson said. "Just the facts, sir."

That night as Allyson Pickering typed up her interview, she wondered whether the game she was playing was worth the shadows she was creating in herself. She thought she had the story right, but she knew that wasn't enough.

Chapter 27

Pittsburgh, November 18, 1975: 11:50 a.m.

Del Porco's Bar and Grille on Larimer Avenue near the corner of Meadow was dark and close. It was known for its extra-good Italian food and other matters.

Its bar ran the length of the room opposite a row of eight booths. A steel door at the back led into a windowless office. From that room, another steel door led into the alley behind the Grille. An air-conditioner had been installed above that door with a pan to catch the drips so they wouldn't fall on people leaving.

Tony Bruno ran the Pittsburgh Mafia from Del Porco's back room.

Tony sat at his uncluttered desk and squared the linen napkin in his lap. Then he straightened the silverware. He noticed the ice in his water glass.

"Paul," he said softly.

Proprietor Paul DeFade had just set a plate of steamed mussels in a tomato-and-garlic broth in front of Tony who nodded toward the glass.

"Sorry, Tony. Augie is sick today, and Markie Boy don't know no better about no cubes."

"I understand," Tony said.

Paul brought him a fresh glass of chilled water.

Tony was particular about his food and its presentation. As a young man, he had thrown a bowl of mussels at a waiter, because the kitchen staff had not debearded them properly. He was equally particular about his business. He used to be a steamroller; now he thought of himself as a hurdler who didn't care if he knocked them flat.

A number of Italian restaurants opened in Pittsburgh after WWII. Their owners were moving out of Italian neighborhoods and finding enthusiastic non-Italian customers. A couple of first-timers considered their restaurants to be as good as the Park Schenley, which Frank Blandi ran on Forbes Avenue in Oakland. None, however, could match the extravagant gold bathroom faucets at Blandi's Louis-XIV-decorated LeMont on Grandview Avenue. Frank hung his $1.5-million restaurant off the edge of Mt. Washington overlooking Pittsburgh's downtown in 1960. When Johnny Carson's wife visited her Pittsburgh family, Johnny hit golf balls toward The Point from the LeMont's roof.

Tony Bruno preferred the simple, southern-Italian cooking Paul DeFade prepared. Flash had its place, he liked to joke, but not in his fry pan. His 50 percent ownership of Del Porco's gave him a legitimate front and a secure back. Tony kept Del Porco's clean—a restaurant where everyone felt safe and was.

"Set another place," Tony said to Paul.

At noon, John Corelli, a tall, broad-shouldered 30-year-old with tar-black hair down to his shoulders and eyes the color of aqua velva, pulled his old Valiant into a space on Meadow Street close to Our Lady, Help of Christians Roman Catholic Church. He had spent many hours in Help of Christians with its three bronze domes, golden bricks and bell tower that housed an illuminated clock. Attendance was at his mother's insistence. Father Bolzano considered John an unlikely future congregant.

Help of Christians was the center of life on Larimer Avenue's piazza, which echoed a typical Italian village. The Franciscans provided its sacraments—baptism, first Holy Communion, confirmation and marriage. In the Larimer neighborhood, you had Help of Christians. You had a few aspiring gentry. You had workers. You had decent folks trying to rise. And you had the Mob.

Corelli sat for a moment, watching the street and sniffing.

John Corelli always defended "*Italianità*," the sense and character of being Italian. He had come to appreciate the Larimer Avenue neighborhood that raised him. But he understood as he grew older that Larimer was a side channel to mainstream America. He had no use for Help of Christians' religion either as a system of beliefs or as a set of rituals asking for outside intervention to solve life's problems. Even as a youngster, neighborhood parents warned their children to stay away from Corelli. They saw his rejection of convention, his volatility, anger and violence. As a teenager he developed a curl in his upper lip that made girls his age and older think of a young Elvis, an Elvis with the same cerulean eyes and black hair that did not come out of a bottle. They also saw someone who might be more than they wanted to try. As he got older, he started looking less like Elvis and more like Bugsy Siegel.

He sat for another moment, watching. Then he got out and walked slowly toward Del Porco's. He waited by the front door for his eyes to adjust to its interior dimness. He felt the eyes of Help of Christians on his back.

As he came through the doorway, he scanned the room, searching for the unfamiliar, the out-of-place detail. He noted three construction workers on a short lunch break at the bar, each with an Iron City Beer. They were gold; no trouble there. The restaurant's eight booths were filled with neighborhood people. Those who knew him nodded as their eyes met.

Corelli respected Tony Bruno for keeping Del Porco's free of loafing wise guys and clean-up hitters. In-and-out was the rule; come in the front, do your business, go out the back. No hanging around; no arguing; no drinking; no scenes. Del Porco's was an oasis of enforced peace and quiet.

It was easy for Corelli to spot a run-of-the-mill slugger. The hitter he feared was the 50-year-old plain-Jane in a pastel pantsuit with a beehive who looked as if she was coming home from a shoe sale at Horne's downtown. Women, he had discovered, were better than men in his business. They were more thoughtful, less emotional and smarter. He liked working with them.

He noted two women about his age sitting opposite each other in a booth near Tony's door. One had long dark hair; the other had long blond hair from a good beautician. The blonde glanced up and caught his eye. She smiled, not too shyly, and returned to her conversation. Not a pro, he thought, just getting a little older. He stopped.

"I'm John Corelli," he said, with a smile directed at the blonde. "Dint you go to Peabody? Your name Janice?"

"Sacred Heart," the blonde said. "And it's Ginny. My parents refused to let me go to a coed high school, especially one with boys like you."

"We both went to the Heart," the brunette said. "We called it 'Our Lady of the Infected Speculum.' My name's Pepper. I'm not married; she has been. Graduated in '65."

Corelli smiled. "I'm sure we know some of the same people."

"There's room here if you want to join us," Pepper said, scooting over.

"Thanks," he said, "but I'm meeting someone."

"Personal?" Pepper asked without embarrassment.

"Aren't you the nebby nose?" Ginny said.

"Business. Sorry. Ladies." Corelli smiled and waved as he moved past them.

"I thought you were going to start doing chin-ups on him," Ginny said to Pepper.

"Did you catch those eyes! How many Italians have eyes like that?"

Ginny thought about this. "Must be Viking shit left over from when the Normans conquered Sicily 1,000 years ago. My Pop is still bitching about it."

"He looks like that guy, Sylvester Stallone, the guy we saw in 'The Lords of Flatbush' last year," Pepper said.

"A hoodlum, you mean, in a black leather jacket," Ginny said, buttering a slice of fresh Italian bread.

"Yeah, so. You can't blame a 28-year-old girl for throwing a line out," Pepper said.

"You didn't throw a line out, hon. You were the bait and the fish, and the rod and reel. You about filleted yourself."

"Well, I could do that, too," Pepper laughed, pursing her mouth.

"It's your business, hon, but he looks to me like the type who'd kiss your doodlebug one night and punch out your lights the next," Ginny

374

advised. "As my friend LaVon -- you know the black girl who works chipped ham and cheese over at Isaly's on the Boulevard -- says, 'Take a later on that dude, girl.'"

"Maybe he cries when he comes," Pepper giggled.

"I wouldn't bet on it," Ginny said. "LaVon would say, 'That boy down.' He doesn't look like the type you would scare."

John nodded toward Paul DeFade who nodded in return and said, "He's in."

John was moving toward the steel door when he saw Jerry Multirosa nursing a white mug of coffee at the end of the bar.

"How's it goin', Jer?" Corelli said to the 50-year-old contract killer, a slight man who carried three guns and two knives even when he went to the bathroom.

"Shit flows downhill," Multirosa said.

"Won't quarrel with that," Corelli said.

"Boss told me to wait here until he was through talkin' to you."

"Are we workin' together?"

"Ain't sure yet. Somethin' dahn in West Virginia again. Where Little Louie and Bonk bought it."

Corelli knocked four times, paused and walked in.

John Corelli wondered why he was not like everyone else. He was good with numbers, good with logical analysis, had a high IQ and didn't panic under pressure. So why wasn't he at least a Heinz bean counter with a wife and two kids, tallying pickles for a living?

It was easy to blame Vietnam for turning him counterclockwise. But Corelli knew that his LRRP service was, as he once put it to himself, "just frosting on my fucking cake." He came to the War in 1965 as a strong, roughneck kid from Pittsburgh's Little Italy. The War gave him an excuse to rationalize his ways. He had come to terms with having a lot of sociopath in him. Vietnam fine-tuned his "talent" and added skills.

The Larimer neighborhood was named for William Larimer, a French-Scots Conestoga wagon-maker of the 1830s. It was a plateau that was separated from other neighborhoods by bridges and railroad tracks. William Larimer built his fortune on the early railroads and went on to be a founder of Denver. His daughter, Rachel, married James Mellon, son of Thomas Mellon of the Pittsburgh banking family. The Mellons sold or rented Larimer land and partly financed their coal, steel and gas ventures with the profits. The founder of Gulf Oil was William Larimer Mellon.

Northern Italians were the first to settle Larimer, followed by those from Naples and Calabria in Italy's toe. Later immigrants came from Sicily, home of the Corellis. His people learned to work quarried granite setts, called Belgian blocks, to pave Pittsburgh streets. By the 1950s, Italians who could were leaving Larimer for the close-in suburbs of Verona and Penn Hills. They wanted nicer housing and bigger yards. They were also fleeing blacks who were edging into Larimer's core from nearby Frankstown and Lincoln Avenues. Northern Italians tended to be the wealthiest, so they moved first; Southerners, like the Corellis, stayed the longest as Larimer began to decline in the 1950s. By 1970, only 1,000 Italians remained.

One who stayed was John Corelli. He had grown up fighting to protect himself from bigger, older kids on Meadow Street. And then he fought to get what he needed or wanted from weaker ones. He would fight for his friends and fight for his neighborhood. He grew up on his corner hustling to buy school clothes, playing sports, skirmishing with the black boys across the bridges and getting laid early.

At Peabody High School, he was taken into The Diablos, a social club of teens that never turned into a gang because of declining membership. Few of The Diablos had Corelli's mean streak though a number affected it. Many had as much reason to be as angry as he, but none were as unpredictably dangerous.

Elmer Flowers, Peabody's principal who had spent his prime years in vocational guidance from which he climbed a very short career ladder, marked Corelli as "trouble" in the ninth grade. He and two older Diablos had stuffed Sheldon Himmelbaum, a five-foot-two-inch freshman, into a trash barrel and rolled him down two flights of interior stairs. When Flowers asked Corelli to explain why a young man with a 135 IQ would endanger the life of a classmate half his size, Corelli said, "Self-defense. He threatened to beat me up." Flowers suspended Corelli for two weeks and resigned himself to future disciplinary encounters, which he hoped would lead to a quick and permanent expulsion.

Corelli stories quickly became part of the school's folklore—Corelli flipping cats off the Highland Park Bridge; Corelli throwing burning biology books at fellow students from the grandstand's top row at home football games; Corelli blowing his nose into the Bible before Miss Bursick's morning reading; Corelli mooning Miss DeFoe during study hall. Becker had witnessed the biology book being flung, and he did not dismiss the other stories.

Becker, like his classmates, developed strategies for keeping out of Corelli's way. Since he was assigned both a homeroom seat and a hall locker next to Corelli, he had discovered techniques as a freshman to make himself invisible, or at least, inoffensive.

Corelli, Becker thought, had imagination of a peculiar kind. He wasn't just an ordinary teenage bully. Becker knew Corelli walked up from the "manual arts" prison next to the basement's boiler room to the third-floor

"Both of us should be suspended or both on probation," Corelli said. "That's the rule. Same punishment for fighting for both. I know the rule."

"I'm not going to debate this with the likes of you."

Well, well, Steve Herndon thought.

"John's right, Mr. Flowers," Becker said, nodding toward Corelli. "I threw the first punch. I know the rule."

In the morning as Elmer Flowers drove his Chevrolet sedan to Peabody, he often pictured himself as a lone soldier holding high the banner of true American respectability. Faculty and students would see him standing there and be inspired. But Flowers had learned to bend when necessary. He glanced at Becker. He wanted to avoid controversy more than he wanted to get Corelli. Perhaps Becker would learn how the world worked, some day. Perhaps not. Flowers didn't care either way.

"You're both on probation for a month. Any more fighting and you're both suspended for a month. Is that clear?"

Becker and Corelli said they understood.

"Now shake hands and go to Mrs. Emery's office and get cleaned up."

The boys did and left. Elmer Flowers turned to read the daily attendance sheets. Steve Herndon felt happy, even light, for the rest of the day.

After Mrs. Emery dressed their cuts, Becker and Corelli walked back to their lockers, sort of together, since they were walking to the same destination down the same halls at the same speed.

"You hurt my hand, John," Becker said. "I didn't deserve that."

"Yeah, well. I don't deserve a lot of things."

Becker didn't understand what Corelli meant.

"You're an asshole, Becker. You should have taken the one-week probation."

"You were right, John. He wasn't being fair."

"You're an asshole, Becker. 'Fair' ain't part of my day. You gotta protect yourself first."

"I did," Becker said, surprised at his surviving boldness.

"Yeah, I guess you did," Corelli said, and walked ahead.

Student opinion, which kept a running tally of fights, concluded that Corelli had won, but Becker had not exactly lost. This spared Becker a real fight with Corelli to his great relief. He knew he could get away with a sucker punch -- and a lucky one at that -- only once. The Diablos agreed Becker was an asshole, but several began acknowledging him as they passed in the halls between classes and in gym.

By their senior year, Becker and Corelli discovered they shared a taste for rebellion. With Becker, it emerged as adolescent bohemianism— discovering Leadbelly and Camus, declaring himself an agnostic, wearing motorcycle boots and harmonizing with Mary to the exclusion of Peter and

Paul. Becker found himself summoned to Mr. Flowers' office for infractions of the never publicized rules, such as growing a mustache (which he darkened with his mother's mascara brush) and general lectures about his sullen attitude, smart-aleckiness and seditious writings. Corelli continued to frighten everyone, though a portion of his anger was siphoned into football, volleyball and baseball.

They began meeting without scheduling at Eat 'n' Park near the Silver Lake Drive-In on Friday and Saturday nights, late. Becker discovered in Corelli a window into a world that was more vibrant, violent, physical and sexual than his own. Corelli found in Becker a friend who liked to talk about ideas and understand why people did what they did. They began explaining each other to their friends with limited success. They lost touch after graduation.

Larimer Avenue in the late 1950s was a street without much mercy for weakness. Fighting was better than punking out. Fighting was how Corelli established himself in the Darwinian hierarchy. But there was, he knew, something more in him than a willingness to hurt and be hurt. It was a lack of pity, a lack of empathy, a word his most recent ex-girlfriend had thrown at him. He sometimes called it, "regression to the mean"—a reference to his deceased father who beat him with his heavy work belt made from harness leather. Corelli knew he had something of a conscience, because he was intensely loyal and reasonably honest with his friends. But he did not deny his fascination with inflicting pain on males of his own species. Maybe he was like that, he thought, for the same reason he had black hair and blue eyes—the crapshoot of who made you and how you were raised. He also assumed it had something to do with being powerless in the largest senses of that idea. At 14, he was supporting himself and his mother, humping produce out of refrigerated rail cars in the Strip District before school.

Corelli watched how things worked on Larimer Avenue. The Mafia wise guys and even the wannabe wise guys seemed to live better and have more control over their lives than the men who went to work with a metal lunch box. The wise guys feared each other but not the big institutions and invisible economic forces that bobbed ordinary people on seas of uncertainty. When recessions hit Pittsburgh's steel industry, the Mob's loansharking went up, bookmaking went up and the number of desperate people coming to Tony Bruno for help went up. Corelli saw that most of Larimer's civilians were never more than a half-dozen paychecks from cascading disaster. No matter how bad the economy, the wise guys always had a cash fold without holding a job. They drove new cars that were always washed and waxed. "Friends" protected them from harmful raids and indictments. In return, a South Side brothel was raided once a year at the end of August and a Hill District gambling joint was given up when the need arose. These raids were evidence, officials said, that crime of the organized variety in Pittsburgh "was well in hand and being managed"— which it clearly was.

Corelli also saw that the Mafia lived by sucking money out of almost every legitimate business in Larimer and other blue-collar neighborhoods. On that steady flow of small dollars, the Mob reached higher and got bigger. It infiltrated unions, businesses, restaurants, bars and supper clubs. It took a special courage to stand alone against the Mob's threats to hurt shopkeepers and torch their stores if they refused to pay protection. One match illuminated community consciousness for many years.

The Mafia was the closest ladder for Corelli to climb. He could choose from gambling, numbers, loansharking, stealing, scamming, prostitution and muscling those who couldn't pay or wouldn't play. He didn't have objections to things illegal, which were, in his opinion, often a matter of who was writing the law. Guys like me, he told himself, don't go to college and don't live quiet like a bookkeeper. He didn't consider himself a criminal. He considered himself a janitor, the man who cleaned things up. He never gave much thought to the possibility he could change the trajectory that seemed to be his fate.

Corelli was drafted into the Army in late 1965 after a couple of years of looking for easy money in hard places. He was curious about combat in Vietnam, though he felt no particular support for the War. It was in his opinion just another high-school football game where he played for his teammates, not the school. John Corelli considered soldiering for Lyndon Johnson's political career a sick joke on guys like him.

Corelli learned the methods of long-range reconnaissance at the U.S. Army's 5th Special Forces Nha Trang's Recondo School, which General William Westmoreland opened in September, 1966. He learned every weapon ground forces were using against each other. He rappelled from Hueys. He mastered small-boat operations, map reading, land and water navigation, fire direction, radio, Morse code and first aid. He was schooled in the objectives of six-man LRRP patrols—gather intelligence, see and not be seen, direct fire but not discharge a weapon and get in and out without leaving a trace. Occasionally, his group was tasked with snatching an enemy soldier for interrogation. When they got a sniper assignment, Corelli by unanimous decision was given the stalk and shoot. On patrols, Corelli never objected to walking point and bearing the risk of each first step on new ground. He'd learned to disguise his scent, because the Viet Cong could smell shampoo and deodorant. His team never smoked or cooked over a fire for the same reason. He learned to move silently, using terrain as cover. His team slept in a wagon wheel, backs to each other, weapons facing out. He ate the dehydrated, 1,100-calorie LRRP rations without complaint. He had even grown to half-like the spaghetti, which was not much worse than what he ate cold out of a can after his mother died.

Returning to Larimer Avenue at the end of 1968, Corelli was surprised to see how the neighborhood had changed. From 5,000 Italians in the early '50s, it was down 75 percent from what he saw. Help of Christians had lost more than one-third of its congregants, and almost half of its aging members no longer lived in the neighborhood. The buildings and streets looked smaller and dirtier than he remembered. Most of the houses were modest two-stories built in the early 1900s with a front porch and a tiny back yard. Kept up, they had always been respectable. When cash was short, they aged quickly and badly. Yards were the first to be neglected. Paint peeled; gutters sagged. Wood rotted.

A number of Italian-owned shops had followed their customers into the suburbs. Corelli missed Minutello's Meadow Street Grill, Turp's Homemade Pizza and Labriola's Italian Market. A handful of old-line businesses hung on despite the demographic tide washing customers away from their shore. He took some comfort in visiting Stagno's Bakery, Henry Grasso Meats and Ralph Moio's Italian Pastry—places he could never afford when he was a kid. Tony Bruno made sure businesses that stayed were protected from burglaries, shoplifting and "bad behavior"—for a very reasonable monthly fee.

Corelli found a few older Diablos still loafing at The Raven hoping for Bruno scraps, but most had either gone into the Service and then left or just left after high school. The remaining Diablos -- the younger brothers of Corelli's friends -- bunched tighter for their own protection as a declining minority. They wore their hair long like hippies, smoked dope and gave the V-sign to the black teenagers who drove down Larimer Avenue at night yelling "Black Power." "V" meant vengeance.

The Raven looked like an Italian social club, but its main business was hosting card and dice games, bookmaking, loansharking, distributing hijacked cigarettes and allocating vending machines, pinballs and slots. Wise guys conceived new scams in The Raven's dimness. Tony used The Raven as daycare for his associates between assignments. As Larimer changed racially, Tony's people forted up in The Raven, declaring that island off-limits to the "invaders." The Raven's doors were locked every night, but there was no need to do so.

The common threads that had once closely knit the people to their neighborhood for better and worse had frayed. To Corelli coming home after two tours in Vietnam, the old was no longer the same. He didn't care for the new, but he cared less for the alternatives. John Corelli felt the loss of place, but it was not with much nostalgia. He did not romanticize the old Larimer.

Corelli rented a second-floor apartment with a private entrance from its elderly owners who lived downstairs. It was on Carver Street, off Larimer. He wanted quiet time. He wanted to be alone to think about himself and straighten his head. He'd seen the wages of patriotism paid by kids just out of high school. He'd seen devastation. Had it made him a little harder? he asked. It felt like it had, but it hadn't transformed him from one kind of person to a very different kind. Killing was a job he had learned well. It demanded being careful with details, which he already was. Just like making a deal, he thought. You researched the target, planned the "event," prepared, sighted in and eased onto the trigger. He knew it could be a living.

The War, he concluded, had done two things to him. It had provided a graduate degree in the skills needed to be an assassin, and it had adjusted his mind to allow him to apply those skills without remorse.

John bought an inconspicuous black Valiant from a used-car lot on Baum Boulevard, because it would blend in to any background. He did not want to be noticed in the months after his return. He started spending time in the Oakland Library, reading military history and Ayn Rand. He wandered into biography and then psychology. He read the Kerner Commission Report that said blacks were living in a world apart from the American mainstream. He agreed with that conclusion and thought the Little Italy neighborhoods of Pittsburgh were much the same. He subscribed to <u>Foreign Affairs</u>, <u>The Wall Street Journal</u> and <u>The New York Review of Books</u>.

He had been transfixed by the <u>Ramparts</u> cover of Special Forces Master Sergeant Donald Duncan, winner of two Bronze Stars, in uniform announcing: "I quit." That story appeared in February, 1966. Had he read it then, he would have dismissed it as liberal propaganda. Three years later, he simply nodded in familiarity. Duncan, like Corelli, had been raised a Roman Catholic, but unlike Corelli, he still took his faith seriously. Corelli understood Duncan's commitment to the religion of his childhood. Duncan had knocked around in blue-collar jobs before going into the Army, and he, like Corelli, had spent most of his Vietnam time on patrol. Duncan wrote: "The whole thing was a lie. We weren't preserving freedom in South Vietnam. There was no freedom to preserve. To voice opposition to the government meant jail or death. …it's not democracy we brought to South Vietnam—it's anticommunism."

Corelli had walked the same path. He had heard of Captain Richard L. Steinke's refusal to board an aircraft to take him to a remote Vietnamese village in June, 1965, because he said, the War "…is not worth a single American life." Steinke, a West Point graduate, was court-martialed as were the Fort Hood Three and Captain Howard Levy, a Brooklyn dermatologist who refused to teach Green Berets how to treat skin diseases. During his tours, Corelli personally witnessed a growing number of "combat refusals," mutinies by an individual or a group unwilling to obey a specific order. John Corelli did not object to killing Vietnamese, "retail or wholesale," as he put it. By the time of his honorable discharge, he had lost whatever belief he had once had in either the commonsense or the effectiveness of it.

One fall afternoon, he drifted into a Shadyside secondhand bookstore where he found himself arguing pleasantly with an earnest Chatham College student about nonviolent resistance. Out came opinions he did not know he had.

"What about civil rights?" she'd asked.

"What about them?" he answered. "The more money you have, the more civil rights you get. Blacks'll have the same rights as whites when they're the same economically. They shouldn't be treated different until then. Whites should help them get there. That's in our interest, too." It occurred to him he had lost some of the racism he had carried from an early age.

He just laughed, but not rudely, when she said that Gandhi's non-cooperation and non-violent resistance would have defeated Hitler.

"Maybe," he said, "if a large majority of Germans did it. But when that majority more or less supports repression, non-cooperation simply means your ass gets thrown into the gas chamber rather than you walk it in yourself."

Nonetheless, on her urging, he left with a Thoreau reader so he could go through "On Civil Disobedience." The essay, she said, was a call for men and women of conscience to make individual judgments about whether or not to obey an order of government, like conscription for war. As he walked down Walnut Street toward his car parked on Negley Avenue, he laughed to himself about being a "man of conscience." Corelli admired acts of conscience -- like Norman Morrison, the Quaker husband and father of three, who immolated himself outside Robert McNamara's Pentagon office in 1965 to protest the War -- but they were not for him.

John typically returned to his small apartment after his afternoon explorations. He lifted weights -- careful not to bang them on the floor -- and then showered. He got into the Valiant and drove throughout the City and beyond. He scouted neighborhoods he didn't know, always aware and patrolling for useful intelligence. He came to realize that he'd spent most of his life in one of America's expendable colonies. He read about the "isms," but they didn't take. Maybe, he thought, he was an anarchist or a libertarian, but he wasn't motivated enough to be baptized as either one. The political systems of the worlds -- "nation-states," was the term he saw in Foreign Affairs articles -- were connected, interdependent and regularly at war. They evolved, adapted and endured in modified forms. War was a way to redistribute unbalanced power temporarily; wins and losses tended not to be permanent.

The individual, Corelli concluded, had to live between the systems as much as possible without being crushed when they moved against each other. Buying in to one system or another was a fool's game. In the narrow space between them, there, he thought, he might survive. He didn't move to the Walden woods as Thoreau did, but he moved away from much of society. The nation-state mind fuck, he decided, was not something he could do anything about.

The constant that survived Larimer's deterioration was Tony Bruno's organization, which, Corelli learned quickly after his return, was stronger than ever. In addition to the old "businesses," Tony had opened a couple of topless bars and three massage parlors. He was expanding into the area's drug trade. The Mafia had found ways to adapt its "economy" to a Pittsburgh that was losing its blue-collar base. "Our money," Tony said now, "can be made not down in no basement but up in the top-floor offices. We need to widen our point of view. We need to look out new windows from high up."

John Corelli did not like Tony Bruno, though they had always been cordial. John considered Tony to be a loyal believer in a parasitic system that was not much different from the one he believed had run the War. John did not trust missionaries or system-believers. Law enforcement allowed the Mafia to operate. That said to John Corelli a lot about The Law and Illegality. Bruno supported the Legal System that supported him. That's what Tony believed in—accommodation between the law enforcers and the lawbreakers for mutual benefit and stable order. It was a system that corrupted everyone it touched.

Tony was not analytical like Robert McNamara or polished like McGeorge Bundy or slick like Richard Helms—the Washington Believers who fed the War its fuels. He simply wanted to impose law and order on the anti-Establishment, disruptive elements so that "real Americans" like him could function as they pleased. That was Tony's patriotism—don't question the leader, give people what they want, make money however you can, work things out with those that had power and get rid of troublemakers like Black Panthers and radical students.

Tony Bruno was a stubby, no-neck brawler who had come up from and out of the Mafia's Old School. He was a made man in the Pete Luparelli family that had run Pittsburgh's Mafia since the 1930s. Pete had won an internal war over bootlegging territories, a war, he later claimed, was necessary "to clear our sinuses." Luparelli had picked up the pieces after John Bazzano killed the Volpe brothers from New Kensington and then had been killed in turn by Lucky Luciano who succeeded in tamping down the Cosa Nostra's "internal confusions," as he put it. Bruno had been a Luparelli solider, then the funnel for his orders and later his chief enforcer. When Luparelli died in the late '50s, Bruno, who had married the boss's daughter, took over and forcibly brought every Mafia outpost in the Tri-State area into line.

In the mid-1960s, Tony was talked to. New York's Five Families sent an emissary representing their Commission to tell him, in his words, that they "…didn't want no war between Pittsburgh and Cleveland over Youngstown and any of that shit in between. You talk it out. Divide it fair. If someone needs to be hit, you do it small and keep it quiet. And clean up your fuckin' act. Dress like a citizen, not no gangster. Stop usin' fuck this and fuck that. We have to make ourselves respectable to keep doin' business. So get a fuckin' tailor and retire the black leather jackets and purple ties." The Commission's message came from its leader, Frank Fagano.

Before he got a tailor, Tony Bruno got a coach. She was a senior English major -- "a nice Catlick girl" -- from Mount Mercy College in Oakland. He asked her "to polish up my English, make it more fuckin' American."

Laurie Mascaro was a pretty, mini-skirted daughter of a major Pittsburgh contractor whose family had washed the dirt from under their fingernails two generations back. She had been to Europe three times by her 21st birthday in addition to family trips to Italy. She knew a bit about French wine and something called sushi. Her mother had taken her shopping in New York—and not to the wholesale stores. Her horrified parents pleaded with her to drop Tony Bruno before she was tarnished with the Mafia label all Italians bore whatever their accomplishments. She listened, but refused. She told them she knew what she was doing.

Despite her Catholic, girls-school education, Laurie Mascaro was aware of the world, kept up with the news, dated a Jewish law student, stopped going to Confession, was on The Pill, supported McCarthy and then Kennedy in the 1968 Democratic primary (and not for their Catholicism, she pointed out) and understood exactly who Tony Bruno was and what he needed.

Laurie threw out the grammar books she had brought to her first coaching session in favor of rote memory and repetition, at which Tony was amazingly good.

"I want to go to the store," she said, "not I want to go to the fuckin' store. Repeat: I want to go to the store."

"I don't want to go to no fuckin' store in the first place," he pleaded. "I'll get delivery."

"Double negative," she said.

"Yeah," Tony laughed. "I got some 'double negatives' who owe me some positive money."

In time, Tony was improved. He could pass in the business world if he was concentrating. When he was angry, however, he reverted to his roots.

Laurie took him clothes shopping at a made-to-order tailor downtown and had him buy "business shoes" at Littles in Squirrel Hill. She taught him table manners, inoffensive small talk and other things she referred to as "decorative accents." She filed off his roughest burrs over six months. She made him presentable in what she called, "mixed company." In public, he was calmer and easier. The street side of Tony Bruno, she never saw.

Her motive? She didn't need the $25 an hour he paid her, or the presents he gave her, or the loyalty he promised her or the careful propositions he made to her. Laurie Mascaro saw Tony Bruno as the raw material for her debut novel.

Tony saw the wisdom in "cleaning up good." Fagano said "gangland-style murders"-- with a bloody body sprawled in a restaurant or stuffed in a trunk like a smelly gym sock -- were "dysfunctional"—a word Tony quickly added to his working vocabulary. The Mob, he realized with Laurie's counsel, had become so much a part of America that it had to clean up its public face to remain there. The old ways of dealing with each other led to newspaper stories, investigations and politicians calling for someone to do something. Clean up didn't mean change; it meant making sure the dirt went down the drain, and the sink was always ready for inspection.

"Any bum," Tony said before Laurie started working with him, "can shoot a fuckin' pistol and kill some fuckin' guy out in the fuckin' street."

After three months of coaching, he put the same thought this way: "Today, we need a craftsman, a skilled artisan like the old Italian stone carvers. Not no gorilla with a piece."

"Not 'not no.' It's 'not any,'" she advised.

"Yeah, not any gorilla with a piece."

"So what are you going to do with Jerry Multirosa?" she asked.

"Yeah," Tony agreed, "Jerry's old-school, a f... problem."

"Good," she said. "Jerry's a problem, but not a fuckin' problem."

"Yeah, he is."

For that reason, Tony approached John Corelli. He sent over Roberta Magnelli to determine whether John wanted to "come in."

Roberta was 30, an orphan with no siblings. Her family came from Milan, but they were Northern Italians without money. By 19, she was on her own, working as a go-go dancer at Tony's clubs. Tony saw she could act, too. She was pretty. She was sexy. She didn't look Italian, at least, she didn't look like him. She was freckled, with auburn hair and delicate features. She was verbal. She was good at patter with the customers. She didn't get scared when drunks acted up. She took judo lessons. Tony had a hunch she might work out for special assignments. A girl, he thought, could get close where a guy couldn't. He'd never used a girl, but he assured himself he had no prejudices against women, of which he was aware. He liked women, even his wife. So he made the approach, and Roberta said, she could use the money and would give it a try.

"So?" Tony asked her.

"Corelli won't talk about his scars."

"What scars?"

"Inside and out," she said. "I didn't see any drugs. He lifts. He reads a lot of books."

"Books! Like religious shit? Like Bishop Fulton J. Sheen?"

"No. Politics. War. Guns. Vietnam. Thick magazines, too."

"What did he want?"

"He wanted the lights out. That's all."

"What did you do?"

"I said, 'Okay with me.'"

"What did you do?"

"Nothing funny. Normal stuff. He does rattle a girl's bones."

"You're a good-lookin' girl. Why did he want it in the dark?"

"Well, Tony, he didn't say. He doesn't say a lot of things you and I might find interesting. I think he feels in control in the dark. I got the feeling his head was somewhere else. Some of those Vietnam vets are still creeped out. I liked him. But he's not like your regular goombahs, like Jerry Multirosa. Corelli's a door, not a window."

"What the fuck does that mean? I mean, what does that mean?"

"He can open and close if he wants, but you're not going to see through him."

"Jeeez, Roberta. You some kind of professor now? So?"

"He said he had no objection to 'helping' you from time to time. He's not interested in being made. He's a thoroughbred, not a nag."

"You like him. I can tell. Is this gonna be a thing?"

"I can work with him. This won't go to bride-and-groomsville."

When Tony invited John to their first meeting, Corelli had agreed the Mob had to do its business behind screens and not in the street.

"If you want a house painter," Corelli said, "I'm not your guy."

"We're done whacking people like that," Tony said. "No more paint jobs. No more smear and splatter on the walls."

"Serious stuff has to end up looking different than the old days," Corelli said. "Jobs can't look like 'Mob hits.' It can't look like you just dumped a plate of spaghetti and meatballs on the floor."

"I need a Raphael," Tony said.

"Raphael—patron saint of travelers, the ill and nurses?"

"Not the Saint," Tony said. "The artist."

That was six years ago.

388

"Siddahn, John," Bruno said with a smile as he reached over to shake hands. "You want a drink, John?"

"I'm good," Corelli said, taking the chair in front of Bruno's desk.

"I'll get you some lunch."

John Corelli sat, knowing it was unwise to refuse Tony's invitation. He, too, liked Del Porco's food.

"Baked anelletti, Paul," he said, "and some Stagno's bread if it came this morning."

"Fresh every morning, 9:15," Paul said.

"Thanks. Water is fine, no ice," Corelli said.

John stretched his hands toward Tony across the table. The thenar eminence in each one was a hardened rind. His knuckles were thick, stubby knobs freckled with small, white calcium deposits. "Knife hands" were the result of roll-punching a concrete block with the fat part of his hand over to the palm and repeatedly plunging them, finger-first, then knuckle-first, into a bucket of dry beans. Stretching kept his fingers and palms supple.

"You look good Tony."

"I been watchin' what I eat and how much, too. Dahn to 255."

"Pretty soon you'll be posin' like Arnold Schwarzenegger."

"Yeah, Five-five, 255. Mr. World. That's me."

Tony settled into his chair and unbuttoned his vest, which Laurie had forced on him when she started five years earlier. She wanted him to look more like a fat banker and less like a sawed-off stump of a gangster.

He had doubts about some of the changes Frank Fagano had ordered.

"What's the difference," he had asked her, "between front-loadin' interest on mortgages like the banks do and collectin' vig on a street loan?"

"Point taken," she laughed. "You are probably richer, but the banker has a downtown office in the sky and eats lunch at the Duquesne Club. Someday, you'll have an office like that. Andy Mellon, Carnegie, Frick, Schwab -- the original Pittsburgh Mob -- they had downtown offices. You can call them The White Hand."

"I look like a fuckin' priest."

Laurie sighed. "Tony...."

"Okay. Okay. I look like a...a...a...."

"Priest," she said.

"Yeah, a priest. Jeez!"

"The Lord helps those who dress themselves well," she laughed.

"Okay," Tony said, getting down to business with Corelli. "I got a West Virginia contract. Two, in fact. One guy...name is Frank Stover. Goes by Biggie, or some shit like that. He used to be a pro wrestler. Works in this coal miner's campaign against Joe Hunt. Him and the troublemakers are puttin' up some wop named Delucci. That bunch is called Miners for some shit or another. Democracy or Freedom. Like I say, some shit. Here's their campaign office address and Stover's home address. He's aht in the boonies, somewhere where the Hatfields and McCoys are screwin' their sisters while they're takin' a break from makin' moonshine. You need to make this look right. Not like something from us. Use Roberta to set him up. Yinz work good together. *Biggie*, my fuckin' foot."

"Okay."

"The other guy is from the Burgh. Becker. Jeffrey Becker. Lawyer. Seems to be the brains behind Delucci, which don't take much if you ask me."

"You sure that's his name?"

"Yeah, why?"

"No," Corelli said.

"No, what?"

"I won't do Becker."

"Why the fuck not?"

"I know Becker. Went to high school -- Peabody -- with the asshole."

"Peabody! So fuckin' what! Half the guys we do, we went to their fuckin' weddings. Becker went to Peabody? I went to Peabody!"

"I was in homeroom with him for four years. Wouldn't feel right."

"John, this Becker. He's a **problem** for me. You understand, a problem. We got a squeeze goin' on Delucci. Becker is likely to get in the way."

Corelli figured out what kind of problem Becker might be for Tony Bruno. "Get someone else. Not for me."

Tony Bruno considered John Corelli's refusal. It was allowed, because Corelli was not a made member. He did as-needed jobs, ones that required a word Tony Bruno had learned from Laurie, "finesse."

"Okay, John. No hard feelin's at this end. It'll probably work better separate. Not on the same trip down there. I'll give the contract to Jerry. Or someone else."

"Yeah," Corelli said, "Jerry could do him. But I'd look for a lighter touch. When do you need this Stover?"

"Three, four days."

"You lookin' into coal miners now? You've had Teamsters' 203 and the Laborers' 1033 up here since the late '50s," Corelli said.

"Yeah, we done good with both of 'em," Bruno said.

"Drivers for <u>The Post Gazette</u>, they're in 203, aren't they? Is that why the <u>PeeGee</u> never writes much about you?"

"Never hurts to have a little leverage on a situation," Bruno said. "The best leverage is the leverage you never have to use."

"Yeah, leverage never hurts," Corelli said. "What exactly happened to Lazarro and Hyskra on that little bat job a couple of months ago? Did you ever get that figured out?"

Corelli had not been able to make sense of that episode. Little Louie and Bonk were two punks Tony used for errands and simple shakedowns. If they put their heads together, Corelli thought, they might be able to change a dollar bill into at least three quarters. Anyone who could set a mousetrap could take out those two. Had they been bait? Had Tony set up his own guys? Was the set up coming from upstairs, from Frank Fagano for some reason?

"We think it was this Biggie Stover that done 'em. Animal! Used Delucci's Jeep. Stover is in my way. He's fuckin' up our 'business plan.'"

"You goin' for an MBA, Tony?"

"Why would a short, fat guy like me be goin' for the NBA?"

"Yeah, I guess it was stretch," Corelli admitted.

"Same pay. Like last time," Bruno said.

"That works."

They shifted to sports and then neighborhood decline as they ate. After 20 minutes, Corelli got up, gave Tony Bruno a half salute and walked back into Del Porco's. As a free-lance, Corelli didn't have to leave through the back door.

John Corelli noticed that Jerry Multirosa gave Tony a few minutes before he went in. Pepper and Ginny were gone.

Before Corelli walked out the door, Paul DeFade gave him a slip of paper with two first names and two phone numbers.

"They're good girls, John," he said. "I've known them since they were little. Know their folks."

"Thanks," Corelli said, "I'll keep them in mind."

He went out. The day had gone gray, a color he liked.

Chapter 28

Middle Ridge, November 19, 1975, 11:15 p.m.

"Hello."

"Asshole."

Becker shook his head and looked at his phone. He had fallen asleep in front of his television and was now trying to clear the blearies. He noticed he had never turned the television on. His living room smelled like pizza, because most of the pie lay in the opened box on his coffee table. He noticed a crust on the napkin on his lap. He looked again at the phone in his hand, the phone that had just said "Asshole" into his ear.

"Who's this?"

"Asshole. Is that you?"

Several people routinely referred to Becker as "asshole" with varying degrees of affection, hostility and justification.

The voice was familiar. Baritone. Pittsburgh accent. Unmistakable.

"John?"

"Asshole."

"I haven't talked to you since graduation. That's 12 years. You okay? In Charleston? Need a lawyer?"

"Listen and shut up. Some people don't like you, because you're unlikable. You've become a 'problem' to these people. I don't need to mention who these people are. They're not bullshitters. They're sendin' a messenger down there to see you. Soon. You don't want to meet their messenger and receive this message. You don't want their 'problem' to get solved."

"What are you talking about?"

"You're workin' for Delucci, right? He's jammed in with these people. You're a problem, because, man, you will like this, you are a way too *independent variable*."

Becker had heard over the years that John Corelli served in Vietnam, came back harder than when he left and did work for the Pittsburgh Mob. Friends from Peabody told Corelli stories at their 10th reunion. One insisted he wasn't *in* the Mafia. He did "special orders," which paid well. He was known for delivering "clean hits," ones that looked like crimes of passion.

"I'm in the way of what? Whose way?"

"You still haven't learned that assholes ask questions they shouldn't be askin'. Why fuckin' this, and why fuckin' that? If you kept your yap shut in high school, you might have made something of yourself. But no.

You had to mouth off. Elmer Flowers could deal with me, but you screwed with his head. Too many questions get you killed."

"Why is anybody after me?"

"Because you're who you fuckin' are. Don't you get it? The bus is rollin' toward you doin' 100, and you're standin' in the middle of the street buck naked. You're too stupid to move your feet instead of your mouth."

Becker was adding and subtracting bits of information as fast as his now-semi-alert brain could function. Corelli warning him. Mafia guy being dispatched to beat him up or take him out. What deal? Was it between Pittsburgh hoods and Delucci? Is that where the last flush of campaign money came from? For what in return? Had the Mob gotten to Joe Hunt first, then switched sides? Or had they captured both Hunt and Jeep? Was the deal that Bruno would help Delucci win in return for the American Bank of Washington and the Union? What would the Mob do with a Union that mined most of America's coal, which fed its steel mills and generated its electricity? The health and retirement fund! How far up did this go in the Mafia world? Were Frank Fagano and Meyer Lansky making a play? Would Jeep roll over on the Union's treasury and its $222 million windfall? Was he that ambitious? What kind of reform campaign was Becker managing?

"John, what should I do?"

"Resign and get the hell out of Dodge. You're a lawyer. Go somewhere quiet. Vermont. Portland, Oregon. Venice, California. Sue the shit out of bad corporations. You'll make a fortune, marry a nice girl who's smart too, then send your kids to the Ivy League. Forget this shit with coal miners. When it's over, Becker, they won't give you the time of day let alone a $9 Timex."

"How much room do I have?"

"Hand in your resignation tomorrow. Make sure the <u>Post-Gazette</u> gets the word. The boys gotta see it in print before they'll believe it. Say some shit like 'the campaign is doin' well and no longer needs my asshole services.' Say you want to spend more time with your dog."

"Is there some way I can protect myself and not resign?"

"Becker, you ain't listenin'. You've been declared 'a problem.' Leave, and you might not be their 'problem' no more."

"Are you the one they're sending for me?"

"Ain't me, babe. Told 'em I spent four long years sittin' next to you in 210. I have too much time invested in givin' you good career advice and watchin' your back. You pissed off a lot of guys for bein' like you are. Poor Elmer Flowers. Why me? he must have asked. It also took some effort to keep you from gettin' your ass kicked at the flagpole."

Becker took off his glasses and rubbed his neck. "Why does everything turn to shit?"

"More whys," Corelli answered. "Every good deed gets compromised."

"Great, I'm talking to a hitman who's a cynical fatalist."

Corelli said nothing.

Becker realized he had stepped over a line he hadn't seen.

Corelli spoke finally. "Everything doesn't turn to total shit. But most everything turns to partial shit over time. Maybe bad shit drives out good shit. Like in economics. I dunno."

"I dunno either," Becker echoed. "I owe you, John. You didn't have to do this."

"Yeah, well, I'm a sucker for puppies and assholes. You're gettin' a pass if you're smart enough to take it. If you make it through, send me the book you'll write about bein' a hippie farmer with a law practice in Lifestyle, USA. How in the hell did you ever end up in West-for-saken Virginia?"

Becker laughed. "I wanted to move history's needle a tad."

"Jesus. You're fucked up. Why dint you try to make money and give a few bucks to the lame and the halt like a normal citizen?"

"Beats me. Life would have been easier."

"Why dint you listen to all the career counseling I gave you for free. Like ain't no one gonna look out for you if you're too dumb to not look out for yourself."

"I remember our sessions at Eat 'n' Park. I learned a lot."

"Food for thought at Eat 'n' Park. You had a lot to learn."

"If you ever need a lawyer, give me a call. No charge for…brothers."

"Asshole."

"I pay my debts, John."

"Yeah, well, I collect debts…and sell Venetian blinds after hours." Corelli hung up.

Becker couldn't stop laughing. Venetian blinds! How did John Corelli ever come up with that?

394

Chapter 29

West Virginia, November 20, 1975

The "Widders Wildcat" rolled out of Bloomingrose Holler to all the mines in McDowell County. From there, pickets drove it into Wyoming, Logan, Raleigh, Mingo, Fayette, Kanawha and Boone Counties in West Virginia, then into East Kentucky, Southwest Virginia, northern West Virginia, southwestern Pennsylvania, southeastern Ohio, northern Alabama, East Tennessee, West Kentucky, Indiana, southern Illinois and even to a few of the new non-Union, open-pit mines in Colorado and Wyoming. Union or not, it didn't seem to matter—all had been running on the speed-up to sell coal while the price was nonsensically high. But for almost three weeks, no one was selling coal high, low or in between. "Stop the speed-up. Stand still for safety." had touched every miner.

The phrase Jeep Delucci had coined at American Eagle -- "Coal will be mined safely or not at all." -- had come to pass without his help. The American Eagle widows had stood it up and given it meaning.

By mid-November, the strike had not weakened even in the mines where strikes never happened.

President Gerald Ford said at a press conference on Friday, November 14th the coal strike threatened to cut off the Nation's electricity supply. He predicted massive blackouts if the strike continued, with cold houses and warm refrigerators. The Federal Energy Office used a computer model to generate employment impacts from the strike. "Three-hundred thousand plus will be thrown out of work as a direct consequence of the strike," FEO reported to the President, "and another 500,000 laid off indirectly."

Labor Secretary Peter McBride asked the Bureau of Labor Statistics to call employers around the country to confirm the projections of the FEO's model. "Twenty thousand layoffs, tops," was the phone survey's answer. Utilities, mills and businesses had sufficient stockpiles to get through another four weeks before significant disruption or layoffs would occur. McBride, a team player, said nothing either publicly or to Ford when the White House kept trumpeting the FEO's exaggerated job-loss numbers. Ford hoped that scare tactics would turn public opinion against the widows. He saw no advantage in obtaining a Taft-Hartley injunction against the ACMU, because he understood Joe Hunt was trying to stop the wildcat strike as much as the employers. A Taft-Hartley injunction, Ford had been told, would harden the strikers, not break them.

The coal companies fought the strike with all the tools they had. They won federal injunctions that prohibited their employees from striking and spreading it through roving pickets. Miners were restrained from public statements and actions promoting the stoppage. Wives and retired miners who couldn't be fired and weren't afraid of jail took their place. Courts cited local unions and individuals for contempt, imposed fines and jail sentences. Freddie Pruitt was sentenced to six months for defying the TRO and "leading an illegal strike." But jailing him did nothing to stop the strike. It continued without pickets, without endorsements and without leadership. The strike to end the speed-up wasn't led by anybody; it just was.

The 10 American Eagle women said nothing, which was more than enough to keep it going. They carried no picket signs, stayed on public property and pulled the early mines just by driving by. No coal company dared target them with an injunction. No federal judge wanted to issue *that* order. Nobody dared to throw these women in jail. The less they said, the more powerful was their non-control control.

The Governor's Mansion, November 21, 1975, 7:03 a.m.

The Governor of West Virginia grimaced.

The Governor leaned toward the mirror as he pulled the skin under his chin tight. He worked the razor up from his Adam's apple to the point of his chin. It was hard to see without his glasses. He sometimes found it hard to see with them.

The Governor didn't like shaving his Adam's apple. A "Brother" in the Porcellian Club at Harvard had informed him during the "punch" inspection of would-be members that its proper name was "laryngeal prominence." "Punchee" Peter Dance Shortbridge, IV, had not been accepted for membership.

The Pore realized "Shorts," as they dubbed the tall underclassman, could not tell a dirty joke comically, a principal admission criterion. They could find in him neither practiced wit nor intellectual sprightliness.

The Fly Club took him, but the Pore's snub hurt. He had never quite gotten over the feeling that what they had said was true. He knew he was not their equal intellectually or comedically. It did not matter that the main activity of the Porcellians was to languidly observe and remark. He, too, had wanted to languidly observe and remark.

The Governor nicked his chin. He dabbed the tiny blood bubble with toilet paper. Then he worked the razor down each cheek. He preferred being shaved to shaving. But having a barber visit the Governor's Mansion each morning would not sit well with his constituents who would find out eventually. Things like that were always found out, eventually.

Bad start to a bad day, he thought. He felt the wildcat strike closing in on him. He knew he was out of sorts and out of options.

Coal production had stopped across West Virginia. "His" mountaineers were up in arms. They sat at home. Governors in other states phoned. They feared their electricity would be cut off. His budget director provided daily estimates of lost tax revenue. The strike could cascade into closures in steel, chemicals and heavy equipment. It could retard home construction, retail and especially Christmas shopping. A work stoppage would not bring the dead miners back to life. It would not lead to a miracle. Any "deal" over the pace of work would have no legal standing. Unenforceable. Even he knew that. So why?

The Governor who had come to West Virginia as a church volunteer learned to never be surprised at the single-minded willingness of his constituents to shoot themselves in their collective foot. If you're poor and pitiful, he thought as he stretched his skin, you don't cut off your cash flow—you try to increase it. If you have a dispute, you settle it before it gets out of hand. This hillbilly way they had of bargaining takes them to shotguns after the first exchange of "Bullshits!" Surely these widows had other means to make their point!

West Virginia, he knew, had always been too raw for his taste and temperament, but it was where he had determined he was most likely to be elected. New Yorkers would have torn him apart. Connecticut would have laughed. Boston would have snubbed him again. Beggars were never choosers. Political beggars were damn lucky to cadge a place out of the weather, self-generated and otherwise.

And now on this unpleasant, unattractive morning, The Governor was forced to think about a jumbled vision of phantom pickets, widows, injunctions, idled coal mines and projections of economic disasters. The White House had called a few days earlier. "Do something, Peter," The President had said. "Lead for Christ's sake!" John-Cee Smithers had called; Roberson from AMSTEEL, even that Buzzard Maggy fellow from Kentucky. The Governor had talked with Joe Hunt—"Ain't me," Joe said. "I want 'em back on the job." The Governor spoke with lawyers, bankers, consultants, experts, county bosses, superintendents, Wall Street analysts and a couple of professors. No one had a solution. It was all happening in the open, but in the shadows of the open, which was impossible because no shadows existed there. No leaders were leading. Everybody was following an unspoken order. When you had 100,000 cooks, getting rid of a troublesome handful didn't fix the spoiled broth.

Goddamn, he swore to himself, as he dabbed his chin. I may be the first casualty of this wildcat strike. If I lean on the widows, I lose. If I lean on the miners, I lose. If I lean on the companies, they'll cut me like they did in my first election. They'll fund my opponent who promises them what they want.

Labor unrest gives West Virginia a bad name. How do miners expect me to peddle their stupid coal in Europe and the Pacific Rim if they don't have the discipline, the character, to go to work every day just like I do? They're too ignorant to understand a sophisticated market economy. Not stupid, necessarily, but ignorant of how the world works. They always want something but are never prepared to give up something. They think the world owes them. The world owes no one anything. Life is a struggle, that I know.

And I gave up New York -- or at least, Washington -- for Charleston! My God. Charleston, the gritty capital of an internal colony that would be better off sliding into the Kanawha River. Ninety-seven muddy miles long and all of it in West Virginia. Who else would have a waterway that's been an open sewer for 175 years?

The Indians -- the Adena, Hopewell and Woodland -- lived in the river valleys of the Kanawha and Ohio until about 1600. They left their burial mounds, which I have dutifully visited, he reminded himself, in both South Charleston and Moundsville. And then, before whites came, they moved their permanent settlements away from even the level river bottoms. Sure, they traveled through West Virginia. They gathered its resources -- game, salt and chert -- and left.

It's hard to keep in mind, he told himself, that 400 years ago, the only people in the Great State of West Virginia were running around in animal skins using stone tools. He'd learned the bow preceded the arrow by maybe 1,000 years. It was used for drilling and starting fires. The bow and arrow appeared about 500 A.D., about the time the Dark Ages were starting in Europe. He wondered why the Asian people who settled the New World never evolved the technology of their Chinese ancestors. Why did they stay stuck in the Stone Age for so long? Not an axle and wheel anywhere before the European arrival. How hard was it to think up a wheel? Well, maybe it had something to do with the absence of horses; that could be. The Governor believed he could have thought up a wheel if he had been an Indian in 1,000 A.D. Why didn't they domesticate animals, like deer, to pull a cart? Why didn't they figure out iron and bronze? Why didn't they make boats and trade with the Asian coast? Why were they happy in their Paleolithic primitiveness? Not a written language anywhere in North America before Columbus. But the first Americans did grow tobacco, bless their hearts; they were smokers. They were sitting on the world's mother lode of natural resources, and they laid around puffing cigars. Joints, too, probably. What was the matter with them?

West Virginia, he thought, had never been on the cutting edge even when it would have been easy.

And then most of the natives left West Virginia in the early 1600s for reasons unknown. Perfectly understandable. To be honest, I don't want to live here either, and neither does Nancy.

Talk to Delucci, Ben Roberson said. See if he can't lean on the widows. Why would Delucci do anything for me? The Governor asked in reply. The more chaos during Joe Hunt's reign, the better for Delucci. That's obvious.

398

Talk to the widows, John-Cee Smithers said. Sure, good buddy, lay this burden on me. This is UNICOAL's problem. UNICOAL and the other operators need to solve it. Not me.

The Governor bared his teeth, hoping to look feral, or, at least, resolute. He could use more feral. He looked at his face. Too smooth. Hair, too fine. He had always wanted to look rugged and square-jawed. He wanted to play rugby but took up tennis, which, he thought, was just as adversarial. Instead of having a bull's head, he had the face of a steer.

Not fair, he thought. At St. Paul's, no one had taken him seriously. He was not athletic, bright or funny. He was just rich, because his family was. Well, hadn't he accomplished more than anyone thought possible given what he had to work with? So let his father swallow his disappointments. His mother had always been kind if not particularly interested.

It's not my damn job to talk these widows into confining their mourning and their anger to their sweaty little trailers. *Mobile homes*; they're mobile homes, he scolded himself, not trailers. Mobile homes that never move! The widows have a right to be ticked off, he thought. Maybe a little ticked-offness will improve things. But these ladies do need to stop this strike. They'll drive coal demand to oil or natural gas. Why don't they understand Economics 101; I do. I got a B in the course. I've read Paul Samuelson's text book. Well, not cover to cover. The parts I was assigned, I read most of those, except for the graphs where one line crossed the other at a point called price—they were a little tricky.

He patted his chin with a clean tissue. They want me to go to McDowell County. It will be a circus of bereavement. They will babble at me like they do in those one-room churches where they gibber and quack at each other in "tongues." Their lay preachers will bawl and stomp about Jesus. He shook his head. Speaking in tongues! Hell, 99 percent of my constituents can't even speak in English.

He squeezed Crest toothpaste onto his electric brush. He began scrubbing his teeth, lower molars first. Now the operators were screaming to use the State Police to break the strike. But cops, even the West Virginia National Guard, can't break up a picket line that isn't there! They can't arrest people for staying home, can they? He moved to his incisors and then his two front teeth. Firm up and down strokes. Where in the hell would Delucci take these poor souls with "Coal Will Be Mined Safely or Not At All." You can't mine the damn stuff safely, not 100 percent safely. Not at all. Great. Not at all. I can't sell coal to the Koreans and the Japanese if it's not at all.

I don't want to go to McDowell County and pat these poor things on the hand and tell them it will be all right. It wasn't ever going to be all right. It will be different, not the same. These people want the same. The same is their prison. They don't understand the only constant in the world is change. They will complain; I will listen with my earnest face on. It will be something out of Homer—bereaved females, wild-eyed with grief, ripping at their polyester clothes, pulling at their lank hair, throwing themselves figuratively on the empty lunch buckets of their deceased husbands.

The Governor spat and rinsed his toothbrush.

Maybe there's some way I can get out of going. But, he reminded himself, avoidance would be bad politically. Show sympathy for the widows. Forget about offering a solution. Urge a settlement without saying anything specific or taking sides. Announce the establishment of a State commission to look into the disaster. I could have a photo taken with that Willie who survived. And then a shot with the ladies. I bet Nancy would come with me. If we helicopter in, we wouldn't have to stay overnight. Stay in Welch! God! There is a motel there, as I recall. Someone will shout at me. Point an accusatory finger. Bellow that my inspectors didn't do their jobs. It was the feds, not my guys. The feds are to blame. Well, the company, too, I'm sure. I don't look forward to widows spilling their guts in my lap.

What can I do about the push for coal production? It's OPEC. Oil price up, coal price rises. That's the root of the speed-up, which is now SOP in the coalfields to take advantage of the inflated prices. Coalfields! Why for Heaven's sake didn't West Virginia produce popcorn or otter haunches? Or even cars? Why did it have to be cursed with coal? Why do human beings have to burrow into mountains like moles and pull out the very rock that keeps them safe?

The Governor remembered when he was angry about all of that, when he first came to West Virginia. Now, well, it just was what was. He wasn't going to change any of it from the Capitol. It just made him sad and bored with the repetitiveness of it. The faces, the accents, the mangled syntax, the misshapen bodies, the peculiarity, the pitifulness. It broke his heart. He would not learn anything knew by visiting American Eagle to be beseeched and accused. The Governor knew all he needed to know about West Virginia's coalfields. Stay the hell out of their family fight!

"It is, however, your duty," he said aloud. You can't just be Governor, he thought, you have to *do* Governor. You have to appear to be doing something. You are not a Porcellian, languidly observing and remarking!

The Governor ran a comb through his hair. It was horn, a Christmas gift from Mother during his first year at Harvard. It was made in France for Taylor of Old Bond Street in London. Ox horn from South America would oil his hair, build it up, maybe, she said, and it didn't snag like the plastic.

Peter Dance Shortbridge looked at his eyes in the bathroom mirror, turned and walked into the bedroom. A nice wife, a nice family. A political base that should, he hoped, send him to Washington.

It was Thursday. The strike had been going on for several weeks. He couldn't wait. He had to suck it up like the man he thought he was.

The grievances of the oppressed. They never ended, he thought, and were always the same.

Nancy Waring Shortbridge was dressed. She brushed her hair. She didn't look at her husband or speak as he passed into his dressing room and took off his bathrobe.

"You should do something," she said into her mirror.

"Yes."

"At least, set up a panel even if you don't intend to do anything."

"They'll have to make recommendations. Yes. I'm planning to."

"I'll go with you if you want. I can comfort the women."

"That would be helpful. Nice of you to think of me."

"Well, I am thinking of them as well," she said.

"Of course," The Governor said.

"And us," she said. "Poor things."

"Yes, poor things…thangs."

"Yes," she said. "Thangs."

Bloomingrose Holler, November 21, 1975, 8:12 p.m.

UNICOAL transferred Bruce "Butch" Boyles from its underground mine near Washington, Pennsylvania, to replace Delmer Estep. Butch arrived at an idle mine—nobody going in, and no coal coming out. No pickets greeted him at the entrance; none were needed.

Butch earned his mine-engineering degree at West Virginia University where he played tight end. UNICOAL liked bringing college football players into management, particularly linebackers and tight ends. They were large, aggressive and followed orders. Butch fit the Company's management-recruitment profile in the summer of 1963. He came across as a smart-enough kid who wasn't afraid to push people. His academics were acceptable. His dad had worked as a supervisor for Aloe Brothers Coal Company, an independent operator near Pittsburgh. Since joining UNICOAL, Butch had moved up to assistant mine superintendent at the Company's largest underground mine. He was scheduled to take it over in 1976. The American Eagle cave-in changed UNICOAL's plans for him. John-Cee decided American Eagle needed a superintendent who could quickly and forcefully clean up the mess and stop the wildcat strike.

Butch's order to move to American Eagle was a surprise, a vote of confidence and a test. Reestablishing American Eagle as a cohesive, productive operation would be a singular credential on his hoped-for rise to Company CEO.

"You can't beat solving a crisis," John-Cee said to Butch, "for proving your ability and value to the Company."

Butch moaned: "Bloomingrose Holler? McDowell County, West Virginia?"

"Running this Company is about solving problems you can foresee as well as those that arise from out of nowhere. I want you to show me how you handle both tasks down there where it's hard. If it wasn't hard, it wouldn't test you, and I wouldn't learn anything."

"How long?" Butch asked.

"We bought a nice, 4,000-square-foot home for you near Welch, rent free," John-Cee said. "It was built two years ago. Move Janey and the kids there whenever it's convenient. Plan on three years, max. Then I'll bring you back to headquarters. Permanently. I promise."

"'Janey Complainey' and the kids will not be pleased with the move," Butch said. "Probably the best thing is to wait until they finish school in June. They won't like switching schools."

"I spent a couple of years at American Eagle myself," John-Cee said. "It's your ticket. Punch it. Get the long wall installed and running coal the way it can. Patch things up with the local union."

"What about the wildcat strike? What do you want me to do?" Butch asked.

"It's the widows, not the miners who are behind it," John-Cee said. "We'll work on them from different angles. I'll be the good cop. You do what you can to divide them. Your section bosses will tell you who's vulnerable to pressure and who might be bought off. I'll dangle cash in front of them. The combination of your stick and my carrot should break it. Every day this strike continues means the strikers are getting weaker. They're running out of money."

"What about Delmer's widow?" Butch asked. "I hear she's the ringleader."

"I'll call her personally. Your job is to make that mine a team again. Every ton of American Eagle coal we can ship will fetch more than $25 a ton. Five years ago, it was $9. Our production cost today is $8. Blessed be OPEC. Put in three years, and I'll make your career. You have my word."

As he drove to American Eagle, Butch thought about ways of being a bad cop with the women who had started the strike. From his conversations with local supervisors later that day, he understood the divisions in the committee—two management wives and the rest hourlies; widows and several with surviving husbands; white and black; young and old; one gray-haired leader, Doris Estep; one second in command, Susie Rutherford; and one cherry bomb, Wanda Smith. Light the firecracker, he thought, and the whole mess might explode and disappear.

The day Butch Boyles arrived, a rock was thrown through Wanda Smith's window just before midnight. Taped to it was a scrap of grocery-

402

bag paper with the message: "Next time, it's a .45. Back off the strike. Bitch."

Wanda loaded Artie's deer rifle and sat up the rest of the night with her back against the rear wall of their living room. She pointed the muzzle at her front door.

That morning, Wanda phoned Susie Rutherford.

"You don't know who done it," Susie responded. "Coulda been a miner who's hurtin' for money. Coulda been one of the bosses. Coulda been the sheriff hisself for all we know."

"Who you think?" Wanda asked.

"Ain't sure. That's the best I can say. Don't want to accuse no one without proof."

"Fuck proof! It has to be that blond-headed motherfucka they jes' shipped down here from up north to run the mine. I'm going up there and straighten out his l'il butchy, crew-cut ass right now."

"No. Let me talk to Doris."

"I ain't puttin' up with no rocks through my window. I ain't no scaredy rabbit of the Klan, and I ain't runnin' from no Pat Boone."

"Doris'll know ifn it was the Comp'ny. You need to keep cool. Remember what we talked about. They gonna work on you."

"Talk to her an' Linda Faye, too. I'm holdin' off, not backin' down."

That night, four men waited in a banged-up, Ford 150 crew cab on a wide out next to the two-lane highway that led from Bloomingrose Holler to Welch. They had daubed mud over the truck's license plates. Each carried a loaded, large-caliber pistol in his pocket or waistband.

They were hunters.

The CB radio, tuned to the seldom-used Channel 40, came on.

"Daffy Duck jes' pulled out in a purty new blue Bronco. Over."

"Donald or Goofy with him? Over."

"Nope. All the Mouseketeers are in the Club House. Over."

"Br'er Bear drivin' along? Over."

"Don't see no Brother Bear. Daffy's runnin' bare and blind. Over."

"Yeah boy. 10-4."

The Ford pickup pulled onto the highway going 15 in a 55-mph zone. The Bronco with high-beams came around a bend a few minutes later.

The pickup pulled over, letting the Bronco pass on the straight stretch. Two miles later, the pickup passed the Bronco where the road curved with a pull-over on the side. The truck swerved sharply to a stop in front. The Bronco had no choice but to brake quickly, yank to the right, pull off and stop.

Danny Workman, Verlon Bailey, Kenny Stafford and John "Jingle" Bell got out. They pulled ski masks over their heads and drew pistols as they advanced toward the Bronco. Jingle carried his son's softball bat in his right hand.

John Bell got his nickname in high school, because he was always adjusting. It stayed with him in the mines and in the Klan.

Butch Boyles was trapped. His first instinct was to ram his Bronco into the rear of the truck to escape. But he realized he wouldn't have enough road grip to move the big pickup if he couldn't get out and lock the front hubs into four-wheel-drive. Trees behind him and to the side blocked escape. He looked in his front seat for a weapon. He found a Styrofoam cup half-filled with cold coffee and an official paper map of West Virginia. The best he could do, he thought, was hurt one or two of them so they could be identified. Subsequently.

"Get out," Jingle said.

Butch got out.

"Which knee you like best?" Jingle asked, holding the bat in his right hand with his .38 in the left.

"I like them both."

Jingle drew close to Butch. They were the same size. He laid the bat against the inside of Butch's left knee.

Butch realized too late that Jingle couldn't swing against either knee from that position. Jingle lifted the bat hard between Butch's legs. Butch went down, balled up as best he could and fought to catch his breath and not pass out.

"Glad you didn't want to play no favorites," Jingle said.

Danny Workman stood next to Butch, reached in his jacket pocket and dropped a baseball-size rock on Butch's face.

"This here rock," Danny said, "found its way into a place it don't belong. Now this here rock is in the right place. You understand what I'm sayin'?"

"What?"

"If that gal is bothered again, you yourself, and that family you're bringin' here, will be held to 'count," Jingle said.

Butch now knew that the two who had spoken were white. He was getting his breath back. His balls ached.

"It was just that Smith woman. She's the one with the mouth on her. Thinks she's Mrs. Malcolm XYZ," he said.

"Don't matter she's a nigger," Jingle said.

"Could be some Black Panther for all I know," Butch wheezed.

"She's a fuckin' widder not a fuckin' Panther," Verlon Bailey said.

"I got more Panther in me than she does," Jingle said.

"Well, that's because of that thang with Dukey," Kenny Stafford added for historical clarification.

404

Jingle leaned over until his face was no more than an inch from Butch's face. "Need to get you lined out, some. Niggers is niggers, an' we should never have brought them sumbitches over from Africa. Don't like most of 'em. But Pins was a brother miner, an' I blocked my ass off for that sumbitch for two seasons. And when Dukey Lambright kicked him in the head during the Logan game, I put Dukey on the ground, and Dukey's my second cousin on my Momma's side. You understand what I'm sayin' to your sorry white-ass face?"

Jingle Bell's public views on race were well-known among both whites and blacks in Bloomingrose Holler. The adaptation of his views to this situation did not surprise his three brother miners. None cared for Wanda Smith who Kenny Stafford usually referred to as "Mrs. Stokeless Carbuncle."

What his friends didn't know was that Jingle loved Wanda and had since their first time together on a pile of ratty mining curtains in the back of an abandoned UNICOAL welding shop when they were in the ninth grade. They kept it up through most of high school, not telling anyone anything, while proclaiming their racial prejudices even when occasions did not arise.

He asked her to marry him in their senior year, 1970. Wanda laughed and kissed him.

"Won't work," she said. "Too much goin' against it down here."

"We'll move," he promised.

"Same there as here," she said.

He begged. She cried, and then she cut it off. Two years later, they were both married to others.

Jingle jammed the bat between Butch's legs with the end jammed into his crotch. "Understand what I'm sayin'." It was not a question.

"Yes," Butch whispered.

"You fuck again with the ladies, you goin' to be deader than Pins," Jingle said, and then he adjusted himself for emphasis.

"I understand. This ends here."

As the four walked back to the truck, Kenny said to Jingle: "WVU needs some tight ends with balls. Not like Daffy back there. Lost to Penn State last month 39, zip."

"Yeah, but Bobby Bowden's got 'em eight and two, and they beat Pitt," Verlon said. "Give 'em a break."

"You think that fucker understands?" Jingle asked.

"I think he got your point," Danny said.

John-Cee Smithers phoned Doris Estep on Saturday morning after talking to Butch Boyles.

"I'm sorry to make this call to you, Mrs. Estep," John-Cee said, "but there are hard things to do in every family. And I've always considered UNICOAL a family. My family."

"Mr. Smithers," she said. "Good morning."

"Good morning. You have to stop this wildcat strike," he said.

"Why?"

"Because it's hurting everyone in the industry, operator and miner alike."

"I'm sure that's true," she said. "That's sort of the idea, isn't it?"

"Mrs. Estep. You know how sorry we are about Delmer and the others."

"I'm sure that's true," she said.

"This wildcat strike can't bring them back," he said.

"I'm sure that's also true," Doris said. "But this isn't about Delmer or the other six who died, Mr. Smithers. It's about the ones who are still working."

"Well, nobody's working right now," he said, "except me."

"Amazing, isn't it?"

"Your committee has a right to be proud of your, well, let's call it, your success. We've gotten the message. The industry will do better. It's, well, Mrs. Estep, it's just not right that a superintendent's wife should be leading a strike against her husband's employer. You know that."

"The miners don't seem to have a problem with me," she said. "They're leading their own strike."

Doris remembered conversations that had felt like this—when teenage boys were trying to persuade her to do something that she didn't want to do but was curious about at an intellectual level.

"Let's say it appears you are the first among equals," he said.

"I'm one of seven American Eagle mine widows. I'm equal to the other six. That's who I am."

"You're also a teacher. The wife of a well-respected UNICOAL superintendent. A leader in the community."

"I'm just like the others, Mr. Smithers."

"What would Delmer have thought about what you're doing now?"

"He'd want me to do what *he* thought was best. We never did agree on that," she chuckled. "I was not the best wife UNICOAL could have chosen for Delmer Estep. After a while, we made our peace with that."

"Have you given much thought to what you will do in the future? Money can be a real problem if you don't have much, and if you don't have a job. Particularly if you have to move. At your age."

So there it was, she thought. He'll get me fired and tie up Delmer's pension.

"I've made contingency plans, Mr. Smithers. Thank you for your concern. The ten of us retained a law firm yesterday. They will be filing

406

suit in a few days. We expect a very large judgment. Very, very large. Very large. Which, of course, won't make things the same as they once were, but it's the best we can do."

"Down the road, Mrs. Estep. 'Very large' will be very, very far down the road, I can promise you that. If at all. The miners put themselves and Delmer and Lee Roy in harm's way. UNICOAL could sue the eight hourlies -- survivors and widows -- for injuring themselves and damaging our equipment and reputation. Management -- neither Delmer nor Lee Roy -- ordered them to vary from the rescue plan. What they did was a rogue act—just like this wildcat strike. They killed themselves. That's how it lines out to our lawyers."

"Sue us, Mr. Smithers. Sounds good to me. How will it look if you win in court?" she asked gently. "Do you really want to leave seven widows penniless?"

"No, no I don't. I want to treat you fair."

"Then the money is a false threat," she said.

"Maybe to you, but not to the others, I'm sure."

"Would you like their phone numbers?"

"I have them."

"Start with Wanda Smith, Arthur's widow. She's the most financially vulnerable," Doris said. "See how far you get with her." Doris laughed out loud at the thought of Wanda Smith trying to hold her tongue.

"I started with you because of Delmer. I was the one who moved Delmer up our ladder. I started with you, because you're the most worldly and the smartest."

"Mr. Smithers. This isn't about smarts. It's about grit. And I surely am not the grittiest. I'd say Susie Rutherford and LeeAnn Dorsey are. Just an F-Y-I."

"Did you know that four miners -- well, let me say, 'individuals of unknown occupation' -- attacked my new superintendent, Bruce Boyles, last night?"

"I hadn't heard," Doris said, hoping to sound truthful.

"This is getting out of hand," he said.

"I did hear that someone threw a rock through Wanda's front window. Taped a message on it," Doris said. 'Stop the strike, bitch, or we'll shoot you.' Words to that effect."

"It certainly wasn't me," John-Cee laughed. "I was in Pittsburgh. You're not accusing UNICOAL of throwing rocks?"

"I'm not accusing anyone of anything," Doris said. "I just know a rock was thrown through her window."

"Could have been -- probably was -- a local miner who has run out of money and wants to return to work," John-Cee said.

"Could have been," Doris said, "but I expect that will be the last incident of that kind against the women of your community."

"I expect you're right," John-Cee agreed. "You know, this strike will get settled eventually."

"I certainly hope so," she answered. "Stop the speed-up, and you'll get your miners back. Your tonnage will make you a lot of money."

"Mrs. Estep, we can't have miners -- employees -- and their wives, for Heaven's sake, dictating how we run our business. We can't give in to extortion. You know that."

"Mr. Smithers, I'm just an elementary-school teacher. And I extort grades from 11-year-olds every year. I'm giving you the opportunity to earn an 'A.'"

John-Cee grinned despite himself. "Never heard a wildcat strike framed that way before."

"Let's talk again," she said, "after things have ripened a little. We're reasonable people. We're willing to work with you."

"Sure," he said, as he felt advantage shift from him to her. "So what kind of money will it take for you to call off the ladies?"

"You're not listening, Mr. Smithers," she said, using her best sixth-grade-teacher's voice, which he heard as the sixth-grade-teacher's voice from his own elementary school.

"Yes, ma'am." It just came out.

"Stop the speed-up, and we'll work out the money with you. I promise."

"I'll get back to you. That's the best I can do today."

"Have a good day, Mr. Smithers."

At the end of the strike's third week, Burton "Buzzy" Maggard said to Betty as he sat in their kitchen over morning coffee that he was "ready to bite the head off a 10-foot rattler if it would get this damn strike stopped."

Betty Maggard had lived through 55 years of coalfield squabbles, the last 30 as the wife of the largest non-ACMU coal operator in the United States. She lived in the largest home in Pike County, Kentucky, with another large home in Lexington, the state capital, and another in Naples, Florida, and one more on 14,000 acres in Montana. She didn't object to wealth, but she never took it to mean more than it was. She never believed virtue radiated off a pile of dollars to form a self-justifying, wrap-around ether. As the daughter of a disabled coal miner from Happy in Perry County, Kentucky, she treated connubial wealth for the little it really was. And had she not been a sumptuous cheerleader on scholarship at the University of Kentucky, she would not have met Buzzy Maggard who swept her into his plans like a man fueling his inner fire.

"Why don't you settle with the ladies?" Betty asked.

Buzzy looked into his coffee, which was as black as his mood. He'd had a team of ridiculously expensive lawyers gunning his clock for weeks.

408

Injunctions, TROs, restraining orders. Jailings. Pickets and more pickets, and then no pickets. And still no one came back to work.

"It'd be better if you talked to 'em, Betty. They don't like us boys."

"Well," she said, without having to say more.

"Doris Estep—she's the one holdin' them together," Buzzy said. "Imagine, a superintendent's woman! That jes' ain't supposed to happen."

"Well, sweetheart, if it's not supposed to happen, why has it happened?" she asked in her best imitation of the affected naiveté she suffered from the trussed up ladies she had to socialize with at the Derby. "Would there be some reasonable reason that's motivating her to step out of her assigned role?"

Buzzy grumbled. "She sees it that way."

"Deal with the ladies respectfully and fairly, and the boys'll come back to work in 24 hours."

Buzzy looked at his wife. "Why didn't none of us think of that?"

"Because," she answered.

Buzzy knew enough to not ask, "Because why?"

"Because you've fought each other the same way for years," she said. "It's not a very good way of settling disputes, but it's what you know."

Thirty minutes later at his office, Buzzy told his secretary, Tina Totten, to phone Pittsburgh.

"John-Cee, this shit is killin' me," Buzzy shouted into the receiver. "I got 400,000 ton settin' on the ground, waitin' on some ragtail to load it. But ain't no ragtails workin'. An' my ragtails are non-ACMU to begin with. I can't even get ragtail scabs to come in at time-and-a-half to scab on my own strikin' ragtails. I got 2,500 empties on sidin's from here to yonder in four states. I got customers on every phone line a-threatenin' to sue me for every penny I wish I had over my failure to perform on supply contracts. My damn lawyers are sittin' in court chargin' me $150 an hour to fart around with injunctions that don't get nobody back to work. Legal fuckin' legal. Legal ain't worth spit in an empty pop can. And I got $25 dollars a ton garn'teed hangin' in front of my big fat nose like some fuckin' carrot that I can't never bite."

"We're all in the same boat," John-Cee said with a calmness born of being bone weary. "We're trying to get it resolved."

"Our boat's is the Tie-Fuckin'-Tanic, and I'm gittin' off. Now what do them widders really want?"

"They want us to stop the speed-up," John-Cee said, "but we can't announce we've stopped something we can't admit we started in the first place. If we say we'll stop it, we're opening ourselves to liability lawsuits over all kinds of injuries and fatalities, not just by my American Eagle miners."

"Then here's what you do," Buzzy said. "Don't admit Jack Shit. You meet with them widders. In private. Just the 10 of 'em. No men, no strikers. No Joe Hunt. No lawyers. You give 'em a fair money deal for their loss, and you tell 'em that you and the other operators will agree -- without sayin' squat publicly -- that we'll slow things down to regular. Which we will. All the widders gotta do is announce they're satisfied with your deal. You make sure they understand you are speakin' with them on behalf of the entire coal industry, not just UNICOAL. I'll get the independents and the strip boys out West lined up for you. I'll come to the meetin' to he'p you out.

"You understand what I'm sayin', John-Cee. You an' me should be down at Hilton Head hittin' golf balls at the fuckin' pond gators and drinkin' too much Jack Daniels, not tied down with this wildcat and givin' up 25 bucks a ton. Get 'em back to the damn face runnin' coal, which is what they want to do, too."

John-Cee considered Buzzy Maggard's idea, which was so simple it made him shake his sleep-deprived head. "I can break this strike eventually."

"'Ventually, you can. And 'ventually I'm a-gonna die, and sooner'n 'ventually I'm a-gonna go broke," Buzzy yelled. "Buddy, I'll tell ya this. Ifn we whip them boys back to work, they're a-gonna get back at us. They're gonna start workin' by the book. Equipment'll be sabotaged. You ain't gonna be happy when a cup of sand gets poured into the engine oil on your vehicles. You wanna buy 100 new electric motors to swap in on your mobile machines? You want things to run dry of lubricants? Buddy, I know how them bobtails thank, because I'd do the same damn thang."

"We can beat them," John-Cee said.

"We lose if we win that way. They gotta go back a-holdin' their heads up."

"It'll look like we're givin' in," John-Cee said without much conviction.

"Damn it to hell. It'll look like we want to make some money and do the right thang at the same time. That's what Betty says."

"All right. I don't know why a good-lookin' and sensible East Kentucky girl ended up with a pirate like you."

"Me neither, but I'm glad as hell she did. You settle this thang, and I'm gonna buy that girl the biggest emerald ring in Kentucky. Maybe bigger than the biggest even in Pittsburgh."

"Maybe you'll even get lucky at your age."

"Well, maybe I will, because I surely am—a lot more'n I deserve."

Chapter 30

Pittsburgh, November 24, 1975, 11:45 a.m.

The Widows Committee from Bloomingrose and Anawalt Hollers stood humbly in front of UNICOAL's 12-story office tower in downtown Pittsburgh. They wore their church clothes. Doris had a stenographer's note pad in her purse. Doris knew shorthand. She whispered to Wanda. "Ready?"

"I ain't gonna huff an' I ain't gonna puff, but we gonna blow this house down," she whispered back. Wanda didn't feel as confident as she sounded. She felt asthmatic and not much like The Big Bad Wolf.

With the exception of Doris Estep, these women had lived in southern West Virginia their entire lives. They rarely left McDowell County. Their lives had been structured by the mine work of their men—fathers, husbands, brothers and sons. A man's work and a woman's life were defined by the Company in the persons of the mine superintendent, office managers and section bosses. Though the women knew the Company from opposite sides, they shared the sense of how it controlled them. Beyond that, they had only the fuzziest notion of accounts, ledgers, spreadsheets, margins, capital plans, contracts, cash flow, taxes, grosses, nets, ROIs and the large forces affecting them individually and collectively.

To the women married to miners, UNICOAL had always felt like an upside-down pyramid balanced on the back of their necks. Beyond Bloomingrose Holler, the UNICOAL pyramid was an abstraction of immense daily power. As long as the Mike Deckers and Willie Rutherfords produced coal each shift, they and their families kept the pyramid's tip suspended. When the Deckers and the Rutherfords wouldn't run coal, the pyramid, like some giant hydraulic press, pinned them into the dirt.

Now they stood in front of the upside-down pyramid. They walked in together, as a group, not holding hands but wanting to.

"I never seen such," Jeannie Lou Burdette said, scanning the three-story atrium on the ground floor. "Look!"

She pointed to a larger-than-life statue of an old-time miner cast out of liquefied coal. He carried a pick over his shoulder and stood in a slouch.

"Looks like my Daddy," Juanita Buchanan said. "Black an' all."

"Looks like all our Daddies," Linda Faye Decker said. "Black an' all."

"Remember ladies, it's the miners who built this building," Wanda whispered.

Their guide was a heavily made-up, middle-aged woman in high heels and a tight dress. She led them past the lobby guard who had been instructed to not ask them to sign the registry. He waved and smiled as they walked by. His Daddy had worked a UNICOAL mine outside of Pittsburgh, and he was rooting for the widows.

"See that," Daisy Jones whispered to Sharon Lewis. She pointed to a large oil painting facing the elevators of a grizzled miner on his knees at a coal face, struggling to turn his five-foot-long breast auger into the coal. "Granddaddy drilled his blasting holes with one of them. He looked like that."

"Mine, too," Sharon whispered back, "tired and poor."

"Think they got any pictures of strikers?" Linda Faye giggled. "Or women?"

"They have photos, I'm sure," Doris said, "not oil paintings and sculptures."

Next to the oil painting were large photographs of excavators used in surface mines and underground long-wall systems.

The women felt their stomachs floating as the express elevator rocketed them to the 12th floor. Fletcher Waddington, the handsome public-affairs vice-president, greeted them as they emerged from both cars. He introduced each by name to John-Cee Smithers, who had been standing behind him. He then introduced the group one by one to Ben Roberson of AMSTEEL and Burton Maggard of Appalcoal. John-Cee then told the women that he was John-Cee, and this was Ben and that one was Buzzy.

John-Cee led them to a dining room where the woman in high heels suggested the ladies might want to freshen up before lunch. She escorted them to the restroom where she handed each a tote bag of personal toiletries and then left.

"'Freshen up,'" Linda Faye Decker repeated, as she judged the heft of the bag in both hands. "Hell, I ain't been this fresh since I was 13."

Jeannie Lou Burdette looked through her bag and said: "Some of mine are in a foreign language!"

"French," Doris said.

"Careful girl with those French fumes," Linda Faye laughed, "I hear they drive men wild."

"That's the one thing I don't need right now," Jeannie Lou replied.

"Do we keep what we don't use or do we leave it in the bag here in the potty?" Daisy Jones asked Susie Rutherford.

"I believe these here are gifts," LeeAnn Dorsey said.

"They're complimentary," Doris said. "Take the bag with you with everything in it when we leave."

When the women were done, their escort led them back to the dining room where they were seated at places designated by name cards. The woman in heels left. The ladies noted they outnumbered the men, 10 to four.

412

"I wish I could get my sixth-graders to have penmanship like the calligraphy on this card," Doris said to John-Cee who was sitting on one side of her.

"I could send a wonderful young woman down to show your kids how to do it," he said.

Buzzy Maggard who sat on the other side of her snorted: "Don't matter none how nice the signature looks if the check bounces."

"I'll keep that in mind, Mr. Maggard," Doris said.

"Now, you call me, Buzzy, ma'am. I'm jes' an ol' country boy. I grew up so raggedy the Methodist charities figured it would be a waste of time givin' the likes of me used clothes."

"I grew up in a middle-class suburb of Washington," Doris said. "Maybe my Methodist church shipped some of my charity clothes down your way."

"I didn't wear none of yers, I'm sure," Buzzy laughed.

"Well, you've come up in the world," she said, as she laid her napkin in her lap. "Appalcoal is a famous company."

"Luck, mostly," he said. "Got some breaks. Some old-timers gave me a hand, showed me the ropes of how to buy old equipment, fix it up and get some more tonnage out of it. I have a wife you'd like. You're both pistols."

"Well, I haven't been called that in a long time, maybe never," Doris giggled.

The other women were glad Doris was taking the conversational lead. She might not be their most powerful talker, but she was most like the men at the table on their side.

"Now, you listen to me, Miz Estep," Buzzy said. "It takes balls…er, it takes real courage to do what you ladies done. You've got my respect. Same goes for the other operators."

John-Cee rose, and tapped his glass with a Swedish stainless-steel spoon that carried the UNICOAL logo. "Before we start…officially that is, since we already seem to have started," he said winking at Doris and Buzzy, "I'd like Mrs. Estep to say Grace."

"Me?" The thought occurred to Doris that this was a sly move to anoint her as spokeswoman, because the boys thought they'd get the best deal from her. "Certainly, I will."

The women extended their hands to either side and made a closed circle with the men.

"We thank Thee, Lord," she said, with her eyes closed, "for all the blessings you have bestowed on each of us around this table and for the food of which we are about to partake. We are gathered here to do right by each other. We mourn for our lost loved ones, but we trust You will guide each of us to speak honestly and as equals in Your eyes and ours as well. Remember our husbands. In your name, Amen."

The women sat a little taller when they echoed their "Amens"; the four men a shade lower as they said theirs.

Doris turned to John-Cee as she adjusted her napkin again and picked up a spoon for her fruit cup. "Several years ago, I had a sixth-grade class with a half-dozen boys who had failed at least one grade, and a couple who had failed two. They were 13- even 14-year-olds in a class of 35. They were open-wide throttle into puberty, girls and acting tough. Not interested in education. And because of that, they were disruptive. I tried everything I could think of, but I couldn't get them to settle down. I couldn't bend them to my will."

"Did you try the paddle?" Buzzy asked.

"Indeed, I did. I had the woodshop make me a one-inch-thick, two-handed hickory paddle that I swung at their rumps like a baseball bat. It did no good. I'd march them out of the classroom. Then I told them to bend over against the wall. And I walloped them with all of my strength. They ignored it. They saw getting paddled as something tough guys endured to come out stronger."

"Principal's office?" Ben Roberson asked.

The entire table was absorbed in Doris Estep's story.

"He had no tools that worked. They wouldn't show up for detention. They looked forward to being suspended or being permanently tossed out of school."

"Could you get their parents to discipline them?" John-Cee asked.

"I met with the parents, more than once. I'm sure their Dads -- who worked for UNICOAL, of course -- knocked them around. But by that time, they were beyond physical punishment. They were feeding courage to each other to defy Authority."

John-Cee then asked what everyone wanted to know: "So what did you do?"

"I told them they could do what they wanted in class as long as they told me beforehand what it was. Well, that stumped them. It forced them to think hard about what they wanted, which they'd never been asked to do before. Until then, they filled their time cutting up and unsettling whatever was. So I got them talking about doing something that might interest them. One started a scrap book on cars, which led to looking at parts and repair manuals, which led him to learn to read better. Another liked cigarettes. So I had him look for information on how tobacco was raised and cigarettes were made. And then he looked a little bit at the cancer pictures. And another boy said he was interested in sex—thought he was being cute. So I got him books about puberty and sex. He's now in nursing school at WVU."

"I see your point," Buzzy said. "You let 'em tell you what was right for them. Then you helped make it happen."

"Yes."

414

"Then you got what you wanted," he said.

"Yes."

The men recognized that Doris Estep had just gotten them where she wanted.

John-Cee Smithers wondered why UNICOAL didn't have a woman like Doris Estep running one of his mines, or the Company for that matter.

After the meal, John-Cee asked Buzzy to say a few words.

Buzzy stood. "Ladies. I was raised up in Pike County, Kentucky, just across the Tug River from Mingo County, next to you all. My Daddy was an ACMU miner. Joined in Nineteen and Thirty-three. He died a Union miner. I myself never had an ACMU card, because the Union had been run out of Pike County. But I woulda been proud to carry one. We was as poor as anybody. You an' me know all the ways to make cornbread taste like somethin' a little richer.

"Now I own Appalcoal, a non-Union operator. I'm jes' like that rich feller Smithers settin' there next to Mrs. Rutherford on one side and Mrs. Estep on the other. Your husbands made their livin' in the coal bidness workin' for us. We make our livin' in the coal bidness sellin' what your men dug out of the mountain. It's a hard, nasty bidness, and I ain't a-tellin' you widders nothin' you don't know firsthand.

"I cannot bring your men back. Ifn I could, I'd spend my last penny a-doin' it. In a minit. B'lieve me, I would. I thank the Lord that Willie Rutherford, Byron Lewis and Mike Decker made it out.

"We know you all are a-hurtin' and' you're mad as a hive of stirred-up hornits. Ya got every right to be.

"We can't make thangs the same for you, but we're a-willin' to make thangs as right as we can.

"Now this wildcat strike is a-hurtin' us. No two ways 'bout it.

"Most of us operators didn't make much money in coal for most of the '50s and '60s. That's when we had to mechanize and cut our work force and labor costs. Had no choice. OPEC boosted coal demand, and prices have more than tripled in the last couple of years. If we can mine coal, we can make a lot of money right now.

"Was there a speed-up? Of course, there was! We all did it. We was tryin' to get as much coal shipped as we could, because we was makin' so much on every ton. We was workin' 'round the clock. Sundays. Holidays. Vacation days. Was we pushin' hard to get the coal? By God, yes, each and every one of us was pushin' your men. And they were getting paid overtime for the extra hours. That time-and-a-half, that double time, was buyin' you new washin' machines, new TVs, thangs you wanted.

"But -- and ladies this is a mighty big 'but' -- this prosperity, these prices, ain't a-gonna last. Coal bidness is seven years of lean for maybe a year or two of fat. The market gets out of whack on the upside, and then prices fall. Regression to the mean is what the fancy-pants economists at the University of Kentucky call it. Prices are going to settle down to historical trend lines sooner or later.

"Let me say it another way. We want black numbers, not red numbers. Black numbers mean we made some money that quarter, or at that mine, or on that shift. Red numbers mean we didn't. Too many reds, and we have to shut down the losing operation if we can't fix it. If we don't try to put up as many black numbers as we can, your men won't have jobs, your Daddies won't have pensions and you and your kids won't have health care and food. When we have the opportunity to run up a string of big, black numbers, we have to do it as fast as we can, because we know the reds are coming to bite our be-hinds pretty soon.

"America has got a lot of coal. But here is the second 'but.' Coal is a rock that we gotta dig out of the ground. And 'cause it comes out of the ground, it has other stuff in it, like mercury and arsenic and sulfur. There ain't nothin' nice and clean about coal. And that's why I think coal in this country is a gangplank industry. More and more folks are going to object to strip mining. And air-pollution regulations are goin' to increase the cost of burning coal so that our customers will likely switch to cleaner fuels to make electricity. I can't tell you when all that's goin' to happen, but it will.

"So we have to make money while we can. We bein' us operators and you miner families. We have to be reliable to make that gangplank stick out as long as we can before we all fall off. If we can't be a dependable and cheap supply of a 'bad' product, then we operators are gonna go under one by one, and we'll take down every miner who works for us. Not 'cause we want to. Because that's the way it'll work.

"There's one winner so far in this wildcat strike. It ain't me, and it ain't none of you. It's the comp'nies that supply oil and gas, like Exxon, Chevron, Gulf and Amoco. It's also the utilities with nukes. It's the hippies with them windmills. You show everybody that coal can't be counted on, they're gonna shift to somethin' else. Oil and gas are reliable, they'll say; coal's a crapshoot. An' then my customers start importing coal from Canada, Australia and South America where production is reliable and cheap. What you think you gonna do if you runnin' an electric utility that needs a hydrocarbon to burn to make steam to turn a turbine? You gonna go with what's cheap and reliable. If it's just cheap, that ain't good enough. So our American coal is cheap, but it ain't reliable, and it ain't clean. We have to stick out that gangplank as far as we can for as long as we can. That's in the interest of all of us in this room. But mind—all of us are a-walkin' on it together.

"Now us boys have given some thought to how to settle this with you. What do you need?"

"Stop the speed-up," Linda Faye said. "That's what kilt our men."

John-Cee started to speak, but Buzzy shook his head.

416

"We -- the industry -- agree to do that," Buzzy said. "It's more important to us to run 100 tons of coal a section than to run 115 tons on the speed-up. That's important to you, too. An' it's real important we stop runnin' no coal at all. It's like what Mrs. Estep said about them bad boys in her class: 'Give 'em what they want, and you get what you want.'"

"How will the men know you stopped for good?" Wanda asked.

John-Cee answered. "First, Mrs. Smith, *we'll tell them* what we're doing. No more compulsory overtime. No more compulsory Sundays. No more working on vacation days and birthdays. No more unrealistic production quotas for each section and for each mine. If there's a safety concern, the supervisors will get it fixed before production starts back. *All that will show them.* They'll see the difference in the first week."

"So what do you all want from us?" Linda Faye asked.

"We want you to announce today if you can, tomorrow at the latest, that your committee has unanimously reached a 'satisfactory' agreement with the coal operators on the safety issues that concerned you," John-Cee said. "Tell the men to go back to work, and they'll see the changes immediately."

"Ain't good enough," Wanda said. "There are men in jail over this strike. Get 'em out."

"They're there because they violated a federal restraining order," Ben Roberson said. "We didn't put them there."

The women just stared at Ben Roberson in silence.

"Well," Buzzy said.

Ben conceded: "Ladies, we will use our good offices to get them out."

"What that mean?" Wanda asked. "'Good offices.' What that mean?"

"Means we'll get them out as soon as it's humanly possible to get them out," Buzzy said. John-Cee and Ben nodded in agreement.

"An' no fines, and they get their jobs back with no penalties," Linda Faye said.

"An' no black list like there was 'gainst the Jehovah Witnesses back during the War, my Daddy tol' me, for refusing to fight," LeeAnn Dorsey said. "Freddie Pruitt and 'em should be just like before."

"Amnesty," Doris said. "Full amnesty. Clean slate. No grudges. No targets on anyone's back."

"Amnesty. Agreed," John-Cee said.

"Back pay for the time lost out on strike?" Jeannie Lou wondered.

Everyone laughed.

"Well, I thought somebody ought to at least bring it up," she said with a smile, both shy and sly.

"Now there's this other thang," Buzzy said, with a nod toward John-Cee. "We want to settle with you widows and with the three who have survivors. First, we'll pay all the hospital and rehabilitation bills if the miner's health fund comes up short with you. Second, we'll pay for the

417

funerals. Third, we'll pay for your kids for four years at a state university and graduate school if they have a mind to go. Fourth, we'll keep Willie, Mike and Byron on full pay until they feel well enough to come back. If they are disabled, then we'll keep them on half pay until they qualify for retirement benefits. Finally, we'll set up a comp'sation fund for all 10 of you. You tell us what you need."

"A million to each of the widders," Linda Fay blurted, "and $250,000 each to the other three."

"Done," Buzzy Maggard said almost before she finished. "Your terms are agreed to."

Linda Faye looked at Doris who frowned. Linda Faye realized that what seemed like a fortune to her the day before might be small potatoes today to the men in this room at the top of the upside-down pyramid.

Susie looked at Doris.

"Maybe, we should discuss this among ourselves," Doris said, hoping the ladies would catch her meaning.

"A million dollars!" Alma Rae said.

"A million dollars!" Daisy Jones said.

Doris realized the committee was split. Maybe six or seven wanted the money right now. The others were willing to chance haggling. The consequences of the committee breaking up over money were too great. They had to stick together. "Deal," she said. "Ladies?"

The women affirmed silently.

"Everyone in?" John-Cee asked. "No objections? No hold-outs?"

Doris scanned her group. "Yes," she said. "Everyone agrees."

"This is a private arrangement," John-Cee said. "No publicity about the money. We'll set up the accounts at our bank, and you can draw it out however you want in any amount to your local bank."

Dessert was served—their choice of chocolate cheese cake, a huge éclair, ice cream or fruit. Buzzy joked with Linda Faye that he knew John-Cee could come up with cigars if anyone wanted one. Ben did.

Everyone shook hands at the elevator.

Fletch Waddington gave each woman a copy of their agreement, signed by the three men representing the coal industry. "The new superintendent, Mr. Boyles, will have your account numbers by the time you get home. Just go into his office and pick them up. He'll ask you to sign a waiver that says you agree we operators accept no additional liability, you willingly entered into this final agreement and you have dropped your lawsuit. There will also be a confidentiality clause that says you promise not to reveal the amount of your UNICOAL compensation. All the arrangements will be set up just as we outlined them. Remember Mrs. Estep took notes as we were discussing things. If you have any questions, I'll pass out my business card now with the statement we want you to read to the press. Sign these agreements before you leave the

418

building, and I'll collect them at the door. This press release captures what your committee agreed to," he said. "I'll get copies to each of you."

It was only a couple of paragraphs. Doris read it slowly.

Then she read it aloud.

> The American Eagle Widows and Wives for Safety Now reached an amicable and comprehensive agreement with the American coal operators today. We are completely satisfied by the terms of the agreement as it relates to safe-mining practices. It is all of what we wanted. The men will see the changes immediately. All fines and prison sentences against strikers will be resolved as soon as possible. The operators agree to amnesty for all strikers. No other penalties will be imposed.
>
> We ladies urge all miners to return to work on their normally scheduled shifts. We thank the men for their support. We won, and so did miners and the operators.

"Ladies?" she asked.

They nodded.

"There will be a press conference for you in the lobby," Fletcher said. "Just read the statement. Don't answer questions. I'll hand out copies of the agreement. But it won't contain the dollar figures for each of you. That's private. No need to put a bullseye on your backs."

"I'd like to see it," Doris said.

He handed her the press documents. She read them. "They're fine," she said. "It's exactly what we agreed to."

Everyone approved, and then, almost by magic, elevator doors opened and took them down.

Ben, John-Cee and Buzzy retired to John-Cee's office.

"Slick as peelin' a boiled peach," Buzzy said.

"You got off cheap," Ben said to John-Cee.

"Seven million, plus $750,000," John-Cee said. "I wouldn't call that cheap. I'd call it reasonable. It's a good day. You did a good job, Buzzy. I knew you'd be our best negotiator. Now let's see if our employees come back settled down. Then we can celebrate."

"What about the speed-up?" Ben asked. "How do you want to handle that?"

"We'll do what we promised," John-Cee said.

Buzzy laughed. "Do you boys know how you eat an elephant?"

"With a knife and fork?" John-Cee said.

"A spoon?" Ben said.

419

"Nope," Buzzy said. "One little iddy-biddy nibble at a time and slowly."

John-Cee and Ben Roberson agreed. A slow nibble.

Buzzy decided he would not share that observation with Betty. Some things, he had realized early on, were better left unsaid in his marriage. He'd get her that emerald ring, even pay retail up in New York City.

The women went shopping and then boarded a UNICOAL plane for a flight to Beckley at 7 p.m.

Doris sat next to Linda Faye who had been uncommonly quiet in Saks Fifth Avenue. Their UNICOAL guide told them to try either the Pecan Ball or the apple pie when they stopped mid-afternoon at the Tic Toc Restaurant in Kaufmann's department store. Excitement ran through them, which they tried to conceal from their UNICOAL chaperone who paid for their meals.

Linda Faye fired up a Virginia Slims and looked over with pain and regret.

"They skinned us on the money," Linda Faye whispered, "didn't they? I fucked us up. How could I have been so stupid?"

"You weren't stupid. One million dollars *is* a lot of money," Doris whispered back."

"Stupid and greedy," Linda Faye said. "I was like a 15-year-old boy with his first girl. I popped as soon as I got in."

"No, it wasn't greed," Doris said. "It was unfamiliarity."

Susie and Wanda overheard. The others gathered in the aisle.

"We didn't know what we were really worth to go away," Doris said. "We should have gone in with a lawyer to help us. We didn't research them. We didn't know our fair market value."

"But they told us before the meeting," LeeAnn said, "just us. No lawyers. Just us."

"We should have insisted on a lawyer," Linda Faye, "to protect us from me."

"Protect us from us, not just you," Sharon Lewis said.

"Now we know why they said just us," Alma Rae said.

"How much more you think we might could have got?" Wanda asked.

"I don't know," Doris said. "One million each for the widows was the number we talked about before we went in. And we all thought that was way high. Maybe it was just right. This is a great deal. One million for each of the widows! We can start fresh, somewhere else, or stay where we are but better. All of us now have choices and flexibility. We don't have to go back. We can go forward."

"We shoulda started at two million," Linda Faye said. "How dumb was I? I'm sorry ladies. The boys snookered us."

420

"This is seller's remorse," Doris said. "Once a seller makes a deal to sell, he, or she, always thinks more could have been gotten out of the buyer. It's natural."

"But we're mountain girls," Alma Rae said. "We know how to dicker. And we didn't."

"We didn't dicker, because their first offer was so far above what we expected," Sharon Lewis said. "That was a smart move."

"We're not dumb, and we're not greedy," Doris said. "We just pulled off the biggest wildcat strike in memory. We got the speed-up stopped. We got college scholarships for our kids, funeral expenses paid, health care and compensation for the survivors. And on top of that seven of us got a million dollars each, and the others $250,000. We will hold our heads up for the rest of our lives. We've done something no one has ever done before. We '*done good*.'"

"Amen to that," LeeAnn Dorsey said. "I will sleep easy tonight, 'cause of what we done in Pittsburgh."

"So we all," Susie said.

The strikers resumed work that night.

The miners had won a victory for safer mining. It was simply a question of how long they could keep it.

A couple of weeks later, Buzzy sent a beautiful carving of an elephant to John-Cee Smithers and Ben Roberson.

"Made from Kentucky walnut; paid for with Kentucky coal," Buzzy's note read. "Nibbling starts after the first of the year. Take your time."

On the same day, he delivered to Betty an emerald ring that was so big he had it brought to their house with an Appalcoal John Deere 544-B front-end loader. He put the Tiffany Blue Box in the three-cubic-yard bucket that was rated to lift 15,000 pounds.

Betty rolled her eyes at Buzzy's joke. She wore the ring to bed that night.

Chapter 31

Anawalt Holler, November 25, 1975

Susie Rutherford got home on Tuesday morning just after midnight. The drive through the mountains from Beckley was starless and cold. She and the others drove home filled with pride, doubt, uncertainty and wonder. A lot of wonder.

Willie was up when she slipped in.

"Mighty proud of you," he said, sitting in their living room. She had phoned him from the Tic Toc.

"I'm wrung out, ain't a drop left in me. Did you make out while I was up there?"

"Me an' the stiff leg are workin' thangs out with the good leg. Sort of like a second marriage."

"Don't wan' hear no talk about that," she laughed. "Let's go to bed, Willie."

"Gimp loves his lady."

The phone rang at 8:30 a.m. She answered. She listened and asked Willie what he wanted to do. "Sure," he said. "We be here."

She heard the knock at their door a little after noon. She answered. "Willie, you got visitors."

Willie was dozing in his recliner with the television turned to ABC's "Let's Make a Deal." A glass of tap water and his medications sat on a portable tray stand next to him. He wore pajamas that were cut off and hemmed where his stump protruded. The oil heater was working hard to keep the room at 72 degrees.

He struggled to lift out of a sleep dream that was deeper than he realized. Something had his right ankle in its teeth and was chewing its way up. He saw his leg being chomped off at the knee. He felt no pain but screamed for help. He saw Pins coming toward him with a peach pie.

"Willie, wake up," Susie said from the front door. "Willie?"

He opened his eyes. He felt dream-sweats in his pajamas. He lifted the comforter that covered his torso. He looked. No right foot. Damn painkillers! Make you bumfuzzled.

Willie collected himself as the visitors stood in his front hall. He rubbed his hand over the soft, bare skin on the top of his scalp. He shook his head to banish the dream.

He hated hot, stuffy rooms. That was Susie's doing. It smelled like a damn hospital.

"You decent?" Susie asked from the hall.

"In a manner of speakin'," he said.

Jeep Delucci, Freddie Pruitt and Jeffrey Becker walked in. Their faces were concerned but with small smiles. Willie knew Freddie, but not the other two. All wore red-white-and-blue campaign buttons: "Dig it with Delucci. Vote MDU."

"This is Jeep Delucci," Freddie said, "and Jeff Becker, the campaign manager. Willie Rutherford."

They approached Willie and shook hands.

Susie brought kitchen chairs into the living room. The men fussed at her for having carried the chairs when they were standing there. They settled around Willie's recliner. Susie stood next to a kitchen chair just inside her kitchen's doorway.

"Can I fix you mens a drink?" she asked. "I have cake and cookies folks brought over that'll last us from here to Christmas…next Christmas. Coffee?"

"Coffee would be mighty nice," Jeep said. "Thank you. Black all around, I 'spect."

"How you doin', buddy?" Freddie asked.

"Better today than the day before," Willie said. "You heard that Susie and the widders settled for good money yesterday, but they can't say what it is?"

"Sure did," Jeep said. "We were tickled to death at the settlement."

"Maybe, we should have gotten more," Susie said from inside her kitchen.

"You did plenty good," Willie said. "Better than anyone ever done with UNICOAL."

"A-men to that," Jeep said.

"A-men," Becker added a beat late. A-men was not part of Becker's working vocabulary.

"How's that left leg?" Freddie asked.

"Lef' is as good as ever. Right could use a hand."

Freddie and Susie laughed.

Freddie explained the joke to Jeep and Becker. "Willie was the kicker over at Elkhorn High School. Punts, kickoffs, field goals and points-after. Willie did it all. Left-footed kicker, only one we ever had. None of that side-footin', soccer-shit kickin'. 'Scuse me, Miz Rutherford. Willie was always straight ahead like Lou 'The Toe' Groza up at Cleveland. Willie's field goal got Elkhorn into the State Championship game in '52."

"Only 23 yards," Willie said. "Weren't that hard."

"Twenty-three yards in the rain, under the lights, in the mud, with the temperature around 30, with little Blinky Moats holdin' for you for the first time and the game on the line with 15 seconds on the clock," Freddie added.

"It was the state colored league back then," Willie said, informing Jeep. "Booker T. Washington up in Charleston whupped our butts in the big game. 'Course three o' their boys went on to the pros in the late '50s. Almost a dozen got football scholarships. Don't imagine there's much call for a one-legged, left-footed kicker these days."

"If you could figure out how to kick without landin' on your ass," Freddie said, "Willie, you'd be a rich man. Put you on 'Hee-Haw.'"

"Me an' Charlie Pride."

"Singin' and kickin' beats minin' coal," Freddie said.

"Most anything legal -- an' jes' about any work that ain't all that much illegal -- beats minin' coal," Jeep said. "'Cept the money."

"Minin' gets familiar," Willie said. "Some say it gets in your blood. I think it's jes' what we knows. So we do what we knows. If we knew different, we'd do that. If different was around, we'd do it. Some of us, anyway."

"You kick with one leg, you'd make the national news," Freddie said.

"Might could kick a little on crutches," Willie said with seriousness. "Maybe could do 10, 15 yards."

Susie brought in a tray of filled coffee mugs with a plate of cookies and bite-size pieces of various cakes that she had prepared before their arrival. She placed the plate on her coffee table in the middle of the group. Each man took a coaster, a mug and several treats on a cloth napkin. Murmurs of approval for the coffee and baked goods rose all around. Willie smiled at her.

"I played linebacker," Jeep said.

"You played against Walter Bishop, didn't you, the boy who carried the ball for Logan High back 'bout eight, nine years ago?"

Jeep knew that Willie knew what he'd done.

"He was killin' us."

"So we heard," Willie said.

Freddie Pruitt knew the story. Only Jeffrey Becker had no idea what Willie and Jeep were talking about. But Becker caught the grievance in Willie's tone.

Jeep's mind slipped back. He remembered what he was willing to do and the lack of shame.

It was the Saturday after Thanksgiving, 1967. A cold, wet, muddy afternoon at Sherman High School's field in Seth. Boone County's Sherman was playing arch rival Logan High—the maroon-and-gold Tide against the blue-and-gold Wildcats. It was the big game for each team. Coal-miner kids from neighboring counties beating the shit out of each other for something hard to express, Jeep thought at the time. Something was at stake, of course. It wasn't just rote habit or adolescent passage.

Maybe it was winning rather than losing. Something had meaning, he hoped.

It was the middle of the fourth quarter, Logan was up by four, 46-42. Delucci could not remember a game when he was colder, wetter, dirtier, more battered or more miserable. He had played the whole game at middle linebacker with Biggie at left defensive tackle. Sherman's defense had been creamed and humiliated.

Delucci felt like he had been a punching bag for three-and-a-half quarters. Logan's All-State fullback, senior Walter Bishop, had run up the middle and off tackle into Delucci time after time. Every four-play series involved Bishop running off his left offensive tackle at least twice. Bishop avoided Biggie at defensive left tackle, because he was the only Sherman player larger and, possibly, as powerful as Bishop.

Walter Bishop had knocked silly Sherman's first-string right defensive tackle, Junior Hiner, at the start of the second quarter. Second-string right tackle, Loy Adkins, smaller and less courageous than Junior, went out with a separated shoulder. Sherman's third-string right tackle -- 157-pound freshman Larry Lively who had acquired the nickname "Deadly" -- was doing everything he could to stay out of Bishop's way. Deadly learned after his first tackle attempt that if he fell backward under the blocker coming his way, Bishop wouldn't hit him. Delucci couldn't blame Deadly; he, too, had had more than enough of Walter Bishop. Sherman had no fourth-string right tackle. Maybe, Coach would put in a cheerleader, Delucci thought; maybe a cheerleader would wiggle her butt, and Walter Bishop would stop running so hard. Until then, Bishop was Delucci's problem with whatever help came from Sherman's right defensive end, who, Delucci had observed, was fully and prayerfully occupied with whatever blocker appeared near him. Sherman's outside right linebacker had developed a highly focused interest in covering Logan's wide receiver who as yet had no pass thrown in his direction.

Whatever chance Sherman High had to stop Bishop depended on Delucci hitting him hard enough to slow him down for a second or two. That would give Biggie and others a chance to get to him. Four could bring him down, two no, three sometimes. If Bishop got into the Sherman Tide's secondary, he was gone. He was faster than anyone in those positions and outweighed the biggest defensive back by at least 70 pounds. Sherman's corners and safeties bounced off him like pinballs off electric bumpers. Bennie Daniels, Sherman's best safety, wondered if Bishop was targeting him because he, too, was black.

Jeep wasn't sure he had another head-to-head collision with Walter Bishop left in him. He knew he was a little dizzy and should take himself out of the game. But his replacement was Deadly Lively's cousin, Glen, a 133-pound sophomore who Walter Bishop would trample like a stampeding bull buffalo, assuming Glen didn't run through the exit gate under the scoreboard after he was told to go on the field.

Before the game, Jeep and Biggie had talked about Walter Bishop.

"He runs fast," Biggie said. "He's too quick for us. He's too big, too strong. He ain't no Walter Bishop out there. He's like the Archbishop of Runnin' Free."

"Archie Bishop," Jeep had said. "We ain't got a prayer."

Seven minutes to go. Logan's quarterback couldn't throw an accurate pass more than nine yards from his five-step drop, so 95 percent of Logan's offense all season had been Walter Bishop. The other five percent was quarterback fumbles. Bishop had scored seven touchdowns with 275 running yards against Sherman, so far. Logan's kicker had missed his first three point-after attempts. Logan had run Bishop into the end zone after his last four touchdowns. Walter Bishop, Delucci thought, was like a big, black locomotive coming down the track full speed, steam blowing out of his stack, whistle wide open, screaming, "Get out of the way!"

Delucci had checked before the game: Bishop was listed as six-five, 260. He was more powerful, faster, quicker and shiftier than anyone at Sherman High had thought possible. Bishop played a different game at a level unknown in West Virginia. Delucci thought he was trying to tackle Cleveland's Jim Brown. No wonder Logan was undefeated into their last league game, despite having a quarterback who couldn't throw and wide receivers who were never expected to catch. The game was close only because Walter Bishop refused to play defense.

Delucci knew Bishop had a scholarship to Number-1-ranked University of Southern California. Bishop told the Logan Banner just before Thanksgiving that he wanted to follow in the footsteps of consensus All-American O.J. Simpson who had promised Bishop he would show him the ropes. Walter Bishop might even be better than Simpson, both thought, but neither said. The story of Walter Bishop's visit and commitment to USC was picked up by every daily and most weeklies in West Virginia, almost all of which lamented editorially about a native son shunning WVU football and its 5-4-1 season that ended on November 18th.

Walter Bishop felt lucky and blessed that his athletic talent had given him a ticket out of Logan County to southern California, a leap that left him dazzled. USC was big-time football, big-time exposure, big-time pro-opportunities. WVU—well, Walter could think of a couple of players who had made pro teams—Joe Marconi a slow fullback who played for the Los Angeles Rams; Chuck Howley at Dallas and Sam Huff with the New York Giants, both linebackers. So much for WVU football in the National Football League.

Walter had a plan to escape the dreary southern West Virginia winters; its coal; and the mine closing that had sucked the life out of the little coal

426

camp of Omar when West Virginia Coal and Coke shut its operations in 1954, leaving his father jobless. He saw a way to escape Superior Bottom, one-tenth of a mile south of Omar, where he and the remaining "colored" lived amid a growing population of abandoned houses; escape the segregation that hung on until the mid-1960s; escape Omar's Big Row where the white superintendent and foremen lived when the mines were operating; escape the coal dust and dirt that blew into his shabby house when the rattletrap Mack and Euclid dumpers hauled strip-mined coal from Stirrat and Sarah Ann to preparation plants; escape the abandoned slag heap outside of Superior Bottom that still smoked like a buried dragon wanting to break free; and escape the peculiar chains of being born black in an Appalachian coal camp. In California, he guessed people might dismiss him because he was poor and from West Virginia but not so much for being black. It was, after all, 1967. All he had to do was to run with a football tucked in his arms.

Every time Deadly Lively hid under a blocker, Bishop barreled into Delucci at full speed. Delucci felt Bishop was looking to hit him rather than juke him out, which he obviously could do. Delucci was giving up 55 pounds. He was almost ready to take himself out of the game. He was angry at himself, angry at his circumstances, angry at Walter Bishop. He didn't want to take more Bishop hits.

Logan was at Sherman's 17. Second down. Another touchdown would put the game out of Sherman's reach.

Delucci held up his hand. Sherman's defense huddled around him loosely. The lights had been turned on. Sherman's players were blowing like winded horses. Their breath showed white, coming out of their face masks. This drive had started on Logan's eight. Bishop had run on each of its seven plays. Jeep's teammates looked at the churned ground, waiting dumbly for him to call their formation. They all knew what the Logan offense would run. The small, quick guys in the secondary had had enough of being flattened by the Walter Bishop pile driver. Their only chance at both tackling him and surviving was to try to grab both his ankles at the same time. He'd stomp them otherwise.

Delucci looked into their eyes. Sherman High was ready to lose. The defense was thinking about ice packs, warm showers and cold pops. Deadly Lively was thinking about quitting high school in the next 30 seconds.

Except Biggie. He looked at Jeep. He was there. He had something left. Biggie was still game.

Delucci looked at his secondary. "Play a 43 defense with Biggie over center. Corners and safeties, forget the pass. We know what's coming. You all point at that sunnavabitch. Deadly, you do your flop so that Bishop maybe'll cut back toward Biggie. You, Biggie, look for him comin' your way."

"Had enough of that Walter Bishop," Bennie Daniels said. "Stick him good, Biggie."

As they broke, Jeep said to Biggie: "See if you can nick him before he gets to me."

"Yeah boy," Biggie said.

The Logan offensive line went into their three-point stances. But before their quarterback could put his hands under center, Biggie stood straight up and shouted: "Hey Archie Bishop, you been duckin' me all game, you sunuvabitch. You run at me, you chickenshit, an' I'll drill your black butt."

No one on either team moved. No one said anything. Everyone knew his name was Walter Bishop. Everyone called him Walter. What did 'Archie Bishop' mean? What was Biggie Stover up to?

From behind him, Delucci heard Bennie Daniels say: "Do it, Biggie."

Walter Bishop said nothing, showed no emotion.

Walter tried to play like Jim Brown who had retired two years earlier with a 5.2-yard NFL-career rushing average, second only to Marion Motley at 5.7. Jim Brown -- a poor black kid from Manhasset, New York, where his Mom worked as a cleaning lady -- showed Walter Bishop how to manage his talent and his person. Manhasset had taught Brown about racism -- he was told not to take the hard courses -- and the window of equity sports offered. It showed him there were whites who believed in fairness and merit. Jim Brown was Walter Bishop's model—never losing his cool, never disparaging an opponent, never belittling anyone; never backing down; and always trying to stand up for what he thought was right. Brown had core strength, the kind Walter Bishop was developing. Brown said what he thought; Bishop believed he would get that chance some day.

The teams settled nervously into their stances. Logan had one running back, Walter Bishop. Logan split receivers on both sides—a useless custom, Jeep thought. Logan's center snapped the ball. The quarterback faked nothing before sticking it in Walter Bishop's gut with both hands. Walter aimed for Deadly Lively. Delucci moved that way. He was ready to be smashed.

Deadly slipped under the left guard who was trying to push him out of the way. As he fell into the gap to his left, Deadly grabbed the guard's jersey and pulled him down on top. Together, they made a big clump in the hole where Bishop was heading. Bishop cut to his right. Biggie sidestepped the center's block and moved toward Bishop who was moving sideways rather than forward to avoid the Lively mess. Biggie was coming fast and hard as he got his arms around Bishop before the fullback could start moving forward again. Their helmets cracked like a gunshot. Biggie held on, and the two stood motionless for a moment, both stunned.

Walter Bishop raised his left leg to begin powering forward. And for that second, he stood with his weight entirely on his right leg, his cleated shoe dug in.

As Delucci ran toward him he thought Bishop looked like a heron. Jeep saw opportunity. He was at full speed when he slammed his shoulder into Walter Bishop's right knee as Biggie held him still. Delucci ran through the tackle as much as he could while holding Bishop's leg. He fell from the impact. He felt and heard Bishop's knee snap with the sound of a tree limb breaking. He did not let go. He felt Bishop's lower leg flop loose in his arms. Bishop screamed once and collapsed in Biggie's arms.

Biggie put him on the ground, gently.

Delucci lifted his head out of the mud.

Biggie nodded toward Jeep and smiled as he got up.

"You got him, Jeep," Deadly whispered, hoping Bishop was not Superman. Kryptonite was not available on the Sherman sideline.

The referees called an injury timeout.

Jeep stood over Bishop whose eyes were open. Bishop had passed the point of pain. He lay motionless. He looked into Jeep's eyes. They both knew. No scholarship, no pro career, no escape.

The Sherman trainer and some helpers tried rolling their new stretcher -- a gift from the Sunburst mine to the Volunteer Rescue Squad -- through the mud. It bogged down. Finally, Logan teammates carried it over to Bishop.

Jeep watched them work on Bishop whose leg below the knee, he saw, was separated at the joint. The EMTs talked to Walter. They told him they were going to immobilize his leg in a way that would, hopefully, not cut into his arteries or nerves. They applied a splint, from hip to ankle, without trying to match up anything. They strapped him down and told him he would be taken to Charleston and then flown to Morgantown for surgery. They gave him a painkiller shot, spread blankets over him, made sure he was not going into shock and told him to keep up his spirits.

The ambulance drove onto the field and sunk to a stop at the Logan 30. Logan players carried the loaded stretcher to the ambulance, which was then dragged off the field by a Logan fan in his D5 bulldozer with its Tulsa winch that just happened to be sitting on a lowboy trailer in the parking lot on its way to a logging job. The ambulance wheels left deep drag-ruts in the gridiron's mud, which no one could do anything about.

Walter caught Jeep's eye as his teammates were about to carry him to the ambulance. Jeep stared back, showing no remorse or pity. The Logan team and some Sherman players kneeled in prayer. Biggie and Jeep stood off to the side. Players from both teams touched Walter on the stretcher and wished him well. Jeep and Biggie said nothing.

Biggie looked at Jeep. "Hell of a smack," he said with a laugh that only Jeep could hear.

"End justifies means," Jeep said under his breath. "Ain't nothin' else can."

"You bagged us an Archie Bishop," Biggie said. "You can mount him on your bedroom wall next to that eight-point buck you shot last year."

"I done what needed to be done," Jeep shrugged. "Let's give credit to Deadly for a flop-and-grab that had to have been his personal best."

"Deadly is a Sherman legend for sure," Biggie sniggered.

Bennie Daniels came over and patted Jeep on his ass.

The teams and the fans clapped as the ambulance was winched toward the sidelines with its engine off.

Logan's offensive line talked in the huddle about getting Delucci for putting Bishop out of the game, but they never had the chance. They missed a field goal on fourth down. Sherman then scored the winning touchdown in 11 plays. With a minute left, Logan concentrated on scoring, not hurting Jeep. Their second-string fullback was an ordinary runner who did little behind an offensive line that had lost heart. When the game ended, the Logan team as one, refused to shake hands with the Sherman players. Several pointed at Delucci. Biggie pointed back.

The instant he decided to hurt Walter Bishop was the first time 17-year-old Jeep Delucci felt power over another human being.

Walter Bishop never ran again.

The Democratic machine in Logan County wanted to show its black voters that it cared about Walter Bishop. After he graduated, they gave him a job sweeping the halls and washing the courthouse floors. When Republicans won a fluke election in 1968, Walter Bishop was the only patronage job they didn't turn over. Politicians of both parties told Walter to wear his Logan High letter sweater at work, which he did to keep his job.

Delucci saw Bishop once after he came back from Vietnam. Walter was walking his mop up and down the corridors. His still powerful arms worked in broad, methodical strokes as he limped from side to side with his patched-up knee in a brace. Delucci nodded to Walter Bishop without saying anything. Bishop never changed his expression as he muttered, "Cheap lick."

"Did what I had to do," Jeep said.

"It was common," Bishop replied and then went back to mopping.

Jeep felt that power again two years later when he was adjusting the front and rear sights on his M16 for a 200-yard shot at a North Vietnamese platoon leader standing alone next to a hooch in a cluster of thatched-roof huts. He was using a standard 55-grain, 5.56x45mm cartridge that caused massive wounding. He was not concerned with the M16's habit of having powder residue jam a spent cartridge in the chamber. He was only planning one shot, then running like a rabbit. He lay prone in grass at the edge of a rice paddy. Woods were behind him. The sun was hot, and he had no shade. He was in the bubble, a calm, quiet place where his only job was to concentrate on his rifle, his target and his environment—the stillness of the air, the leaves on the trees behind him, the comfort of the ground and the wariness he maintained for cobras and green bamboo vipers. He didn't see much difference between putting a shot into the head of a buck and sticking one in the heart of his enemy. He counted the clicks as he adjusted the elevation and windage. He wanted to strike the target dead-center. He would have preferred a scope, but he knew he could make this shot without one. He lined up the middle apex of the iron W of his front sight with the front of the enemy's chest. Jeep never blinked, never jerked and never closed his eyes. He did not know why he could do this without remorse. He told himself: One less of them, one more of us goes home.

"Is Walter kin?" Jeep asked Willie.

"Naw," Willie said. "Jes' interested. Not many of the colored in Boone County."

"We had a couple on the team," Jeep said. "One was our safety, Bennie Daniels. Walter Bishop ran him over. No mercy. That's how he did all of us—white or black, didn't matter. Tacklin' Walter Bishop was like tryin' to stop a loaded coal truck runnin' downhill with no brakes."

"I know Bennie's people," Willie said. "An uncle works down this way."

"Bennie's backin' me in this election," Jeep said.

"Gotta go with who you know," Willie said, and then paused. "You hear 'bout that little trainin' session that Butch Boyles, our new superintendent, got himself after a rock found its way into Wanda Smith's living room? Wanda, she Pins's widder."

Freddie Pruitt laughed. "Jingle Bell!"

Jeep smiled. "I did. Sounds like the situation got straightened out."

"Jingle and three white boys took up for her," Willie said. "Jingle told the colored to let him handle it. Made all of us feel right."

Freddie laughed and turned to Jeep. "Jingle Bell is in the Klan. The other three ain't. But this wasn't about none of that. Jingle blocked for Pins. Same side in football an' minin'. Other kinds of outside is different."

"Jingle is supportin' me," Jeep said.

"So I heard," Willie said.

"Jingle don't like bosses in anythin'," Freddie said. "Got some radical in him."

"Never had no trouble with Jingle or any of them Kluxers," Willie said. "Some of the other colored did. Jes' talkin'-tos. Mostly about sleepin' with white girlfriends. Heard they had the same talkin'-tos with white boys sleepin' with black girlfriends."

"Ain't no place for race stuff underground or in the Union," Jeep said with conviction.

"Knowed Jingle since he was a kid," Willie said. "Showed him how to swing a baseball bat a little up for distance. Never quite figured what he had against the colored."

"Not sure he actually did," Susie added, without elaboration. "Miz Bell, she brought us over a real nice casserole when Willie come home from the hospital. Set right there in that chair you settin' on, Mr. Jeep. Had a glass of sweet tea with me. My Daddy worked with her Daddy years back."

Becker shook his head without shaking it. West Virginia never failed to be more nuanced than he expected.

"Nice to see you out of jail," Willie said to Freddie.

"I wuz out the day after the widders settled," he said. "We all wuz. 'Good behavior,' they told me. John-Cee Smithers had to have put the word out. The law down here is just another division of Pittsburgh headquarters."

"We wuz hopin' yer campaign would support us women and the strike," Susie said to Jeep. "We wuz doin' like you said—mine it safe or not at all."

That surprised Willie, Susie going straight ahead like that.

"I went 'bout as far as I could in publicly supportin' your strike. My campaign issued a statement that I endorsed your goals. If I'd come out for the wildcat, I would have been thrown in jail."

"Freddie went to jail," Willie said.

"I was in the middle of my campaign."

"Freddie went to jail," Susie said.

"It woulda looked like I was tryin' to politick -- tryin' to claim leadership -- off your move. Like I was piggy-backin' on you. It was your play. I didn't want to mix your strike with Union politics. You were doin' fine without me."

"We wuz out there by ourselves," Susie said. "Jes' a bunch of women. 'Cept for Doris, we didn't count for nothin'."

"You counted then and now," Willie said. "Nobody never say different. You women count more 'n anybody."

432

Becker was mentally beating his head with his fists. He had begged Jeep to endorse the wildcat strike.

"You'll win this damn election," he had said to Jeep, "if they put you in jail for standing up for injured miners and widows. You can win sitting in a cell. You won't need another dime in campaign contributions. You'll have more publicity than Joe Hunt could buy in three campaigns."

"It'll look like I'm just a Johnny-Come-Lately tryin' to tag onto these righteous ladies."

"It would be like Martin Luther King in the Birmingham jail. Garibaldi was jailed."

"I don't want to go to jail," Jeep said with finality. "I ain't no Garibaldi."

Becker filed those sentences away.

Jeep looked directly at Willie and then Freddie. "If I had come out on your picket lines and gone to jail, Joe Hunt's boys would have said I was tryin' to get votes. Some of the 'white boys' in the Union would have said it was jes' another Mafia wop goin' to jail where he belongs." Jeep grinned at Willie.

Willie grinned back. "Gotta watch them 'white boys.'"

Where'd that come from? Susie wondered. She knew Willie had never had a conversation like this before. The wildcat strike had changed him almost as much as her. She liked this Willie.

"So's how's thangs at the mine?" Willie asked Freddie as he eyed Delucci. Willie was figuring Jeep wanted something out of him. Why else was he here? Willie supposed he would get the short end of any deal with Delucci. Deals, Willie knew, were never truly even up. The man with more power got the lion's share. But that was okay. The question Willie and every black man in southern West Virginia had about Jeep Delucci had to do with Walter Bishop. Was it football or was it race?

"I'd say, so far, so good," Freddie said. "We ain't bein' pushed hard like before, like when you was inside. I hear the same from other mines. Butch Boyles jes' abandoned your section with the bad top and opened a new one where the top was good like we always knowed it. Everyone feels the ladies won us a big one."

"That good," Willie said. "Let's hope it lasts."

"They make you up a leg yet over at the Beckley hospital?" Jeep asked. "ACMU fund will pay for it."

"I been fitted," Willie said. "I get to tie it on two days from now. Got me crutches and gettin' a chair with a battery motor. UNICOAL's payin' any bills the health fund don't cover. That's part of what Susie and them got."

"I've been told it takes a while to get the hang of a leg, but it'll do pretty good for you," Jeep said. "Had a buddy in the service who stepped on a VC mine. Can't hardly tell when he's got his pants on."

"Gotta take 'em off sometime," Willie added softly.

The three visitors nodded.

"Don't make me no nevermind," Susie said.

Willie laughed. "She married me for my sweet and lovin' nature."

"No sir. I married you for your money."

"Now, woman, *that* is a lie you'll have to explain on Sunday mornin'."

"Disability comin' through for you?" Jeep asked.

"Believe it will," Willie said. "Nobody gonna challenge I only got one leg and can't mine coal no mo'. Susie been doin' the papers. If I'd knowed how many papers it took to lose a leg, 'spect I woulda tried harder to hang on to it. Now I'm 'bout to lose my lef' hand from signin' my name all the time."

The men laughed.

"I've done some disability claims," Becker said, taking a card from his wallet and handing it to Willie. "Let me know if I can help out. I'm a lawyer up in Charleston. No charge."

"Thank you. Susie keepin' on top of it," Willie said. "Don't think they'll be quarr'lsome."

"You got reason to be proud of Susie and all of them women," Jeep said. "They sprung that wildcat and got what they wanted. Took the heat and didn't back down. When I win, I'm gonna hire a couple of 'em in the Organizin' Department. Turn 'em loose on non-Union mines over in Kentucky an' out West."

"Wanda, she was breathin' fire," Willie said, "but Miz Estep and Susie was the two stick-ums in the middle of it. Men down here knows who did what for them."

"It was all of us, Willie," Susie piped up, "not jes' me and Doris. Us womens stuck together for ourselves jes' as much for you mens."

Willie looked at his wife with respect for her new pipe-up quality. "Yes, ma'am," he said. "For yourselves jes' as much, maybe even more."

Becker took notice of how Willie Rutherford referred to "Miz Estep," the wife of superintendent Delmer Estep. Becker would have addressed her as "Mrs. Estep." Willie's "Miz" was not the "Ms." he had learned to say when he dated Allyson Pickering. "Miz" was Appalachian, country, southern, churchy—everything Becker wasn't. What surprised him was the respectful ease with which Susie Rutherford now used "Doris." Something had changed in Bloomingrose Holler, he thought. Susie and Doris were now first-name friends.

Willie, it appeared to Becker, felt comfortable with who he was and where he was. His use of "Miz Estep" now came more from his admiration of Doris Estep's courage in "taking up for the laboring man" than it was a vestige of the enforced submission in which he had grown up. Becker liked how Willie said "Miz Estep." She had earned an honorific "Miz." Becker thought maybe he'd try a "Miz" on someone pretty soon. He liked it better than "Ms." He thought he better keep that to himself.

Willie had lived his 50 years in a segregated coal camp in a state that did not abandon segregation until the mid-1960s. Terms of formal deference learned in childhood tended to stick, Becker thought. He himself still referred to his high-school teachers as Mr. Herndon and Miss DeFoe. He knew nothing would happen if 13 years after graduation he were to slip into Steve and Portia if only in his mind. But it would not feel right. Willie Rutherford, 20 years Becker's senior and a product of a very different time and place, could not know what to expect were he to bust out with a "Doris." Miz Estep was safe as could be in 1975; Doris might still be chancy, though not with her. So Willie called every older woman Miz, white and black alike. It was how he'd been raised, and he saw no reason to change. Miz worked for him; Doris now worked for Susie.

Becker discovered relations between West Virginia whites and West Virginia blacks were more complicated, contradictory and confusing than any he had encountered in the North. West Virginia whites were not united in their opinions, consistent with an industrial northern panhandle and a rural south. While West Virginia practiced slavery until 1865, it broke with Virginia over secession and entered the Union as an independent state in 1863. Over the next century, the Ku Klux Klan and legal segregation were present side by side with the non-discriminatory American Coal Miner's Union, black politicians and black-controlled institutions. There was Booker T. Washington who had been rescued from child labor in the Kanawha Valley's coal mines and salt works after the Civil War by the white, school-teacher wife of a salt baron. There were lynchings as well as biracial efforts to improve working conditions. There was soon to be U.S. Senator Robert Byrd writing to Mississippi Senator Theodore G. Bilbo in 1946: "I shall never fight in the armed forces with a negro by my side. Rather I should die a thousand times, and see Old Glory trampled in the dirt never to rise again, than to see this beloved land of ours become degraded by race mongrels, a throwback to the blackest specimen from the wilds." As late as 1958, Byrd argued the Klan was not responsible for anti-civil-rights violence in the South. But 10 years later, he had changed his views along with many other whites. There was a biracial strike by Charleston sanitation workers for a union contract in the early 1970s and a textbook controversy in the very same county the next year that had anti-black sentiments as well as many others.

Becker had questioned Jeep Delucci about race during his job interview. As Jeep talked with Willie and Susie in their living room, Becker remembered that conversation:

Becker: Will you be running with any black guys on your ticket?

Delucci: You bet. At the Subdistrict level and District level—Lonnie Bailey out of District 29 in southern West Virginia, hopefully; Virgil Shrewsbury in District 30 in northern West Virginia, the same. I'm looking for a couple to run for the International Board with me.

Becker: Do you have guys in mind for the Board?

Delucci: Yes. But I've not asked anyone yet.

Becker: What are your thoughts about the ACMU and black miners?

Delucci: The Union always had good words, pretty good intentions and not enough follow through at the mine level. I didn't see things right when I was in the mines, but lookin' back, I see how it was tilted against them. The Union always stood for treatin' everybody the same on the job and in the Union. We was the only organization in West Virginia that had that policy before the 1960s. I also know blacks were laid off more than whites when mechanization came in. The plain fact now is that there ain't a lot of brothers who are workin' miners, and those few we have are mostly in their 50s and ready to retire. I need guys in their 20s, 30s and 40s. I'd say no more than four or five percent of the Union's workin' miners are black. That's it.

Becker: Did Vietnam change your early ideas on race?

Delucci: That mess changed a lot of ideas. Me an' Biggie went in as ordinary country boys, you might say, sort of rednecky in our opinions. We found white boys like us had more in common with the brothers from Detroit than we ever expected. Sure, we were white, but it was the same boot on both necks.

Stover: We was brought up thinkin' blacks -- we called 'em niggers without ever thinkin' twice about it -- was different than us. We might have been sorry white hillbillies, but their black asses were just naturally a little sorrier. That made us feel better. We could always kick someone lower when we should have been thinkin' about kickin' someone higher.

Delucci: We learned their G.I. blood looked just like mine and Biggie's. Their dead smelled the same. They wanted to come home just like us.

Stover: But you know it's always awkward. Me an' Jeep got good intentions, but we're dealing with years of distrust, broken promises...lots of that. West Virginia always had a lot of southern shit in our pinto beans and bulldog gravy. It's hard to convince a brother that we ain't feedin' off that no more.

Becker: What's bulldog gravy?

Stover: Coal-miner food from the 1930s. Water, flour and grease. Fry it in an iron skillet. That's your meal. You can't eat cheaper than bulldog gravy.

Delucci: I ain't color-blind, Beck, but I'm in a different place than where I come up from. Both of us. It may not be where one of you Yankee radicals from Columbia are. I ain't no Black Panther, but I understand what them boys are sayin' about self-defense, community control, doin' shit yourself, buildin' up your own. That's what I want to do with the Union. I thought stuff, I did stuff, before that I ain't proud of. Can't fix that. Jes' tryin' to do better.

Becker: All of us are working on the same thing. I'm not better than anyone else.

Willie was trying hard to decide whether to trust Jeep Delucci. Was Delucci mine management wearing a Union button?

Willie had seen how coal operators in McDowell County had laid off black miners disproportionately in the 1950s and 1960s. When asked, management said low-skilled labor had to be the first to go. Blacks just happened to fall into that category more than whites.

At American Eagle, UNICOAL had cut two blacks for every white in the same job classifications. Local Union 4355 had never filed a grievance despite grumblings by black miners who still had jobs. Willie's section was the only black-majority crew in the mine. Only one other had as many as two blacks. Darrell Dorsey, Mike Decker and Billy Burdette -- the three whites -- liked the easy, careful way Willie ran their section. Delmer Estep liked the way the section produced coal and kept things tidy. He and Lee Roy Stump figured Willie Rutherford was the exception to the guideline they kept to themselves.

Willie knew first-hand the ACMU had not done enough to make sure that black miners had a fair shot at all jobs. He knew blacks were routinely slotted in for the brute work of shoveling, lifting and toting. While they benefited equally with white miners from ACMU-negotiated contract gains, the Union let management hire preferentially and do the same even with job bidding, which was supposed to be governed solely by seniority and ability to do the job. Willie knew when he bid up to his continuous-miner that he had defeated the never-stated white bias of both UNICOAL and the ACMU. Both could now point to Willie's position to prove the absence of discrimination. And while he was going through this history, Willie knew the favortism he'd seen should be laid on UNICOAL's doing as well as Joe Hunt's not doing.

None of that past could be hung on Jeep Delucci. Maybe he was different, had changed. Maybe the Union was ready to change, a little change. But what about Walter Bishop?

Willie looked at Susie, then he said: "So you gentlemen want somethin' from me. What might that be?"

Jeep looked at Willie. "I want your support. You an' me want the same thangs. I want you to help my campaign."

"Are you lookin' for my support 'cause I'm a famous cripple from the mines or 'cause I'm black?"

Becker cringed since he knew it was both.

Willie went on. "Actually, you already got yourself a black cripple waitin' for you, Mr. Jeep."

"Just Jeep," Jeep said.

"Jeep then," Willie said. "And that be Walter Bishop."

Jeep stiffened.

"Walter's endorsement would win you every black miner in West Virginia and likely the Union, too. Everybody know that story."

After a few seconds, Jeep said: "I guess it's both—because you got hurt, and because you are black, Willie, plus one more thang. I'm lookin' to get black miners to help out with the Union—run for office, take on administrative jobs. I'm lookin' for men in their 30s and 40s with experience who the workin' members will respect, 'cause they're one of them. That's you.

"As for Walter Bishop, everyone was playin' hard in that game. I hit him clean."

"No need to mash him up, permanent," Willie said, unwilling to let it go.

Susie looked at her husband: That's enough, now.

"You went for his knee," Willie said.

Jeep shifted around in his chair. "You're right, Willie," he said. "The game wasn't worth what I done to him. I know that now. Both him and me live with it. You make mistakes when you're young."

"Would you have done him that way if he'd been a white boy runnin' riot over you?"

"Willie!" Susie said.

"No, that's a fair question, ma'am," Jeep said. "I don't know how I woulda done him if he was white. Maybe not the knee. I don't recollect makin' a conscious decision to hit him like that, but I did. I can't go back an' do it different. I wanted to win. The team needed something to change otherwise Logan woulda beat us. If things had been reversed and there was a Walter Bishop for Sherman High runnin' wild over Logan, I think someone over thar would have tried to do him the same.

"You do your decisions, good and bad, then live with the consequences. Maybe I wouldn't have hit him if he'd been white. I meant to knock him out of the game, not cripple him for life, not take away college and the pros. If he'd made the NFL, we'd have been proud of him.

438

All us white boys from Sherman High would have been linin' up to boast, 'Walter Bishop run over top of me.'"

"He up at the Logan courthouse, sweepin' and moppin'," Willie said. "Has a wife and a young boy."

"I know," Jeep said.

"Well, okay," Willie said. "I ain't really the right man for what you want."

"How's that?" Jeep asked.

Willie gave this question his full attention. He shifted his good leg and faced Jeep squarely as best he could. "Ain't me you should be askin' for an endorsement. I was jes' an unlucky miner down in the hole when the roof fell. You best be askin' her, the woman, here. She and the women got the job done. Not me."

Susie shot her husband a puzzled look—Where might you be goin' with this?

Becker saw Willie was right. The women had made things change and won the strike. Jeep should have asked Susie, not Willie. Or better, he should have asked both.

My fault, Becker thought, I should have given better advice. Allyson Pickering would scold me on this, he thought. Now, I'm a racist, sexist opportunist,

Jeep paused. "You're right, Willie. Miz Rutherford, I apologize. I remember my Daddy telling me the Union couldn't organize in the early 1900s in West Virginia until ol' Mother Jones showed up. The Union paid her $500 to get the men to do what the men themselves couldn't get started. Maybe, you'll be our next Mother Jones."

"This Mother Hubbard ain't no Mother Jones, Mr. Jeep," Susie said with seriousness. "I think she was angry, because she lost her babies. I never could have none."

Susie and Willie exchanged a quick glance. After the tests, they both knew it was Willie, not her. Two adopted kids.

Susie added: "I think she saw miners as her children who she was lookin' out for. She turned her loss into greatness. I ain't great."

"You never know how high a balloon will rise until you let her go," Willie said.

"Yeah, well, I ain't no balloon," Susie said.

"Mr. Jeep," Willie said, "you should know Susie is kin to Frank Ingham on her Daddy's side."

"Who?" Jeep asked.

Willie smiled. "I know you know about Frank Keeney, Fred Mooney and Bill Blizzard, the District 17 leaders who organized 10,000 union miners from Kanawha County to march on Logan and Mingo Counties in 1921 to end the enslavement of the miners down here."

"Sure," Jeep said. "The southern West Virginia coal operators ran a police state. If you joined a union, they fired you, evicted you from your company house and blacklisted you from gettin' another job. Made you sign a yellow-dog contract, promising not to join a union as a condition of employment. The sheriffs down here were employees of the operators. Comp'nies always paid below ACMU scale. 'Encouraged' you to buy at the company store next to the mine. If you took scrip to buy from an independent, those stores would cash you out at 80 percent of your scrip's face value, then turn it into the comp'ny and get paid 90 percent. That's what the U.S. Coal Commission found in 1922. Where there was a union, the stores were fairer.

"In Mingo County, I read that 63 percent of the families qualified as 'destitute' in 1933. In 1923, a coal miner averaged about $850 in annual wages; 1929, it had dropped to $590; and in 1933, it was down to $235. That was a family tryin' to live on, let me figure, about $.65 a day! It didn't get better until the ACMU organized the industry in the mid-1930s.

"As long as southern West Virginia operators kept miners poor, they could sell their coal cheaper than ACMU mines. So the ACMU guys armed themselves and fought it out with Sheriff Don Chafin's boys on Blair Mountain and Spruce Fork Ridge in September, 1921. Chafin used private biplanes to drop gas and shrapnel bombs on us, on American citizens! General Billy Mitchell authorized Army planes to gather intelligence on our whereabouts. Federal troops -- 2,100 -- were sent in to stop the war but really to stop us.

"We lost. The ACMU couldn't organize Logan, Mingo and McDowell until the New Deal and the Norris-LaGuardia Act outlawed the yellow-dog contract. By that time, the coal operators recognized their race-to-the-bottom competition was so destructive they had no choice but to level wages across the industry by signing our contract. The gun thugs was finally run out. The Baldwin-Felts Agency closed in '37 after federal and state laws were passed that stopped comp'nies from using private detectives to police their towns."

"That's the highlights," Willie responded. "An' behind the Keeneys and the Blizzards was lots of ordinary folk like Frank Ingham. He was the first colored into Mingo County back in the early 1890s. Worked as a handloader for 30 years. Around Chattaroy Holler. Good worker. Never talked union until 1920. Got fed up, so he took the membership pledge. The Mingo mines were strikin' for the ACMU to represent them. Every union man was kicked out. They was a-livin' in tents down on Lick Creek. Frank was fired from his job at Howard Collieries, which was owned by the N&W. He had worked there 14 years, non-union. Brought in other colored to work in Mingo. His wife taught at the colored school in Chattaroy.

"But firin' him and evictin' him wasn't enough. A deputy arrested him, and they hauled him over to Welch. The Sheriff there, S.A. Daniel, put him in jail. No charge. He wasn't allowed to call his wife or a lawyer. Sheriff and his deputies took him out jes' after midnight. Drove Frank toward Hemphill. Took him out in the woods. Beat him with iron clubs 'til they thought he was dead. Then a deputy kicked him in the face and robbed his pockets.

"Even after that, Howard Collieries told him they'd take him back if he would tell the colored to take the place of white strikers. He refused. He told his boss he didn't want to set one race against the other. The ACMU gave him a job at $4 a day, working in the Lick Creek tent colony, organizin' folks, handin' out food and such.

"Frank Ingham was Susie's great uncle. There was always colored standin' up for the Union. Maybe not in Boone County where there wasn't but a few of us, but down here in Logan, Mingo and especially McDowell."

Jeep stepped in. "I didn't know 'bout Frank Ingham. I'm glad you taught me. All of us come out of how we was raised. We have those ideas an' attitudes. I got to know black guys when I went to Vietnam. Had my eyes opened. If you believe in union -- where everyone's a brother member -- you gotta leave behind your prejudice on black and white. That's why the ACMU prohibited its members from joining the Klan back in 1924. An' I guess you opened my eyes some more about women jes'now. I'm sorry I insulted you, Miz Rutherford. I truly am."

Becker thought that was as good a speech as he'd ever heard Jeep give. Union, race, women—if you changed yourself to be right on one, then you had to change yourself on the others. A slippery slope. Becker grinned.

Susie turned toward Delucci: "Mister Jeep, I'll talk to the women. I 'spect it'll be all of us or nothin'. You'd do better with Doris Estep a-campaignin' for you than me."

"Now that would raise more than a few eyebrows," Freddie laughed. "Miz Estep has always been a fair woman with our wives and kids. Never high-hatted any of us like some. I'm not surprised she took up for Willie and the widders."

"Doris smart," Susie said. "She steel."

"You, too," Willie said.

"I'm glad you'll talk to your committee for me," Jeep said. "An' I'll be happy to meet with you all whenever you want."

"What exactly do you want from me an' Susie?" Willie asked.

"I want you to help me on the campaign and work for the Union if I win," Jeep said.

"Doin' what? Bench warmin'? Politickin' ain't exactly my line of work."

"I told Jeep you weren't a politics man," Freddie said, "but he said you might want to bring some good outa the loss of our men."

"I thinks of them every day," Willie said. "It ain't right, me bein' alive and them seven dead."

"I knew Pins was for Jeep," Freddie said, "but I wasn't sure about you. If you're backin' Joe, then it's my mistake in comin' and no hard feelin's either way, I hope."

"Never did know much about you," Willie said to Jeep. "Least I knows what I gets when I vote for Mr. Hunt."

"Yes, you do," Jeep said. "You'll get the same old, same old. I want the workin' miner to see safety as a real issue in this election. We can get the comp'nies to do better—the ladies showed us that. You know the Union ain't givin' the men the kind of backup you need. I meant what I said, Coal should be mined safely or not at all."

"Most likely that means not at all," Willie said, "Or maybe it means the comp'nies shut down their Union mines and shift to them big, low-cost, non-Union strip jobs out West. So what could I do for you?"

"Maybe work in the safety department. Go around and talk to young miners about safety. Maybe Miz Rutherford can come on board and talk to wives. I'll promise there will be money in the budget for the two of you."

Willie said nothing for a minute. "What I have to do now?"

"If you're able, I want you to come around with me a couple of days. You ain't to blame for survivin' a roof fall. North Vietnamese bullets missed me, hit others. Sometimes you get a break, but most of the time guys like us don't. All I want is for you and Miz Rutherford to talk safety—what the ACMU can do to make thangs safer and keep 'em that way. I want the papers and the TVs to keep hearin' about safety. Hey, man, I'd even feel okay if you went to work for Joe Hunt, talkin' up safety. Safety is my issue. The more the workin' miner hears it, the more he'll think about me for president."

"I can get around enough," Willie said.

"My campaign will pick up your travel expenses and pay both of you as campaign workers. It's not much, but everybody's gettin' the same."

"Jes' like the other white men," Willie said, with a sly smile.

Delucci blinked. His face flushed, and then he smiled. "Jes' like."

Freddie came out with a very small laugh that sounded more like a burp.

Becker had a writer's taste for plot reversals, particularly ironic ones. In his mind, it was now a toss-up as to whether the fisherman was going to land the fish or the fish was going to pull the fisherman overboard.

"White folks ain't treated black folks right," Jeep said. "Down deep, most white folks know this in our hearts. I know it. I can't change history, ours or my own. But I can stick my hand out. You can take it if you want. I want you to see this as a down payment on doin' better."

442

Susie thought she'd better say what she'd been thinking. "I think me an' Willie need to talk this over. An' I need to get with the ladies. It's not right I get somethin' the others ain't."

"I understand, Miz Rutherford," Jeep said. "The campaign would be hirin' you to be more than Willie's legs and driver. More important is you talk to the wives. If I win, you can have ACMU jobs goin' around talkin' safety."

"An' what you want from us now?" Willie asked.

"An endorsement from you and the widders. Jeff has a statement. Very simple and plain. It says you think I would be the best man for ACMU president. That I would push for safety and health on the job, that I would do better for the men. That's it."

Becker reached into his inside jacket pocket and handed a statement to each of them. Becker knew better than to carry a lawyer's briefcase into a miner's home when he wanted someone sitting at a kitchen table to do something. He'd made that mistake several times before a native West Virginia lawyer clued him in.

"Says what you said," Susie said.

"I don't have no problem with this," Willie said, "but like Susie said, give us a day or two to talk this 'round."

"Sure," Jeep said. "Glad we had this time together. Pleasure meetin' you both."

Hands were shaken all around.

"So what you think?" Susie asked her husband after the three men left.

"I think we make a good road show," Willie laughed. "You tell jokes, and I'll do a buck an' wing."

"Grumpy and stumpy," she giggled.

"We don't need his money. We doin' okay," he said.

"But what you think about what he say?" she asked. "'Bout talkin' safety and dust…health…to the miners and the women? Nothin' wrong with that."

"He usin' us to get elected."

"But he's doin' right by the miners and their families," she said. "Who better'n you to talk safety? Why can't I talk to the women and even the men?"

"No reason," Willie said softly. "You be good."

"An' nothin' wrong if both Mr. Hunt and Mr. Jeep talkin' the same on safety and keepin' the dust down. No more black lung—now that would be a Hallelujah Day."

"Nothin' wrong with any of that," Willie agreed. "Better than me an' the leg watchin' TV."

"No need to shrivel up like two old taters with our eyes buggin' out," Susie said. "We'd visit some country we'd never see any other way. Might even do some good for somebody."

"I could tell 'em that every ACMU miner has got a right to withdraw from unsafe conditions -- which is what I shoulda done -- without no penalty. Show them the reasons not to go along with speed-ups. Show them why they should stop takin' chances and cuttin' corners."

"What if the ladies get jealous of me makin' money and them not?" Susie asked.

"Like who?"

"Don't know 'who' yet."

"Talk it over with them like you said. If they object, we won't do it."

"Okay" she said with a few reservations about approaching the committee but not enough to forget the idea.

"We'd be eatin' at restaurants, real ones, not no burgers in the car," he said. "I might finally get to taste a lobster."

"You might finally could."

"I might not like it."

"You might not," Susie said.

"Onliest way to know is to give it a try."

"Thanks, Freddie, for makin' the introductions," Jeep said, as they drove to his house before heading back to Charleston.

"I think they'll do it," Freddie said. "They're good people. Willie ain't no bullshit guy. He'll hold up his end, one leg an' all. Always been like that. Never heard him say so much."

"His wife 'ain't no bullshit' lady, either," Becker said.

"They understand the deal," Jeep said, dragging on his Marlboro. "We don't want a dummy with someone puttin' words in his mouth. He gotta be himself, his own man out there. Miz Rutherford, too in a manner of speakin'. White miners'll respect him for it. The wives will listen to her. She won't be tellin' them what to do, just what happened to her and what she and the others done. Heck of a story.

"Gettin' them to sign on should help me with black miners. It'll offset Walter Bishop. Even a lot of whites in Logan County never forgave me for that hit. Willie can put the word around that I'll do better for them than Joe."

Ah politics, Becker thought.

"What about Walter Bishop?" Becker asked. "Would he endorse you?"

"His people were miners," Jeep said. "I don't know if I could look him in the eye and ask."

"Do you want me to talk to him?" Becker asked.

"No," Jeep said. "That wouldn't set right. That's my job."

444

Becker let it drop.

"Anyone takin' bets?" Jeep asked.

"I think he'll give it a shot," Becker said. "The question is, will he stick it out?"

"You mean flip and go over to Joe Hunt?" Delucci wondered.

"No," Becker said, "just wash his hands of the whole mess."

"Why would he do that?" Jeep asked, without asking anyone.

"Because this campaign started out simple, and now it's getting very complicated."

"Life ain't simple," Freddie said.

"Or fair," Jeep said.

"Or clear," Becker said. "Were you serious about hiring both of them?"

"Yeah, buddy," Jeep said. "You, too, maybe."

Chapter 32

Pittsburgh, November 25, 1975, 4:30 p.m.

John-Cee was bent over his credenza with his back to his door when his secretary, Sally Schreiber, showed Allyson Pickering into his office.

Allyson noted he was wearing a very dark blue suit, which could pass for funereal black in a pinch. Even so, she thought she saw the faintest of stripes. The cuffs of his plaster-white dress shirt were starched and stiff. He wore gold UNICOAL cufflinks and a matching tie clasp. His salt-and-pepper hair was like her father's—smooth, full, combed with a part and cut so skillfully that it was not noticeable. He was very conscious of having to present himself well even when he was at home, relaxing.

John-Cee turned toward her, straightened slowly and came with a smile to shake her hand. She noticed a few lines in his forehead, fewer than 60-some years should normally etch. His right hand was dry, his grip firm. His gray eyes met hers.

Sally Schreiber set up a micro tape recorder on John-Cee's desk between them.

"Ms. Pickering. Nice to see you again. Under better circumstances I should add. We've done what was right for the widows and survivors at American Eagle as I'm sure you now know. You did a nicely balanced piece on the settlement. Thanks for being fair in these circumstances."

She leveled her most reportorial-feminist look into his eyes. "They could have gotten more."

"You don't get, if you don't ask," he said in a tone that indicated he did not want further inquiry. "They didn't. That's off the record. None of what I say is on the record or to be attributed in any manner. Have a seat." He motioned toward a comfortable chair across from his desk. She settled in and took out a tape recorder that she placed next to Sally's. She clicked it on.

"Sally will stay with us, taping the interview for our records. Can Sally...can I get you some coffee, tea, a pop? Have you ever tried Tom Tucker Mint Ginger Ale? Sid Harris from Squirrel Hill invented it. Sid dropped out of school after the eighth grade and started selling soft drinks and ice from a horse-drawn wagon downtown in the early '20s. Dad bought me a pop when I came to the office with him on Saturday mornings. Sid built a nice business on flavored fizz. I remember his sign, 'We don't know where Mom is, but Pop's on ice.'"

"A true Pittsburgher," she laughed. "I grew up in Philadelphia where people say 'soda.'"

"I know that," he said with a wink.

"Oh?"

"Your father and I were at Yale but different years. We were not chums, but we've gotten to know each other."

"He never said anything to me."

"I'm just disclosing. I'm not trying to sway your reporting. Is this interview going to focus on American Eagle or something else?"

"I'm actually interested in two something elses."

"Sure. Just for the record, there's nothing new in the roof-fall investigation. You're up to speed."

He crossed his legs. She crossed hers.

She started. "How much are you involved in the Frank Stover deal? Stover...he's called Biggie. He's Delucci's best friend and a consigliere of sorts."

John-Cee frowned. "Right, the big guy. I remember him from the fracas at American Eagle. He could handle himself. What deal?"

"UNICOAL's purchase...or lease...of the mineral rights under Stover's 3,200 acres on Kayford Mountain."

"This is the first I've heard of that."

"Really?"

"Yes, really. Property acquisitions come to me only when they involve special circumstances like CEO-to-CEO negotiations. I'm familiar with the area at the head of Cabin Creek and over into Boone County. Great coal. We have mines in that area. UNICOAL would, I think, be the high bidder if that property were available. It would fit with our transportation infrastructure and markets. Now you've raised my curiosity. Talk to Wayne Slack—he's our acquisitions guy. Where did you hear this?"

"I got a call from an anonymous source who said he was knowledgeable. He didn't sound like a West Virginian. He *speculated* you were trying to aid Delucci's campaign by funding it indirectly."

John-Cee Smithers laughed, actually slapping his thigh. "Buying coal rights is about as indirect as I can imagine. UNICOAL is officially, unofficially and in all other ways absolutely neutral about the ACMU election. Anyway, why would I prefer a young, aggressive reformer who will cost me money in the next contract negotiations to an old comfortable shoe like Joe Hunt? New shoes pinch until you break them in. Remember this interview is off the record."

"Because the future is Delucci, not Hunt," Allyson said. "It might be better to give him his first contract now while coal prices are at record highs than fight with him down the road when prices slip back. Helping him now starts to build a long-term relationship for negotiations. It could be very strategic."

"An interesting idea," John-Cee said. "Of course, you might say we should support a smaller contract now so we're not killed when prices fall, and we can't afford inflated labor costs."

Allyson understood his logic.

"Your anonymous source is giving me more credit for subtlety and strategic thinking than I deserve. Any sale or lease of minerals should be recorded in the Boone County courthouse on the day the money changes hands. You can't do these things secretly. You can check it out."

"I didn't say you *had made* the deal," Allyson said, "only that this source said you were negotiating toward one."

John-Cee raised his hands in front of him in a what-can-you-do gesture. "Speculation is always worth what it's worth, and what it's not worth."

"You could postpone closing the deal until after Friday, December 5th when the ACMU votes. You could record the sale on Monday, the 8th, for instance, which would give Delucci the money to pay off his campaign debts without tarnishing him before the election."

John-Cee smiled. "We could, indeed. But why should I assume that money UNICOAL would pay to Stover ends up in Delucci's campaign?— just to play out your theory. You are a lot cannier than I am. I think a Hunt supporter is playing you, trying to damage Delucci through rumor. But let's stop pooling our ignorance." He reached for the phone on his desk and punched in a three-digit number.

"Wayne, it's me. Are we negotiating with a Frank Stover in Boone County for mineral rights, either sale or lease? Kayford Mountain. 3,200 acres. I see. But you know the property? Sure. Right. Have we ever approached him? What would you lease it for? That much! Okay. A reporter, Allyson Pickering from The Post-Gazette, is in my office. She might stop by to talk with you. Thanks."

John-Cee hung up. "Wayne Slack is on the third floor, 325. He knows the property. It's the one I thought it was. He says every coal operator east of the Mississippi does. It's a gem—three surface-mineable seams and two deep ones. All thick and never been touched. Great qualities; high Btu, low in sulfur. If Stover now wants to deal, Wayne says we should grab it. Stover was approached by several companies, us included, when he inherited the land several years back. Said he wasn't interested at any price. Wayne said he will contact Stover 'pronto' to see if he's changed his mind. We would like to do a deal as would at least a dozen other operators. But the idea the Stover property is in play with UNICOAL right now—no, not to our knowledge. I wish it were."

Allyson frowned. "So it's fair for me to say UNICOAL denies it is currently negotiating with Biggie Stover for his coal rights but would be very interested were they to become available."

"Yes. But I want you to say it like this in your story: 'UNICOAL has not been and is not negotiating with Frank Stover for his coal rights.' I don't want you to use or imply the word 'deny,' because it would confirm it with my competitors. If Stover is interested in selling or leasing, I want UNICOAL to be first in line with the cash. I don't want to wake other

448

bidders through your story. Any of us would be tickled to get that coal. The bids would be dog-eat-dog if we couldn't lock it down before it became public knowledge. Stover would come out very rich by anybody's standard. All of that is off the record except the 'not-negotiating' sentence."

Allyson had been lied to before. She wasn't sure whether John-Cee was the most recent example. She knew the anonymous source could be trying to use her to degrade Delucci's campaign as Smithers had suggested. Or the deal could be going down just as the source surmised. "I agree," she said.

Allyson took a two-page, stapled photocopy from her bag and handed it across the table.

"I'll summarize," she said. "It's on UNICOAL letterhead. From Wayne Slack, Acquisitions to Bert Battles, Operations. Date: November 3, 1975. Slack describes the Stover 3,200 acres, summarizes the U.S. Geological Survey's estimates of proven coal reserves, refines that with UNICOAL's estimates and proposes to pay 'whatever it takes to button it up, preferably on an outright purchase of all subsurface rights, but a 20-year, renewable lease at the minimum.' Slack says 'we should be willing to pay as much as $4-a-ton royalty on a lease.' That's twice the going rate, he points out."

John-Cee said nothing. He relaxed in his chair. He dutifully read the memo and handed it back to her. "I've never seen it. But it sounds like Wayne's on the ball if this is authentic. Wouldn't you agree?"

"I would."

"Where did you get this if I may ask?"

"In the mail at the paper. No return address. The same day I got the phone call from the anonymous source."

"This is proprietary information. Not for public consumption. You shouldn't have it."

"It looks authentic," she said.

"I repeat. This is not public information. If it's real, it was stolen from my building. In any event, this is preliminary. I've been sent hundreds of such memos over the years. It's simply flagging a 'possible' opportunity. It does not say we're in negotiations with Stover."

"Why would UNICOAL pay above market to Stover?"

"Allyson! At this moment, we're not paying him anything! If we were to make a deal, we'd pay high -- and, at the same time, as low as we can -- because he's sitting on a black gold mine. My company would want what he has. That's our business. These statements are not for publication.

"Off the record. It doesn't matter that much whether we pay two bucks a ton royalty or three, four or five. With steam coal at $25, the royalty is a chip. It's a pass-through cost on a long-term utility contract."

"But why are you giving Stover all this money *now*…during the election?" she asked while trying to keep the accusatory tone out of her voice.

"I'm not '*giving*' him anything," John-Cee said. "If, IF, IF we did a deal, I would be paying him for the resource he owns. That's not a gift; it's a commercial transaction. I would make a good return on the investment even after paying him top dollar. Under a lease, we would provide him with an upfront fee, but he would not get any tonnage royalty until we mine the coal. That's several years down the road, maybe more. I doubt he would sell both surface and minerals to us outright, but that's what we would prefer. Leasing is messier when the landowner doesn't like what we are legally entitled to do with the surface.

"This memo doesn't say we've made an offer. It doesn't say we've been in contact with him. It doesn't say anything about timing or when a deal is to be closed. It doesn't say there is a deal. It simply says what I said to you—UNICOAL would pay as much as we could afford to get that coal. Every coal operator would look at it the same way. All of this conversation about Stover, his coal and our interest in it is absolutely off the record."

"But if you did buy his coal…"

"What a landowner who sells or leases us his coal does with his money is his business, not mine," John-Cee said. "Let me say as clearly as I can, UNICOAL is NOT trying to influence the outcome of the ACMU election in any way, shape or form. We are neutral; we'll negotiate a labor contract with the winner. That can be on the record. If we buy Stover's coal, it's a simple business deal. It has nothing to do with the ACMU election."

"Sometimes," Allyson said, "one thing leads to another."

"One thing can lead to another thing or nothing at all," John-Cee laughed. "Now you've got me wondering a little bit about how Mr. Delucci would repay his friend Biggie were he to lend the campaign a large amount to get through the last month?"

"It could be a gift," Allyson said, as she immediately came to the thought that Delucci would *have* to use ACMU money to repay Biggie. How else could he come up with several hundred thousand?

"A gift -- a contribution -- from Stover to Delucci's campaign is clean," John-Cee said. "But a loan to the campaign would be expected to be repaid. On the other hand, Stover could forgive the loan. Hell of a nice friend who'd do that."

"A rich friend could," she said.

"A rich friend could," John-Cee agreed.

"Clearly, I need to think about Delucci's money more, more…"

"Comprehensively and factually?" John-Cee offered.

"Yes," she said. "It has more dimensions than I realized."

"Your leaked memo, there," he said, pointing his nose at her document, "it's a non-starter. UNICOAL is not trying to fund Delucci's

450

campaign through a purchase or lease of Stover's coal rights. I hope you don't publish a stolen document.

"Let me say one more thing to you as your father's contemporary and, maybe, a friend to you in the making.

'You and I are different generations. I grew up in the 1930s, served in The War and went to Yale. The '30s were tough on everyone, even the rich. You were in college in the 1960s. Everything was easy. Societies get hooked on conspiracy theories when things are hard *and* when they're easy. In your time, the government lied about the Vietnam War. The Warren Commission did not pursue some leads I thought deserved investigation. The CIA intervened in domestic politics. Then came Nixon, Watergate and cover-ups. You lived through some genuine conspiracies and a lot of 'could-be' conspiracies. That's how your generation thinks; the times shaped your perceptions of big organizations, like governments and corporations. Sure, some businesses try to fix prices or apportion markets. They are the exceptions, not the rule. What you're driving at -- that I'm trying to buy the ACMU election to put Delucci in -- is Baby-Boomer paranoia.

"I am not some sinister capitalist ruler jerking hidden strings that control ACMU officials. That picture comes from editorial cartoons in the Communist newspapers that we find distributed outside our mines from time to time by the true-believer sons of Cleveland dentists and the daughters of Long Island stockbrokers."

Allyson brushed her hair back from her forehead and laughed. "I interviewed a few last year during the wildcat strike over the right to strike."

"We would have industrial anarchy if every local union had a right to strike over every grievance that it didn't want to submit to arbitration," he said.

"You might be surprised. I'd guess they would police themselves and not strike over every little thing. After all, every shift that doesn't work is a shift that doesn't get paid. I doubt it would be used frivolously."

John-Cee leaned back in his chair. "You had another 'something' to discuss?"

"I do," Allyson said. "What do you think of Joe Hunt?"

John-Cee leaned forward. "I'm trying not to laugh," he said, and then gave up. "We are so far off the record that I will deny I've ever talked to you."

"Okay," she said.

"He's been an average union president. Maybe a little better than that. He has made some improvements for his members in contracts. He's been honest with his members' money—no stealing for himself that I know about. He's not charismatic. His leadership failures come from…well, in the cattle business, which I dabble in on our Ligonier farm, it's called a lack of 'backgrounding.' He's not educated. I'm not sure he ever entered high school. He's not an autodidact. A lot of the financial stuff in contract negotiations is over his head. His understanding of the coal business -- my side of it -- comes from being a working miner years ago, which is not the equivalent of having an MBA. He knows coal from the bottom up but not its money from the top down. He wants to do the best he can. He hasn't been too bad for them overall. He's loyal to the Union and its members. We hoped he could stop the wildcat strikes, but they've increased each year since 1969."

"And Delucci?" she asked.

"Again, off the record. He's a question mark. He's young and full of himself. Probably smarter than Joe Hunt. But really just a high-school graduate from Boone County. Which speaks for itself, I suppose. I've met him twice. He's taken some night courses at West Virginia Institute of Technology. Economics. Vietnam vet. That's good. Probably a labor Democrat, something like the Autoworkers. May be a socialist. Who knows?"

"Can you work with him?"

"We'd have to. I understand him even though we're different. Young guys want more. As candidates, they sell hope. They promise more than they can deliver. 'Coal will be mined safely or not at all.' Hell, mining can never be 100 percent safe. Sitting in this chair is not 100 percent safe. Old guys, on the other hand, want change on the margin, but not where they shit…excuse the graphic nature of the observation. Me, included. In any event, the Bituminous Coal Companies Group can only afford a contract we can afford. So who wins won't make a lot of difference in outcome, but it will in the process."

"Do you have a preference?"

"A small one. But I won't share that with you. From the operators' perspective, both Hunt and Delucci present risks—instability risks. Joe is old and losing his grip. But he was nothing short of a genuine hero at American Eagle. It took moxie for him to make honest statements about us after that tragedy. I won't forget that in the next round of talks. But he's out of touch with his young guys who are *my* future. Coal miners don't follow their leader the way they used to. The discipline is gone. Wildcat strikes destabilize our operations, our deliveries, our customers and our cash flow.

"Delucci, on the other hand, presents the risks of the unknown. How will he handle pressure and dissent? What happens if he wins but his Board remains stacked with Joe's cronies?

"Look. The unionized sector of the coal industry is declining. The ACMU represents a slice that's shrinking faster than the pie is growing. Coal's future is in surface mines in Wyoming, Montana and Colorado. The ACMU is clustered in high-cost, Appalachian deep mines. We in the

452

ACMU sector have to keep our cost of production competitive with non-Union mines that don't carry our expenses for pensions and health care. Their labor cost is at least one-third cheaper than mine. We have to reposition toward long-wall systems underground and big strip mines to stay competitive.

"In one sense, UNICOAL's interest is to have every gram of coal organized under a single ACMU contract. If labor costs were uniform, then the most efficient companies win. That's me, underground and surface. We want a guy who can unify the Union and get them to understand the situation we collectively face. We want the guy who can shake my hand and make a deal stick. If the Union dissolves into chaos, we lose too."

"Here's the other thing I want to ask you," Allyson said as she paused for effect. "Did Joe Hunt kill a superintendent -- Frank Gallagher -- at the Fricktown mine back in the early '30s during a strike?"

"That's an AMSTEEL mine, not UNICOAL," John-Cee said.

"I know."

"You should ask Ben Roberson. He might know something about that."

"Since you're the leader of the most important coal company in the industry, I thought I'd ask you. Off the record, of course."

"I've heard that rumor," John-Cee said. "Most management people have. AMSTEEL investigated but never developed proof against Joe. It could have been him, or Sonoski or any of the other strikers. I never had occasion to ask Joe directly. Why do I care?"

"Water under the bridge, huh? A murder under the bridge?"

"I'm worried about today and tomorrow, not what happened 45 years ago. Which reminds me. Delucci has a campaign manager, Jeffrey Becker. Now there's someone you should look into."

"What's his story?" Allyson asked with as straight a face as she could assemble.

"He's a lawyer, for one thing. Went to Columbia and their law school."

"I'm sure that makes him guilty of low crimes and high misdemeanors," she laughed.

John-Cee laughed, too. "It wasn't Yale, so who knows? He's some stripe of do-gooder radical. What's *his* agenda? Why is he working for peanuts when he could be making big bucks chasing ambulances or extorting honest businessmen like me?"

"I've talked to him," Allyson said. "I didn't realize he scared you."

"If he's the guy pulling Delucci's strings, he scares us. Smart scares us in a different way than stupid does. But everyone has a history. Becker has left tracks."

"As does everyone."

453

"I'm surprised that Joe Hunt's campaign hasn't brought this up. I assume it will."

"What has Becker done, exactly?" Allyson asked. "What 'do-good' has he done?"

"Well, I don't know what he's *done* 'exactly.'"

"Would the coal companies prefer him to be a 'do-badder'?"

"Very funny. It's more a matter of what he thinks, who he associates with, what he believes and what he might do if he's given a high position in the ACMU. We do know he was on an SDS mailing list at Columbia. Coal miners are patriots, not communists."

"I see," she said. "I guess I have as much as I'm going to get today. I would be interested in knowing more about him."

John-Cee smiled. "Oh, I think you got more than you thought you were going to get. By the way. I hear you have your eye on The Washington Post."

Allyson blinked. "And how did you come by that rumor?"

"You have sources at UNICOAL. We have sources. I mention it, because I don't want you to go off the deep end with this Stover business and get burned to mix metaphors. So thanks for coming by."

John-Cee held out his hand, palm up.

Allyson gave him her tape cassette.

Once Allyson gathered her things and left the office, Sally gathered her tape recorder and smiled at her boss.

Allyson rode the UNICOAL elevator down to Grant Street and walked into the first bar she saw.

I'm scrambled, she thought. I'm getting mixed signals. He's lying about Stover. But maybe he isn't. If there is a deal, he'd deny it, which would be a lie. He could be setting me up to keep it under wraps or to reveal what isn't there. Why would he want me to run a piece that diminishes Delucci if he thinks Delucci is the better future for the companies?

"Shit," she said.

"Not available," the bartender said "until later, much later."

"Gin and tonic," she said.

Becker's going to get dumped on, she thought.

After the second drink, her hands stopped shaking a little.

John-Cee picked up his direct dial line and punched in a number.

Ben Roberson at AMSTEEL picked up.

"As our Negro brothers say," John-Cee said, "'I got her nose open.'"

Then John-Cee called Buzzy Maggard at Appalcoal.

"Hi-yew," Buzzy said. "Didya give that gal reporter a taste?"

454

"She's chewing on it as we speak."

"Now, boy, you know my heart. Don't start stirrin' me up with that type language. Betty would get all shook up if I come home in that frame of mind. Mess her hair an' all."

"Bless her heart," John-Cee said.

"Whose?"

"Betty's."

"I do," Buzzy said.

"I'll keep in touch."

Chapter 33

Charleston, November 26, 1975

The American Coal Miner's Union was about to begin a news conference at the Holiday Inn on the polluted Elk River just a few hundred feet from where it joined the polluted Kanawha. It was 10 a.m. on Wednesday. Joe Hunt stepped to the podium. Television lights came on. A dozen reporters sat on banquet chairs with notebooks poised.

"I got a real short statement," Joe said, adjusting his reading glasses.

"Today, the wildcat strike was officially called off by the American Eagle Widows and Wives for Safety Now after meetin' with leaders of the coal industry several days ago.

"The ACMU is pleased a satisfactory agreement was reached. Mining will be safer. The widows and survivors will be properly taken care of. UNICOAL will pay for the funerals and set up a college fund for the children. All miners who were jailed have been released. All charges have been dropped. The ACMU supported the widows in their goal for safer mining.

"If you have questions about this agreement, you can ask Foster Shives, ACMU counsel, who's standin' over there.

"We hope a new day is breakin' in our industry on which both miners and operators depend. I'll take questions."

"Mr. Hunt. Charlie Frazier of <u>The Charleston Gazette</u>. Did the Union help negotiate this settlement?"

"We supported both sides in reachin' an agreement. We endorse it. That's really all I need to say. Coal miners made their point and won a good deal for them ladies and themselves, too."

"So is it fair to say the ACMU facilitated the deal?" Charlie persisted.

"We did some thangs behind the scenes but not in front of all of you. That's how deals get done—in private. Just for your information."

Charlie Frazier suspected Joe Hunt had been frozen out of the negotiations. He felt no need to pursue an admission or denial.

"One last follow up, Mr. Hunt. Did the ACMU give any type of assistance to the women's committee during the strike? Like financial support or legal advice?"

"No comment to that one," Joe said smiling at his deft handling of a set of issues that could explode in his face like a box of blasting caps whether he said yes or no.

"Julie Cogswell, Mr. Hunt. Have the operators agreed to end the speed-up?"

"It's like this, Miss. They ain't gonna say they're stoppin' what they never would say they was a-doin' in the first place. Let's leave it that the

widders got what they and the ACMU wanted on safety. Time'll tell if
thangs are changin' for the better down in the hole. I think they will. These
ladies did somethin' no one ever done before. I take my hat off to 'em."

"Owen Paige, Joe. AP, as you know. What lessons should the general
public learn from this wildcat strike, its causes and the way it was settled?"

"I take thangs as they are," Joe said, looking at Owen who he trusted
more than unpredictable Charlie Frazier. "The coal industry is the way it is
today, because of the way it was in the past. We drag along a lot of hard
feelin's. Maybe the lesson is we don't have to fight the past to solve our
today problems. But if you're a-askin' me why we fight, it's because that's
how we was raised up. Ain't sayin' that's good. Just sayin' that's what
was—so that's what is. Maybe it's best to forget some of the past in order
to have a better future."

"John Babcock, The Washington Post, Mr. Hunt. You lost the
nominating round of local unions. The polls show you losing the election
if it were held today 47 percent to 40, with 13 undecided. Do you think
this settlement will help your campaign? And what do you plan to do
differently over the next few weeks to gain enough votes to win on
December 5th?"

Joe squinted through the television lights to get a better look at
Babcock. "Polls is polls. I got facts. My poll last week showed me ahead
48-44," he said, making it up as he said it. "An earlier one showed me with
46 to 39." This "fact," too, did not exist.

"Can you show me those polls?" Babcock asked.

"No, I cannot show you them polls. They're internal. Private. I paid
for them personally. Classified, you might say."

"Will you release a summary at some point?"

"I just gave you the summary. Now here's what I want to say. You
people in the press are a-rootin' for Delucci, because he's young and
handsome and skinnier than me and calls himself a 'reformer.' And you
paint me as a big ol' fat guy who don't know nothin' no more and prob'ly
never did. Jes' a dumb-as-a-duck coal miner out of his league and out of
touch with the times. So out with the old and in with the new, whatever the
new is. And why? You people are wired up to support the fresh face, the
underdog, the David, the kid—because that's news and no one roots for ol'
Goliath. News ain't interested in old or even what is. News is only
interested in new, the noisier the better. You live on fresh conflict. So you
write your stories that way. You pick around looking to widen a sore,
which you make into news. Then you jump on it like a pack of coy dogs
on a fresh dead groundhog. That's what I want to say.

"And now that you asked me about the election, here's one more thing
the Union's membership should know. Jeep Delucci's campaign manager,
Jeffrey Becker, is from all the reports I've received in the last two weeks
some sort of communist-socialist who wants to do who knows what with

our great Union once he gets into our headquarters. This Becker is not a coal miner. His people ain't miners. He don't come from the coalfields. He went to school up in New York City where he was in that SDS-crazy-people group of students. Maybe he takes his orders from the Kremlin. Or Peking, which is in China. Or Castro down in Cuba. Or maybe he's runnin' with the Snowmen, the Weathervanes, whatever they call themselves now. 'Blowin' in the wind' got tossed over for blowin' up bathrooms. I'm told he was best friends with that Gondleman kid. And then Becker mysteriously shows up in West Virginia. He's a radical and an agitator and an outsider and a lawyer who's trying to force his ideas onto my Union's rank and file. You vote for Delucci, you're a-votin' for Becker's brand of communism or whatever this Becker is. Becker is an enemy of coal miners and all we've ever stood for. Now I'll take one more question."

A dozen hands shot up with a clamor of "Joe!" They wanted to know more about this accusation.

In the confusion, Joe pointed toward Allyson Pickering before he recognized her.

Shit, he thought, her again. Serves me right for givin' girls equal opportunity.

"Allyson Pickering of The Pittsburgh Post-Gazette, Mr. Hunt. I have one question: Did you murder AMSTEEL Superintendent Frank Gallagher on the night of February 26, 1933 or the morning of February 27th during the ACMU strike at Fricktown, West Virginia?"

The room hushed and then rustled like new wind. Heads turned toward Allyson. Lights swiveled toward her and focused. Reporters shook out their cramped fingers and raised their notepads. American Eagle widows and wives were forgotten. Even Jeffrey Becker was shunted into the background.

Joe blinked. He shook his head, trying to clear it. He felt his temples pounding. He stood still.

He remembered. The smoky light of Gallagher's coal-oil lantern. The rotten odor of rotting people. The ache of hunger—its diarrhea, weakness, dizziness, cold. The rat he felt gnawing at his organs. The two clicks of Gallagher's thumb cocking his double-barreled shotgun. The impulsive swing of his Daddy's hammer. Its weight; its speed. The feel of the blow as steel met bone, like a ball hitting a bat in its sweet spot. The rasp of Gallagher's last breath.

"I'll repeat the question. Did you murder Superintendent Frank Gallagher during the ACMU strike at Fricktown?"

Skis moved to Joe's side. "It's that Pickering girl. She's for Delucci. Don't answer. Let me handle it."

Joe felt his Daddy's hammer in his hand, which allowed them to survive. He felt it in a young hand, at the end of a strong arm. Where was that hammer? Left it in Daddy's Fricktown house, probably still in the shed. Suddenly, the years seemed to lift from Joe Hunt. He saw opportunity.

"Miss Pickering…a reporter with a license to kill," Joe said and stopped. He gave her a short dismissive laugh.

A tight smile lifted his heavy face. He focused on a light—a bright light outby the last open crosscut in his mind's eye, a light that might free him from Siciliano, a light that might get him elected as his own man, a light that might let him earn it fair and square. He ran toward the light.

"I didn't do nothin' wrong, 'cept maybe trespass. It was an accident. He did it to himself.

"It was the winter of 1932-'33. We was a-starvin'. I know none of you know what that really means. It's a slow dryin' up, shrinkin' down. It's thinkin' slower and slower. It's not carin' no more. We was dyin' in them tents from no food and no warmth. Simple as that. Those ain't jes' words. An' why was we a-doin' this to ourselves? Because we couldn't earn enough at the lower wage rates to live, and we knew it. It was starve on strike or starve at work. We'd been like that for months. We was a-strikin' for our very lives. Wasn't like this widders' wildcat. It was live or die back then.

"Gallagher found me huntin' around dawn that mornin' on Fricktown land, which used to belong to my people, the Hunts. Up on the mountain, way high where no one goes. I hoped there might be a squirrel or a rabbit left up there. Gallagher had his shotgun leveled at me. Told me to get the hell back to the tents. Didn't say nothin' about trespassin'. I turned to go back to the camp, and then for no reason he swung the barrel of his gun into my back. Spun me around. My safety was off. Told me to give him my shotgun. I said no sir. Daddy and me couldn't hunt without no gun. He grabbed the barrel with his free hand and yanked it toward him. When he did, he pulled the trigger against my finger. My gun fired and hit him in the belly. I wasn't aimin' or nothin'. I didn't pull the trigger. He tried to jerk my shotgun out of my hands. I knew he was dead. His belly was opened up. I left him where he lay. Don't know why no one never found his body. I never said nothin' to nobody.

"Now you ask me if I'm sorry. Not a bit. It was my gun that killed him, but he killed himself by makin' the accident happen. So I ain't feelin' guilty. I ain't a backin' down from the truth. I ain't mourned one minute over it. Gallagher was the cause of his own death.

"Now I'll say one last thang. It was the times that killed Gallagher, not him tryin' to jerk my gun away. It was The Depression. The operators needed to cut wages to stay in business. They were tryin' to survive jes' like us. You can call it 'capitalism' if you want. It was a-livin' in tents during four winter months. It was hungry beyond hunger. You was dyin' some every day you was livin'.

459

"It was an accident. Not on purpose. I didn't try to kill him, or intend to, or plan to. None of that. Just an accident of the times. And in them long-ago circumstances, he'd do the same thang, and my gun would go off accidental the same way. Why did he hit me and grab my gun? Because that's what a superintendent did with a green-as-spring ramps, teenage handloader who was tryin' to feed his hungry family by huntin' on Comp'ny land that used to be his.

"Miss, I hope you wrote down every one of them words I just said. But I don't expect you to understand what them words were like when they was alive. I wish to God I never had to learn what they meant."

Joe gave Allyson one final, disdainful look, paused and then walked straight through the reporters' line of scrimmage. Larry Sonoski was right behind him, doing his best to suppress a grin over two homeruns in one inning. Joe gave Allyson an unfriendly, slightly triumphant smile as he passed. Skis and several Union buffalos formed a moving cordon around Joe as they worked him toward the exit. Shouted questions from reporters bounced off unanswered, so reporters started yelling questions at each other.

Skis understood Joe's instincts. Maybe, he thought, Joe had just squeezed himself a pitcher of election lemonade. Maybe he had made himself free of the Mob. The Becker accusation had been planned. Joe had done it well. The Gallagher story--those dice had now hit the wall. That go-for-broke gambler, the doer who was the Joe Hunt that Larry Sonoski knew when they were kids, he was back.

Skis whispered to Joe: "Damn fine story."

Reporters surged toward Allyson, knocking over two television cameras and a sound man.

She stood and held up her hand to quiet the crowd. She was amazed they shut up. "No questions, please. We all have the same stories."

They started shouting questions at her again. She shook her head, gathered her things and walked into the lobby, followed by her colleagues lined out like a comet's tail.

Julie Cogswell sidled over to Foster Shives who was standing by the microphones as he tried to make sense of what had just happened. "Not for attribution," she stated. "Was that question about Gallagher from The Post Gazette an ACMU plant?"

"No comment."

"No comment, meaning that it was, or no comment, meaning that it wasn't, or no comment, meaning that you don't know, or no comment, meaning that you know but don't want to say?" she asked.

"No comment."

460

"Who fed Pickering that information? Who put her up to it?"

"No comment."

"Who you for, Foster?"

"No comment."

"What does Joe have on Becker?"

"You heard what he said. Becker was SDS at Columbia when they brought that great institution to its knees. He's trying to infiltrate the ACMU. Maybe he has his sights set on all of America's organized labor. With those people, the sky's the limit."

"Okay, he was in SDS seven years ago when he was in college. Any other incriminating evidence?"

"Be a reporter. Do your job."

"Joe said he'd seen recent reports on Becker. Can I see them?"

"No. They're private investigations. And it wouldn't surprise me if you were in SDS, too. All you people think alike."

"Foster, red-baiting Delucci over Becker will undoubtedly get you some votes. It's a matter of what you give up to get them."

"We're not giving up anything *I* can think of."

"Probably true," Julie said. "Anyway, when you have something you can release with a straight face on either Delucci or Becker, let me take a look at the same time you feed it to the big boys. Give a coalfield girl a break. Here's my card."

Foster looked at it and said: "Go away."

"Foster, do you know anything about those two guys in a Cadillac with Pennsylvania plates who happened to do a swan dive off Lens Creek Mountain?"

"No."

"Do you think Delucci was behind it?"

"Dig up the facts. He had motive, means and opportunity," he said.

"Was Joe Hunt campaign money or ACMU money in their pockets?"

"Go away."

"Should I take that as an affirmative?"

"Go chase your tail."

"I am," she said. "Where's Joe getting his campaign money, Foster? He'll need three or four hundred at least."

"Reports will be filed on time with the Department of Labor," Foster said, "after the election."

"Do you think Delucci will keep you on as General Counsel if he wins?"

"Ask him."

"You're general counsel to the American Bank of Washington. Would you say it's been a good investment for the ACMU? Is the Union getting a fair return from the Bank for its members?"

Foster stared at her. He decided she knew nothing.

"It's been a safe and conservative investment for the Union," he said. "It's not a campaign issue between the two candidates."

Julie had now exhausted her knowledge of the ACMU's ownership of the American Bank of Washington. If she had the time and resources, she thought, she would do well to learn more. But a one-woman show in Boone County knew her limits.

"Thanks, Foster. Keep me in mind. I'll take you to lunch at the Main Street Café the next time you're in Madison."

"Sure," he said, knowing that she knew the last place he wanted to be seen was having lunch with a trouble-sniffing, pain-in-the-ass, self-righteous journalist like Julie Cogswell who ran around with more chips on her shoulder than he could count. "I did like your Dad," Foster said and walked off.

He didn't think much of you, Julie said to herself.

Allyson called in her Joe-Hunt-confession story from the pay phone in the Holiday Inn's lobby. She made sure reporters gave her privacy. She told the transcriptionist to slug it, "Joe Hunt," and then composed the piece as she went through her notes. Davey Bloom came on, listening.

"Jeez Louise," Bloom said.

"He's denying murder," she said. "But it doesn't add up. If he left the body where it fell on the mountain, surely it would have been found. The bones and the clothes and the gun would not disappear. If nothing else, the gun and the bones would have stayed around. Unless somebody moved them."

"There were only two witnesses," Davey said, "according to his telling. One is dead, and he's the other."

"My guess is Gallagher's body and his gun were burned in the commissary fire," Allyson said. "That would explain the absolute disappearance of all the evidence."

"And if that's the case, then Joe's story doesn't hold up," Bloom spoke slowly, but he was thinking quickly. "The other two possibly knowledgeable people -- Gus Olin and Sonoski -- aren't talking despite what you've told me. Joe will clam up now if he has any sense, or, at least, if he listens to a lawyer who does.

"A prosecutor with no evidence may or may not bring a charge. At the most, it might be involuntary manslaughter. But I don't think it's even that since Hunt, according to Hunt, wasn't negligent. And I'm not sure it was even misdemeanor trespass if the AMSTEEL land wasn't properly posted or whatever the hell was required back then. Gallagher, according to Joe, didn't tell him to stop hunting or get off AMSTEEL land though I'm sure that was implied. He just said something to the effect of 'Go home.' or 'Get back to your tent.'

462

"It was an accident in Joe's telling of the tale—no intent, no scuffle. I don't think the local prosecutor will bring charges on the basis of Joe's statement. And if they do put money and manpower into an investigation, it's not likely to turn up something since no one else knows anything. No one's going to turn against Joe Hunt today. No one's going to confess to what we think is the truth."

"I bet Gallaher found him breaking into the commissary where food was stored. I bet Joe killed him there and then started the fire," Allyson said.

"That's a lot more plausible than the squirrel-and-rabbit story," Davey admitted. "Proving it is another matter."

"There could have been someone with Joe," she said.

"Sure, there could have been," Bloom said. "Probably was. That old sonofabitch still has some political magic. His constituents will not hold this against him. He may have just pulled victory out of the jaws of defeat by confessing to an accidental killing that wasn't accidental."

"Good for me," she said, deflated. "I just helped elect a murderer."

"You don't know that," Davey said. "What you know is there's still a loose thread in your hand that didn't unravel the camouflage net when you pulled it. That's what you know."

"I want to stay on this," she pleaded.

"Where can you take it?"

"Let me see if I can find another thread. There are other people who went through the Fricktown strike. Maybe the Company did its own investigation."

"I'm sure they did. And if they found anything, they would have turned it over to the prosecutor and insisted on a murder indictment. AMSTEEL wasn't trying to protect anyone in the tent camp. Joe Hunt was just a kid with a strong back. They would prosecute him for murder just to send a message to the strikers. Wouldn't really matter if he'd actually done it. No, hon, they came up empty."

"I have one other source who might talk," Allyson said.

"Who?"

"The Union's lawyer, Foster Shives."

"Why would he crap on his only meal ticket?" Davey asked.

"Because he may think Delucci is a better bet for him than Joe Hunt. I've talked to him a couple of times. He sounds like he's trying to be neutral, which I'd say is a quiet vote for Delucci. He's worth a visit."

"A guy playing both sides of the street for his own benefit might say anything," Davey said. "Anyway, Joe has improved his reelection prospects through this 'confession.'"

"Let me check it out."

Davey Bloom thought a moment before he said something that he'd been reluctant to tell her.

"Maybe he'll say something about those two Pittsburgh boys who met their end a few weeks ago. Danny Manifesto on the City desk has organized-crime sources on the street and with the cops. He says he's heard they were not made men but thugs who got low-brow, strong-arm work—shakedowns, extortion beat ups and collections, that type of thing. They have minor records. Street talk ties them to the organization."

"Mafia? You think Hunt is tied up with the Pittsburgh mob?" she asked, truly surprised by the possibility and intrigued that another thread was now dangling in front of her.

"Somebody was paying those two guys to do a small, surgical rough-up job. I'd ask Shives about that more than what Joe Hunt might have done 40 years ago. Are you sure you want to follow this?"

"Yes."

"This is not playground, hon," Bloom said. "You fuck with the Mob, they'll fuck with you. This Mafia link might be something or nothing. I felt I should tell you what I found out."

"Thanks."

"Yeah, well we'll see about that. I want you to call Art Greiner, a Pittsburgh P.D. detective. He keeps tabs on Tony Bruno and the local hoods. Has contacts in northern West Virginia and over in Steubenville. He knew Paul 'No Legs' Hankish and his underboss Buddy Jacovetti. They ran prostitution, gambling and Wheeling Downs, the track out there. Greiner will know how to learn something about Lazarro and Hyskra."

"Okay. Leave Greiner's number on my desk."

"Now the last thing is about this Becker. Hunt called him 'some sort of communist-socialist' and Columbia SDS. Anything else?" Bloom asked.

"It's just campaign blah-blah," she said. "The young guys call out the old guys for being sellouts. The old guys call out the young guys for being communists and radicals."

"Well, sweetheart, there are actual card-carrying, fire-breathing Communists. I've interviewed some. They used to come to Pittsburgh to organize steel workers—I use 'organize' in a manipulative sense. Several showed up at Fricktown in '33. There was a college girl. Nice looking, as I remember. Old money; high class. Like you. She would have made a murderous commissar. There really was a Communist Party that wanted Soviet-style government here. Of course, it doesn't amount to much now. And despite McCarthy's exaggerations and falsehoods, there really were some Communists working for the federal government in the '40s and '50s. The Rosenbergs -- at least, Julius, for sure -- really was a spy who helped send secrets to the Russians. So maybe this Becker is something more than a liberal idealist."

"Davey, you have to learn to stop calling me 'sweetheart.'"

"You're right, hon. I'll try."

464

"Davey, sugarplum, most students at Columbia in 1968 were against the War," Allyson said, "and most of them were not communists. Becker was against the War and the draft like a lot of boys his age. Back then, SDS had a lot of different kinds of kids in it. The Communist Party was not a factor. My guess is Becker was not an ideologue from what I've seen of him."

"Since Hunt put it out there, you better check Becker out."

"Will do," she said."

Davey Bloom thought about this. "Isn't Becker an old boyfriend? Am I remembering right?"

"Yes."

"Does Hunt know that?"

"No."

"Can you cover Becker like a reporter, a professional?"

"Yes."

Davey listened to her voice. "You better come off this story."

"No. You'll have to fire me."

Davey let his silence say what he thought. Then he hung up.

Allyson stopped at the front desk and asked for advice. After making a stop at Delucci's headquarters, she drove her rental car to Charleston's one semi-fancy grocery in South Hills. She bought a pound of fresh shrimp, two pounds of filet mignon, salad and two slices of strawberry cheesecake. She went across the street to the ABC store and bought an expensive red wine.

Although she'd never been there, she now knew where Jeffrey Becker lived.

Chapter 34

Middle Ridge, November 26, 1975, 7:33 p.m.

Jeffrey Becker pulled his three-year-old Datsun station wagon into his open garage. He wondered about the new Chevy sedan parked in his normal parking spot. He didn't recognize the car or the Ohio plates. Was this Tony Bruno's messenger? Was it guys from the campaign needing a place to stay? He took his new SIG Sauer P220 out of his briefcase and readied it for firing. He had bought it the day after Corelli had called with his warning. He had fired 20 practice rounds at a soup can from 20 feet without making a scratch. He hit the can from eight feet away, three out of 10 rounds. Forty-five-caliber slugs would, the salesman promised, stop a grizzly, assuming, Becker thought, I can hit the damn bear before he bites off my head.

Becker came around the garage corner to the front porch of his house. He saw her rise from the rocking chair.

"You're home," Allyson said. "I was starting to get chilled."

"Allyson," he said.

She noticed the pistol in his hand. "I come in peace."

He put the safety on and tucked the pistol in his briefcase. "Things have gotten tense."

"I came after Joe Hunt's press conference. I didn't see you there. I'm glad it's not that cold tonight. I didn't want to wait for you in my rental car with the motor running. Your place was not that easy to find."

"You drive out to Davis Creek, then right on Middle Fork, then two miles up the dirt road to Middle Ridge, then...."

"Becker, I'm obviously here," she said. "Dicey Shuck gave me directions. I told him I was an old friend. He licked his chops."

"You made his day. He thinks I'm lonely. I didn't know Dicey knew where I lived. I'm not sure what to say. You are here."

He stopped short of the porch steps. He loosened his tie, which was already loose.

She weighed giving him a social kiss and then decided against it. She was not the social-kissing type. Becker, even less so, would have probably sneezed in her ear.

"This is a pretty place," she said in a chatty voice that Becker did not remember. "Probably nicer when I'm not in the dark."

"So am I," Becker said.

Allyson ignored that crack. "It's remote but convenient to downtown Charleston. Nice view of ridgelines from this height, I imagine. Big trees. No neighbors. No barking dogs. Cute little house. Firewood drying on the porch. Motorcycle in the garage. Apple trees. Fall foliage must have been lovely. I guess you still have some of Mandy's farm in you even with a law degree."

"That was a long time ago," Becker said.

"I see you weren't a terminal hippie," Allyson said. "Good for you."

"I liked building stuff with Rick. I spent a year there after you left. They let me inside when it got cold. Then I went to law school. I never saw you on campus."

"I was gone by the time you came," she said.

"I looked…for a while."

"I'm sorry Becker. I just couldn't book passage on the Good Ship Hippiepot," she said, shifting her weight. "I gagged every time I caught an image of myself as a New Age woman, whelping children by kerosene light in a drafty log cabin attended by a Sarah Lawrence dropout in 12-pound Limmer boots whose soles left mud spoor on the hand-planed floorboards. I didn't want to exchange tofu recipes with other Aquarians and cluck-cluck over 10-grain breads that were impossible to chew. I didn't want to garden until I detested anything with chlorophyll. I'm too snide to be a true-believer. It would have been acting, not being."

"There was that aspect to it, sure" he countered, "but we were fumbling on new ground, trying to be different and better than where we came from. Comedy, I guess, is the price of reinvention."

"Do you hate me?" she asked.

"I don't think hate is the right word."

"Are you angry with me?"

"Not any more," he said.

"I didn't behave well."

"You dumped me."

"It was…complicated. I was afraid of getting stuck," she said. "Other things, too."

"You were afraid to love me. You were afraid to give up something to get something. I was of less value than your agenda."

Allyson brushed her hair back from her face. "We're certainly moving right along, aren't we?"

Becker said nothing.

"I brought supper. I'll fix it. You'll like it."

Becker walked up the two porch steps. She stood directly in front of him. "Where is this going?" he asked.

"Into the kitchen," she said, "for starters."

"And for finishers?" he asked. He felt it all coming back.

"It's only food," she said. "We can talk over supper. I'll cook."

"Allyson, I dunno…."

"You used to call me, 'Pick.'"

"That was then."

"Becker, I need to go to the potty."

He shrugged. "The front door's open. No need to lock it. Go straight through to the back. It's next to the kitchen."

She gathered her purse and the wine. He picked up the grocery bag. He opened the door for her with his free hand. She walked in, stopped and scanned.

"Nice fireplace. Piano. Comfortable. Lots of windows. Do you have a girlfriend?" she asked.

"I thought you had to go."

"I'm going," she said, standing in place, looking at him.

"I've dated a couple of women since I came to Charleston after law school."

"Sleepovers," she stated, "don't count for much in your book. I take that as a no, no girlfriend."

"You can take that as a no," he said.

"So why?" she asked, as she settled onto his sofa.

"It either happens or it doesn't. 'You can't hurry love.'"

"'You just have to wait.'"

"It's true," he said. "It's either there or it isn't there."

Allyson brushed her hair over to the side of her forehead. "I'm not sure I ever expected a thunderbolt," she said. "Or deserved one. Or even wanted one."

"I'm not sure what to say about that," he said. "I take it you're single."

"There's a guy in Pittsburgh. He's with Scraife National Bank. He manages assets—stocks, bonds, that sort of thing. Kennedy Brown. He lives well. Says he loves me. Wants kids. Decent guy. Wants to get married, soon. He'd be a good dad and a decent husband."

"Sounds like you found a better version of Trip Pennington," Becker said with more of an edge than he meant.

"Safe, Kennedy is," she said. "He has a pool table in his basement, but I've not seen him try to jump on it, yet." She snort-laughed at the memory.

Becker smiled but didn't laugh. "He may be saving that for your honeymoon."

"Oh, there's the kitchen," she said, trying to look around a corner without success. "I'll freshen up first."

Becker went over to the thermostat and turned up the heat.

Becker went into his bedroom and changed into a t-shirt, jeans and sneakers. When he came back, Allyson had taken off her suit jacket and was patting two minced garlic gloves into softened butter, which she rubbed into their steaks. She ran them under his broiler. She set out the other food on the dining-room table. She was half-way through a glass of burgundy.

"It doesn't look like a college kid's kitchen," she said. "You have good knives. Wusthofs. Wine glasses. Plates. Bowls. Spatulas. A mortar. A pestle. Spices. Good for you."

"I'm not a college kid."

"Have you gotten the back-to-the-land business out of your system?"

"I'm here rather than in an apartment. I'm not in New York or Washington. I guess where I sleep says something about where part of my head is. I like woods. I like mountains."

"Woods scare me," she said, "especially at night."

"You need a map, compass and flashlight," he said.

"We may be talking about different things," she observed.

"Life is woods," he said.

"Oh Becker. That would get you a strong C+ in freshman Metaphors. Steaks are ready, medium rare on the rare side. I'll serve. Sit," she said, "stay."

They ate slowly and talked. She worked down her third glass. He nursed his first. He wanted his wits to hang around.

Becker could not forget she had ended them badly. She had walked out, cut it off, sharp and cold, with no warning. Maybe, possibly, probably, certainly—it would not have worked had they given themselves a genuine shot. Too many things had been tugging at what they shared. They were too young to know how to handle the uncertainty of each other. They had not settled into what they would become. They could never quite harmonize her upbringing and his. They could joke about their differences but not forget them. He could never fully endorse her ambition. Becker knew he would always bear the hurt, because, regardless of everything, he had loved her completely. It would never be the same with anyone else. He was afraid to expose himself again.

Allyson poured a fourth glass.

"You were always the better drinker," he said.

"You never tried," she said.

"Never felt the need to," he said. "I'm not sure we want to go into who tried and who didn't."

"Are we friends?" she asked.

"We were once. Now, how about acquaintances?"

"That's better than enemies."

"You look the same," he said. "Still as pretty as I remember. A little harder around the eyes. Aren't we all?"

"Oh, Becker. You have such magic with words. Women must just melt."

"I've left puddles," he laughed. "I've stepped in a few."

"I've been lucky," she said. "I've had decent jobs so far. Nothing has gone terribly wrong. Many things have turned out reasonably well."

"'Things' have a way of evening out," he said.

"Always the optimist. Well, yes, I've seen that. I suppose full disclosure requires me to tell you that I have a trust fund."

"You say it like you're confessing to a venereal disease."

"It's not infectious. Daddy told me when I graduated. I got it in September, just after I left Mandy's farm."

"How nice," he said neutrally.

"I get a check every quarter. I give to causes. Save this monkey, save that dingbat. Daddy manages it. Daddy has always handled it since he and Boo set it up, with her money, too, Andrews money. His people had something to do with founding Scraife National. Her people owned a big piece of the Philadelphia National Bank. They also had interests in coal companies before WWII. Anthracite coal in Pennsylvania."

"Scraife is my hometown bank," he said.

"Mine too."

It sounded to Becker like Allyson wanted to be forgiven.

"I'm glad you're not squandering it," he said, for lack of anything better to say. "You always projected, let's say, financial comfort. I thought you were a pretty good catch even without money in your pocket. What do you own? A coal company? A bank?"

"I don't know," she said. "It's blind, so I'm not allowed to know. But Daddy's told me, after I asked, that he put his own money in UNICOAL, AMSTEEL, USOCO—the oil company that bought Amalgamated Coal. Tax-free municipal bonds, General Motors, utilities, banks. 'Blue chips,' he calls them. So I suppose some of the same is in my account."

"I don't spend any of the trust's earnings on myself. I live on my salary and give away at least 15 percent of that to women's health, small presses and food kitchens."

"Maybe you should have Walton sell any coal stocks in your trust now that you're covering the industry," Becker said with as much suggestion subtracted as he could from an obvious suggestion.

"I've thought of that. You're right. I said something to Daddy, but he said now's not the time to sell coal. I don't ask what's in there. If I sell out, it won't be for a dividend."

"I agree, Allyson. You won't sell out for money. So what might capture your flag?"

"Prestige among my peers, maybe. Recognition."

"What about love?" he asked. "Would you compromise for love?"

"No," she said. "Look. I'm just a bleeding-heart Quaker. It upsets me to see bag ladies in downtown Pittsburgh. I live simply. My refrigerator is never full. I drive an old Bug."

"I'm not judging you," Becker said.

"I do enough of that," she said. "As we get older, we seem to talk more about money."

470

"We had a free ride in college. That's why we didn't talk about money. What you have to do to make money is the last secret parents keep from their children. There is never another Santa Claus after that is revealed."

"I guess I still am riding free," she said. "So what gets you up in the morning?"

"The alarm clock," he laughed. "Delucci has a good chance of winning. If he did, it could inspire reform movements in other unions. Then who knows what might happen? Maybe a McGovern will beat a Nixon next time."

"So '60s radicals end up as reformers."

"I never fit the mold, even then. Too much gadfly."

"Where's Joe Hunt getting his campaign money?" she asked.

Becker startled. She had shifted without warning. She was now a reporter probing a source.

"I don't know anything for a fact," Becker said. "I've heard he's hitting up companies that supply the Union with goods and services, hotels where the ACMU held conventions and Foster Shives' law firm. He spent hardly anything during the nomination round. Now, he's running TV ads everywhere, billboards, yard signs and radio spots. He's buying votes wherever he can. It's like someone dumped Fort Knox in his lap. This is not for quotation or attribution or to be used."

"How much could he shake down?"

"Jeep figured, maybe, 100 grand total. But this looks to be four or five times that much. Maybe it's his own money and Sonoski's. We can't figure it. Maybe you can. Do it quickly. If it's dirty money in some way, we need to let miners know about it."

"And speaking of rogue elements, how does it feel to be outed by Joe Hunt as an agent of the international communist conspiracy?"

"It was only a matter of time. I told Delucci all about Columbia when he asked me to help his campaign."

"The accusation will lose Delucci votes."

"We prepared for this. We'll do a statement first thing Monday. You know what I did and didn't do, and why. I broke a University window with a bag full of library books."

"It won't matter what you say to set the record straight or deny what you weren't then," she said.

"He has my signed letter of resignation. If he wants to throw me overboard in a close race, I won't blame him. No hard feelings from me. I'd probably do it were I him."

"Sure you would. Do you keep in touch with Gondleman, Cobb, Sedgwick, Fishbein—the Columbia people who went underground?"

"Nope. The last conversation I had with Gondleman was just before the '68 bust. I'm amazed the FBI can't find him. He would have had a hard time hiding in a closet from himself. His mug shot hangs in the downtown post office."

"I wonder how he manages," she said. "All of his IDs have to be fake. He can't work jobs that demand a valid Social Security number."

"I suppose he has to move before his false ID betrays him. I'd guess he's working temporary day jobs that pay cash and don't ask questions. Work that draws illegal migrants and ex-cons."

"But he'd need help wouldn't he?" she asked.

"He'd need safe houses where he could disappear when the FBI got close. His parents are probably getting money to him. Yes," Becker said, "he'd need people willing to take him in."

"I never saw him as somebody serious," she said.

"He was a Johnny-one-note," Becker said. "The times changed, and he found himself out at the far end of his political twig. Gondleman was not your cup of tea."

"Ick," she said. "Would you give him shelter?"

"No. I might help him move along. I oppose what he's done, but I'm not willing to turn him in. I don't claim there's any consistency to what I'm saying."

"Would you have taken in fugitive slaves or Jews running from the Gestapo?" she asked.

"I don't know. I hope I would have. They were victims. Rooky brought this dopey underground existence on himself."

"It could have happened to a lot of us," Allyson said.

"That's true. Celebrity is addictive. Now, he's just a memory. The Weather Underground is a cult, talking to themselves and not anchored in reality. In another decade, some graduate student will track Rooky down for an oral history. They trashed the student movement. Rooky didn't have the courage to leave when they decided to pursue terror tactics. He should have."

"In a few ways, it was the best of times," she said, "and the worst."

"I don't remember much of the best. I do remember you walking toward the cops on 114th, reassuring them you were a pacifist and wouldn't hurt them."

"It worked," she laughed. "They put me on a bus, took me to a Harlem police station and then let me go, because I hadn't done anything they could charge me with. Walking down West 114th with a black eye was not a crime."

"Yeah, it was."

"I bet I could find Gondleman and do a series for the paper," Allyson said.

"Don't," Becker said. "He's not worth it, and he wouldn't trust you to protect his cover."

"I'll give it some more thought."

472

"Are you still a feminist?" he asked.

"Yes, but lighter than before. I don't think men are the source of all problems with women, just a lot of them."

"It's hard to be married to a guy when you think that way."

"Depends on the guy," she said. "Men are changing for the better. We -- feminism and women's liberation -- forced them to."

"I agree on both counts. But it's been tough. A lot of divorces. Breakups. Us."

"Us," she said. "To some extent. There were other factors."

"Like what other factors?"

"It's getting chilly back here," she said. "We could have dessert in front of the fireplace."

"I assume you want a fire in the fireplace."

"A small one," she said. "Enough to see what we're looking at."

He got a fire started, then cleared the dishes and washed them. She retrieved her luggage from the rental car and changed into running shorts. She sat on the couch in front of the fireplace where she was warmed. Later, she handed a plate of cheesecake to him after he'd finished fiddling with and poking the burning wood. She sat next to him, her legs stretched out in front, parallel to his.

No, No, No, he told himself.

"I'm sorry," she said. "I know I wasn't fair to you. I know I hurt you. It hurt me, too."

Becker raised his eyebrows. "It was a long time ago."

"You were right about us," she said.

"I'm not looking to revisit the past," he said.

"Neither am I. Whatever is, is right now. And tomorrow."

She put her left hand lightly on his right thigh.

Becker jumped.

She moved her nails lightly down toward his knee, then up.

"What are you doing?" he said.

"Making amends," she answered.

He felt flushed, aroused and overwhelmed with her.

She put his hand on her bare thigh.

He knew she had him. Allyson led them into his bedroom.

Later, as they lay next to each other, she rolled next to him so that they touched from top to bottom: "I love you, Beck. I never stopped."

"It's the wine that's talking," he said.

"Fuck you."

"You just did," he said.

"And it was how I remembered us," she said.

"Agreed."

"I'm glad," she said.

"I didn't want this to happen," he said lamely. "I'm an idiot."

"Glad that's settled," she laughed. "We were young. We have history. It's true what I said, about loving you."

"But it doesn't work for us, day to day," he said. "We tried."

"That wasn't normal trying," she said, raising her voice. "It wasn't normal trying in normal circumstances. That was hippie make-believe."

"This Trip guy…"

"Kennedy Brown, not Trip."

"He's 'normal,'" Becker said. "He's your guy, not me."

"I want you," she said. "Come here," she said, reaching for him.

Becker tried to nudge the pinwheels out of his brain. She slept next to him. He looked at the clock. A little after 9 p.m.

He had missed her. She lit him up. It was what it was. He knew it. She knew it. This is bad. I'm more than a normal idiot, whatever that is. An idiot squared. Or cubed.

Allyson stirred. She opened her eyes and turned to him.

"Hey," she whispered.

"Hey."

She kissed him.

"My brains are on the floor," he said. "No more."

"You win more with a trifecta," she whispered.

"Uncle."

"Maybe later? This is fun. I miss you."

"I can't move," he said.

"I can."

"Allyson…what do you want?"

"I want you to go again. And if that doesn't interest you. I'll do the heavy lifting. Just lie there and tell me."

"Stop! Stop humming."

"Uh-uh."

He put his hands on her cheeks and lifted her up. She didn't go willingly and returned. He felt his eyeballs being pulled out of their sockets.

She rested her face on him. "I like this. So?"

Becker got control of his breathing, and then he said: "No, I'm not aware of any."

"What?"

"No, I'm not aware of any."

"What are you talking about?" she asked.

"I'm answering your question," he said.

"What question?"

474

"The question you haven't yet asked, but will."

"I'm just a girl who can't say no. What question are you talking about?" she asked.

"Do I know of any involvement by Jeep Delucci in the highway killing of Lazarro and Hyskra, the two guys from Pittsburgh?"

Allyson didn't say anything for several long minutes. She shifted, so that she was lying next to him face to face in the dark. They listened to each other's breathing, trying to interpret what the other's breath was saying.

"I think I should go," she said finally.

"I guess you should," he said.

"It's true what I said—about loving you."

"Sure," he said, "it's true. You love me in a way. And I love you. And we had something good working once. And I can't shake free of that. But you want to get to the other side; I don't give a shit about the other side. The other side is a trap. Ambition like yours kills."

"Who's running away this time?"

"Me," he said. "I know where you and I will end up. You'll break my heart again. Better not to get started."

"So what was this?" she asked.

"This was showing us what we lose, what we give up to keep ourselves functioning."

"I don't want us to stop," she cried. "Don't end this way for these reasons. Don't punish me now for what I did then. Stop using your head instead of your heart."

"Instead of my dick, you mean."

"Not fair," she said.

"Well, you did approach me along that path. Anyway, I can't stop using my head," he said. "Neither can you. That's why you would have asked about Delucci sooner or later."

She lay still and quiet. He said nothing.

"Okay," she said, swinging out of bed.

"I'll sleep on the couch," he said. "Or there are places to stay in Charleston."

"I'll drive home tonight."

"It's a long, five-hour drive," he said. "It's almost 10."

"It'll do me good."

She put on her work clothes. She collected her suitcase and purse.

As he walked her to her car, she kissed him: "I'm sorry, Beck. I'm sorry this didn't work."

"Me, too."

"You and I will drag this with us. It'll screw up both of us," she said.

"It has and will."

"So why are we doing this to each other?" she asked.

"Because the alternative is worse," he said.

Allyson drove the new, lonesome I-77 north to Cambridge, Ohio. Then she ran east on I-70, past Consolidation Coal Company's surface-mining shovel, The Mountaineer. With each dip, the huge electric machine, she had recently learned for a story, was removing 100 tons of rock and dirt that lay over the Pittsburgh No. 8 coal seam. The Mountaineer had to clear off several hundred feet of overburden to get to the five-foot-thick coal bed. Passing this roaring, 16-story-high tower of light in the darkness of southeast Ohio had to be, she thought, the high point of her sad drive back to Pittsburgh.

She cruised through the wide-open-but-very-safe Wheeling, West Virginia. The City had been the domain of Big Bill Lias, a 400-pound Greek who turned his hometown into a national center for Mafia-controlled prostitution and gambling. Lias died in 1970, but Allyson heard Wheeling was still as safe as a monastery for people who wanted to lose their money or get laid.

Allyson turned north onto Rt. 19 at Washington, Pennsylvania. Once in Upper St. Clair, she wound her way to Kennedy Brown's Tudor Revival on Salem Drive. It was 3.20 a.m.

She let herself in with her key.

Ken stirred when she padded into his bedroom.

"I'm here," Allyson said softly. "I'm home."

She took off her clothes and slid next to him.

He sensed something different.

She reached for him.

"I love you," she said.

"Good."

"I accept your proposal, gladly," she said.

He laughed. "I suppose I should ask you officially since you've already agreed."

"No need," she said. "I'm in."

"I have a ring," he said.

"Later," she said. "I don't care about rings." She reached for him, and he reached for her.

476

Chapter 35

Cinderella Holler, November 27, 1975, 8:45 a.m.

The television was now always on in the den, which smelled like the end of a long sickness. Its fake-walnut paneling was funereal. The couch with the transparent plastic cover had been moved out. The curtains were drawn against the cold.

Jeep sat on the edge of the rented hospital bed looking at his father's watery, sunken eyes. Jim Delucci had grown gaunt. His hip bones were visible through the white sheet. The skin of his face had shrunk against his skull.

"Glad I could give Mom a break," Jeep said.

"Thanks for that," his father said. "Juanita's carrying my load, for sure. Can!"

Jeep placed the Maxwell House can next to where his father was propped on three pillows. Jim struggled to eject the thick, black phlegm at the bottom of his throat. He moved it like a very old man working his way up a staircase with each step requiring the landing of both feet and a little rest. When he got the gob into his mouth, he spit it out in dribbles.

"Wipe."

Jeep handed him a moist towelette.

"Feels like I'm trying to cough up 50-weight motor oil that's been left out in January."

"Sorry, Daddy. Wish there was something I could do to make this easier."

"Take me up on a strip job and leave me."

"Can't do it, Daddy," Jeep said.

"Then load me my gun, an' by God I'll do it."

"Amounts to the same thing," Jeep whispered. "Can't."

"It'd be the right thang to do, honey."

"Doin' right thangs ain't simple," Jeep said. "Wrong is always simpler. I'm sorry."

"Wrong is simpler at first," Jim said after laying back on his pillows. "Right is easier in the end, harder at the start."

Jim reached for <u>The Charleston Gazette</u>. He picked it up in hands that had trouble picking it up.

Jim rattled the front section that carried Joe Hunt's confession. "Guys like Joe built the Union back in the '30s. I got in at the end of '37. The Union had been here for three or four years. The real rough stuff happened before me. So what if Joe kill't that superintendent 40 years back? They was a-tryin' to kill us. I remember my Daddy in '30, '31, '32, '33.

Workin' one or two days a week if he was lucky for food, poor as it was. We was hungry every day, every one of them years, every damn day."

"Joe might have pulled a win-the-election rabbit out of his hat," Jeep said. "Doubt many miners will think less of him."

"I sure as hell don't," Jim said. "Ya know, Jeepy, there was some guys in the Union back then -- *paesanos* -- who said everythin' should belong to everybody. Not comp'nies like we have. They was a *tribu* -- a tribe, sorta -- what believed in killin' the big bosses. They were secret, underground boys, not like a political party. Git ridda the priests, the Mussolinis, the Rockefellers. Had roots in It'ly. But they was also *antiorganizzatrice*, thought the Union was a compermize with the cap'alists. Opposed negotiating a labor contract, because they wanted to keep the right to improve working conditions and comp'sation whenever they felt strong enough to do so. Wanted to strike whenever they thought they had the upper hand. Some had been in the old Wobbly outfit, which I heard Daddy talk about. Some was like Sacco and Vanzetti—anarchists who never had no problem with a-killin' them what was a-killin' us. Neither did my Daddy, or me, too. Daddy knew 'em, but never joined. By the time I come up, they'd been run out of the mines and the Union."

"You think his story about Gallagher will lose him any votes at all?"

"Shit no, son. Even the lay preachers who work in the mines will let that particular bygone stay long gone. It'll win him some votes amongst the undecided, 'cause it shows the sorry bastard had some bone up his fat back once upon a time. But…"

"…but?"

"But no miner is gonna believe that fairy tale he told about squirrel huntin'."

"I figure it the same way, Daddy. You think the law'll git after him?"

"The law got nothin' to work with. No corpse—not a bone or a tooth. No murder weapon or witness. They got a statement from Joe Hunt that was not under oath. But there ain't no conviction without proof. The big coal comp'nies up there --AMSTEEL, in particular -- will tell the prosecutor to lay off, 'specially if they think Joe might beat you. Last thing they want is an ACMU president who spends his time screwin' around with a 42-year-old murder rap that ain't goin' nowhere."

"Becker tells me I should say nothin' about it."

"'Bout all you can do, Jeepy. A man can't load coal ifn he can't lay a shovel into it. And you don't have no shovel."

478

Chapter 36

Charleston, November 27, 1975, 9:02 a.m.

The phone rang on Becker's desk at Delucci's campaign headquarters on Washington Street. Becker looked out his window at the brick wall of the adjoining wig shop. Snow was falling between the buildings. A good wig might lift his spirits, he thought. Thursdays were always tough. He picked up.

"It's Dicey," Dicey Shuck said. "Girl reporter's on the phone."

"Julie Cogswell?"

"No, I think it's the one from Pittsburgh. Don't hear no holler in her voice."

"Shit."

"Yeah, I know."

Becker picked up. "Becker speaking."

"Jeffrey, I'm calling you on a professional basis."

He laughed. "Not in the market for what you're selling."

It took a couple of beats for Allyson to catch his insinuation. "That's beneath you."

"No it isn't. I'm about as low as I can get. Why do I want to talk to you about anything?"

"I'm a reporter covering a story. It's up to you to decide whether information you provide will benefit your client."

"Go ahead."

"Does the Delucci campaign, does Jeep Delucci believe Joe Hunt or his agents were involved in beating up Vernie Skeens?"

"We don't know any more about that than what The Charleston Gazette reported. That amounts to nothing more than the West Virginia State Police are still investigating."

Allyson persisted: "The two Pittsburgh men who attacked him have apparent Mafia connections up here. Does Jeep think the Mafia was involved?"

"I have no idea what he thinks about that," Becker said. "What are the *apparent* Mafia connections?"

"A source told me Lazarro and 'Bonk' Hyskra did jobs for Tony Bruno, the head of the Pittsburgh family, the old Pete 'Needles' Luparelli family. Like punching and kicking people."

"I have no information on that subject," Becker said. "By the way, you need more than an unquotable source to prove something."

"Does Jeep think these two Mafia associates were trying to intimidate his voters on behalf of Joe Hunt?"

"I don't know what he thinks about those two, or whether anyone was behind it." He paused and then lied some more: "I've never talked to him about that."

"Never?"

"Nothing beyond sharing facts as I knew them when I learned them."

"I see," she said, seeing more than she wanted behind his denial. "Okay, does the campaign have an opinion about Joe Hunt's revelation that he was 'involved' in the death of Frank Gallagher during the Fricktown strike?"

"The authorities may want to review the matter. We've only heard Joe's side of the story. Gallagher's side will never be known. There's zero forensic evidence. A lie-detector test, while not admissible in court, might shed some light. Was Joe offering this confession in an off-the-wall attempt to win votes? Who knows?"

"Good Jeffrey, a half-genuine answer, finally. Let's try this. Did anyone from Delucci's MDU campaign play any part in the car wreck on Lens Creek Mountain where Lazarro and Hyskra were killed?"

"That is the question from the other night. As you and the police know, Delucci's signature Jeep was stolen to make it look like Jeep had something to do with it. And as you and the police also know, I was with Jeep at Murad's until after 12. Other witnesses have corroborated our presence there. The State Police told Jeep that he is not being investigated as a person who might have been in his Jeep that night. Someone tried to frame him in my opinion. And maybe the mugging of Vernie Skeens was the first act in a two-act play to discredit Jeep and his campaign."

She laughed. "Let me get this straight. You think somebody sent those two guys to Logan and then had them killed to pin the two murders on Delucci?"

"It's a theory," Becker said from his best lawyerly persona. "The only fact I know is that I don't know what's behind it."

"Frank Stover -- Biggie -- could have 'stolen' the Jeep and pushed them off the road," she said. "That would have sent a stop-it message to whoever was behind the attack."

"That cheap-shot accusation disguised as a hypothetical has absolutely no basis in any evidence you have," Becker said. "And I want you to quote these exact words in your story." His right hand started to shake. "Anyone, including you, could have stolen Delucci's Jeep that night."

"Well," she said, "there have been no other beatings of Delucci's supporters. How do you explain that?"

"Coal miners are patriotic Americans who respect the law and support law enforcement," Becker said. "The only violence in this campaign has been committed by two thugs who have no connection to anyone in the ACMU election as far as I know."

Becker hoped that statement might possibly be sort of true.

480

"So who do you think was driving the Jeep that night?" she asked.

"You," Becker said with as straight a face as he could muster over the phone line. "You need a big story, and you'll do anything to get one to feed your ambition."

"Fuck you," she said.

"We've been down that road," he said. "More than once."

"You ruined it, not me," she shouted.

"That's not how I remember it." Becker felt himself sliding into "his stuff" with Allyson once again.

"You cut it off," she said.

"Not true."

"This time, not the first time," she said.

"Is this what you now think passes as a 'professional' interview by a professional reporter?"

"Fuck you," she said.

"Not any more. You need to take the Allyson show to another audience."

"Okay, Becker. So tell me. Where has Jeep Delucci gotten the money to fund his campaign over the last few weeks?"

"Not my department. I can't help you with that."

"Is it from the Mafia? Could they be funding both candidates?"

"The deep end in which you are now drowning doesn't have a bottom," he said. "Your own fantasies will kill you."

"Is that a non-denial denial?"

"Your questions do not deserve a response," Becker said with as much official indignation as he could dredge up from his own doubts. "A denial gives your wholly-imagined theory a smidgen of credibility it doesn't deserve. My advice is this: Either be a reporter and get the facts or move on to something else. Stop trying to boost your career on the cheap and lazy."

Allyson ignored his words since it was the best way for her to proceed. "One last question. Is there anything to this story that the American Bank of Washington is being sold?"

"Where did you hear that?"

"I can't reveal my source."

"More rumor. More anonymous sources. Go fish in another hole. I'm done."

Allyson composed herself. "You know what I think? I think you suspect Delucci and Stover hatched a plan to run those two Mafia thugs off Lens Creek Mountain. My guess is someone on Hunt's side connected with Tony Bruno who sent them to Logan County. They were told to administer a small beating, nothing more. A little rough stuff would signal MDU supporters to come back to Joe or face the consequences. And then Delucci figured he better stop this intimidation by sending a counter message to both Hunt and his own allies. I don't know who actually did the phony theft of the Jeep, but it has to be someone Jeep trusts with his life. Probably Stover. And I think Delucci kept you from knowing, because he doesn't trust you. And I think you're thinking exactly what I'm saying."

Becker had to smile. She had always had him.

"You have no witnesses, no evidence, no documents, no testimony, no 'nothin' to back up your guesses," he said. "Prosecutors often tell juries stories when they don't have facts to prove a case. Stories are plausible when you create them with motive and an internal logic. That's all you have, Allyson. A story, by the way, that occurred to the West Virginia State Police as well. Their investigation found no evidence to tie anybody in the MDU campaign -- including Jeep and Biggie -- to the wreck. That's the salient fact. *No evidence of any connection.* This 'guess' of yours doesn't really even rise to the level of a story. It's nothing but hunches. Maybe woman's intuition?"

He figured that would get her.

She didn't rise to the bait. "Becker, I hope you are not involved in this."

"It wouldn't matter to you if I were," he said. "You're sliding down this hill, gathering speed. You want a platform, a national megaphone. You always have. You think it's yours by divine right. Your ambition will leave damage in its wake."

Allyson let silence fill in the hole. "Becker," she pleaded.

He said nothing.

"Becker...I miss you."

"Right."

"We had glue."

"Yes, we did."

"Becker...."

"Goodbye," Becker said.

"I told Kennedy that I would marry him."

Becker closed his eyes. "Best wishes," he said and hung up.

He put the receiver down on its base. He placed his left hand over his right wrist and squeezed to stop the shaking. It helped, a little.

Allyson figured it the same way he had. His suspicions were now hers.

Somebody had fed her something about the Bank, but she didn't yet know that Chickie Siciliano was the buyer. The rest of her hunches would require a lot of dangerous digging. Maybe she would nail it, maybe not. If she got the story before December 5th, it would go national.

Allyson Pickering, it seemed, had volunteered to be the reporter Mort Blatnik wanted to break this story.

Ambition was driving her into the sharks. Ambition of a different sort, he now realized, and self-preservation were driving him as well. Just how much willful ignorance did he want to live with?

Thursday, Thursday, not so good to me, he thought. Or her.

Charleston, November 27, 1975, 8:05 p.m.

Becker accepted the cold Heineken Dark from Andrea Warner. He forced himself to smile, though he had nothing to smile about. Her husband, Thaine, sat in a large recliner drinking the same. Thaine rarely smiled even when something was funny. He never seemed to smile at Andrea who, Becker believed, had never been either funny or much fun. She projected an air of permanent disapproval.

Becker knew the Warners from their common membership in the West Virginia chapter of the National Lawyers Guild, the organization of left-of-center lawyers who ranged from liberal and progressive to socialist and communist, to the chronically dyspeptic and dysphoric. The majority of its 25 members were young lawyers who had moved to West Virginia in the late '60s and early '70s to work on labor, environmental and poor-people issues. A handful of native eccentrics rounded out the roster. The Warners graduated from the University of Pennsylvania's law school in 1970 with a keen-but-patient interest in social change and an intellectualized sympathy for revolutionary upheavals.

They chose to live in an integrated, lower-middle class neighborhood in Charleston's West End. Their two-story house had been built in the '20s. It was a sturdy, unremarkable brick. In Becker's opinion, it was suited for armed defense. He'd been there several times over the years for Guild meetings, followed by nourishing potlucks.

The living room was close but comfortably appointed. Thaine faced a new Montgomery Ward, 25-inch, solid-state color television. Becker sat at one end of their white linen sofa with Andrea at the other. Toys lapped at their feet.

"The kids are upstairs," Andrea said to her husband. She had majored in theater at Cornell. After being kicked around for a year on Broadway, she fled to law school.

"Contained?" Thaine asked.

"For the time being," she said. "They're watching 'Welcome Back, Kotter.' Their favorite show is 'Emergency!' on Saturday night."

"That's better than 'Saturday Night Live with Howard Cosell,'" Becker said. "He's dreadful."

"But he defended Ali publicly when he claimed conscientious-objector status," Thaine reminded all.

"Yes, Cosell defended Muhammad Ali," Becker said dutifully. "That doesn't make him a good broadcaster, just a decent guy on that issue."

Andrea nodded. "Jonathan, the four-year-old, says he wants to be a fireman. Ellen still wants to be a cowboy or a MASH doctor in Korea."

"No lawyers?" Becker asked.

"We're not encouraging either one to follow in our footsteps," Andrea said.

"The Guild will be disappointed," Becker said. "The Warners were supposed to be good for at least one legacy."

"Not that we're discouraging them going into law," Thaine added. "My Dad pushed me into the profession, but he never figured I'd turn class traitor."

"That's what a sociology major will do," Andrea added.

"It was more Vietnam than Veblen," Thaine said. "I guess I made my peace with a little conspicuous consumption."

"My Dad wanted me to follow him into the scrap business," Becker said, "until I got into Columbia. After that, he wanted me to stay away from any business he was in. I did run a cutting torch in the summers during high school. Chunking out rusty girders"

"A genuine working-class hero," Thaine laughed.

"It was the kind of semi-mindless grunt work where you had to pay attention to what you were doing or you'd get hurt. I dragged the cart around with the two tanks. Made the cuts. Breathed the fumes. Occasionally, I got to work the cranes with the magnet or the claw. It was hard work in the heat. I never felt ennobled."

"Heretic," Andrea said.

"You've never been doctrinally reliable," Thaine said. "We know that. So what's up?"

Andrea knitted her fingers around a mug of herbal tea.

Becker wanted to smoke, but the Warners were a no-smoking house. He knew Thaine smoked when Andrea couldn't catch him.

"I'm having doubts about what I'm doing with Jeep's campaign," Becker said.

"You mean the politics of what you're doing, working for reform in a union setting?" Andrea asked.

"No, not that part of it."

"Well, *that* is a difficult question in these times," she said emphatically. "Whether to work for reform or against it. Whether to work in electoral politics, or as a third party, or totally outside electoral politics."

"Our view is working on behalf of the working class is what we should be doing, whatever form it might take," Thaine said with the no-budge finality for which he was known.

"I understand your perspective," Becker said, "but, I guess, I'm not sure where the 'real' interests of the working class are right now."

"You're not saying that Joe Hunt should win because he's the better unionist, are you?" Andrea asked.

"Of course not," Becker sputtered.

"Delucci has more potential for progressive working-class leadership than Joe Hunt," Thaine said. "Clearly!"

"Yes, sure," Becker said. "It's like this. What if Jeep is not exactly who I thought he was when I signed on? Not exactly who you think he is."

"You're being opaque," Thaine announced.

"I'm being unclear, because I'm swimming in murk," Becker said. "I have questions."

"Such as?" Thaine asked.

"What I mean is, what if he okayed the murder of those two guys?"

"What do you know the cops don't?" Thaine asked.

"Nothing," Becker said. "I was with Jeep that night at Murad's. He could not have done it himself. But maybe Biggie or somebody else did. I did not hear Jeep say to anyone 'Kill them.' But I did not hear him say 'Don't kill them.' They were discussed, but nothing was decided. At least, I saw no decision."

"A no-call does not prove a murder," Thaine said quickly. "A no-call is a no-call."

"I know that," Becker said. "He and Biggie talked it over in the campaign office early that night. I sat in on it. They talked about striking miners shooting at company guards in the old days when the trees leafed out in the spring."

"So?" Thaine said. "No evidence of Delucci's involvement. No suggestion he authorized use of his vehicle. It's unsolved with no leads. And what if he did agree? Self-defense, if you ask me."

"Not in the law," Becker said. "A small detail, admittedly. It's accessory to homicide. Probably conspiracy."

"Self-defense in a broader sense," Thaine countered.

"This is old news," Andrea said. "I wouldn't lose sleep over it. If Delucci did have a 'working knowledge' of it, that's no reason to bail out. It shows focus, commitment, strength."

"What if these two Pittsburgh guys were Mafia?" Becker asked.

"I don't get it," Andrea said. "Do you think Joe Hunt made a deal with the Mafia to beat up Vernie Skeens?"

"It wouldn't trace back to him and his campaign," Thaine said.

"So what's in it for the Mafia?" Andrea asked.

"Well, Joe could have paid them for their services," Thaine said impatiently.

"What if it's something bigger?" Becker asked, mostly to himself. "What if the Mafia is now funding Joe's campaign?"

"Like the Teamsters," Thaine said.

"Right," Becker said. "They fund Joe's campaign, then they're inside the Union."

"All the more reason why we want Jeep to win," Andrea said.

Becker took a long, deep breath. "And what if the Mafia has also started funding Jeep's campaign?"

"What!" Thaine swore.

"You're kidding!" Andrea said.

"I don't know," Becker said. "Jeep has recently gotten a lot of money from somewhere. The first lift, I was told, came from Biggie taking out a mortgage on family land. Maybe…"

"Maybe that's where the second lift came from," Thaine said. "More of the same. Borrowed against collateral."

"So how is Jeep going to pay back those loans whether he wins or loses?" Becker asked.

"How much are we talking about?" Andrea asked.

"Two hundred for the first round that I know about, sort of," Becker said. "I'm guessing about three or four more recently, which I know nothing about."

"My God, Jeff," Thaine said, "He'd have to squeeze it out of the ACMU."

"Doesn't squeeze mean steal?" Becker asked.

"Let's not sit too high on our horse," Andrea said.

"He could touch up friends, appointees, vendors," Thaine said, draining his beer. "Maybe he and Biggie had savings."

Andrea looked at her husband. She spoke to Becker: "I hope you didn't go into this election thinking you'd come out with your virginity restored."

"When they interviewed me, they said they would worry about the money," Becker said. "The topic of my being reflowered was not raised."

"We don't know the Mafia is funding Delucci, do we?" Thaine asked hopefully.

"This has to stay in this room," Becker said. "Apparently, Joe Hunt made a deal to sell the American Bank of Washington, the Union's bank, to a Mafia front in the District, a guy named Chickie Siciliano who's working for Tony Bruno out of Pittsburgh. I got that from one of the former ABW directors who had just been booted off the Bank's board. Mob-friendly local business guys are coming on as replacements. Sold for $222 million! That's more than double or triple what it's worth. My guess is Joe got campaign money as part of his agreement to sell."

"So Joe's a crook," Thaine said. "Why does that tarnish Jeep?"

"What if Siciliano is hedging his bet?" Becker asked. "He gives Jeep the money he needs to stay in the race in return for Jeep agreeing not to make the sale of the bank an issue either during the campaign or after."

"You don't *know* this," Thaine said. "Maybe Biggie will just forgive the two loans and pay off his bank by selling some land."

"What you say is possible," Becker said. "And I don't know anything for certain, but…"

"But…?" Andrea said.

"But what if the Mob also wants to use the ACMU's health and retirement money the way they used the Teamsters Central States? Rip it off for their 'investments.'"

"You don't know this either," Thaine said.

"Correct."

"What if the Mafia is planning on getting most of its $222 million paid for the Bank out of the Union?" Becker asked.

"How?" Andrea asked.

"Squeezed," Becker said. "Slowly."

"If Biggie's funding Jeep, he'd have to sell his land to a coal company like UNICOAL or AMSTEEL," Thaine said.

"So Jeep gets into office on the dollars coming from either the Mafia or the coal operators," Becker said. "Great."

"Whether Delucci wins or loses, the sale of the Bank means the Mafia has its hooks in the Union," Andrea said.

"And if the Mafia captures the Union that's the end of Jeep's ideas on union democracy—members voting on contracts, due-process rights, accountability on Union finances and fair play," Becker said. "It's Hoffa at the Teamsters redux."

"Unbelievable," Andrea said.

"Have you asked Delucci about this?" Thaine asked.

"No."

"Then, it's just speculation," Andrea said.

Becker bristled. "No. The sale of the ABW to Siciliano's group isn't. A big chunk of cash into Delucci's campaign a few weeks ago isn't. Cash into Joe's campaign isn't. Two dead guys on Lens Creek Mountain isn't." Becker threw up his hands.

Thaine looked at his wife.

"This isn't for us," she said.

Becker looked at Thaine who was two years older and described himself to a select few as a "revolutionary." "I'm not asking you to *do* anything."

"Look, Jeff, we're idea people, not guerrillas in the hills shooting fascists," Thaine said. "We're intellectual workers, revolutionary facilitators. We read—books, articles, manifestos, memos, cases, labels. We're smart about words and concepts but not particularly about people. Ideas to us have an intrinsic historical rightness or wrongness, based in our theories about how relations between the classes operate. We think a 'correct idea' will win eventually. But Delucci and his campaign are largely about people and less about ideas. He's not about a correct theory."

"Okay," Becker allowed.

"What Thaine's saying," Andrea explained, "is we're lawyers like you. We use the law to help people and do what we think is right. You should have known when you joined the MDU campaign that Delucci was an ambitious politician, a guy driven less by ideas and more by his own self-interest. He's not like us. History may work through him, but he's not looking at it that way."

Thaine added: "The Deluccis of the world slip ideas into gear, but they're never smoothly synchronized with the interests of the working class. So there's a lot of grinding, slippage and wear. Correct ideas get changed, even deformed. You can't expect more of Delucci than for him to do what he's going to do. He's not historical like Andrea and me."

"Thaine and I accepted our limited roles as change-agents when we chose to be lawyers," Andrea said. "Sometimes we can nudge the law correctly; sometimes, not. We made our decision to express our politics through the law. You did too, I suppose."

"I saw the law as a tool," Becker said, "which could be used for some things but not everything. I wanted people to tell me how to use it, not me, the lawyer, tell them. But I'm now in a position of not using the law for anything. If union reform starts out corrupted, it's pointless to do it. If I do nothing, I'm a part of the swindle."

"We rarely have the luxury to be highly moralistic about the work we do," Thaine said.

"I'm being put in the position of an accomplice," Becker said.

"Don't be so prissy and self-indulgent," Andrea scolded.

"The question is whether you are doing something that moves the forces of History in the correct direction or not," Thaine said. "We don't get to pick our moment in History or who its flawed agents might be."

"Look at my practice," Andrea said. "I do child custody, divorces, Social Security disability and black-lung compensation cases. It's not revolutionary work, but it's politically useful. I get to talk with a lot of regular people."

"And it *is* a living," Thaine added. "I do the same. It pays for the new idiot box, which is nice for Sunday football games. We try to pick up some union work, small AFL unions. Tame stuff. Nothing cutting edge. But it is advancing the working class, such as it is. We do political work in the community—talking, educating and answering quick legal questions for free."

"Maybe I should do contested divorces for rich people rather than play a part in what may be happening in this election," Becker said.

"No," Thaine said.

"Thaine is correct—no," Andrea said.

488

"You need to be disciplined about this work," Thaine said.

"Why *are* you managing Delucci's campaign" Andrea asked.

"I wanted to leave a small scratch on the mirror of history."

"Very poetic," Andrea said, "but diamonds cut glass, and you, Jeffrey, are not one of history's diamonds."

"Right, as always, Andrea," Becker said. "Whether or not I leave a scratch really doesn't matter. What matters is that I gave it a swipe."

"You're such a liberal idealist," Andrea said. "It's so weird to still hear these ideas being spoken."

"Should I try to answer these questions I have?"

Thaine went to the kitchen and got a second beer. "I wouldn't. Let the class struggle sort it all out."

"What does that mean?" Becker asked.

"It means, let the process decide the outcome."

"You're not guilty of anything as long as you're ignorant of whatever might be going on," Andrea said."

"That's ridiculous. I'm not ignorant," Becker said.

"Hey, look," Thaine said, "if you want purity, go teach Latin at St. Paul's and wear a bow tie for the rest of your life. Grow up!"

"What Thaine means," Andrea said with more gentleness than she typically invoked when telling others what her husband meant, "is that it's important to do what you can with what's at hand even if it's not what you think is best."

"No what Thaine means," Becker said to her, "is that an ideological end justifies scummy means. The idea of Heaven or utopia justifies murder. That's Stalinism." He put his empty bottle down on a coaster and got into his jacket. Then he went into the kitchen and tossed the bottle into the recycled glass bin.

"Don't go," Andrea said.

"I'm sorry I worried you with this. Bad decision on my part. Keep what I said in this room, please."

"Of course," Andrea said. "Thaine?"

"Yes, I understand," Thaine said.

"Jeff, I'm glad you talked this over with us," Andrea said.

"Me, too," Thaine said.

"Thanks for the beer."

Chapter 37

Charleston, November 27, 1975

Peter Dance Shortbridge walked into the second-floor family quarters of the Mansion ready to eat a late supper.

The Governor was pleased the three-week-long wildcat strike was settled. He was glad the American Eagle widows and survivors had gotten satisfactory settlements, whatever they might be. He predicted to himself this money would bring 100 drooling scammers and 200 coalfield Romeos to their doorsteps.

With the strike ended, coal sales on the spot market might surge. The price for both thermal and metallurgical coal was rising, not falling as economists predicted. With renewed production, West Virginia would be collecting more tax revenue, and miners would start pumping their paychecks into the State's businesses. In another week or two, everything would settle into familiar routines. Coal would be sent out on trains and barges. Miners would be making payments on houses and pickup trucks. The poor would be scraping along as they always did, waiting for the next ripple of life to break their loose grip on stability. Normalcy, The Governor thought, would return to West Virginia, a normalcy that produced chronic abnormality in his private opinion.

Nobody had been killed during the strike—that was good. And nothing had blown back in his face. He could not take credit for the negotiated settlement, but he hadn't gotten in the way. He hadn't said anything dumb or shot himself in his political foot. Sometimes, he thought, even I catch a break. He poured a glass of white wine from the decanter on the sideboard.

In his briefcase, however, well, he needed to talk to Nancy.

"The kids are eating in the den," she said as she walked in. He pecked her; she pecked him.

He tried to read her mood. If touchy, he would be especially polite and inoffensive during their meal. The Governor understood his ability to read Nancy Waring Shortbridge's emotional semaphores was below average. But all women were like that, at least, he was like that with all women. He had thought her to be smart and calmly objective when they were dating. He had never seen her volatile, or cross, or aggressive, or mean, or emotional, or pig-headed or small-spirited. She had shown all those sides as the years passed. Maybe a little crazy was just part of adult womanhood; how was he supposed to know? He was The Governor, not a psychiatrist for women.

He learned she was very sensitive about her looks. Her face had grown less cut after two pregnancies. Her figure was too full for his taste, which he would never say to her. Two weeks ago, he noticed she had shortened her hair and added blond streaks or frosting, or whatever that stuff was called. He hated streaks, or icing or whatever it was. He took it as a sign of middle age. Of late, she seemed to be losing patience with him. He hadn't changed. He didn't understand why women changed while men like him didn't.

They sat at opposite ends of a triple-pedestal, four-leaf, Regency mahogany table. His mother had shipped it from New York on his inauguration. She called the 24-seat table "The Old Board," because it came from what The Governor called "Mother's ancestral stash." He hated it. When he sat at its head, it felt as if he was playing goalie at one end of a hockey rink while his wife guarded his opponent's net. "It's just wasting in the storage barn, Peter," his mother announced in rejecting his objections. His mother hated family furniture in storage.

Opal Smoot, the long-serving head of the Mansion's kitchen staff, brought their supper out on a cart, kept warm under Edwardian sterling silver dish covers from James Dixon & Son. His mother had shipped them as well, because they were "just tarnishing from staff neglect in the barn. Your people can keep them bright." Opal was miffed that the Shortbridges had snubbed "her" West Virginia dish covers.

"Wasn't our good silver good 'nuff for them?" she'd asked her husband, Franklin, who replied, "Guess not."

But Opal did admit: "I never had to ask him: 'Is you quality, or does you stack?'" Franklin laughed at her joke. Both knew this Governor had never stacked.

Opal came with the Governor's Mansion, but it was more accurate to say the Governor's Mansion came with her. She ran the show, knew everything and forgot nothing.

"Thank you, Opal," The Governor said. He peeked under the cover. "Good, I'm in the mood for grilled salmon and string beans. Could I have a rasher of bacon, please?"

"A rasher of one strip," Nancy interjected.

"One strip, yes, Miz Shortbridge. I'm watchin' his heart, too, ma'am," Opal said. Then she said under her breath: "Made peppermint ice cream for you today, Gov'nah."

The Governor's wife was both miffed and resigned to her husband's juvenile weaknesses. At least, he didn't chew bubble gum in public.

"If I wasn't already married, Opal, you know you would be my first choice."

Opal kept her eye roll to herself. "You never know about these things, Gov'nah," Opal allowed as she retreated through the door into the kitchen. "Never do know."

"You might not be *her* first choice," Nancy observed under her breath.

The Governor paused. He heard her tone. He sounded high alert to himself. Was this about peppermint ice cream, one strip in a rasher or two, or the continuing unspoken grievance of having married above herself financially but below herself intellectually? Was this about him being Governor and on his way, or her not being Governor and not on her way except by his side? Was this her first jab in an impending fight? He hoped not. He fervently hoped not.

"So how did it go today?" he asked with more neutrality than any mediator could muster.

"I cut the ribbon on the new elementary school in Belle. It perks up the town...a little. Everyone thanked you *in absentia*."

"Belle," he said.

"Well, it isn't very belle."

"Yes. It isn't very," he repeated.

"The DuPont chemical plant permeates the air there," she said. "The head of the PTA whispered to me to avoid the iced tea served at the coffee-cake reception. I can only imagine what DuPont is dumping into the Kanawha River at their Belle plant."

"Yes. I've seen some reports. Benzene is bad. It smells sweet. The EPA and my guys work with DuPont in a manner of speaking. They don't like us telling them what they can and can't do. It's an old plant, built in 1926. I don't want them to leave the State. Their Parkersburg plant may be even worse on water. They could, you know, just shut the whole darn thing down. It could make tax sense for them."

"Did you know that DuPont makes phosgene at Belle—poison gas. Its for polyurethane and pharmaceuticals. But the PTA woman said the odor today was something else. She wasn't sure what it was."

"The locals are used to it, I'm sure," The Governor said. "The smell, that is. They work there; they know. Don't you remember what we were told the first time we were driven through Nitro on I-64 past the FMC, Monsanto and Pike chemical plants? 'That stink is jobs. That smell is money. Take a deep breath. This is what keeps the Chemical Valley alive.'"

"I do remember," she said. "It made me wonder whether we made the right decision to come here. Cancer rates are significantly higher in Charleston and Kanawha County than in the State and nationally. I so loved Palo Alto."

"Charleston's getting a little better. We know more about pollution now than we did even a few years ago," he said. "DuPont says all the excess cancer is mostly caused by unhealthy lifestyles—biscuit-and-gravy diets, tobacco, lack of exercise, risky behaviors."

Nancy Shortbridge looked at her husband in hope he had been trying to make a joke.

"Monsanto makes the components in Agent Orange. Dioxin dust is all over Nitro," she said after accepting that he hadn't been. "And Oscar Pike blows up his plant at least once a year."

492

"He *is* like Old Faithful. Oscar doesn't like regulations that impede his 'sovereign right' to operate his business the way he sees fit," The Governor said. "He belongs in this Valley 100 years ago. I've had to sit through several of his rants."

"Chemical Valley!" she spat it out. "What's it doing to us, to the kids? Shortbridge kids are not immune to chemicals in the air and water. Cancer doesn't know us from all of the Dwayne and Dreama Shiftlesses who live a mile from here."

"Everything doesn't cause cancer," he said.

She slowed: "Peter, we can't escape what's around us. It's worse than strip mining, because it's everywhere. We both know that. Saying nothing about something you know is dangerous to us condones and absolves it. Doing nothing lets it continue."

"You wanted me to get elected, didn't you?" he asked pointedly and with some anger. "Shutting up about stripping was the price I paid to get the coal operators to stay out of the race. You knew that. Same with the chemical companies on air and water. You told me to make the deal."

"Go ahead, blame me!"

"I'm not blaming you. I'm just saying we both knew what I was doing. If I double-cross them now, they'll take away our future. Anyway, we know enough to not drink tap water in West Virginia. Problem solved."

"For us," she said.

"Look, Nancy. The food's getting cold. We're not going to reinvent the wheel here. Shall we start eating?" The Governor picked up his salad fork.

She sat still.

"Well, that was my day. You?" she asked.

"Nothing much. I met with the usual folks from the Legislature on the budget for next year. There *was* something that came in today that might interest you."

She raised her eyebrows.

"A report from the Criminal Investigation and Prevention section of the State Police arrived. Bob Redbone -- Colonel Bob -- brought it by."

"And?"

"They concluded the Lens Creek Mountain episode six weeks ago was a double homicide. Those two Pittsburgh fellows—somebody deliberately pushed them off the road using Delucci's Jeep."

"Wait," she said. "Who were they?"

"You mean their names?"

"No, Peter. Why would I want to know their names? Who *were* they, sociologically, occupationally? Why did they beat up that coal miner in Logan?" She heard herself straining to be patient.

"They're associated with a reported Mafia leader named Anthony Bruno in Pittsburgh. Maybe it's Alberto, not Anthony. It's one of those

Italian first names -- Angelo, Alphonso, Anzio -- something like that. Mother had an Italian gardener for years, Pasquale. Wouldn't use a power mower. Cut the whole lawn with a push mower. Huge biceps."

"Peter."

"Took him two days. Yes. The two were described as doing 'odd jobs' for this Bruno fellow. But they don't appear to be full-fledged Mafia members, according to Colonel Bob."

"So why," she asked, "were these two Mafia men from Pittsburgh in Logan? They didn't just wander into southern West Virginia and pick out a Delucci ally randomly. Who sent them? Who was paying them?"

"Colonel Bob said his FBI sources believe Bruno would have sent them. They don't appear to be independent contractors who freelance for whoever pays them."

"So why would this Bruno want them to beat up a Delucci supporter? Did Joe Hunt get Bruno to do this for him? Did the FBI check to see whether they could find a payment from Hunt or the Union to Bruno?"

"Yes, they did. They found no money trail between Hunt or the Union and Bruno's accounts. They looked."

"It's cash, Peter! Cash doesn't show up in checking transactions."

"I know that."

"Does Colonel Bob think Bruno did this on his own? His good criminal deed for the day? A whim? As a 'favor' to Hunt? What's a Mafioso's motivation in this? Why did he send them to beat that guy, but not too much, just a little?"

"Colonel Bob doesn't know why this was done this way."

She thought about that answer. "Shit like that doesn't just happen, Peter. This was not a couple of local rednecks fighting after getting drunk at a bucket-of-blood beer joint."

"I'm sure you're right, sweetheart. We simply don't know what was going on or is going on. At least, they didn't kill this Skeens fellow. Broke his arm or his nose. Something. Kind of a warning shot if you ask me."

"They were making a point by *only* breaking his arm. And then a counterpoint was made when their car was pushed off a mountain."

"I'm afraid the police have no suspects in the two Lens Creek homicides, murders, I guess, is how I should put it."

"Any suspected suspects?" she asked.

"It wasn't Delucci. He has a solid alibi and disinterested witnesses to support it, including Jeffrey Becker. The lawyer who's running...."

"I know who Becker is," she said. "Delucci's campaign manager! 'Disinterested!' Obviously, Becker would tell the cops Delucci had nothing to do with a double murder. What do you expect? Becker's a paid alibi!"

"My cops interviewed at least a half dozen witnesses at that Washington Street bar. They saw both Delucci and Becker there until around midnight. The cops say the car crash happened between 10 and 12, probably around 11 p.m. Neither Delucci nor Becker could have been in the Jeep when it was used in the crime."

"They got someone to do their dirty work," she said.

"It's possible," The Governor said. "But there's no witness to the actual crime, Colonel Bob said."

"Did the cops interview Delucci and Becker?"

"Yes, both of them. Nothing."

"They're smart," she said. "Of course, they provided nothing. They'll get away with it."

The Governor picked at his fish. "Someone might get away with it. The cops have no way of showing Delucci was behind whoever was in his car. There's no evidence to even suggest that. So why are you so invested in this? They were just two Mobsters. Who cares, really?"

"You should care, for one. Delucci is a young politician. He's a pretty face for a West Virginian if you like his type. He's a good public speaker. He's a liberal Democrat like you. His pro-labor credentials in a working-class state are, shall we say, more authentic than yours. If he wins this union election, he might be coming after your seat, your career."

"He doesn't have any money," The Governor said. "He's just a coalfield kid. How would he fund a primary run against me? He'd never be competitive. He couldn't buy the slates the way I can."

"If he's Union president, he'll steal the damn money out of the ACMU!"

The Governor looked at his cold string beans. He pushed several into a bundle with his fork. Then he pushed them back, separating them. He knew that voice. "Well, it is a free country. I can't stop Delucci from becoming a candidate in the future."

"But you *can* push Redbone to connect Delucci to the two murders."

"But Colonel Bob and the FBI were unable to make any connection between Delucci and the two homicides. Look, I brought the report home. Read it tonight if you're so interested. There's no evidence connecting Delucci to the car wreck."

"Peter, his personal vehicle did the killing! That is not a coincidence. Use your head!"

"Delucci reported it stolen that night," The Governor said with a little testiness.

"Someone in the Delucci campaign used his Jeep while he and Becker were manufacturing a defensible alibi. They wanted to make it look like it was Delucci at first blush, but then suspicion would point away from him after investigation. This is smart. Becker probably cooked this up."

"There were no witnesses, Nancy, to either the crime or whatever planning preceded it."

"It's the witnesses who did it! Why don't you have the Kanawha County prosecutor convene a grand jury. Get Delucci and Becker to answer questions. See what comes out. Offer Becker immunity in return for testifying against Delucci. If you want an apple to fall, Peter, you have to shake the fucking tree."

"Very good trope," he said.

"Listen to me. You can't be Passive Petey about this. A prosecuting attorney can get a grand jury in this State to indict a lollipop for oral sex!"

"Shhhh."

"It doesn't even matter whether Delucci and Becker did anything criminal," she said. "What's politically important in the public's mind is that a prosecutor figures they did. Put them on trial. It doesn't matter whether they're convicted. What matters is they've been forced to defend themselves. What matters is they've been indicted, which means the State of West Virginia thinks they're guilty of a crime like murder. Put them on trial, and you may get one to turn against the other. That's the way you'll find the guy who was driving the Jeep that night."

"I see your argument," The Governor said, staring at his half-empty wine glass. "But the Kanawha prosecutor has to have some reason to allege that Delucci was involved. That's my point. We have nothing to work with!"

"It doesn't matter! He has Delucci's car as the murder weapon. That should be enough!"

"It isn't. That's what the report says."

"Were there any signs of forcible entry into the Jeep? Like a broken window."

"Yes. The driver's side window was broken out."

"...to make it look like a car theft," she said, her voice rising.

"Well, if it looks like one maybe that's just what it was," he said. "And the ignition was hotwired."

"To show it was a theft," she said, "not an inside job."

"Well, they found a magnetic key holder tucked inside the front bumper with a key in it. If it was an inside job, wouldn't the guy have used the key, which he knew was there?"

I can't fix stupid, Nancy thought to herself.

"If it was an inside job," she said, "the guy would *not* have used that key, because that would have shown it was an inside job."

"Well, yes. I suppose. Right. It certainly could have happened as you say. But isn't it more likely someone from Hunt's campaign stole Delucci's Jeep to pin the murders on him? Doesn't that make more sense than Delucci setting himself up to provide an alibi?"

As he finished, The Governor realized Nancy had the more plausible explanation.

496

"That's a superficial theory," she said, violating her rule of never talking down to him. "How could a Hunt guy know where Delucci left his car? How would he know that Delucci and Becker would stay at the bar until midnight, leaving the Jeep parked and ready to be plucked?"

"Well, probably not," The Governor conceded. He palmed his forehead, hoping to rub out a pain that was building fast.

"What I would do," Nancy said, "is bring Delucci and Becker in front of a grand jury on a conspiracy charge involving an as-yet-unknown third party who actually did the murders. Nothing bad can happen to you from that. Promise Becker immunity."

"Let me think it over. This is a Kanawha County matter, not something for my Attorney General. I don't want my prints on any of this."

"Will you actually follow through?"

"I will think about it," The Governor said.

Nancy Waring Shortbridge told herself to curb her tongue. He moved her sometimes from frustration to overwhelming anger, which she knew she had to keep under control. And then she blew.

"Peter. As you know," she said in a low, menacing voice, "I do not want to spend the rest of my life in this God-forsaken dump of a city. This place, this State, makes me crazy. Everything is upside down, inside out and always backwards. Breathing the air is dangerous. Drinking the water. Driving these fifth-rate roads in a fourth-world colony!"

"Keep your voice down."

"It is down. It's like living in a sheltered workshop where the clients are too stupid to know where they are and why they're here."

"Honey, the staff! It's not that bad."

"No, Peter, No. I've put in five years here. Your promise -- our deal -- was 10 and out, one way or the other. The Senate seat will be vacant in 1978. I want my ass sitting in Georgetown in January, 1979. To run for the White House, you have to do the Senate first. A governor of West Virginia amounts to nothing in national politics. You're just an amusing oddity, a rich kid slumming in a Brooks Brothers suit with a jug of moonshine for a prop. National voters have to have a reason to take you seriously. You have to get Senate credibility. Any idiot can be elected governor of West Virginia."

"Thanks."

She did not pause. "I don't want to see Delucci's name on the Democratic primary ballot in 1978. His or anybody's but ours. That Senate seat belongs to me. I've earned it. We've earned it. It's our time."

"Let me think about this report a bit more. I just got it this morning."

"Peter!"

"Honey, if I'm perceived to be targeting Delucci, it could backfire with the voters. They'd want him in 1978, not me. Anyway, I don't think I

497

am that much against Delucci. He'd be better than Joe Hunt. Don't you think?"

"I give up," Nancy said. "I don't care whether Delucci would be better than Hunt. I care about you, about us, about getting on with it, about getting out of here."

"I'm not worried about the Senate seat. I'll line up the county machines. They didn't knife me like the first time I ran for governor, because I paid the 'Shortbridge premium.' The local thieves honored their bribes.

"I patched things up with the old fossils. I stopped talking about abolishing strip mining. Smithers and Roberson put the word out that I would work with them. I keep their taxes low, shut up about stripping and give them just a little *pro forma* grief about air and water pollution, coal ash and waste dams like Buffalo Creek. That's the bargain that successful politicians have to make here. I don't press them too much, and we get on with the plan.

"My money would kill Delucci in a Democratic primary just like Kennedy money killed Humphrey in 1960. And Delucci would have a narrow base of support in a general Senate election. West Virginia has elected pro-labor governors and senators like me but never an actual union man."

"I don't disagree with what you just said. But I'm a girl who strips risk out of investments."

"Including me," he observed without rancor.

"Yes, including you, us."

"The best thing for us is to sit on this report. If Delucci wins, maybe I can get a prosecutor to take it to a grand jury and bring Delucci and Becker in."

"So what about the quaint old notion of duty?" Nancy asked. "There were two murders. You are, after all, The Governor."

"Timing, Nancy, timing. I can take Delucci down after their election if that needs to be done. No need to do it now. I don't want to look opportunistic or self-promoting. I shouldn't be seen as meddling in their election. I have to be subtle."

She snorted but said nothing. Then: "Does Delucci have a friend, someone like that Luca Brasi in 'The Godfather' who does Corleone's dirty work? Might that someone be the third party, the driver?"

"There is this big kid named Stover, Frank, I think, who grew up with him. Served in Vietnam together, I'm told. He was a pro wrestler around Charleston. He's Pancho to Delucci's Cicso Kid. Maybe him?"

"Did the cops question Stover?"

"Yes, I looked."

The Governor rose and retrieved the report from his briefcase. He thumbed into the Index.

"Hang on. Page 43. Stover says he drove home to Boone County, leaving Delucci's headquarters about 7. His wife confirmed his arrival about 8 p.m., 'or thereabouts, I wasn't runnin' a clock on him.' Then he read 'some' in a Louis L'Amour western and went to bed around 11, maybe a little later. I like those westerns, too. Not sure how you break that alibi if an alibi it is."

"Was there any physical evidence in the Jeep—like hair, or fingerprints, or anything when they found it?"

"Jeep left prints and hair. Naturally. But nothing else on the steering wheel or the driver's side. Wait. There was something. They found boot tracks, size nine, the report said, next to the Jeep. I've seen that Stover. He'd wear a size nine on one toe."

"Peter, murders just don't happen! Someone did this! Someone knows about it. Probably more than one someone! Who has more motive to take those two out than Delucci and Becker? I would call in the pros from the FBI."

"Redbone would pitch a fit," The Governor said. "Whatever physical evidence our cops found has already been turned over to the FBI for analysis. The murders don't seem to have violated any federal laws, so there's no justification for getting the FBI involved. I don't think their civil rights were violated unless the murders were racially motivated, which I doubt since the two victims were white."

"DO SOMETHING, ANYTHING! GODDAMN IT!"

The Governor looked at his string beans, then the kitchen door. If these were magic Jack beans, he thought, he could escape her, climb a stalk and find a goose that laid golden eggs. Forget the golden eggs; escape would be good enough. No, no, he thought, you can't throw cooked beans out and expect a stalk. Stalk-growing beans have to be the little, dry things you stick in the ground. He heard rustling behind the door—maybe his rasher. Opal was back there, along with her four kitchen workers, listening while pretending not to. Opal, he hoped, would make sure their lips were sealed even though their ears were wide open.

Opal brought out The Governor's bacon.

The Governor had suffered Nancy's flailings before. He had come to accept a marital fact: His wife was embittered by having to crew a boat with an undersized sail to launch her ambitions. In light wind, it didn't go very fast. In heavy wind, he pointed into it and luffed.

Nancy would get control of herself in a bit. He just had to talk calmly and wait.

"Thanks Opal," he said as she turned to go back through the kitchen door.

He waited. "Honey, I don't care if Delucci had those two men killed. The world is better off without them. I don't like Mafia criminals—like those greaseballs I had to pay in Wheeling and Clarksburg."

"Peter, don't be your father. Take your balls out of your pocket!"

"It's time to use my head, not my cannon," he said with deliberate restraint.

She considered that image without comment.

"This is like living in a William Hamilton cartoon," she said with resignation.

"Who?"

"William Hamilton. He draws for The New Yorker about people like you, us, I guess. Andover. Yale."

"Oh him. Mother finds him distasteful. Why mock the people who make America successful? I would never foul my own nest!"

Wrong horse! The words lit up like neon in her brain. He's the wrong fucking horse. You can't be a pussy and be president. You have to believe in something, some damn thing, care about it enough to risk everything.

She found her composure. Sometimes she could get him to do the smart thing and sometimes not. She tried. What else could she do with him?

"Let's finish. Then you can eat your peppermint ice cream," she said.

"Thanks," he said. "That Pancho was real funny, don't you think? I liked him better than Cisco."

Chapter 38

Charleston, November 28, 1975, 9:30 a.m.

"Mr. Becker, this is Charlie Frazier over at <u>The Gazette</u>. The AP is carrying a story by Allyson Pickering at the <u>Pittsburgh Post-Gazette</u> this morning. Have you seen it?"

"No," Becker said into his office phone.

"Can I bring a copy over for your comment?"

"I'll send someone over to pick it up. That'll give me a chance to try to get a response from Jeep to whatever she's written."

"You might show it to Mr. Stover as well," Charlie said.

"Why is that?"

"Well, Mr. Becker, Mr. Stover is a major part of her story."

Shit, Becker thought. Shit!

"I'll try to get back to you," Becker said. "Can't promise anything right now. Jeep isn't here. Neither is Biggie…Mr. Stover."

"I'll be working on a local follow-up until eight or nine tonight," Charlie said. "We'll be running something in tomorrow's paper."

"I have your number, and you have mine."

Becker figured he should be sitting when Dicey Shuck handed him the sealed <u>Gazette</u> envelope 30 minutes later. He read the headline:

Did ACMU Candidate Delucci Okay Two Murders?
UNICOAL Offers Pal $2.5 Million For Coal Rights

"What!" he said before reading the first paragraph:

> CHARLESTON, WVa.—Mineworker presidential candidate James "Jeep" Delucci from Boone County, W.Va., may have played a role in an unsolved vehicle wreck that claimed the lives of two Pittsburgh-area residents, George "Bonk" Hyskra and Louis "Little Louie" Lazarro, around 11 p.m. on October 5th, according to a source with knowledge of Delucci's reform-oriented campaign in the American Coal Miner's Union.
>
> West Virginia law-enforcement investigators believe the two men attacked Logan County, W.Va., Delucci-supporter Vernon S. Skeens at his home earlier that evening. Skeens suffered a broken arm and nose.

Sources within the Pittsburgh Bureau of Police have long-believed Hyskra and Lazarro were low-level enforcers for western Pennsylvania organized crime, commonly known as The Mafia.

Delucci's 1974 CJ-6 red Jeep was reported stolen that evening. West Virginia State Police determined his vehicle was used to push the Pittsburghers' Cadillac off fog-shrouded Lens Creek Mountain. Both men perished at the scene of the fiery crash about a 30-minute drive south of Charleston on Rt. 119.

The Jeep had been "hotwired," and the driver's-side window broken out.

Delucci's Jeep was later found some 20 miles from the crash scene. An indentation on the Jeep's front bumper matched an indentation on the Cadillac's rear bumper.

West Virginia investigators found no evidence Delucci was in his vehicle at the time it rammed the Cadillac driven by Hyskra.

A number of witnesses placed Delucci at Murad's Grill in Charleston from approximately 7:30 p.m. to midnight. Delucci was accompanied during that time by his campaign manager, Jeffrey Becker, a Charleston lawyer and Pittsburgh native.

A source requesting anonymity said "Jeep could have authorized the use of his vehicle to attack Hyskra and Lazarro, but there's no evidence that he did. Anyone could have stolen his car to commit a crime that was set up to point toward him as the perpetrator, including you [this reporter]."

West Virginia police have been unable to develop any leads as to the Jeep's driver. No evidence has been found to suggest any person was in the Jeep at that time other than the unknown driver.

West Virginia authorities consider these fatalities to be a double homicide.

Investigators are searching for the identity of the Jeep's driver as well as an explanation for why Hyskra and Lazarro attacked Skeens.

Pittsburgh detective, Art Greiner, said: "These two guys [Hyskra and Lazarro] don't do this kind of stuff out of the blue or for kicks. Someone told them what to do to Skeens, how to do it and when to do it. Someone paid them. Someone had a reason to start something like this in the middle of this mineworker election."

At this time, no one in either Delucci's Miners for a Democratic Union or the Hunt campaign is under investigation.

West Virginia Governor Peter Dance Shortbridge may release to the public a state police report delivered to him a week ago. The investigation failed to develop any leads as to the driver of the Jeep or the motives of Hyskra and Lazarro, according to Harold Huffer, spokesman for the Governor's office.

Joe Hunt, embattled ACMU president, said he had "no [expletive deleted] idea why them two gun-thugs attacked Brother Skeens. That sure as hell wasn't my doin'."

Hunt offered no opinion as to who might have been involved in the deaths of the two Pittsburghers.

Larry Sonoski, ACMU staffer and close adviser to Joe Hunt, said: "Delucci is the only guy I can think of who had a clear motive to hurt them two after what they done to Brother Skeens. That ain't sayin' Delucci was behind it. It's just sayin' he would be the guy I'd think of first. I'm sure he wasn't drivin' his Jeep. But we don't know yet whether he had something to do with it, which the Kanawha County district attorney should look into if you're askin' me, which I guess you are."

Delucci, president of ACMU District 17 based in Charleston, won the September 29th nomination round with 57 percent of vote. He and Hunt now face each other in a run-off set for December 5th.

Hunt has been Union president since 1960 and has run unopposed in every election since.

Delucci was unavailable for comment.

The Post-Gazette has also learned that Frank "Biggie" Stover, a long-time friend and close Delucci adviser, may have been offered $2.5 million by Pittsburgh-based UNICOAL for the subsurface mineral rights beneath his extensive landholdings on Kayford Mountain in Boone County.

The status of negotiations, if any, could not be determined as of yesterday.

Stover, a coal miner and former professional wrestler known as 'The Coalfield Avenger,' is widely thought to be Delucci's principal financial supporter.

Johnson C. Smithers, UNICOAL CEO, and a land manager on his Pittsburgh staff, confirmed the Company's interest in buying or leasing Stover's coal rights in his 3,200 acres. Smithers noted the Stover property was highly desirable and well-known among coal companies.

ACMU staffer Sonoski said: "Now it comes out that the biggest coal operator might be funding Delucci's campaign against President Hunt. UNICOAL must think it'll get an easier contract with Delucci than with Joe. Who am I to say that ain't true?"

Stover was unavailable for comment.

Becker wanted to smack Allyson in the mouth.

How could she write that Jeep "may have played a role" in two murders? And then attribute it to a knowledgeable source in his campaign? Her finger pointed directly at Becker. How her story got through an editor in the absence of supporting evidence left him stumped. This wasn't reporting news; it was circulating incomplete information, guesses, possibilities and innuendos.

Becker put his head down between his legs to control the nausea. After a minute, he lifted up with his eyes closed.

Becker never saw the fist that landed between his ear and cheek.

His last conscious memory was Jeep Delucci's tortured screaming: "JUDAS!"

November 28, 1975, 10:05 a.m.

Not awake, Allyson saw a clapper going berserk in the bell of her head. It stopped. Then it started again. Phone. She was pretty certain it was her phone. It was ringing, or worse—clanging with accusations.

Screeching. Phone!

She picked up.

"You Goddamn used me," Becker shouted at her. "You lied about what I said, and how I said it. You got a story off your back. How could you do that? What kind of reporter are you?"

"Time? What time is it, Jeffrey?"

"It's time for you to make this right with Delucci. That's what damn time it is. I DID NOT tell you that Jeep 'okayed' those killings! And I did not say that he 'may have played a role' in them. It's time to write the damn truth."

"Okay. I'm sorry," she said with no remorse.

"'Sorry' doesn't hack it," he said. "You didn't make a reportorial mistake or a factual error. You did this deliberately."

"Maybe I can fix it," she said and then paused. "I was fired yesterday."

"Good. Somebody in that newsroom has some sense, belated as it is," Becker said.

"I'm a little wasted right now."

"I hope you are permanently unemployable by every newspaper in the country."

"Davey Bloom, my managing editor, fired me. He said he couldn't trust me or my writing. I drank too much last night. I feel like Trip when he landed on his head."

Becker ignored their resurrected memory. "Bloom and I are on the same beam. You're out of control. Personal ends don't justify deceitful means. Have you turned into Nixon?"

Allyson was gathering her wits but not very efficiently. "I believe 100 percent that Delucci okayed the attack on those two if that's any consolation. For me, it is. I also believe with the same confidence that Stover drove the Jeep that night. I got this story right even without the proof that would have satisfied you. You are deliberately keeping yourself in the dark. You don't want to know the truth. You are not morally better than I am."

"You set me up, Allyson. You distorted what I said to make your story."

"Delucci and Stover killed them. Am I supposed to cover it up or ignore it like you're doing?"

"You don't know that! Believing is not knowing. Knowing is a higher standard. Surely you understand that! All you had was my statement that all of us are capable of murder in certain circumstances. That's an opinion about the evolutionary history of *homo sapiens*. It was not said to you as a reporter; it was said to you as a… as a…an old friend…, something like that."

"I was interviewing you over the phone," she said. "Reporters are always reporters," she said. "Don't give me the ingénue."

"You just slept with your source! That's the only reason you even got my opinion about evolution."

"You and I know what happened," Allyson said.

"All you have is hunches. No witnesses, no confession, no physical or circumstantial evidence that ties Stover to using the Jeep that night. No evidence of any kind that even suggests Delucci approved of anything.

You have shit! Which you just threw against a very public wall. You smeared Delucci, and you all but named me as your inside source. All bullshit!"

"I'm a reporter. It's my job. Was my job, I guess."

"That's not reporting. That's make up."

"But I'm right about this, aren't I?"

Becker said nothing, then: "Believe whatever you want."

"Wrong about methods, I admit; right about the truth. And on that Biggie Stover story -- about UNICOAL trying to buy his coal to fund Delucci's campaign -- John-Cee Smithers set me up. They baited a hook with just enough information to get me to swallow the lie. I guess they want Hunt to win one more time," she said. "I feel used. Stupid. Dirty. Tricked."

Becker said nothing. Finally, "Pick, what happened to you?" he asked softly. "What changed you? Where's your Quaker honesty?"

She considered this. "I dunno," she said. "I assume your job is hanging by a narrative thread. I'll call Jeep if you want."

"He hasn't fired me yet. Just punched me out."

"If you quit, you get free."

"Right. I'll go back to my two-room law office over The Peanut Shoppe. I can look forward to going home every night lightly coated with oil and heavily papered with unpaid bills."

"We both have ambition. Isn't private practice in the vapors better than being a silent witness to corruption and murder?"

Becker said nothing.

"I have this blind trust fund."

"So you said."

"I'm pretty sure it has coal stocks in it—AMSTEEL and UNICOAL, among others. I can 'confess' that I was trashing Delucci and you to benefit the coal operators and my own financial self-interest."

For a moment, Becker was stumped. "That is ridiculous nonsense. Look, I appreciate your instinct for Quaker self-sacrifice, but a confession like that would be transparently, laughably and demonstrably false. You'd just open yourself to more ridicule. Not of your finances, but why you would try to pull off such a dopey contrivance."

After a moment of consideration, Allyson said: "You're right. Another bad idea from me. Smart girl, bad judgment."

"I suppose we're both after something better for ourselves," he said.

"I don't see much of a difference between us," she said. "You're welcome to think that you're 'gooder.' But you're making up a story, too, to get something you want."

"I'm not telling lies," he said.

"You're not telling the truth," she said. "Anyway, I'll call Delucci and see if I can make this right for you with him since that appears to be what you want."

Becker stared at nothing in his office.

"I think I'll work this story some more on my own," she said.

"Don't!"

"Have to. It's the one way to prove I'm right."

November 28, 1975, 11:15 a.m.

Davey Bloom hated these calls. They represented failures. His, in particular. They made him feel old and in the wrong.

The phone light kept flashing at him. He frowned his world-weary frown, the big one he saved for special occasions like weddings for people whose marriage wouldn't work. He thought about retiring. He picked up.

"Bloom."

"This hyar's Biggie Stover in Charleston. Is this the editor up there?"

"This is David Bloom. I'm managing editor."

"You the boy who run that shit on me and Jeep yesterday?"

"I'm responsible for Allyson Pickering's work," he said.

"Now you listen at me. It says hyar that UNICOAL offered me $2.5 million for the min'ral rights under the land that my Daddy left me up on Kayford Mountain. That ain't so. That land ain't for sale to no coal comp'ny at any price. Never was, never will be. My Daddy and Momma are buried up there, and theirs, and theirs before them. I do a little loggin' for cash to handle taxes and such. No commercial loggin'. No minin'. Hell, I coulda sold them min'ral rights a hundert times for more than that. Don't want to."

"Mr. Stover," Bloom said, "has UNICOAL *ever* made an offer to you for those coal rights?"

"A bunch of operators talked to me when I first inherited the property. I told all of 'em no. UNICOAL has said nothin' to me since then. That land is how West Virginia was before the minin' come in a hundert years ago. That's how I aim to keep it. That girl of yours never asked me."

"Allyson Pickering."

"Her. Now them UNICOAL people could have faked up an offer and showed it to her so she would write a story about Jeep an' me like we was in the pocket of the operators. I think UNICOAL tarted up a paper to help Joe Hunt who's been sittin' quiet in their laps for years. That paper they fed her ain't real."

"I see. Mr. Stover, I fired Allyson Pickering last night after I read the piece."

"Deserved more than that. That Pickering girl, she's a- tryin' to waste Jeep an' me. Ambush us."

"'I don't follow," Bloom said.

"She has to be workin' for the comp'nies, is my opinion," Biggie said. "She as much as said that Jeep ordered the killin' of them two thugs, and that UNICOAL was financin' Jeep's campaign through the backdoor, through me. There ain't a single piece of proof of what she's sayin' in her story. She has to be gettin' somethin' out of runnin' this shit. People don't do thangs for no fuckin' reason."

Davey Bloom wanted to run that one on the PG's masthead:

People don't do thangs
for no fuckin' reason

"We are running a full retraction and an apology in today's paper," Bloom said. "She maneuvered her piece into print through a new assistant editor while I was out. The story about Hyskra and Lazarro wasn't sourced properly. Not enough facts. I was…am…ashamed."

"That's a-closin' the barn door after the horse is three mile down the road. Folks down here are sayin' that me an' Jeep killed them two."

"I'll try to get the retraction and apology on the AP A-wire. I'll send it down to The Charleston Gazette and every West Virginia daily."

"Ain't good enough. We got us an appointment with Stanley Preiser to sue your ass for libel."

"I know Mr. Preiser," Bloom said as tonelessly as he could.

"Well, you best be fixin' to know him some better right soon."

"Truth is a defense, you know," Bloom said

"You people don't know squat about truth down hyar. You ain't never gonna learn squat about it, because you ain't one of the fish in this sea."

Biggie hung up.

"Shit, shit, shit," Bloom swore. Stanley Preiser was the best lawyer he had ever seen in a courtroom. Stanley Preiser, a native Charlestonian, could persuade a jury of astrophysicists that the sun was nothing more than an ink spot with a flashlight.

Twenty-five minutes later, his phone rang. Bloom closed his eyes, sensing it was from West Virginia.

"Bloom."

"Mr. Bloom, this is Jeffrey Becker, James Delucci's campaign manager. I'm a lawyer. I grew up in Pittsburgh."

Davey reached for his aspirin bottle and a Tums. "I know of you, Mr. Becker. I assume this is about Allyson's story and not a friendly call about whether the 'Stillwers' are going to win a second Super Bowl in January."

508

"Allyson did not quote me directly, but she misused something I did say to her to convey a meaning that I had not meant to convey and never did convey."

"I canned her last night after I read the piece," Bloom said.

"I know. I talked with her this morning. I did not say what she insinuated I said. I have no information or knowledge that Jeep had anything to do with the two fatalities on Rt. 119 that night. The cops found nothing linking anyone in our campaign, including Jeep and Biggie Stover, to those deaths. The investigation is still open but not active. That's my understanding."

"Yes, mine too. You were not quoted in her piece."

"Doesn't matter. Jeep knows she talked to me, knows about the past between us. He knows I was the only one she talked to. Delucci and Stover now think I'm a traitor or a double agent trying to tube their campaign."

"We're running a retraction and an apology today," Bloom said. "She told me last night that she interviewed you. Her notes were sketchy. They seemed to have been put together after the interview."

Becker laughed. "'After the interview!' First, she slept with me; the non-interview interview came later. Allyson was my college girlfriend. All I said to her was 'anyone' could have been driving the Jeep that night, including her, and any human being is capable of murder in the right circumstances."

Bloom exhaled and groaned. "She fucked up."

Becker laughed again. "Yes, in a daily newspaper. That stuff is now all over the coalfields. People believe what they read in the papers."

"I am not totally surprised by her behavior," Bloom said. "Maybe it's Vietnam. Your generation didn't have a good enemy like Hitler and Tojo. You had Johnson and Nixon—wrong on the War but they were not genocidal dictators bent on world conquest. You didn't have a chance to see right from wrong in the way my generation did. In your time, wrong kept being called right; and right kept being called wrong. And then there's Watergate, and every reporter wants to be Woodward and Bernstein. In her, it's a bad combination of screwed up ethics and ambition that wants too much, too fast. Other than that, she's a nice kid. I hope she learns and lands on her feet."

"She says she will pursue this story on her own," Becker said.

"Bad idea. She'd be out there with no institutional cover, such as we are. But here's the thing, Mr. Becker. Somebody murdered those two Pittsburgh hoods. They just didn't flap their wings off that mountain, hoping they could fly home in their Cadillac."

"Agreed," Becker said. "Joe Hunt could have set this whole thing up. Got those two to go down to Logan and then had them killed on the way back to Pittsburgh. One of his guys could have stolen Delucci's Jeep to frame him for the homicides."

"'Could have,' I suppose," Bloom said. "Not very plausible. There are lots of couldas in the world, Mr. Becker. Newspaper editors like me deal with couldas every day. Maybe Joe Hunt and Larry Sonoski are a lot more cunning than I've ever known them to be. Delucci is the obvious suspect, because he has motive. That's an opinion, which will not be in this paper, because it's just an opinion. I'd be real careful down there, Mr. Becker. Real careful."

"And her story on Biggie Stover is total bullshit."

"Yes, agreed," Bloom said.

"UNICOAL seems to have fed her a bogus story to have it look like at first they were trying to wreck Jeep," Becker said. "But UNICOAL knew it would come out as false pretty soon. So the beneficiary of a bogus frame-job against Jeep is Jeep, not Joe Hunt."

"And why would one of Pittsburgh's leading corporate citizens want a young, so-called radical to deal with rather than an old, familiar hand?" Bloom asked.

"I have no idea, but I assume they're looking far ahead and want to start now with a young winner and not prop up an old loser who won't be around much longer. None of what I just said is on the record. It's not for attribution, not for background and not for anything else that makes its way into your paper in any manner or form. I told Biggie to get Stanley Preiser to sue you. I'm sure you don't want to deal with him on a second suit."

"That is correct," Bloom said. "Perhaps UNICOAL is playing the long game. That's why they prefer Delucci, the better of their bad choices."

"Ask John-Cee Smithers. Send me ten copies of the paper with the apology and retraction overnight," Becker said and gave him his address.

"Good luck, Mr. Becker."

November 28, 1975: 11:34 a.m.

"Some lady on the line," Dicey Shuck said.

"Who?"

"Says she's a reporter. Not the Pittsburgh gal. Sounds local."

"Put her through."

"Becker," he said into his phone. He hoped his brain would stop spinning like a crazed electron expelled from its atomic orbit.

"Jeff, this is Julie...Cogswell. You know, the local, independent girl reporter who told you to duck the first punch."

"Good advice," he said. "I remember it well."

"And me?"

"I remember you, too."

"'Well'?"

"Well."

"Dinner today?" she asked. "I'm in town, close by."

"You want to do lunch!" He laughed. "As what?"

"I'm sorry?" She hadn't set herself for a blunt question.

"As what?" he repeated. "This is not such a great time for me. Lunch between us as what? What are we?"

"We? What do you want us to be?" she asked, although she wasn't sure she wanted him to give her an answer.

"Not sure," Becker said with a curtness he knew he would regret. "Getting back to business, I don't have anything to say to the press right now except Allyson Pickering's story was not based on facts, evidence or my statements. The Post Gazette ran an apology and retraction. I'll get you a copy. She's been fired."

"She seems to have shaken her own snakey self out of the tree of knowledge," Julie said, trying half-heartedly not to smirk.

"Along with most of its limbs and branches," he added.

"She's a little too Vassar for my plebian taste," Julie said.

"Bryn Mawr, she and her mother," he said. "Her aunt Maude is Vassar."

"A pee out of one pod is about the same as piss out of another. I know you and she have history."

"Yes."

"Current?"

"Of various types," Becker admitted.

"I'm not her, not Allyson."

"That's a credit not a debit," he said.

"Maybe. But first loves hit hardest, stay longest, hurt deepest and mean the 'mostest,'" Julie said.

"So?"

"So, I guess I don't think you know what you want. That's a plenty good reason to leave 'As what?' at just casual dining."

"You're right on all counts," Becker said. "I'm not going to argue you into anything."

"We're different," she said. "I don't think we have much of a chance over the long term. And you're not exactly prime rib right now."

"Not even potluck."

Julie paused. "You're more like a covered dish. If you win, won't you get a job with Jeep at headquarters? I don't want to move to Washington."

"Who knows? I doubt it after Allyson's story."

"Is it likely you would move?"

"Beats me."

"Well, give me a call, I suppose, if you care to."

"Sure," he said. This wasn't working out either. Why hadn't he just said yes to her invitation?

November 28, 1975, 7:52 p.m.

"It's mother, dear."

"Mother dear," Allyson kidded flatly. She got up from the chintz wingchair in her living room and began walking back and forth with the phone cradled between her shoulder and ear. Her bare feet made little slaps against the red-oak floor. She was dressed in pajama bottoms and the comfy Bryn Mawr sweatshirt she had slept in. The streetlight outside her second-floor apartment near Elmer and Myrtle Way in Shadyside backlighted her drawn curtains without getting through. She stretched and untangled the coiled handset cord as she walked over to the television and turned it off.

"How are you?" Boo asked her daughter.

"Fine."

Jane Pickering strained to discern how much discomfort was embedded in 'Fine.' "Uncle Bob called and told me you had some, shall I say, 'disagreement' at the paper."

"I was fired."

"Uncle Bob ran into John-Cee Smithers yesterday and…."

"What do you want to know, Mother?"

"First, I want *you* to know your father and I will do whatever you want to help you through this."

"Thanks. The offer is generous and appreciated," Allyson said, wanting nothing so much as to not need help from her parents at age 30.

"Second, I suppose we are curious as to the circumstances of this incident. We know the Block family at the paper, back to Paul, Senior. Dad knows both Paul, Junior, and Billy. St. Paul's, Yale—that sort of connection. Uncle Bob knows Billy Block quite well."

"Please do not intervene with the publishers about this. Davey Bloom made the right decision."

"Blume?"

"He's the managing editor. My boss. Ex-boss."

"I'm friends with a Virginia Bluhm, that's her maiden name, of course. Her people were in machine tools, whatever they might be. You knew her daughter at the Baldwin School, Sally."

"That's B-L-U-H-M. This is B-L-O-O-M."

"Oh, like The Bloomsbury Group?"

"Bloom, Mother. Like Leopold."

"Really. Wasn't Leopold a conversion Protestant and then a Catholic in the book? My memory has gaps these days. Well, the Blocks always were ahead of their time. Good for them. Did you get along with Mr. Bloom?"

"Yes, Mother, I did."

"Then why did he do this to you?"

"He didn't. I did it to me. I blew it," Allyson said, lighting an unfamiliar Winston and sipping from her fourth half-full glass of wine as she paced. She coughed. The smoke was harsh; harsh felt right. She tapped the cigarette into a china saucer.

"Should I get your father on the phone?"

"No. Just announce the bad news to him in your own way."

"I don't understand," Boo said.

"I tried to punch my own ticket."

"Allyson, dear, parlez-vous Anglais?"

"I lost control of myself, I guess. I pushed a story beyond the facts I had. I made something up that I think is true, but I couldn't substantiate it. And I found myself in a conflict of interest with a source. It's a mess. I'm to blame."

"Did this involve the coal miners of Appalachia, the union story you were working on?"

"Yes."

"You know your father did some legal work for UNICOAL some years ago and knows John-Cee Smithers from college."

"Christ, do our chain links never stop?"

"These 'chain links' can be very helpful. They're a gate, not a fence. I can't imagine what type of conflict of interest you would have with coal miners."

"I slept with a source."

"Allyson! A coal miner! Really. Well, I suppose, that's very broad-minded."

"No, Mother, not a coal miner. It was the man running the reform candidate's campaign. Do you remember Jeffrey Becker? From Columbia."

"Becker?"

"The tepee, Mother. I was sleeping in a tepee with him at a farm in Massachusetts the summer before journalism school."

"Oh. Him," Boo said.

"Him."

"But that was years ago. Surely, that doesn't count against you now."

"No, it doesn't. But I slept with him before I wrote a story on the union election. Last week."

Boo blinked. Allyson heard the blink over the long-distance line. Boo was trying to examine with Darwinian detachment this old-new Becker bug in her garden. What she really wanted to do was to crush it and throw the carcass over the fence out of sight. "Oh, I see. Well."

Allyson waited. She had years of experience interpreting her mother's "Wells."

Boo cleared her throat.

"Are you beading Becker's moccasins again?"

Allyson laughed, the first time in two days, or two weeks or two months.

"Nice, Mother. Becker is quite respectable these days. He's a lawyer and rents a pretty little place in the country. He wears suits—stripes, solids. I've even seen him in a three-piece. He wears cordovans like Daddy."

"Well, I'm sure they're not *exactly* like your father's shell cordovans. Probably Florsheim's version. Not the Edward Green shoes made from the hide of a horse's rump."

Allyson shook her head. "Becker no longer wears a loincloth. Not when he's wearing Florsheim's cordovans or, for that matter, when he sleeps."

"Oh my. You will not provoke me, Allyson. Indeed. May I ask whether there is a goal in your renewed interest in this individual?"

"You should have been a dentist, Mother."

"Women my age no longer have time for circuitousness. I am being nosy though, aren't I? I'm just getting more and more dreadful each year. I know. I know."

"I'm beyond being offended," Allyson said.

"It's not easy for me to discuss…sex…that is, relationships… men… with you."

"Bathrooms, too."

Boo had never given any thought to bathrooms as fodder for conversation. She had redone hers once, and Mr. Sowers, the plumber from Germantown, cleaned the lines every fall. And then Boo realized that Allyson was not talking about bathrooms.

She giggled, a little uncomfortably. "Well, yes. You're right. My generation is more private; repressed, the Freudians would say. It did have its advantages though."

"One of which was you never got yourself into a mess like this," Allyson added.

"I have done a lot of things, dear. Some I should have done; others probably not. I think, now, all in all, it's best to paint on the biggest canvas you can face each day rather than the smallest. You'll make big mistakes, that's true. But in the end, you'll have something more than a few crusted brushes and a perfect miniature."

"Thank you, Mother. That makes me feel better."

"Mistakes are part of learning how to live. We all make them. Would you like to come home for a bit?"

"I don't think so. I may need to do some traveling."

"Do you need anything?"

"I have plenty of cash. The Pile keeps growing."

514

"I'm not entirely comfortable with your reference to your trust as a 'pile.'"

"More bathroom boogie-woogies?"

Money was not what Allyson Pickering needed at that moment. Unemployment would not be hard to weather with her savings and trust checks. And she could have a lifetime free ride were she to marry Kennedy Brown. In the worst of circumstances, she could get a distribution from The Pile if she needed to buy a house or flee the country. It amazed her how easy a lot of unearned money made life.

"And what about that young man you're seeing, the banking boy?"

"Kennedy Brown. He wants to marry me, smudged as I am."

"'Smudged!' I doubt that."

"Let's say I'm mulling his offer."

"'Well, dear, mulling is better than stewing. Allyson, let me be frank. You are of that certain age. Your bearing years are now and coming to an end. Love is…well, if it's there, that's nice. But marriage has many foundations that are equally important, several maybe even more so."

"He's fun in bed."

"That, dear, is not a good reason for marrying a man."

"Point taken, Mother."

"I didn't mean that this aspect is unimportant."

"I understand your concerns. I told him I wanted to get this ACMU story straightened out. I want a good name. Then I can give his proposal the attention it deserves. I'm leaning toward yes."

"Grandchildren would be nice."

"At a distance," Allyson added.

"In small, but not irregular, doses. We would certainly like to meet Mr. Brown and his parents who…?"

"…are acceptable," Allyson said. "His father is high up in Brown Brothers Harriman. He's not a *Brown* Brother, however. His mother went to Smith."

"Well, I suppose," Boo said. She did not think her Bryn-Mawr-driven opinion of Smith needed to be introduced into this conversation. In any case, Allyson knew her opinion of Smithies—too many tight sweaters festooned with pearls of dubious lineage.

"Are you applying for other newspaper jobs, dear?"

"Not yet. I need to go back to the canvas with different brushes."

Jane Andrews "Boo" Pickering reflected on this for a moment, "Wear a smock, dear."

Chapter 39

Pittsburgh, November 28, 1975

John Corelli believed in planning for many reasons.

Planning reduced risk in his business, which he called his "capital ventures." Planning was insurance against the unknowable. Planning was quality control. Planning minimized errors and limited the effect of any that might be made. Planning prevented the unexpected to the extent possible. Planning prepared for the unexpected. Planning was a promise to his client that he would get full value for his dollar. But, as John pointed out to Tony Bruno, "to be honest about it, there ain't no 100-percent guarantees in either life or death."

Corelli liked to plan. He liked the methodical analysis it required. He liked making decision trees. Planning was a process where focused intelligence could be applied to problems of management and logistics. Strategic planning won wars even though he agreed with Helmuth von Moltke's observation: "No plan of operations extends with certainty beyond the first encounter with the enemy's main strength." For that reason, Corelli also agreed with the Prussian General's companion idea: "Strategy is a system of expedients."

Planning had to be flexible, adaptable and alert. It had to change nimbly with feedback. Planning forced the planner to think through the universe of decisions, outcomes and consequences, expected or not. If you didn't plan, he concluded, you didn't win, except by luck, which could never be counted on. Professionals never trusted in luck, which, in Corelli's opinion, deserved its frequent adjective, "dumb." Planning separated the master craftsman from the dingbat do-it-yourselfer. Planning was choreography, the creative dance of his business.

John Corelli started the Stover plan with the right vehicle.

Before dawn on Monday morning, the 24th, he had stretched his hands into a pair of surgical gloves and stole a new, dark-red Bronco from Triangle Ford's lot on Pittsburgh's Baum Boulevard. He bolted on counterfeit plates and taped on valid stickers before driving along Penn Avenue toward downtown. Then he made a sharp right turn onto 40th Street. He crossed Butler Street—a grimy strip of neon-eyed shops, dark taverns, warehouses and home-improvement companies shoehorned into ratty storefronts. On his left was Arsenal Park. He turned right onto Eden Way, a double line of decrepit row houses built on a narrow 19th-Century lane. About one-third of the dwellings had been abandoned, another third were falling apart; and the final third were hanging on by the fingertips of their inhabitants.

Butler Street ran the length of Lawrenceville, parallel to the Allegheny River. Composer Stephen Foster's father, William, founded the neighborhood in 1814, naming it after Captain James "Don't give up the ship!" Lawrence. With its flat land and easy access to water transportation and, later, railroads, Lawrenceville became the site of many of Pittsburgh's early iron-working companies and foundries. Their employees were housed near their work, first in cabins and then in two-story, brick tenements. The typical 19th Century house on Eden Way was 14 feet wide, with six rooms and a total of 754 square feet. Each had a privy in its back yard.

The federal Allegheny Arsenal built in 1814 was a mainstay of the community's growing metal-working economy. On its 30 acres, a significant portion of the ammunition federal troops used during the Civil War was manufactured—some 40,000 bullets a day.

Allegheny Arsenal was said to have been a target of a raid J.E.B. Stuart was rumored to have been planning in the summer of 1863. Two earlier Confederate probes had come within a day's ride of Pittsburgh. In the short-lived Stuart panic, some 6,000 Pittsburghers were put to work erecting 37 fortifications, redoubts, cannon positions, trenches and moats in a 12-mile-long circle around the City. Among these was Fort Croghan, a battery on Black Horse Hill above Stanton and Morningside Avenues where Jeffrey Becker played war as a kid in the surviving trenches. The Stuart threat vanished after Lee's Gettysburg defeat.

Along with the Arsenal, Pittsburgh's Fort Pitt Foundry and Knap Rudd Company made a majority of the Union's cast-iron cannon, huge siege howitzers and mortars. Seventy-eight of the Arsenal's workers, mostly teenage women who were loading cartridges, were killed in an 1862 explosion. Fifty-four unidentifiable bodies were buried in a mass grave in the nearby Allegheny Cemetery.

The Arsenal was sold at auction in 1926. Much of its land was then sold and the remainder turned into a neglected park between 39th and 40th on Butler Street. By 1975, Lawrenceville had lost most of its industry and manufacturing. Those who could move out, had. Eden Way had never been a garden.

John Corelli drove the stolen Bronco slowly in the murky dawn. Eden Way was a "Way" in name but no more than a pot-holed and functionally abandoned alley. His eyes were adjusting to the morning's dimness. That adaptation, he had learned, took 15 minutes minimum for total blackness. He watched dark windows more than the occasional lighted one. Unexpected trouble usually came out of darkness.

The two-story houses, almost mirror images, faced each other on a street so narrow that only one car could safely move through at any particular moment. Windows faced windows, stoops faced stoops. Houses shared a common wall that transmitted sound in both directions. Tiny fenced yards -- the original location for the privy and pile of winter coal -- squared up behind their respective houses. Once or twice in every block, sagging multi-colored, aluminum window awnings broke up the brick facades. Poles carrying electric and telephone lines spread their cross arms over the street. Old cars that needed a paint job, many non-essential parts and a number of essential ones were parked along the north curb. There were no secrets in Eden Way; there was no place to hide them.

Lawrenceville had fallen close to the bottom of the City's barrel. Eden Way was one of its many streets whose residents made do as best they could. It was a place where a young unemployed man with a wife and baby made frayed ends meet by "throwing a pint" as often as permitted.

Corelli stopped in the middle of the third block under a weak street lamp. Broken asphalt covered 100-year-old cobblestones. Both were heaved by years of the freeze-thaw cycle and pocked by water-filled holes the City was always intending to repair. Eden Way was still.

He stopped in front of a dingy, double-wide garage door that had been inserted in the ground-level wall of three adjoining houses.

The electric door began retracting on greased rollers in greased tracks that made for a quiet opening. Corelli turned and flicked his headlights twice. A flashlight inside answered three times. Corelli then eased the Bronco inside as the door came down behind him, quietly. The garage was unilluminated.

John had been there before. He knew houses on either side had been "acquired," then hollowed out like this middle one and turned into a garage. He cut the engine. He waited to get the feel of the space. In front of him, he saw the lighted tip of a cigar. He smiled. Harry "Extra" Sobczak was always on time.

Harry was a slight balding man in his late forties who looked like a young Sinatra who had aged badly. His face was deeply creased, sour and suspicious. His hands were terribly outsized for his body. His fingers were as thick as the kielbasas he loved. Three fingernails were smashed flat. His knuckles were scarred from years of cheap wrenches slipping off rusted nuts and bolts. He bore a perpetual odor of petroleum products on his clothes and skin.

Extra had started honest enough, fixing cars in front of his parents' house on Eden Way. He'd prop the wheels on the high stone curb so he could work safely underneath. He kept his scratch-together tools in his parents' living room for lack of any alternative. After six years and with his parents dead, he'd had enough of working in the gutter. He approached the Lawrenceville branches of Mellon Bank, Pittsburgh National Bank and 2nd Federal Savings and Loan for money to convert his house into an auto shop. The loan officers looked him up and down. They didn't see an entrepreneur with six years of OTJ experience. Rather, they saw a poorly educated, blue-collar guy who was more likely to blacken his collar over time than whiten it. They didn't even bother to write him a rejection letter.

So Extra got in touch with one of Tony Bruno's "loan officers." He got cash the next day. Neighbors on either side agreed to sell their houses to him within the month even before he knew he wanted to make them an offer. He later learned his "loan officer" had, in his words, "touched base with the neighbors." The interest rate Tony charged was reasonable. The only catch was that Extra had to do whatever Tony Bruno asked whenever Tony Bruno demanded it. Bruno's work came in a couple of times each year, like this job for Corelli.

Extra walked toward the Bronco. He moved slowly for a thin man. Corelli heard the soles of Extra's work shoes scuff against the oil-soaked sand on the concrete floor. Corelli got out and stood in the unlighted garage.

"Extra," he said in greeting.

"Johnny C."

"I need this Bronco by this time Friday. I'll be out of tahn until then. That gives you time. You sure you got everything on the list?

"Yeah. I got it all," Extra said, pulling on his cigar so that it glowed. "Got the plates, the registration, the sticker, lifters, knobby tires that'll get you through a swamp and enough paint for a complete job. White, for Chrissakes, over a red Bronco! Jeez."

"Grind out the serial numbers and change the locks first thing," Corelli said.

"Locks is extra."

"Change the fuckin' locks, Harry." Corelli grinned and shook his head.

Extra grumbled deep in his throat. He didn't like giving freebies, not even to Tony Bruno who did not consider them freebies. When he was sprawled in the gutter on his back, he cursed his need to offer half-price rates to get any work from his neighbors. He hated not being able to charge for "the little shit that mounts up, a nut here, a bolt there, a minute spent adjusting an idle screw." He had resented every dollar lost. Extra took no offense at the nickname Tony hung on him. It was his motto, his business philosophy: No free lunch, not no more.

"Remember, I need two sets of West Virginia plates and registration and stickers," Corelli said. "Two."

"Yeah. Clean plates is extra, you know," Harry said with determination. "I gotta charge Tony what it costs me for them plates. It's harder to get 'em out of West Virginia, the Moundsville pen, than in Pee-A. Why is that? How do I fuckin' know why is that?"

"Richie Polizo in Wheeling has the contact inside," Corelli said. "Shouldn't be more than $50 to him and $100 to you for each set. Not $250. I wouldn't mark Tony up if I was you."

"Yeah."

"Now listen, Extra. I'll get this Bronco back to you Saturday morning. You chop and shop it. We split what you get even."

"I'm takin' all the risk," Extra complained. "I need sixty."

"I stole the fuckin' car. That's my share. No car, no 50 for you. Tony pays you fair, and none of it goes on your books. You don't like 50-50, then I'll take it to Grosso in Verona. Or maybe you want to do this work for nothin'? All of it."

"Yeah. Okay, 50's fair, I guess." Extra leaned down and stubbed out his cigar on the Bronco's new front tire. He would sell the set of five as "new, driven not no more than 10 miles and never in the potholes of winter."

John Corelli understood greed, though he never found much appeal in it. "Okay," he said. "Up the door, Harry."

Parked in front of Extra's entrance was Roberta Magnelli, sitting in the driver's seat of a beat-up, 1971 AMC Gremlin she had stolen that morning on Frankstown Avenue in East Liberty.

"Perfect. Nobody will look twice at this piece of shit," Corelli laughed, "unless they get close enough to smell it."

He noticed her surgical gloves on the steering wheel. She saw him nod. "Good girl," he said.

"Not a girl anymore," Roberta said.

"Yeah, well," he said.

"Not good anymore, either."

"Some conditions improve over time," he said. "Yours has, for instance."

"Let's hope this wreck gets us back to within walking distance of your place. It objects to going into fourth gear and then staying there."

"You got money for bus fare, hon?" he asked.

"Yeah," she said.

"Me, too. Be prepared."

"Corelli, you were never a Boy Scout," she laughed.

"I was given the Good Citizenship medal at Larimer Elementary School in the sixth grade."

"*That* says a whole lot about your competition," she laughed.

"I had to beat out a couple of goody-two-shoes girls."

"What'd you do, bribe the principal? Threaten him?"

"Didn't have to do anything," Corelli said. "Just mentioned to Mr. Weever that my mother might like to see it come to me. I was big for my age. He was small for his."

Corelli had scouted the terrain, scoped Biggie Stover and developed a plan. He bought topographical maps of Kanawha and Boone Counties at Moore's, the Charleston bookstore across from the Kanawha County

Library. He found Stover's house in Boone County. He traced alternative ways Stover might get home from the campaign's headquarters. He respected the way Stover parked, pointing out in the alley behind the campaign office. The alley, he decided, was the best capture point.

Corelli then found the place he wanted to go. He drove there in a stolen car at night. He crossed the Kanawha River from downtown over the South Side Bridge and wound up Bridge Road through the old-money section of Charleston's South Hills. He drove down to a "T" in blue-collar Loudendale, which was strung out along both sides of Davis Creek. A left at the T would take him past Kanawha State Forest and eventually into Boone County. A right turn soon brought him onto a one-lane, dirt road that ran through an overgrown and abandoned stretch of flood-prone bottom land. This road forded Davis Creek seven times in ever deeper and trickier crossings before it reached another section of paved road about 10 miles from the T. The paved road ended at Rt. 214 in the Davis Creek neighborhood. He found a secluded turnaround between fords five and six, more than a mile from the nearest inhabited house.

Corelli staked out the alley behind Delucci's headquarters. He noted that Becker and Stover parked in two reserved spots behind the storefront. Delucci either walked from his Quarrier Street apartment or found a spot for his now-returned Jeep on or near Washington Street where it could be seen. This section of Washington Street was downwardly commercial and parking spots were not hard to find. Dicey Shuck fed the parking meter for Jeep. Delucci, Stover and Becker usually left after 7:00 p.m., but not together.

Corelli focused on Stover who was as easy to recognize as an ICBM standing in a library reading room. Stover walked with physical confidence. He kept his eyes moving, scanning. One night he lifted the hood of his Blazer, checking with a flashlight. Becker had a mustache and longish hair, though not close to shoulder length. He wore a suit one day and jeans the next with a loosened tie.

When it was dark enough on his second night of observation, Corelli slipped next to Stover's Blazer. Wearing surgeon's gloves, he picked the driver's door using his jiggler tryout keys. If the jigglers didn't work, he had a professional lockout kit in his car. The Blazer's power steering, automatic transmission and power brakes would make his plan easier to manage. Corelli found a loaded pistol in a false speaker in the driver's door. He found another in a rigid plastic holster bolted under the driver's seat and an AR-15 semi-automatic under the back seat. The boy's not a fool, Corelli thought, and he'll be carrying.

On the third night, Corelli drove the run-down end of Capitol Street, the red-light strip that was two blocks from the Daniel Boone Hotel where politicians bunked when the Legislature was in session. The Boone's location made coupling logistics convenient for both street sellers and hotel buyers.

Corelli left the untraceable clunker he was driving in the Kanawha Valley Airport's long-term lot and paid cash for a ticket to Cleveland where Roberta Magnelli would meet him. They would drive to Pittsburgh. In the air, Corelli went through his plan, step by step.

John Corelli picked up the now-white Bronco from Extra's garage at 6:30 a.m. on Friday, November 28th. He stopped at a pay phone on Butler Street, next to Teamsters' Temple 249 across from Allegheny Cemetery. He left the motor running and the headlights off. He got out, dropped in a dime and dialed. A woman answered. He said nothing. They rang off.

Fifteen minutes later, Corelli pulled to the curb in front of the Stanton-Negley Pharmacy in Pittsburgh's East End. Roberta stood in the shadows of the building. Snow swirled. She opened the Bronco's door and slid in a suitcase. She wore blue jeans and running shoes. She had a black knit hat over her now red hair and a bright-red down jacket.

"I like you as a redhead," Corelli said.

"Magnelli's a Swedish name, didn't you know? It's the diminutive of Magnuson."

He laughed. "'Diminutive!' Enjoy it while you can. It's going back to black when we get home."

"Brown, not black. I'm a brunette."

"Brown, sure. You got all the stuff?" Corelli asked.

"Sure."

"All of it?"

"Don't worry, hon. All of it. Lunch, too. And snacks."

"It's about a five-hour drive. I'll fill up the Bronco and the two cans in the back when we're out of the City. Get some sleep. We'll do it tonight."

The snow stopped as they arrived in Charleston about noon. He drove to Davis Creek on Rt. 214 and then through all the fords to check their water levels. He did not want the white Bronco to be seen going into the dirt road from the Loudendale side twice in one day. Somebody might become curious about a new, unfamiliar Bronco in that neighborhood. Davis Creek was running no more than a few inches over the fords. That was a bit of luck, Corelli thought, since they could now use any two-wheel-drive vehicle for their second car without having to worry about getting stuck in high water.

They returned to Charleston and parked in the unattended lot along the north bank of the Kanawha River next to the Union Building and the South Side Bridge. They had their pick of more than 100 cars. They stole a 1970 Ford Galaxie that looked as if it could have used more than a little tender loving care. They drove it out of the lot, slipped on Extra's second set of

West Virginia plates at a nearby Kroger and waited until late afternoon. They gassed it up from one of the two five-gallon cans. Around six, they drove both cars in the dark to the remote site on Davis Creek that Corelli had picked out. They came in from the Rt. 214 side, not the Loudendale side. They left the Galaxie with a note on its windshield: "Broke Down. Throd a rod. Gone for recker." They drove back to Charleston in the white Bronco.

After eating the supper Roberta had packed, they drove down the hooker strip on Capitol Street. Then they drove up Capitol Street, then down again. They wanted to be seen in the white Bronco.

Corelli was dressed in a dark winter jacket, jeans and boots. He wore sunglasses and a straw cowboy hat that nearly filled the front seat. On his hands, he wore vinyl gloves the color of his flesh.

Roberta had changed into a white mini skirt, tank top, short leather jacket, high-heeled leather boots that came to her knees and sunglasses. She was working under a waist-length, parakeet-blond wig. In her suitcase, she had a change of clothes. She let a fringe of red hair peek out behind her ears.

"Good hair," Corelli said.

"Right. It's Dynel, a fiber from Union Carbide. Seventy-five bucks! It weighs three pounds! The place I had it made promised it was resistant to carpet beetles, mildew and fungus."

"Good to know," he said. "Your clothes are perfect."

"It's amazing the funky shit you can find at Goodwill," she said. "Maybe the skinny-ass, pink-and-green ladies from the country clubs play a little late-night-hole-in-one. This rig is not cheap. This is a Gucci 'Hobo Bag' just like what Jackie O carried. The sunglasses are Gucci, too. No one will notice the crack in the glasses or the stain on the bag."

"You'll be the classiest piece of trash on the street," Corelli said. "We've been noticed. This Bronco will be remembered. My hat; your hair, outfit. You."

Corelli double-checked his shoulder holster. He carried a Smith & Wesson Model 29 Quiet Special Purpose Revolver with a 1.375-inch barrel. It fired six .410 cal. internally silenced bullets. The AAI Corporation had refashioned this pistol for the short, slim soldiers who crawled into Viet Cong tunnels. The QSPR 29 had been field-tested, but it never entered official service during the War. Corelli had palmed it off a dead tunnel rat. It fired a shell that contained 15 tungsten balls, effective in very close quarters. The 29 was Plan B, the backup. Plan A was to use his Ern Solingen 6/8 straight razor—Swedish carbon steel, extra hollow ground with red stamina scales. He preferred no noise to limited noise. He carried three pairs of police handcuffs.

Roberta pulled on white gloves that ended above her elbows. "Makes me look like a fuckin' debutante," she said.

"I wouldn't know whether they do or don't," Corelli said. "I never had a shot at any of them. Anyway, you do spruce up the local scene."

She put on cherry-red lipstick and made her mouth bow.

"Save some for me," he said.

She got out, carrying her shoulder bag. She pushed out her chest, cocked her butt to the right and pursed her lips like Marilyn Monroe.

"It's damn cold!"

"Just another burden honest workin' women have to bear," he said.

"You got some time, darlin'?" she asked in as coquettish a voice as she could muster.

"Later, I will. You sure stand out from the competition," he said, cutting his eyes down the block at the four early birds.

"Doesn't say much for me. Scags, I figure," she said. "They'll show a little leg but no arms."

"Ain't my taste," he said. "Now be careful. You're new meat. I shouldn't be more than an hour. You're on your own till then. I'll be in his black Blazer. I'll have him pull over in the middle of the block. I'll be in the back seat. Hang out on the end of the block until 7:20 or so. Don't crowd anybody. Don't get in a fight over turf with the regulars. Make sure your colleagues remember seeing you get in Stover's Blazer. Make sure they hear it."

"Got it." She walked slowly down Capitol Street as if she was trying to swipe buildings on both sides with the swing of her hips.

She's switching her ass like a race horse, Corelli thought. The girl's got balls. Roberta Magnelli was still in training, but Corelli knew she could get good, fast. She'd always have a nice figure, a pretty face and the advantage of surprise. He hoped she didn't have a soft heart. She was smart, too smart in a way. Where did she come up with, "diminutive?"

Shedding his cowboy hat and sunglasses, Corelli parked the white Bronco in the Union Building's lot and walked the few blocks to the alley behind Washington Street. He slipped into position behind Delucci's headquarters. Becker came out at 7:05 p.m., got into his unlocked Datsun and drove off.

Corelli eased over to Biggie's Blazer. Still wearing gloves, he unlocked the driver's door. He removed Biggie's two pistols from their hiding places and stuck them under the back seat with the AR-15. He left a locksmith's key in the ignition. He clamped one set of cuffs on the right side of the steering wheel at four o'clock and a second set at 10. He closed the door but did not relock it. He spun the Blazer's front hubs from Free to Lock. Preparation took no more than 90 seconds. In his pocket, Corelli had a small paper bag filled with dry brown rice. He resumed his hidden position in the alley.

About 10 minutes later, Biggie came out. He waited a few minutes, looking, listening. He walked to his Blazer and reached into his pocket for the key.

As Biggie looked down to fit the key into the lock, Corelli moved behind him.

"Hold still, Biggie," Corelli growled in as low and quiet a voice as he could manage. "I got a snubby 29 pointed at the small of your back. This ain't a stick up."

Biggie stopped. The guy knew his name. He figured the shotgun pistol was cocked and equipped with a flash and noise suppressor. The car key was in his right hand. If the guy was close enough, he might surprise him with a quick key in the eye. His pistol was holstered under his left arm, beneath his zippered winter coat. He couldn't get to it with his left hand.

"I'm 10 feet behind you," Corelli said, anticipating Biggie's thought, which would have been his own.

"Maybe," Biggie said.

"Danny! Okay. Danny," Corelli whispered above a whisper. He threw the paper bag about 15 feet behind Stover so that it slid with a soft scraping sound.

Two, Biggie thought. Just like on Lens Creek Mountain. They'd take his .357 in the holster, but he had back-ups in the Blazer if that's where this was going.

"Unzip your coat, Biggie and take your gun out of your holster. Hold it with two fingers by the barrel and put it on the ground. Use your left hand. Your LEFT hand. Then kick it over to the front of the car. Danny you pick it up after Big Boy gets in."

Biggie unholstered his gun, dropped it on the ground and kicked it to the front of his Blazer. Damn poor way to treat a good weapon, he thought. This clown knows more than the last two. Probably watches TV cop shows. Biggie judged he could get to one of his pistols once they were in his car.

"Open the door, it ain't locked," Corelli said. "Now do each step as I tell you when I tell it to you. Okay, now get in. *Don't close the door*. Take off your watch and put it on the dash. Put your keys next to it. Now put your right hand on the steering wheel at four o'clock. Roll the window down with your left at the same time. Come in a little, Danny."

Corelli moved toward the Blazer. "Turn the car on. There's a key in the ignition. Turn on the heat. Hit the headlights, low beams. Now, lock your right wrist to the wheel, then the left. These cuffs are special long so you'll be able to steer. I want to hear two clicks. Now show me. Yank hard, Biggie, on both. I want to see those wrists staying inside the cuffs. HARD!"

Corelli watched the test.

"Do it again, harder."

It might be possible for a gorilla like Stover to break one nickel steel cuff, maybe the right one, but not two at the same time. Even a gorilla would not be able to break the extra heavy steel chain link that Corelli had welded in. Mr. Rodney Unthank in Peabody's metal shop would be pleased with his work. Anyway, Corelli thought, he'd have plenty of time watching Biggie struggle with the cuffs to prevent his escape.

Biggie thought he might be able to break the cuffs. Might could. But he would only have one chance. He'd have to lift up and out, like a front dumbbell raise while sitting. He wouldn't be able to bring his legs to bear. He would have to break both cuffs in one flash-fast motion and then grab his gun under the seat before the guy shot him. Not likely.

Corelli picked up Biggie's gun and slipped it in his jacket pocket. "Your pistols—the one in the speaker hole and the one under the seat, I got 'em. The rifle in the back, too."

Biggie realized his best chance had been when he was standing in the alley facing his Blazer. He should have not gotten in. He now understood the guy with the gun was a pro. He had known the Blazer had one key for opening the door and another for the ignition. He had swept the Blazer for weapons.

Corelli opened the passenger door and rolled down the window. He climbed into the back seat and positioned himself directly behind Biggie.

Biggie looked in his rearview mirror for the man who held his life in his hands. He couldn't see much.

"It'll be cold with the window down," Biggie said.

"Yeah, it'll keep us alert."

"What do ya want?" Biggie asked.

"You an' me are gonna have a serious talk."

"About what?" Biggie placed the accent as northern West Virginia or southwestern Pennsylvania. Not a local.

"Patience," Corelli said. "Cooperate and you'll get out of this in one piece. Drive down Washington to Capitol and make a right at the Daniel Boone onto the strip. No speedin'."

"What are you," Biggie asked, "some kind of hotel dick?"

Corelli laughed in spite of himself."

"What about Danny?" Biggie asked.

"Don't worry about nobody you don't know. He'll follow."

Biggie found he could drive without much trouble while shackled to the steering wheel. He drove to Capitol Street. He kept glancing in his mirror for a glimpse of his captor, but the dash lights were dim and the streetlights weren't very illuminating. Try to get him talkin', Biggie thought.

"The Boone ain't what it once was," Biggie said as he turned onto Capitol. "Used to be glamorous. FDR stayed there, Eisenhower, the Kennedys. Elvis stayed there this July when he did a concert at the Civic Center."

"Elvis—a fat guy with his nose open for shit," Corelli said.

"How do you know that?"

"How do I know he's fat?"

"How do you know about 'shit'?" Biggie asked.

"I hear things from people who know. Vegas, other places. Travels with a doctor who feeds him what he wants."

"You hear thangs from Vegas. Does that mean you're with Chickie from Dee Cee?"

"Pull over in the middle of the block."

"Or are you from that Pittsburgh guy who sent them other two down here?"

"See the blonde. Pull in front of her."

"That your girl?"

"Yeah, but she's yours tonight." Corelli ducked down so he could not be seen. "This weapon is right behind your back, pointed at your heart. Do what I say, and you'll get out of this."

The strip was heating up at 7:25 p.m. Roberta had seen a half-dozen second-tier ladies join the starting third-string in the hour she'd been hanging out. The girls sashayed slowly on the sidewalk, or leaned provocatively against street light poles. Pickup trucks started to drive by around seven. Some slowed, and a few stopped in hopes of early-bird discounts. Well-dressed businessmen from the Daniel Boone navigated these shallows on their way to the Merry-Go-Round Bar for supper. They chatted up the women, several more than half-seriously.

"Leave the engine running," Corelli told Biggie who stopped.

Roberta worked her way the few steps to the open window and leaned in. She stuck her ass out and shifted her cheeks. The strip was watching. This was the new girl's first score. Two pimp brothers -- sitting in their purple, 1975 Cadillac Coupe deVille with an ultra-padded, white-vinyl top -- sat up and watched. They agreed to move on her when she returned with cash.

"Lookin' for a friend, big feller?" Roberta asked in a voice freighted with a not-too-bad imitation of the country-and-western singers she'd accompanied that morning on the radio. "I do love your Blazer. My name's Cun...try Cathy. Get it? What's yours?"

Biggie said nothing.

"Biggie!" she squealed. "Oooo, I do hope you live up to your name, butta'cup. I love big guys. You a cop, Biggie?" she asked.

"Say no, real loud," Corelli prompted.

"No."

"You wouldn't lie to Cathy would you? I'm lookin' for a friend tonight. Why you too? Imagine that! Fifty is a gratuity. Completely voluntary. You say it might take a while. Let's play this by ear. We got us a date, you an' me, Biggie."

"Tell her to get in," Corelli said.

"Get in," Biggie said.

Roberta got in the Blazer. At least five of the eight women on the strip had heard the entire conversation between Roberta and mostly herself.

"Drive out to Loudendale," Corelli said. "Turn right at the stop sign at the bottom of the hill. You know where I'm talkin'?"

"Yeah."

Roberta sat close to the console and the four-wheel-drive shifter that separated the two bucket seats. She put her hand on Biggie's right leg and ran it up lightly toward his groin. She was still wearing her white gloves.

Biggie drove the Blazer along the narrow, twisting two-lane road that wound up to and through the wooded ridgetops of South Hills, known as "The Hill." The former Indian trail linked the columned Greek Revivals and late Georgians the local wealthy had built on Loudon Heights overlooking the Kanawha River before The Depression. Past them, the road ran down the back side of The Hill through the new chateaus and cedar moderns built in the late '60s and early '70s. Even lower, it passed split-levels, ramblers and ranchers from the 1950s.

"Pull into the store," Corelli said at the intersection of Bridge and Oakwood Roads. "Park by the retaining wall."

Roberta got out and made a scene walking into The Hill's boutique gourmet market, which had previously served as a small, neighborhood grocery. She got two six packs from the cooler and then flirted with the middle-aged proprietor who was about to close. She looked him full in the face, tossed her blond wig to and fro and leaned low over the counter to examine the two wines he suggested. He took a long, unsettling look despite being a regular church-goer. She hooker-walked out five minutes later with a large shopping bag.

"They had a pretty good wine selection," she said in the Blazer. "I asked him to recommend a good West Virginia label. He admitted he didn't know of a single winery in the state. So he came up with a Napa Valley merlot, Stag's Leap '74. Said it was only known out there. Said he found it on a buying trip last year. I also got two six packs of Stroh's for the Biggie boy."

"You couldn't do better than that cheap shit?" Corelli asked.

"The guy will remember the flashy hooker with taste, at least in wine, and the guy who wanted Stroh's."

Corelli smiled, impressed.

Roberta let her mini-skirt ride up as Biggie drove down the long hill to Loudendale. He declined a beer.

"Drink it!" Corelli ordered.

Roberta pulled the ring and dropped it in the can. She handed it to Biggie's right hand, next to the steering wheel.

As they descended, they passed a rock outcrop that greeted visitors with: "Creekers Eat SHIT."

Charleston's Old Money was ambivalent and sometimes sensitive about West Virginia's "treasonous" origins and their permanent estrangement from the fullness of the lost life in Charlottesville and Richmond. Among themselves, Old Money Hillers would now and then snicker gently but with forbearance about their connections to the unfortunates who lived jammed next to each other up the narrow hollers and down in the knife-cut creek bottoms. The Creekers did the work that made the Hiller fortunes, which both sides understood and never forgot. Charleston's "First Families" considered mingling with their fellow Scots-Irish and English cousins in the hollers as a limited obligation. The men looked forward to the occasional "mixed" companionship of coon hunts where they could drink whiskey, chew tobacco, tell lies, piss anywhere and laugh at the stories they told on themselves. Their wives drove along Davis Creek to get to Berry Hills Country Club where the Loudendale/Davis Creek families served them food, toted their bags and groomed the grounds. They also supplied The Hill with quilts, honey, picked blackberries, split firewood, landscaping and backs for moving family furniture in, out and around.

Old Money on The Hill thought "Creekers" was a crude, talking-down term and told their children not to use it. When George Washington High School was built on The Hill in the early '60s, it had to take in Loudendale students, which rubbed both sides the wrong way. The Hillers were tracked into the college-bound academic programs; most of the Creekers were distributed into general courses and shops. Dating between the groups was rare. It was the children of the aspiring middle class who had just made it onto The Hill who felt the need to publicly differentiate themselves from Creekers.

"What's a 'Creeker'?" Roberta asked Biggie.

"Guys like me," he said. "Redneck trash to them who painted that sign."

"At the stop sign, turn right," Corelli said. "I've spun your hubs. Country, you shift him into four-wheel drive when the hardtop changes to dirt. You'll be goin' through the crick. Go slow through the water. I don't want no stallin' out in the middle. You stop when you see a Ford Galaxie that looks like it belongs in a junkyard."

529

The road soon turned into a dirt lane with blackberry canes scraping the Blazer's sides. They passed a lighted, shacky place on the right, then nothing but scrub brush and stunted trees. The water was not high enough to flood the Blazer's engine even had Biggie floored it.

Biggie understood they were going to kill him.

He cursed himself for not making a move in the alley. He who hesitates gets dead, he thought.

"What have I done?" Biggie asked. "Why are you doin' this?"

"Ain't my business," Corelli said. "Probably has somethin' to do with this union election. This 'reform' shit that you're peddlin'."

"You workin' for Siciliano?" Biggie asked.

"Ain't your business," Corelli said.

"It's about money. Gangsters are tryin' to screw decent coal miners who're tryin' to play it straight."

"I didn't make the world, Biggie. Life ain't fair," Corelli said.

"You an' me come up outa the same place, I 'spect," Biggie said. "No money in the cookie jar. Worked when you were a kid. Went to Nam. Came back with your eyes opened."

"Ain't gonna help you," Corelli said. "You're a problem. I'm the solution."

"You'd probably vote for Delucci if you were a miner," Biggie said.

"Probably would. But you ain't gettin' nowhere with this," Corelli said sympathetically. "A job's a job."

"This is killin'. This ain't honest work."

"I killed in Vietnam for a paycheck. Same work; a lot better pay."

"Special Forces?"

"No."

"What province?"

"Nope."

"What year?"

"Nope."

"Did you ever have anythin' against them VC?"

"Nope. I was told to figure out where the little people were and then help kill as many as we could."

"Why?" Biggie asked. "You reckon they was goin' to swim the Pacific with AK-47s in their teeth and take over L.A.? Then Vegas? Then Tony up in Pittsburgh?"

"The dinks I ran into had the Chinese copy, called it a type 56 assault rifle. Had a hooded front sight and a folding pig-sticker behind the muzzle. I saw them haul 152-mm Russian howitzers down the Ho Chi Minh trail and up mountains by hand. Women workin' just like men. Swimmin' the Pacific would be a piece of cake. We weren't going to beat them workin' like they was. They were willing' to lose 20 for our one, which counted like 100 here at home."

530

"Lurp," Biggie said.

"That ain't gettin' you off the hook. Look. Up there. See the Galaxie. Pull in next to it. Your driver's side, next to the Ford's. Put it in neutral. Leave the motor runnin'."

Biggie stopped.

"What's your favorite station?"

"WKAZ. 95.0."

"Top 40," Corelli said dismissively

"What about WKWS country?" Roberta asked. "That's what I listened to."

"Put on whatever you want," Corelli said to Roberta.

She went to 96.1 WKWS and found Barbara Mandrell singing "So pack your rusty razor. Don't bother with goodbye. Your cup runneth over. But mine is always dry."

"'Standing Room Only.' Well, at least, it wasn't 'Convoy,'" she said.

"That's a big 10-4, fur shure," Corelli said dismissively. "Let's get this over with. Get his wallet, cash and credit cards and put them on the dash. Go ahead and do him."

Roberta got his wallet off the clip chain on his belt. Then she reached over with her hands still gloved, unbuckled Biggie's belt, unbuttoned his jeans and unzipped his fly.

"Pull down his pants," Corelli said.

Biggie didn't cooperate, but he didn't kick at her either.

Roberta pulled his penis from the steam pocket between his legs. She took off her gloves. Her hands were warm and knowing. Biggie felt himself swelling between them.

Biggie strained against the cuffs. He knew his life's seconds were ticking down. He tried to think of a way out. He wasn't afraid of dying, even like this. But he didn't get the point. He didn't deserve to be killed for the little he'd done. This was a waste. Brenda would be pissed. Him gone, and no kids.

Roberta reached between Biggie's legs and planted her middle finger firmly below his sack. Then, slicking her tongue, she rubbed it against the soft, sensitive underside of his erection. Corelli touched the end of his pistol against the back of Biggie's head.

Biggie felt himself swelling. This is crazy, he thought.

He felt panic coming, mixed with sex against his will.

Roberta took him in her mouth and moved slowly. There was no sensuality in her effort, and still Biggie felt his mind centering on his prick. He felt himself rising. He pushed up and deeper into her. She felt his belly tighten, his muscles strain. Sweat popped on his forehead, he was breathing harder and faster. He gasped. His wrists burned against the cuffs. He felt the cuffs holding him. Then, deep within, he felt himself coming.

She felt it, too. He grunted. Without warning, she pushed hard against him and moved her lips fast.

Biggie came.

Corelli reached around with his straight razor as he pushed Biggie's head forward to reduce blood splatter. Roberta pulled away, back to her seat.

Corelli slashed quickly across Biggie's neck, catching the carotid arteries on either side just below the jaw line. It was over in a second.

Blood flowed immediately onto Biggie's chest. It felt like a bad razor nick. He felt himself losing consciousness. He kicked at Roberta. He thought of hogs he had shot in the head, hung on a tripod and slit their throats. Their blood drained into the dirt. His last thought—This is for shit.

Roberta spit onto Biggie's thigh. Corelli handed her a Chicopee wipe for her hands. She opened a Stroh's and washed out her mouth. She flicked some beer around Biggie's face. She wrapped Biggie's right hand around the can, then let it drop to the floor.

"Good job," Corelli said.

"Good job yourself. I don't have a drop on me."

"Had to get under the great black beard of his," Corelli said. "All right let's clean for prints," he said handing her a half dozen wipes from the package he had in his jacket pocket. Do your seat, door handle, window handle, dash, shifter, radio. Leave his prints on the wheel. Cut the radio and wipe the ignition. Take my key out and put his in. Keep your wig on until we get out of here. Don't want any of your own hairs left. I'll get the cuffs before we go. Cops might be able to trace them."

They worked quietly and steadily. It took 15 minutes to kill Biggie and clean the Blazer. Corelli opened the cuffs with separate keys. In the Galaxie, Roberta changed out of her costume into clothes she had in her suitcase. Corelli put the two sets of cuffs in a heavy-duty, plastic trash bag along with Roberta's costume—shoes, wig, clothing, gloves, sunglasses, Gucci bag, even her false eyelashes and lipstick. She emptied five beers on the ground and put the empty cans into the bag. She threw in the wipes she had used to remove her heavy makeup and clean the Blazer. Corelli added his hat and sunglasses. He put Biggie's four weapons in the bag. He left the Blazer's glove compartment open. He pocketed Biggie's cash and credit cards, then tossed his wallet on the ground next to the Blazer. He put the sealed trash bag in the Galaxie.

"I'm starting to feel like a person again," she said.

"We'll go out the other side," he said, "not the way we come in."

He drove the Galaxie slowly toward the last ford. He kept his headlights on low. They emerged onto the hardtop with tires dripping. Corelli drove at five mph with his foot lightly on the brake to burn water off the drums. Wet drums meant no braking.

Corelli understood their safety depended on how convincingly he had made it appear that Biggie Stover's murder had nothing to do with coal-miner politics and everything to do with a pimp murdering a john as part of a robbery. To do that, he had to work the cops against themselves.

Corelli knew cops. He read about them and studied them. They believed in themselves. They believed that fear would persuade America to defend itself against a growing army of criminals. Cops would contest every inch of ground they had a reasonable chance of protecting. They personalized solving crime. Unsolved crimes -- cold cases -- were more than a loss. Even lazy detectives viewed them as an insult, an inch of law and order lost, a robbery of part of their identity.

Corelli based his plan on the way he believed cops thought about crimes. Investigators were inclined to fit new cases into familiar models, into crimes they had solved before. Good cops recognized this tendency in themselves, but only a few succeeded in controlling it. Careful investigators trusted small details more than big, showy clues. The small details Corelli left would lead them to conclude that an out-of-town prostitute and her pimp had robbed and murdered an innocent local out for a quickie. That was a crime West Virginia cops could sink their teeth into.

Although the odds were on his side, Corelli knew there was always the chance that Biggie Stover's file would land on the desk of a detective just pig-headed enough, just imaginative enough, to doubt the readily found details.

Corelli knew one Pittsburgh homicide detective like that, a cop who tugged at a case until he found the one hanging thread that unraveled the whole blanket of contrivance and misdirection. Art Greiner. A dangerous man in Corelli's opinion, a guy who loved those odd early morning times when the churning of his subconscious popped open his eyes with some hot insight that melted a case frozen in place. Corelli shrugged. There was something funny about Greiner that Corelli couldn't identify. But it was unlikely an Art Greiner would get involved in Biggie Stover's file.

Details: The ladies on the Strip would relate the overheard conversation with Country Cathy, the new girl with a blond wig covering red hair and a leather Gucci bag. They would report hearing her say "Biggie." They'd mention his black Chevy Blazer. They'd say her pimp was driving a new white Bronco with West Virginia plates. Her pimp was wearing shades and a big cowboy hat. They were sure to mention her price, $50—that would not have been forgotten, because it was above market for street work. The two local pimps would swear up and down they didn't know either her or him.

The police would find Biggie's four weapons missing from where Brenda told them to look. But they would find his empty wallet, beer can, footprints of the girl and the pimp and tracks of a Ford Galaxie that had broken down at the pull-off that afternoon. They would not find any witness to a white Bronco passing through Loudendale toward Rt. 214 that evening. Several people would mention they saw a black Blazer with two people in it roll by.

The police would find Biggie with his pants down and semen on his leg. They'd find big bruises on his wrists, indicating a taste, they'd figure, for bondage. Brenda would deny Biggie had ever done anything "kooky" with her, but the cops would assume some guys had secrets, and, maybe, Brenda did, too. The pimp must have followed them. No out-of-town pimp would know this forgotten, hard-to-get-to section of Loudendale, but someone like Biggie would. They'd infer that Country Cathy cuffed him and then the pimp cut him from behind. They'd find the receipt for the Stroh's and the wine on the passenger-side floor in the paper bag Roberta had left. The proprietor would identify the blonde hooker: "She's hard to forget, officers." Try as they might, they'd never find the pimp's white Bronco. Extra would have it parted out, repainted and sold a couple of days after Corelli returned it to Eden Way.

If things went Corelli's way, these details would become "facts," which would drive the investigation into a dead end that had nothing to do with an election in the American Coal Miner's Union. The cops would spend their time looking for Country Cathy, her pimp and a white Bronco—all of which had disappeared.

Corelli would dump most of the trash bag's contents into the old coal-stoker furnace at Del Porco's. He'd clean out the ashes and run them through the stoker a second time. Then, one night, he'd toss them off the Highland Park boat launch into the Allegheny River. The Chrome-Molybdenum alloy and high-carbon steel from the weapons would be given in a sealed cardboard box to a friend of Tony's who would melt it with other scrap at the yard where he worked. When heated to 1,800 degrees F, the induction furnace turned gun metal into molten liquid ready to be cast.

He'd give Biggie's watch to Tony who would get it to a fence in New York who would leave it on a bench for a junkie dupe to steal and then get caught when he tried to pawn it. Presumably, the watch would be traced back to Biggie since it had his name engraved on the case. The pawned watch would buttress the robbery-pimp story. Biggie's credit cards and license would be sent to a wise guy in Los Angeles who would drop them in a ganged-up Mexican neighborhood. The finder, he hoped, would run up as much as he could as soon as possible before the alarm bells rang. Corelli wanted to watch Pedro trying to pass himself off as the bearded, six-foot, six-inch Frank Stover as shown on his West Virginia driver's license.

They drove the Galaxie back to the parking lot by the Union Building. Even at 9:30 p.m., some 20 vehicles remained. After checking for surveillance, they parked the Galaxie as far from its original spot as possible. The owner who had reported a stolen vehicle, the police would conclude the next day, just forgot where he had parked his forgettable heap. Why would a car thief steal that piece of shit? they would say to themselves as they closed the case. The homicide guys who had heard about a Galaxie with a bad rod in Loudendale were not likely to be talking to the car-theft cops who had stopped working the Union Building's parking lot.

Corelli and Roberta gathered their things and got into the white Bronco. Roberta turned on the radio. "I left the other six pack for the cops. I took the bottle of wine."

"Sounds like a plan," Corelli said. "After we kill it, we'll wipe it, burn off the label and break it. By the way, I like you better when you look like yourself than when you were a tricked-out blonde."

"Was this redhead thing necessary?" she asked, shaking her newly dyed hair.

"I want the hookers to report a redhead under a blond wig. The cops will be looking for a woodpecker."

"I'm a red riding hood," she said.

He laughed. "You look good Red."

"There's no accounting for taste, Corelli. You just sweep a girl off her feet."

"I've always been suave," he said as he drove toward the new I-77 entrance.

She paused. "You know he didn't seem like a bad guy."

"I doubt he was. Probably a good citizen."

Roberta settled into her seat. She looked over at him. "John, did we do the right thing down here? I mean," she laughed, "'thang.'"

"It's done," he said quickly. "Forget it."

"You know what I mean. He was like us. Like he said. Came from nothin'. He was just trying to help miners live better."

"We are soldiers," Corelli said. "We do what we're told and don't question the order. Then we get paid—a lot more than a soldier does. After a while, if you're still around, you retire and consider yourself lucky. If we didn't do Stover, Tony Bruno would have sent Jerry Multirosa. He sent us, because we know how to do it without creating problems afterward."

"I don't mind taking out a scumbag," Roberta said in a soft voice, "but this one bothers me."

"Don't go girl shit on me," Corelli said. "No soft heart."

"What if Tony told you to do me?" she asked.

"I wouldn't. I already turned down a job on a guy I knew in high school. Hope you'd extend me the same consideration."

"Would you protect me? Get me away to some place safe."

"Maybe. It depends on why he was goin' for you."

"There is another thing," she said. "What am I going to say at confession?"

Corelli started to laugh and then swallowed it. "Do you mean this Sunday? At Help of Christians?"

"Well, some Sunday," she said.

"You didn't have intercourse with him," Corelli said. "So that's one sin you don't have to worry about."

"Blow jobs don't count?" she asked.

"Well, I wouldn't mention that," he said. "This was business, not sex."

"I *was* an accomplice to murder," she said. "You can sin in business just like personal."

"Naah, it's on me, hon," Corelli said.

"If I am sincere, I will be absolved and forgiven at confession," she said.

"You can't be a hitter during the week and a confessing sinner on Sunday. It's one or the other."

"Yes."

"I absolve you, and I forgive you," Corelli said.

"You're not a priest," she said.

"I am better than any pie-in-the-sky church," he said. "My absolution means more than words from a priest who always gives absolution as long as he thinks you're sincere. I rarely give it and never to myself."

"John, you're weird," she said. "Did you ever think about doing something straight instead of this?"

"Sure. Got any suggestions?"

"Maybe. Security?"

"Like guarding money?"

"Okay. Maybe just do wise guys; no more citizens."

"Whacking wise guys is more risky than disposing of civilians," he said.

"But there would be some redeeming social value, so to speak," she said.

"Don't kid yourself, hon. For every hard-ass criminal you eliminate to improve the human herd, there's a line waiting to take his place. You and me are replaceable. Wise guys figure that killin' is a hell of lot easier than diggin' ditches."

"But we're doin' the shit work for the guys who leech money off the little guys who are just tryin' to make it. We're helping bad wops steal from good wops...or good hillbillies in this case."

"No one said life ain't rigged. I don't see any difference between shootin' a gook because Lyndon Johnson tells me to and shootin' a citizen because Tony Bruno tells me to. What's the difference between two criminals who have that power? Both are bad; 'wrong,' if you want to get churchy about it."

536

"If it's wrong, then maybe we shouldn't do it. Don't forget Canon 983.1, which I learned in Catechism class. It says the priest can't betray a penitent in any way, including revealing a crime. That's in case you change your mind about going to confession."

"Listen to me, Roberta. Our shit stays in one toilet, the one we share. That's always been the deal. No talking. No confessing."

She didn't like the tone of his voice. It scared her. Shut up, she told herself.

"That's the deal," he said. "Come closer."

She leaned over.

He reached across his chest into his holster.

She flinched.

"Here," he said. "It's rubbing into my chest. This Bronco seat is a tight little bucket."

She took the snubby 29. "Funny little gun."

"Not when you're hit with the shotgun shell that's inside it," he said. "About this other. We're not in the question business. If it doesn't suit you, get out now. If it does, don't think about it."

"You're right, John. I'm okay."

They drove straight through to Pittsburgh that night where they dropped the Bronco at Extra's garage. They drove Corelli's Valiant back to his place. They drank some of the Stag's Leap and went to bed. Roberta slept soundly.

John Corelli did not. He was walking on the pebble that Roberta Magnelli had put in his shoe.

Chapter 40

Kayford Mountain, November 30, 1975

It rained on Biggie Stover's funeral, a dispiriting winter drizzle that converted itself into a dreary shower as the preacher began and threatened to turn into a downpour as he finished.

Friends had come that Sunday morning to dig Biggie's grave in the Stover Family Cemetery above and behind his house. They used shovels, picks, mattocks and rock bars. They rejected using a backhoe. Two feet down, they hit a sandstone ledge. Cursing, they chipped at it with rock bars and picks. It was hard, tedious, discouraging work—digging a big hole for a big friend. When they finished, they sat on a tarp at the lip of the grave with their boots dangling over the abyss, drinking beer, smoking, talking of revenge and getting soaked beyond caring.

Hartwell's Funeral Home erected a graveside tent for the mourners, spread a ground cloth and set up folding metal seats in rows. The rain dripped through the canvas enough to be annoying. A neighbor had built a rough coffin from air-dried poplar boards he had stickered and stacked in an outbuilding five years earlier. A humble, unplaned coffin had been Biggie's stated desire in the will Brenda read for the first time about an hour after police called her.

At one o'clock, eight pallbearers dressed in camouflage and hunting gear carried the extra-extra-large coffin from the four-wheel-drive hearse to the grave. Mourners walking behind on the rain-slicked path in their church shoes held on to each other. No one wanted to end up in the mud at a funeral. The pallbearers struggled with Biggie's weight, bumping their hips into the casket and getting out of sync with each other. They struggled to lift Biggie onto the black-draped dolly next to the grave.

Ezra Powell, the preacher from Brenda's Glorious Word Primitive Full Gospel Church, spoke about the mystery of the Lord's ways. To his credit and at Brenda's request, he did not ask of Death, Where is your sting? She felt a lot more than a sting. Ezra made it short and said nothing about the circumstances of Biggie's passing. He had never liked her husband, because Biggie told Brenda that Powell was "nothin' more than a voodoo-pushin' jackanapes who wouldn't do honest work."

As the coffin rested on the dolly, Jeep took out a permanent marker and wrote a message on its lid. The ink bled into the rough-cut wood. Friends and family followed. The pallbearers -- Bennie Davis, Deadly Lively, five miners and Jeep Delucci -- slipped four slings under the coffin, lifted it over the grave and, to a count, lowered it hand over hand. The coffin came to rest on two short skids.

Brenda sat in the first row, leaning against her mother who had given her daughter her own widow's veil.

When Biggie was in the ground, Jeep stepped to the head of the grave and spoke to the crowd of more than 200 mourners.

Me and Biggie go back to the beginnin'.

You were my best friend. You saved my life over there. I would trade places with you in a heartbeat.

This ain't right. To be murdered like that. I wouldn't do a damn varmint thataway. Nobody would.

No one should ever think Biggie got himself into this situation with that lady. Biggie wasn't that kind. I know. Biggie was set up. This is about our campaign and the election. Pure and simple.

This is cold-blooded murder I'm talkin' about.

We're coal miners. We have it better than our Daddies and Mommas had it, and they had it better than theirs. We ain't starvin' no more. We got a roof over our heads, a couple of cars, a pickup. Our kids ain't eatin' commodity peanut butter like some of us had to. The sheriff don't come to throw us out of the comp'ny house if we take the Union pledge.

The American Coal Miner's Union made our lives better. But the Union ain't like a comp'ny. The Union ain't no better than you an' me, our Daddies, our Mommas, our wives, daughters and sisters, all the women that stuck it out with us through all that thin and so little thick.

Now we say the Union done made our lives better and minin' coal safer. But the fact is we done it, workin' together, workin' through the Union. We -- you an' me, everyone here, everyone before us -- we done it.

Now what's happened is the miner has got it pretty good. We've gotten fat and lazy. When things got better, we stopped doin' for the Union and started expectin' the Union to do for us. The Union became somethin' up thar in Warshington, somethin' like the Social Security, somethin' that sends you a check every month and then tells you who to vote for.

The Union became somethin' outside of you an' me. It became somethin' apart from the membership. And Joe Hunt slipped into that. He thinks he's the Union, not the people here around this grave, not the people goin' underground, not the women who keep us goin'.

Joe Hunt thinks the Union is like that mountain yonder. It's supposed to look like one of them Egyptian pyramids with him at the top and a whole bunch of workin' miners down at the bottom.

Me an' Biggie, we saw it just the opposite. We want the mountain upside down, workin' miners at the top, runnin' the show.

Biggie and me figured Joe Hunt would throw some rough stuff our way—like beatin' up Vernie Skeens who's a-standin' right over there. We figured he'd get money from somewhere to buy votes.

But we never figured he'd get the damn Mafia into this election, which is what he's done. He's takin' their money and puttin' it against us. If you ask me, it's the Mafia that done Biggie like this. They killed him 'cause he was a-tryin' to stand in the way of these crim'nals from gettin' hold of the Union.

You and me, we're coal miners. We ain't stupid, an' we ain't weak. But we sure ain't used to dealin' with the likes of them boys.

Now we've come to a fork in the road. They done hurt us bad. Hurt Brenda. Me. Us. It's a hurt that won't heal up. We can quit. Or, we can stick it out to the end and give it our best shot.

I ain't sayin' we can win. But I am sayin' that if we quit now, then we've lost our pride in ourselves. That pride is what got our folks though the strikes and evictions an' blacklists and mine disasters and gun thugs.

Brenda Stover, my heart is breakin'. This shouldn't be. Me an' you and Biggie should be sittin' on your porch 50 years from now, dandlin'grandbabies an' tellin' lies.

Maybe 50 yars from now, you an' me will be sittin' on your porch tellin' the truth about what happened back here in 1975.

Boys, I'll tell ya. This train ain't rollin' in the right direction. An' it's up to us to shut that motor down and turn it around.

Shut it down an' turn it around.

Delucci stared into the grave, stared without moving. Tears fell from his cheeks into Biggie's hole on Biggie's coffin resting in Biggie's mountain.

540

No one moved. The miners hunched their shoulders against the cold and rain, having left the tent to the women, children and retirees.

Finally, Brenda stood and walked over to stand next to Jeep. The rain flattened her veil, and she shook off several men coming to her with umbrellas. Her eyes were red and puffed, and she wanted to remember this moment of misery.

> Life ain't fair, and it ain't easy.
>
> You grow up in a coal camp, you learn that right quick.
>
> I'm 26 and a widow after five years of bein' married. I waited for Biggie when he was over in Vietnam.
>
> We was just startin' out. We wanted kids. He was talkin' 'bout settin' up a camp for kids back here on the mountain. A camp for miner's kids in the summer.
>
> He was good to me. I loved him.
>
> And…that time I threw a skillet at him, which you all know about, I didn't try to hit him. He knew that. My goodness, how could I miss the big lug unless I was tryin'?
>
> They killed Biggie because he was doin' right. The Union treats us like you and me are the enemy, not the comp'nies. If we lose the Union, the comp'nies will beat us down.
>
> They took Biggie away from me, but if you men and ladies, too, don't stick together, they're gonna take away a lot more than that.
>
> If you stay with it, count me in. I'm in. All in.
>
> Shut it down an' turn it around.

Brenda walked to the side of her husband's grave, took a spade and stepped it into the loose fill. She then pitched the dirt on top of her husband's coffin. It landed with a wet, smacking thump. She handed the shovel to Delucci and started walking down the hill to her house, alone.

"You all come down an' have coffee and a bite when you're through up here," she said over her shoulder.

Brenda Stover's one helluva tough cookie, Becker thought.

One after another, mourners came to take the shovel that Brenda had used and add their bit to filling the hole and backing the promise she had made.

Delucci, Becker and several others stood off to the side. Jeep shook hands with the men and thanked the women for coming.

Willie and Susie Rutherford were the last in line. He greeted them.

"Mr. Jeep," Susie said, "we ready to do what you need."

"Thank you, Miz Rutherford, Willie. I'll call you tonight."

Delucci and Becker got into his Jeep for the slow ride to Biggie's house. Jeep cranked the motor and turned up the heat. He cracked his window and fired up a Marlboro. They sat without moving.

"What Mafia?" Becker asked, though he knew.

"A guy named Tony Bruno from Pittsburgh."

"I know the name," Becker said.

"They're buyin' the Bank from the Union. They gave me $500,000 in cash. That's what we've been using since the nominatin' round. I'm guessin' they gave Joe the money he's been spendin' against us."

"I suspected as much," Becker said, "after Allyson Pickering told me that was her hunch. You never told me where the money came from, and I never asked."

"Me an' Biggie went up to Dee Cee a couple of weeks ago. A few days earlier, they had threatened me with a gun to my head. Said if I didn't take their money, I was dead. What was I going to do? In Dee Cee, we went to a meeting at Chickie Siciliano's house. Front guy for them. I guess they figured Biggie wouldn't play ball, but I would. They knew about you, too."

"Me!"

"Told me to fire you from the campaign. Biggie said no. Becker, you better be careful."

"I had a call from a guy from high school. He does freelance work for Bruno. Said the same thing."

"You should resign."

"What are you going to do?"

"Sweat it out, I think," Jeep said. "Killin' Biggie was a message sent to me to play ball."

"Go to the cops," Becker said.

"I got nothing, no proof, nothing on paper, no tape recording. Squat."

"You got their money."

"It came in cash. And Mafia is not printed on the bills. They'll simply deny they gave me anythin'. Biggie was my only witness. Foster Shives is on their side, too."

"Shit," Becker said.

"No lawyer ever said it better," Jeep said with a little laugh.

"Withdraw from the campaign?"

"Can't do that," Jeep said. "Not after Biggie. It'd be pissin' on his grave."

542

"Give me a cigarette," Becker said.

"You don't smoke," Jeep said, tapping a Marlboro out of his pack.

Becker accepted the cigarette and the light. "I'm starting."

"This may get rougher," Jeep said.

"I don't think they're after you," Becker said. "They want to use you, assuming you win. If you lose, they use Hunt. Win-win."

"Do you think I should have called their bluff when I was sittin' in that car with a pistol against my head?"

"They would have hurt you, not killed you. Hurt, you're under their thumb, because you're scared of getting hurt again and worse. Dead, you don't give a shit. So they'll threaten your family. People close to you. Biggie is a warning, not that you're next, but someone else would be next."

"Might be you that's next," Jeep said.

"Probably," Becker said.

"So what do I do?" Jeep asked.

"Stay in. Stick it out. Win the damn thing."

"Then what?"

"Then, we'll.., I don't know, we'll see," Becker said.

"You should drop out officially. I accept your resignation. I'll get Dicey to contact the papers. That should give you protection."

"Do want me to come on as general counsel if you win?"

"Let's see how this plays out. I'm thinkin' of your best interest."

"Okay," Becker said.

"I got something to do in Logan. I'll be back in Charleston as soon as I can."

Book Four

Chapter 41

Pittsburgh, November 30, 1975

Allyson Pickering had holed up in her Shadyside apartment for three days. She hadn't gotten out of her pajamas. She told Kennedy Brown she didn't want any company when he called.

"'It ain't me you're lookin' for, babe,'" she sung a little off key owing to the booze.

"We are not a Bob Dylan song," Kennedy said with obvious control. "Let's wait until this thing that's troubling you sorts out. Then we can come to the table without pushing a dead skunk ahead of us."

"Perfectly rational," she said, "as always."

"Rationality is not a vice," he said. "It's not a character flaw."

"You're right. I'll call if I become more rational." She hung up.

Allyson didn't take a shower. She had stacked the few dishes she had dirtied in the sink, unrinsed.

She cried, and she swore. She smoked, and she drank. She looked at old pictures of herself in Wonalancet. Of her and Becker at Mandy's farm. Of her in journalism school. She was seeking a centered place in her past from which to start again.

She got dressed and spent all of Sunday at the central Carnegie Library.

On Monday morning, December 1st, Allyson showered, dressed like a reporter, put on war paint and walked into The Pittsburgh Post-Gazette building. She took the elevator down to the morgue, which upper management had recently renamed The Library.

Ruth Ann Rapucci, the head librarian, greeted her. Allyson had always liked Ruth Ann, a fleshy woman in her early 50s with graying hair who never gave up her 1961 lacquered bouffant. Ruth Ann possessed an encyclopedic knowledge of the paper's clips, which she had been collecting and filing since graduating from Oakland's Schenley High School. She liked her job. Reporters valued and trusted her.

"I heard, Allyson," Ruth Ann said. "Sorry."

"Davey did the right thing," Allyson said. "No hard feelings. I'm going to freelance a couple of articles. May I use *your* library?"

"Sure. I don't see any harm in that. You're a member of the general public."

Allyson gave her three names -- Anthony "Tony" Bruno, George Hyskra and Louis Lazarro -- and one subject file, Pittsburgh Mafia.

Ruth Ann began pulling a few old folders and microfilm reels, which she put on Allyson's desk.

Allyson looked through the files as Ruth Ann waited.

"Do you know Bruno?" Allyson asked her.

"I know who he is," Ruth Ann said. "The other two, no."

"I'm looking for an answer. Why did Lazarro and Hyskra go to West Virginia to beat up a coal miner several months back? The miner was a Delucci supporter. He's the reform candidate in the ACMU. Why would these two go there to do that? Who's behind it, and why?"

"Maybe the other candidate, Joe Hunt, hired them?"

"Maybe."

"So you think Tony Bruno sent them. Why would he do that?" Rapucci asked.

"I don't know," Allyson said. "Maybe, Hunt paid Bruno for their services. Maybe there's something in the clips that will give me a clue."

"If my memory serves," Ruth Ann said, "Tony Bruno did a little time for something or other when he was just out of high school, then nothing. Maybe it was getting in a fight. He's always attracted rumors. No indictments that I recall. He's now on the board of several charities and civic organizations. He owns a couple of pizzerias and car washes. Some of his relatives have a wholesale produce business down on the Strip. Italians know about other Italians."

"Do you know any other names I should check out?" Allyson asked.

"Well, Pete Luparelli was the head of the local gangsters in the '40s and '50s. His nickname was 'Needles,' because he learned to crochet in prison. He came out of Prohibition with a lot of money from bootlegging and speakeasies. Pete always had numbers, gambling…that sort of thing. And then there was Al Machete after Luparelli."

"That's his real name, 'Machete,' like the sword?"

"Yes," Ruth Ann said. "Bruno took over quickly from Machete who was a big knife but not very sharp from what I've heard."

"Is Tony the local Mafia boss for the national organization?"

Ruth Ann offered a small smile. "It's 1975. The Mafia isn't around the way it was under Luparelli. I guess Bruno's a local contact."

"There are very few clips in the Mafia file," Allyson said.

"The paper hasn't done many stories about it. I'm sure they still do bookmaking, maybe loansharking, that sort of thing. I think the Kennedy Justice Department backed them down in the early '60s. Then Jimmy Hoffa disappeared at few months back. Whatever's left of them -- and good riddance, I say -- aren't nice guys, but they're not the gangsters they once were."

"I'll see what I can find," Allyson said,

"Whatever Bruno's doing, it's buried and probably doesn't amount to that much anymore. That's what I hear. But what do I know? I sit in this basement eight hours a day. Let me know whatever else you're looking for."

In the library, Allyson started with stories from Pittsburgh papers in the late 19th Century. She traced the roots of the Pittsburgh Mafia -- La Cosa Nostra (LCN) or "Our Thing" -- back to the fears, vulnerability and uprootedness of poor Italian and Sicilian immigrants fleeing stagnant, feudal societies. They washed up in alien industrial workplaces and dreadful urban slums where they had few defenses against criminals, employers and police. She found copies of English-only contracts for five-year indentures that bound x-signing, immigrants to Andrew Carnegie's steel mills and Rockefeller's coal mines in return for "free" ocean passage. The newcomers found America's open-hearth furnaces and coal pits as tightly controlled as the wheat-growing *latifundia* they had fled.

In Pittsburgh's Little Italys -- East Liberty, Larimer, Bloomfield, the Hill District and Homewood -- Italians were easily extorted by the The Black Hand (*La Mano Nera*) that appeared in the early 1900s. The immigrants understood The Black Hand. Those small businessmen and landlords who resisted paying for "protection" found their businesses bombed or burned.

Established Presbyterian Pittsburgh hated the shabby Italian Catholic newcomers who couldn't speak English without adding a vowel to every noun and verb. But their loathing and dismissals were tempered by fear that all Italians were members of The Black Hand, or, at least, had connections to its thugs.

Allyson read lurid pre-WWI accounts of Black Hand involvement in extortion, gambling, prostitution, loansharking and an occasional murder—all of which occurred among Italians. Prohibition swept the Black Hand gangsters into the mainstream. Some Irish and Jews worked with them in the '20s and early '30s, particularly "Pittsburgh Hymie" Martin, a spats-wearing rumrunner who also provided murder for money. The Pittsburgh Mafia appeared to involve fewer Jews in major operations than the New York, Chicago and Los Angeles mobs.

Allyson found no mention of anyone like a Meyer Lansky, Moe Dalitz, Bugsy Siegel or Sidney Korshak in the clips. But she did find one story that mentioned "The 40 Thieves," which was an informal group of small-time Jewish bookies, gamblers, scammers, con men, fences, protection racketeers, fraudsters, swindlers, loansharks and shady bookkeepers. The story implied the Thieves knew each other and would work together as needed, but they never structured themselves into a leader-led organization.

Bootlegging in Pittsburgh during Prohibition was an Italian-Sicilian operation with Jews and ethnic whites working the retail end as bar owners in working-class and poor neighborhoods. The Presbyterians and Episcopalians bought their alcohol from "connections" and drank at home and in private clubs. The Prohibition-era Mafia -- successor to the Black Hand -- provided alcohol to anyone who could buy it.

The Mob's Old-World methods became channeled into the mainstream of America's consciousness in these years. In Pittsburgh's Allegheny County alone, more than 200 gangland murders were recorded between 1926 and 1933, with only half being solved. Most of this mayhem was over control of bootlegging.

The American Mafia was strengthened after Benito Mussolini forced Sicilian Mafiosi to flee. Carlo Gambino and Joe Bonanno settled in New York. When Pittsburgh was made one of 24 American Mafia families under Lucky Luciano's Commission in the mid-'30s, the shooting wars among rival Pittsburgh factions wound down. One organization emerged.

By the '50s and '60s, the Mafia was a substantial presence throughout western Pennsylvania, eastern Ohio and northern West Virginia. It was run after WWII by Needles Luparelli and soon, following his natural death and the forced departure of Al Machete, by his son-in-law, Tony Bruno.

Allyson learned Bruno had been arrested in the '50s -- assault and bookmaking -- with no convictions. After marrying Josephine Luparelli, the arrests stopped.

A decade later in 1965, Tony's name appeared on the <u>Post-Gazette</u>'s business page when Pennsy Beer announced he was one of its new owners. The story stated the brewery had been on the ropes because its small physical plant could not be expanded, and it carried a union contract with high labor costs. Within three months of Tony's involvement, adjoining landowners sold their property to Pennsy Beer for additional plant space. The brewery workers union renegotiated its contract prior to its expiration. Pennsy suddenly found its brew in demand at taverns all over the Tri-state area. Pennsy kegs replaced other brands for bar drafts after two recalcitrant owners found their Budweiser kegs laced with kerosene. One anonymous bar owner was quoted as saying he had been told by "the 'sales guy' from an unnamed vending company that "my monthly lease fees for my jukebox, cigarette machine and pinball game would double if I didn't go along with taking the new Pennsy keg-and-bottle quota. If I don't take their beer whether I can sell it or not, the bar'll be torched. The sales guy didn't have to say it. He just left me his lighter as a reminder."

Allyson also found Bruno headed Steel Town Construction, which obtained major contracts from the public and private sectors.

By the late 1960s, Tony Bruno, operating the Mob from Del Porco's on Larimer Avenue with a downtown office for Steel Town Construction, had become a civic stalwart. Local skeptics conceded he was an up-from-his-own-humble-beginnings ruffian who could get projects built on time and within budget. Laurie Mascaro had polished him enough to pass a perfunctory inspection. It was rumored that each of Tony's construction projects carried an "unrecorded cash tax" that went directly into his hands. Some of it stayed, and the rest went up his chain of command. The tax was the kickback contractors paid to work on Tony's projects. Its cost was passed on to the developer and, ultimately, the customers. When Tony's mother died in 1965, several judges and prominent politicians attended her funeral. Tony was named to the board of Oakland Hospital and the Pittsburgh Art Gallery though he had never evinced an interest in any art other than pin-up calendars. He figured a hospital connection might come in handy.

At lunch, Allyson cornered the PG's crime reporter and asked him what he knew. Danny Manifesto told her what she had already learned with a few additional pieces of information. He had heard -- but never confirmed -- the U.S. District Attorney once thought Bruno was involved in a money-laundering scheme through his car washes.

"Whatever they did to investigate didn't seem to be enough to support a conviction," Manifesto said.

"Anything else?"

"Tony Bruno protects himself and is protected. He stays behind -- and out of sight of -- all the conventional Mafia criminality. He's set it up with so many layers of corporate covers that the paper trail never leads back to him personally. All of the crime stuff he does is oral; no paper. He gets his office, house, phones and car swept for bugs weekly. He takes 'birdwatching' walks with the wise guys in Frick Park. He carries a pair of binoculars, says he's looking for a 'rare federal protected species, the yellow canary.' He has an office at Del Porco's Bar on Larimer Avenue.

"He has one well-known habit—a regular poker game with the Barsky boys, Nate and Maxie, and whoever those two can sucker in. It's held on the first Saturday night of the month in a room over the kitchen at Mandelbaum's Deli on Murray Avenue in Squirrel Hill. Apparently, Tony Bruno has a taste for corned beef, good pickles and weak poker players.

"There's still strong-arm activity in town -- you know, collections, extortion, protection money -- and some contract work. When I asked around, I learned that Lazarro and Hyskra did his scut jobs. I've heard there's a Vietnam vet who does his 'complicated' jobs. Don't have a name. I've also heard Tony's moving into trash hauling and scrap yards."

Scrap? Allyson thought. Wasn't Becker's father in scrap? Or as Boo put it with such freight: "His father is in that business, and his mother does the scraps books."

"Has the PG done anything on Bruno within the last five or 10 years?" she asked.

"Nope," Danny said.

"Why?"

"Interesting question. I've asked to be given time to follow these leads, but Davey always said he's too short-handed to free me for a big project. Then he gave me his riff on needing to feed the dragon every day."

"I got the same lecture," she said. "Do you think that's the reason?"

"I like Davey," Danny said. "He's a good editor. I'd say he's been told to focus on other stories, 'positive' stories. You know the PG is having money problems and declining subscriptions.

"One other thing. There's a Pittsburgh Police detective, Art Greiner, who seems to keep a weak eye on Tony to the extent he can. I think he keeps files. I haven't seen them. Greiner might be willing to talk to you."

"Davey mentioned him. Thanks, Danny."

"I wouldn't go into this if I were you. You'll be poking around on your own. No PG. No protection. Tony Bruno is a real Mafia boss. I heard he was once asked by Frank Fagano, the New York Mafia chief, why Pittsburgh was such a good Mob town. 'Because,' Tony reportedly said, 'we got three rivers and almost 40 bridges.'"

"'Bridges,' like for throwing bodies from?"

"'Like for throwing bodies from.' You'll be waving your ass like a slow-moving target in a shooting gallery," Danny said.

"Mixed metaphor," she said without humor.

"You get my point," he said.

"Maybe I can wave my ass faster than you think."

"The question is," he said, "will it be fast enough?"

Ruth Ann Rapucci left her desk 15 minutes after Allyson walked out of her below-grade library. She hurried three blocks to a pay phone on Smithfield Street. She dialed the number printed on a 3x5 index card.

A gruff male voice: "441-5863. Who's this?"

"Ruth Ann Rapucci, from the paper."

"Hold on. I'll get him. He's eatin'."

This was a good thing, she thought, that she was doing for herself and her family.

Art Greiner had been talking with Allyson Pickering since 3 p.m. in a far corner of the open stacks at the Oakland Carnegie Library next to the Carnegie Museum of Art, which was next to the Carnegie Museum of Natural History.

"Good choice. Wise guys don't read much Plato after lunch," he had told her when she suggested that they meet in the main reading room by the card catalogue in mid-afternoon.

"How will I know you?" she had asked.

"I'll be wearing a black fedora with a stupid little feather in the band."

"What's a fedora?"

"It's what your Dad probably wore in 1953," he answered. "I'll be carrying a black overcoat. I look like a gangster."

"Just what I need. I'll tie my hair in a ponytail with a red ribbon."

"I know your type."

"What *is* my type?" Allyson had wondered.

"Oh, you know," Greiner had said, "Probably tall and pretty. Maybe a little boney. Good teeth. Decent figure. Educated. Earnest. A missionary, maybe, 100 years earlier."

"Fuck you," Allyson said.

"You sound like my kind of girl," Greiner said, "Mzzzz. Pickering."

Allyson spotted Art Greiner immediately when she entered the main reading room. He was built like a Hollywood thug. His face was broad, long, boxy and unrefined. His crewcut marked him as a '50s loyalist. His suit fit badly; his shoes weren't shined. His tie would have been grateful to have been selected last at a Goodwill close-out sale. He carried a black overcoat and a funny little hat in his hands. She nodded to him. He jerked his head toward the stacks. She went straight back to her desk without stopping. He followed a few minutes later. They settled in at the far end of the shelving. He sat on a window ledge. He stuffed his coat next to hers on the 345 shelf, criminal law.

"Corelli," Greiner said without introduction. "John Corelli. Local talent. That's who you got to watch for. He bats cleanup, but I never could catch him in a box score."

Allyson wasn't exactly sure of Greiner's meaning. She looked at him—a middle-aged man with an unfashionable haircut in a baggy suit. His mouth was drawn down in a way that projected universal doubt. He was tall and wide. He didn't look bright or curious. He had, she thought, "cop eyes," always looking for the rock with something under it.

"You mean he cleans up messes Tony Bruno leaves behind?" she asked.

"Not exactly, hon. Corelli moves the runners around to home and leaves no mess," he said patiently. Art Greiner figured he was going to have to be Allyson's training wheels on her first ride down Mafia Street.

She frowned and shook her head. "I don't follow."

"I'm guessin' here," Greiner said. "My guess is Corelli does some of the important killings for LCN central. I'm guessin' they go through Tony." Greiner thought for a second or two, then added: "You might not want to put no more guesses in your reporting."

"I agree," she said.

"Are you by any chance already on Tony's shit list, hon?" Greiner asked. He rubbed his eyes as if they were tired of looking for hidden things.

"How could I be? He doesn't know me from Adam's house cat."

"You should keep it that way," Greiner said. "If you keep askin' questions, you're gonna pop out on his radar like Jayne Mansfield's bazzongas at a 3D drive-in movie. You probably never been to a drive-in…with a boy."

"I wasn't allowed to go to a drive-in when I was in high school," she said, "but I've been to a lot of mopey movies with subtitles. I'm sure boys try the same things wherever."

Greiner smiled, then snorted out a laugh. "You ain't as bad as you look."

"I look bad?"

"Wholesome."

"I wish," she said.

"Classy-wholesome," Greiner concluded. "Anyway, I'd stay away from Corelli at all costs. As for Tony Bruno, I'd do the same. It's too dangerous."

"I don't care," she said.

"That's bein' foolish, not brave," Greiner said.

"Just give me a little information to get started."

Greiner saw that Allyson was pursuing her ideas with or without his direction. "Tony, I suspect, has arranged for a certain amount of protection in my department. He might contribute to some of our judges and politicians."

"You mean he pays them off?"

"One way or another," Greiner said. "He helps palms-up Patsy Brennan, our lowly-regarded mayor, with home remodeling through one of his construction outfits. Charges her way below market. I've heard he's helping my own chief, Pete Bolkovic, buy property out in Sewickley through Josie's -- that Pete's wife -- chicken-shit lawyer brother out in Munhall. Bolkovic puts it in Eddie Pavlik's name, not his own. Eddie transfers title for one dollar a couple of years later. Pete throws Eddie a couple of grand for his signature and his recreational interest in white powder."

"This Eddie Pavlik.., he skis?" Allyson asked, surprised.

"Yeah," Greiner laughed, "Eddie does a lot of downhill. The last time I saw Eddie in court, he was representing a DUI. He actually asked the judge for a 'coke break.'"

"Does Bruno have an arrangement at the PG, too?"

"Probably not. Unless, he has something on the publisher or the editor. Like a thing for one of Tony's workin' girls. But I never picked up anything like that."

"I never heard any office chatter about Davey Bloom, the editor, or the publisher," Allyson said, "but the paper avoids investigating local organized crime."

"The thing you have to realize about Tony is his influence goes where you don't expect. He is asked to do favors for very respectable people. He's asked to help kids get into college. He contributes to a lot of good things in the community. Sometimes he does a favor without being asked as long as the person knows who did it for him. Like maybe he gets the Teamsters drivers at the paper to stay on the job when their contract expires. Being helpful is the way he infiltrates normal society. You accept a guy who helps you out. So we lay off him. If you bring down Tony, you might bring down people you wouldn't think are connected. It would be like opening up a madam's little black book."

"Does he have his hooks in everybody?"

"Not everybody, hon. The thing is, you don't know who is and who ain't his friend."

"This is depressing."

"If I was you, I wouldn't stick my pretty little silver spoon into Tony's minestrone. He's in the bigs; you're in the junior league."

She laughed. "Very good, detective."

"Let someone who has some cover and who ain't hangin' onto a dead tree branch by her eyelashes take a run at the LCN."

Allyson caught herself starting to pout.

"Corelli don't make mistakes, hon. He don't leave tracks. Or he leaves tracks that don't lead nowhere. I respect folks who are at the top of their profession. Which ain't you right now. I'm not tryin' to be mean. You are what you are."

"I *am* damaged goods," she said. "Maybe I can make things right if I nail this story."

"You were fired, we might say, under a cloud. And now you're muckin' around in a lion's cage."

"So why did you meet me?"

"Curiosity. My business is to know who knows what, how they know what, who's interested in knowing what, who thinks he -- or she -- knows what and what that person might do to find out the next what."

"So if what's on second, who's on first?"

Greiner laughed. "Okay. That was okay for a girl who don't know a can of corn from a dying quail."

What the hell is he talking about? she wondered. "Quail—you keep both eyes open and lead the bird."

Greiner laughed.

"Daddy," she said. "He shoots."

"So now you know that Tony runs the local LCN. And John Corelli works for him, sometimes. So what's your story?"

552

"Humor me a little more," Allyson said, without waiting for his assent. "This LCN, as you call it, wants control of the American Bank of Washington, which the ACMU owns. My guess is they're looking for a cash-rich union to take the place of what they're losing with the Teamsters. To make sure the Bank and the ACMU fall in their lap, Bruno may be funding both Hunt and Delucci. Both have gotten big slugs of cash in the last several weeks from who knows where? Don't start with Who's again."

He laughed.

"I think the Mob has already bought the ABW. It gives them a self-service laundromat for their dirty cash. The Union's pension and health-care fund gives them easy money to buy legitimate businesses."

"Tony dresses like a business guy now and can talk different than he used to," Greiner said. "But buying a bank ain't a pitch in his wheelhouse. Somebody bigger is behind that. Tony don't have the brains to run a bank or the bucks to buy one."

"Well, how hard is it to steal the purchase price out of an acquired Bank? Isn't that what the leveraged-buyout types do?" Allyson asked. "My types."

"Same idea, different vocabularies," Greiner said. "It ain't hard to steal, but it does take brains to steal over many years without getting greedy or caught. A good crooked business has to balance makin' enough money to let the wise guys milk it without killing it. It's harder than it looks."

"If it's not Bruno with the brains, it's somebody with the brains," Allyson said. "Somebody is doing this. It's not nobody who's doing this."

My God, I'm starting to sound like these cops and robbers, she thought.

"You're right. It's not nobody."

"I'm also guessing," Allyson said, "that federal bank regulators under President Ford don't have to be told to look the other way."

"Don't know about them," Greiner said. "I'm just local eyes and ears. I'm sure Tony and his friends have contributed to both parties, mostly Republicans in '72. I can't see Giancana or Marcello handing a couple of million to a righteous Methodist like George McGovern. McGovern isn't flexible. Nixon was. Ford is."

"I've been in the clips at the paper and here," Allyson said. "I called friends who are reporters at The Washington Post."

"What did you find?"

"You have to know Gerald Ford's record to understand why he won't stop the Mafia from moving into the ACMU and the Bank."

"What do you have?"

"Ford never had a problem with the Mafia in Michigan," she said.

"If the Mob got to Ford," Greiner said, "it was through the Teamsters and the Detroit Partnership, the Mafia family closest to his home in Grand Rapids. Ford's too young to have known The Purple Gang, which ran organized crime in most of Michigan during Prohibition. But I'm sure he knows Joe Zerilli who has led the Detroit Mob for years, along with the Toccos and Giacalones. They took over from the Jewish Purple Gang after Prohibition.

"There's a Republican money guy, Max Fisher, who, I'm told, was a runner for The Purple Gang carrying money into Canada to buy booze from the Bronfmans. Fisher is Ford's principal financial backer. These old connections don't necessarily vanish over time. Fisher's father was in the oil-distribution business. When Prohibition ended, Max built a chain of gas stations, then went into real estate, United Fruit and philanthropy. Very respectable today."

"I didn't know that," Allyson said.

"A lot of respectable people today were involved in bootlegging and the rackets when they were young," Greiner said. "People do what they have to do to make it."

That comment puzzled Allyson. She dismissed it.

"Ford wants the Teamsters' endorsement in 1976, like Nixon in '72," she said. "Teamster money came to Nixon for pardoning Jimmy Hoffa at the end of '71. The deal was that Hoffa agreed to stay out of the Teamsters. Frank Fitzsimmons, Hoffa's successor, didn't want him back. But Jimmy wanted back in."

"I've heard," Greiner said, "Hoffa wanted the Mob to repay their loans; Fitzsimmons didn't. So the Mafia, too, wanted Jimmy kept out of the Teamsters. They solved their Hoffa problem a few months ago."

"Ford had to know about the connection between the Mafia, Teamsters and Nixon," Allyson said. "He's not going to squirrel up a Mob play for a bank before the '76 election or, I think, after. He needs Teamster votes and cash to offset the stench of the Nixon pardon."

Greiner nodded in agreement. "From my humble perspective, Ford and the FBI don't really want to solve Hoffa's disappearance, because that will lead back through the Teamsters to the Mafia. Hoffa found alive or dead is a problem. Hoffa not found is not a problem; he's just a mystery. The RICO Act still hasn't been used against the Mafia after five years. That tells you a whole bunch about Nixon, Ford and the FBI. Still, there's no law against crooks operating a legitimate business legitimately, including a bank. But operating on the up and up is not what they have in mind."

"This is overwhelming," Allyson said, "I can't go in all these directions."

"One more thing is I wouldn't count on Clarence Kelley to sic the FBI on this bank deal," Greiner said. "Kelley was police chief in Kansas City, Missouri, for years. He got along just fine with Nicolas Civella who ran the Mafia there. Civella used Teamster money to set up the Tropicana casino in Las Vegas. And that's just one of a dozen or so casinos the Mob owned in the '50s and '60s using Teamster money—Flamingo, Stardust, Desert Inn, Riviera, Hacienda, Golden Nugget, Sahara, Fremont, Sands, Dunes, Caesars Palace, Circus Circus and the Thunderbird. They're the ones I know about. It's something like $250 million that came from the Teamsters to buy these places for the Mafia. And Bobby Kennedy's crusade against the Mob and the Teamsters never curbed their Vegas holdings.

"Then Howard Hughes started buying Mob casinos in the late '60s. But, and here's the big but—Mob guys like Moe Dalitz at the Desert Inn continued to manage the casinos after their sale to Hughes. Howard, apparently, wanted to own everything and all the land around everything, but he didn't much care about whether he was getting a square deal on casino income as long as he could pay as little tax as possible. Dalitz skimmed cash from the count room and the slots. The FBI estimated they skimmed more than $300 million from Hughes's seven casinos. Hughes bailed on Vegas after four years. Didn't like atomic testing 65 miles away. Offered Nixon a $1 million bribe to stop them. Nixon didn't take it."

"Where am I?" Allyson asked. "Oh right. Kelley at the FBI made his peace with the Kansas City crooks years back, so he won't investigate the Mafia and the ABW deal."

"Kelly hasn't done much on organized crime since he took over from Hoover in 1973. Maybe, he'll do more with Nixon out of the picture. The wise guys learned with the Teamsters to keep their thieving under the radar. This bank buy will look clean. It'll be a slow bleed."

Allyson grimaced. "No one cares enough to stop it until it gets so bad that it can't keep being ignored."

"Like an ingrown toenail," Greiner said.

"But it makes sense to cut the nail before it buries deeply into your flesh, doesn't it?" she said.

"No one ain't sayin' no to that," Greiner said, shifting his weight and uncrossing his legs. "An ounce of prevention is worth more than a pound of boo-hooing after the *facto*."

"Another Greinerism."

"You can beat back the wise guys here or there, but you can never shake free of them," Greiner said. "They see stealing as an honorable trade—a full-time, lifelong business. There will always be people who steal, because stealing is part of human nature. Every society -- every culture, race, religion and ethnic group -- has thieves. Anyway, hon, you got nothin' new on them. You know what's already out there."

"I'm looking," she said, "for the right thread to pull. I want it to go all the way to the top. Maybe Corelli is that thread."

"Bad idea, hon. Pull on him, and you'll get yanked."

555

Allyson intentionally paid no attention to that warning. "I'm guessing Corelli and a woman killed a man named Frank "Biggie" Stover a few days ago near Charleston. Stover was Delucci's best friend, his consigliere in the campaign. I think Stover pushed Lazarro and Hyskra off the road. I have absolutely no proof that Corelli killed Stover. But it fits with Bruno funding Delucci's campaign. Bruno had Corelli kill Stover, because he wouldn't go along with mobbing up the ACMU. Delucci, I think, was going along for whatever reason. Maybe, his life was threatened. Stover, from what I've picked up, was the ethically stronger of the two. If I can tie Corelli to Stover's murder, maybe it will lead back to Bruno and whoever pulls his strings."

"You have three dead guys and a brain full of hunches," Greiner said. "I need a cigarette."

"You can't smoke in library stacks," Allyson said with exaggerated primness. "Didn't you learn anything at Harvard?"

"'Harvard.' Right. Except we called it Arsenal Washington Vocational Technical High School in Lawrenceville. I was in Manual Arts. I took machine shop—a LeBlond Regal metal-working lathe, power saws, milling machine, 25-ton press brake, measuring tools, blueprints, clamps, shanks, mallets. If you ever need to mill a shaft with a keyway, I'm your man."

"Give me your business card. How did you become a cop?" she asked.

"I got bored in Billy Schmidt's Machine Shop. I guess I had some smarts. Well, that's a lie. I was curious about how things fit together and why. Solving a problem in a machine design ain't a lot different than figuring out who did a crime."

"Do you have anything in your files that can help me?" Allyson asked.

"Like you, I have more guesses than answers," Greiner said. "My files are my life-insurance plan. I need to keep them mysterious. I might be considered expendable otherwise. Surplus."

"I don't understand."

"Leverage comes from what you have on people as well as what they perceive you have on them."

"Oh," she said.

"Tony doesn't want out what he thinks I know. If he whacks me, the files would open like Gomorrah's Box."

"Hope was left inside *Pandora's* Box when she let out all the evils," Allyson said.

"Who?"

"Pandora, not Gomorrah," Allyson said gently. "Pandora was the first woman in Greek mythology, like Eve. She was cobbled together as punishment for Prometheus stealing fire. She's described as a beautiful, deceitful, seductive, money-grubbing evil whose descendants would

556

torment man forever. Men cooked up this story. It was handy to blame women for the world's miseries."

"Naw, girls ain't *that* bad."

"Thanks. Anyway, Pandora opened a jar, not a box. All the world's evils escaped, and then she locked hope inside it."

"False hope is worse than no hope," Greiner said.

"That's uplifting," she said.

"Well, what can I do? Greiner means 'quarrelsome' or 'ornery' in German. What I'm saying is you got no hope of bringing down the American Mafia with a story that no one will act on. It's too big a bite. If you go after Tony and the guys above him, you have to make sure you kill everybody over and under."

"'Kill'…as in *kill*?" she asked.

"Kill as in getting them off the street," he said. "Permanently. It ain't gonna happen. Best not to try."

"But I might be able to stop them from taking over the Union and stealing its money."

"That's possibly possible."

"So where does that leave me?"

"Nowhere you want to be."

"Let me see your files."

Art Greiner reached under his suit jacket and pulled out his .38 Smith & Wesson police special. He pointed the revolver's barrel at Allyson's eyes. "I got an FBI load in this. More powder. More stopping power. Soft-lead, hollow point. You want me to pull the trigger now and save Tony the aggravation?"

Allyson swallowed hard, almost a gulp. Her eyes fixed on the black steel and his big, heavy hands. She peered down the barrel into blackness. She had never seen a revolver close up. The oxymoron -- "real live pistol" -- ran through her mind. She looked at Greiner.

With gentleness, he said: "You could put everything I have in your story, and, if the cage is the same as now, the rats still run free because the door is open. Their cage doesn't shut tight like Pandora's Box."

"I need to see them," she said.

Greiner slowly cocked the hammer. It clicked. Allyson flinched. She looked into Greiner's eyes.

"No," he said. "If you're that desperate, you'll just get yourself killed. I'll tell you some things. But you need to be a reporter and confirm either with hard evidence or a knowledgeable source, preferably more than one."

"I agree," she said.

"I have bits and pieces linking Bruno to the five New York Families," Greiner said. "The LCN calls their leadership 'The Commission.' Bruno's the head of the Pittsburgh family. It's one of two dozen or so around the country. Tony reports to Frankie Fagano who's the big cheese. Chickie

Siciliano is their front in Washington, but he's not a player in any of their big-money decisions. He's a public layer between the bosses and the political world. They never had an official family in Washington, because the District never had much of an Italian immigrant population on which to feed.

"I have stuff that associates Bruno's boys with local drugs, arson, protection, bid rigging in his construction businesses, gambling, money laundering, bookmaking and girls…but not enough to get a jury verdict. This is normal LCN activity. A lot of my 'evidence' is hearsay. Tony doesn't leave paper trails. He uses a good lawyer dahn at The Frick Building. Hy Crammer has stacked up more shells between Tony Bruno and his rackets than a beachcomber with a collection fetish. Tony doesn't use banks for most of his cash. He uses checking accounts only for legit business—paying the rent, like that. He cleans his cash through his car washes, bars, pizzerias, massage parlors and strip clubs. Who the hell keeps a straight set of books in massage parlors and strip clubs? Tony wants to look respectable these days."

"Maybe that's the way to take him down," Allyson said. "Publicity. Peel the clothes off the emperor of crime."

"Maybe," Greiner said. "But the publicity has to land on fertile soil, clean soil, on people willing to take him to the finish line. Our local soil is not clean and fertile; Tony farms it. And don't forget, people have to trust what you write. That's a little bit of a problem, hon.

"Now about Corelli. I've seen him go into Del Porco's, but that doesn't make him a hit man. I have a snitch who says this and says that about Corelli doin' work for Bruno, but it's just a snitch sayin' this and that. I don't have anything that nails him.

"You're probably right that Stover was somethin' other than a pimp robbery. That's a good cover for Corelli. But finding evidence to make that case stand up like hair on Brycreem is a whole different kettle of fish."

"Greinerisms are better than Yogi Berra," Allyson said. "We agree that I have to prove the truth."

"Proof is a necessary evil in my business," Greiner grinned. "I did call down to the Kanawha County homicide unit this morning after you rang me up and asked about Stover."

"And?"

"Every hooker in the state and their mother saw a blonde -- not a local -- named Country Cathy get into Biggie's Chevy Blazer. She called him by name. Shouted her price. Stoned as they were, the girls remembered $50, what, maybe, they were supposed to remember. Her pimp had a cowboy hat and drove a new white Ford Bronco with West Virginia plates.

"Stover's throat was cut, clean as a whistle. It happened down in some creepy crick bottom. The cut was no butchered up thing. His pants were down; his wrists had been cuffed to the steering wheel; he went out happy.

558

A beer can has his prints. Receipt from a grocery store where she bought beer and wine was in the car. His money and cards were gone. Three hidden guns—gone. No trace of Country Cathy or her pimp, or the cowboy hat, or their white Bronco. No Pee-A license plates were seen down there around that time."

"Does that tell you anything?" she asked.

"Too much is pointing toward a pimp robbery," Greiner concluded. "I expect the credit cards will show up and the guns, too—more 'evidence' of a pimp robbery, selling the plastic and fencing the guns. But Country Cathy and her pimp don't have a history in West Virginia and probably anywhere else. They came from nowhere, for one night, for one client named Biggie Stover and then vanished into the mists like Brigadoon. Pimps and hookers move around, but they don't disappear. Robbing johns is their business; they don't eat if they don't rob."

"So what do the Charleston cops think?"

"They admit it could have something to do with the ACMU campaign, but they're 'persuaded by the evidence' that it was what it appears to be—pimp robbery. They'll file Stover's murder as an open case. They'll continue to be nagged by it, but it'll be one of the four out of 10 that'll never be solved. I need a cigarette."

"This is not right," she said, surprising herself at her own naiveté. "It's getting away with murder."

"Yeah. Life's a bitch, isn't it?"

They sat in the stacks next to criminal law for a few minutes without saying anything.

"So what do we do next?" she asked.

"'We?'"

"We," she said. "Look. I can pull what we have into a story. A spotlight on Tony Bruno is exactly what these crooks don't want. It could force them to back off. And maybe you can link him and Corelli into the Biggie Stover murder with the Pittsburgh connection."

"But you're out of the Post-Gazette. They're not going to run your stuff."

"Charlie Robb at The Pittsburgh Point will."

"Who reads that little thing?" Greiner asked.

"Everyone at the PG, for one thing," she said. "It's independent. It'll do the stories the PG and the Pittsburgh Press won't. If I do the story right, the PG won't be able to ignore it."

"Yeah? Maybe. You're forgetting that some number of people in authority have to follow up on your publicity. I need another cigarette. Some number of that some number don't want to follow up on your publicity."

"So?"

"The first thing is your personal security if you are so stupid as to pursue this losing proposition. As soon as Bruno hears you're stickin' your toe in his pot, he's gonna turn up the heat. You got a gun?"

"No! I'm a pacifist."

"All right. I'll bring one around tonight. Nothin' says pacifists can't have a gun around. You undoubtedly don't know how to shoot."

"I do, too. Skeet. Daddy taught me to use a 12-gauge shotgun at clay targets. He shoots quails and ducks."

"Rilly."

"At the Corinthian Yacht Club on the Delaware River," she added in a quick, low whisper suitable for a library. "And in New Hampshire, near our summer place."

"Im-press-ive. You know pistols, hon?"

"No."

"Point the damn thing and pull the trigger as fast as you can. You got locks on your door and windows?"

"Sure. The door has a lock. Windows—they're the old-fashioned double-hungs with a lever catch."

"Where do you park?"

"On the street wherever I can find a place."

"Notice anyone hangin' around or followin' you?"

"No."

"Well, start payin' attention. Tony's guys don't look like they belong in Shadyside unless Bruno has given you to someone smart. Look for a guy in a windbreaker or a soft, black-leather jacket—that's the usual dress."

"Okay."

"But it could be a girl—this Country Cathy in a different get up. Like a Pitt girl or a beatnik."

"It's 1975," she laughed, "there are no beatniks."

"Okay. A flower-power hippie-dippie."

"Where have all the flowers gone? I understand. I'll pay attention."

"Corelli's a big guy. Looks like Elvis, except hard. Don't open your door without knowing who's on the other side. Now, anyone local know you're interested in Bruno?"

"No," she said.

"Where did you get the information you have?"

"Mostly from the clips here and at the PG. From an old boyfriend named Jeffrey Becker who was running Delucci's campaign. He may still be. I may have gotten him fired. Unfairly."

"Didn't you talk to Danny Manifesto at the paper?"

"Well, sure. He and Bloom gave me your name."

"And who helped you in the PG's morgue?"

"Ruth Ann Rapucci. She's been there for years. She likes me."

560

"Rapucci. Yeah. Well, we'll see. Anyone else?"

"I've read what I could. Books, articles, hearings on the Mafia. I haven't interviewed anyone around here about Bruno or Corelli."

"Now here's what you do. Leave them two to me. I'll get together what I can from sources that you don't know about. I'll work on the Biggie Stover thing. You concentrate on whatever you can find out about the bank deal in Washington. Now if this Biggie Stover ran them two losers off that mountain then that buttons up their murders. But we don't know who sent them and why, and we don't know whether anyone else -- Delucci, this Becker boyfriend of yours…"

"Ex-boyfriend. Very ex."

"Right. Ex-boyfriend who still seems to be camping out in your head…whether him or Delucci ordered Stover to eliminate Lazarro and Hyskra. If not a direct order, then did either one have prior knowledge?"

"Becker says no."

"And Nixon said he wasn't a crook. Guilty people always say they're innocent."

"So do innocent people," Allyson protested. "What else can they say?"

"What I'm sayin' is you never know what you'll find when you start digging into characters, shady and otherwise. Maybe Stover acted entirely on his own like Oswald. You may find this very ex-boyfriend had knowledge of this double murder that you think Biggie Stover pulled off. At that point, you have to decide whether you're all in on all the truth, some in on all of the truth, some in on some of the truth or none in on none of it."

"I see," she said.

"So?"

"I can't honestly say what I'd do if I found that Becker was somehow involved in a murder…or two. That's not who he is. Anyway, Becker isn't the story, whatever his role. If it's too hard, I can just not write about him."

"Okay. You'll cross the ex-boyfriend bridge when the water's over the dam," Greiner said.

"Right," she said. "*If* I come to that dam, I'll see about crossing the bridge."

"Everybody comes to a place like that sooner or later."

"Art, I'm running out of time. The election is on the fifth. Today's the 30th. I need to start writing Tuesday at the latest."

"Let's see what you have by tomorrow. I need a damn cigarette."

"Me, too."

Greiner gathered his topcoat off the shelf. He held his fedora. He felt tired.

"Oh, detective, there's one other thing," she said.

"Yeah, what?"

"The spot on your tie," she said, pointing. "There."

He looked down, then bent his head lower. He saw no spot.

She kissed his cheek and whispered. "I'm charmed. Thank you."

About 8:30 p.m., Greiner rang Allyson's bell. She came down from her second-floor apartment and opened the solid-wood door.

He stood in front of her. "What did I tell you about security?"

"No one's hanging around. No one's following me."

"You don't open the door without knowing who's on the other side. Better yet. Don't open no fucking door that you can't see through."

"All right. Sure."

"Here," he said, holding a pistol in his hand. "This is an M1911 Colt .45. Big slug. There's a seven-round magazine in the grip. Use two hands on it like this. You pull the trigger, and it's ready to fire the next round. You have to rack the slide for the first round, like this. Keep it racked like I have it now. You'll forget to rack it in a pinch. Grip it with your thumbs horizontal so they don't get in the way of the slide. This gun is ready to fire. Stand with your feet apart, lean forward a little. You'll handle the recoil better. Just point and shoot."

"I hope my neighbors don't see this."

"You want me to come up and check your place?"

"No. Let me get accustomed to having this thing in my apartment."

"Keep it close."

"Okay."

"It's not going to hurt you sitting on your night table. It might save your life."

"Dear mother. What would The Haverford Friends Meeting say about this?"

"Check in with me tomorrow."

"Okay. Thanks."

Art Greiner didn't like this set up one bit. A smart girl with no street smarts. A dark alley behind her place. A back stairs up to her second floor. A downstairs landlord who was asleep. An old street with old incandescent streetlights. Lots of big trees along the sidewalk. High hedges in front of small lawns. Cars parked on both sides of the street. Very little traffic, either cars or people. In late November, this block buttoned up by eight. Allyson's Shadyside was an urban innocent, a neighborhood that did not bleed like Homewood or The Hill District. It was, he knew, a gentrifying enclave that valued old sidewalks, old trees, old lighting, old houses, old foreign cars and new money.

"Shit," he muttered to himself, as he walked the block, front and rear.

Art Greiner had a hunch, and he was willing to invest a little time betting he was right.

562

He had dressed warmly. Heavy topcoat, black. Fedora, black, with no feather. Trousers, dark blue. Thick socks. Hunting boots. He kept his revolver in his right hand in his coat pocket with the safety off. He took a post, concealed in the narrow walkway between Allyson's house and its neighbor.

Shortly before midnight, a late-model Buick strolled the block. It was a very long car with the new egg-crate-style front grille. One guy in it, the driver. It slowed in front of Allyson's house.

Looking for the house number, Greiner thought.

The Buick moved past and circled again about 10 minutes later. No parking spots were open. He'll park as close as he can, then come up the back alley, Greiner thought.

Greiner moved toward the alley. He couldn't see her back stairs from where he was. He figured the guy would come from the direction his car had been heading. Greiner considered crossing the alley to get a full view, but he didn't want to risk being seen.

He didn't hear the footsteps. He saw a man moving carefully across his narrow rectangle of vision.

Art Greiner took four steps into the alley with his gun drawn in one hand and a six-battery flashlight in the other. He came within five feet of the man's back.

"STOP! I'm a cop. Hands up. Now turn around, to the left."

The man did as he was told. He was wearing a windbreaker over a heavy sweatshirt.

"Jerry Fucking Multirosa," Greiner said, after switching on the flashlight. "Of all people."

"I ain't doin' nothin', Artie."

"Well, exactly what *are* you doin' in this alley after midnight?"

That stumped Jerry for 30 seconds at Greiner's count. "Real estate, Artie. I'm lookin' at real estate. Thought I might move to a better neighborhood."

Greiner snorted. Even Jerry laughed a little.

"You carryin', Jer?" Greiner asked.

"Well, yeah. You know me. For security. You never know when some criminal might try something. Man has a right to defend himself against whatnot."

"Yeah, 'whatnot.' You never know who you might run into in a back alley on a cold winter's night," Greiner said.

"Just exactly, Artie. I got a permit for your info."

"For all three you're carryin'?"

"One license does for all of 'em. You know that."

"You're a convicted felon several times over, Jer."

"C'mon, Artie. I had a little help in filling out the application," Multirosa allowed.

"I'm sure you have a paper that looks like a permit, but maybe one of your three ain't one of your regulars, I'm guessin'. You wouldn't be drivin' an Electra?"

"No law against Buicks, is there?"

"You bring any friends with you, Jer?"

"Naw. I look for real-estate deals by myself. Fixer-uppers. Shadyside's comin' up."

"I thought you said you wanted to move."

"Well, I could swing either way, live in or rent out."

"You wouldn't be lookin' for a girl by any chance?"

"Naw, Artie. I'm married. Which you know. Hookers is different. But, no, not no full-time girlfriend. What kind of girl would I find out here with the garbage cans anyway this late?"

Greiner saw Multirosa shift his feet. Jerry didn't like being cornered in an alley with a flashlight pointed in his face.

"Let me have your guns, Jer. Put them on the ground, barrels facing you."

"Aw come on Artie. You know me. I know you. We got no beef over nothin'. I ain't gonna cause no trouble."

"Just the same old friend. Humor me. Now slide them over to me with your left toe."

Greiner picked them up one at a time with his flashlight hand and dropped them in his pockets.

"What else?"

"Well, I always carry a knife or two. You never know when you might need to peel a apple."

"'Peel a apple,' like on 'The Honeymooners.' Very funny. Were you gonna cut her first, Jer?"

"Who?"

"The girl."

"What girl?"

"The girl you were lookin' for in this alley."

"Hey, Artie. I'm not that hard up, lookin' for alley cats in the middle of the Goddamn night."

"They don't have alley cats in this neighborhood, Jer."

"They got cats. They just don't meow as loud," Multirosa said. "Anyway, Teresa still puts out—Christmas, my birthday, not hers, our anniversary and sometimes on a Friday night if I bring home supper, somethin' she likes. She don't put out on Friday if she don't like what I bring home."

"Good to know," Greiner said, "Now, do the same with the knives. Then I want you to put these cuffs on that I'm gonna toss over to you."

564

A light came on in Allyson's apartment. Greiner looked up. He saw her standing at the window, looking at them. He waved and gave her a thumbs up. She started to lift the sash. Greiner shook his head, No.

Jerry Multirosa looked up and asked. "Who's that girl, Artie? You know her?"

Greiner shook his head. "You shoulda been a stand-up comic, Jer. Now do I need to read you your rights just in case I decide to arrest you?"

"Naw, Artie, I know 'em good. I could read 'em to you from memory."

"Okay, now you and me are going to take a ride."

"Where at?" Jerry asked, as he eased the knives toward Greiner and then clicked together the old-fashioned steel cuffs. "You ain't takin' me dahn to the station, are you?"

"Over to Tony's house out in Shaler Township."

"No, Artie! That's a rill bad idea. Tony'll be asleep. Him and Josephine. And his kids. He'll be pissed, rilly pissed."

"I'm sure he will. My car's out front. You and I will walk around to it."

"What about my car?"

"Like you said, Jer. This is a good neighborhood. No one is likely to steal your hubcaps. No one around would know what to do with Buick caps. They all drive Volvos and shit like that."

"Don't that girl drive a VW bug?"

"What girl, Jer?"

"Uh…that girl you was wavin' to. Uh…she looks like the type that would drive a VW, not a Volvo."

"Come on. Let's take a drive."

"This ain't right, Artie. Tony's gonna be pissed, us showin' up undenounced. You got me doin' nothin'."

"I got you doin' exactly what I thought someone like you would be doin'."

"What's the charge, Artie?"

"Disturbin' my piece."

Art Greiner rang the bell. A dog barked and growled inside. A minute passed, then the porch light came on. Tony Bruno, dressed in a bathrobe and bare feet, holding a leveled AR-15, opened the door.

Tony recognized his visitors: "What the fuck?"

"I tried to tell him, Tony, not to come here. But he cuffed me and drove me out here against my will. Like I was kidnapped! And he got me for doin' nothin'."

"It's 12:45 in the fuckin' mornin', Greiner," Tony said.

Greiner looked at his watch. "It's like this, Anthony. I could arrest Jer for loitering, and sneakin' his punk-ass around, and peepin'-Tomin' and conspiracy with you to commit murder and shit like 'at, but I thought maybe yinz and me might work this out without me havin' to write up a lot of paper and you havin' to pay Hy Crammer a lot of money to keep you out of jail."

"I'm listenin'. Well, come in. I'm freezin' standin' here."

Tony penned his Rottweiler in the kitchen. The dog whined to be included. Greiner uncuffed Multirosa and returned his arsenal. They took off their winter garments. The three sat in an expensive and almost-never-used living room on plastic slip covers.

"You wanna drink?" Tony asked.

"Whatever you're havin'," Greiner said.

"Me, too," Jerry said.

Tony went into the kitchen and came back with three chilled ceramic glasses and a bottle of Villa Massa Limoncello. He had put on slippers. They settled into their seats.

"The girl, Anthony," Greiner said. "You gotta see her like a cop. She's off limits."

"I hear she's diggin' around about me."

"Who you hearin' from?" Greiner asked.

"Here and there," Tony laughed.

"Rapucci, your girl at the paper?"

"Who?" Tony said without much effort to conceal his source.

"Pickering's lookin' into Lazarro and Hyskra. And some coal miner named Biggie Stover," Greiner said.

"I wanna know who fucked up Little Louie and Bonk more than anybody. I have a right to know, don't I? Who you think it was, Art?"

"Probably Stover. I'd say it's best to think the score's even up."

Tony frowned. "I got two dead, and they got one. That ain't square. So what is she after?"

"Your two equals Delucci's one. That's square, 'cause they weigh the same on the scale."

"Like a bathroom scale?" Jerry asked. "Bonk was a big guy."

Greiner and Bruno ignored that comment.

"As you know, there is an election that happens on December 5th," Greiner said. "Coal miners."

"We ain't interested in coal mines, coal trucks, barges, stoves and whatever they do with that shit. I shoveled coal into my parents' furnace when I was a kid. Every day when it was cold. Couldn't get the dust off me. Probably got black lung. Nobody has an interest in none of that. Nobody's goin' for that business. Just bein' straight with you, Art."

"Anybody interested in the ACMU?" Greiner asked. "Wanna make it like the Teamsters?"

566

"Unions are part of our port-folio," Tony said without apology, "even after that little runt Bobby Kennedy raked us over with the Teamsters. Unions ain't no secret."

"Tony, if the feds ever start looking hard at the Teamsters Central States, they're gonna find loans that will stink worse than a week-old fish on a Miami Beach bench. The feds may start looking hard at Fitzsimmons and the Teamsters what with Hoffa vanishing. What Fitz is doin' with dues money and pension funds—that's shadier than anything under a spreading chestnut tree and dirtier than the village smithy."

"Teamsters is Teamsters," Bruno said. "They've been ours for years. You know that; everybody does. We'll be okay if Ford wins."

"Fitzsimmons was born and raised in Jeannette in Westmoreland County," Greiner said. "Do you know him?"

"Sure. Fitz is a good boy," Bruno laughed. "Hoffa's probably on some island with dancin' hula girls. I wouldn't be surprised if Fitz didn't pay Jimmy to disappear himself to get out of his hair."

"Right," Greiner said skeptically.

"We work with a lot of unions. But who wants to get in bed with fuckin' coal miners? Strike over this, strike over that. Got no discipline."

Greiner figured the more denials Tony Bruno used, the closer he was getting to the truth. "They got a bank," Greiner said.

"You think Frankie Fagano needs a bank? You think we want federal snoops proctolin' us 24 hours a day, countin' the pennies up our wazoo? I keep my money in a sock. Don't like banks. Banks are run by fuckin' criminals."

Art Greiner smiled. "Anthony, *you* are a fuckin' criminal."

"Yeah, well, you're a fuckin' cop."

"Criminal and cop don't rest in the same spot on the moral seesaw," Greiner said.

"Seesaw, like in the playground?" Jerry asked. "You need to balance each other otherwise the see don't saw right and the saw don't see right."

"Not many like Jerry around," Tony said.

"Let's be honest, Anthony," Greiner said. "You ain't no good guy, no matter how much cash you dump into Help of Christians."

"Well, you ain't ready to be no saint neither," Tony said. "I play the system from outside working inside. You assholes support a corrupt system from the inside. My business ain't no different than U.S. Steel. We're both lookin' to make money off somebody's sweat with as little of our own tossed in."

"Anthony, you were a punk hoodlum when we were in 3rd grade at St. Raphael on Chislett Street. You cheated; you stole baseball mitts; you shook down little kids for nickels; you bullied weaker kids; you spent half your time in the principal's office getting your ass paddled by Sister Gretchen."

"That broad shoulda batted cleanup for the Pirates back in the '50s," Tony said. "She hit harder than home-run-king Ralph Kiner."

"She called you 'Little Anthony and the Imperial Margins.'"

"Well, I called her…don't matter. And stop callin' me 'Anthony.'"

"Your business is makin' money by stealing it off people who are tryin' to play straight with life," Greiner said. "You are a giant leech. You produce nothin' of value. Your business falls apart if you don't threaten and kill people who refuse to play ball. The world would be a better place without you."

"The world would be a better place without a lot of people," Tony said. "We ain't the worst of the worst by a long shot."

"I agree with that," Jerry Multirosa added. "Little Louie was worser than me. Me and Bonk was about even, I'd say."

"Art, you tell that bitch to stay away from my shit," Tony said. "I can't guarantee nothin' if she don't."

"If somethin' happens to her, Tony, people'll be comin' after you, personally," Greiner said. "Legal-wise and maybe not legal-wise. She's got family connections. Hit her, and it'll be front-page news for months. She comes from money. She's not one of the scag girls down at your Magic Fingers Massage. Take this as a friendly heads-up."

"Talk about threatenin' people with violence!" Tony Bruno said. "And for the record, my girls ain't scags. They're fuckin' cheerleaders."

"Yeah, Tony's right," Jerry added, "they bring cheer." Jerry laughed at his own unexpected wit.

Greiner laughed. "And every one of them just turned 16 and is a virgin to boot."

"Every one is at least 18," Tony said, "not no underage 16. I know the law."

"I saw a couple I figured was 20, maybe 30," Jerry said. "I don't think they was still virgins, not with two kids each. How would that work? Like artificials?"

"Back to Pickering," Greiner said. "You and me, Anthony, do we got us an understanding on what your limits are?"

Tony Bruno resettled himself in his captain's chair. "Yeah."

"Okay, then," Greiner said. "No Corelli. Don't pop the girl."

Tony Bruno looked at his slippers. "So how do I get her to lay off?"

"She doesn't have anything on yinz that's not already out there," Greiner said. "She can't hurt you on the bank deal, because she doesn't have enough time to put a story together. And my guess is no one will run her stuff now that she's been fired for bein' a bad reporter."

"She could fuck up a lot of shit, with writin' this an' writin' that," Tony said.

"Then lean on her outlets, not her," Greiner said.

"How will I know where she's tryin' to peddle her lies?"

Greiner laughed. "Do what the FBI does. Tap her phone."

"All right," Tony said. "I'm gettin' one more drink, then I'm goin' back to bed. Nothin' on TV this late, not even Chiller Theater with Chilly Billy Cardille."

"I love Chiller," Jerry piped up. "Saturday night. Monsters, dead people walkin' around alive. I keep lookin' for someone I did. Creeps me out."

"My best to Josephine," Greiner said as he rose. "I still can't understand why she married a low-life like you and not a low-life like me."

"Maybe she didn't want to scrape by on a cop's wages," Tony said. "And I'm better-lookin'."

"The fuck you are," Greiner said. "You're Italian. Needles wanted her to marry Italian. That's why."

"That didn't hurt."

"Me being Catholic wasn't good enough," Greiner said. "I even believed in it back then...unlike you."

Tony paused and then said: "Some day, Artie, when we're both old and droolin' in wheelchairs next to each other, we're gonna be rill friends again like back on Chislett."

"Depends on what happens between now and then. C'mon, Jer, I'll give you a ride back into Shadyside. No cuffs this time."

"You think I want to be seen ridin' around with yinz? Everybody'll think I'm one of your snitches."

"Well..," Greiner allowed.

"That ain't true, Tony! Artie's fuckin' with your mind. I ain't no snitch!"

Tony Bruno laughed and walked them to his door, his AR-15 at his side.

Allyson was getting closer to Tony Bruno and Biggie Stover, but she knew she hadn't nailed the story. She knew that Art Greiner had saved her life. She decided to try to put it together while there might still be time to get something in print somewhere.

Chapter 42

Logan, W.Va., December 1, 1975

Jeep parked on Stratton Street at 7:40 a.m.

Jeep saw him walk into the alley and enter the building's side entrance. At eight, he unlocked the main front door. Jeep was waiting.

Walter Bishop looked up.

"Walter," Jeep said.

Walter Bishop nodded.

"Walter...."

"What you want, man?"

"I want to apologize," Jeep said. He was startled by Walter Bishop's size and persistent muscularity.

Walter Bishop stared at him.

"I'm sorry. It was high school. I..."

"So you saw the blindin' light on the road to Damascus, is that it?"

"I jes' lost my best friend, Biggie. Murdered. It was over this election. It made me think about makin' things right as I can for what I done."

"See that push broom over there," Walter said. "See that mop and that bucket on wheels. That my life. I have to wear my letter sweater every day. You done this to me."

"I didn't plan it. It was on purpose, I admit that."

"You can't change what you done."

"You're right. I can't."

"So what you want?"

"I want, I want you to know I wish I hadn't done what I did. I wish I could change it, for both of us."

"I need to get to work," Walter said.

"You woulda been like Jim Brown or OJ," Jeep said.

"Mighta been better."

"I carry it with me," Jeep said.

"You an' me, we carry it diff'rent," Walter said, turning toward his tools. "Can't change a mistake that's permanent."

"Guess not," Jeep said.

"If you lookin' fo' fo'giveness, it ain't comin' from me."

"Not forgiveness," Jeep said. "I made mistakes. I jes' wanted you to know. I'm sorry. I wish I could make it right."

"You wantin' my support for your election, ain't you?"

"I'm better than Joe Hunt. Better for miners like your Daddy. Better for the brothers. I changed in Nam. I ain't who I was back on the field that day."

"I heard about Stover," Bishop said.

"Yeah," Delucci said.

Walter Bishop looked at the push broom in his hands, and then he looked at the floor. "Yeah, you might do right. You losin' ain't gonna fix me none."

"Thanks," Jeep said.

"I need to get started," Walter said. Then he stopped. "What Biggie mean by 'Archie Bishop'? That's what he called me on that play."

Jeep grinned. "The night before the game, we decided you were so good you should be named the Archbishop of Football. That's where Archie Bishop come from."

Walter Bishop shook his head. "Archie Bishop."

"Archie Bishop," Jeep said softly.

"Archie Bishop," Walter said and began working his broom with a very small smile on his face.

Jeep drove to Charleston, cursing himself for what he'd done years before. He wondered how he would have responded had that broom been in his hands for the rest of his life.

Middle Ridge, W.Va., December 1, 1975, 6:47 p.m.

Young woods, brush and blackberry brambles closed in on both sides of the dirt road near the top of Middle Ridge. A waning moon provided a little light. Wet snow fell slowly.

A thin man with a small mustache and a heavy, three-day beard crouched beside a large, leafless forsythia in front of Jeffrey Becker's house. A woman about his size knelt beside him. They both held automatic pistols.

They'd discovered that Becker's place was the next-to-the-last house, about a mile from the road's end. They were watching his bungalow for something that would disrupt their plan.

After turning around their old Plymouth sedan, they had parked about 50 yards beyond Becker's driveway. They'd noticed a car parked another 100 yards beyond where they left theirs. Neither could be seen from Becker's house.

"Might be a commuter park," the man said.

The woman looked at him. "Why would you park your car here and not at home, at the last house?"

"Maybe someone is sharing a ride?"

"Doubtful," she said.

As they huddled by the forsythia, the man whispered: "I'm cold."

"Who isn't?" she whispered back. "Suck it up."

"I bet it's no more than 27, 28 degrees," he said. "Fahrenheit. It's been 20 minutes. No one's in there. I say it's safe to go in."

"Maybe," she said.

"The porch light is on to scare off burglars," he said.

"We're not burglars," she said.

"I haven't seen anybody moving inside. No sounds. No dog. No cat. No light inside. He's not there," he said.

"Maybe."

"It's snowing for Chrissakes!"

"You won't melt," the woman said.

"I'm worried about freezing, not melting."

He forced his eyes to squint at the house one more time. The moon was little help.

An old International pickup truck sat in the sloping driveway but not in front of the open two-car garage. The truck, no more than a dozen feet from them, looked like something from the late 1940s, the man guessed without real interest. A chunk of firewood scotched a rear tire.

"No emergency brake. Leaves his garage doors up," he said.

"Defenses down," she said. "Too trusting. Stupid."

The December air stirred a wind chime on the porch. The man tightened his grip on his gun. His bare fingers were now numb from pressing against its cold steel. He pulled his cap lower on his forehead.

"I wish I had earmuffs," he said.

"Jesus," she said. "Earmuffs! Would you like me to knit you mittens and sew them on your jacket's cuffs with elastic ribbons?"

"You can sew? Who would have guessed it? I'm going in," he said.

He scuttled from the bush to the front of the house and stopped. He peeked through a bedroom window. He moved toward the back. She followed. They stopped at a red door. She looked through the next window with her flashlight. A breakfast room with windows on three sides opened into a kitchen. He put his hand on the door knob and turned.

"It's unlocked," he said.

If it turns, it's unlocked, she thought, but said nothing.

He opened the door. A little squeak sounded as loud as a bugle in the rural silence.

He hesitated. She slipped inside. He followed.

"Close the door," she said.

They waited, allowing their eyes to adjust to the different shade of darkness. They could make out the kitchen.

"Wipe your feet on the mat," she whispered.

"Living room, bedrooms and bathroom must be on the other side of the kitchen. I can see a hall, maybe," he said, wiping his feet. He moved toward the hall.

She nodded. She heard nothing. She smelled nothing. She saw nothing to make her suspicious, which she had trained herself to be. She stood straight, motioning him to go forward.

572

He took out a penlight and twisted the head to turn it on. She shook her head, but he did not turn it off. He walked slowly across the kitchen toward the hall that led into a living room. He could see a picture window on the far wall. A bathroom opened to the right. A bedroom opened to his left, the one they'd passed going toward the back door. A phone was mounted in the hall. A built-in ladder led to an attic hatch in the ceiling. The house was temperate from a propane stove.

He could make out a high-backed, upholstered swivel chair in the living room, facing the window with its back toward him. He moved forward two steps. He could see a fireplace to his right with open space to his left. A couch and coffee table were to his right. He saw a piano to his left. Not much furniture. Books sat on block-and-board shelves on the far wall, framing the window.

He moved into the living room, gun raised in his right hand, penlight in his left. She came in behind him. He looked right; she looked left.

They took a step deeper into the living room. Nothing stirred.

The man stood straight and took a deep breath. He unzipped his jacket. He lowered his gun and put his penlight in his coat pocket. The woman did not lower her gun.

The chair began to revolve, turning in their direction.

A woman sat in it, about 12 feet away. She turned on the floorlamp next to the chair. They saw that she had leveled an Uzi 9mm submachine gun at their waists.

"Shoot the bitch," the woman said under her breath to the man standing beside her. He did nothing. No one had ever pointed a gun at him before.

The woman in the chair shook her head once.

"You're not Becker," she said. "Who the hell are you two?"

"Who are you?" he replied.

"I asked you first."

"I asked you second," the man said, "and most recently."

The woman in the chair had to laugh. "Jesus Christ. Clowns!"

"We're friends of Becker," the man said.

"Friends? Sneaking into his house with guns drawn."

"Yeah, well you're sitting in his chair with an Uzi…waiting to what? Ambush him? Are you working for Joe Hunt?"

"Are you working for somebody I might know?" the woman in the chair asked. Maybe, she thought, Bruno had sent two teams for Becker, working independently. Unlikely, she decided.

"Self-employed," the man said.

"*Kill the bitch*," she whispered to the man. "*Shoot her!*"

"Contract work?" the woman in the chair asked.

"We work for The People," the woman next to the man said.

"You work for the people? What the hell does that mean? Which 'people'?"

As the woman in the chair ended her question, the other woman fired three times as fast as she could pull the trigger. The first struck the woman's thigh; the second, her chest; the third, her neck. The Uzi dropped to the floor.

The gunshots made Rooky Gondleman stumble back into the kitchen where he came to rest against the sink.

Louise Draney walked over to the woman. Blood had splattered over the chair, lamp, window and floor.

"What a mess," she said.

"You killed her! That lady! Weez, you killed that lady," Rooky screamed. He pointed his gun at the dead woman slumped in the recliner.

"What do you think she was going to do to us, you idiot?"

"She was...talking...to me."

"Let's get her outside," Weez said. "Then we'll try to clean it up."

"Where?"

"Outside means out of inside, out of here," Weez said impatiently.

"Where outside?"

"How would I know where outside? Bury her somewhere in the woods."

"Me? Who is she? What was she doing here?"

"She was waiting for Becker. She was going to kill him?"

"How do you know that?"

"What do you think she was doing with that Uzi, Bobby? Plucking her eyebrows?"

Louise Draney walked over to the chair and reached into the pocket of the woman's unbuttoned parka. She tried not to get blood on her clothes or hands. She found a wallet and keys. A driver's license: "Roberta Magnelli, Pittsburgh, Pennsylvania." She put the wallet and keys in her own pocket.

"Maybe she was Becker's girlfriend. He's from Pittsburgh. Or maybe she was guarding him."

"She was waiting to kill him," Weez said, with more certainty than she now felt. "Probably over the miners' election. Come on. You take her arms, I'll take her feet."

"What if she was guarding him?" Rooky pleaded. "You might have killed a friend of his!"

"Too late for reevaluations. Shut up and help me," she said.

Rooky put his gun in his jacket pocket. He'd never met a dead person face to face before. The warm blood made him woozy.

Weez found a lantern-style, six-volt flashlight on the window ledge in Becker's kitchen. They carried Roberta Magnelli out of the living room, then through the center hall, kitchen and breakfast room. Weez stopped, opened the door, looked around and signaled for Rooky to lift again.

They carried the corpse several hundred feet, flicking on Becker's light close to the ground to help them find their way. They saw they were leaving a blood trail.

"Here," she said. "Bury him in this little flat spot in the scrub trees and brambles. Go back and find a shovel and a pick, or something. Look in Becker's garage. Or in a shed. Hippies have those things for gardening. Get it down as deep as you can. I'll clean up the house. Dig it in the dark. Don't use his flashlight."

"Why am I digging the grave?" he asked.

"Because you're the boy," she said.

They walked back to the house, single file. He found digging tools hanging in the garage, including a mattock and a pick.

Weez stood in Becker's breakfast room and watched Gondleman sneak back toward the body in the snow, carrying tools she remembered her father using. I just killed a human being, she thought. She closed her eyes and leaned against a wall calendar.

Her mind went back to Newton, Iowa. High school had not been hard. She was nice looking, but no thunderbolt in anybody's calm. She was 5-9 in heels, a little heavier in the middle than she wanted to be, but not that much. She was more shapely than pretty, more smart than come-hither, more serious than coy. She had dated. She had danced on Friday nights. She had gone pretty far but not all the way. She remembered the night of a late August picnic with Craig Starrett in Maytag Park under a tall elm before she left for college and he, the Army. They stirred each other, but neither had protection, so they joined in a circle that got hotter and then stopped abruptly. She remembered the friendly darkness, the comfortable coolness, the feeling that something special would happen. It was a good time, a touchstone. A couple of 17-year-olds trying new things.

Nice, she thought, it had been nice. When was the last time, she asked herself, I had nice? What good am I doing? Where is this going? Why is the revolution so hard? Weez strode into the kitchen and got cleaning utensils and liquids from under the sink.

It took Gondleman with frequent breaks 90 minutes to dig a grave deep enough and long enough to accept Roberta's body. The ground was cold and wet, but not frozen. Snow fell steadily. When he finished, he rolled her in. She landed on her face. He thought about turning her on her back, which is how people were buried normally, he thought. But who gives a shit? He turned her over anyway. Snowflakes landed on her face. He covered her with 18 inches of loose dirt and rocks, then stomped it down to keep the grave's surface level with the ground. The grave felt mushy as he tried to pack it down with his boots. He dragged brush over the grave. "I'm sorry," he said, as he picked up the tools to leave, "that this happened. You understand these things more than I do since you were waiting to shoot Becker, I hope."

When he returned, Weez had gotten Becker's living room, floors, window and furniture as clean as she could. It was almost 9 p.m. Both were sweating from their work. She went into the kitchen and brought them water in two glasses that she held in paper towels.

"Sit," she said.

"We're dead," he said, sitting.

"Not yet, Rooky. But you need to be clear that this is exactly the kind of shit you always get us into."

"Me! You shot her, not me!"

"See! You don't understand your objective situation. Relying on friends, rather than comrades in the struggle, puts us at risk. Failing to scope a rest spot puts us at risk. Failing to look into the right window got us into this mess. Your carelessness will kill us."

"You're always shifting the blame to me, always justifying whatever you do with whatever's at hand."

"You're an undisciplined, bourgeois anarchist!" she said.

"You're a beneficiary of white, female skin privilege!"

"You're a pig! And a sexist. And a white, middle-class temporizer."

"You're a dopey Maoist like Schlonsky!" he said.

"You're a little fascist prick who wasn't even that good at chess!"

"You're a crazy lady who kills people and an idiot!"

"You're a man!"

"You're a double idiot!" he shouted.

"Sorry. I misspoke. Boy."

They had run out of familiar accusations and sat on Becker's couch, facing the swivel chair in silence with only a small table lamp casting a soft, shadowy glow in the room.

"Becker'll never help us now," Rooky said.

"We can go before he gets home," Weez said. "We'll drive her car somewhere and dump it. It must be the one we saw parked beyond where we parked. He won't know that we've been here. He won't know about her. Snow will cover the blood outside."

"He'll know something went on in his living room when he sits on that wet chair and takes a breath."

"I'm leaning toward going," she said. "Or we can stay and not tell him."

"That's a lie," Rooky said.

"No, it's not telling him something. We're not lying about it."

"Stalinist!"

"I'm not going there with you again," she said.

"This is your shit, not his," Rooky said.

576

"WHOSE SHIT?"

"Yours…and mine. Legally."

"'Legally'! Some revolutionary," she said. "I can't believe you said that."

"Okay. Our shit. But it's not Becker's. You don't drop a corpse on somebody. People just don't do things like that. Not even people like us."

In spite of herself, Weez Draney laughed at his unintended humor. Shaking her head, she said: "My mother would insist on a hand-written note, and maybe, if she had time, she'd leave a coffee cake wrapped in Alcoa foil."

"Or we can stay and tell him," Gondleman said. "The place in Baltimore won't be ready for a few days. We need to rest for a while. Won't he know something's funny from all the cleaning and smells?"

"Maybe he'll think a woman like me likes to tidy up after boys," she said. "Kind of my way of welcoming him home. A little present."

"You welcoming anybody strains the imagination," he said.

"I'll charm him," Weez said.

Rooky said nothing.

"You don't think I could bedazzle a man?"

"Should we turn off the light?" Rooky asked. "It's easier for me to imagine that unlikely possibility in the dark."

"It would be wasted on you," she said.

Louise "Weez" Draney, daughter of a moderately liberal Methodist minister and skeptic, grew up in Newton. As a rising junior at Cornell College in Mount Vernon -- the first college west of the Mississippi to graduate a woman -- she had joined several hundred other students in 1964 to work in the Freedom Summer Project. Thoreau's "On the Duty of Civil Disobedience" lay next to her hair curlers in the small Samsonite vanity she carried to McComb, Mississippi.

The Freedom-Summer orientation program at Western College for Women in Oxford, Ohio, had scared her but not enough for her to leave. She was prepared to die. She stayed even after word reached the group that James Chaney, Andrew Goodman and Michael Schwerner had disappeared on their release from the Philadelphia jail in Neshoba County. They vanished soon after they left the Oxford training session.

In the College's Kumler Chapel, one of the black organizers who had been working for a year in Mississippi told the group: "Goin' to Mississippi is goin' behind the enemy's lines. You'll have friends here and there, all of them black, but you'll never be safe on the white side of town, never, even in a group. You can trust most black folks, but not every one of us. We have our snitches for The Man. Don't kid yourself, those three are dead. It's time to decide what you want to do. An' let me be honest. We want white faces in Mississippi this summer. We want you to bring attention there, publicity from out-of-state. We want whites next to us, because maybe it'll make the Klan think twice before killin' us. Somebody'll put a stop to this Klan shit once the bodies of rich, white northern students start turnin' up. Don't wan' none of you good people dead, but that's just the fact of what we're about."

The night before Weez left for the drive south, she gave herself to an 18-year-old who had just graduated from his segregated high school in Jackson and was entering Alcorn State University in September. Neither had a condom. She used a diaphragm, which she had acquired at the end of her freshman year. Two weeks later in McComb, she noticed the yellow discharge of gonorrhea. She had it treated when she returned to Iowa in early September. Her first takeaway from a man in Freedom Summer was the clap.

Newton was a company town, run by the Maytags who built washing machines and dryers. Everybody either worked for Maytag or depended on those who did. Louise Draney believed the plantation South with its racial and class divisions would be no more than a few steps more obvious and oppressive than her hometown. She was wrong.

With two white northerners, she slipped into McComb, a town just north of Mississippi's border with Louisiana. Their leader was a black high-school student who was driving a beat-up '53 Chevy with Mississippi plates. He had joined the Council of Federated Organizations, one of the groups sponsoring Freedom Summer. The four were tense as they drove south on Rt. 51 and turned off Rt. 98 onto 550 through the still-steamy night. They were heading for the safety of Burglund, the black neighborhood on the other side of the Illinois Central tracks.

"That place," driver Jimmie Lee Patterson said, motioning toward Hudgey's Diner, "it's a Klan hangout. Stay away from it."

McComb, that summer, was a center of Klan violence against COFO workers, local black supporters and all efforts to register black voters in Pike County. A group of 11 white men, including Emery Lee, a former U.S. Army demolition expert at Camp Aberdeen, bombed 16 houses and businesses and burned 13 others in McComb over eight months. Civil-rights workers and supporters were harassed, arrested, shot at and beaten with brass knuckles.

Weez Draney was assigned to teach in a "freedom school" where the kids wanted to learn French, which was denied them in their segregated high school. The unending terror filled her consciousness, but it left her hardened. She stuck it out, inspired by the resilience and courage of the black families who fed and housed her, protected her and bore the brunt of the Klan violence and the retributions of their white employers. By the time she returned to college, Weez hoped her 33 "Freedom Kids" could find a bathroom on the Champs-Élysées. It was the first time Weez had been close to poor people or black people.

578

On a few occasions, Weez went with registration volunteers to visit black sharecroppers in rural areas. She was appalled at their circumstances, the shabbiness of their tumble-down shacks surrounded by cotton fields; the nose-clearing smell of urine in their mattresses; the flies on their food; the fat, barefoot women eating Arglo Gloss Starch or clay dirt, baked and seasoned with vinegar and salt. Weez hated local whites for creating and benefitting from this misery. In the privacy of her own thoughts, she couldn't understand the sharecroppers for quietly adapting to their imprisonment.

Leave. Get out, she shrieked to them in her mind. And then she berated herself. These people were trying to change their condition, to make a genuine revolution from the bottom up, to overthrow 350 years of slavery, segregation and repression. They sustained themselves on next to nothing and were willing to offer her "ice sweet tea" with or without ice on their front porches of unpainted, weathered, rough-cut planks. She admired their simple dignity and knowledge, their ability to transcend the ugly meanness that lay on top of them. She was drawn to their "authenticity," their seemingly unbreakable connection to each other in spite of the poverty and the oppression -- a word that acquired lifelong meaning for her -- she could not have stood for a week let alone decades. She found herself more comfortable in their one-room churches than she had ever been in her father's. A few agreed to go to the courthouse and try to register to vote. Most were too scared of the inevitable physical and economic retaliation to challenge how things were. But the movement knew that a few fed-up souls might be enough to force a change. "A few" could do it. A few could inspire others and force a change—that was the lesson she drew from her three months in Mississippi in the summer of 1964.

She graduated in 1966, hating America's racism and the War her President was waging in Southeast Asia. After Mississippi, she gravitated toward the Students for a Democratic Society and was elected one of five members of its National Organizing Collective in 1968. It took her many months to feel not completely uncomfortable around the alienated, wealthier kids from the two Coasts and the big cities who formed the SDS core. They tended to see her stereotypically as representing rural whites, heartland farming and a close-to-working-class pedigree they lacked. They asked her about pigs and tractors and corn—in that order. How flat is Iowa? Are all women blondes? Is everybody white?

Weez knew who she was—the lone daughter of a struggling, church couple who were comfortable in Newton and at peace with the quiet lives they led. She hated working outdoors in the hot Iowa summer. Only once had she joined the Newton teens who trooped out to the fields to detassel the pollen-producing flowers of one seed-corn variety to promote hybridizing with the other variety planted in the same field. Detasseling produced a cross-breed that created dramatically higher yields. She had spent one hot day detasseling as a 13-year-old and vowed never again. At least she knew what detasseling was. She told no one in SDS she had won the Betty Crocker Homemaker Award in high school. Stanley Schlonsky kept calling her "Comrade Cornhuckster."

"We're Hawkeyes," she said. "Cornhuskers are Nebraska."

"Well, all those square states are the same when you get down to it."

She began calling him "Comrade Schlongsky" until he realized she was not offering a compliment.

As the War escalated, Weez and the SDS leadership escalated their protests. On November 14, 1967, she was one of 2,500 demonstrators who scuffled with New York City police near the Hilton Hotel on Manhattan's Sixth Ave. They were protesting hawkish Secretary of State Dean Rusk who was receiving an award from the Foreign Policy Association, a group of business executives, policymakers and academics, including Columbia University President Grayson Kirk. Following Rusk's arrival, two hours of melee ensued that raged between 42nd and 55th Streets. The crowd tried to block the limousines from depositing their guests at the evening's festivities. Weez managed to throw balloons filled with fire-engine-red paint against the rear of a mounted cop's horse, a Chock Full O' Nuts window and one leg of her own. Weez refused to help rock the taxis of theatergoers that evening, because she saw no "revolutionary meaning" in that action. The terrified occupants looked like her parents, except much better dressed. Several dozen demonstrators were arrested. She watched a Columbia student -- known for his "let's-go-wild-in-the-streets" politics -- get arrested. His name was Robert Gondleman; he went by his college nickname, Rooky.

Weez grew angrier and more confused as the War continued and SDS led itself into talk of "armed revolution." She found in herself a growing feminism that became more intense as SDS grew more militant. Her struggle with the War, racism and imperialism now merged with a constant struggle against sexism, patriarchy and male supremacy in her revolutionary organization. She found herself both hostile to and working with SDS men who held themselves in higher regard than all women, save for Paulette Rotz who had become the pusher-queen of their war against government and capitalism. Rotz, she saw, used her good looks and sexuality to gain influence over the men her feminism belittled. The only woman to rival Paulette's sexual draw among the men in SDS's sleep-with-everybody group was a drop-out French horn major from the Peabody Conservatory of Music who also played the sousaphone.

Weez and other SDS women formed the Women's Brigade to smash monogamy, bring the War home, overthrow patriarchy, end imperialism and raise their consciousness through brawling. She slept with men and women, with whoever asked her, because they were "comrades in communism." Smashing monogamy, she came to understand, carried with it a chronic genital itch that required visits to free clinics.

Sex, drugs and Revolution carried her through 1968 and 1969. She followed the Weathermen into the Weather Underground in the spring of 1970. While proclaiming the need to take down the State by force, she found herself missing the simple days of pacifism in McComb. Nostalgia was one more thing she had to shed to be a revolutionary.

Weez had proven her political commitment. She had participated in various violent confrontations—the Chicago protests at the 1968 Democratic Convention and the Days of Rage a year later. She had stolen jeans and ripped off the telephone company. In June of 1970, she helped plant 10 dynamite sticks on the second floor of a New York police station. Though surprisingly distinguished in rifle marksmanship, she was no better than average in public speaking, karate and oral sex. She refused to admit that she was just average in Marxism.

Weez was not unattractive in a slightly-washed-out-blonde, Midwestern way, but she did nothing to increase her appeal. This was a protest against what she observed in the Weathermen: The prettiest sisters in the organization were more prized than the rest, by both men and women, even though everyone professed to be non-discriminatory when it came to sex and everything else. She sometimes felt that she was the kid in fourth grade who was always picked last for softball and then deported to right field. Weez had come to be seen as useful and competent but not especially desirable. Even in their version of classless communism, she realized, everyone was not equal to everyone else. She wanted to be more appealing but considered that a political weakness. Her face thinned and sharpened. She cut her hair short. She wore glasses in steel frames. She thought about starting to jog but was afraid cheese fondues would soon follow.

Even as the Weather Underground embraced "revolutionary war," Weez accepted her role as a stable presence in a group that was as explosive as the hydrogen gas she had accidentally ignited in a high-school chemistry experiment. Her peers thought her to be responsible and dependable but not friendly or even comradely. She was not one to share her feelings. SDS men did not like her, and her sisters found her remote and stoic. A Boston native said she was "farmy like the oppressed woman in that Grant Wood painting...with the guy holding the pitchfork, which is the phallus if you ask me on which Weez's life is impaled."

In 1972, the remaining underground fugitives decided Weez Draney should shepherd Rooky Gondleman, four years her junior and one of the Underground's remaining "name celebrities," to prevent his capture and keep him functioning. She agreed she would probably do better at this unpalatable task than the other women. She said in the public square of her women's group that she resented having the "Gondleman burden" placed on her shoulders but would do what needed to be done. She felt like her Dad when he did something distasteful that made him look better than he knew he was.

Weez did her assignment well. They had not been caught in the three years she had herded Gondleman from one temporary spot to the next. He was inept at physical labor, so she concentrated on finding him jobs like stocking shelves and dishwashing. She calculated their phony credentials and Social Security numbers would work for no more than three months at each stop. So she moved them from one urban area to the next, using sympathizers for crash pads, finding cheap furnished apartments and interacting with as few people as possible. With each other, they tried to be polite through the strain of not really wanting to be with each other. Weez had sex with Gondleman when she decided she wanted to have sex. Her feelings for him were, she thought, "functional and operational." She believed she was living the life of an American revolutionary and someday, someday, her sacrifice would be recalled and honored.

"You're not my revolutionary Prince Charming," she told him bluntly one night as they rode in the unlighted back seat of a Trailways bus to Portland, Oregon. "You're not Che."

"I thought girls stopped looking for Mr. Perfect when they learned he gave Cinderella the crabs after the ball."

"He did not give her the crabs!" she said with both a laugh and an edge. "He gave her his hand. You, of course, would not know the difference."

"No difference! Both a Prince and a louse are objectively parasitic!" he said triumphally.

"Very good," she said, shifting her sarcasm toward their shared ideological prison. "I'm not defending my bourgeois images. They are what they are. I get rid of those I can. Still, you look for your ideal and settle for the closest you can get. Everybody's looking for the perfect mate, the perfect romance, the one Romeo. Even revolutionary people like us."

"People like us settle for compatibility and complimentary assets," he said.

"A low bar," she said.

"A revolutionary cares about making the Revolution, not personal happiness," he said correctly.

Rooky tried to see the two of them as others might now see them. He—skinny, somewhat haggard looking, plain, spindly, unathletic, pale, unskilled, bored and intellectually dormant; she—unforgiving, unfriendly, menacing glasses, stern countenance, a hard edge in her voice and hostile to men to whom she now felt superior. Neither laughed very much. Both felt smothered. They still dressed in jeans, sweatshirts, boots and thrift-store castoffs. We're dogs, Rooky thought. Arf.

582

"People hope, sure, but, I guess, settle," he added to make peace.

"You shouldn't take this personally," she said, lamely and with a kindness that he rarely saw.

"We've been together for three years. If it's not said personally, how else are you saying it? It can't be anything but a commentary on me."

"I'm just being honest."

Rooky weighed his next thought before he said it. "You're being stupid like a teenybopper. Happy ever after is a myth. Dreamboats can't exist with radical politics. Prince Charming is a Disney mind-fuck. I don't want to be Prince Charming. Prince Charming doesn't exist, never has. I exist. Look! See! Me!"

"You've confirmed my opinion."

"And while we're rating ourselves, do you think you come across as Cinderella? Snow White? Raquel Welch?"

"That's who you want…Raquel Welch? Talk about unrealistic expectations!"

"Look. This is our life. *Our life.* We're surviving out here by our own wits. The FBI can't find us. It's not what either of us might want. But we could, if we tried, make a life together."

"I guess we have," she admitted, "though from my perspective it was a politically necessary arrangement."

"It would improve if you put some effort, some time, into it," he said.

"Time? Effort?"

"You could pay a little more attention to me," he said with an embarrassed hesitancy. "As a person, not as a political task."

"I'm sure I could. Other things are…."

"…more important to you."

"It's hard to be with you, Bobby, when my feminism says you are my gender enemy, regardless of how nice, how helpless, how progressive, how once-famous you are."

"We're stuck with each other," he tried it as a joke.

"Not on each other. With each other. Yes."

"I don't see much of an alternative," he said.

"No, there isn't any that I can see."

"So maybe we should try to make the best of it," he said.

Weez thought about his offer. It was genuine. It wasn't slathered with Marxist goop. It came from Gondleman's heart, an organ with which she had limited experience by intention.

"I know this is wrong, and I'm being stupid. But I'm not ready to give up completely on the dreamboat," she said finally. "My guy is not Tab Hunter, but even a revolutionary woman has a right to hope for the right match."

Then she took from her bag Susan Brownmiller's, <u>Against Our Will: Men, Women, and Rape</u> and turned on the overhead reading light.

"I don't think I benefit from a 'culture of rape,'" Rooky said, as he went back to looking out his window into nothing.

"That's because you're a man," she said, turning off the overhead light. She didn't want to see either him or her own reflection. They sat together in silent darkness, wondering about their past, present and future.

They heard a car drive up and park as they were almost ready to leave. A car door opened, then closed. They heard the back door open. A light came on. They heard stuff being dumped on the table in the breakfast room. The kitchen light came on. Then the one in the hall. Becker walked into his living room holding his new pistol. He turned on the overhead light.

"Beck, it's me, Rooky...Gondleman," he said from the couch as he got to his feet.

Becker turned sharply, his gun pointed at the unexpected.

"Me, Rooky. From Columbia."

"Gondleman," Becker said, "it's you."

That's all I need now, Becker thought. He hadn't anticipated this moment, but he was not surprised by it. How many friends did Rooky Gondleman actually have, not counting his parents who felt obligated to help their fugitive on the FBI's 10 Most Wanted List? Sooner or later, those in the political underground used up their safe houses and friends willing to take risks. Then they came calling on second-tier friends, then third-tier acquaintances.

"It's you," Becker repeated, pocketing his gun. He walked over to his recliner and switched on the floor lamp. "Smells funny in here. Who are you?"

"Louise Draney. Weez."

"I've heard your name. Do you need money?"

"Never hurts," Gondleman said.

"We need a place to rest and lay low," Weez said.

"For a while, just a little while," Gondleman added quickly. "Couple of days. Maybe a week."

"Okay. Stop right here," Becker said. "You are in my house seeking legal counsel, not fugitive shelter. We are talking as an attorney to clients. This is a professional relationship. You have come to me as a lawyer for advice and counsel. Our conversation is protected by attorney-client privilege."

"I told you he'd be a pig," Weez spat. "Let's get out of here before he calls the rest of the litter."

"I'm protecting all of us," Becker said. He got the feeling Weez Draney was not worth the investment it would take for him to tolerate her.

"Right," Weez said.

"Your picture's in the post office," he said to Gondleman.

"Makes me look too studious. We're revolutionaries, not criminals. I should be, we should be, in a hall of fame."

"America isn't quite ready for you, Rooky," Becker without laughing.

"I'm talking down the road," Gondleman said.

"Most Americans don't make a distinction between a bank robbery in the name of The People's Revolution and a bank robbery for the purpose of buying a sailboat and sunning yourself in Tahiti."

"You understand the difference, don't you?" Gondleman asked.

"I understand your rationalizations."

"You're afraid to make your values explicit like we do," Weez said.

"I do what I can in that department," Becker said. "I think you're discrediting the Left opposition to Nixon and Ford. Blowing up urinals won't win you converts."

"Toilets," Rooky said. "Not urinals. Toilets for women. There's no place to hide stuff in a urinal. The Pentagon and the U.S. Capitol, that was me, us."

"Shut up," Weez said.

"I don't want to know and stand corrected, toilets," Becker said. "Why are you here now?"

"We need a place to disappear," Rooky said. "We're not hot, exactly, but we have to keep moving."

"How 'not exactly hot' are you?"

"No one's following us," Gondleman said.

"Are you carrying anything I should be made aware of as your lawyer?"

"No," Weez said.

"Yes," Rooky said, "Guns and stuff. Legally purchased."

"What guns?"

"Shotguns, pistols, an Uzi. All legal, except maybe the Uzi," Rooky said.

"What stuff?" Becker asked.

"Shut up," Weez said to Rooky.

"Two cases of dynamite, blasting caps, switches and timers—all legally bought in Kentucky with cash."

"Rooky, you couldn't put a bomb together if your life depended on it," Becker said.

"You don't know me these days. Anyway Ronnie Fliegelman can."

"SHUT UP!" Weez shouted.

"This is privileged conversation," Becker said in his best lawyerly voice.

"See...'privileged,'" Rooky said to Weez. "It means confidential."

"I don't want you to stay here," Becker said. "I'm a campaign manager for..."

"We know about Jeep Delucci," Weez said. "Reformer. He's the current liberal Band Aid for the working class."

"Spare me," Becker said. "I don't need a lecture on how you are making a revolution by smashing the State's plumbing fixtures. It's not safe for you here, let alone me."

"Can we stay the night, at least?" Gondleman asked.

Becker stood by his upright piano with his arm on top of its black carcass. "I'd rather not. People from the campaign drop by without phoning first. All kinds of stuff are going down in the election, which is this Friday. One of our guys was killed last week. A Mafia guy from Pittsburgh is corrupting the election. It's dangerous for you to stay with me. This Mafia guy might be sending someone here to shut me up. That's why I have this gun; it's why I came into my own house holding it. Let me make a call. Are you sure you don't smell something funny? Bleach maybe."

"I cleaned a little before you got here," Weez said. "Women's work is never done, you know."

That didn't make sense to Becker, but he didn't pursue it.

Becker walked into the hall, took the phone off its hook and dialed.

"Andrea, this is Jeff."

"It's late. What's going on?"

"I have two…friends, clients really, who dropped in unexpectedly just now. They need a place for the night."

"Let me get Thaine on the phone."

"Beck, hey," Thaine said, coming on. "Andrea told me you were on the line."

"See, my guest bedroom is filled with campaign stuff," Becker lied. "You might enjoy talking to these folks."

"Out-of-town people?" Andrea asked.

"Yes."

"Old friends?"

"There's a college connection," Becker said.

"Would we know them?" Andrea asked.

"You might have heard their names."

"Sure," Thaine said.

"No!" said Andrea.

"We have room," Thaine said.

"No," said Andrea. "Not enough lead time. The spare room's a mess. Sorry. End of discussion."

"I understand," Becker said and rang off.

Becker walked into the living room where Rooky and Weez had heard his conversation.

586

"No go," he said. "Pay cash at a motel. I'll give you the money." He went over to his swivel chair, sat down and turned toward them on the couch.

"We can sleep in the car if we have to," Rooky said. "It's parked on your road. We've done it before."

"Where are you heading, oh, better not tell me." Suddenly, Becker shot out of his seat. "This chair is wet! Did you spill something on it before I came home?"

"No," Weez said. "Maybe there was water on my jacket when I sat down. From the snow."

"You must have been standing out in it for a long time to get it this wet," Becker said.

"Sorry about your chair," Weez said. "It'll dry out."

"Smells like Mr. Clean, Lysol, or something," Becker said.

No one said anything.

"It was blood," Rooky said. "Then Weez cleaned your chair."

"What blood? Whose blood?"

"I shot a woman who was waiting to kill you," Weez said.

"Weez killed her in your chair," Rookie added.

Becker felt his eyes widen. "You killed a woman in my house, in my chair, just before I got home? Are you crazy?"

Gondleman broke in. "She had the Uzi. Roberta Magnelli. From Pittsburgh. I buried her in the woods. I used your shovel and pick and some other thing. She was sitting in that chair, waiting to kill you. Weez shot her. With a pistol."

"You buried her behind my house? Are you fucking nuts?"

"I saved your life, asshole," Weez said, calmly.

"She didn't know who we were," Gondleman added.

"Well, that's good news," Becker said. "Just think what she could do with that information after you got through with her."

"She was pretty," Rooky said. "Maybe 30. Long brown hair with some red in it. Weez surprised her. Me, too. She would have shot us. Pretty woman with an Uzi. Doesn't make sense."

Becker's head cleared. "Magnelli. Don't know that name. Wait a minute. It might make sense."

Country Cathy, Becker thought. The faux hooker who set up Biggie. Corelli said he had rejected the contract on me. But this Roberta Magnelli, she could have taken it.

"You're right," Becker said softly. "I think she was waiting for me and would have shot both of you as well. My guess is she works for Tony Bruno, a Mob guy, who wants me out of Delucci's campaign."

"What do we do now?" Gondleman asked.

"Well, it's clear," Weez said, "your old college friend doesn't want us here. So we should go."

And take the body with you, Becker thought. He forced himself to think more like a lawyer and less like a transfixed squirrel as a tractor-trailer sped straight at him.

"All right. Assume that Roberta worked for Bruno," Becker said. "Bruno's not going to report her missing. She'll just vanish like Hoffa. No one will say anything to the cops up there or here. So drive her car as far from my house as you can. Don't leave any of her ID in it. Maybe she drove a 'clean' car down here. Fake plates. No serial numbers. Then drive away in a different direction. I have $600, $700 in cash here. That'll get you somewhere."

"What will you do if the body is found?" Gondleman asked.

"I have no idea," Becker said.

"Roberta would be like the 'The African Queen' rising from the depths," Gondleman said.

"To blow me out of the water. That's a helpful analogy," Becker said. "I'll deny I had anything to do with her murder, that's the first thing. Leave it at that."

"What about the chair?" Gondleman asked.

"I have a brush pile out back. I'll burn it first thing in the morning, then scrap the metal frame up at my Dad's yard. There's no reason why cops should suspect me of having anything to do with Roberta Magnelli's disappearance."

"Are you going to turn us in?" Weez asked Becker. "Point the finger at us. Pick us out of a lineup?"

"I hope I would not do that."

"People named names in the '40s and '50s to save themselves," she said.

"I hope I'm better than that."

"That's it?" Weez asked. "That's all you can promise us? I saved your fucking life!"

"I'm not going to jail for murdering this Mafia assassin. Which I did not do," Becker said. "I'll protect you as much as I can. I don't want to perjure myself too much. So just go."

"I'm sorry, Beck," Gondleman said.

Becker said: "I should say, Thanks."

"Me, not him," Weez said.

"Thanks, Louise," Becker said.

"It's been a memorable visit," she said, gathering her gun, the Uzi and her flock of one.

Becker handed Gondleman the cash he kept in a drawer under the ironed-and-never-used linen napkins his mother insisted he take with him to West Virginia.

"I want to talk to him in private before we go," Gondleman said to Weez.

588

"Are you going to cut a deal and sell me out?" she snapped.

"No, something personal. You may recall the concept."

"Out in the garage," Becker said.

They put on their coats and walked outside and into the garage. It was black and smelled like engine drippings. Becker didn't turn on the light. They couldn't see each other's eyes.

"What?" Becker said.

"I'm thinking of turning myself in," Rooky said. "Running and hiding is pointless. We're not doing anything except not being caught. The only charges I know of are those in Chicago for the Days of Rage in 1969. I hope there's a statute of limitations."

"Are you asking me to represent you?"

"Yes."

"I can help, I guess," Becker said. "But you'll need a lawyer who's licensed in Illinois to take your case. A criminal guy, criminal defense. Someone who has experience in both local and federal cases. I can find someone."

"Thanks."

"Rooky, why did you go off the deep end?"

"The War. The draft. The celebrity. Paulette."

"Paulette Rotz?"

"She was an enchantress. The Weather leadership was almost entirely male, except for her. She was the final authority. None of us could resist her. She'd do anything. Then, we were her prisoners. We had to do what she wanted or she'd kick us out of her bed. She was like heroin. I couldn't get enough of her. None of us could. And on top of that, she was smart like a lawyer and always the most radical. It was the card I played at Columbia, except she had sex, which made her radicalism so powerful."

"Boys marry for sex," Becker said. "I suppose it leads us into other troubles."

"She was not like the other women in Weather, like Weez," Gondleman said. "She talked about feminism, but she didn't bitch and whine about it. Her feminism took her into the leader's position. The other women were lesser. They couldn't figure out how to do it like she did. Paulette acted male but without diminishing her femaleness and sensuality. She was stern; the others came off as hostile. They went along with sex out of political duty; Paulette had fun with it. At least, it seemed that way. They tried to ape her, but it came out different and lame. She was like Helen of Sparta. She had a power to make men do crazy shit. The thing about Paulette's feminism -- that Movement males are misogynists, that we didn't value women equally, that they did the shit work and we postured -- all that is true."

"You're not the first guy in history to let his zipper do too much of his thinking."

589

"Do you think I can skip jail?"

"It depends on the exact charges and the circumstances. The prosecutor will try to get you to flip on your comrades," Becker said.

"No," Gondleman said, "I won't do that. It's funny how this works. I'm a criminal for fighting with a Chicago cop and bombing some bathrooms. But Nixon, whose policies caused 20,000 deaths of U.S. soldiers after peace terms were agreed to, he gets pardoned."

"Our system adapts," Becker said. "Ford gave Nixon a full, free, and absolute pardon for all offenses against the United States that he committed, may have committed or took part in during his two terms. Nixon resigned before he could be impeached. A pardon in advance of a guilty verdict acknowledges that Nixon was guilty. But you'll get nowhere arguing you should get off because Nixon got off."

"What's my best shot without flipping?"

"Statute of limitations on the local stuff, tainted evidence on any federal charges," Becker said. "What about Weez?"

"She has no interest in coming up," Gondleman said. "I won't testify against her if that's what you're asking."

"Are you romantically involved?" Becker asked.

"I'd call it 'business, not personal,'" Gondleman said, with a grim chuckle. "You are more her type."

"ME!"

"She likes tall guys who are older."

"I'm flattered, of course," Becker said in an effort not to offend Gondleman. He changed the subject. "You know that you and the Weather people destroyed the SDS that could have become a national student union. It could have had a lasting impact."

"We weren't into liberal reforms, incremental changes," Rookie said. "We were about clearing the deck to see what happened next."

"Nixon happened next. George Wallace. Cambodia. The Christmas bombing. Kent State. Watergate."

"Can't go back and do it different. I have to live with it."

"And so here we are," Becker said.

"Time for us to go. Thanks," Gondleman said. "I'll get back in touch after your election is over."

Becker watched them drive off in two vehicles, their red tail lights fading into the white-flecked night. Snow covered their tracks.

A line he was required to memorize in 10th-grade English with Miss Mildred Reedy came to him as he peered into the emptiness they left. It was from Thomas Gray's "Elegy Written in a Country Churchyard":

The plowman homeward plods his weary way,
And leaves the world to darkness and to me.

590

Rooky is not going home; he plowed a field made barren by his own hand, Becker thought. Now I share his darkness.

Becker went inside. He moved the chair to his burn pile. He went into the kitchen and opened a can of tuna. He walked into his living room, turned on the television and hoped his brain would go to sleep. The thing to do with Roberta Magnelli, he concluded, was nothing and hope for the best.

Hell of a night, he thought.

He owed his life to Weez Draney.

As she drove Roberta Magnelli's car down Middle Ridge, Weez Draney considered Jeffrey Becker.

With Roberta buried behind his house, I now have leverage over him, she realized. His life is in my hands. Keep his secret, and he goes ahead. Reveal it -- anonymously, of course -- and his life goes haywire. I can now get things out of him. Money. Legal help. Maybe…a baby.

Chapter 43

Washington, D.C., December 1, 1975

Gus Olin left Fricktown early in frigid darkness. He didn't mind getting out of bed at four. It reminded him of his working days. His plan was to beat the Monday morning traffic in Montgomery County on his way into downtown Washington. It snowed as he drove through West Virginia and western Maryland. Even with a 4:30 a.m. start, he knew the weather might slow him enough to hit the thick of rush hour. He drove at a steady 40 mph, with snow blowing behind his Chevy pickup. It had gotten colder that night.

The best laid schemes of mice and men often go to shit, Gus thought. That was why he was driving through bad weather.

Snow had never bothered Gus except when cold brought a rapid fall in barometric pressure. Every coal miner paid attention to that. Lower pressure allowed more methane to gush from working faces. A ton of coal in the Pittsburgh seam typically contained about 200 cubic feet of methane. When a face gassed out normally as it was cut, the ventilation system would sweep the methane into the return and then to the surface. When gas came out fast and the ventilation was poor, an explosion could easily result.

When methane reached five percent by volume in an air mixture, it became explosive. Fans typically pushed at least 3,000 cubic feet of air per minute past working faces to keep methane below one percent. In the gassy mines of northern West Virginia, some fans had to flush as much as 9,000 cubic feet past a face.

A cold snap's quick two or three point drop in barometric pressure could increase the methane release underground in an hour or two. Gus remembered the fear he felt when he saw a mushroom-shaped cap in the open flame of his safety lamp, because it signaled a combustible five-percent mixture. He always stopped everything until the flame dropped into a spear point that meant a two-percent mixture, which was permissible before 1970. The 1969 Federal Coal Mine Safety and Health Act lowered the permissible limit to one-percent methane. By then, Gus was out of the mines. He had no idea whether every section in every underground coal mine was in compliance 100 percent of the time. He had his doubts.

It had only been seven years since Consolidation Coal's Number 9 Mine in Farmington, West Virginia, exploded at 5:30 a.m., on November 20, 1968, killing 78 of the 99 miners underground.

Farmington was 12 crow-flying miles from Fricktown.

Fricktown worked the same Pittsburgh seam as Number 9. It was known as a gassy mine since its opening in 1909. "Hot mines," they were called, for their gas volatility, not their temperature. Late fall and early winter were the most dangerous times. Investigators had not agreed on what caused the Farmington explosion. Gus figured it was inadequate ventilation. It was also likely somebody had done something to elevate the methane risk. The drop in barometric pressure that evening had boosted the methane emission. A methane pop could trigger a big methane blast that, in turn, could have ignited a massive coal-dust explosion. If someone had disabled the safety buzzer on a ventilation fan, the miners would have had no warning if it stopped pushing air. Gus figured something like that had happened at Number 9—someone did something unsafe to keep production up. Got the '69 safety act in return for those 78, Gus acknowledged.

Mornings like this spooked him. He knew the killer methane was leaking out of a million cracks in 500 hundred coal faces—invisible, odorless, tasteless. One stupid spark, one match to one cigarette as dumb as everyone knew that was, would make the next "tragedy-in-the-mines" headline. It wasn't his neck any more, but coal still held his mind.

Gus made decent time until Germantown. Then the I-270 traffic caught him just as the snow, thick now, wet and sticking, slowed his progress. Gus had placed a dozen 40-pound concrete blocks in the bed of his truck for traction. He pumped-braked just in time when a new Mercedes in front of him skidded into a Peugeot. Not bad reflexes for a geezer, he thought. Fender bender, no injury, no need to stop to help the pinstripes. He drove on in silence, herky-jerking with the others.

Gus had studied the road map. He was not opposed to trying something new every once in a while, but this morning was not one of those "onces." So he drove straight down the gut, down Connecticut Avenue. He knew that route from 1969 when he and dozens of miners had come to Capitol Hill to lobby for the safety bill that also provided a little compensation to black-lung victims. It's funny, he had thought to himself at the time, that taxpayers are expected to "compensate" miners disabled on the job. Why not let the people who buy coal pay the full freight? So what do I know? he'd asked himself. If you made coal pay all of its costs, it might become too expensive to use to boil water to make electricity. A devil's bargain.

Gus found the Hirshhorn Museum at Independence and 7th without much trouble. It was hard to miss the new, flying-saucer building. Parking at 10 a.m. was another matter. The plows had already locked in the curb-side cars. A cop was sticking tickets on the imprisoned vehicles. Gus passed up a spot on a side street and put the Chevy in an indoor garage. He accepted being reamed for two bucks an hour, which was better than a ticket. As he walked toward the museum, he noticed he was the only person wearing a red Mackinaw and a red-plaid hunter's cap with ear flaps. Most of the men he passed wore Chesterfields and rubbers. They were cold; Gus Olin wasn't.

Gus bought a ticket and went to the third floor. He sat down on a bench facing an oil painting the size of a garage door. Naked hippies were smoking marijuana.

Gus didn't smile when Skis came in a few minutes later and sat next to him. Skis blew his nose into a handkerchief. He was wearing a Chesterfield and rubbers. He jerked his head toward the lolling hippies: "This is the only picture here I understand," Skis said.

"I was at that Guggenheim building in New York that looks like a collapsible campin' cup," Gus said. "Think it's called an 'inverted ziggurat.' You can't expect modern architects to build the Parthenon over and over again. You gotta keep an open mind, Skis."

"Sure, 'open mind.' If I had dripped my paints like that one over there, Miss Shenk would have flunked my first-grade ass. The guys that dot up everythin' like grease spatterin' out of a skillet are real popular."

"I saw a bronze statue of a coal miner on my way up," Gus said. "'Bout the size of a quart of milk."

"Size always says somethin' 'bout who counts for how much."

"There was an English guy," Gus said, "Henry Moore, a sculptor, son of a Yorkshire coal miner. Some of his are outside."

Gus looked around. They were alone, except for a security guard who stood some distance away, straddling two galleries.

"Snowin' much at home?" Skis asked.

"More down here," Gus said. "I'm worried about the methane."

"Bad time for it," Skis said. "You see the papers about this Becker workin' for Jeep?"

"Saw it in the <u>The Morgantown Post</u>."

"Commie," Skis said.

Gus huffed out a laugh and brushed his hand across his face. "Every college kid who supports unions ain't a Commie. You yourself were helped by three of them when they come to Fricktown with food that filled your belly when you were hungry."

"I remember that pretty girl from a fancy college. Wonder what happened to her?"

"Probably got tired of tryin' to sell to workers what they weren't buyin'," Gus said. "It was sort of like those fellows who come around peddlin' siding and windows. Their philosophy seems to be: If they ain't lyin', we ain't buyin'. Do you actually believe that stuff you put out about Becker?"

"Joe hired a consultant to do up a report. Becker knew Gondleman, the Weatherman, at Columbia. Becker broke a library door at a demonstration on campus. Then he was at the Pentagon in October, '67, tryin' to make the building flap its wings or some shit."

594

"That's it? Do you really think that's Commie stuff?"

"That's enough to raise questions, don't you think?"

"Christ, Larry. You did more 'commie' stuff at Fricktown in one shift than that."

"Yeah, well. That was different."

"Where'd Joey get the money for his campaign?"

"Donations. Retirees. Some from workin' miners. A few miscellaneous donors—a lawyer or two who the Union uses, people like that."

"Where'd he get the big money, Skis. This is Gus, the guy who kept your ass safe when you were too green to wipe it."

"A guy named Bruno, in Pittsburgh. Tony Bruno," Skis said, tapping out a cigarette.

"Ain't allowed to smoke in here," Gus said.

Skis replaced the cigarette. "Yeah, I know."

"Mob guy, I reckon," Gus said. "He wants the Union."

"He already bought the bank," Skis said. "Joe figures once he gets reelected, we'll show Tony Bruno the door with a big thank-you."

"Is Bruno where the two goons come from that beat up Vernie Skeens?"

"I guess. Don't know nothin' 'bout that. Joe might have made some arrangements with Bruno."

"You sure you had nothin' to do with that?"

"Wasn't me, Gussie. It could have been Joe," Skis said, "but coulda been a freebie, Bruno on his own. I don't have no knowledge it was Joe."

"Does Bruno have his hook into Delucci, too? Is that where his campaign is gettin' funded?"

"Jeep come up with a whole boatload of cash from somewhar a little after Joe did. Bruno's probably givin' money to both sides."

Gus lowered his head and raised his eyebrows. "Do you really think you're gonna kick Bruno out once you win?"

"No," Skis admitted. "I think we got in bed with the Devil, 'cause that was the only way we could win. I don't think Bruno's the kind that stops screwin' us when we say 'Enough.'"

"So how does this end up?"

"He'll try to turn us into the Teamsters," Skis said. "Sweetheart contracts. Steal all the money he can. Corrupt the union. Phantom jobs. Bad loans. He'll want us to use his accountants and lawyers."

"He'll butcher the men, steal their money," Gus said.

"Joe an' me will fight him," Skis said. "You know us."

"Joey could end up 'disappeared' like Jimmy Hoffa if he stops playin' ball," Gus said. "You, too."

"We ain't dead, yet," Skis said.

"'Yet.'"

"Our cards have been played," Skis said. "Me an' Joe are old men. Don't matter for us no more, Gussie. What else can we do?"

"Make it right. You clean up your own place. Like I showed you in the mine."

"How?"

"Aint gonna be easy or pretty," Gus said. "Do you have documents, copies of checks?"

"The money -- $500,000 -- came to Joe, personally, in cash. Five big suitcases! All twenties. Thousands of them. I told the campaign bookkeeper to send Jacksons to our guys in the locals. No checks. The rest went to advertising, salaries and office. I worked up the list of who got how much. I got that list."

"I never thought it would be this bad," Gus said.

Skis looked at the hippies in the painting. The naked girl wasn't even very pretty. "Do you think Delucci would be better?"

"My guess is that Bruno has the kid in his other pocket like you said," Gus said. "To be honest, I think Joey has run his race."

Skis looked at his friend, a man who had been as much a father to him as his own. "I know."

"I'm the same," Gus said. "Not much gas left in my tank. Suckin' fumes."

"You got Edna. You got your place. Your garden. Your books. A decent truck. Pension. Social Security. Black-lung check. ACMU takes care of your medical."

"We gotta pass down somethin' good," Gus said. "Leave things a little better. Don't want to pass down meat stinkin' with rot."

"How?"

"You an' me will find a way," Gus said. "An' will bring Joey along. That's how."

Chapter 44

Anawalt Holler, December 2, 1975, 7: 15 p.m.

"Thank you all for coming," Willie Rutherford said to the women who were working themselves into whatever comfort they could find on the kitchen and dining-room chairs crammed into his living room.

"How yo' leg, Willie?" Wanda asked.

"Which one?"

The 10 women appreciated his now-familiar humor.

"Willie, you cloggin' yet?" Linda Faye Decker said with a poker face.

"Thumpin' and stumpin," he said.

"All right, ladies," Susie Rutherford said. "I'm behind this meetin'. So I guess I should call us to order."

"Now, honey, how orderly do you think gals like us can be, considerin' our disruptive origins?" Linda Faye asked.

Susie laughed, her frame shaking a little. She put her hand to her mouth. "Well, you know what I mean. Willie, tell 'em."

"We went up to a funeral in Boone County," Willie said. "For Frank Stover, Mr. Jeep's friend. They call him 'Biggie,' which he most certainly was."

"I saw Biggie at American Eagle," Jeannie Lou Burdette said.

"Me, too," Sharon Lewis said.

"My goodness," LeeAnn Dorsey said.

"Hard to forget the likes of him," Wanda Smith said. "Black beard an' all."

"Ladies," Doris Estep said, grinning. "Willie."

"Biggie, he worked in Mr. Jeep's campaign," Willie said. "He was murdered. The story goin' round is he found himself a gal on Capitol Street one night and her pimp killed him in his own car. I don't put no store in that. That Biggie boy wasn't the cattin'-'roun' kind from what his friends say. We figures it like Mr. Jeep said. Mr. Biggie was kilt to get him out of the election. There was talk about the Mafia helpin' Joe Hunt. Maybe the Mafia was behind this killin'."

"Don't know nothin' 'bout no Mafia," Wanda said. "Like that Godfather dude?"

"They're organized criminals," Doris said. "Eye-talians. They prey on their own, and now they're moving into the mainstream."

"Why do the Mafias want to poke their nose into the Union election?" Alma Rae asked.

"Money," Susie said.

"Money," Willie said. "They want to get at our pensions and health-care fund. So here's why we called this meetin'. Me an' Susie think Mr. Jeep be better on safety than Mr. Joe. We think the young boy'll fight for safety and against the speed-up comin' back. And we think he'll fight off the Mafias more than Mr. Joe. If you all agrees, then we should call up the folks we met during the wildcat and tell 'em the widders are backin' Mr. Jeep."

"I bet we have 250 phone numbers from the strike. All the way out to Colorado and Wyoming," Linda Faye said.

"I think I should step out," Doris said. "Alma Rae and I shouldn't be seen mixing in your election."

"What you all think about that?" Susie said.

"You were in with us then, you're in with us now, whether you like it or not, whether you step out or not," Linda Faye said.

"We could not have got as far as we did without you, Miz Estep," Daisy Jones said. "You and Miz Stump helped put money in our pockets. You made the mines safer."

"You have a right to say what you think," LeeAnn Dorsey said. "Earned fair and square."

"Ain't like it was before, Miz Estep," Wanda said. "You wif us, and we, the same, back to you. You ain't jes' comp'ny no mo'. You diff'rnt. You done widened out."

"My, my," Doris laughed. "'Done widened out,' indeed I have. In many respects."

"I turn this meetin' over to Doris," Susie said.

"Doris, you're like the Mother Jones of management," Linda Faye laughed.

"My Granddaddy said he met Mother Jones up at Paint Creek, during the shootin' war in 19 and 12 and 13," Juanita Buchanan said. "Kanawha County kept her jailed up at Mrs. Carney's Boarding House in Pratt for 85 days. Granddaddy said 50 of us was kilt, not countin' the starved. Strike lasted for more than a year. The comp'nies ran folks off. That's why he come to McDowell County."

"I read about that strike," Doris said. "I always wondered whether that miner, Cesco Estep, was kin to Delmer. Cesco was killed in Hollygrove when they ran that armored train up the Creek firing two machine guns into houses and tents."

"Imagine shootin' machine guns at women and children," LeeAnn said.

"Or men for that matter," Doris said. "Fellow citizens, human beings."

"That's why the Union's been important. They don't do that shit no more to us. Stuff, not shit, I mean," Linda Faye said looking at LeeAnn Dorsey who went to church services at least three times a week.

"I have two kids," LeeAnn grinned, "I know there ain't no difference."

598

Doris went on: "Cesco's real name was Francis. He was shot in the face. His wife emptied his gun at the train as it went by. Delmer told me this story. I suppose there *was* a family connection, but he never said."

"There's plenty more coffee and cake," Susie said, as she circled with a plate of baked goods.

"Don't eat them sour-cream, chocolate-chip bars, ladies," Willie snickered, "'cause they taste awful and will make you fat as whales."

"Right," Wanda said. "Willie, you don't need two good legs to stand up for your ol' greedy self."

"I was thinkin' of what's best for all you," he grinned.

"Didn't you win a blue with these a couple of years back?" Alma Rae asked.

"Yes'm, I did. The '71 fair."

"Ladies?" Doris asked. "We sort of have a motion on the living-room floor. Do we need to talk more? Hearing no talk and with all mouths full of chocolate-chip bars, I'd say we're ready for a yea or nay. For? Against? Ladies, it's unanimous. To the phones! Just tell them that we women are behind Jeep Delucci, because he will be better than Hunt on what we care about."

"Amen," said LeeAnn Dorsey.

"Amen," the others responded.

December 2, 1975, 9:47 a.m.

Jeffrey Becker got to the Delucci campaign office later than his usual 8:15. It had taken time early that morning to thoroughly clean his floors, lamp, door knobs, light switches, throw rugs and everything else on which he found the ghosts of blood splatters and possible fingerprints. At the brush pile, he doused the chair with an entire can of charcoal-lighter fluid. He threw on the cloth and paper towels he and Weez had used. The brush burned hot and fast, the chair took longer. He pushed the crisped fragments of fabric into the flames with his shovel. Becker saw himself in a movie, destroying evidence. He saw himself sitting in a different kind of chair.

Becker figured he was safe through the election. It would take a day or two, or even more, for Bruno to figure out that Roberta Magnelli had not killed him and was not coming home.

But Becker was now at permanent risk of finding himself in a calamitous jam if Roberta's remains were discovered. How would he explain that? His life would be a shambles. He would be convicted of concealing evidence of a crime at the very least. He would be disbarred. He could go to jail for a long time. Gondleman and Draney now held his life in their hands.

He thought about talking with a lawyer. Thaine and Andrea Warner were out. They'd advise him to do what was best for the working class, which would not be of much help.

Becker was on good -- but not close -- terms with two criminal-defense lawyers in Charleston who would, he thought, advise him to do what he would advise them to do in this predicament: Notify the cops about the body and turn in Gondleman and Draney.

Murder was a crime, he said to himself. Keeping it under wraps was aiding and abetting murderers who, by the way, had saved his life—a "small" complicating factor. Is self-defense by proxy a defense in court or anywhere else?

Becker walked in the back door of the MDU's office. On his desk was the early edition of The Charleston Gazette. He read the headline above the fold:

Delucci Campaign Manager
Is Communist, Hunt Charges

Becker sat. He closed his eyes. He tried to capture a moment in his past where he felt things were going mostly right rather than all wrong.

The Gazette had reprinted a feature from The New York Times written by Burton Sniderman, their beat reporter on coal and Appalachia.

The story was accurate. Becker had been at Columbia University. He had participated in the demonstrations in the spring of 1968. He had known Rooky Gondleman and had attended a couple of SDS meetings. He had broken a window in a locked Low Library door, which allowed the crowd to occupy the president's office. After the Columbia melt down, Gondleman and a few others had thrown themselves into street fighting and then politically motivated bombings. Becker had not been any part of that, which Sniderman mentioned. Hunt was quoted as saying Becker was "an anti-War hippie who wanted to hurt our brave fighting men in October, 1967, by making the Pentagon fly away, maybe as far as Mars." Sniderman's piece found no connection between Gondleman and Becker after Columbia.

Well, Becker thought, events of yesterday have eclipsed today's news.

Joe Hunt was quoted: "This Becker is an outsider with a Communist-type agenda for my coal miners and my Union. He's a lawyer, which says a lot about him. He don't come from no coal-minin' family, not even the comp'ny side. He was against the War in Vietnam. ACMU members should ask, 'What's this Communist up to in the Delucci campaign?'"

When Sniderman asked Hunt how he knew Becker was a "communist," Hunt said: "'Cause he's good friends with that terrorist Robert Gondleman who's a weather forecaster, or some ____, and wants

600

to destroy the American way of life and turn all of us into Soviet robots. I bet Becker gives money to Gondleman on the QT. Go ask him if he don't."

Indeed, I have, Becker thought. $665. Just last night.

Becker walked back to Delucci's office. He knocked.

"I'm here."

Becker walked in and sat. "We're getting close to the finish line."

"Yeah boy," Delucci said, leaning back in his chair. "Look, Beck, I'm sorry about punchin' you. I lost my temper. I know you didn't tell Pickering me an' Biggie killed those two hoods."

"While you're in a forgiving mood, did you read the Times story?"

"I did. I see you're tight with a gen-u-ine communist," Delucci said.

"As I told you, I knew him in college. Most everybody knew him by sight. I talked to him. We had a class together. We were not social friends. The story got the facts it printed right. I did break the window, but I did it to protect Grayson Kirk. The crowd would have mobbed him. So I smashed the window with my book bag to divert the demonstration inside."

"Your book bag!" Delucci said laughing so hard Becker thought he would roll into a fetal ball. "Your fucking book bag! Who the hell breaks windows with a poke of books? You use a rock or a brick for Chrissakes. Fuckin' intellectual. Jeeeez!"

"All I had was my humble book bag. Grayson Kirk should have thanked me. By the way, 15 pounds of books in a bag is a pretty good weapon. It was not a planned act of vandalism, I should add."

"Becker, you're a riot."

"Yeah, so Joe Hunt says."

"Half our membership was more rowdy than you at that age," Delucci said.

"Your members are far more advanced."

"Probably got laid sooner, too. Anyway. So after my campaign manager terrorizes Columbia University with his bag of books, he crosses interstate lines to Dee Cee so he can launch the Pentagon into orbit. Is that it?"

"At the time, October, '67," Becker said, "there was talk among the Zennies, Yippies and hippies of levitating the Pentagon. They weren't into breaking windows. I'm a window man."

"What do you mean, 'levitatin'? Like everybody liftin' on the count of three?" Delucci shook his head.

"Abbie Hoffman's idea was to focus the minds of 100,000 protesters surrounding the Pentagon, then sing, dance and chant. He said the Pentagon would turn orange and then its evil spirits would be exorcised while the vibrating building floated off like a hovercraft on acid."

"You can't be serious?"

"I did not share his vision or his politics," Becker deadpanned. "I expressed doubts based on what I recalled from high-school physics. I didn't join the lift-off team. Incidentally, the protest organizers wanted a permit to lift the Pentagon 300 feet into the air. The Authorities agreed to a three-foot lift. That was in the permit."

"You can't be serious?"

"It was absurdist theater," Becker said. "The hippies' smoke and mirrors was bullshit just like the smoke and mirrors of the Pentagon's PR guys. Hoffman and Jerry Rubin believed that turning opposition to the War into a big goof was the way to strip off the veneer of truth from the White House lies. I thought they were crazy."

"All we heard in Nam was that the 82nd Airborne and some U.S. Marshals kicked ass."

"They did. That night. They were armed. We weren't. By the way, I was never a hippie. I wasn't part of the levitating crew."

"So how far up did they get it?" Delucci asked with all the seriousness he could muster.

"There were reports that it shook a little."

"Coal miners ain't gonna understand this levitatin' shit," Delucci said. "Now if you had thrown a pie in Westmoreland's face, a lot of grunts over there would have cheered. Or you could have mooned Nixon. Or shot him."

"I didn't shoot anybody, ever."

"But you have a gun with you now, like I told you?"

"Yes," Becker said. "It's even loaded."

"Praise God," Delucci laughed. "Let's hope Tony Bruno was makin' idle threats."

They weren't idle, Becker thought.

"Maybe you could levitate Joe Hunt out of ACMU headquarters. Get the old crowd together for one last stoned lift off."

Becker rolled his eyes.

"Some revolutionary," Delucci snickered. "I'd say at least half the infantry when me an' Biggie was over there saw no reason for the War and couldn't understand why we didn't hold the land we took from the VC and the North Vietnamese. Their side was willing to throw more people at us than we could kill fast enough to make them quit. Totally fucked. Most of the guys who came into the mines after Nam won't care that you were against the War. The WWII vets, the Korean vets will. 'Course nobody will understand levitatin'. If you didn't like a building in their wars, you blew it to shit with artillery. No one tried to turn it orange and send it on its way. Were you arrested in either place?"

"No."

"Pussy."

"I was against the War. I hated it. It took over my life. What to do if I was drafted? How to stop it? I almost don't remember a time when it wasn't in my head affecting everything I did. And it only ended this April. Dead: 58,000, 153,000 wounded, 1,600 missing. $140 billion, $140,000 for every enemy killed. For what? Vietnam is now one country with a Communist leadership. Does that now threaten the United States?"

"You're preachin' to a choir boy," Delucci said. "The dinks will spend the next 20 years tryin' to recover from what we done to them and their land. Thirty, 40 years from now, they'll be our good friend and ally against China, their usual enemy."

Becker took a breath. "The point is, Jeep, I did not then and do not now share Gondleman's ideas, which is why I'm working for you and not hiding from the FBI."

"So this is bullshit about being pals with Gondleman?" Delucci asked.

"I knew him. I talked to him. Not political pals, then or now. We had different politics."

"Don't give him money?"

"Don't give him money," Becker lied.

"Don't help him stay underground?"

"Don't help him stay underground," Becker lied.

"Ain't no Underground Weatherman in disguise?"

"Ain't no Underground Weatherman in disguise," Becker said.

"Ain't no communist tryin' to take over the Union?"

"Ain't no communist tryin' to take over the Union," Becker said.

So now, Becker thought, I've just lied to Delucci about Gondleman, because…because...because telling him what happened last night is too complicated to explain. And if I told Delucci, he would then be part of my cover up. Or he would always have something on me. And how can I turn those two in after they saved my life? Would I have turned them in if they had just shown up looking for a safe place? Probably not? Why? Because Rooky's more a fool than a criminal. Weez Draney, on the other hand? But even her, nope. You are a truly stupid shit, Becker said to himself. The Weather Underground should shut up and disappear. But turning them in to the government that waged a war based on lies, ran COINTELPRO and break-ins, did Watergate and pardoned Nixon—I can't do it.

And so that ends me up in the classic liberal befuddlement: try to do something 'good,' and you find yourself doing something questionable, even indefensible, to get there. Why does everything turn to shit?

"Would you turn him in if he showed up on your front porch?" Delucci asked.

"Would you turn in Joe Hunt if you had evidence he killed that superintendent during the Fricktown strike?" Becker answered.

"Probably not," Delucci admitted. "No."

"Same," Becker said.

"All right. Then screw it," Delucci snorted and waved his hand against the gnat-like accusations whizzing around. "We don't answer Joe's charges in person. We issue a press release. You write it. Call Joe's smears 'last-minute, campaign mud-slingin' by a desperate candidate who's losing the race.' Poor ol' fuck don't know no better 'bout how to run honorably. Now, of course, don't say he's a poor ol' fuck. Say this is like what the comp'nies pull in negotiations to divide and weaken us. Coal miners have been through diversions before. *Etcetera*. Get it to me this afternoon."

"Did Sniderman call you for a quote?" Becker asked.

"Called, but I was out. Did he call you?"

"Dicey never gave me a message that he called," Becker said.

"Good. Your press release can set the record straight in your own words," Delucci said.

"I need to talk to you about another thing. This Mafia thing," Becker said, closing his eyes, then opening them. "This high-school friend I mentioned to you at Biggie's funeral works for Bruno sometimes. He told me to drop out of the campaign if I wanted to stay alive. I took his warning seriously."

"You did resign, sort of," Delucci said.

"With these Hunt charges about Gondleman, maybe I should disappear."

"If you vanish, it will give legs to Joe's bullshit. It will look like you're guilty. I'll lose. If your life is in danger, that is a reason to get out. You could say you were ill and had to rest. Not very convincing. If you quit under a cloud, it kills my campaign. You'll have a hard time shakin' the charge whatever you do next. Maybe you can stay around without being seen. Like an unofficial adviser."

"What will you do with Bruno and Siciliano if you win?" Becker asked.

"I dunno," Delucci said.

"Go to the U.S. District Attorney in Washington or Pittsburgh," Becker said. "Expose Siciliano's contributions. It's not illegal to take cash even from them for your campaign. So far you've given them nothing in return. You're clean and would be a cooperating witness. Then you can run the Union free and clear. They'll be fighting in court and in the press. That's my best legal advice."

"What if they kill me?" Jeep asked.

"Then you'll be dead and will no longer be troubled by these problems," Becker said. "How's that for insightful legal advice?"

"I want to be shut of these problems and still be alive," Delucci said. "There's a lot of good I can do as president. I patched things up with Walter Bishop. The widders are callin' around for me."

"That's good."

"This election ain't worth your life, Beck."

"You have my signed resignation letter. But it will look like I'm guilty, and you've been a dupe."

"You're right."

"What do you want me to do?" Becker asked.

"You've gotten me to the point where I think I can win. Why risk your life? We can announce together you've done what you were hired to do, and now it's time to get back to your law practice."

"Over The Peanut Shoppe."

"Alive and over The Peanut Shoppe. Bruno doesn't want you gettin' in their way. He doesn't need you dead. He needs you shut up and not near me and the Union."

"What do you want, Jeep? Do you want to go to the feds and get clean or do you want to see what happens, what you can do on your own?"

"Ain't sure," Jeep said.

"Do you want me as ACMU general counsel if you win?"

"Sure. But I've lost one friend already. I don't want to lose you, too."

"If you go to the government, bring me back on. I'll take my chances just like you. If you don't go to the feds, then I'll go back to practicing law. It's up to you."

"About going to the District Attorney," Delucci said, "I guess we'll see what I decide, won't we?"

"I guess we will," Becker said, hesitantly.

Chapter 45

The Governor sat on his toilet's lowered lid scratching his nose.

Pleasant vapors from the walk-in shower lingered in his bathroom. He thought about cutting his nails but decided to put it off for a day or two. He'd get a manicure; the Vietnamese lady would come to him. He considered a pedicure but decided against it. What would West Virginia voters think of that if it got around?

He had draped his bath towel over the lid to keep his bottom warm. His mother had insisted he continue to use his monogrammed towels when he went to Harvard despite the teasing he had endured in prep school. She delivered a new set to Nancy when they were married. He admitted he liked his mother's towels. They were 750-gram weight, which he supposed was as good as towels got. They had stitched hems with a zero-twist yarn made of Turkish cotton. She told him they were woven in a humble Portuguese town at a tiny plant that still used Jacquard punch-card looms from the late 1800s. He liked them because they were big, fluffy and water-absorbent; his mother cared as much about their provenance. He sat directly on the NSW monogram to show he was a regular guy when it came to using his wife's towels.

The Governor was troubled. He didn't like the rumors.

Where were Joe Hunt and Jeep Delucci getting all the cash they were spreading around the West Virginia coalfields? "They're spending it, quick and thick," his political director had reported.

The Governor knew he was plenty savvy about West Virginia elections. You gave money to the county boss who distributed it to the heads of loyal families, poll workers and drivers. You bought votes by bribing particular people who could and would bring a package of votes with them.

But that's not what he'd been hearing about the ACMU election. Cash was coming in from both sides to buy individual votes, directly. As much as $25 a vote from both Hunt and Delucci. How would they deal with double-crossers? The Governor estimated each side was putting in at least $200,000 in ads, above the vote-buying.

And then there was this murder of Frank Stover. It certainly could be what it seemed—a robbery of a John. But Stover's death during this election in circumstances that didn't fit what the cops knew about his habits didn't smell right to The Governor. No hooker had been found. No pimp had been found. No white Bronco pimp car had been found. No murder weapon had been found. Stover's credit cards turned up on the West Coast with a 17-year-old Mexican kid. Backtracking that lead hit a dead end. The Kanawha County investigators had no theories other than the obvious one and increasingly less interest in a case they were not solving. Stover, the Governor had been told, was Delucci's spine. Oh well, The Governor, concluded, it was better to stay out of fights between the natives. They had their own ways of resolving conflicts. You didn't see Frick and Carnegie shooting at each other.

Then there was this story about Jeffrey Becker. The West Virginia Bar had concluded Becker was of "good moral character." The Governor estimated at least one-third of the lawyers he had run across in West Virginia were scumbags who were incompetent cheats. The "good ones" tied legal language into slipknots to defend whomever they were billing. If Becker had a criminal record as a student radical, the Governor felt the Bar examiners would have found it, assuming they had looked, which they probably hadn't. It wasn't illegal to have been against the War; even the Governor had come around to that position by 1973 when America signed the peace treaty. He, of course, had kept this to himself. And there was, presumably, a statute of limitations in New York City that would let Becker escape prosecution for breaking a window in 1968.

And you couldn't jail Becker for having known Gondleman in college. Hell, The Governor himself had known several communists at Harvard. They were, he recalled, intense, voluble fellows from New York City with chips on their shoulders, verbally nimble and not ready to be asked into the right clubs. One was heir to a major department-store fortune. The Governor had even roomed beside him at prep school. He was a rich kid with guilt, a syndrome The Governor's mother encouraged her son to rise above. The kid drove a classic Jaguar, a red '56 XK-140, with rear spats and "matching numbers," which The Governor assumed meant something important. And when he thought about the Lefty gadflies he had known, there was the Peabody from Massachusetts and that Alcott from Connecticut. Those two had been for civil rights before it had become *de rigueur*. Surely, he had spoken to both of them from time to time about one thing or another. He was sure he had heard each of them espousing. The Governor was certain that involuntary listening to unpopular opinions, even revolutionary opinions, was not a criminal offense.

The Governor focused. Becker might have kept in touch with Gondleman since Columbia and might have sent him money through a conduit. But, as far as The Governor knew, no Weatherman was in West Virginia. Colonel Bob Redbone told him almost all SDS students had rejected the Weathermen. These accusations from Joe Hunt were last-minute politics. Accusations, The Governor knew, didn't have to be true; they just had to have been made. That's what Nancy said.

Like that story he'd been told in his first race about George Smathers who was running against his mentor, Senator Claude Pepper, in the 1950 Florida Democratic primary. Smathers supposedly said: "Pepper is known all over Washington as a shameless extrovert! Pepper has a sister who was once a thespian! Pepper practiced...*celibacy* before his marriage...and nepotism with his sister-in-law in sinful New York. He matriculated with women in college, and his brother is a practicing *homo* sapien." Smathers denied making these statements, but The Governor understood their appeal to voters. And once they're circulating, accusations acquire legitimacy, deserved or not.

The Governor stood and began brushing his teeth while looking at himself in the mirror. Leadership, he repeated to himself, is knowing when to decide to decide and when to decide not to decide. Stay out of this ACMU election tar pit, Shortbridge. He recalled his mother telling him: "Step in dog doo-doo, Petey, and you walk around smelling like dog doo-doo. It's the same, whether the doo-doo is from an AKC champion best in show or a mangy mutt from the pound." She never felt the need to show her son her meaning; telling, she hoped, would suffice.

I'm not quite ready to decide to decide, let alone to decide on a decision, The Governor decided.

Charleston, W.Va., December 2, 1975 7:15 p.m.

"Knock, knock."

Becker looked up from his desk at Delucci's headquarters where he was going through phone messages he had not answered, because he was officially out of the MDU campaign. "You!"

"I need to talk. I'm scared," Allyson said. She came in and sat on the one chair in Becker's office. She wiggled out of her heavy coat. She saw no hooks or hangers, so she laid it on the floor with her gloves and scarf. She saw maps on the walls, books, paper piles and campaign clutter.

"I'll try not to drip," she said.

"Why did you drive all the way from Pittsburgh? Go back. Get out. Leave me alone."

"Someone tried to kill me," she said.

Becker put down the clutch of messages and looked with concern at the woman he once loved.

"A Pittsburgh detective who's been helping me guessed that Tony Bruno would send someone after me. He stopped the guy. Behind my apartment. At night. I saw them in the alley."

"Good," Becker said. "I'm glad you're alive. Maybe you'll stop digging your hole deeper. Go marry Trip, or whatever his name is. Have babies. Set up a feminist collective in the Junior League. Raise their consciousness. Win a country-club golf championship. Burn the black book with the orange lettering as a protest against Old Money. And convert everyone to Quaker pacifism."

608

"I'm not that bad," Allyson said. "You know that."

"I thought so at one time," he said. "Well, you still have your looks."

"You're a sexist pig, Becker." Allyson Pickering, however, was not upset he'd said that.

"On purpose, not from ignorance," he said.

"Bruno is behind the Washington gang that bought the Union's bank. Siciliano is just a front," she said.

"So I've been informed."

"By whom?"

"Anonymous sources," he said.

"And Bruno was behind sending Lazarro and Hyskra down to Logan to rough up Skeens."

"Proof?"

"Inference."

He shook his head. "Not good enough. Still, we figured it the same way. Maybe Hunt paid for it, maybe not. Bruno may have sent those two as a freewill offering."

"And Greiner -- he's the detective -- thinks they were bait to get someone from your campaign to retaliate. Then their murder could be pinned on Delucci."

"I've heard that theory," Becker said.

"And Greiner thinks Biggie Stover ran them off the road."

"Dead men can't defend themselves," Becker said.

"And Greiner thinks Bruno was behind Stover's murder," she said.

"That fits."

"And Greiner thinks Bruno has funded both sides in your election."

"Proof?" Becker asked.

"No proof. It's just what he thinks."

"And does Greiner also think our planet is a cube around which the sun travels in a square orbit?" Becker asked.

"He hasn't said. And he thinks Bruno will get his hands on the Union's money, including the health and pension fund."

"The Mafia is always trying to infiltrate legitimate businesses and unions. Their business is stealing."

"So what are you going to do?" she asked.

"I'm going to finish a press release and go home. I might live large, drink a beer and go to sleep."

"You're going to do nothing?"

"Going to sleep is doing something. Right at this moment, yes. That's it."

"This information could swing the election."

"Which way?"

"Well, I'm not sure," Allyson admitted.

"It could swing Jeep and me into federal court for violating the Racketeer Influenced and Corrupt Organizations Act, not to mention state court on murder and conspiracy charges."

"Yes, very possible."

"Maybe you should let us work this out. We have a plan," he lied.

"Which is?"

"I'm not going there with you," Becker said. "Twice burned, thrice shy. Anyway, it's too late for a story to have any effect on the election. Time has run out."

She sagged in her chair. "I guess it has."

"And, furthermore, I've resigned from the campaign."

"So what are you doing here?"

"Tidying up. We sent out the release yesterday. That should keep me safe."

"I hope so."

"I would be out if Jeep wins," Becker added. "Mutual decision."

She doubted that.

"One last thing," she said. "Just before I left, Greiner told me Rooky Gondleman was arrested at a rest stop just outside of Baltimore. A Maryland state trooper said he recognized Gondleman in the men's room where he was brushing his teeth. Found a bunch of bomb-making stuff in the trunk of his car."

"No search warrant," Becker said. "That evidence might be admissible if the officer had probable cause. A clever defense lawyer should be able to keep it out."

"He was building bombs, Becker! He wasn't assemblying Legos."

"It doesn't matter. What matters in the courtroom under the law is whether the cop found the stuff legally. Gondleman probably possessed legal materials, legally purchased. He probably gave the cop a false name and ID. Why did Greiner mention Gondleman's arrest to you?"

"I told him I'd been at the Columbia protests in the spring of '68 when you and I began keeping company. I told him mounted cops wanted to chase me down the street. I left out the beer bottles. He thought I might have known Gondleman."

"Did Rooky say anything?"

"Nothing that Greiner has gotten from his FBI contact."

"Anybody arrested with him?"

"No. Do you know anything about this?"

"Nope. Haven't seen Rooky since the spring of '68."

"Do you think Gondleman will talk?" she asked.

"He'll request a lawyer who will tell him to say nothing. He will fight a battle between his fears of prison and his commitment to his friends. I don't think he has the character to take a long jail sentence. But the

610

charges against him from the late '60s are not big deals. I don't think he's been charged with bombing anything."

"Do you think he'll cut a plea agreement?"

"Rooky is a chess player when you take off all the rhetorical clothes. He knows how to set traps, to sacrifice for the greater gain, to follow a strategic plan. The goal is to win the game. How he defines winning will determine what he does to get there."

"Do you think he'll give up his friends?"

"No. His lawyer will tell him in their first conversation that the government will probably have to abandon any big charges against him, because they likely rest on illegally obtained information under COINTELPRO. I don't think he'll have to rat out his friends to get off."

"So you think he will walk away from all the bombings he did?"

"I think he'll get a pass on most of what he did. He might serve a little time or get probation."

"Amazing. A kid goes to jail for a joint, and Gondleman goes free!"

"God Bless America," Becker said. "And now you've suckered me once again into talking to you. None of what I've said is on the record. None of it is to be used in any way."

"Look. I have no story that's ready to run. Do you want what I have? Put it out as a press release. I brought my files with me. They're in the car."

Becker assumed he knew whatever Allyson knew in broad terms. Given Jeep's compromised position, Becker reasoned no publicity was best. Reporters, given new leads, would dog the scents until they uncovered what was twitching their noses.

"Nope," he said. "I don't want to see your files. I'm *in absentia* for the rest of the campaign. Give them to Jeep if you're so hot to give them to somebody."

"Well, no. Jeep is…"

Becker said nothing.

"…involved, too," she said.

Becker did not respond.

"You're protecting yourself," she said. "You have knowledge of a crime. Maybe more than one."

"Think whatever you want," he answered.

"You don't trust me, do you?"

"Not anymore."

"You don't love me, do you?"

Here we go again, he thought. He shrugged.

"Not even some?" she asked.

"It's like this. Those summer months were the best time in my life. And then you ended it. So my heart wants that good time back. But my brain knows it would not have worked then, and it would not work now. My brain says my heart doesn't want to be broken twice."

"I was happy then, too."

"All evidence to the contrary," Becker said.

"Could we try?"

"Too late. I made that offer to you once, and you left me sitting in a tepee."

"Princess Bra-burner has matured."

"What is the Princess now?" he asked.

"Damaged merchandise. Looking for a friend in the wilderness. Becker...."

"What?"

"I don't need to hurt you now."

"There's a confidence-builder."

"I want you to know I'm different. I could live with you now without loading all that resentment on you."

"That's something, I guess."

"I've changed."

"We all change. I don't want to roll my life dice again on what you just said. I don't trust your words. It hurt too much the last time when you crapped out on me."

"So you'd rather live half-alive than...."

"Yes," Becker said. "I would. And there's also stuff you don't know. We don't have a clear shot with each other now."

"Complications. Unknowns. Mistakes. Secrets. Bad ideas. Hurtful words. It's all part of learning and getting older."

"You're not going to seduce me again," he said.

"I haven't even started trying that."

"Go back to your Trips."

"Kennedy."

"'A rose by any other name smells as sweet.'"

Allyson gathered her things. "He doesn't smell."

"We do. You and me."

"I won't bother you again with my feelings. You know, Becker, we are simply hurting each other."

"I always thought it would work better with you than anyone else," he said. "But it would end the same way. At least, I tried the first time."

"Yes, you did," she admitted.

"I wasn't running away from us. You were."

"I was pulled in two directions. I'm not that way anymore. We have history; we have glue."

"Glue dries out," Becker said. "There has to be something more in the present than just the past. You have to be in 100 percent with each other.

We're not there. The campaign story -- what you think you know -- is between us."

Allyson had her coat and gloves in her hands. She started crying. "You're in my head. You're in my heart. Why can't I be happy?"

Becker felt himself fumbling at all levels. "This Kennedy—he sounds great."

"Oh shut up."

"Can I take you to lunch tomorrow?" he asked for lack of any other idea to make her stop crying.

"No!"

"I'm sorry, Pick."

"Give me what I want," she said, pulling herself together.

"No," Becker said. "I don't want to be kicked in the teeth again."

Allyson rose and put on her coat, scarf and gloves.

"Well, it's nice to see that you're famous," she said. "Twenty-four column inches in The New York Times."

"Perhaps your parents took it better than mine," he said.

"My father said the one communist he knew at Yale ended up making a ton of money on Wall Street betting against the blue chips during the Depression. My mother is rooting for Kennedy Brown as the best of those I have presented over the years."

"Go with him," Becker said.

"Goodbye, Becker," she said and left.

Becker closed his eyes. He felt a headache storming in from the rear. He could go to a movie. He could go to a movie every day. He hoped there was a better cheap office available than the one still for rent over The Peanut Shoppe.

Becker went home and fell asleep. It was snowing. Anything could happen in West Virginia when a cold snow was falling.

Pittsburgh, December 2, 1975

"Tony. This is John Thomas Stuart."

"Yes? It's 9:30…at night."

"I'll be downtown in about 45 minutes. Meet me at the Frick Building. Corner of Grant and Fifth. We've used lawyers there in the past. I'll have a rental car. Get in when I pull up to the curb."

"Yes," Tony said and hung up.

"Shit," Tony said, as he got dressed.

"Where are you goin'?" Josephine asked from her side of their bed.

"Out," Tony said.

"Out, I knew. Where out?"

"Business out," he said, pocketing a pistol from his sock drawer.

"Why the gun? You're worried. I can feel it."

"That's indigestion from the raw garlic you always put in your Amatricana sauce."

"Garlic is good for us."

"Garlic has killed half the Italians in Pittsburgh," he said.

"Garlic?"

"Yes, Josephine, garlic is good for us. I'll be back around midnight. Don't wait up. You're my love."

Tony dressed quickly and thought at the same speed. John Thomas Stuart! Lawyer for Philip Bombardo, the éminence grise of the Genovese family in New York. Stuart! Partner with Gary Swiney and Arnold Gradué in Stuart, Swiney and Gradué, P.C., the special-projects Mafia firm. If Stuart was here, he was coming from Bombardo and, more importantly, Frankie Fagano, chairman of the Five Families.

Scozia was John Thomas Stuart's given name. He looked like a WASP who had been finished at a New England prep school. He dressed like one, acted like one and married one. But Tony knew that John Thomas Stuart's Dad, Enzo, had worked the New York docks with a cargo hook in his hand, both on the job and off when the wise guys needed him. Mafia money had put Enzo's one bright kid through Brooklyn Law School on the understanding he would change his name and represent the Mob exclusively.

Tony parked his Cadillac in Scrip Way, the alley behind the Frick Building. He walked to the southeast corner of the intersection and waited beside a street-level window. He pulled up the collar of his jacket against the cold. In a few minutes, John Thomas Stuart rolled up Grant Street in an Impala and stopped.

"Tony," he said, through the lowered window. "You'll catch your death of cold out on a night like this."

"Yeah," Tony said, getting in.

"This won't take long. I'll drive while we talk. What happened?"

"I'm not sure. I sent Roberta to do Becker, and she never come back. Fucking disappeared."

"Left?"

"Why would she run out on a job? The girl ain't like that."

"She must be dead," John Thomas said.

"Her car turns up in Highland County, Virginia, in the George Washington National Forest, 200 miles from Becker's place."

"Where is this county?"

"Between Charleston and Washington. I asked around. Don't have more than 3,000 people. It's trees an' baaa-baaas an' moo-moos. I figure whoever did her, took her car and dropped it there clean. Probably on their way from Becker's place to wherever they were going."

"Why didn't you send Corelli?"

"I wanted to," Tony said, "but John said he knew Becker from high school or some shit. He refused the contract."

"Do you think Becker killed Roberta?"

"A lawyer kill her? Naw. Something happened we don't know."

"'Something happened.' Bombardo and Frankie figured that out— 'something happened.' They have a million dollars in this coal miners' election and several hundred million in buying their bank. 'Something' is not supposed to happen!"

"I can't make Corelli do a job. I've lost three people so far. The girl was pretty good. The other two would not make the varsity."

"We can send someone from New York if need be."

"I'm down to Jerry Multirosa for Becker," Tony said. "And he didn't get that girl reporter done."

"First I've heard of that."

"Art Greiner, a local detective, stepped between Jerry and the job."

John Thomas Stuart said nothing for a few minutes. Tony lit a cigarette and dropped the window one-third of the way.

"Greiner…isn't he one of yours?"

"Sort of," Tony said. "We have an understanding, kinda. He lays off most of our interests, but I don't do certain things. Him and myself go back to elementary school. His girl married me, not him. I think Artie got a soft heart for this girl reporter, Pickering. He told me I have to think of her like she's a cop. No messin' her up."

"What does she have?"

"Depends on what Greiner gave her," Tony said, "if anything. He has files on me and yinz in New York, too. He didn't say he gave her anything, and I think he didn't. I don't see why he would. But he could. But that would go against our understanding, me and him."

"What understanding?"

"I stay out of heroin, and he lays off the rest of my shit. Marijuana, he don't care about. No whackin' civilians—I guess he cares about that too. That's why he stopped Jerry Multirosa from whackin' her. I promised him we'd lay off the girl. It was that or he was going to come down on me, personal."

"How much do you think she knows?"

"She might be able to connect our cash goin' to both Hunt and Delucci. But that don't mean nothin'. There's no limit on contributions to union elections. She probably has some information on the bank sale to Chickie. I doubt she has anythin' on who done Biggie Stover. She'll connect Lazarro and Hyskra to me, but that's a big so-what? She can't prove nothin'. No one can. Those two ain't gonna rat me out. Stover was the guy who done my two mutts in my opinion."

"Frank gave this work to Bombardo who gave it to you, Tony," John Thomas said. "A coal miner, a lawyer and a girl reporter. You managed to get one of the three and lost three of your own in the process. There's no percentage in doing our business like that."

"I'll get Corelli to do the girl."

"No. Greiner's protecting her now. You have to live up to your arrangement with him. It's worse for us if you don't."

"What about Becker?" Tony asked.

"I've talked to Clippinger about him. If Delucci loses, we don't need to do anything about Becker. I saw in the paper that Becker has resigned from the campaign. If Delucci wins, we will persuade him that he can be president of the American Coal Miner's Union without having Becker around."

"Persuade how?"

"You will show him the error of his ways if he wants to bring Becker back."

"I can do that," Tony said.

"You might want to bring in Chickie and Clip on those discussions with Delucci if he wins. So hold off on Becker for now."

"Okay," Tony said. "I'm sure Delucci knew what Stover was going to do. Maybe he ordered it, maybe not. My bet is Delucci okayed it in advance. That's what I'd do. Our whacks are authorized. My people don't go around freelancin' people off cliffs when they get an itch to see a flyin' car."

"After the election, we'll find out what Delucci did with your two Western Union boys," John Thomas said. "That will give us more leverage on him."

"I don't know for sure that Delucci gave Stover the go ahead," Tony said.

"You don't have to know it, Tony, to make what you don't know work for you. You just have to say it in a way that makes Delucci think you believe it. It doesn't have to be true, it just has to be in front of his nose. What matters is you tell him you believe what you're saying, regardless of whether you do or don't."

"I'm followin'," Tony said. "If he didn't do it, he'll give up the truth. This is good."

"Delucci doesn't want to be in court defending himself against a double murder after his election. He wants to come across as a clean new face without baggage."

"I understand. Shit don't have to be true. Shit is useful whether it's true or not."

616

"There you go," John Thomas said. "Hold off on Pickering. I have another way into her, which I'll check on tomorrow morning. As for Becker, let's see who wins. Right now, we don't want to call attention to our business. Leave him alone. Got it?"

"Got it."

Weston, W.Va., December 2, 1975, 10:30 p.m.

On the drive to Pittsburgh on the new and mostly completed I-79, Allyson stopped for gas in Weston. At the pay phone, she dialed Kennedy's number.

"Hello," he said.

"Will you still have me?"

"I've been down this road with you before. What's changed?"

"I have. I've grown. I've learned. I'm free of the past."

"No hemming? No hawing? No 'Get-Out-of-Jail-Free' cards? No reconsiderations? No backing out?"

"Yes," she said.

"No crazy crusades against Mafia guys?"

"Yes," she said. "Babies, too. We can start trying tonight when I get home to your place."

Maybe she would tell him she couldn't have children; maybe she wouldn't.

"Where are you?" he asked.

"About three hours away. Weston. On the new Interstate."

"I'll be up when you get here," he said.

"All in," she said.

"We have each other's back?"

"Yes."

"Do you love me?"

"Yes," Allyson said.

"Deal," he said.

"Deal," she said, hoping it might turn into one.

Chapter 46

Washington, D.C., December 2, 1975

Joe Hunt paced his office floor. Little of the gray light of a winter's morning entered his office from the big windows behind his desk. The gloom matched his mood. He heard the bustle of Union headquarters beyond his door. His campaign staff had been in and out all morning seeking direction from him and Skis, his campaign manager. Joe had been answering questions since 7:30 a.m. It was now almost 10, time for the meeting.

It had gotten colder overnight. It was snowing. Joe knew Washington residents resented physical inconvenience that impeded business as usual. Greed, Washington could handle. Spinning and lying, it could handle. But bad weather threw the Nation's Capital for a loop. Joe now embraced a Washingtonian's right to be aggravated about local weather.

Joe had never understood why ACMU headquarters was heated with fuel oil and not the coal his members mined. It had something to do with a local smoke-pollution restriction, Foster Shives had explained. It was just one more thing that annoyed Joe. And his own house in Arlington was heated by natural gas. That was another thing. There were now a lot of things like those two things. His was a despair from a thousand annoyances.

Joe was suspicious of this meeting Delucci had requested. Joe wanted nothing to do with his lawyer, Becker, who was also coming.

Skis had talked Joe into the meeting by saying, "Let's see what they have in their hand. Delucci wants something, and they're gonna give us something. Won't hurt to see what their deal is."

"I saw on TV the cops arrested Becker's buddy, Gondleman, in Baltimore," Joe had said. "Maybe it's about Becker. Maybe he'll confess."

"To what?" Skis had asked. "Becker knew Gondleman. That's it. We knew there wasn't much to it before Shookoff threw Gondleman against Becker to see if any of that would stick to Delucci."

"Well, you, me and Gussie were called communists. Didn't hurt us none," Joe had said.

"You can look at it that way," Skis had said, "I guess."

Joe walked stiffly, back and forth, feeling his age. His belly sagged over his belt. When the weather changed, arthritis gnawed at his joints. Joe knew that handloading on his knees in cold water had wrecked them. His doctor recommended replacements. Joe had a hard time imagining walking around on a couple of plastic U-joints. Better to just tough it out, he concluded. He tried to make himself limber and pain-free by remembering a time when he was both. Occasionally, he'd shake one leg and then the other. Shaking didn't relieve the ache. He remembered when he could jump, run, kneel, squat and even duck walk. Joe spit into the Styrofoam cup he carried for the purpose of spitting into. A spitcup was classier than an aluminum pop can, but not as classy as his old coal scuttle, which, he had been told, was a genuine antique.

Skis came in. It was his job to figure Delucci's motives. Was this a meeting called by a guy who thought he was winning or losing? Skis sat at the mahogany conference table near the front of Joe's office. He lit a Marlboro.

"Nice flowers," Skis said, indicating the vase on the conference table.

"Fakes," Joe grumbled. "Better lookin' than real ones. Edie gets them. She says they dress up the place."

Skis examined this meeting like a man searching for flaws in a rough gemstone. A sure loser wouldn't propose a meeting unless he had a surprise. A sure winner had no reason to talk with a sure loser. Skis figured Delucci saw the race as close just the way he saw it. Jeep had to be coming with something, with some deal.

Campaign adviser Marvin Shookoff came in, hung his overcoat on the stand in the corner, took off his galoshes and sat next to Skis. Marv loved being the fly on any wall. He liked to watch big boys carve each other with their big knives. Marv was pumped.

"That meatball's got somethin' on me," Joe said. "I can feel it in my joints."

"That's a weather change you're feelin'," Skis said. "Let him show his hand. Patience."

"Patience...shit!"

Marv straightened his tie, which never seemed to stay straightened for very long. His socks were wet from the sidewalk slush despite his rubber boots. He stretched his thickening neck. His shirts kept getting tighter. He now admitted he had a heavy build. He had promised his wife, Rachel, he would go on one of her liquid diets soon. But the liquid he was looking forward to was a Scotch at lunch that came with a steak.

Marv wiped his forehead with a Brooks Brothers handkerchief that was too fancy for wiping sweat. He sweated a lot even when he wasn't hot or worried. It's just how he was. He no longer bothered to apologize for something he hadn't caused. He felt classier wiping sweat with a classy product. He guessed he might be more sensitive to stress than he appeared even though he was built like a pachyderm. His doctor said it was "hyperhidrosis," which affected hands, feet and armpits. But also my forehead and stomach, Marv said. "Probably genetic," his doctor had said. "Or something to do with your flight-or-fight mechanism. Nothing much to do except wipe." Every time Marv had to shake hands with someone important, he'd wipe his right hand against his pants. Politics was the

619

wrong business for a man with a sweaty handshake. Marv Shookoff rose above himself, making himself into what he thought was lemonade. Nothing stuck to a light-footed fly on a wall. As a kid, Marvin Shookoff's nickname was "Shifty".

Joe's secretary, Edie Morse, buzzed him, signaling his visitors had signed in.

Delucci came through the door, followed by Becker and Art Greiner. The six shook hands awkwardly.

Skis motioned they should take seats at Joe's conference table.

"Nice flowers," Jeep said.

"Edie changes them fresh every week," Joe said. "I know who Jeep is, but who are you?"

"Art Greiner. Security," Greiner said with a tight smile. "Also do a little research."

"Where'd you say you were from?" Skis asked.

"Dint."

"He's from Pittsburgh," Delucci said.

"Ex-cop?" Joe asked.

"That's my day job. I moonlight on my own time."

"Are you here in an official capacity?" Skis asked.

"Volunteer and unofficial," Greiner said. "This is a private meet. I know some things."

Greiner looked at Jeep, who nodded. Greiner took out a gadget from his large brief case.

"What's that?" Joe asked.

"This is a radio-frequency scanner," Greiner said.

"He's lookin' for bugs," Jeep said. "All of this conversation is off the record."

"There ain't no bugs in my office," Joe said. "Me and Skis are coal miners, not the CIA. Look all you want. Let's get on with this."

"Clean," Greiner said, putting his kit back in his case.

"So you 'know some thangs,'" Joe repeated to Greiner. "What kinda thangs you know?"

"I know about the sale of the bank to Chickie Siciliano who's frontin' for Tony Bruno and the Mob. I know about the $500,000 in cash that Bruno gave to Siciliano who gave it to you through his Dee Cee pals— Wyndham Clippinger, Chris Chaconis, Jackpot Ginsberg and Moe Kazin. They didn't ask DeFazio to chip in; he's just a poor, corrupt Teamster district director. Those ABW directors are frontin' for Siciliano. These boys are plannin' to do with the ACMU what they done in the Teamsters."

"So far you know shit," Joe said. "Nothin' illegal about me sellin' the Bank for a big price to help my members. Nothin' illegal about campaign contributions. I have no obligation to them five once the Union no longer owns the Bank." He waved his hand dismissively.

620

Greiner felt no need to explain further.

"And you're Becker," Joe said. "I see your ol' buddy, Gondleman, got his ass busted while he was brushin' his teeth in the toilet. Wasn't he the one that blew up a urinal at the Pentagon a couple years back?"

"It was a women's bathroom," Becker said. "Most don't use urinals from what I'm told."

"Very funny. Didya learn to be a smartass breakin' windows at a university any coal miner's kid would have given his right nut to go to?"

"Think whatever you like," Becker said. "I'm no longer with Jeep's campaign. Just here as a friend. Your bullshit won."

"Who are you?" Delucci interrupted, looking at Shookoff.

"Marv Shookoff, political consultant. I help unions. I'm working on Joe's campaign."

He slid his card across the table toward Delucci. It read: "Shookoff, Glickstein and Kruncher LLC."

"What kind of consulting do you do, Mr. Shookoff?" Becker asked with inoffensive politeness.

"Usual stuff. Campaigns, polling, media, strategy, research, tactics. The whole schmear."

"You're the one who came up with a Gondleman connection for me?" Becker asked.

"Yep," Marv said with a grin. "Read quotes from his speeches The Columbia Spectator carried in '67-'68. FBI has an amazing file on him."

"You have his FBI file?" Becker asked.

"No thank you. I'm not going there," Marv said. "I did locate some campus conservatives who said you knew him. That's where I heard about you and the mighty book bag."

"Then you know I didn't support the Weathermen who split off later."

"Of course," Marv said with a grin and a chin wipe. "My job is just selling the sizzle, son. I don't even need a steak to do that, just a picture, just a word that creates a memory. We're all liberal Democrats in this room. We're more the same than different."

That thought made Becker sick. "You're sort of a hired clogger."

"'Clogger?'" Marv responded. "Like one of those hillbilly dancers?" Marv had never thought of himself as light-footed.

"Sure, clogger—you're hired to create blockages."

"Yeah, I guess so."

"But you also get hired to eat them out," Becker said, "headfirst."

"Well, I am certainly not a Communist," Marv said.

"You've also established neither am I despite the words you put into Mr. Hunt's mouth."

"Enough," Joe said. "This meetin' ain't about Becker and Gondleman."

"Ground rules, just so everybody knows," Skis said. "Whatever anybody says in here to anybody or about anybody or about anythin' don't leave this room. Just like contract negotiations. No leakin'. No talkin' to nobody."

"Agreed," Delucci said.

"Whadda ya got, Jeep?" Joe growled.

"We got us a problem, Joe. A *mutual* problem."

"You got *you* a problem," Joe smiled. "Shookoff here says his last poll says it's me 59 and you not but 35. And them 59 are as solid as a virgin block in the Pittsburgh seam."

Delucci laughed. "Isn't that the poll where you asked, 'Which candidate is older?'"

"That's a reliability question," Marv said defensively. "I've been working for unions since the late '40s. I know how to win an election. You'll see on Friday that my numbers are good."

"Your ass is gonna get kicked on Friday," Joe said.

"That's assumin' all your votes stay bought the way you paid for 'em," Jeep said. "As I recollect, I beat you pretty good in the first round."

"We underestimated you," Skis said. "That's not happenin' this time when it's for keeps."

"Runnin' with the big dogs ain't like runnin' with the pups, is it?" Joe smirked.

"More fleas that's for sure," Jeep responded.

"And distemper," Becker added.

"Well, I'm sure you learned something from this experience," Joe said, sitting back. "Six years from now, who knows? I'll be ready to retire. You'll have a straight shot at my office as long as you don't do nothin' stupid over the next few days. In fact, I'll give it to you straight, Jeep. You've run a good race against me, and I ain't gonna run again. It's yours next time. I'll even break you in. Appoint you to this an' that. Show you how this town works. Introduce you to the players on The Hill and in the Labor Department. Bring you into negotiations. You're a smart guy. Got a little college. Fought for our country like you should. I got no beef with you. I ain't holdin' no grudge over that sucker kick you give me at American Eagle. Have no objection to turnin' the Union over to you. Another six years will give you time to get more experience. See, I ain't mean."

"So what do you want me to do, now? Drop out of the race?"

"That's the track I'm goin' down," Joe said.

"Funny, you should say that. I was going to propose the same to you."

"Me!"

"Your poll is bullshit," Delucci said. "Shookoff drew your sample from names your people in the districts submitted. And I got 35 percent

622

from your own supporters. I'll win the election. That's why you want me to withdraw."

"Now just a minute," Marv Shookoff said. "I've been doing union polls for almost 40 years. I know how to build a sample properly. I know how to write questions that are value-free."

"I'm sure you do," Becker said.

"Did you do what he said?" Skis asked.

Marv wiped his forehead. Then he wiped his chin. Then he wiped the back of his neck. "I know what I'm doing with election polls."

Skis looked at Joe. They, too, had wondered about the 59-35 results after losing the nominating round. Marv had explained the difference by noting that local unions had one vote each in the nominating round while individual members voted in the general election. That explanation made little sense to either Joe or Skis. Maybe that's why Marv had submitted his final bill yesterday with a request for immediate payment. They now realized that Shookoff anticipated Joe losing the election.

"It's a toss-up," Skis said. "We both have spent a ton of money over the last couple of months."

"The money," Delucci said. "Yours comes from Tony Bruno, a Mob boss in Pittsburgh, through Siciliano."

"Siciliano's a business guy here in town," Joe said. "Real estate, parking lots, restaurants, that type of thang."

"Banks," Jeep said.

"It was a good deal for the Union," Joe said. "That cash will guarantee pensions, health care, widows' benefits. Shit like that. Maybe even college for the kids."

"Siciliano's gang will drain the purchase money out of the Bank and the Union," Greiner said. "It ain't free money, Mr. Hunt. He'll take loans from the Union that will never be repaid. You'll have to hire his guys. He'll squeeze it out of you in a dozen ways. Your Union will end up payin' them to buy your Bank. That's how these guys work."

"Badly done deals can be undone," Becker said, "with publicity plus prosecutorial scrutiny. Deals done with the Mafia are bad deals no matter what you get at the start."

"You mean the feds will get on their asses?" Skis offered.

"Right," Becker said. "RICO was set up to deal with just this kind of situation. The guy behind the crime, the guy who orders it, can get nailed now."

Delucci cleared his throat. "The Bank ain't why I'm here, Joe," he said. "The election is."

"Yeah?" Joe said.

"Bruno gave both of us money. You jes' like me. Probably the same amount to each, $500,000."

"Yeah?"

"Why do you think that is?" Delucci asked.

"He figures one of us will win a two-man race," Joe laughed.

"And then what?" Delucci asked.

"And then he gets what he wants," Skis answered.

"No matter which one of us wins," Delucci said, "he's set himself up to get access to the Union's fund, the $222 million and the Bank's ability to clean up dirty money."

Joe turned his head and stared at his desk, behind the conference table. His eye fell on the old coal scuttle, the one from Fricktown. The one he spit in, because he hated the memory. If Coy Hunt had only hung on to his mineral rights, then Joe Hunt knew at this moment he would be a retired farmer, taking it easy, piddlin' around on a John Deere tractor and watching his kids and grandkids take over. He wouldn't be jammed up like this. There would have been no mining on Black Creek. No Fricktown. No Gallagher. No Delucci. No Siciliano. No American Bank of Washington. No Marv Shookoff.

No big desk. No being important. No having waiters know who he was. No having pretty women laying out for him. No signed photographs of John Kennedy, Lyndon Johnson and Richard Nixon on his wall.

"And like with the Teamsters," Greiner said, "they'll make the Union favor certain coal employers and penalize others. They'll have you sign sweetheart contracts if the employer pays them a bribe. With coal prices as high as they are, they'll threaten selective wildcat strikes and slowdowns if a company won't pay them off. Eventually, they drive out the employers who won't be corrupted. Your members will lose jobs. More non-Union companies will spring up. You'll start organizing with ball bats and dynamite like in the '50s."

Joe rubbed his eyes.

Skis looked out the window. Snow, more snow.

They sat silently for a long moment.

"I got Bruno to do Vernie Skeens," Joe said softly while looking Delucci in the eye. "I figured you'd hit back at them two. I woulda done the same. I figured you might get caught squarin' thangs up."

"That was pretty clever," Jeep said.

"But I didn't have nothin' to do with killin' Biggie."

"I figured it that way," Delucci said.

"I specialize in old Irish mine superintendents," Joe said.

Everyone broke up. Joe looked around sheepishly.

"Self-defense," Skis added.

"Self-defense," Delucci repeated.

"Same with them two Mob boys Biggie done up on Lens Creek Mountain," Joe said. "Self-defense."

Becker, Delucci and Greiner looked hard at Joe.

624

"That push that night. Biggie done it in your Jeep. An' you, Jeep, you knew what he was a-doin'.'"

"Just how do you come by that?" Delucci asked.

"Third cousin on my Momma's side," Joe said.

Jeep looked confused.

"Dicey Schuck, that ol' crumpled-up retiree who works phones at your headquarters."

"Dicey!" Jeep swore.

"Says he heard you fellers talkin' it over. Then he helped Biggie switch vehicles that night."

Becker was stunned. He now knew Delucci had authorized the ambush. Everyone in this room now had that information, including Greiner, who had something on all of them if he wanted to use it.

"Dicey is not enough for court," Becker said. "Just hearsay against Jeep. You could get Biggie for it, but he's already been gotten to."

"So why didn't you use it?" Jeep asked Joe.

"Well, you haven't beat me yet. And if you did, the International Executive Board could vote to remove you for 'moral turp'tude,' which is in our Constitution. So it made sense to wait and see."

Delucci gathered himself. "Self-defense," he said.

"Self-defense," Joe said. "Got no problem with self-defense."

Self-defense, Becker thought. Roberta Magnelli and Weez Draney. Self-defense—a rationale for all seasons and perfectly legitimate in most.

"So why doesn't Dicey take this information to the cops?" Becker asked.

"He's afraid he'll have an accident on Lens Creek Mountain if he does," Joe said.

"Bad road," Jeep said. "Anything can happen, day or night."

Joe Hunt gained respect for Jeep Delucci after that comment. He'd probably do okay as president.

"So this Tony Bruno's he's got both of us," Joe said. "Maybe we should both withdraw."

"That would get us off his hook," Jeep said, "but there's nobody in the Union who would do better than me in fightin' Bruno off."

"I could do that, too," Joe said.

"Too old," Greiner blurted out on behalf of both Delucci and Skis who had the same thought.

"But that's exactly why I'm the right guy to take Bruno on," Joe said. "It don't matter now for me. Either way, I don't have many more trips up to the face left. That's the advantage of bein' old. I don't have nothin' to run after forward no more."

"We both made mistakes with Bruno."

"I was taught you clean up your own place," Joe said.

Marv Shookoff had heard more than he wanted to hear. He'd worked for Hoffa and then Fitzsimmons at the Teamsters. He knew Siciliano and those he had named to the Bank's board. This was too sticky for a guy who didn't want to get stuck, he thought. Sonoski had paid his bill. He was out. This mess would sort out one way or the other. He didn't need business badly enough to stay in. He wiped his hands on his pants.

"Okay," Jeep said. "We'll see what happens Friday."

"Friday," Joe said, rising.

Delucci, Greiner and Becker gathered their things and left. Shookoff did the same.

Joe sagged in his chair while Skis lit a cigarette.

"What's this about bein' too old to care?" Skis asked.

"Doctor told me last week I had the sugar an' some blockage."

"Why didn't you tell me?"

"I jes' did. I got time."

"Shit."

"Yeah, shit," Joe said.

Baltimore, December 2, 1975

"I'm here to see Gondleman," Ira Aptsky said. "I'm his lawyer."

The desk sergeant looked over his glasses. "Show me ID and sign the book. You local?"

"No."

"Didn't think so. If you were Bal-mer, I'd know you."

"Dee Cee."

"You know he bombed a police station in New York. You know that don't you?"

"You don't *know* that, Sergeant, and neither do I."

"I'd fry the little fuck if it was up to me."

"I'm glad it isn't up to you."

Gondleman came into the small interview room and wiggled into a seat while his hands remained cuffed in front of him. The table at which he sat was bare. The walls were bare. The floor was bare. The ceiling was sound-proofed.

Ira Aptsky walked in. Tall and thin, he wore his hair a little long and carried himself with an air of informality despite his three-piece suit. He put his brief case on the table.

"I'm your lawyer. Ira Aptsky, with a T. National Lawyers Guild. I do criminal defense in Washington. I'm also licensed in Maryland. Brooklyn

College. NYU Law. Nine years of experience. Grew up in Queens. Stuyvesant High. We probably know some folks in common."

"Rich Jew from Forest Hills Gardens or duplex Jew?" Gondleman asked.

"Multi-family, rowhouse Jew. 102-08 62nd Road. Dad sold buttons in the garment district. Mother taught elementary school. Grandfather on Dad's side was in the Party back in the early '30s."

"I said nothing to the pigs."

"First rule of revolutionaries," Ira said. "Say nothing to the 'pigs.'"

"Okay."

"But you might want to consider saying something at some point. Here's the situation as I see it. You have many potential federal and local charges they could pursue—conspiracies to commit one felony after another, bombings, possession of various bomb-making materials, drug possession, crossing state lines for who knows what, auto theft, falsification of documents, bail jumping. I needn't go on. Most charges have yet to be filed, so we don't know your situation until they are. What you have going for you is that the nasty charges are likely to be based on evidence I think I can get tossed."

Ira sat back in his chair.

"Why?" Gondleman asked.

"Illegally obtained. FBI bugging, mail opening and so on. COINTELPRO. Your Constitutional rights as an American citizen were violated. I think I can get the big charges dismissed. Something like resisting arrest or littering from '68, '69, they might stand. Depends on what they are and what the statute of limitations is on each one. I'm not sure the search at the rest stop will pass muster."

"I hate Amerikka."

"Let's keep that under our little red Mao cap in your present circumstances, eh?"

"How did you get to be my lawyer?"

"Luck has always followed me," Aptsky laughed. "An anonymous woman called the D.C. Guild chapter. Asked for a volunteer to defend you."

"Who's paying you?"

"As far as I know, no one. That's not exactly true. I'm paid to do criminal defense for indigents by The People, otherwise known as the State of Maryland."

"You could have said no. Why are you my lawyer?"

"Because even *fercockta* political people deserve to be defended even when the charges are true. That's the beauty of America."

"Do you think I'm *meshuggeneh*?"

"I don't think a revolution of the type you want is going to happen in this country, and you're not going to build a revolutionary movement by blowing up stall dividers and soap dispensers."

"We didn't want to harm people."

"Some Lenin, you are."

"It's not easy running from every cop in the country for five years. It was an off-duty cop who recognized me. We beat the FBI."

"Good for you. If the evidence against you is not tainted, then I need to talk to you about a plea deal. Whether you care to do one or not, that's up to you."

"What will they want me to give up?"

"The whereabouts of your fellow Weatherpeople. Sources of money when you were on the run. Places and people who gave you shelter from the storm. Who you traveled with. Methods you used to obtain false IDs and Social Security numbers. People you contacted while on the run. What you did—bombings, arsons, accomplices. Where you got weapons and bomb materials. Who made the bombs. Whether you had foreign help. Names, dates, amounts. Crimes you were part of."

"No. I won't."

"Let's think about whether or not to cross the plea bridge if we have to come to it," Aptsky said. "How are you being treated?"

"Okay. I'm in the general population. They're being very careful with me."

"Good. I can request solitary confinement if you're scared."

"Of course, I'm scared," Rooky said. "Wouldn't you be? My peer group is not the cream of Wall Street criminals."

"How tough are you, Rooky?"

"I could use some protection."

"I have a friend who does criminal defense in Baltimore. Mostly drug cases and violence. She knows how the jail runs from the prisoner side. I'll ask her to talk to the brothers who run the place, to keep you left alone."

"Thanks."

"You may have to deal with some white, right-wing nuts who hate bomb-throwing commies."

"There's one guy so far."

"No one is going to stick his neck out for you. You have no friends in there. The Aryans want to have nothing to do with you, because they don't think you're white. To them, you're a Jew banker who runs the world. The blacks don't want you either despite your protestations of 'solidarity with the oppressed revolutionary black proletariat.' Don't buddy up to the blacks even though you think they are the vanguard of the revolution. Stay out of any alliance with anyone, that's your best strategy. You're not going to get bail so you'll have to make the best of it for a while.

"Keep your mouth shut. Don't try to convert anyone to Marxist-Leninism. If someone gets in your face, don't back down. The predators among the 'oppressed' criminal element hunt for weakness. They'll try to extort you for money and *drek*—cigarettes, candy, cans of tuna, drinks. Don't befriend anyone unless you are willing to cover his back at the expense of your own. Don't accept favors from anyone, because they'll always want something in return. Everyone will know who you are—the bombings, the FBI list. So you'll have some inmate credibility. Criminal cachet of a sort. Don't talk to anyone about your past. The cops will work snitches on you. Don't act like a smarty pants. Don't make eye contact. Don't be a schmuck. And one other thing. If you play chess, make it close, but let your opponent win without being obvious about it. Better make it a draw, that's less suspicious."

"So while I'm doing all that, what will you be doing?"

"I'm going to see what you're charged with, and then see how much of the evidence I can get thrown out along with the charges that depend on it."

"That's it?"

"If we're lucky, you'll walk quickly. If there's a trial, I'm your lawyer if you want me. Do you need anything? You can make collect phone calls to my office. Don't call anyone else, like comrades. Parents are okay. Send me a list of books, and I'll order them to be sent to you directly from the publisher. Be sensible about this. They might let some political stuff through, but don't count on it. You're not going to get a copy of The Anarchist's Cookbook past the censor."

"About half of what that kid -- William Powell -- wrote will get you killed," Rooky said.

"Good to know, I'm sure," Aptsky said. "I'll file it under dishes that give me heartburn."

"Do you have other clients like me?"

"You're the only one of your type. Let's put it that way. I'll put a little money in your canteen account. Use it sparingly. You *do not* want to come across as rich. One thing you might do is help prisoners without counsel write their appeals. Do this for both whites and blacks, regardless of their politics. That will make you too valuable to cut up. I'll get your identification number at the desk when I leave. Do you want me to contact anyone on your behalf?"

"Call my parents, I suppose. Tell them I'm fine and not to visit. Call Jeffrey Becker, a lawyer in Charleston, West Virginia. Tell him I got nothing to say."

"Becker, okay. Were you with anyone when you were captured?"

"Yes."

"Who?"

"Why do you need to know?"

"I might be able to set up a communication channel between you and your friend through some people."

"Just tell them that Rooky Gondleman won't break."

"You're not going to be tortured," Aptsky said. "The Baltimore cops, even the FBI, they're not the Gestapo. You might be isolated to soften you up. Twenty-three hours a day. No TV. No contact with other prisoners. It works on your head. Do math problems or play chess with yourself. Read. Your best tactic is not to engage in conversation of any kind with interrogators. Don't trust any prisoner who starts asking you questions about what you did. Don't boast. Quiet works best. Exercise. Even though you look like a college kid, let your new colleagues use their skewed imaginations to embellish your chops as a bad-ass."

"Can I give you a letter for someone?" Rooky asked.

"No. All of your mail has to be looked at going out and coming in. I'm searched, coming in and going out. I'm not a smuggler."

"If you establish a channel to the Underground, I want to give a message to my, well, I guess she's my girlfriend."

"Which is?"

"Don't worry. John Wayne is cool."

"'John Wayne'—that's you?"

"Inside joke."

"I'll see what I can do. I'll be back in a week or so as soon as I know what they have. I'll leave my card with the front desk. They'll check it for dope and then give it to you."

"Okay," Gondleman said, rising awkwardly from his plastic chair. "Thanks for helping out."

Aptsky smiled. "Can I drop your name when you Stalinists come to take me off to the Gulag?"

"Sure," Rooky said. "We'll probably meet in the same camp."

"Maybe you're not as loony as you've appeared," Aptsky said.

"The War's over. I'm close to 30. I could go back to school and get a degree. I was good at math. Maybe teach."

"In enough time, your past won't be forgotten or forgiven by those you hurt. But its sharpest points might wear down to nubs."

"'Radio Electronics' did a story on a personal computer kit called the Mark-8 last year," Gondleman said. "I was reading up on remote controllers at the time. I could build one of those. Maybe I'll go into computers."

"I'll look around for some magazine articles on…what are they called again?"

"Personal computers. PCs."

"Do they count numbers like an adding machine or calculator?"

"And other things. They remember stuff and organize stuff. You type on them."

630

"Anything else?"

"A corned beef on rye with Swiss, chopped liver, Russian dressing and a pickle."

"On visitor's day. They let food in. I'll give it a shot. Remember no talking. Later."

"Thanks," Rooky said. "Later."

Chapter 47

Pittsburgh, December 3, 1975

At 9 a.m., Kennedy Brown entered the office of Sewart Morgan, chief executive officer of Scraife National Bank.

"Have a seat, Ken," Morgan said. "This is my friend John Thomas Stuart from New York. John's a lawyer who represents an important group of clients. They do business with us in New York and other cities, including here."

Kennedy Brown didn't think he was being either fired or promoted. So what else might this be about? He sat up straight and crossed his right leg over his left. The New York lawyer sat next to him.

"This is about Allyson Pickering," John Thomas said, turning toward Kennedy.

"Yes?"

"I'll be blunt," John Thomas said. "She's pursuing stories she should not be pursuing. I am aware of the circumstances of her leaving The Post-Gazette. These interests of hers have put her in personal danger. I'm not being melodramatic. Her life was spared as a matter of good fortune when a Detective Greiner stopped what in all likelihood was an assassination."

"What!"

"She's making certain people uncomfortable. Well, let me just say it plainly, organized crime."

"Who are you?" Kennedy asked.

"I'm a partner in Stuart, Swiney and Gradué in Manhattan. We're a boutique firm -- three partners, seven associates -- that handles delicate business matters and criminal defense for a handful of clients. I specialize in negotiating work outs like the conversation we're having today."

"How do you know about Allyson?"

"Her recent investigations into coal and banking have come to the attention *of acquaintences* of my clients, which is why I'm here. My clients thought you and Sewart should have that information. Sewart and I thought it best to approach her through you rather than directly. We understand you're close."

"We are to be married."

"Wonderful," John Thomas said.

"Well done," Sewart said. "I know her father, her family. Quakers. Business Quakers."

"Sewart and I are interested in protecting her and you," John Thomas said. "The stories she's pursuing…well, let me cut to the chase. They are not worth her life and yours. That is the information I want to share with you."

"You're threatening…."

"No, no. I'm sharing information my clients have come upon. My clients are not threatening anybody. We're trying to be helpful communicators. Proactive intervenors. Allyson would have been killed the other night had not Greiner intervened. The elements who sent that killer will undoubtedly do so again if she doesn't drop her freelance investigation."

"Who is after her?" Kennedy asked.

"A local bad actor, Tony Bruno," John Thomas said.

"I've heard the name," Kennedy said. "He on a board of something."

"He runs the local Mafia affiliate," Sewart Morgan said, "and he serves with one or two legitimate organizations. It's not a bad idea to have danger close to you where you can keep an eye on it."

"So the gangsters really are trying to take over the miners' union. Allyson's right," Kennedy said.

"Being right is no defense against criminals," Sewart said.

"You want me to get her to stop."

"Yes, for her own good and yours," John Thomas said. "I'm simply relaying what I believe is an accurate assessment of the situation. If she continues, Bruno and those elements I mentioned will respond as they are wont, as they have already tried. This crusade, this story, is not worth her life, is it? Or yours?"

"No," Kennedy said. "It isn't."

"The Bank wanted to pass this information on to you," Sewart said. "We want nothing bad to happen to our employees and their families. You have a bright future with Scraife."

"Do you know why she is pursuing this story?" John Thomas asked. "Is it money? Is she in debt?"

"No. Money has nothing to do with it."

"What then?" Sewart asked.

"Redemption is my guess," Kennedy said. "She wants it to come out that she wrote the truth even before she knew it was true."

"There are other paths toward redemption," John Thomas said. "Perhaps I can smooth the way for her at The Post-Gazette or another daily. I know people. I also know people who know people."

Kennedy realized he did not know who John Thomas Stuart really was.

"The Scraife Bank," Sewart said, "wants this to end now, quietly and immediately. I will be watching to see how you handle it."

"I understand," Kennedy said.

"Good," Sewart said.

"Sorry to have met you under these circumstances," John Thomas said. "Perhaps we can do business together in the future in a more pleasant context."

"Thank you for the information," Kennedy said. "Thank you both."

Kennedy Brown rose and left.

A few minutes later, John Thomas Stuart followed him out, drove to the airport and returned to New York.

Sewart Morgan hoped Kennedy Brown was bright enough to see a loaded pistol when it was aimed at his head from three feet away. Such a bright young man, Sewart thought. Very promising.

Thirty minutes after Kennedy Brown walked out of Sewart Morgan's office, he stopped shaking. He willed himself to approach this problem as he approached investments—rationally, logically, linearly, analytically, methodically. He doubted a direct appeal would get Allyson to back off. He came up with one person who might know what to do.

He reached for the phone, looked up a number and dialed.

Fricktown, W.Va., December 3, 1975

In Pittsburgh, Ben Roberson fumbled for the phone. It was 4:57 a.m. He tried to turn on the light by his bed, but he couldn't find the phone and the switch at the same time. He chose the light, then the phone. He hoped it was a crank call. Even a heavy breather. It wasn't.

Willie Rutherford heard it on the six o'clock WJLS newscast out of Beckley. He didn't wake Susie. He got into his recliner and pulled Susie's crazy quilt over his head. Then he started to tremble.

At the same hour, Gus Olin was working a crossword puzzle from the Sunday Post-Gazette at his kitchen table. He heard it on Morgantown's WAJR. They used to sound the mine whistle, he thought.

Skis called Joe Hunt at 7:03 a.m.

"Fricktown blew," Skis said.

"Shit! Methane," Joe said. "You think they firebossed it right?"

"They'll say they did."

"Flame safety lamp woulda told the men if the gas was too rich at the face."

"They use methanometers now," Skis said. "Gizmos with a needle."

"Don't matter what they use, 'cause they didn't use it. Or somethin'. How many was inside?"

"Hoot-owl, maybe 60," Skis said.

"Production or maintenance?" Joe asked.

"I'd guess they're runnin' three production shifts with prices like they are. They'll fix equipment when they have to."

634

"You talk to anybody?" Joe asked.

"Not yet. Figured we might wanna go up there."

"Yeah. Get somebody to drive. We may be up home for a while. We're gonna know a lot of them boys."

"We'll know their Daddies for sure. We'll pick you up as soon as we can."

The Governor was informed by his chief of his staff as he dug into his egg cup.

The Governor had always been a two-minute man. His father before him was a two-minute man. He asked Opal Smoot on his first day to tell the chef to use a timer.

The Governor preferred the pointy end of his egg up, with the fat end down. He cut through the top with an egg scissors his mother had given him from her collection. The scissors had a rooster body and did a neat job. The Governor did not want to make a mess of his soft-cooked egg by butchering it with a butter knife or spoon. Nancy could pull off both of those tricks, but he never got the hang of either one. She could also wiggle one ear. He couldn't even make a scary face.

The Governor recalled stopping in Fricktown during his campaign to use the town hall's restroom. He remembered it was cleaner than he expected.

It would be cold in Monongalia County. He'd take boots and wear two sets of socks.

Visiting mine disasters came with the job, but he hated having to serve as the comforter-in-chief. The women would be crying. Their kids would try not to. He would be asked questions. His answers would be unsatisfying. Real answers would jeopardize his career and his marriage. Somebody in the crowd would blame him and his mine-safety agency. He couldn't understand why miners weren't more careful. Perhaps, more education would solve their problem. There's an answer he could give, more education for miners.

Jeep Delucci heard about it when he phoned his headquarters before 8 a.m. Dicey Shuck answered.

"Fricktown blew jes' before five," Dicey said.

"I'll get Becker, and we'll drive up."

"I thought he was out," Dicey said.

"He'll be with me unofficially. As my lawyer."

"Oh, I see," said Dicey, meaning he didn't. "You takin' the Jeep?"

"It's cold on a long drive," Jeep answered. "But it would be good to be seen up there. Yeah, I will."

"Had some family up thataway," Dicey said. "Some Glovers. Mighta been workin' that hoot owl."

Jeep hesitated for a few seconds. "Some Hunts, too?"

"Some Hunts too."

"Joe told me," Delucci said.

"So fire me," Dicey said, with a short explosive laugh. "I'm a volunteer. Won't cost me nothin', and I'll save the gas money."

"No," Jeep said. "Stay on the phones. We'll talk about this after the election. I might have a job for you after Friday."

A job was the last thing Jeep Delucci had in mind for Dicey Shuck.

Tony Bruno heard something about a coal-mine disaster in West Virginia as he was parking his Cadillac in front of Del Porco's. One more screw up with coal miners, he thought. Frankie will lay this on me.

Julie Cogswell saw the morning news on WCHS, Channel 8, ABC-TV in Charleston. She didn't want to report on another mine disaster. One a year was more than enough. You see one, you've seen one too many.

She threw some clothes into her suitcase, tossed her sleeping bag into her pickup and headed to Fricktown.

Allyson Pickering was arguing with Kennedy Brown over breakfast when they heard it on WDUQ, public radio.

"I'm going to Fricktown," she said.

"Is there something I just told you that you did not hear or understand?"

"A mine disaster is just that. It's not about the election or the Bank."

"You don't have an outlet for a story."

"I'll try Charlie Robb at The Point."

"That's 50 bucks, Allyson."

"So."

"You don't need 50 bucks, Allyson."

"So."

"You're too late to influence the election. You can't get anything in print today. Continuing with this investigation is dangerous and stupid," Kennedy said as calmly as he could. "You're poking killers in their eyes."

"Wallets."

"You don't need to be self-destructive. There was nothing ambiguous about Bruno's threat to us. My point is that we are a team. That's what we agreed the other night."

"So," she said.

"So we think about what's best for both of us, for the team."

"It's hard for me to walk away from this injustice," she said. "People are getting screwed."

"Your life will be taken. Are you not processing that information? Stop!"

636

She said nothing and did not stop.

Becker was awake at 5:15 a.m. He lay in bed, trying to restore a semblance of order in his mind.

What if Gondleman broke? Some things -- like a dead Mafia hit lady in his back yard -- tarnished you forever regardless of any official exoneration. The West Virginia Bar might lift his law license. Was he a party to Biggie Stover's double murder on Lens Creek Mountain in a legal sense? Was he shielding Delucci and obstructing justice now that he had heard Jeep's confession in Joe Hunt's office? Was he conspiring? Should he turn Delucci in? If Joe Hunt lost would he have the Union's board take the election away from Delucci? What would a rational man do with Roberta Magnelli in a shallow grave behind his kitchen, courtesy of two of the FBI's most-wanted fugitives, one of whom might spill his guts at any second?

Becker drifted back to an early August morning in the tepee. Just a bit of zip in the air. He could taste the coffee that was percolating on the small grill over the campfire. Allyson snuggled next to him.

He wrenched himself back.

"You're an idiot, Becker," Becker said to himself.

He heard about Fricktown on the 6:30 a.m. news.

He packed, got in his car and met Jeep for the drive north.

Davey Bloom arrived at the PG's office a little after 8:30 a.m. His metro editor met him with the AP wire story. Davey grabbed a kid reporter and got in a PG car.

Philip Bombardo, known as Philly Squint, heard about Fricktown on the Philadelphia news and called Frank Fagano in New York at 9:15 a.m.

"The miners are blowin' themselves up. What's that to us?" Bombardo asked.

"Maybe something; maybe nothing; maybe in between; maybe we don't know," Fagano said. "Tell Tony to keep his eye on this. No surprises."

"No surprises," Bombardo said.

"No more fuck-ups," Fagano said.

"No more fuck-ups," Bombardo repeated.

John Corelli saw television footage of the Fricktown mine when he was working an elliptical at Scotty's Gym. The KDKA report reminded him of the casualties he'd seen in Vietnam. And then he thought of Roberta Magnelli. It was his duty to find out what happened to her. She was his trainee, maybe a future partner. He liked her more than most. He was fairly certain that Jeffrey Becker hadn't killed her. But somebody had, and Becker probably knew who it was.

"It's me, Allyson," she said into the phone.

"How lovely," Boo said.

"Is Daddy there?"

"Are we no longer exchanging the customary pleasantries, which are, I believe, still customary?"

"I'm sorry, Mother. It's urgent."

"Yes, I'll get him on the phone. Is anything wrong?"

"I need to talk to him…privately."

"What's this about, dear?"

"Can't say."

"Oh, it must be about our 40th anniversary coming up," Boo said knowingly. "I understand. Here's your father. I'll busy myself in another room. I won't listen."

"Good morning, sweetheart," Walton Pickering said. "I heard the news about Fricktown. Terrible. Just terrible."

"I'm going there as soon as I get off the phone with you."

"I've known Ben Roberson since Yale. He's a decent fellow. Not a knucklewalker like some in coal. AMSTEEL's a decent company. Ben has always been a good egg. His father had a tough shell."

"Daddy, I don't know what to do."

"About what?"

"My life has been threatened. Ken's too."

Walton knew the situation from having talked to Kennedy Brown after his meeting with Sewart Morgan and John Thomas Stuart. Walton had been thinking it through when she called.

"By whom?" Walton asked with as much incredulity as he could muster.

"A Mafia boss here in Pittsburgh. And in New York. A lawyer named John Thomas Stuart came to town yesterday. Ken was called into a meeting with him and Sewart…"

"I know Sewart Morgan. I know him well."

"…at Scraife. Stuart said he was relaying information he picked up from a concerned client that my life, and Ken's, will be ended if I keep digging into this story about the Mafia and the American Bank of Washington. The ACMU sold the Bank to the mobsters."

"I'll look up John Thomas Stuart when I get to the office. What exactly did he say to Ken and Sewart?"

"I don't know exactly, because I wasn't there. But Ken said the message was clear: If I continue to follow the story or do anything with what I know, they'll kill us both."

"Kill! This came from New York?" Walton asked.

"I think so. Apparently, New York Mafia families have accounts with Scraife that neither the Mob nor Sewart wants to end. Maybe Scraife is laundering some of their money. That's just a guess."

"My word! Well, Sewart was always a little too easily swayed."

"The Pittsburgh leader is Tony Bruno. He seems to be the one who ordered the murder of Biggie Stover who was Delucci's closest friend and adviser. A Pittsburgh detective named Art Greiner has been helping me. He actually saved my life."

"My God!"

"Bruno sent a gunman to my apartment, but Greiner intercepted him. I don't think this threat out of New York is something Greiner can fix."

"This story is not worth your life," Walton said.

"Maybe it all will blow over if Delucci's wins."

"I don't think so, Allyson. You are a threat to their core interests, not just the Pittsburgh branch. You've stumbled on something to do with their illegal cash, which is the beating heart of their operation."

"That's my thought too," she said.

"You could go to the U.S. District Attorney in Pittsburgh," Walton said without enthusiasm. "The RICO Act is designed to reach up to the ones who give the orders but get others to do the crime."

"But buying a bank isn't a crime," she said. "Contributing to union elections isn't a crime."

"The law doesn't act prophylactically," he said. "A crime has to happen before it can be prosecuted."

"Daddy, how do you know about criminal law? Don't you do business? Contracts, negotiations, finance?"

"You don't do business in Philadelphia without eventually rubbing up against the local Mafia boss, Little Nicky Dicka, who answers to Phil Bombardo who runs the Genovese family in New York. Bombardo is known as Philly Squint because of his thick glasses. Mr. Squint puts others in front of him to bear whatever scrutiny the government brings."

"I thought you just did silk-stocking cases with the old Main Line families."

"You'd be surprised at who works with whom."

"If I went to the U.S. District Attorney, I'd spend the rest of my life in witness protection, darning and damning socks in Podunkia, USA."

"I agree," Walton said. "So the best thing to do is drop your investigation today and get that information to this Bruno fellow immediately."

"They also want Ken to guarantee them -- and Sewart, I guess -- that I've dropped the story. Maybe I could pick it up after the election."

"No. They don't want your story out, period. If they sent one person after you, they will send another," Walton said. "Tell Ken you're dropping the investigation."

"It's my life line. If I drop it, I'm just a cheap-cheat reporter who made up a story."

"Then come home immediately."

"No. That puts Ken at risk, and it's simple to find where you and mother live. I need to go to Fricktown first."

"You need to get yourself into a safe place."

"They'll find me wherever."

"Then go to Wonalancet."

"Wonalancet is part of wherever, Daddy."

"Let it go," he said.

"Even if I stopped, I'd always be a threat. Giving into them won't protect me."

Walton hated choosing between bad alternatives. "I'll call Sewart as soon as we ring off. I've represented Scraife in Delaware where the holding company is registered. The Pickerings have connections to Scraife. In the meantime, stay in the open. Don't hide. Stay in public as much as you can. Don't stay at home or Ken's place. Pay cash for a motel, not a credit card. Call me every hour."

"I can do that. Thank you, Daddy."

Allyson's call to Walton Pickering provided him with no new information. He had already been thinking.

"Watch out for the damn dinosaurs," Gus Olin had told the two boys when he first took them underground. "Miners die when them big, old boys fart."

Young Joe Hunt looked up with his open-flame carbide lamp. Larry Sonoski was staring at the fossilized skeleton of a lizard-like creature perfectly preserved in a patch of roof slate. The boys were loading coal that Gus had just shot down. Skis traced the undulating fossil and stepped off two paces to gauge its length. In his first week underground, he had seen fossils of sea shells and leaves but nothing like this.

"Where we're standing had to have been a flat swampy place, probably at sea level, with a lot of vegetation, animals and dinosaurs," Gus had said. "Back a-ways, maybe 150 or even 200 million years."

"But the Bible says God did everything in six days, and that t'weren't but a few thousand years ago," Joe said. "How'd these dinosaur critters get here before that? How did Noah get every critter on his Ark? Like kangaroos that he didn't know about?"

"You can wrestle those questions with the preacher, Joey," Gus laughed, "I'm just sayin' when the plants and animals rotted out, they left methane. Same stuff that's in your farts. Light it up and Boom!"

"You can blow yourself up by lightin' a fart?" Joe asked. "Come on. I ain't stupid."

640

"It'll light," Gus said. "But there ain't enough oomph to send you to wherever. Here at the face, there certainly is enough. And you gotta use them safety lamps I showed you to measure it. You can't smell methane, taste it or see it. Mix it with air, and a spark sets it off."

"Okay," Joe said.

"And remember," Gus said, "You get yourselves an electric-battery cap lamp out of your first paycheck. Them old-time Justrite carbide lamps you're wearin' throw good light, but they can ignite the gas. Fartin' dinosaurs are best avoided."

"Should we touch that lizard for good luck?" Skis asked. "I heard that's what you're supposed to do."

"You can if you want," Gus said. "Some do; some don't."

"Won't hurt," Joe said, touching it.

"Won't hurt," Skis said, touching it.

"You boys count on your selves, not superstitions, to keep you safe," Gus said.

The boys laughed as they ran their hands along the fossil.

They bought the new battery lamps from the Fricktown commissary out of their first pay. They did as Gus told them, because they knew he would keep them as safe as they could be doing work that never would be safe.

Three generations of miners had worked in AMSTEEL's Fricktown mine. It lay beneath almost three square miles of mountain land Coy Hunt had once owned from its surface to the core of the Earth. AMSTEEL had purchased the remaining surface rights in 1914 from Coy and Lucinda's heirs for a dollar an acre. "It's a fair price," Lawyer Chilton said, "since there's not much left to take off, and it was pretty sorry to start with, except for the coal."

Fricktown miners had dug out more than 75 million tons of that coal over the years. The mine's tunnels and "rooms" where the early miners had picked, blasted and shoveled had long been worked out, walled up and abandoned. As many of the coal pillars as possible had been "robbed," causing the roof to collapse. These "old works" were labeled "gob" on the mine maps. Methane accumulated there.

In the summer of 1975, AMSTEEL introduced a new "long-wall" mining system into a big block of coal -- 1,200 feet long by 600 feet wide in a seven-foot thickness -- at the far southwest corner of the Fricktown property. To make the block ready for the "wall," tunnels were driven on four sides to handle in and out airflow, access and coal haulage. A continuous-miner cut in two tunnels on each short side of the block. One tunnel provided fresh, intake air and another on the opposite side of the block was used to remove dust-laden, methane-rich outtake air. The tunnel next to the intake was used for bringing in miners, equipment and materials. A conveyor was set up in the tunnel next to the outtake air to belt the coal to the surface. The four side tunnels were connected at the far end of the block -- close to and parallel with the Fricktown property line -- by a fifth where the wall's machinery would be installed. Once set up, the wall would cut coal in retreat from that connecting tunnel. The long wall would move back through the block of coal toward the mine's main workings.

The wall itself was a machine with two rotating shearers that, together, sliced a seven-foot-high path along a 1,200-foot track. The cut coal dropped into a panline that carried it out to the belt conveyor. A 1,200-foot-long line of huge hydraulic roof supports kept metal shields in place over the machine and the men running it. As the long wall cut into the block, miners moved the roof supports over the operation. The roof behind the supports soon fell where the coal had been removed. The two shearers could take off as much as a two-foot-wide swath in a single pass. Long-wall mining would typically remove between 80 to 100 percent of a coal block compared with 50 to 75 percent in the room-and-pillar method using continuous-miners. People working on a long wall were supposed to work under supported roof all the time.

The wall was a hugely expensive system and unfamiliar to the Fricktown crews. British technicians came over to train them to operate both the cutting machine and the roof-support system. The techs told them to "keep your ventilation up, because the shearer kicks up a good bit of fine dust, and the long face liberates the gas, fast."

At the end of their first production shift, the Fricktown crew was astonished by the amount of coal they had produced. Fricktown management, from the section boss up to the superintendent, beamed.

But there was a hitch. The block being mined lay in a far corner of the mine, more than two miles from the portal. The wall, management discovered, would cut coal faster than the conveyor could belt it out. The most expensive solution was to punch in a new portal closer to the wall. A less expensive alternative was to install a wider conveyor belt with a greater capacity. Either option would take months to implement.

While AMSTEEL's mining engineers in Pittsburgh penciled out costs and feasibilities, Fricktown management decided to jury-rig a temporary "moving" dump in the belt tunnel. That would allow the wall to produce coal at capacity. This fix used a continuous-miner and roof bolter to double the width of the far end of the return tunnel to 24 feet. The wall would off-load the freshly cut coal into this "retreating" dump room. A self-propelled scoop would then load the coal onto the existing conveyor at a rate that belt could handle. The dump was an extra and inefficient step, but it would work well enough until AMSTEEL could install a larger conveyor.

642

The British reps frowned when told of the temporary fix. They had warned AMSTEEL of the mismatch between the old belt and the new long-wall shearer. Now they worried aloud about roof control over the extra-wide dump room. AMSTEEL engineers in Pittsburgh talked it over with Fricktown personnel. Orders came down that evening. Make the dump area only as wide and as long as necessary to pile the coal and operate the scoop. Then retreat it along with the long wall. Bolts should hold up the roof long enough for coal to be loaded safely onto the conveyor, Pittsburgh said.

The ACMU safety committee complained to Buck "Hink" Hinkle, Fricktown superintendent. "It's too wide," they said.

"It's free coal," Hink replied, "on the outside of that return tunnel. We'll only be in there a shift or two in each dump room. Bolts can handle the extra roof ride."

The safety committee grumbled but went along. They didn't want to walk out over an "imminent danger" they couldn't prove was "imminent." They liked the overtime pay Fricktown's coal sales were dropping in their laps. Buck mentioned the likelihood of cash incentives for the wall's crew—bonuses tied to exceeding a production target.

Before the hoot-owl shift began, Buck Hinkle told his long-wall section boss, Dudley Nipper, to have his continuous-miner advance the first dump room "three or four feet deeper toward the property line, then spread her out. No use leavin' good coal to rot."

The crew spent the first part of their shift moving the wall's roof supports and cleaning up spilled coal. When they finished their 30-minute dinner break, Dudley relayed Hink's instructions to Cloy Casdorph, his continuous-miner operator.

"Won't that be close to the line, Nip, like almost on it?" Cloy asked.

"A good four, five foot off, I reckon," Dudley replied. "Nothin' in front of you 'cept coal."

Cloy checked for methane and then energized his miner. With slowness borne of caution, he eased the machine into the seam toward the property line.

No AMSTEEL mining had ever been recorded in that corner of the property. It should have been solid coal, virgin coal.

It wasn't.

Two feet forward, he broke into unmapped old works—gob!

Before he could de-energize the miner, Cloy Casdorph's cutter bits struck a piece of metal in the breakthrough. The spark ignited methane trapped in the unknown tunnel. Cloy Casdorph was blown out of his seat and killed instantly.

Fire raced down the two return tunnels. The now-heated air in the returns expanded, shooting the firestorm into other tunnels and crosscuts.

A shock wave built in front of the fire, stirring up coal dust and mixing it with air. The fire triggered a coal-dust explosion that was far more powerful. That blast rolled down the returns and main entries toward the portal. It combusted good air and left poisonous gasses up one tunnel and down the next.

Fricktown's carefully designed ventilation system of fans, masonry stoppings, overcasts, undercasts and temporary canvas curtains was mangled. Its belt conveyors were twisted. Mobile machines were damaged. But the British long wall survived since almost all of the explosive force had occurred outby of where it sat. Main entries were clogged in places with roof falls and wrecked machinery but not totally blocked.

Here and there, miners had managed to duck into a crosscut when they heard the run-away roar screaming down the tunnels at more than 500 feet per second. The mine filled with poisonous combustion gases. The explosion left fires burning in the coal.

Each miner carried a 30-minute self-rescuer that protected against deadly carbon monoxide, one of the byproducts of burning coal and methane.

Of the 60 underground, three got out. Twenty-three survived the blast, huddled in two, separate groups.

Those near the dump room hoped there might be breathable air in the mined-out place Casdorph had penetrated. They knew mining had once occurred there. Its tunnel might give them an escape to the surface. They looked into the void. They noted a few timber props and no roof bolts. They couldn't see an opening in the small tunnel. Now numbering 19, they decided to use their 30 minutes to barricade themselves near the headpiece at the opposite end of the long wall from the dump room where they hoped good air might still be coming in, at least a little. The other four survivors were in an older, distant part of the mine.

The 19 made a pocket for themselves behind canvas curtains in the intake tunnel. They nailed the curtain into the roof and weighed down its bottom with cement blocks. One painted MEN HERE on the canvas with a grease gun.

After their self-rescuers were spent, the survivors took them off, one man after another. Their faces cooled. They sat against the ribs, slowly and quietly inventorying their food and water. They knew they could collect water from roof drips. They'd divide their food equally.

If the air was still heavy with carbon monoxide, they would start to slip away into deep, irreversible unconsciousness. They said little as they watched each other for drowsiness, resigned to being each other's canary. As long as good air held out, they might make it for as long as a week. The consensus opinion—they were alive. Their survival depended on how quickly rescuers could get to them. The consensus, unspoken bottom line—they had a few hours if they were lucky, real lucky.

Gus was waiting at the AMSTEEL gate when Joe and Skis arrived about noon. Joe told the driver to park and get some coffee at The Moose across from the mine entrance. The Red Cross had set up its canteen in the most convenient, most heated and most bathroom-rich building they could find—the Fricktown Moose Lodge 1445. Women of The Moose were helping Red Cross volunteers prepare food and clean up.

"How many?" Joe asked.

"They're sayin' about 57," Gus said. "Sounds right. Three got out before the explosion rolled 'em."

"Any communication established with survivors?" Joe asked.

"Not yet. The phone lines to the surface got burnt up."

"Who do we know?" Skis asked.

"I know most of 'em," Gus said. "Danny Stalinsky's boy, Jackie. Buddy Nelson, Jinks Humbles. Your sister's grandson, Dale. Mike DiVitale. Jasper Glover. Trent Elkins. Al Nucci. Babe Tonkovich. Mackie Sensabaugh."

"Lord! Mackie's almost as old as me," Joe said. "What's he doin' underground?"

"He was set to retire this month. Forty-seven years in. He was mechanicin' on a continuous-miner section. This explosion, I suspect, happened on the new long wall."

"Why do you think that, Gussie?" Skis asked.

"'Cause I heard they was makin' a big dump room in the return near the tailpiece. The wall ran coal faster than they could belt it out. So they were dumpin' it straight into the room and spoon-feeding the belt with a scoop."

"Never seen one of them long walls in action," Joe said. "AMSTEEL and UNICOAL showed me how they worked. They had slides and this model that moved back and forth under the movin' roof chocks."

"Wouldn't they have done methane checks?" Skis asked.

"Sure," Gus said. "Everyone knows Fricktown is hot. They would have checked before they started up. They wouldn't have run the wall if methane was over one percent."

"So how?" Skis asked.

"Not sure," Gus said. "I got a notion, but it's just a guess."

Joe and Skis waited.

Gus decided to keep his hunch to himself for the time being.

"That crackerjack rescue team from over at Consol's Blacksville Number 2 set up a base about 200 feet in from the portal. Workin' their way in. Air's bad. Some top is down."

"Is the hoist okay?" Joe asked.

Gus hesitated: "They removed the hoist in 1953. Cut a portal directly into the seam."

"I guess I'd just forgotten that."

"Did the guys have air packs?" Skis asked.

"Doubt it. Just self-rescuers for carbon monoxide."

"They ain't worth shit if you're two mile in," Joe said. "Don't give you air long enough."

"So why didn't you write air packs into the last contract?" Gus asked. "You *are* the president of the ACMU."

"Why?" Joe repeated in a tired voice. "Because the operators come to the negotiatin' table with only so many dollars they're willing to spend on labor. That's why. If I get a dollar more on pension, I don't get to spend that dollar on air packs. The operators' pie is only so big. 'Bout all you can do in negotiations is cut it up this way or t'other. I was hopin' MESA would require air packs and take it off my plate."

Gus cut his eyes toward Skis who was looking at the December sky in Fricktown without nostalgia.

"Are you supportin' Delucci?" Joe asked.

"Maybe," Gus said.

"You an' me goes back a long ways," Joe said.

"No denyin' that, Joey."

"It hurts me that you're goin' against the Union."

"I'm goin' for the Union but maybe against you."

"You kept me alive when I was a kid. Now you want to kill me off."

"For Chrissakes, Joey. You'll retire at full salary for the rest of your life."

"I ain't talkin' 'bout money."

"I know," Gus said. "You're talking about feelin' important. Mixin' with the big shots. Sharin' your dinner bucket with Senators and such. Easiest thang in the world is for a poor sunuvabitch coal miner to get hooked on 'Yes-sir-Mr.-Hunt' shit."

"You think Delucci's gonna be better'n me? You think he's goin' to go over to the White House in his knee pads and safety toes? You think he's gonna work for a miner's pay? You think he's gonna bring his 30.06 to the bargainin' table and shoot the cap'list enemy sittin' on the other side?"

"In time, I imagine he'll turn into jes' as much of a disappointment as you or anybody else, including me. Between now and then, he might have a better chance of makin' our pie a little bigger than you do."

"If he starts that 'union-democracy' shit, the Union'll fall apart," Joe said. "Nobody will ever agree on nothin'. Nobody will be able to lead nobody. Every contract will be voted down. You don't never hear nothin' 'bout 'comp'ny democracy.' Them operators run their outfits like the Russians run Poland. Big shots in furry hats call the tune, and every little sunuvabitch in the hall has to go out on the floor and dance the boss's polka."

646

"Better to give the men a chance than not to," Gus said.

"They'll want to vote on everythin', from contracts to when every bloody-fingered, slate-pickin' breaker boy up in the anthracite can take a leak."

"Ain't used breaker boys since the '30s," Gus said.

"Well, shit, I was just makin' a point. A point don't have to be sharp as a tack for Chrissakes to be a point."

"Everybody makes a mistake or two on a new job," Gus said. "I figured you would make a mistake or two at headquarters. That's how you learn."

"I *have* learned up there," Joe said. "You got leaders, and they're only as good as the followers behind 'em. The men have to stand solid when I say 'Stand solid.' Can't have any 'but this' and 'but that.' An' if the Union's business ain't run right, like a business, the membership is bein' cheated."

"Looks to me, Joey, like you've gotten yourself into some monkey business with our Bank, and, at the same time, you've eased yourself out of bein' in the Union business."

"Gus, you was always too smart to be a coal miner," Joe said.

"Nope. I ain't no smarter than you, Joey, or anyone else. Difference between me and you is I never had no ambitions to go higher. If you got no ambitions, you're as free as you're ever gonna be in this life."

"I sold the Bank," Joe said. "We got a big price."

"I heard you sold it to the Mafia," Gus said.

"Their money spends same as yours, Gussie," Joe said. "Your trouble is you ain't a believer in what a man tries to do. No man succeeds in bein' perfect. We all fuck up, some. But if you want to get anythin' done in this world, you gotta get in and mix it up. Not spend your life warmin' the bench, watchin' and waitin' for somethin' to happen that never will. Commentin' on the passin' scene is jes' bein' a gasbag. This game we're in won't end up in a Russian Revolution. America ain't Russia."

"When you put it that way, you sound almost honorable," Gus laughed.

"'Honorable!'" Joe shouted. "I'm talkin' reality, and you're talkin' 'honorable.' Them two don't play on the same side of the ball most of the time."

"Thing is, Joey, you've forgotten the men," Gus said. "They ain't individuals to you no more. They're members. Or dues-payers, or 10,000 of this kind or 3,000 of some other. When they don't do exactly what you want, they become the 'enemy.' You're President of the American Coal Miner's Union. So you think president makes you better."

"Someone's got to lead. Someone's got to be president. I make the hard choices. That's why I *am* different."

647

"You're different," Gus said, "because you forgot who you are and what you come up from. You ain't been underground in 15 years, I bet. You don't flop on a tool belt when you get to work. You don't duck walk into your office under low top. Your ceiling don't drip down your back. You don't work on your knees in water. You can't remember no more what feedin' off the bottom is like."

Joe paused. "I remember some, Gussie. I didn't try to end up this way."

"I know that, Joey," Gus said gently. "It would have changed me too."

Joe looked at Gus, straight on. "You've always been a friend to me and Skis. You kept us safe. We've always looked up to you, respected you as a man and a Union brother. I've never known you to slack off your share of the job. Shit, you're right. I have slipped. I'm 67. Maybe I ain't smart enough no more. Maybe I'm too old. Maybe I can change. Maybe I can't."

"Thing is, Joey, the job changes the man—you, Skis, Jeep Delucci, me. You become how you spend your life."

Joe thought about that. "I'm goin' in," he announced.

"Not for me," Gus said.

"Not for you," Joe said. "For me."

"Well, nobody's goin' in right now," Gus said. "Not yet."

"I'll get some overalls in the bathhouse," Joe said.

"What's your idea about this explosion?" Skis asked Gus.

"I think maybe we mighta had a hand in it," Gus said.

"US!" Joe exclaimed.

"Us."

An ambulance, lights flashing, pulled in front of the three old men, temporarily blocking their view of the portal. They moved around it, down the familiar road.

"Is that a tipple?" Joe asked, gesturing toward a new five-story complex of sheet-metal structures, bins, tanks, conveyors and towers that stood above a double-track railroad siding.

"New wash plant," Gus said. "We now need to get out as much sulfur here at the mine as we can so the utilities can burn it with less sulfur-dioxide pollution. If you keep the oxides of sulfur down, you lower acid rain and make the air healthier for people to breathe."

"We've been fightin' EPA air regulations on coal for five years," Joe said. "Regulatin' coal pollution will shift electric generation to nuclear and oil. That'll take jobs away from my members."

"Joey, both miners and people need clean air," Gus said. "You can't be for good air underground and bad air above it."

"Yeah, I can," Joe said. "It's like this: I have to be."

648

Gus shook his head. "Coal's a 19th-Century industry walkin' down a road that keeps gettin" closer to a dead end. Coal's dirty. When a power plant burns it, particulates -- we used to call it soot -- come out. It gets in people's lungs and makes it harder to breathe. Kills people before their time. Coal also has tiny amounts of arsenic, mercury, lead and cadmium. They increase cancer. Coal smoke hurts people away from here. It also hurts people like us who live with the dust and use water that's dirtied up with it. We put up with it all these years, 'cause it's our meal ticket. But other folks are sayin' no more. There will be cleaner energies sooner or later. They may not be cheaper up front, but they won't cost as much in paying for our bad health from coal, like cancer, heart disease, lung problems. How far the coal road sticks out in front of us is anybody's guess. But 'ventually, coal's gonna get to its end."

"Some coal miner, you are," Joe said.

"Jes' sayin what I think'll happen. ACMU better start organizin' other energy workers—oilfields, refineries, nukes, uranium, even windmills and shit like that. Otherwise…"

"Otherwise, what?"

"Otherwise, there will be just a few coal miners and no more ACMU," Skis inserted.

"I figure coal mining will have mostly vanished in another 75 years," Gus said. "We're dinosaurs. We're the team of pullin' oxen about to be run out by the John Deeres. We done played our part. Next."

Men in white hard hats, miners and agency officials were clustered in front of the portal. Rescue teams carrying oxygen packs and safety equipment stood together, waiting for instructions. Heavy machinery was ready. Scoops could bring supplies and men into the mine, clear rubble and tram it -- and bodies -- to the surface. Technicians took samples of the mine's air to determine its constituents and toxicity. Excitement surrounded a big drilling rig that just pulled in. One Fricktown crew was setting up a fan to draw air out of the mine. This would help the intake fan that was pushing air inside. Reporters and television crews were looking for interviews. Families bunched together against the December cold, and the bad news they expected to hear.

In The Moose, women had grown quiet before anybody knew anything for sure. Their teenage sons stood next to the stage where every Friday night Bingo numbers were called out to their mothers, aunts, married sisters and old men thinking they might have a pinch of luck left in their lives. The boys stubbed out their cigarettes in a sand bucket, one of many placed around the Bingo tables. The girls sat on folding chairs with the older women, legs crossed, shooting looks of suspicion and anger at every man who spoke with hushed authority. Retired miners drank their coffee at

649

the Bingo bar, which was getting ready to start serving alcohol at noon. They stood in bunches, talking low. Some blamed AMSTEEL, some their fellow miners, some the gassy coal, but none the profession. A few thought it was God's will, but most of those who believed God had done this on purpose kept it to themselves.

In her own mind, Nancy Waring Shortbridge rose to these occasions. She also wished she had a magic wand that could change ugliness into prettiness, even banish misery altogether. She would make sad people happy and remove their hurts the way her mother discretely and inoffensively shooed off uninvited relatives from their beach house. Instead, she took the next woman's hand in hers and said she was so very sorry as she tried to get comfortable in her heels. Through the window, she caught a glimpse of The Governor's helicopter sitting by itself in the parking lot of the Fricktown Moose.

Peter was better at this consoling; she acknowledged that. He was totally sincere in his concern. He did not blame them for their lot. He did not ask why they did not leave for something better. He once told her that he considered miners to be soldiers, and "we, their commanders, should expect them to take casualties." She saw him standing with the Fricktown local-union president and a management person, the three in earnest, honest conversation. His eyes never wavered from those who came up to him. His hand never trembled. His words of comfort were never boilerplate. He always mixed a "sorry" with an expression of hope, with light at the end of the tunnel, with it's in God's hands now. He remembered a couple of names, men who had helped in his last campaign, men who had taken his money and not cut him from their slates. He was never obtrusive, never hovering. Where had he learned to do this? How does he get it just right? Does he actually give a shit? she wondered.

West Virginia's First Lady said her sorrys to an older, barrel-shaped woman who she guessed was 50 but looked over 70. The woman wore a house dress and snow boots. She reminded Nancy Waring Shortbridge of the peasant wives in the art she'd studied in college—Van Gogh, Jean Francois Millet, Pissarro's haymakers. They were thick, worn down and largely spent, but still tough enough to do stoop labor.

She also remembered the fisherman's wife who looked like this woman. Nancy had to barter with her during her family's vacation in the Cyclades Islands. Nancy wanted the woman's decorated "frying pan" made of green schist. She later learned it was probably used as a plate and more than 3,000 years old. She bought it for $10 American, a five and five ones. Nancy understood without having to ask that it had been looted. In a single passing moment of guilt after buying it, she half-hoped it was a fake. In 1959, it was not hard for a pretty American teenager to smuggle an antiquity home, concealed from both custom inspectors and her parents.

She now kept it in a curved-glass curio cabinet. She told Peter she bought it on the Navajo reservation on a cross-country drive when she was in college. As she stood in The Moose, she guessed it would sell for about $25,000 at Sotheby's.

Nancy felt something under the sole of her shoe. She moved her foot and looked down. It was a piece of gray metal, the size and shape of a quarter.

The woman whose hand she still held noticed the Governor's wife lift her foot. "It's a Bingo chip, Mrs. Shortbridge. It's bad luck to step on one."

"Oh, I'm so sorry. I didn't mean to...."

The woman bent down and peeled it off the floor. "The men save 'em for us. Knockouts, they call 'em, from electric boxes. You know when they wire something into a panel."

Nancy smiled and nodded as if she and her husband helped each other install 200-amp breaker boxes every weekend.

The woman rubbed the chip between her fingers and thumb, then on the hem of her dress. "We like the metal ones. They don't fall off the cards like the plastic. You better keep this now," she said. "I cleaned it up for you."

"Oh, I...I couldn't."

"We need us a miracle, ma'am. Don't take a miracle away from us."

"No, I'd never do that."

"This here is yours now."

"Yes, I'll treasure it."

"Come back when this is all over. Friday nights. Seven p.m. You'll probably win."

"Oh, I'm sure I wouldn't," The Governor's wife said.

"Well, hon, I'd say you already have."

Linda Faye Decker drove her new Oldsmobile Cutlass north out of Clarksburg. She was following Doris Estep's 10-year-old Chevy sedan.

"Now you Linda Faye, you tell me again what exactly are we gonna do when we get there?" Alma Rae Stump asked.

"Be seen, darlin'."

"And fly our flag," Susie Rutherford added.

Alma Rae shifted in the back seat between Susie and Wanda Smith, smoothing out the wrinkles she imaged might be attacking her new permanently pressed skirt. She'd never touched black women before, and now here she was thigh to thigh between two who made her feel good about herself.

"Be the comp'ny's conscience," Willie added from the front passenger seat where he had stretched out both legs.

"That slippy-slidy-talkin' Buzzy Maggard sunuvabitch."

"Wanda, honey," Linda Faye said.

"Don't you 'Wanda honey' me Linda Faye Decker. You done heard him jes' like me. He promised us: 'Ain't nothin' gwine be on paper, ladies, but me an' the boys'll do you right. No mo' speed-up. Back to normal. Ain't gwine to kill no mo' minin' men from speed-up. No ma'am.'"

"We don't know that this Fricktown mine was speedin' up," Alma Rae said.

"Heard they was runnin' one of them new long walls," Willie said, blowing his Tiparillo smoke out of a quarter-opened window. "Don't know enough about them walls to know about sparkin', but everybody know they do run a lot of coal real fast."

"American Eagle men say UNICOAL has been livin' up to what Mr. Maggard promised us," Alma Rae said. "Doris heard the same."

"You right," Willie said

"If they can do it at American Eagle, they can do it at Fricktown," Linda Faye said. "We'll find out soon enough."

"Same shit, everywhere, all the time," Wanda said. "Never changes. We jes' go roun' an' roun' like mice runnin' on the inside of an ol' tire. They throw you a crumb to keep runnin' in their loop. If you stop runnin', you die. Or get kilt."

"Well, I never been much outa McDowell County so I wouldn't know about mice in this tire you're talkin' about," Alma Rae said. "Well, I do go Christmas shoppin' over at Bluefield and Beckley where they have a McDonald's an' all. An' that time up in Pittsburgh at UNICOAL, of course. But that was different."

"That don't count, honey," Linda Faye said. "Or maybe it counts more than all the other ones put together."

"Fricktown ain't gonna be no different than Bloomingrose and Anawalt Hollers," Willie said, sounding more certain than he was.

"Got Eye-talians up there," Wanda said.

"Hunkies, too," Linda Faye said.

"Honkies?" Wanda asked.

"Hunkies, honey, not honkies," Linda Faye laughed. "Hunkie people come from Russia, Poland, places like that. Well, I guess hunkies are honkies if you wanna look at it that way. Me, too."

"You different," Susie said.

"No, I ain't different," Linda Faye said. "I jes' had to thank about thangs more lately. When you start askin' questions about one thang, you start naturally rollin' into questions about other thangs. Lots of thangs."

"White folks ain't treated black folks right," Alma Rae said. "We all knew that, deep down. But it was jes' how thangs was down here. It was how we was raised up an' all."

"What it was," Linda Faye said as she passed a truck that Doris had just passed, "it was easier and more convenient to believe 'all niggers are

652

dumb' than to believe us whites was all wrong. But Mike knew it wasn't right. He'd tell me stuff 'bout what went on in the mine. How you all got more than your share of the jobs with bad dust and water. How you could only rise up only so far."

"Yeah, that true," Willie sighed and then chuckled. "I was biddin' on 'lectrician job when the top come down. Pins, he say I wouldn't get it. Glad Mike talked to you 'bout us underground. By the bye, he ever tell you 'bout the 'potion'?"

"Uh-uh," Linda Faye said. "What potion?"

Willie grinned and cut his eyes toward Susie and then Wanda.

"Lawd, Willie, you can't be tellin' that," Wanda said.

"What story?" Linda Faye insisted. "Come on, Willie. Now you brought it up. We're all friends and equals. 'Course since it's my new car and I'm a-drivin', I'm the most equal, which means I get to say when we need to hear a story."

Susie shook her head. A lot had happened during the last few months. And now this.

Willie smiled. "It was like this. Pins and me was sittin' in the dinner hole 'bout two years ago. Mike was there. Billy Burdette. Darrel Dorsey, Timmy. Petey Jones. Couple of others. Me an' Pins was off to one side a bit. Now this young Schooley boy, Roy Lee Schooley, he come over from another section and sets down besides Pins.

"'Hear you a potion man,' he say to Pins real low so the others couldn't hear unless they was tryin' real hard.

"Now Pins, as you know, was always lookin' for a way to make a buck or two on the side, so he says, 'What you need?'

"So Roy Lee, he say he jes' got hisself married to that little Mooney girl, Sheryl Ann Mooney, and he havin' a time settlin' her. Seems he a little quick on the trigger."

"Bes' stop right there," Susie said.

"Oh no, he ain't a-stoppin' right there," Linda Faye said. "We're gettin' to the good part. My car, my rules."

"I thought we was all equal now," Wanda said.

"On most thangs," Linda Faye said, "not all thangs. Now Mister Willie Rutherford, you proceed with your tale about this white boy with his hair-trigger popgun."

Willie dragged on his Tiparillo and blew smoke out the window. "Well, Pins, he don't say nothin' for a little bit, jes' nods his head up and down. Now Roy Lee, he gettin' anxious. He ain't never talked to Pins before 'bout much of anythin' though they knew each other up at the high school. Pins pours himself some mo' coffee. Still ain't sayin' nothin'.

"'I hear you all can fix up a potion,' Roy Lee say.

"'Naw, man,' say Pins, 'that just voodoo shit. Don't work for white folks anyway.'

"But Roy Lee he know what he think he know.

"'Come on man,' Roy Lee say, 'he'p me get her settled in right.'

"So Pins he say, 'Well, I ain't gonna turn down a friend and a neighbor who be needin' a favor. I might could try an' fix you up a little somethin'. No guarantees, of course. Could be mighty pow'rful. Comes out a little different each time. Might be too much for a white girl. No offense intended.'

"'How much you want for that powerful potion?' Roy Lee asks.

"'Oh my goodness, Roy Lee,' Pins say, 'I ain't doin' this for money. Tell you what. If it work good, you give me whatever you think it be worth. If it don't work, you don't owe me a dime.'

"Roy Lee agrees and leaves. I'm about to pee in my dinner pail. Pins jes' settin' there a-grinnin' an' a-nibblin' on the Little Debbie that Wanda packed. Pins, he jes' as cool 'bout this like Roy Lee had been talkin' about nothin' mo' than some ol' snow shovel he used last winter. So Pins he go home that night. He know he ain't no witchdoctor, but if Roy Lee wan' a potion bad, then Pins is the man to fix him up one. So he go into Wanda's kitchen and he take a little honey for slick and mix it with a little cream and some Vaseline and a few sugars. Then he put in a smidge of vanilla. Then he decide he need somethin' to make it look sassier. So he shake a dash of red color in. He put this mess in a little jelly jar and tapes it closed. Uses 'bout 20 yards of black 'lectrician's tape.

"Couple of days later, Roy Lee comes back over 'bout the same time, an' Pins say, 'Now Roy Lee. You jes' dab the tee-tiniest bit of this potion on yo' pecker before you start messin' with her. You hear me, Roy Lee. Jes' the littlest smitch. This here shit be straight from Africa. My people brought the secret recipe over on the slave boat. Ain't never given none to no white man befo', so I don't know what it'll do on a white pecker. Might make you last an hour, even two. She might start doin' who knows what. There 'nough potion in this jelly jar to last you two, three years. Maybe five. Now don't you go wearin' out that po' new wife.'

"Then Pins rolls his eyes white like in them ol' movies so that Roy Lee'll know for damn sure he's gettin' into some very serious potion straight outa the African jungle where them 500-pound go-rillas do their nasty."

"My word," Linda Faye said.

"So Roy Lee, he grabs this jelly jar and runs back down the crosscut like Pins jes' gave him the one and only key to the new Playboy bunny house that's jes' been set up in his section.

"Well, sir, ladies, I mean, the next day, Roy Lee come struttin' back to our dinner hole wearin' the biggest shit-eatin' grin you ever saw. Pins stay cool. Roy Lee, he say, 'Man that potion work like a charm. Like to kill me, but she all settled now.'

"So Pins, he say, 'I told you that you'd only need a dab.'

654

"'Dab!' Roy Lee shout, 'I used half the damn jar on her las' night.'"

The women exploded in laughter.

"And then Roy Lee give Pins a hundred dollar bill an' orders two mo' jars!"

"Bless her heart," Alma Rae added with a grin more knowing than she would ever acknowledge.

"Ooooh Sheryl Ann, you poor baby," Linda Faye cried through her tears. "Maybe I should pull over for a minute of silence."

"Bought us a color TV with that 'potion' money," Wanda said in a deadpan tone. "Still in the living room. Works good. Gets three channels clear."

"Men'll believe anythin' about sex," Linda Faye said.

"They simple as pie," Wanda said. "They all got a squirt gun, an' they all want to squirt in the same places."

"Sake alive all my time!" Alma Rae exclaimed.

"WANDA! That is enough," Susie said with a grin she was unable to suppress.

"White men'll believe anythin' 'bout the colored," Willie said. "They got some strange goin's ons in their heads 'bout black men, that fo' sure."

"But it's all true," Wanda kidded, "if they got the potion."

"Willie, honey, them Fricktown miners are gonna be mighty jealous when you are driven up in my car with four fine-lookin', sex-talkin' babes," Linda Faye said.

"Willie, you are going to get rich selling potions some day," Alma Rae said.

"Him! I should make the money," Wanda laughed. "Don't you know, Pins, he tried every one of them damn potion formulas out on me."

"Lordy!" Alma Rae exclaimed. "Really?"

"Really?" Linda Faye said.

Willie looked back at Wanda.

"I ain't splittin' no profits with you, Willie Rutherford," Wanda said. "Potions is my ticket."

Ben Roberson closed his eyes and let the shower head drive hot water over his face. He did not want to end this cleansing moment. His hands fell against his soapy sides. Then he forced his mind to focus, to think through what needed to be done.

Gert was in her bathrobe when he stepped out of their large shower stall. She handed him his oversize Turkish bath towel that had been her gift on one of their early anniversaries. He loved it. He refused to let her buy him a new one. It was one of the comforts that made life pleasant. She placed a mug of coffee on the vanity.

"How bad is it?" she asked.

"Buck Hinkle said 60 were underground when the blast hit."

"My God! Sixty! Are...are they all dead?"

"Three got out. We could lose all the rest. Christ, I hope not. It should never have happened. That mine's been gassy since the day the first pound of coal was taken out. Everyone knew it. That's why we've always kept up the ventilation. No short cuts. No skimping. Hasn't been a big explosion there since the '20s."

"I should come with you," Gert said.

"No need to," Ben said. "It'll be rough."

Ben brushed his teeth and slipped into his boxer shorts and undershirt. He hadn't minded how his body had aged. He wasn't fat, and he hadn't lost his hair, which was now a distinguished gray. He sat on their bed and slipped on his socks. Gert handed him a freshly starched white shirt. Then she started getting ready.

"It's funny," Ben said. "About two years ago, the AMSTEEL board was undecided about Fricktown. It's an old mine with a lot of infrastructure problems and expenses. It had long hauls from the face to the surface. Still, the seam was thick, and the coal was high in Btus. It was good for both coking and steam. But it was high in sulfur, which meant that we had trouble selling it to electric-generating plants. If they had scrubbers, they could use it and stay within the air-pollution limits. If they never put in scrubbers, they couldn't use it without getting into trouble with the EPA. For making steel, it's almost the best damn coking coal this country has. Ninety percent of Fricktown's coal goes to coke.

"Until the early '70s, we never cared much about costs at Fricktown because the coal was so good. All we cared about was production. We could pass along the higher cost in our steel products, and the utilities could do the same with their electric rates. Fricktown's job was to get the tonnage out and rail it up to our coke ovens in Donora. But overcapacity in American steelmaking, foreign steel production and weak demand forced us to look at Fricktown's costs.

"We decided to put in a new wash plant and buy a British long wall to boost production of a cleaner product. The long wall produces coal more cheaply than every other underground method. That cheapness comes from using fewer miners and producing more coal for every dollar of invested capital and hour of labor."

"Fewer miners?"

"Right. With the long wall, Fricktown will produce more coal than before with about 40 percent fewer miners.

"What made Fricktown feasible going forward was the huge amount of the Pittsburgh seam that we'd never touched. There's maybe 1,200 acres of virgin coal scattered around the edges in big blocks. And we have more reserves on adjacent properties we bought years ago.

"Fricktown coal has been the foundation of AMSTEEL for more than 75 years. I know those people just like Daddy did. I played with them when Daddy took me with him on his inspections. The whole place depends on us, several hundred working miners and maybe 1,500 retirees, disabled and widows. If we could modernize the systems and make money, I would have been ashamed of myself if I had walked away from them. I think we did the right thing for them and us."

"You did," Gert said.

"But if we had backed out of Fricktown, this would not have happened. This is on me," he said.

"You're not a clairvoyant," she said, handing him his suit.

"I wish I was."

"When's your car coming?" she asked.

"About 15 minutes."

"I'm going with you."

Ben knew Gert was not asking for permission.

"I'm glad to walk in to any room with you. But you'll probably be on your own a good bit."

"Fine. I'll talk with the women."

"Take clothes for a couple of days. Casual, not dressy."

"I'll be ready," she said.

"You always are. Best woman I ever knew for getting out the door on time."

"One more thing. Were we doing anything wrong? Something risky that might have caused this?"

Ben paused. "Somebody did something wrong. If the ventilation was correct, even a Red Hat sneaking a smoke with a Zippo wouldn't have ignited the gas. I hope to hell it wasn't us."

"I won't get underfoot. I'll find something useful to do. You'll need a friend down there."

Ben took her in his arms. "You're quite a girl."

The AMSTEEL driver stopped at the Fricktown mine office. Ben kissed Gert in the back seat. He had called Buck Hinkle on the car's analog phone to say Gert would be with him. He asked that at least one person be available at all times to accompany her. Hink's wife, Angie, was waiting. The drive from Pittsburgh had taken two hours. Ben spent it talking with Fricktown personnel and mine-safety officials from West Virginia and Washington.

Ben met his headquarters people at the office door: Bob Townsend, vice-president for coal operations; Jim Ferguson, head of human relations; Don Browski, head of safety and health; and Conley Bonney, head of public affairs. Buck led them into the conference room where hot and cold drinks and a coffee cake were waiting. A mine map covered one wall. A blank flip chart with a green marker stood at the head of the conference table. Pittsburgh sat on one side; Fricktown on the other. Ben Roberson, Junior, took his seat at the head of the table.

Hinkle gave everyone a brief summary and update. "Sixty underground. No communications yet. Three out. I have to assume some of the 57 are dead. But we also have to assume that some survived from that many. The explosion seems to have started at the load out for the long wall in the belt return. The three continuous-miner sections were operating at least one mile away. A fresh-air base has been established about 200 feet in. We're working on the fans. We don't want to feed any active fires in the coal so we keep checking for how much smoke is coming out. Four rescue teams are on the property. Each is developing a different approach. The new drilling rig is ready as soon as we say where. We can get a six-inch breathing hole drilled quick once we know where survivors are. The rig also has a 30"-diameter, Hughes tri-cone bit, like in oil drilling. With that wide a hole, we can lower a capsule and hoist them out one at a time. But it takes a while to drill that wide, 300 feet down. From what I've seen, the mains to the different faces are blocked here and there. Good air will be short. That means we're on a very fast clock for survivors. We had the wall running for only one day. Then this."

"Hink, are you saying the wall blew it?" Ben asked.

"If not the wall's shearers, something, let's say around the wall or associated with the wall. That's the best guess I have right now."

"Was there a cigarette pat-down pre-shift?" Bob Townsend asked. Bobby, as he was generally addressed, was a short, muscular and aggressive mine engineer who was the whip hand in AMSTEEL's coal operation. One of his assignments was to make AMSTEEL's metallurgical coal competitively priced in the open market. In the coal division, his nickname was "Squash," a game he was said to play without a racket.

"We pat down every shift," Buck said. "Company policy. But somebody coulda sneaked a smoke. There's a hundred ways to get a cigarette and a match underground. But even the cherriest Red Hat wouldn't be dumb enough to light one up in the returns."

"Hell, the cutting bits on the wall's shearer could have hit an iron ball in the roof," safety director Don Browski said. "That could have popped gas at the face."

"Sure," Hink said.

"Anything non-permissible inby on the continuous-miner sections?" Browski asked, referring to older, now-illegal, electric-mining machinery whose sparks could ignite methane.

"Nope, not a thing. Got rid of all that stuff in 1970 when the '69 safety law came in," Buck said. "Sold that shit to the dog-hole operators in East Kentucky. Got more than what they were worth, which was not much."

"The long-wall face, was it fire-bossed?" Browski asked.

"As far as we know," Hink said. "Here's the log. Called it in like he was supposed to. Air flow was normal. Both volume and velocity. Methane was well under one percent. Took another reading after dinner. Same."

"Welding? Electrical work?" Bobby Townsend asked.

"Nothing scheduled. No call in of a breakdown," Buck said.

"It couldn't have been the wall," Don Browski said. "The Brits have been using that shearer for more than a decade in their deepest, gassiest mines. There's never been an ignition recorded. That's why I recommended we buy the damn thing for Fricktown from a safety perspective."

"Well, we were also running a continuous-miner back in the belt return," Hink said.

"What for?" Ben asked.

Buck explained the reason for enlarging the return to handle the surplus of coal the long wall produced. "We also had a scoop loading onto the conveyor."

"That would have produced a roof-control problem, too much span," Browski said, "not a methane problem."

"Pittsburgh checked off on the dump-pad fix," Hink said in case some in the room had forgotten.

"Bobby?" Ben asked. "Did you sign off on Hink's plan for a dump pad?"

"Yes," Townsend said. "I also authorized the purchase of an eight-foot-wide conveyor belt, because our four-footer can't handle the wall. The retreating dump pad was temporary. It'll take a couple of months to get the belt here and running."

"I didn't know," Don Browski said, closing his eyes at what he saw coming at them.

"Not me," Jim Ferguson, human resources, said.

"Neither did I," Conley Bonney said. "We have a PR problem here."

"We have a responsibility issue here," Ben said. "We did something 'knowingly and willfully' that was out of compliance. We knew a double-wide dump pad would never have been approved. We can't deny it, because as soon as the rescue teams get back in that return, they'll see it's too wide."

"Now hold on," Hink said. "They were glue-bolting the roof with six-footers on a tight pattern. It wasn't a roof fall that caused an explosion. I'd bet anything on that."

"We could seal that section of the mine," Squash Townsend said.

"That would arouse suspicion, and I'm too old to go to jail," Ben said. "The best thing is to lay it all out."

"Then I'll go to jail," Hink said, "with Squash over there."

"Not necessarily," Ben said. "The Ford Administration isn't sending coal people to jail under the '69 safety law. More likely, they'll hit us with a big fine. But the federal law does have criminal penalties for a knowing and willful violation. I should get Legal down here."

"It wasn't the dump pad," Buck insisted with increasing desperateness. "We were extra, extra careful with the roof. The roof was good. No problem with it."

"Nothing happened to Consolidtion Coal's managers when Number 9 blew at Farmington in '68," Squash said, "but that *was* before the Coal Act came in."

"Seventy-eight dead at Farmington is why we have that law weighing us down," Browski said.

"We are better for it," Ben said. "Every mine operator has the same new costs, and all of us just pass them on. The regulations fall hardest on the small coal companies, not us. High coal prices give us the room to be safer."

Ben started thinking out loud. "My guess is it had something to do with the continuous-miner. Not the shearer on the long wall, not the battery scoop, not the bolter in the return."

"It was non-sparking, permissible equipment," Buck insisted. "I have records to prove we sold all the crap."

"I know I shouldn't ask this," Ben said, "but who did you sell our 'crap' to?"

"Buzzy Maggard's boys," Buck said. "They planned to paint it up and resell it quick to the raggedy-asses opening raggedy-ass dog holes to take advantage of the high prices. They figure they'll be in and out before they ever get inspected or fined. One told me that he was going to buy one miner that's permissible and show it to the inspectors. Then run the two they've hidden that aren't. Lots of ways to cheat."

Ben closed his eyes and rubbed his forehead. Would it always be such in his business?

After a minute, he walked over to the mine map. He used his finger to locate the returns for the long wall. "I don't see anything on the map to indicate the belt return is extra wide at the far end."

"Well, see, we didn't put it on the main map," Hink said. "I think we might have patched something in as a change order on an as-built supplemental map, somewhere."

Ben understood what Buck Hinkle was not saying. "Anything else?"

"We did want the miner to dig out a little forward, toward the property line," Hink said. "Still on us, of course."

"Forward?" Ben said.

"We were just going to drive the dump room a little deeper toward the line. It would give us more room, more safety and get more coal."

660

"That would not have passed an inspection," Ben said. "There'd be another discrepancy between our plan and our practice."

"We were inspected the day before we started the wall up. No citations," Hink said.

"And then yesterday you had the miner digging the dump pad forward?" Ben said.

"We wanted to run coal while prices are so good."

Ben closed his eyes and rubbed them. He knew Hink's argument; he'd used it himself many times. He looked again at the mine map. He squinted. He penciled in the dump-room enlargement with the extra feet forward toward the property line.

"It wasn't the dump room," Hink pleaded. "It had to have been something else."

"If AMSTEEL screwed up, gentlemen, I am to blame," Ben said. "If Fricktown management screwed up, I am to blame. The rule applies to everyone in this room, everyone who works for me. We, as a company, are to blame if we screwed up. Understand?"

The men in suits from Pittsburgh and the men in work overalls from Fricktown sat silently in reluctant agreement.

"Is this where the dump pad was, all the way over here where I marked it?" Ben asked, with his finger on the mine map.

"Yes," Hink said. "That's it. The coal was as pretty as a beauty queen when we took the first cut."

"How far from the property line was the connector tunnel between the wall's headpiece and the tailpiece?" Ben asked.

"We surveyed it out very careful," Hink said. "We started 10 foot back from where our property line was. Left a bunch of coal in place in that 10 foot just so there was no question. My surveyors were dead certain about the property line's location. To make the dump room a little bigger, I told the miner to cut in four foot, maybe five, deeper toward the boundary, then stop. That would have left a good five feet of solid coal between us and the next guy."

"Hold on," Ben said, "Let me get my glasses on. Okay. Now I can see fine. Olin! Gus Olin owns the adjoining property. Is that right?"

"Sure," Hink said. "Old timer. He lives here in town. Never would sell or lease his coal rights to us. Owns 75 acres in fee. Offered him big money. Must have asked him a dozen times over the last 15 years. Funny old guy."

Ben Roberson shook his head, and smiled. "Gus Olin -- that 'funny old guy' -- is smart enough to run any coal company in America," he announced to his managers, "including AMSTEEL. And he'd probably do a better job than every one of us in this room."

The AMSTEEL men were stunned. The Fricktown managers knew Gus Olin, or at least had heard the name. None had ever given much thought to the retiree in the Mackinaw they saw buying groceries in the Fricktown IGA. The Pittsburgh contingent was totally baffled. Who in the world, they wondered individually, was Gus Olin?

"He's just a retiree," Hink said. "Worked his own room, shot-firin' and handloadin' back in the old days. I think he retired in the early '60s. Had 35 or 40 years of service. I can check his records."

Ben raised his eyebrows at the ignorance that assumptions can foster. "I've known Gus since the late '20s. Dad told me to spend time with Gus, because I would learn more from him than anyone else. Dad knew I would be a better coal operator for knowing him. He's an autodidact—self-taught. You go in his house, it's like walking into Carnegie Library. You want to talk about particle physics, Spinoza or the Chicago school of economics, talk to Gus."

Buck Hinkle thought he might have heard of one of the three discussion topics Ben had just mentioned, all of which Gus could explain to him. Spinoza, Hink wild-guessed, might be an Italian dish, maybe a special desert.

"Wasn't he a radical or something?" Hink asked.

"I'm sure he is. He went through the '32 Strike. Wouldn't blame him for being radical after that or before for that matter."

"Gallagher?" Hink asked.

"Dad thought he knew what happened to Gallagher about a week or so after the commissary fire," Ben said. "We found a scrap of melted gold when we sifted through the ashes. Figured it was either his wedding band or his pocket watch. Our informer in the tents said he believed it was Gus and one of his helpers -- Joe Hunt or Sonoski -- who killed Gallagher, because he saw Gus pass up the soup kitchen for a few days right after the fire. A fellow with a family who's starving doesn't do that, even the noble ones. But that was the only evidence we had against Gus, and that wasn't evidence that would stand up. The snitch also saw blood on Joe's pants the day after the fire. Joe said it was rabbit.

"Dad guessed Gallagher caught them stealing food from the commissary. Maybe they killed him and set the fire. Dad thought it was unlikely that Gallagher was shot, because the mine guards would have heard. That story Joe told at his press conference about squirrel hunting and accidentally shooting Gallagher was 20 pounds of horseshit. Gallagher would not have been patrolling for squirrel hunters, because no squirrels were left. And if, for some reason, he had been killed there, surely someone would have found his remains.

"Somebody knows what really happened. Dad talked to Gus, one to one, after the War. Gus denied killing Gallagher even after Dad said he wouldn't prosecute. So, given that the strike had ended, and nothing could bring back Gallagher, and we had no proof of anything, well, it seemed best to let things heal. The miners were back underground on acceptable terms. The market was picking up in the late '30s. We needed Fricktown miners working a few days a week more than we needed those two in court defending themselves against charges no one could prove. A trial might have started up the strike all over again.

"And the interesting thing to me was that for all of Gus Olin's radical ideas, he was the best guy in this ACMU local for us to work with. I don't mean he was our patsy. But Gus understood our financials, our business, our industry as well as Dad or I did. You could always sit down with him, show him your numbers as long as they were honest. I could discuss whatever the problem was, think through alternatives, weigh the costs and benefits and then come to an agreement both sides could live with. He would have made one helluva ACMU president, which is why John L. Lewis never let him get above being a local officer."

"You never said anything about him to me when I came here," Hink said.

"Gus was retired by then. I wanted you to find your own way."

"So how do we handle this media-wise?" Conley Bonney asked.

"I'll do it. This is my company. But first, I want to talk to Gus."

"Gus! We have 57 men in the hole!" Conley said. "What if the press hears about the dump pad?"

"Then I need to talk to him as quickly as Buck can get him here," Ben said. "So move!"

Jeep Delucci and Jeffrey Becker had been talking with Fricktown miners for about 30 minutes when Becker saw Julie Cogswell walk toward the heated mine garage where chairs and tables had been set up for the various rescue teams and agency personnel.

A hand-written sign had been tacked onto a carpenter's sawhorse by the huge garage doors: **FOOD AT THE MOOSE**. Men in mining clothes and boots, their belts heavy with anonometers, methanometers and pineapple-sized self-rescuer cannisters tried not to look bored with the waiting. Each had an air pack close by. A KDKA-TV van pulled next to the garage, and its crew began setting up. A smaller van from WQED Pittsburgh public television had arrived earlier. They were doing a long, three-minute feature on mine safety. It might be turned into a documentary if funds could be found.

Becker noticed children were playing around the Governor's helicopter in the bare spot where the downwash had cleared the snow. The two pilots were explaining to a boy and a girl how a helicopter could fly without wings when God's birds couldn't.

Becker, finally, caught Julie's eye. She smiled and headed toward them. She was dressed in a red down parka and boots with furry wool trim. L.L. Bean, he thought, uncommon in West Virginia. She held a reporter's notebook and carried an over-the-shoulder satchel that held a tape recorder, camera and wallet.

Becker met her on the salted asphalt drive that led into the garage. She seemed to be looking past him. He didn't want to slip on an icy patch and land on his face.

"Again, we meet," he said. "Similar circumstances."

"Worse," she said.

"Yes. Of course. I'd hoped you would have called for lunch, or something."

"Jeffrey, I did call."

"You did? I don't know why I didn't get the message."

"For Jeep," she said gently. "I called for Jeep."

"Oh. Did you get your story from him? He didn't say anything to me."

Julie looked at him straight on. "It wasn't for a story."

"Okay," Becker said. "Then?"

Julie smiled at him. "We're an item."

"Huh?"

"Jeep and me."

"Oh. I didn't know."

"I know that. Very recent."

"Oh."

"Did you notice his blue eyes?" she asked.

"Of course," Becker said. "He's used them on a lot of girls before you."

"Coal miners are not Hollywood handsome as a rule," she said.

"Surely, there's more than that."

"Obviously. What do you take me for? Jeep and I, we know each other. I dated boys like you, but I won't ever understand who you really are. I don't know your 'fixin's.'"

"My 'fixin's'?"

"Jeffrey, do you like grits?"

"No," he said, having never tasted them owing to their unappetizing name. He even wasn't exactly sure what they were. Maybe something like chitterlings.

Julie could tell Becker was confused. "Grits are poor-people's food. When the old water-powered gristmills ground corn, the coarse meal that didn't fall through the screens was called 'grit.' You boil whole-grain grits -- not the instant kind -- until they absorb about four times their volume in water. Add salt and lots of butter. Serve with red-eye gravy if you have a little ham or bacon drippings. Or bulldog gravy if you have nothing at all."

"I like cornbread," Becker said belatedly.

Julie smiled and touched his cheek. "Jeep and I share West Virginia bodily fluids from before the womb. You and me? What you have to remember is I hold a grudge, fairly or not."

664

"Against me?"

"Against the people who prosper off our backs."

"Me?"

"Unknowingly, unwillingly, unconsciously, unfairly—you."

"Nonsense! This is stupid West Virginia, pinto-bean nationalism," Becker sputtered. "Every Yankee, every person who went to a fancy college, is not your enemy. What do you think I've been doing on this campaign? Was that wrong? Was that oppressing you?"

Julie smiled sweetly, which was not her habit. "Jeffrey, do you know the song -- 'Take Me Home, Country Roads' -- John Denver?"

"Sure. It's West Virginia's unofficial anthem."

"Anything wrong with it?"

"Schmaltzy," he said. "'Younger than the mountains…teardrop in my eye…yesterday, yesterday.'"

"Bill Danoff from Springfield, Massachusetts, wrote it. He had never set foot in West Virginia. He wrote it in Georgetown."

"Okay?"

"The Blue Ridge Mountains are not in West Virginia."

"Right."

"The Shenandoah River blesses us for just a few miles."

"Maybe he wanted to write the Potomac but needed four syllables. Your point being?"

"Even our identity -- and a false one to boot -- is shipped in from the outside and stuck on to us. That 'schmaltz' runs in on a track parallel to the one hauling our coal out, which is the only reason we are valued. If we didn't mine coal to keep the TVs fired up, we'd be walled in on our Appalachian reservation and left to rot in our miseries. That song offends me, but, apparently, not you."

"Other stuff offends me more than a song that gets some geography wrong."

"It's the little stuff that wears me down, Jeffery. I can get set for the big things, but the little things snipe out of the blue. Now stop pouting. You'll find someone. Lots of girls would like to run with an up-and-coming lawyer. You're a good catch."

"Right."

"Come on. Remember what Benjamin Franklin wrote: 'In the dark, all cats are gray.'"

"That's one way of looking at romance," Becker said.

"Franklin wasn't talking about romance, dopey."

"I figured," he said.

"We can be professionals and friends," she said.

"Sure."

"Oh, I see Jeep coming over. Anyway, you never know how things work out," she said as she walked past him.

"Yes, you never know until you do," Becker said under his breath. Then he remembered he hadn't followed Julie Cogswell's advice. Duck the first punch! He'd caught hers flush on his nose, and it hurt.

Buck Hinkle found Gus Olin when he recognized Joe Hunt from the photographs of the ACMU president that appeared in Coal Age from time to time. Gus was standing next to Joe who was talking with the ACMU District 31 president for northern West Virginia, Eddie Mullins, Fricktown's Local Union 4566 president, Wade Samples and a couple of safety committeemen.

"Wade, Eddie," Buck said in greeting.

"Hink," Wade said in return.

"I'm Buck Hinkle," he said extending his hand to Joe Hunt who took it. "Fricktown superintendent."

"Joe Hunt."

"Ben wants to talk with Gus Olin," Hink said, "up at the office as soon as possible."

"About what?" Joe asked.

"Don't know," Hink said. "I'm just the boy with the message."

"Sure," Gus said, starting toward the office without Buck. "I'll catch up with you and Skis in a bit, Joey."

Gus walked through the mine office where a platoon of Pittsburgh and Fricktown officials stood, staring silently at him.

Gus stopped. "Gentlemen?"

"He's in the conference room, next to Hink's office, back there, last door," Squash said. "I'm Townsend, vice-president for coal ops."

"Gus Olin, AMSTEEL retiree," Gus said. "I know the way."

Gus knocked before opening the door.

Ben walked over to him, and they shook hands. "Sorry to see you in these circumstances, Gussie," Ben said.

"Long time, Benny," Gus said.

"Edna?"

"We're both doin' as well as we can expect to do at our age. Mrs. Roberson?"

"Gert came with me. She's fine. When things settle down maybe we can have a meal together, somewhere."

"Sure," Gus said. "The barometric pressure dropped fast from the cold. Gas built. We know how that works. But the intake air should have diluted it and taken it out."

"I have a theory," Ben said.

Gus raised his hands in a helpless gesture. "Me, too."

"Look over here," Ben said, leading him to the map on the wall. "This is the block where the long wall started. Here's the property line. Our best guess is the methane ignition happened in the belt return. The wall had just

666

started a day before. All the methane and ventilation readings were good at the face."

"In the return too?"

"Don't know about that," Ben admitted. "Look here. You own on the other side."

"I know. Seventy-five acres. Came from my granddad, Jacob, through Arvil to me."

"Hink says they were supposed to leave a 10-foot-wide safety buffer between you and me," Ben said.

"Wouldn't doubt a superintendent's word," Gus said.

Ben raised his eyebrows at the light jab. "But...." Ben said.

"But?"

"But Hink told the miner to drive the return five feet forward to get a little extra coal and make the dump room bigger. They were supposed to leave 10 foot, not five, between us."

Gussie closed his eyes.

"I'll write down my theory in one word on this pad," Ben said. "You do the same on that one."

"No need," Gus said. "Bootleg."

"Bootleg," Ben repeated.

"During the Strike," Gus said, "I punched my Dad's tunnel farther into our side of the hill to get out a little coal to keep the tents from freezing. I didn't have your maps, so I stepped it in with a 12-foot-long, cloth carpenter's tape. I stopped driving my entry short of where I thought the boundary line would be. It was a one-tunnel operation. Pushed my one little cart by hand on some old rails scavenged and straightened from your discards. Me an' the boys, Joey and Larry."

"You could have crossed over -- bootlegged -- onto me. Not on purpose."

"I could have," Gus said. "I was guestimatin' where the line was. But not by much."

"There still should have been coal between us," Ben said.

Gus had figured it out. "Joey shot a last face when I wasn't in there. He didn't understand we weren't supposed to advance any more. He thought he was doin' us a favor by havin' the coal ready to load when we come in the next time."

"A mistake!" Ben said. "An innocent mistake."

"If you had an idea that my old mine was over on you, why didn't you tell your men to drill test holes ahead and to the side of where they was minin'? That would keep them safe from breakin' into a water-filled mine or a gas pocket in the gob."

"I didn't know Hink was mining out a dump pad or pushing toward your line. If we were mining right up to our property line, we would have been drilling test holes ahead of mining like you say. We assumed we were safe. We both know that assumptions kill."

"Learned that right quick underground," Gus said.

"Dad had a notion you might have crossed the property line," Ben said. "I'm sure he thought the few tons you were taking weren't worth fussing about. Dad wanted to break the Strike, but he really didn't want anyone to die from starvation or freezing. Still, he knew he had to put enough hurt on you to get you back on acceptable terms. He knew you would stay on your side of the line. A couple of other boys…"

"Oral Lee and Jimmy Wayne Daubenspeck…"

"…were more than likely taking out as much of Dad's coal that winter as they could. But Dad didn't want the headline: 'Mine operator wants striker babies to freeze.'"

"Some did," Gus said.

"Some did, I know. Which is why he put up with those two bootlegging his coal," Ben said.

"If I left old works on the Fricktown line, gas would build up with not much place to go. It wouldn't show on your map as a gob area," Gus said.

"How did you ventilate?"

"Didn't much," Gus said. "Built a fire at my portal to draw out the bad air, but we had no way to get good air up to the face where we were blasting and shoveling. We went in after the fire drew out what it could. Then stayed as long as we were able to catch our breath."

"Did you crosscut any?"

"A little, but the air was even worse in a crosscut. We did do a Tee at the end of the tunnel. Not much of one. My guess is your miner punched through where Joey shot the face."

"I think you're right," Ben said.

"But the methane would have needed a spark from something. Those new continuous-miners you had to buy a few years back don't spark like the old ones."

"The cutter bits on the drum could have hit something you left," Ben said. "A rail, a lunch pail, a wheel on your car, a shovel, a…."

"…an iron pick," Gus said.

"A pick, sure."

"I always cleaned up my place before I left," Gus said. "I always took my tools home so they wouldn't rust or disappear."

"Any damn piece of metal," Ben said, shaking his head.

"If, like you say," Gus said, "the ignition started in that return, guys on the long wall might have missed the worst of it. The explosion would have blasted outby to the surface, not inby toward the face."

"I'm following you," Ben said.

"So we might get to survivors quicker by going in though my old tunnel than by working through the bad air and rubble in the mains coming in from your portal. I'd guess it's two miles back to the long wall from your portal. Maybe 300, 325 feet from my opening to your dump room."

"Is your tunnel usable, passable?" Ben asked.

"Maybe. I was in there a couple of years back when I was still a young feller. Scratched out two ton off the ribs just for me and Edna to mix with the wood. Didn't go in all the way. There wasn't no reason to take any more of my coal after the Strike ended. I remember Ben, Senior, agreed to give us miners free house coal in our 1934 contract after he signed with the ACMU."

"My, My, how we coddled you," Ben laughed. "Dad was the first steel company with captive mines to sign with the Union."

"'Coddle' was exactly the word I would use," Gus said, rolling his eyes.

"Could we get equipment into your tunnel?" Ben asked.

"Not on its best day more than 40 years ago. It's too narrow. We kept it tight so the ribs would support the roof. No roof bolts. Didn't have them back then. A few timber props here and there. But it's only five or six-feet wide, so we might be able to still get up there. It's worth a shot."

"Who?"

"Me," Gus said.

"Gus, you're 80 some. You can't go crawling around in an abandoned mine!"

"And the boys, Joey and Skis."

"You're crazier than hell," Ben said. "The 'boys' are almost 70! Joe Hunt wouldn't last 150 feet."

"We'll see. Anyway, it's my little mine. Private property—and all the rest. I say who goes in, and who don't. Those two are my helpers. It's my pick I'm guessing that was the cause of this. My mess. I clean it up."

"Let me get a couple of the rescue teams in there," Ben said.

"No."

"They have training. They have equipment."

"I have the experience. The boys and me know that tunnel. I'll not put another man at risk."

"Gus…"

"If it's blocked, we come back out. If it isn't we go in as far as the dump room in the belt return. If it's too much for us, we come out. What we need are three sets of clothes and equipment—including boots, air packs, caps, whatever fancy stuff you now use to measure carbon monoxide, oxygen and methane."

"We still use a flame safety lamp," Ben admitted, "along with methanometers."

"We need at least 19.5 percent oxygen if I remember," Gus said.

"A little more is best. I could set up a fan for you outside to push air in."

"It'd take too long to get a fan up there with a generator, then level a pad and secure them somehow. There'll be snow and ice on the north side of my hill. I might be able to get a four-wheel-drive pickup with chains and a winch up there."

"I'll get a chopper to bring equipment in," Ben said.

"There's no place to land or set up. Too many trees. This is a jackleg dog hole from 1933. It's not a multi-million-dollar AMSTEEL operation. Look, Benny, this is either going to work or not," Gus said. "And we'll know right quick whether we can get in. And if we get back in there, we'll sound a bell or an air horn to let survivors know they got a way out. If the coal's on fire, we're comin' out. We can't handle fire."

"I'll get you what you need. I'll get a pickup and drive you up there myself."

"No, you stay here. They'll need you to make decisions."

"Yes, you're right. Okay. Gert can do it," Ben said. "The girl was raised on a cattle farm in the Colorado Rockies. She knows about pickups in winter driving."

"Gert'll do," Gus said.

"I'll get a truck with a CB so she can keep in touch. Meet me over at the bathhouse as quick as you can."

Becker went over to Willie Rutherford who was waiting for someone to come to his table. The McDowell ladies had fanned out in twos, talking to local women and their families.

"Thanks for coming up, Willie," Becker said as he sat with his coffee. "Can I get you a refill? Doughnut? Sandwich?"

"I'm good," Willie said, indicating an array of a half-dozen, heaped plates Susie and others had left in front of him.

"Thanks for the campaigning you and the women have done. Do you think this explosion came from a speed-up?"

"I think the comp'ny was shortin' somewhere on somethin'," Willie said. "Mighta been not enough air at the face. Mighta been not enough rock-dustin' to keep down the coal dust. Somebody makes explosions happen either by doin' somethin' wrong or not doin' somethin' right."

"A safety committeeman told Jeep just now they were dumping coal from the long wall in an extra-wide return tunnel. He said they were using a scoot to take coal from a pile and put it on a conveyor."

"Scoop run on batteries. Wouldn't cause no spark."

"Scoop, sure."

"More likely, they was runnin' a continuous-miner back there in the return. Somehow, someway that miner set off the gas."

"Do you think there was a violation of the federal safety regulations?"

"Couldn't happen no other way. If you keep the air up and the methane down, you can't get no explosion even if you sparkin' like Reddy Kilowatt."

Becker nodded. "I just wanted to say I'm proud of what you and the women have done for miners. You all did something good."

"We gave it our shot," Willie said, "but this Fricktown, I dunno. Seems like all we done was go back further from where we started."

"The politicians can't continue to ignore you, the women, and now this," Becker said.

"We'll see," Willie said. "Politicians are pretty good at not seein' what they don't want to look at. It's plenty easy to ignore guys like me even when we're mashed up. But you never know how a hand plays out until it do."

Gus found Joe and Skis asking questions of the safety technicians as they checked their equipment. He pulled them aside.

"This shit's gotta stop," Joe said to Gus. "Fifty-seven guys!"

"You remember my old mine we worked during the Strike?" Gus asked.

"Sure," Skis said.

"That coal kept us alive," Joe added.

"We need to go back in there," Gus said.

"You think we can get to survivors through your back door that nobody knows about?" Skis asked.

"Benny knows about it. Senior knew about it. Benny's over at the bathhouse getting us equipped. His wife is gonna drive us up there."

"Jesus!" Joe said. "Why are us three doin' this?"

"Because," Gus said slowly, "I suspect we drifted close to or maybe a little over into Fricktown coal by mistake. And, it was us that left the metal the Fricktown miner hit when he was diggin' out their dump pad."

"Jesus!" Joe said.

"We're responsible?" Skis asked.

"Maybe. Probably."

"Maybe we can make it up if we can get them out," Joe said.

"That's the way it lines out to me, Joey," Gus said.

"Same here," Skis said.

"I suppose it would win me the election if we got them out," Joe said.

"That it would," Gus said.

"Do you have any idea what's in that ol' tunnel?" Joe asked Gus.

"A little. I went in there 100 feet or so back a few years for a quick look-see. But not all the way to the end. Come on. Let's get dressed."

"Like old times," Joe said.

"Pullin' Fricktown chestnuts out of the fire one more time," Skis said.

"Fifty-seven chestnuts we put in," Gus said.

"Fifty-seven," Joe said, shaking his head.

Becker knew he needed some coffee. He stood on Main Street opposite The Moose. It was snowing a little. He noticed that Fricktown's four-room houses were now aluminum-sided and added to. Chain-link fences separated them. They differed in color but not in relation to each other. They were still strung along the highway and the creek, still stepped up in lines on the contours of the hills, still an appendage to the mine.

The mountains around the town were bleak and dingy. Scraggly tree trunks stood black against the white snowscape. It looked and felt ugly, as only a dreary winter day can be. Muddy pickups drove by Becker in opposite directions. Lookers were arriving. An occasional late-model sedan with black-wall tires rolled in representing a public agency. Becker noticed an old man standing next to the AMSTEEL entrance sign. He was shaving perfect cedar curls with his pocket knife. They fell into the snowy mud. Becker thought of Roberta Magnelli in her grave. He waited for a gap in the traffic that would allow him to cross. Gaps for safe crossing were rare.

An old Pontiac sedan slowed to a stop. The window rolled down.

"Get in, asshole."

Becker shook his head in semi-disbelief.

"What are you doing here, John?" Becker asked, slipping in on the passenger side.

"Looking for you, looking for answers. Let's go for a ride."

"I'm here with Jeep Delucci."

"I figured. This won't take long."

It occurred to Becker this might be his last ride.

Corelli drove slowly.

"I need to thank you for my life," Becker said. "I now carry a pistol. See." Becker pointed to his shoulder under his winter jacket.

Corelli grunted. He stopped at a dumpster a mile outside of town.

"Hot in here, don't you think?" Corelli said, leaving the engine running, reducing the heat and opening his window. He lit a Marlboro.

"You look the same as 12 years ago," Becker said. "Hair's longer."

"You don't look the same."

"Yeah, well. I heard you were in The War."

"I was."

Becker figured his best strategy was to talk. "I ran into Ralphie Calderone outside the Circle Bar on Walnut. He said you were a LURP. Two, maybe three tours. Hard years."

"What would you know about it?"

"What I've heard."

"What would a beautician know about it? Ralphie spent his time giving buzz-cuts at Ford Ord."

"Also heard you went to work for Tony Bruno after you came home."

"Naw. I was a handyman."

"Handyman?"

"Cleaned out basements for old ladies. I also helped several young ones reset their thermostats. They kept asking me to 'unthaw' their pipes."

Becker laughed.

"Did you leave Delucci's campaign like I told you?"

"I left the other day. We sent out a press release."

"So what are you doing here with him?"

"Observing. Unofficial lawyer."

"That won't fly with the boys. So let's cut to it. What happened to Roberta Magnelli?"

Becker took a deep breath. "I didn't have anything to do with it. I wasn't there when it happened. From what I was told, she was sitting in my living room at night, waiting to kill me. Then out of the blue, totally happenstantial, two people showed up. They walked into my house, surprised her and one of them shot her before she could shoot them and me."

"I ain't horsing around with you, Becker. If you want to tell stories, write a novel. What really happened?"

"What I said."

"Who were these two people who appeared as if by bullshit magic?"

"You're not going to believe this. One was Rooky Gondleman."

"That Weather jag off?"

"I knew him at Columbia."

"And the other?"

"His girlfriend. Her name is Weez Draney."

"Weas, like a weasel?"

"Weez."

"Wheeze? Like she has asthma?"

"Louise. W-E-E-Z is her nickname. She's also in the Weather Underground. Couple of years older than Gondleman. Not real friendly."

"It was the girl, wasn't it? She did Roberta."

"That was what they told me."

"Girls have an advantage."

"Gondleman is in jail. I don't know where Weez is. They have been underground for four or five years. I hadn't seen Gondleman since 1968. Was Roberta your girlfriend?"

"She thought she was moving in that direction."

Becker thought better of pushing John Corelli's feelings on that subject. "Gondleman came to my place to rest for a few days. No advance notice. Just showed up, hoping I'd let them stay."

"Roberta didn't have time to scope you and your habits," Corelli said. "In that situation, it's always better to have two shooters. When you don't have time to do your research and plan, you often get surprised by how things happen. Roberta wasn't expecting anyone but you. That's how your two bozo friends got her."

"They aren't 'friends.' I treated them as legal clients so the conversations would be confidential in court if things came to that."

"Where were they heading?"

"They didn't say. I heard that Gondleman was arrested near Baltimore. Weez wasn't."

"Where's Roberta? My guess is she's around your place."

"Are you going to kill me, John?"

"Might."

"Why?"

"I knew you'd start asking questions first thing. Just like in high school. A real nebby-nose."

Becker laughed. "Haven't heard that one in a long time."

"Tony Bruno thinks you are totally out of Delucci's campaign. He's not going to put up with this. You won't get a pass."

"I did resign. If Jeep loses the election, I'm out. Tony then has Joe Hunt, the Bank and the ACMU free and clear. If Jeep wins, then we'll see. Plenty of lawyers up there would love to take my seat on his train."

"You're not listenin', asshole. If Delucci wins, you're going to be out voluntarily or non-voluntarily. Did you not understand what I told you? Did you not understand the message that Biggie Stover delivered? Did you not understand why Roberta was waiting for you?"

"I understood. Did you kill Biggie?"

"Do you really want to know?"

Becker shook his head, since he now knew.

"If you stay with Delucci as a winner, you will be whacked. Tony's put an X on you, which doesn't stand for exception. The reporter from Pittsburgh, he's Xed her too."

"Allyson," Becker said. "Allyson Pickering."

"Her. The last thing an LCN *padrone* wants is publicity, particularly a clear explanation of how his money is made and handled."

"A Pittsburgh detective named Greiner is watching out for her. That's what she told me."

"Greiner is well known to Bruno," Corelli said.

"What's that mean?"

"What kind of lawyer are you anyway?"

"Underutilized, underpaid and underappreciated."

"Well, you've always had a thing for the poor and oppressed. Even in high school, you couldn't pass a boat without rocking it. I remember you tried to get the principal to spend the income from our senior class play to pay for prom tickets for kids who didn't have money. The class would have voted for it if Elmer Flowers hadn't adjourned the meeting before we could vote."

"It was my first civics lesson," Becker allowed. "I was ripe for the '60s. I can't explain why."

"So you go to law school to change The System. And what do you discover? That lawyers for the poor don't get paid very much. That most of your criminal defendants are scum who did what the 'pigs' say they did. That your right-on poor people lie to your face. That The System ain't fair, and people aren't equal in the eyes of the law. That the legal issues poor people have are small and depressing, not big and noble."

"The details of what you've just described are familiar to me and discouraging," Becker admitted.

"So Crusader Rabbit decides he's going to help these hillbilly miners march on the White House and Wall Street. Is that the plan?"

"When you put it that way, it sounds pretty stupid and manipulative. I thought getting something better was better than sticking with something 'badder.' Delucci is better than Hunt. Not that Delucci is perfect."

"Delucci ain't perfect," Corelli snorted. "And even if your miners did take over their union, they'd end up being no different than Joe Hunt. No different than Nixon and Ford, the lesser crook who pardoned the greater crook. In Russia, from what I've read, the Bolsheviks were worse than the Czar who was bad enough. <u>Animal Farm</u> got it right."

"You're right. Reform falls short of promises. You can argue that we regress to the human mean. But over time we seem to be getting better at least in defining what's better and what isn't. So should I get a job murdering people for the Mafia?"

"You don't strike me as the next Bugsy Siegel," Corelli laughed. "Good assassins are stone-hearted. They're not impulsive or hot-blooded. They're methodical and detailed. Smart hitters don't drink, gamble, do drugs or call attention to themselves. The punks are loud; the pros are quiet. Any jag off can pull a trigger. An unsolved murder is art. You'd be okay on the thinking part, but I don't see you pulling the trigger."

Becker felt himself shiver. "Are you a made man?"

"No," Corelli said, "I'm no thief."

"Well," Becker said in spite of himself, "you do steal lives."

"Look, the LCN is all about stealing, whether it's swindling, shylocking, extortion, gambling or fixing races. They all come from the same motive: It's getting money that don't belong to you that you don't have to work hard for. I do honest work. I get paid only if I do the job. I don't make money off money. I don't live off the sweat of others. I don't trick people into thinking I'm doing for them when I'm really doing for myself."

"That's right, John. The only thing you do is kill people for a guy who does all the things you've just listed."

"Complicated things are complicated, not simple," Corelli said. "Cigarettes kill people all the time, innocent people. All perfectly legal. The guys who make my Marlboros, the guys who own the cigarette stocks, nothing happens to them. Why should anything happen to me? Why is killing a lot of innocent people legal, but killing one or two gangsters isn't? The guy with the law can kill you every bit as dead as I can. In some ways, deader. Anyway, the Mob mostly hits its own."

"Biggie Stover was not a criminal. He wasn't one of yours."

"An unfortunate casualty. He put himself in the way."

"Biggie was a decent guy who didn't do anything wrong."

"Life is funny," Corelli said. "Death and taxes are guaranteed, not fairplay or good results."

"You're making excuses," Becker said.

"I'm a hell of a lot more moral than Robert McNamara. I'm small potatoes, just a common sniper."

"It's a difference in scale, not kind," Becker said.

"A difference in scale is a difference in kind," Corelli said. "Does it really matter whether you die sooner or later?"

"Sure it does. The '60s would have been different had Oswald not killed Kennedy. *You* don't have the right to decide when someone dies."

"I don't."

"But you hire out to a man who does for all the wrong reasons. It's not self-defense."

"We all hire out to somebody," Corelli said. "Nobody ain't free. When you work for somebody else, you do what the boss wants done, the way the boss wants it done and when the boss wants it done. Otherwise, you don't work for nobody. If the boss wants you to stomp the guy below you, you stomp the guy below you. Otherwise, you get stomped."

"But you can choose who you work for."

"Don't matter who. It's the same shit. If you want to eat, you do what you're told. If you work for Delucci, you do what he wants you to do, not what you want to do for him."

"Sure," Becker said, "all organizations are pretty much the same. But what they're about is different. There's a difference between extortion and nursing, between selling dope and selling tulips."

"The bottom line is everything is about money—profit, salary, wages. Don't matter whether you're a wise guy or a civilian, school teacher or common thief, capitalist or communist."

"But why shoot a good guy like Biggie Stover and not a McNamara?"

"Wouldn't fix anything to kill the McNamaras. Those guys are like the Chinese army. You nail one, and there's another coming up right behind."

"You think like Gondleman. He'd argue it doesn't do any good to kill the individual in authority."

"Gondleman's been underground for a few years by choice," Corelli said. "I've been underground my whole life and mostly not by choice."

"You know, John, if you wanted to fix some small thing in the world, you could…you could take out Tony Bruno."

"Take out Tony? Okay, what's it worth to you? How much?"

"It's worth a lot, but I'm not paying you to kill him."

"If his friends found out, they'd whack me. It's not a packet of chewin' gum you're askin' me to swipe from the Woolworth's."

"Just a thought," Becker said disingenuously.

"You want me to do your dirty work for free while you keep your hands clean. You're not even offering gas money."

"You're right. I'm not leading from the front. But you would be doing coal miners, the Union, Pittsburgh and America a public service."

"Nah. Crooks are crooks," Corelli said. "Wise guys fill their own gaps. Tony and Siciliano are following orders from Frankie Fagano. The Commission needs to find a replacement for the Teamsters. That's what this is about."

"That's how I figured it."

"So you want me to kill Bruno to get you off the hook. I'll tell you what, Becker, you and me will take him out. But you need to pull the trigger at least once. You can pull it after I kill him. How's that?"

"I don't think I'm capable of being an assassin. Maybe I could."

"He'll be dead, asshole. You're not killing him!"

"Legally, I'm not sure."

"Legal. Legal. Legal. Figures," Corelli said. "I had to watch your back at Peabody. Legal didn't watch your back and won't now."

"The point is, John, Stover was not a bad guy in any sense of the word. A bad guy told you to murder a good guy, which you did."

"Which makes me what?"

"On the wrong side of things."

Corelli looked through the windshield at the grim hillsides that ran to the edge of the road. "Well, Becker, I guess I figure it that way too."

"I don't like Weez Draney," Becker said. "She means nothing to me. But what will be accomplished by evening the score with her for Roberta?"

"Globally nothing," Corelli said. "But keeping score is one way of going through life. Where is Roberta? No bullshit."

"They buried her in the woods behind my house. Gondleman said he dug a grave. I don't know exactly where. I don't want to know. I could probably find it. To be honest, I'm not highly motivated to memorialize a woman who broke into my house to kill me on Tony Bruno's orders."

"Understood," Corelli said. "We come at this from different angles."

"I need to get back," Becker said, hopefully.

"Right."

Corelli made a U-turn.

"Give Bruno some thought," Becker said. "We're a long way from Homeroom 210 at Peabody High School, aren't we? So what are you going to do?"

"I'm going back to selling Venetian blinds. I got a hot prospect in Altoona."

"Altoona, home of the Horseshoe Curve on the Pennsylvania Railroad."

"Yeah, that's it," Corelli said. "You get through the Curve, and you're heading back in the same direction that you came from."

"But you're not going backwards."

They drove into Fricktown, each thinking his own thoughts.

The Governor was wearing out. He'd been on his feet for more than an hour. His legs were tired of being stood on. His hand was limp from being shaken earnestly. His back was sore from keeping itself straight. His mouth was weary of comforting. His brain was tired of sympathizing. His heart was tired of bleeding.

He stood next to the coffee urn in the Bingo hall of the Fricktown Moose, holding a Styrofoam cup of boiled coffee. He was feeling used and useless. He had hoped his presence in the AMSTEEL garage would calm the situation, but it had not. They still hadn't agreed on a rescue plan, given the lack of information. The MESA people had taken control of the rescue and were offending Fricktown managers, ACMU miners and his own West Virginia safety people. The Governor had been left out of the conversation though not physically.

The Governor's head hurt. He saw no happy ending at the end of his day. He saw no fix, no compromise and no deal that would make things come out decently. He suspected some portion of the blame would ultimately be stuck on him. How unfair was that? Did anyone think The Governor wanted a coal mine to explode? It would become The Governor's disaster, because it happened on his watch. To be fair to himself, how could he watch for something like this? Everyone knew, of course, the West Virginia mine-inspection program was largely a *pro-forma* exercise. No one had great expectations of the state inspectors, and none were disappointed. That's what The People wanted! he said to himself. Did they really want him to close every mine in the State? He was glad the feds were the ones mainly responsible. Takes one monkey off my back, he reasoned. Maybe President Ford would step up and take responsibility. Right, he thought, and maybe Nixon would run off to Tahiti in flip flops with Bella Abzug in a bikini.

Bad coffee irritated The Governor. Bad luck irritated The Governor. Bad outcomes irritated The Governor.

Bad press irritated The Governor's wife.

678

The Governor announced he needed a break and wandered over to the bathroom. He came out and looked for her.

Nancy Waring Shortbridge noticed him wandering through the tables. He looked dazed. He needed help. She made her way to him and pecked his cheek.

"How's it going?" he asked.

"Not much I can do except pat hands. You're better at this than I am," she said. "You're good."

"Only for about an hour," he said. "Then I start thinking how all of life is absurd and what's the point? My hour is long up. I'm tired and bored."

A line had materialized behind them as West Virginians waited politely for a chance to say something to The Governor.

Mrs. Roscoe McAllister, first in line, pleaded with him to have "the State gravel my road before Roscoe's fun'ral so I can get him up the hill to bury and not have the hearse slide around like butter in a hot fry pan."

"Now, now, we don't know what's going on with Roscoe in there," The Governor said. "Let's not bury him until he's dead."

That did not come out quite right, Nancy thought.

"Well, it purely wouldn't hurt to gravel my road, one way or t'other, would it now?"

"No, certainly, it wouldn't," The Governor said.

Nancy took her hand. The Governor nodded.

"It's Poor Fork Road off Dry Run above Palestine," Mrs. McAllister said.

"I'll be sure to speak to the state road commissioner personally," The Governor said, as he indicated to an aide to take the relevant information.

Next came Woodrow "Woody" and Starlene Clatterbuck who, she said, just wanted to "thank you and the Missus for comin' all the way from Charleston to be with us in our troubles, an' by the way, our boy, Randy, who everyone calls Raunch, who got that football scholarship to Glenville State we told you about four years ago, is doin' real good an' says he wants to go into cooperative extension with the State, which, maybe, you could he'p with later on, you know?"

"We're so pleased that Raunch is doin' so well in school," Nancy said. "It's so important that West Virginia keeps its brightest students at home after they graduate."

"He's third-string all-conference," Woodrow "Woody" said. "Right guard, like the armpit spray."

"I'm sure that will help him in extension work," Mrs. Shortbridge said.

The Governor said it was a pleasure seeing the Clatterbucks again and thanked them for their work in his last campaign.

"And thank you for that $250 to drive Starlene to the polls," Woodrow "Woody" said.

"Yes. Well, have Raunch write me a letter when he graduates, and I'll put him in line for an opening."

"You want it printed or typed?" Woodrow "Woody" asked. "He can do cursive if you want."

"Whichever way Raunch feels most comfortable," The Governor said.

The Clatterbucks thanked The Governor and Nancy. They walked away, smiling amidst the sadness.

Next came Clovis Parady who wanted to let The Governor know that he could be counted on again to "work the folks over at Snakey Run next 'lection and dint think it would cost all that much more than last time." The Governor shook hands with Clovis and thanked him for his continued support. As Clovis slipped by, The Governor gave Nancy a pained look.

The Governor wanted to rest. People just didn't realize how much standing a sitting politician had to do. So he found himself nodding here and smiling there, frowning appropriately, trying not to promise something he didn't want to do, offering prophylactic condolences and invoking God in whom he hadn't believed since before prep school. He thanked each person for taking the trouble to spend a few moments with him and Nancy "at a time like this and please write me about your concern—Make sure to write PERSONAL on the envelope so I'll read it myself first thing. Or you can talk it over with my assistant who's sitting at Table 2."

Now in the third year of his first term, The Governor had learned that much of what was expected of him was to shake his head at the appropriate time and follow the advice of a fellow Democrat on the West Virginia Supreme Court, which was to say, "Ummhmm, ain't that sump'in'" when the routine irrationalities and miseries of life in The Mountain State were unburdened on him. However, the Justice warned, when a genuine tragedy presented itself, he might be tempted to say, "Ummhmm, ain't that awful." The Justice observed that "'sump'in's could be cast like crumbs to ducks with no harm done to either the ducks or the tosser. But "them 'awfuls' could get you in trouble and make you more enemies than a fat worm in a pond of piranhas." "Why is that?" The Governor had asked. "Because somebody in this State is almost always the cause of some other body's 'awful.' And more than likely, that somebody who's causin' the awful is more important than that somebody who's complainin' to you."

Despite this advice, The Governor had once let slip "That's just dreadful!" as a UNICOAL helicopter flew him over a surface mine in Kanawha County during his first campaign for the governor's office. The operation was employing a mining technique originally termed "mountaintop decapitation," which the industry quickly renamed "head of the valley fill." The Governor's honest outburst found its way onto the front page of <u>The Charleston Gazette</u> about a month before he lost that election.

The first body was hauled through the Bingo hall past the doughnut table a few minutes later. It was deposited in the banquet room, which was serving as the transitional morgue. The next two were hauled directly into the banquet area after The Governor suggested using a different route.

The Governor had been spared death, save for the comely parting of a maternal grandmother during his college years. The plague of the Vietnam War had spared him as if he were an Israelite in the land of Egypt. During 1966 to 1971, the War's bloodiest days, no one he knew had been conscripted. Two who had gone in survived the misery of the Washington delta and the small-arms conflicts of the Georgetown bar scene.

The Governor could not avoid watching death pass by. The commotion assaulted him. He could not help seeing the Fricktown volunteer rescue squad in red jumpsuits rolling bodies through The Moose. He heard mothers, wives and daughters screaming, then rushing forward and shouting "Is it?" The keening began, which disoriented him. It assaulted his sense of propriety and breeched his sense of quiet privacy. Loud, indecorous, unmediated—this working-class grief knocked him off his pegs. He felt Nancy's hand squeezing his in support.

The Governor would remember Nancy flailing at him, grabbing at his jacket, before he toppled face-first onto the linoleum floor of the Bingo room in The Fricktown Moose.

Chapter 48

Fricktown, December 4, 1975

Allyson listened to KDKA driving south from Pittsburgh. Then she picked through a couple of Morgantown stations, hoping for updates. She got to Fricktown in mid-morning and passed Shorty's Gulf on the corner. She saw him standing next to the cash register. She waved. He waved back; Shorty remembered the VW girl who had gone out with Franco Harris. Allyson parked off Main Street, close to the old iron bridge over Black Creek. Walking around the corner, she ran into Davey Bloom.

"Davey!"

"Allyson!"

Neither knew whether to shake hands, hug or stand stupidly doing neither.

"I miss you, Davey," she blurted, surprising herself.

"Did you land yet, hon?" he asked.

"Freelancing," she said.

"This is Ross Loende," Bloom said. "I'm breaking him in. Allyson Pickering."

Allyson shook hands with Loende who had heard the newsroom gossip about her.

"So you're still sniffing for buried bones in this dog pound?" Davey asked.

"You could put it that way."

"Maybe some time later, we could bring you back on."

"For what? Garden clubs and fashion shows?"

"Maybe we could get you to Washington as the PG desk. Just a thought, hon."

"I'm spoiled meat," she said. "I stink."

"Yeah, well, stink eases off after a year, maybe two. I might be able to get it through the ownership if you promise to be a good girl. Ownership seems uncommonly forgiving in your case."

"That's more than I deserve," Allyson said.

"Of course, it would be easier if your various conspiracy theories actually prove up."

"Truth is a pretty good defense," she said.

"You ain't there, hon."

"You're right, Davey. I'm not. I've also been warned to stop poking around."

"What kind of warning?"

"It came through my boyfriend, I guess, maybe. He was my fiancé, not sure now. Anyway Kennedy works at Scraife downtown. He told me a

682

lawyer flew in from New York. Says his clients have a lot of accounts with Scraife, and they heard something. He tells Ken that he should get me to stop digging if he knows what's good for both of us. Says he's heard the Mafia will kill us if I don't."

"Jesus!" Bloom said.

"Mary and Joseph! Don't leave them out," she said. "I need all hands on deck."

"New York—that's Frank Fagano, head of The Five Families," Bloom said. "He's the top guy above Tony Bruno."

"I'd guess it was New York money that bought the ACMU's bank in Washington," Allyson said.

"Yes," Bloom said, "Bruno's not big enough to handle that."

"I suppose they'll install some sleeze like Allen Dorfman at the Teamsters pension fund to run it," she said. "Dorfman gave $250 million to mobsters to build hotels and casinos in Las Vegas. The ones built in the '60s were connected to Meyer Lansky. These unsecured loans were never repaid!"

"An ugly story," Davey said. "Ordinary truck drivers had their pensions ripped off so the Mafia could build casinos for free."

"The second dip," Allyson said, "was skimming in the counting rooms. The skim gave the Mob untraceable, tax-free cash. Their Vegas enforcer is Tony "The Ant" Spilotro. The accountant who handles the skim might be Lefty Rosenthal at the Hacienda, Stardust, Marina and Fremont. That's what I've picked up."

"Stop, stop. You're doing it again!"

"Davey, there *is* a Mob. You know that. They do steal money. They do corrupt unions. They do kill people. They are not fictional characters. They are not nice businessmen who do nothing but pray to the Virgin Mary on Sunday and give cookies to crippled orphans on Christmas."

"It's proof, Allyson. P-R-O-O-F. It's still the same thing with you and this story. Wanting truth is not knowing truth."

"I'm just giving you background, context," she said defensively. "If Delucci took over, he might disclose information that Joe Hunt wanted to keep hidden."

"I doubt it. Why would he tarnish the organization he would be running? He'll bury whatever he discovers."

"I suppose you're right…again," she said.

"You might get something out of your old boyfriend—the Becker kid who's running Jeep's campaign."

"That's a dead end in every sense."

"You never know, hon. Old flames never go out all the way. Blow on it and see what happens. It takes you back to a simpler time in your life. But if it didn't work out the first time, the odds are it won't work out the second."

"An uplifting note. So?"

"So use him as a source if you insist on gambling with your life on this story, which I hope you don't."

"Before you told me not to use him," Allyson said. "You said either I would end up exploiting him or he, me."

"That was then. You are no longer employed by a reputable newspaper or anybody else. People use other people. It *is* our business."

"I think he left the campaign."

"He hasn't left what he saw, what he knows."

"I don't need the money," she said.

"Good," Bloom said. "Then my best advice is to forget coal miners and mobsters. Marry this banker. Have a couple of kids. Move to Fox Chapel. Join the League of Women Voters. Run bake sales for peace and go door to door collecting for cancer. Or you and the banker can move to Washington and hobnob with The Leadership. You belong up there more than you belong in Fricktown on its worst day."

Allyson felt tears welling up. She turned her head away.

Davey Bloom hated when he made a woman cry. Once said, his words could never be deleted from her memory or his. Apologies never worked. This was just a conversation between an editor and a former employee. Why cry over *bupkes*? Who cries over goat shit?

"Ah, come on, Allyson," he said. "Stop. Please."

Allyson wiped her eyes with the sleeve of her coat. She preferred an inelegant gesture to fumbling in her bag for a tissue. "Yes," she said.

"I can't fix your life," he said. "I could never fix my own."

"Yes," she said.

"But look. Do a freelance interview for us with Delucci if he wins. I'll run it under a pen name just like in Hollywood with blacklisted writers. Pay's the same. Management will soften, then you can come back."

"Stick me on obits and be done with me," she said.

"Nope. You're too good for that. Keep in touch. I'll do what I can."

"Thanks."

Davey Bloom and Ross Loende walked through the falling snow toward the mine entrance where they saw a gathering.

"So that's Allyson Pickering," Loende said. "She looks like the girls who wouldn't go out with me in high school."

"Never fault a woman for having good judgment and good looks."

"Do you think she has her hands on what's going on?"

"Sure. Her ideas are plausible," Davey said. "This death threat against her—that's entirely believable. Killing is just another Mob negotiating tactic. When words fail, bullets don't. That's why the paper never went after them. We reported their arrests and intramural killings, but we never dug deeply into how they operate. That news is not worth the risk of antagonizing them. You don't win a fight when you bring a pencil, and they bring a .38. Even when you win, you lose too much."

"Their eraser trumps our pencil," Loende said.

"Yeah. In the short run, the sword is mightier than the pen," Davey said.

"Do you think she'll quit?"

"Would you?"

"Sure."

Davey looked at his new labor reporter with one eyebrow raised. "I don't think she will."

"Is this a road?" Gert Roberson asked in honest ignorance as she inched the Dodge Ramcharger up the slope, slithering between rocks and saplings in an old bench cut that gained elevation through switchbacks.

"Yes, ma'am," Joe Hunt said.

"Gert, please."

"Yes, ma'am, Gert. It used to be, anyways. Sort of a road."

"Who built it? General Braddock on his way to the Battle of the Monongahela?"

"No, ma'am, Gert," Joe said. "Gussie's people laid it out and cut it in with hand tools."

"Daddy fashioned a horse-drawn pan scraper out of a junk water tank he found at your dump," Gus said. "On its best day, it was just a rough-as-a-cob, mule-and-wagon road. More mule than wagon to be honest about it. It's growed up and gone downhill since. During the Strike, it was all foot, 'cause we had to eat the mule. Carried coal back to the tents in burlap feed sacks on our backs."

"We were so hungry I was ready to eat the wagon," Joe said.

"I'm sure that was hard to get through," Gert said.

The three gave unvoiced agreement. No one wanted to go back there with Mrs. Ben Roberson, Junior.

"How much farther?" she asked.

"This good section ends about 150 yards yonder up the hill," Gus said. "Then we're gonna take the chainsaw out in front of you and cut a path for the last couple hundred yards. Saplings mostly. If we bring out survivors, we may need to get them into vehicles with as little walkin' and carryin' as possible."

Gert crawled the borrowed SUV over what her best judgment told her was the roadway. The foreman who had volunteered his vehicle to Ben Roberson had chained up all four wheels.

Gus sat in the passenger seat while Joe and Skis rattled around under the removable top. Equipment borrowed from the Fricktown mine lay under their feet, at their sides and behind them.

Gert wanted to maintain a steady speed and avoid spinning her wheels. Three inches of snow covered the ground. If she could get to the old mine and turned around without hanging up, she could follow her own tracks down even through deeper snow.

"Worse comes to worst, you can walk from here if I get stuck," she said.

The thought of walking a half mile, uphill over icy ground, made Joe Hunt grimace.

"Do the best you can, ma'am, Gert," Joe said. "You're doin' real good so far."

"I learned on a '35 International half-ton pickup," Gert explained. "My winter job before school was to drive hay out to the cattle. I had to get up hilly, ice-slick pastures. Cattle would follow me anywhere. Hauled stovewood and firewood off the mountain with my Dad on weekends. Four-wheel drive and chains make things a lot easier than that."

The men were impressed.

"Is there a place to turn around up there?" she asked.

"Maybe," Gus said. "We can help you with a push or two if you lose traction."

It occurred to Gert that she might have more traction with the three old men sitting in the Ramcharger than with them outside trying to push.

"Wherever you go," Gert said, "you always need a turnaround to get back home."

"It feels to me like I'm comin' home right now," Joe said.

"Mr. Hunt, you're doing a very good job over that axle," Gert smiled into her rearview mirror.

"If you need dead weight, ma'am, I'm your man," Joe said.

"We all are," Gus said.

Gus unlimbered the chainsaw a few minutes later and began clearing the overgrown road. Joe and Skis threw his cuttings down the slope. They made a narrow passage with a steep drop on the outside edge.

Joe tried not to look out of breath. He wasn't spent, but the years of not doing physical labor came at a cost that was obvious after 10 minutes. The closer to the mine they got and the steeper the grade, the more he stopped to collect his wind and reinstall his stamina. Skis was slighter and in better shape. Gus who still cut and split firewood every year was sweating but had a lot left. He watched Joe bend under his efforts but said nothing. He remembered when Joe Hunt could load twice as much coal twice as fast as he could.

"Coy Hunt, my granddaddy, used to own all this," Joe said to Gus, so that he could take a rest.

"Yep. My Daddy, Arvil, bought it after he come back from France in 1919," Gus said to Gert. "Coy and Lucinda Hunt kept one small piece out

686

of the mineral and surface sales to AMSTEEL. Coy's widder needed money, my mother told me. Mrs. Hunt was glad Daddy could buy it with his military savin's, 'stead of givin' it over to AMSTEEL. No offense meant. By that time, she'd seen what Coy had done by sellin' his min'ral rights. Lucinda hated Fricktown and the mine."

"Men made those decisions," Gert said. "On both sides."

"Granddaddy Coy killed hisself," Joe said to Gert, "up on the mountain. Couldn't bear to live with the shame of his mistake."

"Mountain folks back then had no idea what their coal rights were worth," Skis said, "or what would happen to their land after they sold 'em."

"'...visiting the iniquity of the fathers on the children and the children's children, to the third and the fourth generation,'" Gus said.

"*Exodus 34:7*," Gert said.

"Wasn't so much a *sin* of the father," Skis said, "as simple ignorance."

"They didn't know what they didn't know," Gus said.

"Dint know what they couldn't know," Joe said.

"I never thought eating from the tree of knowledge was a bad idea for either women or men," Gert said.

They arrived at the old tunnel about 2:15 p.m., after an hour of working in the cold.

Gert told Ben they were at the entrance though it was unlike any portal she had seen during her 35 years of marriage to a coal-company president. At first, all she saw was a tall thicket of blackberry canes. Behind that, she could make out a black hole, a doorway without a door. Gus cut the canes with the chainsaw, and everyone stomped the mess into the snow.

"Here it is," Gus said, putting his chainsaw back in the Dodge.

"Right where we left it," Joe said.

"Ain't much," Skis said.

"Was never meant to be," Gus said. "Jes' a way to survive."

It's darker in there, Gert thought, than the inside of Dick's hatband, an expression she'd learned from her South Carolina-born grandmother. Gert never knew exactly how dark the inside of Dick's hatband was, but she had always assumed nothing could ever be blacker. This hole scared her, because it looked blacker than she could imagine.

Gert inched the Dodge back and forth to turn it around. The three men offered directions and suggestions, which sometimes helped.

With the Dodge facing downhill, the men unloaded. They changed into orange coveralls with reflective stripes, waterproof jackets, knee pads and 16-inch-high rubber boots with steel toes. They put on hardhats with battery lamps. Each carried a special air pack -- a self-contained, breathing apparatus that resembled scuba gear -- along with their miner's kit of tools and safety instruments hung on their leather belts. Gus had a pickax and square-nosed shovel. Skis carried a large first-aid kit and a light-duty roof jack. Joe looped two extra flashlights on his belt and carried a six-pound miner's sledge with a hammer face at one end and a point at the other to break up big chunks. They carried food and water in backpacks.

"Here's the plan," Gus said. "We don't have the strength or the materials to remove rubble or timber up this entry. So we're just going to slip our way in as far we can and see if we can make contact with survivors. If she's blocked, we come out. If there's fire, we come out. If the air's bad, we put on the packs. If we're short on air, we come out. There's no point in getting ourselves in a jam or worse."

"This shit weighs a ton," Joe said.

"It'll weigh worse when we start crawlin' on our knees," Gus said. "But it's only but 300 feet, maybe a little more, all the way to the back."

"I can do that," Joe said, feigning confidence in conditioning he did not have.

"Maybe just me an' Gus should go in, the two little guys," Skis said.

"No," Joe said. "My neck ain't worth more than yours."

"Gert, we're going in on a straight line," Gus said. "If one of us shouts, you should be able to hear it out here if there's no blockage. If we can get through to the Fricktown side, you probably won't be able to hear us. We might be out in 10 minutes or a lot longer. Just depends. If we will be more than three hours, I'll send Skis back to let you know what's going on. I have 2:35."

"Same," Gert said.

"I was in a few years ago," Gus said to Joe and Skis as the four stood in front of the portal. "Remember that little mine wagon we made out of chestnut boards. It was still usable. Dabbed some grease on the axles, and she rolled like a B&O express. Had to stub in the roof at a few places with oak posts. Them yellow locust posts we put in were still solid after 40 years, least as far as I went. They were decked out with furry white funguses like they were dressed for a weddin'."

"A weddin' for ghosts," Joe said.

"Did you check for methane?" Skis asked.

"It was about two percent, but that's still below explosive."

"Shouldn't be no methane in there now," Skis said. "The explosion on the Fricktown side should have popped our gas."

"We need to check for blackdamp," Gus said to Gert. "It's a mixture of nitrogen, carbon dioxide and water vapor that takes the place of oxygen. We can't breathe that. And then there's whitedamp, a mixture of carbon monoxide and hydrogen sulfide."

"If there's fire burnin' on the Fricktown side," Joe said, "it might be pullin' over good air through our tunnel. That would mean we'd have good air when we're in Fricktown coal."

"Might could," Gus said as he entered.

688

"It's time," Joe said, switching on his cap lamp.

"I guess ol' times seem better after they're long gone," Skis said, doing the same.

"Three broke-down, old miners goin' underground one last time," Joe said with a grin that Skis hadn't seen for many years.

"I'm sure I've seen sorrier crews," Gus said. "But none come to mind."

"C'mon," Joe said, "minin' is jes' like ridin' a damn bicycle."

"When's the last time you was 'ridin' a damn bicycle'?" Skis asked Joe.

"Now duck goin' in," Gus said. "Remember the seam squeezed down to about four feet here at the portal then gains height as it goes toward the Fricktown line."

"Shit," Joe said, "I scraped my back. Guess I'm bendin' higher than I once did."

"Look," Gus said, "there's the rail car. Load your stuff. We'll push it in as far as we can."

"I remember boltin' this wagon together," Joe said. "The three of us. The old chestnut boards were probably somebody's johnny. You showed us how to smith the corner braces at a splayed-out angle so it'd hold more."

"Comp'ny trick back in the old days when they paid by the car, not the ton," Gus said, putting his equipment in the cart. "They used to side up and side out one-ton cars to hold 2,300 to 2,400 pounds each. You take a man who loads five cars a shift, that's about 350 pounds extra a car, or 1,750 pounds of free coal to the comp'ny a shift per man, times 300 shifts a year—that's, let's see, 525,000 pounds of free coal, which is a little over 260 tons, times 200 miners, that's 52,000 tons of coal a year the comp'ny never paid us for. The first ACMU contract made 'em weigh the damn coal honest or pay by the hour. We got our own checkweighman to make sure the tonnage was tallied fair."

"I'm amazed you can still do that arithmetic in your head," Joe said. "I remember you explainin' this to us when we first went in."

"I remember quoting *Leviticus 19:35* to Ben, Senior, just before the Strike," Gus said.

"I'm a little rusty," Joe said.

"It amounts to don't use dishonest standards when measuring length, weight or volume," Gus said. "Ben, Senior, said it wasn't dishonest to pay a 2,000-pound rate for a 2,400-pound car as long as us miners knew about it."

"I remember the screen trick Daddy told me about," Joe said, "before the Union come in. Comp'ny would pay only for lump coal, 'cause it held heat longer and wasn't as messy. Folks wanted lump for their furnaces and stoves. Comp'ny announced they wouldn't pay us for bug dust and fines.

689

They set up screens to keep the lump and drop out the other. Well, Daddy understood that was sort of fair. But then they started makin' the screen holes bigger. That let nut coal, chestnut and slack drop through into the no-pay pile along with the dust. And then they turned around and forced their miners to buy back them droppin's for their house coal. People jes' forget how they done us."

"Well, we did 'em back a time or two," Skis said, "sneakin' a little slate in with the lump, parkin' the loaded cars under a roof drip so it'd weigh more on the scale."

"The score never evened up," Gus said. "They always owed us. You jes' carry them kind of debts on your books."

"An uncollectible debt," Joe said. "It was a big day when John L. Lewis got them to pay us by the hour."

Their talk lapsed as they started pushing the car. Gus and Joe got behind while Skis walked ahead, clearing debris from the narrow tracks. Gus played out a safety line that he ribboned off every 50 feet with fluorescent tape, marking distance from the entrance.

At 50 feet, Gus stopped. "Let's try that gas gizmo."

Skis unhooked the methanometer from his belt. He held it up. "Needle is way over on the left side of the scale. One percent; no problem."

Gus unhooked the anemometer from his belt. The small disk fan rotated slowly. "About 100 cubic feet per minute comin' in behind us."

"That's about what you'd get standin' in the checkout at the Fricktown IGA," Joe said.

"It's somethin'," Skis said.

"Need a minimum of 3,000 cfms at every workin' face," Joe said. "I put that language in the '69 Safety Act."

"You done good on that, Joey," Gus said.

Skis, who had drafted that language and pushed it through the Congressional committees, busied himself with refocusing his cap lamp. Then he pulled out a small glass tube with an aspirator bulb at one end.

"What's that?" Joe asked.

"Probably a damn canary," Gus said.

"The chemical stuff in the tube changes color, dependin' on how much carbon monoxide is present. A man wouldn't be able to walk after only an hour of breathin' air with no more than four one hundredths of one percent CO. Three-tenths and your dead within an hour. At one percent CO, you turn that cherry red 'cause your hemoglobin is combining with the CO, not oxygen. You die in a minute or two at one percent. We put on the air packs at two or three one hundredths. We're okay right here."

"If we run into whitedamp," Gus said, "it'll be on the Fricktown side. We'll smell the hydrogen sulfide."

Joe cut his light onto a floor-to-ceiling red-oak prop whose fibers were shredding due to the weight of the roof rock above it. "Housekeepin' could use some work," he said and then spat tobacco juice on the post. "Let's go."

As Joe pushed the cart with Gus, he acknowledged to himself that he had, as Gus had said, forgotten.

He'd forgotten the feeling of being an ant with an unpredictable boot poised above him. He'd forgotten how it felt to have thousands of tons of rock suspended over an emptiness that he himself created. He'd forgotten how it felt to be betting that the jaws in which he was working would not snap shut. He'd forgotten, too, the beguiling peacefulness of an idle mine. His aching knees, thighs, back and neck now reminded him of what else he'd forgotten. And if they weren't enough, he'd rasp his back on the low roof or knock his hardhat against it. What he remembered was how to forget all of that so that he could do the job, come out and do it again the next day.

Gus had been right, Joe thought. I've known it for a long time. Even Jeep Delucci had been right. My time has passed. I fucked up. Hadn't meant to but had just the same. Lost my bearings up there. The thing was, Delucci, too, would forget in time. Maybe he had already started.

So what's left for me? I owe Siciliano and Bruno. They have the Bank, and they'll come after the Union. They got me cornered. Once, I might have been strong enough, maybe, to prevent a takeover. But now, I don't know. If I don't play ball, they'll make me vanish like Jimmy Hoffa. That would scare Delucci and everyone at headquarters into doing whatever Siciliano wanted. If I lose, then I'm free. Then it's Delucci's problem. If I lose, I'll move to Florida and chase golf balls and young widows. I hear they do most of the chasing.

Joe saw himself in Florida, sitting next to his phone in an air-conditioned living room with the shades down, hoping for a ring. He would be killing days, waiting for time to take him.

Joe spat into the dust on the mine floor and crawled through it, not caring. He'd crawled through worse.

Gus tied a second ribbon at 100 feet. The track was good enough, and the roof had not caved. Here and there, Skis had to shovel the tracks clear of coal that had peeled off the tunnel's ribs.

They stopped for a breather at 150 feet.

"How much you figure this cart weighs?" Joe asked.

"About 250 pounds, unloaded," Gus said. "Maybe 100 pounds of equipment in it."

"Slight uphill grade goin' in," Joe said, sitting with his back to a rib and his legs stretched straight across the tracks.

"Yes, slight," Gus said. "That's why there ain't no water in this tunnel. I dug it that way to let the water drain out by gravity."

"I remember that old squatty Chow dog of yours, pullin' this wagon in and out for a time," Joe said to Gus.

"For a time," Gus repeated. "Red was give to me as a pup. Good dog."

"Nice dog," Skis said. "Had that blue-black tongue."

"Didn't complain about doin' his job," Gus said.

"Yeah, well, he wasn't a-draggin' no watermelon between his front feet and his hind like me," Joe laughed.

"Good dog," Gus said.

No one mentioned they had eaten Red in March, 1933, and then boiled his bones for soup.

"We're okay on carbon monoxide," Skis said, putting the measuring device in the rail car.

"I'm ready," Joe said, resuming his place behind the cart.

Just beyond the 250-foot ribbon, they came to a roof fall that covered the track. Skis crawled forward to scout for an opening and test the roof. Gus and Joe came in behind him. They cut their lights through the rubble pile, along the ribs and toward the jagged hole in the roof.

"I'll give her a try on the right," Skis said, as he took off everything that hung from his miner's belt except his lamp's battery.

Skis scooted debris behind him as he wiggled forward through the crawl tube he was making. Gus and Joe followed his progress with their lights focused on the soles of his boots. Then they saw his boots disappear as he squirmed left into the center of the tunnel.

"Shit," Joe said, "I'm twice his size."

"Fried chickens comin' home to roost, Joey," Gus said.

They saw Skis' light coming back through the hole about 10 minutes later.

"The fall goes about 15 foot," Skis said, plopping out of the hole onto the mine floor. "First six feet are a little tight. Joe can make it. Wagon has to stay here. You hand me the stuff, and I'll move it through. I walked in another 50 foot or more. I seen where the Fricktown miner broke through onto Gus. I didn't go up there, 'cause I figured I might need an air pack. I'll open her up some more for Joe."

"The crawlspace should let more good air through from my side," Gus said.

"Unless I cork it up," Joe said.

"Maybe you should stay here, Corky," Gus said.

"No. I'll slip through," Joe said, "like a young slickery turd."

"That's one way of lookin' at yourself," Gus said. "Joey, you hand me stuff, and I'll work it up to Skis."

Twenty minutes later, they had completed shuttling their equipment through the roof fall. Gus was on the far side.

It was Joe's turn to squirm through. To prevent a snag, he unclipped his cap lamp and battery and pushed them ahead. He got on his belly and lifted up on his knee pads and elbows.

Too hard, he thought. Don't have the strength in my arms and shoulders to do it that way. Just have to sniper-crawl on my belly, pushin' with my left toe while movin' my right knee up, then drag up my left leg while keepin' it straight. At least, it's not hot. Bad enough as it is with the sweat runnin' into my eyes.

Five minutes later, Joe popped his head out of the rubble. "'Here's Johnny.'"

They organized their equipment and strapped on air packs without deploying the facemasks. They made their way through the last part of their old tunnel where the seam was six-feet high.

At the breakthrough, they stopped. Chunks of coal were underfoot. They stepped over the pile.

"Blow your horn, Gabriel," Gus said.

Joe blew three blasts on the air horn, then three more.

They listened for shouts or metal pounded against metal.

"Again," Gus said.

Six more blasts. No response.

"Take your readings," Gus said.

"Methane's okay," Skis said, "Air flow about the same. CO's up. Better start using the packs. They give us two hours. We should take the first-aid kit, water, flashlights and whatever tools we can carry."

Air packs meant, they knew, less chance of finding survivors.

Joe spat out his tobacco reluctantly.

The three put on the face masks with the Y-shaped cartridge that protruded like overgrown buckteeth. They edged into the Fricktown return entry. Their cap lights immediately found the continuous-miner. Its tracks had been blown off. Its orange paint was blistered and singed a mottled Halloween black. Gus went over to the man on the ground and shook his head.

"Cloy Casdorph," Gus said, "Okie's youngest. Not much left."

Gus and Skis went over to the ruined shuttle buggy.

"Skip Harless," Gus said. "Ray and Twila's boy."

"Hard to recognize them with their faces burnt like that," Skis said.

"Yeah, it is," Gus said.

As Joe walked around the front of the continuous-miner, his foot touched something hard on the floor, hard in a different way from the coal. He bent over. His cap lamp spread a tight circle of light at his feet.

He picked up the curved head of an iron pick. It still had the broken stub of a hickory handle through its eye, as snug as ever.

Joe ran his hand over the prying chisel at one end and the point at the other. And then his finger found the shiny, two-inch-long groove that the Joy's carbide cutting bit had gouged into the cast iron. He brought the pick head close to his light. He found nothing on one side. He turned it over.

$\mathcal{G}$ O

Joe ran his finger over the initials Gus Olin had scratched at the mine's smithy in the 1920s.

It's my pick, Joe thought, the one Gus gave me when I started work. It's the pick I left at the face and never went back for.

Joe hung his head and closed his eyes.

How does something like this happen more than 40 years later? he asked himself. What are the odds, the damn odds? Gussie should have been Union president, not me.

Joe walked over to Gus who was standing with Skis by Casdorph's body. With masks on, they could still talk understandably in the silence of the dead mine.

Joe handed the pick head to Gus. "It's the one you give me. I left it in the hole the last time we was in."

Gus examined the pick head. "It's one of mine," he said, giving his answer some quick thought, "but I'm not sure this is the one I gave you. It's possible I took yours home and left my own by mistake. Can't say one way or the other."

Joe peered at Gus through his mask. Was Gus deliberately climbing on the hook with him or was this honest uncertainty?

"Mine had a point and a pry chisel," Joe said. "Not double pick points."

"Mine, too," Gus said. "Could've been you or it could've been me, Joey. But here's the nub—this was my hole. It was my responsibility to housekeep the workplace."

"It was me, us maybe, not likely, but maybe," Joe said.

"Don't matter at this point," Skis said.

"Yeah, it does," Joe insisted.

"Let's focus on the survivors," Skis said. "I don't know exactly how these long walls lay out, but my guess is the explosion would run down the returns and not back up the intake mains that much. Survivors who were workin' the wall might've forted up somewhere along it. Others could have found them. We're not goin' to be able to get all the way over to the

694

old continuous-miner sections where most of the guys were, but we should check for survivors over as far as the headpiece.

"Worth a shot," Joe said.

"We'll have to walk that whole face," Skis said, looking at Joe. "We'd have to share our air with survivors to get them out."

"Will share what we can. Twelve-hundred feet," Gus said. "That's what I understand."

"What if the hydraulic hoses got burned up?" Skis asked. "The roof canopies could be collapsed."

"Maybe they make the hoses fire-resistant," Joe said.

"The hydraulic fluid won't burn with all the PCBs in it," Skis said.

"Boys, we're poolin' our ignorance," Gus said. "We'll know soon enough if the canopies are down. Maybe they have some kind of automatic lock-in that happens when the electric is cut to the hydraulic pump. If the jacks are down, we'll have to head back. No choice about that. Joey, you gonna do this?"

"I'll make it," Joe said.

"Okay," Gus said. "We walk the face, check the headpiece and intake for survivors. We have an hour and 45 minutes left until we have to be back in the good air in our old tunnel."

"Time isn't exactly on our side," Skis muttered.

"Time ain't never on no one's side," Gus said.

"Come on," Joe said.

Skis led them under the long wall's canopied walkway. The coal face was on their right. On their left was the line of hydraulic roof supports whose cantilevered shields still supported the rock roof over their heads. They moved slowly under the jacks. They saw no damage to the machinery.

"Take a reading," Gus said to Skis.

"CO's up. Poisonous. Maybe a couple of hours of survival at this level."

"Let's finish this," Gus said.

As he moved along the unfamiliar long wall, the story, as Joe told it in 1933, came back to Gus.

It had taken them the better part of a day at the end of March to undercut, blast and hand-push about 1,500 pounds to the outside. There, they shoveled the coal into feed bags of about 60 pounds each, which they would take back to the tents -- two bags per man per trip -- and distribute to those who had run out. Each tent was warmed by a small cook stove with a pipe through a thin square of asbestos board sewn into the canvas top.

Joe had volunteered to stay and load the last of the coal into the rail car, which would give them a head start the next time they came in. It meant they wouldn't have to load in unventilated air from a fresh shot. "Won't take me long," Joe said. Skis offered to stay with him, but Joe told him to go out with Gus.

Earlier, Joe had borrowed Gus's pick, because he'd broken the helve on the first one Gus had given him. He laid the unusable pick near the face so he wouldn't forget to take it home for repair when he left. It was easy to forget things like that in the blackness. He loaded the car.

On his own, Joe decided to shoot the next lift to save them time when they next needed coal. Using Gus's pick, he knelt in front of the face and started undercutting a V-shaped groove, with the mine floor serving as its level leg. A V-cut let the coal fall when detonated. Gus made the boys promise never to "shoot from the solid" without an undercut even though it was easier and faster. Shooting from the solid required more powder to fracture the coal, created more dust, weakened the roof and left pieces smaller than the preferred lumps. Joe advanced the V by picking it out as he lay on his side and reaching in under the overhanging coal. When he had notched the V three feet in and a foot high at its mouth, he stood up. He took his five-foot-long breast auger and drilled two holes. He poured black powder into two paper cylinders. Then he tamped them into his holes with a wood rod. He pierced the end of the charges with a copper spear and inserted an ignition squib in each one. He packed the drilled opening with clay, then lighted the squib. It was a good shot. The coal broke in easily loaded chunks. Gus, Joe figured, would be pleased with his initiative, though he'd be scolded for blasting by himself. Joe thought he'd done a good job, even a good deed.

Joe gathered Gus's pick and auger. He walked the length of the tunnel. He was hungry. He hoped he'd find something to eat in the camp. As he was putting on his winter jacket by the entrance, Joe later told Gus, he realized he'd left his broken pick near the undercut where the shot coal had buried it. Joe was tired and weak from hunger. He had not wanted to make another roundtrip to the face to retrieve his broken pick. He apologized for breaking one of Gus's housekeeping rules—take care of your tools and they'll take care of you. Joe knew Gus was right about that. Tools lasted longer, worked better and even safer when they were clean, sharp and tight. Joe knew Gus would have gone back and dug the damn pick from under the coal no matter how tired and hungry he was. He would have taken it home, sharpened the point and fitted it with a new hickory handle.

Gus couldn't spare himself from these habits of craft. More than habits, they were like the fixed tiller of his personality. Joe and Skis had memorized the rules, because they'd seen them prove themselves. A half-done job is not plenty good enough, so do it right the first time. A stitch in time saves nine. Don't quit in the middle of a hard job. Do it fast, and you'll do it over. Many shortcuts end up taking twice the time.

When Joe returned to the tents after dark, he told Gus about the pick. Gus considered walking the two miles back to his mine that night but decided that level of obedience to his own work ideology was too rigid even for him.

"Forget it for now," Gus said to Joe. "We'll get it first thing the next time we're in."

"You want me to go back and fetch it out? I will."

"No. We'll find it when we clean up your shot. Won't be long until we need some more," Gus said.

The end of March and the first days of April in 1933 were unseasonably warm. The tents did not need to be heated. Gus, Joe and Skis did not have to bring more coal to the strikers.

The settlement was announced at the end of the first week in April at ACMU headquarters in Washington.

The 2,000 strikers busied themselves with moving back into their Fricktown rentals. Work started at the mine the day after the settlement. Gus had no need to reenter his mine. He had spare picks. The coal Joe shot in late March, 1933, was never disturbed. The broken-handle pick lay beneath it.

Gus remembered Joe and the pick. What Joe did or did not do, what Joe did or did not remember, didn't matter. Gus knew it had been his responsibility.

They got close to the long-wall's headpiece with an hour left on their air packs. Skis checked for carbon monoxide.

"Bad," he said, shaking his head. He blasted the air horn, three long, three short.

Nothing.

They found the ventilation curtain a few minutes later.

MEN HERE

They stopped. They knew what was behind the canvas barricade.

I'm too old for this, Joe thought.

Skis closed his eyes.

Gus shook his head.

Joe moved the line of concrete blocks holding down the front of the curtain. Gus and Skis followed him in.

They counted 19 men, sitting together, facing each other, boots to boots. Their skin was bright red. Each had scribbled a goodbye on a paper napkin. Their spent self-rescuers lay next to them.

Carbon monoxide had mixed with their hemoglobin so their blood could no longer carry oxygen. At low CO, they would have felt tired and dizzy. Their judgment would have drifted. At higher concentrations, they would have slipped into unconsciousness without nausea, convulsions or a feeling of suffocation. Death could have come in minutes or as long as an hour.

Joe felt weak. He sat on the floor with his back to a rib. Skis sat next to him.

Joe picked up a fist-sized chunk of coal and peered at its bright, shiny surface. He hefted it in his hand.

Gus went around identifying those he knew. He gathered the napkin notes.

"Time to go," Gus said.

Joe got up, with difficulty. He went from miner to miner, touching their cheeks.

"No," Joe said. "I belong here."

"That ain't gonna bring none of 'em back," Skis said.

"Don't care," Joe said. "Don't wanna go back to that election shit. I want to be better'n that. Don't wanna go out as a criminal. I can go out as a hero, maybe. Leastwise I'm better for it."

Skis said nothing.

"Started in Fricktown," Joe said, "so I should end in Fricktown. Right exactly here is where I belong."

Joe Hunt took off his air pack and face mask.

Gus came over.

"No one gives a damn 'bout me," Joe said. "I got no one. Don't matter."

Gus took off his air pack, removed the face mask and sat down. "Take this," he said to Skis, indicating his tank, "you might need it to get back. I'm stayin' with President Hunt."

Skis said nothing.

Joe moved next to Gus.

"If I hadn't gone back an' shot that last face," Joe said, "likely they would have never died. No pick. No spark. No explosion. Nothin'. If I hadn't shot it, none of this."

"But you did," Gus said.

"I was tryin' to be good, shootin' it down ahead so we would spend less time in bad air. I wasn't tryin' to be lazy or bad."

"No one can fault you for good intentions, Joey," Gus said. "Sometimes good notions end up makin' bad consequences, things we can't predict."

698

Joe Hunt found no comfort in those words.

"It was my fault," Gus said. "I mismeasured. Maybe I drove my tunnel too close to Fricktown coal. If I had stayed more short of the line, what you did would not have caused anything to happen. This is on me."

"So it's you an' me, Gussie, like with Gallagher."

Gus took Joe's hand. "You an' me, boy. Skis, you tell 'em that Joey an' me have had enough. Tell Edna she is a fine woman and a fine wife. I'm sorry I never done better by her than Fricktown. There's life insurance in the file that'll set her up. Tell her I've always loved her as much as I could. And tell her thanks. You got that?"

"Yeah, I got it, Gussie."

"I love you like a brother, Skis," Joe said. "Nothin' changes that. Tell Delucci to fight hard for the members every day. Maybe some good'll come of this. Now go."

"Take their notes," Gus said. "Go!"

"I should stay," Skis said. "I belong with you two."

"No," Joe said, "we need someone to tell what happened in this hole, to tell the truth about Tony Bruno, about me too. We're appointin' you. Go!"

Skis felt his eyes welling up. He looked at Gus and Joe. "You're my best friends, my brothers."

"Go, Larry," Gus said, softly. "Tell it straight. Give Edna the pick head. She'll understand."

Skis stood in front of them. "Coal," he said, as he kicked the rib. He gave them a half salute and left.

"You afraid?" Gus asked.

"Naw. It's my time."

Once he got to the dump room, Skis dropped the two air packs, found the pick head and carried it back through the old tunnel.

Gert was waiting. "Are Joe and Gus behind you?"

"They stayed."

"Stayed where?" she asked.

"With the men," he said.

"Helping the survivors," Gert said. "How hard will it be to rescue them? I'll get Ben on the CB. He'll get the teams over here."

"No rescue needed on the long wall, Mrs. Roberson," Skis said softly. "No survivors. Nineteen gone."

"Nineteen!"

"That's what we found. Don't know about the other 38."

"Oh, this is dreadful. Nineteen!"

"Now 21."

"Oh my," she said. "Gus and Joe? They were killed, too?"

"They stayed," Skis said.

"'Stayed?'"

"They felt responsible. It was Gussie's mine. Joe left this pick head at our face. That's what the Fricktown continuous-miner hit. That's what sparked the explosion."

"This thing," Gert said, touching the rusted iron. "How dreadful!"

"Mining's a right sorrowsome way to live a life," Skis said.

"I need a moment alone," Ben Roberson said when Gert told him what Gus Olin and Joe Hunt had done.

Gert went to hug him, but he gently pushed her back. "Not yet."

He went into the superintendent's bathroom. He came out a few minutes later. "I just had to wash my face and hands."

"I'm sorry," she said.

"Where's Skis?"

"He went to tell Edna and give her the broken pick he brought out. The one Joe left in there."

"Left it! That's why they stayed. The miner struck the pick and ignited the gas in Gussie's tunnel."

"Yes. That's what Larry said."

"Dad knew that Gus and a couple of others were grubbing out a little coal for the tents. He said it wasn't worth fussing about. He told me. I knew it, too."

"Oh my."

"I'm responsible as well," Ben said.

Gert went over to him and put her arms around his neck. "Stop! You didn't send Gus and Joe in. They could've come out. Enough."

Ben looked his wife in the eye. He shook his head. "I've had enough."

"Meaning what?"

"Meaning it's time for me to retire. No more coal business. We can spend six months at our place on Jupiter Island and six months in Pittsburgh. We have plenty of friends in Florida. People we've known for 15 years."

"What will you do? You're only 68."

"Play golf. Read. Take you shopping. Carry your bags. Take you to the places I've promised. Spoil you rotten."

"Not that I'm objecting to a life of leisure, but what about AMSTEEL? All you've done and your father, too? It's always been the Roberson name standing behind and in front of the Company."

"What's the difference if I leave now or two years from now? Someone will step in. Benjie probably. Our son knows the marketing end and the environmental rigmarole."

"Would you be bored?"

"Life is full of risks. Being bored in retirement seems a pretty small one. Hell, maybe, I'll get a real-estate license and sell condos to snow birds."

"You? Praising commodes and interior accents! I want to see that! It's not like we need the money."

"Or maybe I could take vacationing families on rides," Ben said with a soft, introductory slide in his voice.

"On what?"

"Well, I'd have to buy a sailboat," he allowed.

"Oh, I'm starting to see how this goes," Gert laughed. "Not some dinghy. Something with a roomy head, a sit-down kitchen and sleeping quarters for at least four."

"Six," he said tentatively.

"Maybe 30 feet?" she said.

"Maybe 51, it'd be roomier, particularly in the galley. Like a two-masted Morgan ketch with an inboard diesel."

"You've given this some thought, I see."

"A little."

"Can one person handle that big a boat?"

"Two could," he said, "in coastal waters. I'm not talking about cruising the world. Maybe over to the islands for the winter. I can hire crew to help, over and back. If that's too big, I could settle for a 41-foot, two-masted ketch."

"I see," she said. "You've lost ten feet, and I've gained 11. A compromise. So why do I feel that you wanted a 41 all along?"

"It'd be fun," he said, "and it would certainly fill up my day what with varnishing and polishing and fixing and painting and repairing and…."

"I see," she said. "Would you be running away?"

"Some," he admitted. "I can't fix this, Gert. I can't bring any of my men back. I can't do anything about Gus and Joe. I think we've lost all 57 miners. Let me give AMSTEEL a clean slate. And I promise we'll give the families a big pile of money, bigger than the UNICOAL widows got."

"I just have one question," Gert said. "Was a speed-up behind this like the widows said on the news?"

"Kind of," Ben said. "Our Fricktown people were taking a shortcut to get coal out now rather than work with a bottleneck from an old conveyor. Buck Hinkle didn't want to run the long wall at half capacity for the months it would take to get a bigger belt set up. It was a temporary patch, to get from now to then. Production comes first, always has, and always has to.

"We were close to the property line. We were supposed to leave a 10-foot-wide buffer of coal, but Hink cut into about half of it. Gus's tunnel was close to the line, maybe even a little over. We were not sufficiently conservative. Hink tried to get a little extra coal that belonged to us. We probably weren't in Gussie's coal when the mining machine hit the pick. If I had known what my crew was planning to do, I would have stopped them or, at least, warned them. I could have told them we might break into Gus's old, gobby tunnel, but nobody told me what they were doing. That kind of decision doesn't rise to my office."

"It's not your fault," Gert said.

"Gussie Olin wouldn't steal coal from me."

"He probably stole food from the commissary during the strike," Gert said. "You told me that."

"I suppose," Ben said. "I've not been hungry a day in my life, let alone starving. Who knows what any of us would do to feed ourselves and our families?"

Gert closed her eyes. "Coal has been good to us," she said, finally. "The industry is better for what you've accomplished in your career. You can leave with your head high. A Morgan 41 sounds like my kind of boat."

Ben accepted the 10-foot shrink.

"I'll sell most of our AMSTEEL stock before I announce."

"Six months of Florida winter sound fine to me. I don't want to give up Pittsburgh."

"Sure," he said.

"What about Fricktown? The operation? The people?"

"The coal's still there," Ben said. "The long wall is probably okay. The mine would be a distress sale right now. No one wants to buy a killer mine that's half cemetery. Except Buzzy Maggard."

Gert shook her head. "Vultures are beneficial to the environment. They clean it up."

"He would pay 40 cents on the dollar, maybe less. A little cash up front, then pay the rest out of production. He'd walk away from the ACMU contract and its health and retirement obligations. Cut wages by 25 percent for starters."

"But the miners would still have jobs, wouldn't they?"

"Yes," Ben said, "they would still have jobs, some of them anyway. I'll try to have AMSTEEL keep Fricktown. Buzzy is a last resort. Very last."

"Nothing stays forever," Gert said, as she moved around him and started kneading his shoulders and neck. "We have a plan, a new plan. You're all knotted."

"I'm a lucky guy."

She winked. "I'll be a boat bunny…at my age."

"I can work with that," Ben said.

Before they left Fricktown, the UNICOAL women and Willie Rutherford found their way to the Olin house. Cars were parked on both sides of the narrow road. Earlier visitors carried food up to the porch and then inside. A name was taped on the bottom of each platter and casserole. Most had known the Olins their entire lives. They climbed the concrete steps that Gus built in 1948 on his summer vacation.

A woman in her mid-70s answered their knock. Behind her, the McDowell group could see the living room filled with people like themselves, wanting to say something to Edna though not sure of what those words would be. They heard the hum of muted conversation. Occasionally, a cluster would laugh over a Gus Olin story.

"We're from McDowell County," Linda Faye Decker said. "From UNICOAL. American Eagle. The widows."

"Come in, please. We know who you are. My sister is sitting in the kitchen. I'm glad you didn't bring any food. There's no space left anywhere."

"We would have, but we didn't come direct from home," Linda Faye said. "We drove up yesterday to, I don't know, I guess bring some comfort, or some such, to you all. We went through the same."

"We just wanted to express our condolences to Mrs. Olin," Doris Estep said. "Just in this short time, we've heard a lot about Mr. Olin and her. We'll just stay a minute."

"Stay as long as you like. We are friends. Food's in the dining room. I'm Ruth, Edna's kid sister. Ruth Godby; she still calls me 'Bitsy.' I'm glad you stopped by. It will mean a lot to her."

"How is she doin'?" Linda Faye asked.

"They've been married for 60 years. Gussie left a big hole."

"Those holes never close," Doris said, "but I hope they get smaller and fill in over time. I lost my husband, Delmer, with the others."

"Gussie and Edna were proud of what you did," Bitsy said. "We all were. I heard Gus say, 'Men get angry, but angry women get results.'"

"We just started the ball rollin'," Linda Faye said.

"Lot of hands pushed it along," Susie Rutherford said.

Bitsy led them through the crowd in the living room and dining room. The house was not unlike the ones UNICOAL had sold them in the '50s. The difference they noted was the shelves built along every wall. They were crammed with books, not knickknacks or photos of kids.

Edna was sitting in her favorite kitchen chair with a cup of tea in front of her. She had a black shawl around her shoulders. Edna was sad but composed. She had always understood Gus. She was not surprised that he had chosen to stay with Joe Hunt.

People stood and talked in the kitchen, giving Edna support by their presence and subdued conversation. Individuals rotated in and out of the two other chairs at the table. A 36-cup coffeemaker from the Fricktown Ruritan Club supplied the flow of visitors. Miners and retirees had set up in Gus's workshop where they drank Iron City beer and whiskey, both of which, everyone understood without it being mentioned, were to be consumed outside. Platters of cookies and slices of various cakes were passed to the table as each new pair rotated in. Edna held an old-fashioned, cream-colored silk handkerchief in one hand. It was a keepsake from a Vassar graduate from more than 40 years earlier.

Edna had placed the rusted pick head on top of paper towels on the table. Gus's initials faced her. The pick lay between her and the carousel holding prescription medications and substitutes for salt and sugar. She hadn't decided whether that pick was a curse or a medal of honor. Or both, and then some. So there it was, as Gus had intended, present and accounted for, waiting for her to make up her mind.

Bitsy introduced the UNICOAL group to Edna, as they each said their name and offered condolences.

"Thank you for driving all the way up here to be with us," Edna said. "Very kind of you. We, Gussie and me, we were inspired by what you did with the strike."

"Do you want to sit, Willie?" Linda Faye asked.

"No thanks, I'm fine," he said, turning to face Edna directly. "See, ma'am, I jes' lost my right leg."

Edna waited a few seconds. "Well, it can't have wandered far. I hope you find it before you leave."

No one said a word for the moment it took to register her comment, then the room erupted. Edna sat primly, allowing herself a grin.

"Yes, ma'am," Willie laughed, "I'm sure I'll catch it before it causes you any trouble."

"And when he does," Susie said, "I'll switch it good for takin' off like a plunderous pup."

"Must have been lookin' for a prettier little lefty to stump around with," Linda Faye said.

"That picture doesn't have a leg to stand on," Doris muttered just loudly enough to be heard.

Edna's tight smile widened.

"That's an ol' undercuttin' pick," Willie said. "Daddy had one out in his shed. They was used before my time."

Edna then recounted what Skis told her about Joe Hunt leaving his buried pick under the blasted coal.

"Don't know what to say," Linda Faye said.

"Gus was 86," Bitsy said. "Joe, almost 20 years younger."

"Gus wanted the end of his life to mean something," Skis said from the doorway. "Same with Joe. Most of us don't get that chance."

"I understand why he did what he did," Edna said. "He might have had another good year or two until the sugar took me. At our age, it's today, maybe tomorrow, but you're not even sure about getting to midnight, let alone, passin' it with a smile that's tryin' to cover up a hurt."

"Everyone loses someone, sooner or later," Linda Faye said.

"He felt it was the right thing to do," Edna said.

"Time comes for everyone," Wanda said.

Edna leaned back in her chair. "Funny you should say that. That's exactly what Gussie said to me when he came back to the tents with food for us." She paused. "He said it about Frank Gallagher."

Edna looked at Skis but spoke to everyone in the kitchen. "Gussie and Joey had broken into the commissary for food that night. Gallagher caught them coming out of a window. Joey hit Gallagher with a hammer. Killed him. Then the two of them put Gallagher inside the storeroom and burned the place. That's the truth. Doesn't matter to tell it at this point with both of them gone."

Edna kept her eyes on Skis. He acknowledged her gift.

"Those were sure hard times," Willie said. "Daddy said they made him feel like a rat trapped in a barrel he couldn't never climb out of."

"It's a wonder more of us didn't die in the tents," Edna said. "Babies and the old ones were passin' on from the cold and starvation. Gussie's coal saved a-many of us."

"Glad all that's gone," Skis said. "Union done it."

"The Union, the men, the women and even the kids," Edna said. "We did what we had to do. We weren't special."

"Bad work, bad times and bad luck," Skis said.

"And now it bites you again," Doris said, shaking her head. "After all this time."

"You mine coal for a livin'," Edna said, "it turns around and mines you, too, Digs out what's of value and leaves not but a husk."

They heard a knock at the door. Bitsy answered it. She came back with two visitors.

"Edna, I'm so sorry," Ben Roberson said, coming over to her and kissing her cheek. "I helped Gussie with his plan. I should have said no. It was my fault."

"I'm sorry, Edna," Gert said, hugging her. "We thought the world of Gussie."

"Thank you for coming over," Edna said. "It means a lot to me. Going in to the old mine and then staying was Gussie's idea. I don't blame you, Ben."

"I will do all I can for you and the others," Ben said. "Better than UNICOAL."

The American Eagle contingent flashed looks among themselves. They now knew that $1 million was short of what they might have negotiated.

"That will help," Edna said.

Ben suddenly realized he was standing in a kitchen half-filled with UNICOAL survivors.

Doris Estep caught his eye. "No need to say any more, Mr. Roberson."

Chapter 49

West Virginia, December 4, 1975

"You won," Becker said, as they sat in Delucci's red Jeep in front of The Moose.

Both the AMSTEEL mine complex and The Moose were lit from top to bottom in the cold of the early evening. Official vehicles with flashing beacons mostly went—police, rescue vans, ambulances. The hearses, however, sat dark and silent, waiting to be filled. They didn't need pulsating flashers. Everyone knew to get out of their way.

"It's hard to lose to a stiff," Jeep said. He lit a Marlboro and cracked his window. "Even if Joe would win the vote tomorrow, I'm elected. In a couple of years, it won't matter that I crawdaddied into the president's chair. My ass'll be sittin' there—that's what matters."

"God Bless union democracy," Julie Cogswell said from the back seat.

"God Bless," Jeep said. "I'm hungry. Let's get some supper. My celebration. I'll pay. There's a restaurant on Main Street."

"Call your dad," Becker said.

"You did him right," Julie said, rubbing the back of Jeep's neck.

"I guess I did. I will, soon."

Becker looked out his window at a steadily growing pack of hearses. "I'm going to take a little walk," he said. "I need to clear my head."

"I'll hold the phone to his ear," his mother said.

"Daddy, I won," Jeep said at his end of the line. "I won the election. I'm president."

Jim Delucci sucked at the nasal cannula even though it pumped oxygen automatically. "Fffffuhl." His throat clogged, and he struggled to clear it. "Fffaaaargh." He coughed, then coughed again.

"Ol' Joe went into the Fricktown disaster and decided to stay. Him and an ol' timer he knew, Gus Olin. Suicides."

"Clean?" Jim wheezed. "You clean, boy?"

"Sure, Pop. I'm clean."

"Owe?"

"No, Pop. I don't owe no one."

Jim coughed up more phlegm. "Money? Where'd you get the money?"

"Biggie gave me some. Took out a loan against his land."

"How'd you figure you'd pay him back?"

"From salary, I guess," Jeep said.

"Rest?" Jim whispered. "Where?"

"The rank and file. Liberals in New York. Some people who want to do business with the Union."

"Mob?"

"Naw, Daddy. Not Mafia money."

Jim knew his son. He heard the lie in Jeep's voice. Jim didn't have to see him to know it.

"Daddy? You still there? The black lung's gettin' real bad ain't it?"

He heard his father growl up phlegm and spit it onto his bib. Jeep knew it was black with coal dust.

"Cob...eatin' the comp'ny cob! Shtttt...."

"What, Daddy? What?"

"Shoot me, for Chrissakes!"

Chapter 50

Pittsburgh, December 4, 1975

John Corelli had thought for some time that were he ever to adopt a child, it would be a Vietnamese war orphan. That might even things up a little.

By official count, he had nine confirmed kills with the Remington M40 and Redfield 3-9 scope he'd stolen from a Marine sniper outfit. By his count, maybe 13 if he counted those without a spotter verification. A lot of Vietnamese kids were left without dads and a few without moms. Biggie Stover was tugging at him in a different way.

He drove the slow, two-lane way from Fricktown to Pittsburgh, through Prosperity. He looked forward to the panoramic explosion of Pittsburgh's pop-up Emerald City when he drove out of the Fort Pitt Tunnel.

Turtle driving gave him an excuse to think about something other than driving.

Corelli had never had a problem killing Viet Cong and North Vietnamese soldiers. One less of them meant fewer arrows being shot at the cowboys—that's how he had weighed it when he'd been there. In the year or so he'd spent decompressing after coming home, he began to believe the Indians had a good argument, probably a better one than the cowboys.

Working for Tony Bruno, he understood, required suspending all rationales other than one: It was a way to make a good living at something he did well without working very hard and spending much time at it. Killing hadn't bothered him when it was confined to the Mafia's internal shufflings.

But the Stover job was making him think about what he called "the core issues of my profession." It didn't feel like business as usual. It felt like murder, murder of an innocent.

Maybe Becker was right, John thought as he drove. Maybe it was time to scratch a mark on the other side of his cosmic ledger. Maybe it was time to slide back toward the better side of the line. Biggie Stover did not deserve to be killed; Bruno did.

With the right planning, he might be able to lay it off on Philly Squint Bombardo who, people would assume, was making his move to take over all of Pennsylvania.

Would he feel better if he did Tony? Maybe, he thought, it would make him feel something, which would open other possibilities.

He knew Roberta would have liked that.

Walton Pickering called his old friend Sewart Morgan and told him that he was flying in from Philadelphia and would get to Scraife about 4:30 that afternoon. Morgan agreed to have the relevant parties together at five.

Scraife National Bank was as much Walton's as it was Sewart's. Their grandfathers had founded it just before the Civil War, tapping capital in both Pittsburgh and Philadelphia. They named it after the largest of their three investors, Angus Scraife, who they eventually bought out. By the time their sons took over, branches had been established in both cities. Both Sewart and Walton had gone to work for Scraife upon graduating Yale, but Walton found himself bored while Sewart found himself fortunate to have his life laid out on a golf course that guaranteed he'd always shoot par or better. Walton left Scraife on good terms and became a respected lawyer. Sewart Morgan in 1975 was even for his round and finishing his 18th hole.

Walton Pickering was not surprised that his life had been easy. At times, he wished it had been harder. His parents had been disappointed that he'd not stayed at Scraife, but they willingly and effectively smoothed his way into Philadelphia legal circles. They retained their Scraife stock, which Walton inherited in the late '40s. He sold about half for diversification.

By the 1960s, Walton was glad he had bailed on banking. He had represented banks over the years and found their younger people had forgotten the wreckage that greed and high leverage had produced in the '20s. Walton's generation was prudent, held mortgages and lent money where borrowers and risks were known. The MBAs the banks hired in the '60s and '70s were free-market libertines, focused on gaining high salaries and big offices. These beneficiaries of stability and regular economic growth had stuffed risk and a trader's mentality into a balanced system of borrowing, lending, saving and investing. In morals as in money, Walton observed, easy erodes good.

In law, he saw a parallel—associates in the blue-chip corporate firms willing to do anything for as much money as they could wrest from the partners for their long hours in desperate indenture; personal-injury lawyers starting to advertise for clients; partners milking fees from cases they should have settled; companies stonewalling regulators through their lawyers to avoid cleaning up their spills, wastes, products, workplaces and operations.

With Watergate, Walton believed Nixon had soiled the entire Nation and besmirched the legal profession of which they were a part. Walton understood that pardoning Nixon might be the wiser of two bad choices, but it left him ashamed and with the conviction that the future would not be as good as the past. He pulled back from some work at his firm, cashed out stock positions and put his affairs in order.

As the 1970s started, Walton began seeing himself as a dray horse pulling a loaded wagon of nonsense and garbage. In the early winter of 1975 at 59, Walton Pickering was disgruntled with the world as he knew it. The way his mind worked was out of favor. Prudence and somber reflection were considered old-fashioned. His word would never be "situational." He refused to represent corporate clients he felt were dishonest. Walton had lived his life on the principles of reliability, trustworthiness, duty and honesty. He was as methodically linear as a marching band on a Kansas blacktop. He was as unadorned as a carpenter's rasp. What he saw around him were norms of a lesser kind.

The Mafia threat to his daughter was out of bounds. He had a small problem with gangsters killing gangsters, because it ran counter to his faith's universal prohibition against taking life. But exceptions, he had told himself, could be understood if not approved.

Walton had on several occasions represented clients whose businesses were being targeted by Nicky Dicka's Philadelphia Mafia on approval of Philly Squint Bombardo. The first case involved the City's largest industrial laundry; its Mob-controlled Teamster drivers were refusing to deliver linen to a supper club that balked at using Dicka's higher-priced garbage service and meat supplier. The second was a shakedown of a general contractor building federally funded highways. Both clients caved.

Walton met Nicky Dicka at the Old Original Bookbinder's on Walnut Street over a third case—a demand that a local hospital use a drug wholesaler the Mob preferred. Dicka, in his late 30s, was a scowling, volatile presence whose face reflected a mean core. He appeared with two associates in work boots and black-leather jackets.

Walton, the patrician in a tailored suit, rose when Dicka came to his table where he was about to start eating a cup of Bookbinder's snapping-turtle soup at three in the afternoon. Walton extended his hand, which Dicka dismissed. They sat. The boys in boots loitered near the kitchen entrance, pretending to be invisible except to Walton.

"Your hospital works with my drug guy or shit will happen," Nicky said without preliminaries.

"What kind of 'shit' are you planning to deposit?" Walton asked.

"Like shit you don't want to know."

"Like an unexplained fire in the hospital's power plant?"

"Anything can happen in a power plant," Dicka said. "Lotsa old electric wires runnin' everywhere like chickens with their balls cut off."

"Like cars in the parking lot being broken into, keyed or stolen?"

"Lotsa young punks around who do that for kicks," Dicka said. "Don't know whatsa matter with kids these days."

"Like hospital food not being delivered on time?"

"Refrigerator trucks break down; can't serve spoilt food to the sick. Ya gotta feed them cancer people fresh. No one can count on nothin' no more."

"Like nurses getting late night phone calls?"

"All kinds of perverts out there. You'd be surprised."

"Like doctors being sued frivolously for malpractice?"

"No one ain't perfect 100 percent of the time."

"Like administrators being roughed up, or even shot?"

"The world's fuckin' crazy. Ya can't even walk down the street safe no more."

"I see." Walton said. "Mr. Dicka, let me say this. If any 'shit' happens to my client for his refusal to buy your overpriced, adulterated drugs, I'll get the U.S. District Attorney to file a RICO suit against you faster than your dirty hands can steal a nickel out of a blind man's cup. See that lady at the next table with the big purse on the floor? That's my secretary who taped this conversation. And there's a second recorder on the seat next to me under this table. Now get up and get out of here! I like my soup hot. And the three fellows dressed like waiters, they're private security. My *armed* private security."

Nicky Dicka decided to avoid Walton Pickering's clients in the future.

Tony Bruno told his driver, Chuckie DeFelice, to pull up to the curb on Oliver Street in front of Scraife National Bank.

"You want me to park right here, Boss?"

"Yeah," Tony said.

"It's almost five o'clock. Rush hour. Busses ain't gonna like it."

"Fuck busses," Tony said. "Nobody rides busses."

"A cop will want me to move."

"Give 'im a Jackson," Tony said, peeling five 20s from his money clip. "Just loaf here. Keep the motor runnin' so you don't freeze nothin' off. This shouldn't take more than half an hour."

Tony Bruno never considered waiting for a reply. He opened the Cadillac's back door and stepped onto the wintery sidewalk.

He noticed the fountains in Scraife Square Park across from the Bank had been shut down to prevent freezing. Tony liked to see the fountains shooting upwards. It reminded him of Las Vegas. Scraife Square Park would look a lot classier, he thought, if colored lights could be shot through spouting water all year round. Maybe, they could use antifreeze in the fountains, which sounded to him like a pretty good idea. Maybe, he thought, he'd stop at McIntyre's Bakery across the street and pick up a couple of dozen cherry- and apricot-filled soft cookies before he went home.

A Pullman Brown UPS truck pulled in behind Chuckie DeFelice, blocking a fire hydrant. Seconds later, the UPS driver leaned on his horn.

712

He motioned for Chuckie to move forward so he could make his delivery without being ticketed.

Chuckie looked in the rearview mirror and shook his head.

The UPS driver honked again.

Chuckie lowered his window and stuck his hand out with his middle finger raised.

The UPS driver swerved hard into traffic, nearly clipping Chuckie's outstretched hand as he passed.

As Chuckie yanked in his hand, his eye glimpsed an older man in a Chesterfield coat with a black velvet collar. He was carrying a long leather bag as he walked on the sidewalk toward the Cadillac. He stopped next to Tony who had stopped to watch what would happen between Chuckie and the UPS driver.

"Mr. Bruno?"

"Yeah, that's me."

"I'm Allyson Pickering's father."

"Yeah, I'm supposed to meet you in Morgan's office. We can ride up the elevator together."

"You're nicely dressed, Mr. Bruno. Your topcoat hangs well on your frame."

"Yeah, I dress nice. A guy in Rome does my shoes by hand. Takes a year. A New York tailor makes my clothes. I'll give you his address if you want. He's got my measurements, which maybe have gone up some from 255."

Walton Pickering pivoted the soft leather bag in which he had cut a hole for his hand. It came level with Bruno's unmissable belly.

Tony froze.

"I have your measure, too, Mr. Bruno. You don't threaten girls! You don't try to kill my daughter," Walton said and then fired both barrels from his father's 12-gauge, side-by-side.

The force of two slugs crashing through Tony Bruno's thick middle knocked him back into his Cadillac. He collapsed in a scrambled, bloody heap next to the front tire.

"Thatta boy," Walton whispered to the Purdey.

Chuckie DeFelice knew instantly that Tony was dead. He spun the Cadillac into traffic with Tony's blood smeared on its whitewall.

Plugger, Walton said to himself, that's what they called me at camp. Scooter and Hugh and Poopy—they'd understand. They'd be proud.

A portly guard in his late 50s stumbled out through the Bank's doors with his gun drawn. He stopped, bug-eyed. "What a mess! I never seen nothin' like 'at."

Walton stood his bagged gun in his hand with the barrel facing down.

"Excuse me, sir," Walton said to the guard. "Would you like my firearm?"

A woman with her Kaufman's shopping bag spilling on the sidewalk finally found her voice and screamed. A crowd gathered, then backed away, staring.

Walton hated to let the Purdey leave the family. But this business with Bruno—well, Walton just gritted his teeth and resigned himself to sacrificing the gun as well as the plain, soft-leather bag an Amish saddlemaker in Lancaster had made for his father. The original Purdey gun case with accessories and cartridge bag would stay with Boo who would ignore it to the best of her ability. Maybe, Walton thought, after everything had run its course, there might be a way to have the authorities return the Purdey and the damaged bag. Maybe the Amish could repair the bag; they were very clever when it came to mending. Allyson might want both as keepsakes. He'd ask one of his law partners to handle negotiations with the authorities after his case was resolved.

The Purdey, he thought as he assisted the guard, was the most suitable way to end a threat to his daughter. Nothing valuable comes cheap, he told himself.

"Ummma," the guard said to Walton. "Put up your hands! I have a gun! In *my* hand! It's loaded, too!"

"He's dead," Walton said. "Better call this in, officer. Do you want me to put up my hands holding the gun or otherwise?"

"Ummma," the guard said.

"How about this?" Walton said as he offered the shotgun to the guard with the barrel pointed at his own waist.

"Yeah, I need to call this in."

The guard took the bagged shotgun in his left hand while his right held his revolver. Then he realized he had no hand left to deal with Walton who was standing in front of him, hands raised and looking at the cathedral-like front doors of the Scraife National Bank. Walton remembered his grandfather and Sewart's had ordered them from a cabinetmaker in Connecticut. They installed one set in Pittsburgh and its twin in Philadelphia.

"The Purdey's not loaded," Walton noted with a reassuring smile. "I fired both rounds. Here let me hold it for you. Then you can keep your walkie-talkie in one hand and dial with the other as you guard me with your pistol."

Walton gently took the shotgun.

The guard called for assistance and fumbled around his belt for handcuffs that he never carried.

A second guard came out with revolver drawn. They conferred.

"Please," the first guard said, indicating he wanted the Purdey returned to him.

Walton handed the gun back. "Please be careful with it. It belonged to my father."

714

"Yes, thank you," the guard said, as he cradled it in his arms. This was a damn fine story for the guys at Fritzie Zivic's bar on Butler Street that evening. He'd buy the first round. He might be in line for a reward. Somebody would buy him a round, maybe two. They might see him on TV. Everybody at Fritzie's knew who Tony Bruno was."

Walton stood there thinking the world as he had known it had disappeared. Scum like Bruno drove in chauffeured Cadillacs. Gangsters, bankers, you could no longer tell the difference. He did not want to hear the excuses and rationales Sewart would have offered. It was clear to Walton who was in bed with whom and why—money.

Where were the good people? The respectable bankers?

When did anything-goes start? Who had poured acid solvent over America's morals, leaving them etched and disfigured?

Tony Bruno had forfeited his moral and legal rights when he sent a gunman to kill Allyson, Walton believed. You get to kill that which is destroying civilization and targeting your family. *Leviticus 19:16*: You're not supposed to stand around like a double-dimmy dodo when your neighbor's life is at stake. That has to go double for a daughter. Justice is a defense. Not just justice, Walton thought. Self-defense is a matter of survival in a new age.

"Do you know that's Tony Bruno," the second guard asked Walton, "in the gutter?"

"I do hope so," Walton said, adding they should not disturb either Bruno's body or the scene.

"Perhaps we can move inside where it's warmer?" Walton proposed. "I'm chilled."

The guards agreed.

Walton Pickering knew he had done the right thing.

The Governor and Nancy were driven to Morgantown Thursday evening after what he described to her as "my momentary lapse" the day before. Bad weather had prevented a return helicopter flight to Charleston. "We'll make the best of it," he reassured her. "We're tough; we can rough it for one more day."

She couldn't scold him either for fainting or spending an extra day in Fricktown as bodies were pulled from the mine and news of Joe Hunt's death spread. She did, however, note this "spell of his," as she put it to herself, on his invisible permanent record card, which she filed in her head despite her conscious effort not to.

Fricktown hadn't been that bad. The four-unit motel had been better and cleaner than she expected. It was, that is, a deli-thin cut above her anticipated tacky and yucky. She took notice of the new plastic tulips the manager had placed on either side of their bed. As she shut her eyes and sought sleep, she could not help but estimate the number of Friday and

Saturday night couplings that had taken place on this same mattress on these very sheets. She wondered whether bed bugs still menaced travelers. When The Governor was in the bathroom, she looked between the mattress and box spring for little things running for cover.

The 20-mile ride to Morgantown over ice-slick coalfield roads was not an experience that either The Governor or Nancy wanted to repeat.

Three-axle coal trucks loaded with as much as 180,000 pounds had run for years over asphalt roads designed for 30,000 to 70,000 pounds in trucks limited to 80,000 pounds. They had pulverized pavement already weakened by cheap construction and annual freeze-thaw cycles. Potholes had been reamed out to as deep as 12 inches. Each time a wheel assaulted a pothole, the cavity spread. Bridge weight limits were routinely exceeded, leaving the metal crossings with names like "Old Shake, Rattle and Roll."

The Governor had received a report from "State Road" Commissioner Chauncey "HalfLane" Swandell that a survey done in the winter of 1974-1975 across West Virginia's three-dozen coal-producing counties showed 75 percent of coal trucks were running above their weight limits.

"Can we do something about that?" The Governor asked.

"Sure," HalfLane said. "Let me set up portable scales at important intersections. I'll paper their asses with tickets and fines. Then you pass a genuine tax on coal haulers, and I'll fix every pothole and bridge in the State. Your own budget office knows the cost to State government of having a coal industry is more than we collect in their taxes. By the way, do you want to be reelected?"

HalfLane earned his nickname by paving the most rural roads in West Virginia only a lane-and-a-half wide to save money. When two cars passed, both had to steer onto their respective dirt shoulders. Two eight-and-a-half-foot-wide coal trucks passing in opposite directions with their side mirrors winged out was always a game of chicken.

The Governor had requisitioned a State Police driver and car for the night drive to Morgantown. Nancy did not care for traveling in the dark in the best of circumstances. She wanted to be able to see far ahead. The Governor did not care for the twists and turns of West Virginia's country roads.

"The State just paved over the old horse-and-wagon trails without factoring in the speed of automobiles," The Governor informed his wife as she cringed in the back seat next to him. "That's why we have all these blind turns and curves that aren't banked right. It would cost a fortune to correct the original sin. So we don't."

She took his hand in hers as they fishtailed up a slope. It seemed to be snowing harder. Flakes were blowing straight into their headlights as they headed northwest.

716

"Where are the salt trucks, Peter?" she asked.

"Working the Interstates first," he said. "Got chains, Ronnie?"

"No sir. No budget for them."

"So there," she said to her husband.

"Call over to your dispatcher and make sure we have a room," The Governor ordered. "Stick to the two lanes, not the one-and-a-halfs."

"Do you know who Morgan was?" Nancy asked her husband.

"Who?"

"Morgan. *Morgan*town."

"Don't have a clue."

"I know," Ronnie said. "I'm Sergeant Decker. You know Deckers Creek? On the south end of Morgantown where it joins the Monongahela River?"

"Don't believe I do," The Governor said.

"Well, my Decker side -- Tobias and his brothers, John and Garrett -- settled there in the spring of 1758. Indians came the next year and killed eight. Garrett, my kin, wasn't there when they came. I guess that's obvious since I'm here 'stead of not here. Deckers Creek isn't much now. Ran a railroad up there, the Morgantown and Kingwood line around 1900, linked up to the B&O. Put up manufacturing plants along the creek. Now it's filled with sulfuric acid that runs down off the strip jobs. It was an open sewer for a long time. Still is over toward Masontown and Preston County."

"You were saying something about Morgantown," The Governor said, conscious that his wife was not interested in visiting open sewers.

"Sure. Zackquill Morgan started it after us Deckers were there. Couple of cabins. Zackquill was a colonel in the Revolution. Came from Berkeley County in the Eastern Panhandle."

"I know where Berkeley County is," The Governor interrupted.

"Sure. No offense meant. Morgan Morgan was Zackquill's father, and some claim he was the first white settler in what's now West Virginia. That'd be about 1731, but I think there were Germans around Shepherdstown three or four years before that. Zackquill probably settled out here around 1780, 10 years or more after us Deckers came back. He got a charter for the town in 1785. Ran a bar. They called it a tavern. Shoulda been Deckertown, not Morgantown, is what I'm sayin'."

"History is full of anomalies," The Governor said.

"Ambiggities, too," Sergeant Decker said.

The Governor and his wife looked at each other.

"True," she said. "Ambiggities."

They drove in silence to the Hotel Morgan on High Street, a 50-year-old dowager that despite showing her threads offered a more suitable ambience for a sitting governor than the Econo-Lodge. Hotel Morgan still smelled faintly of cigars, sex and back-room deals from its glory years in the '20s.

As requested, freshly bought nightclothes were waiting when they entered the eighth-floor suite. Extra-large pajamas for him, rather than extra-long; a flannel gown and booties for her.

Each held their nighttime apparel in front of them. Side by side, they stared into a floor-length mirror.

She frowned. "I told Ronnie I'm between an eight and 10 in most things, depending on the cut and the designer. But I like it roomy, so maybe a 12 or 14. These are 18s! I'll look like a saggy baggy elephant."

"No one will notice, including me," The Governor said.

"*I* will notice."

"I'm sure it's the best they could do with a short lead time," The Governor said. "Probably had to open K-Mart after hours for the Pj's. Look, Nance, mine are too big, too, except they're too short. They look like pedal pushers."

"Honestly," she said, "what I put up with!"

"We're public servants. Just make the best of it for one night," he counseled.

"Do you know what I want?" she asked. "A fresh ripe peach! The kind we get from South Carolina in June. Warmed by the sun, juicy, hand-picked. I just have peach taste in my mouth."

"Room service is not going to have a ripe peach at 10:30 on a snowy Thursday in December. You'll have to live with disappointment."

"I already do. Would you call room service and at least ask?"

"No. It will get around."

"What will get around?" she asked.

"You, being a *prima donna*."

"It's just a peach. I'm not asking for a brandied apricot frappé for Chrissakes."

"Do you want me to have Ronnie go look for a store with a peach at this time of night in this weather?"

"When you put it that way, I guess not," she said.

"It probably wouldn't be much of a peach in any case," The Governor said with the idea of comforting his wife. "I'm sure Morgantown is not a prime destination for winter peaches. They ship them into Charleston from Chile in the winter. How good would you look after being packed in a crate for 4,000 miles with a bunch of other unripe women?"

"You do have a way with words, Peter. It's just that all I can taste right now is coal grit."

The Governor poured himself a Scotch from the room's cash bar. "Want something?"

"Do they have wine?"

He looked. "Yes, indeedy. They have the red and the white."

"Well, for heaven's sake, Peter. What kind of reds and whites? What labels? California? French?"

"They have the red, dear, and they have the white, dear," The Governor repeated.

"The white, dear," she said, rolling her eyes.

"I can't stop thinking about what we've just been through," The Governor said as he sat in a chair and put his bare feet on their bed. "I don't understand these people. It's almost Asian the way they put so little value on life. There's a deep darkness in their souls, like Druids or something. I don't think people like us can ever really understand them. They're not like us. We can work with them, manage them, lead them, but understand them and share common values, I think that is beyond us."

"Well, they did choose you as governor. Do you think that speaks poorly for them or the opposite?"

"I think I represent, maybe, a Christmas present that unexpectedly dropped down their chimney. They see me as shifting their lives onto a different curve, not just a little up on the same curve."

"You mean your dollars falling on them like leaves off a magic money tree?"

"That, sure. But something else. They think I can save them from their entrapment. They hope that some of my family's good fortune will rub off. I'm a good-luck charm."

"You're family's 'good fortune' was rubbed off their backs, so to speak," she said.

He ignored her jab, which she had thrown before. "They think I will bring jobs, more coal jobs in particular. Promise them jobs, and they'll vote for you, for anybody. I can't create jobs."

"We all learn to live with hopes falling short. And I'm not sure they ever saw you as their Messiah. You bought their slates and their votes just like the natives. Except you paid above market."

"You pay here just like you pay at home," The Governor observed.

"It's so ugly," she said.

"Where we come from, we buy what we want subtly, not brutally, not openly," The Governor said, "except when we have no choice. We put apparent distance between ourselves and our pocketbook. We scrub up our money, dress it up, trick it out, disguise it, ignore it, hire others to make it grow and give it away. It's no less our medium of assigning importance to things and people than theirs."

"I wish politics was a meritocracy," she said.

"It isn't," he said. "It's grubby, dirty, West Virginia pay-to-play. Were it a meritocracy, we wouldn't have come here for one thing. I wouldn't have been elected. I had no choice but to play their game with more money than they played with. I was elected, *because* merit had nothing to do with it."

"With the money, don't you suppose you could have been your own man?"

"Not as long as the corrupt system holds the power of election. By paying to be slated, my money continued the corruption. It made the faction bosses stronger. I should have introduced legislation to abolish slating, which is nothing more than legal corruption. If you pay to be slated, corruption has captured you. Politicans who corrupt the system aren't going to change it. I know that. I've made my bargain with it."

"This is a place of bad choices," she admitted. "Good deeds are punished; bad deeds are rewarded; and in between deeds run this world."

"All they have is coal. Mining is their dope. They can't get off it. Junkies will do anything to get it—ruin their land, their air, their water, their health, their very lives."

"Peter!"

"It's true," he said. "Everyone's hooked—the companies, labor, local economies, the State's taxes, the media. As long as they stay hooked on coal, they won't ever change their reality or shift to a better curve."

"Could you have done something?" she asked.

"I could have said what I thought," he said. "I could have laid out a plan to transition the state, all of the coalfields, to a better mix of industries. I could have said to coal companies—mine it cleanly, mine it safely and stop wrecking the environment. I could have said to the utilities, buy the pollution-control equipment that will let you burn more coal without killing people and poisoning America. I could have proposed taxing coal and chemicals fairly to fund the transition, to retrain miners, to fix the damn roads. I could have moved state facilities into the coal counties to provide alternative jobs. I could have…"

"Stop," Nancy said. "They would have run you out of West Virginia just like they did Bill Marland 20 years ago. He favored desegregation in 1953, a severance tax on coal to improve roads and schools, a state income tax, industrial diversification and all the things you would support. He wound up an alcoholic in Chicago, driving a taxi for the Flash Cab Company."

"But that was in the mid-'50s when coal was down," The Governor said. "Now it's up. I could have tried."

"They would have blocked you in the Legislature," she said. "They would have killed you in a reelection campaign."

"I guess so," he said. "But my landing would have been on a feather bed, not like Marland's. Did you ever sleep on one? We had a handmade feather bed in the Adirondack attic. It came from the ancestors. I think it was Austrian. I was allowed to take naps on it."

"Peter, focus."

"Yes. It made sense to make peace with the coal people," he said. "That was my deal with them. Power for complicit peace."

720

She spoke before she thought. "Peter, you can call coal a narcotic, but it's also true that we were, I guess, some of the pushers. We pushed these people into giving up their timber, their oil, their gas, their coal, their land, their air, their water, their health. We offered jobs that paid them to give those things -- and their rewards -- to us. Then we kept pushing coal even though we knew it was bad. We're not unlike the cigarette companies and the tobacco lobby. We profited off their self-destructive needs."

"They have to make a living," he said. "What else can they do? They're not educated for anything else."

"They could have been like poor farmers in Vermont or Maine. Like swamp Yankees—even that would be preferable."

"Subsistence farming, maybe," he said. "They'd certainly be better off if coal had never been discovered under their feet. They'd be poor, but they wouldn't be degraded and corrupted. They'd be self-sufficient, little yeomen on their little farms. They'd be picturesque. Tourists would be their economy. They could act quaint like the Amish but cuter, because they dance and sing."

Nancy paused. "Does it seem right for people like us to tell people like them that they should give up what little they have in favor of living like primitives on the 1800 frontier?"

"Anything is better than what we saw this week," he insisted.

"Maybe you could bring in nicer industries," she said.

"I've tried. The coal companies oppose diversifying their captive economies. They want surplus labor hanging around, because it keeps their employees in line and provides skilled replacements whenever needed. And, to be honest, no outside company is interested in locating in a zone of repugnance."

"What's a zone of repugnance?"

"I learned that phrase last week when I was briefed by my agriculture commissioner, Farley Chew, on manure pollution from cattle. A zone of repugnance is the spot where a cow drops its dung. They don't eat around that spot, because it's repugnant by their own act.

"The coal counties of West Virginia are a zone of repugnance for the rest of the country," he said. "It's best to just write them off, because I can't do anything for them. I have to do triage. Help the places that have a fighting chance and forget places like Fricktown. Let them die as they've lived. Coal! Hell, in 100 years we'll be running everything on solar power. The coalfields will be abandoned. They'll be like Dresden after the fire-bombing except the people here won't rebuild like the Germans did. They don't have it in them. Coal gives them two ways to live—producing the thing that ruins them or living off their mailbox, because they're no longer useful."

"Do you think you're governor of a hopeless shit hole?" she asked.

"I'd abolish the whole damn industry if I could," he said stoutly. "No more coal heroin in West Virginia. A Marshall Plan for part of the State and a Morgenthau Plan for the rest. Deindustrialize the coal areas that have been sacrificed. Turn them back into woods and pasture. Figure a way to get land back in the hands of the little people. West Virginians would be better off on a net basis just the way African natives would be better off if they stopped mining diamonds in South Africa and copper in Zaire."

"My best advice is to keep these thoughts to yourself," she said.

"The truth of the matter is that the American coal industry will die for economic reasons. The energy market will eventually reallocate itself to safer, cleaner and maybe even cheaper fuels to make electricity. And it's Nixon who helped get this started when he set up the EPA. In time, people will dollar value clean air and their health more than a few bucks less on their monthly electric bill. That's when the market backs out coal."

"What will happen in West Virginia?"

"More miseries than you can imagine," he said. "No jobs. No income. No taxes. Population loss. Self-destructive behavior. Entropy will rule."

"Can you do something?"

"No," he said. "The market will be too powerful. We will be out of here by then."

"That wasn't exactly your platform as I recall," she chided lightly.

"God no! I can't say what I really think. That's my secret tragedy, isn't it? The price I pay for political success is political impotence."

"That's one way of looking at it," she said neutrally.

"West Virginia could have become a playground for Cleveland, Pittsburgh and Washington. Maybe we can still attract yuppies on weekends."

"I'm not sure my college chums would drive from Connecticut for a tennis game and drinks on an abandoned strip mine," she said. "Maybe it would have been different if the big corporations hadn't come in the way AMSTEEL did in Fricktown."

"Not a chance. The worst operators in this State are the locals. They exploit their workers worse than our kind do. The outside companies have national reputations that modulate their greed. The big operators have the money and staff to comply with the safety and environmental regulations. The little natives don't have the money to put into hiring staff and getting new equipment. And if they had the money, they don't want to spend it on things that don't make them more money. They like to rip and run, because it's cheaper. They grew up cutting corners. They 'don't know no different,' as they say. It's capitalism, Buzzy-Maggard style."

"He's dreadful. Betty, his wife, is nice," Nancy said.

"He's a poster boy for how not to do things," The Governor said.

"They harm themselves, because they hate themselves," Nancy said. "The worst hillbilly jokes are told at Charleston cocktail parties. What do a

722

West Virginian and a bottle of beer have in common? Answer: They're both empty from the neck up."

"That's bad, not even funny," he said. "After 18 holes, here's one I heard at the bar in the locker room. 'Why don't West Virginia girls play hide and seek? Answer: No one would look for them.'"

"I thought the answer would be they're too inbred to know the difference," she said.

"It's like Zaire," he said. "Dad made me spend my junior-year summer volunteering at a church clinic in Kinshasa. That whole country was upside down in how things happened. Nothing worked the way it should have, and most of the time nothing worked at all. You had a handful of locals making fortunes off western companies while 99 percent of the population had to scratch like chickens in manure for a few undigested seeds.

"The only thing that worked consistently was failure. It was expected. People were comfortable with it, had adapted to it and were suspicious of getting better. And the way they managed to get up and go to work every day was simply to pretend that reality was something other than what they saw, smelled, tasted, heard and touched. If that didn't do it, they hid from reality. The few rich hid behind their bogus titles, their desks, their front gates, their armed guards. The poor souls who came to the clinic were beyond pretending. They hid in religion, fatalism and despair. Same way in West Virginia."

"People with higher technologies always get what they want from the less advanced," Nancy said. "I learned that in a college economics class on emerging nations in the Third World."

"And the advanced countries cook up ideologies and religions to prove that God has given them the right to do what they want."

"If the Congolese had the money and the power, would they have treated white Belgian miners more decently than they were treated?" she asked.

"No."

"Then if West Virginia hillbillies had somehow found the technologies to build steam engines, steel mills and electric-power plants, would they have treated northern city people sitting on coal better than we've treated them?"

"No," he said.

"After what we've just seen," she said, "do we really want these people running the world? Isn't it, them or us?"

"Some choice. They would declare the pinto bean the National Vegetable. They'd put a short-bed Chevy up on blocks in the White House Rose Garden."

"And a broken refrigerator on the South Portico," she said. "Polyesters and velour. Bell bottoms. Leisure suits. Life lived in trailers with a non-functioning school bus as a lawn ornament."

"Ignorance and intolerance," he said, "there's a beast in their soul."

"Maybe," she said, "it would be better if we let them run their little hole in the planet, and we ran the rest."

"Won't work," he said. "We need their little hole and all the other little holes. Their world is ours, even though ours will never be theirs. That's the connection coal makes between them and us."

"It's so hard on us," she said.

"We're paying our dues here," The Governor replied. "Think of it that way."

"I know," she said. "We -- the government -- have to keep giving them crusts so they will vote for us. We use tax dollars to compensate them for being ripped off. But charity is so demeaning, and it keeps them dependent on us."

"But that's what we know, what we do," The Governor said. "Lest you've forgotten, I am selfless, idealistic and motivated by nothing more than my concern for their welfare. Nothing I do is about self-advancement. Nothing I do is about getting elected to the Senate. I get up every morning and the first words out of my mouth are: 'What can I do today to help the good people of West Virginia.' I play Santa Claus with an empty bag and a big Ho Ho Ho."

"Do you think any of them actually believe our bullshit?" she asked.

"Everyone believes somebody's bullshit," The Governor proclaimed. "They believe it enough, because they get a little something in their mailbox each month. 'Our bullshit,' as you put it, is better than no bullshit to believe in."

"Life is nuanced," she said. "We have to make the best of it."

"God, how I worry about them," he said.

"Me, too," she said. "Peter, I'm hungry. I'm resigned to no peach."

"Hey, Nance," he said, lowering his feet to the floor and leaning toward her. "Do you think Ronnie could find us a strawberry pie in Morgantown?"

"A slightly better chance with that than my humble peach," she answered while stifling an involuntary pout. "Frozen, I suppose. God, how I hate frozen strawberries. I have enough mush in my life."

"Remember that strawberry pie you made up at The Cottage on Bay Pond. That was the first time I took you to the Adirondacks."

She concentrated, then snickered low and thick. "Oh, that pie!"

"Must have been 12 years ago," he said.

"It was a ready-made shell. Out of the freezer case. With that dreadful Chinese-red goop they sell in the fruit section. I've never made a crust from scratch."

"I hulled the strawberries," he said with pride.

"Yes, Peter, you hulled the strawberries."

"And I whipped the cream," he said.

724

"Peter," she laughed, "that was Cool Whip I had you beating. I wasn't sure I knew how to whip real cream."

"Cool Whip—the truth comes out after all these years."

"I'm sorry I confessed," she said.

His voice dropped to a whisper, "I like Cool Whip."

"I don't."

"Remember what we did with the Cool Whip?"

"Don't remind me."

"I bet Ronnie could find some Cool Whip at a convenience store," he said.

"Peter, I'm a wife and a mother of two!"

He nuzzled his nose into the soft crook of her neck. "I'm pretty sure The Governor of the Great State of West Virginia could get a can of Cool Whip if he asked for it."

"Oh, okay Peter. Let's see if The Governor of the Great State of West Virginia can actually produce a can of Cool Whip on a cold-as-a-bitch Thursday night in Morgantown."

"With or without strawberry pie?"

"Gentleman's choice."

"Are you betting for or against me?"

"For, I guess," she said. "After all, if I'm in for a dollar, I have to be in for a dime."

In Unit 2 of the Fricktown Motel on Thursday night, Julie Cogswell said, "That was full of vim and vigor."

"You made me see stars," Jeep said. "Jeez!"

"Wanna go again?" Julie asked.

He lay inside her with his weight on his elbows. "The incoming president of the American Coal Miner's Union isn't quite finished."

"I'm patient," she purred.

"Most evidence to the contrary," he said. "I like you."

"That's good. I'd hate to think you didn't."

"You know what I mean," he said.

"Well, actually, no. What *do* you mean, Jeep?"

"You know."

"I don't know. Do you want me to move with you to Washington? Do you want to live together? Do you want to get married and have kids? Do you just want me to come by every once in a while to send you on a rocket to the Milky Way?"

"We could make it together," he said. "I haven't ever said that to any other girl."

"Why? Because we like to sleep together?"

"Sure," he said. "And because you understand what I'll need to do and have to be as Union president. You've been around. You ain't no virgin

725

when it comes to coal-miner politics. You know I'm not a perfect guy and won't be in the future. But I don't knock women around, and...."

"That's a start."

"...I wouldn't stop you from doing what you want. Hell, I'll git behind and push. I can open doors for you."

"So far you have. You seem to think my arms stop working as soon as you see me approach a doorway."

"Okay. Open your own doors. I don't have a problem with that. Have a career—fine with me. Girls on top—great!"

"Working mother?"

"No need to. I'll have plenty."

"There we go," she said.

"Don't you think it's a little early to start a fight about that? Wait. I'll make it easy. Workin' mother—I'm good with it."

"Secrets?" she asked.

"Ain't no secrets. Someone always knows."

"Biggie Stover?" she asked.

"Mob people from Pittsburgh killed him, the best I know. The boss who ordered it is Tony Bruno. He forced me to take a big wad of cash for the campaign; then he had Biggie killed. I guess he thought if he whacked Biggie, I wouldn't give him no trouble."

"Are you going to give him trouble?"

"These guys have already bought the American Bank of Washington from Joe Hunt. The papers will be signed next week. Can't do nothin' about that. But the Mob ain't gettin' into the Union's money."

"How much did he force on you?"

"Five hundred."

"My God!"

"But, Julie, here's how it went down. He gave Joe the same amount to protect his investment both ways. Becker knows this. Now you do."

"Okay. Now something else. Did Biggie kill those two guys who roughed up Vernie Skeens?"

"I believe he did," Jeep said.

"Did you approve it?"

"Do I approve? Sure. You know how this works down here. If Biggie hadn't retaliated, my support would have melted away. If you don't stand up for your guys, they won't stand up for you."

"No, I was asking, did you give Biggie go-ahead approval?"

"What difference does that make?" Jeep asked, pulling out.

"Ooohm, you didn't have to leave. The welcome mat is still on the front porch."

"Is there some reason why you need to know?"

"No," she said, now knowing the answer.

"Good. You wanna talk about Dee Cee?"

726

"In a little bit. First, I want to go around the lane again," she said.

"Rider or pony?"

"Both."

As she moved toward him, Julie Cogswell knew she would not share her future with Jeep Delucci.

"Becker?"

He knew the voice at the other end of the line. He put on his glasses so he could better hear what would be said. He sat up and turned on the light by his bedside phone. The room had grown cold. Since he was up, he decided to throw another stick or two into the bedroom woodstove.

"John," Becker said. "It's 11:30. At night."

"You're right on top of things, Becker. Did you hear?"

"What?"

"Tony Bruno got himself whacked dahntahn about five in front of Scraife National Bank."

"Dead? You mean Bruno's dead?"

"That's what whacked means, asshole."

"I'm afraid to ask."

"No, it wasn't me. Some old guy blew him away with a fancy shotgun. Both barrels. Smack in the gut."

"Why?"

"I guess 'cause he didn't like Tony sendin' Jerry Multirosa after his kid one night. Multirosa didn't get the job done."

"Who's that?"

"He's a sluggo who works for Tony. A generalist."

"Do you know the name of the man with the shotgun?"

"Pickering."

"Jesus! It's Allyson's father, Walton. He's a lawyer. From Philadelphia."

"That's him. I thought you'd know the family. You can never tell about lawyers," John Corelli laughed. "Very cautious, most of the time. But they can go off and do something crazy. Like you."

"This wasn't crazy. Walton knew what he was doing."

"Sounds like it from the reports. Very cool. Got close. Then he blasts Tony into his Caddy."

"Allyson was the reporter for the Post-Gazette..."

"I know."

"...who I dated years ago. Is she okay?"

"Yeah, a detective named Greiner got in Jerry's way. She was grubbin' for dirt in Tony's business. If you dig in shit, ya can't whine about people not wanting you around."

"Does this mean no one's coming after me?"

727

"I'll see what I can find out. Could be yes, could be no. Your contract's still out. But my guess is that Fagano now wants no publicity about their run at the Union and that bank. If you get whacked now -- after Lazarro, Hyskra, Stover and Tony himself -- somebody federal would *have to* investigate. There would be too many bodies to be ignored. On the other hand, somebody coming for you may not have gotten the stop-at-third message yet."

"Do you have any idea who that might be?"

"Maybe. Might be Richard Kuklinski. He does contract work for Fagano through Roy DeMeateo out of the Gemini Lounge in Brooklyn. Kuklinski's a big guy, 6-5, 300 pounds. Losing his hair. Stone cold. Doesn't drink or smoke. Charges at least 50 grand. Uses guns, cyanide, pool cues…whatever's handy. Very methodical. Creative. Motivated by money. Doesn't miss."

"What should I do?" Becker asked.

"Get out of Dodge. Fast. That will give you time to see how all of this shakes out."

"Okay. Thanks. "

"And by the way," Corelli said. "I'm thinkin' about sellin' math."

"Math? Is that a new street drug?"

"Math is math! Teachin' high school!"

"Oh."

"I can pick up a degree in three or four years. The feds will pay for most of it. I have money to live on."

"Have you had enough?" Becker asked.

"Maybe. I might keep my hand in to, you know, pay some bills."

"Would you stay in Pittsburgh?"

"I could move to where I don't have history."

"I could hire you to be an investigator. I'm a lawyer with no practice to speak of, so I'm using the verb 'hire' in the very future optimistic tense."

"You don't think I'd be a good math teacher?"

"You'd be great!"

"Well, it's just a thought," Corelli said."

"Thanks, John."

"I don't know why I do these things," Corelli said. "Must be a character flaw." He hung up.

Becker dressed quickly and drove to Smileys Motel on MacCorkle Avenue in Saint Albans, west of Charleston. He got there just before the front desk closed at midnight. He checked in after parking his Datsun station wagon behind the main building.

He called Allyson.

She picked up.

728

"I heard," he said.

"Daddy was protecting his little girl," she said shakily.

"Yes, that's what he was doing. You've been drinking."

"Yes, I've been drinking also crying. Becker...look what I've done! How could I have messed up so badly?"

"You wanted it too much."

"What 'it'?" she asked.

"Recognition. Importance. Serious journalism. Fame, maybe."

"Those things are not an 'it.' They are not bad things."

"They come at a cost," he said. "What you really wanted was to be loved. That's what is behind your ambition."

"Is Dr. Freud done?"

"Yes."

"We all want some kind of 'it,'" Allyson said. "Jeep wants a better Union. You want more fairness. Bruno wanted more money. Joe Hunt wanted no more Fricktown misery. I just wanted to write."

"You wanted to write from a big platform for important people who would make you important," Becker said before he could keep his mouth shut.

They said nothing for almost a full minute.

"What can I do?" she asked.

He gave this the thought it deserved.

"You know the Dunkin' Donuts on Grant Street across from U.S. Steel?"

"Sure."

"Meet me there at one on Monday."

"For what?"

"For a coffee and a doughnut," Becker said. "And I have an idea."

"Okay," Allyson said hesitantly. "Becker, maybe I should have stuck with you. I left Kennedy Brown."

"You have a better chance with him if you ask me."

"That's mean," she said. "Don't be mean to me. Not now."

"Have you talked to your father?"

"No. They said I could tomorrow."

"Your mother?"

"Yes. Boo says that she's 'bearing up.' Her Quakers are trying not to frown and scold silently in her presence."

"What about that detective...Greiner?"

"He said he'll get me in tomorrow to see Daddy."

"Bring him on Monday."

"This is awful, Becker. I can't feel worse than this. I need to change my life."

"You can't change yesterday," he said.

"Tomorrow. I can try to change tomorrow."

"I'll see you Monday," he said.

"Becker. Welcome me."

"I'll try. We'll see."

Chapter 51

Charleston, December 5, 1975

On Friday night as the last returns were reported, MDU supporters gathered at the Charleston headquarters to celebrate their victory. Dicey Shuck set up an open bar on his front-office desk with kegs tapping Miller and Budweiser and three rows of liquor bottles with mixes. It appeared that Dicey was the father of a graduation boy. Food trays were placed on every raised flat surface. Visitors brought covered dishes. Cigarette smoke rose to the ceiling mingling with celebratory cigars. Alternating country and blue-grass cassettes provided background. More than 100 miners and their wives filled the seven rooms with high spirits. Everyone who had helped was claiming a piece of their victory—Vernie Skeens from Logan County; Biggie's wife, Brenda; disabled miners; working miners from as far away as Illinois; and several from the McDowell County widows. Four local lawyers were in the crowd, along with a couple of college professors and a half-dozen West Virginia legislators. A West Virginia underdog had finally won. No one could think of another union where an insurgent reformer had beaten an entrenched incumbent. Maybe, they hoped, Miners for a Democratic Union might start a cleansing wave that would roll through the American labor movement.

Jeep Delucci had made history.

Jeep was in his office with his feet up on his desk, basking. Miners from the campaign, his local union and campaign staff were telling stories from times when they had thrown in against the Establishment and lost. They had a lot of those stories."

Jeep rose, "Gotta take a leak. Be right back."

As he worked his way to the bathroom, he caught Julie's eye. He smiled and motioned for her to close the distance through the throng.

"I need a kiss," he said into her ear.

She smiled and kissed his cheek. "Last one," she said into his ear.

"Whadda you mean?"

"I'm not going with you, Jeep," Julie said.

"Why not?"

"Well, for one thing," she said, "you haven't asked. And for another, I don't want to go as a player to be defined later."

"Then let's get married."

"No," she said.

"Why not?"

"Because it wouldn't work. And I don't love you. And you may end up in jail. There's another reason, but three is the best I can do right now after two beers."

"Okay, I guess," Jeep said. "It's a kick in the pants if you ask me."

"Better now than later," she said. "I'm not the right girl for you."

"All right," he said, without conviction.

"Good luck. I'll watch what happens."

"'Good luck,'" Jeep repeated, more to himself than her. "A dump out of the blue is a hell of a way to celebrate."

"Consider it an opportunity," she said. "There are a thousand girls who'll line up for President Delucci's inspection. I wanted to tell you face-to-face. Bye."

"Bye," he said with a shrug as he wondered what exactly he had done to deserve this decision. Women, he concluded, were just really hard to figure, particularly the ones he liked.

Jeep made a note to call Stanley Preiser early tomorrow. Julie's remark about jail spooked him. Preiser was the best criminal defense lawyer in West Virginia, possibly in the country. Becker was not right for criminal defense. Becker was loyal, but in this case Jeep suspected more to ideas than him. Being president of the American Coal Miner's Union would be hard enough without a federal indictment on his back. Jeep knew he had to get Preiser between him and the Justice Department. Preiser would run any charges into the dirt.

As Julie moved through the crowd to the front door, she passed Becker's office. His door was closed. She knocked and opened it after she heard him grunt.

"Hi," she said.

"Noisy out there," he said.

"With good reason. You boys pulled off something truly amazin'."

"Yeah," Becker said. "It helped that Joe Hunt 'withdrew' before today's vote."

"You would have won fair and square," Julie said.

"'Fair and square' got lost in the shuffle," Becker said.

"I know."

"What do you know?"

"I know about the money that Jeep had to take from the Pittsburgh Mob. I know about Jeep and Biggie and Lens Creek Mountain."

"Are you going to publish your pillow talk?"

"I don't think so, but anything's possible. It depends on where all this goes." She sat down and brushed the hair out of her eyes.

"And where do you think it should go?" Becker asked.

"What are you drinking?" she asked.

"Some shit like Sprite or Fresca. I need to keep my wits about me. So where do you think this should go?"

"Probably the same place you're thinking, which is why you're barricaded in your office when this joint is lifting off."

"Why would I want to mess up all this good work, all this potential, all this promise? How many times does the bottom unseat the top?"

"And how long does it take for the new top to become like the old top?" she asked.

"In this case?"

"In this case," she said.

"I dunno. Maybe it will all work itself out for the best."

"I don't think so, Becker," she said. "Ends don't justify means even here in the heart of coal's darkness."

"How certain are you of that simple principle?"

"Pretty certain," she said. "I'm sure I should stick in some 'except thats,' 'wheretofores' and 'notwithstandings' so a lawyer like you can understand its lack of complexity."

"Maybe this is a time when the end *is* more important than the means."

"I don't think so, Becker," Julie said. "Anyway, that's why I just told Jeep I wasn't going with him."

Becker stared at her blankly. "I thought you two were serious. He told me he was. You didn't want to move to Washington? Is that it?"

"You're not listening, Becker. Jeep is compromised."

"Hell, Julie, everyone who breathes is compromised."

"He had a choice," she said.

"He had *no* choice. A guy named John Corelli put a gun to his head. He either took the money or his life would have been taken and Joe Hunt would have won."

"He could have taken the money and not spent it. He could have reported it to the cops. He could have exposed the whole thing to a reporter. I don't want to live with what comes next in his life. West Virginia is full of guys who started out nice and honest and ended up awful and corrupted."

So you want me and you -- the two of us -- to jump out of this plane together without chutes?"

"You do what you want," she said. "There is no 'two of us,' no me-and-you together in this. I don't want you to get the wrong impression. It's the right thing for me. You, too, I think. But that's just an opinion. We are not a package. Do what you think is best for you."

"Like Brenda Stover, you're a tough cookie," Becker said trying to laugh.

"Fairly indigestible."

"I thought you cared for him."

"Jeep is slicker than a yolk in a barrel of whites," Julie said.

Becker laughed. "Never heard that one before."

"It just came to me in a moment of sublime inspiration," she answered. "The thing you have to understand about the poor-as-dirt oppressed is that every so often we beget someone special—a John D. Rockefeller, Carnegie, John L. Lewis, Frederick Douglass, Lincoln, Grant, Harriet Tubman, Nixon, Delucci. They grow up with a peasant's shrewdness. They figure out how to use that and their intelligence in the larger world. Ambition drives them, ambition to climb out of their birth hole to a better place. They're mixed bags. They do some good, but they often have a dark side. Jeep's that way. I got close enough to know. He'll do some good for miners and a lot of good for himself. I don't want to watch it happen. If I stayed, I'd always be fighting his instincts. It wouldn't have worked."

"How are you so smart about this stuff?" Becker asked.

"'Cause I was dumb about it for a long time," she said. "And the other thing is you and Allyson. That doesn't look like it's over. Anyway, I'm not your type."

"How do you know that?"

"Because I know you, and you don't know me."

"Okay, I guess," he said.

"I don't care for her much," Julie said. "She's a girl who had it too easy for too long. Might she be out of Timothy Pickering, the guy who wanted New England to secede in the early 1800s?"

"I believe so," Becker said. "I saw an oil painting in her parents' house, which I was allowed to visit once when they weren't home. She doesn't like to talk about The Ancestors. She grew up in Philadelphia. Her forebears started as New England Congregationalists and ended up as Pennsylvania Quakers. Old family with a lot of old money. She was vested in America. She didn't want to be, but she couldn't shake it or make peace with it."

"Maybe you were her rebellion against all of that."

"She was dating a guy named Trip when we started. He was the right sort; I wasn't."

"Come on, Becker, you were punching above your weight with her. I'm not trying to be mean. Just saying."

"I had as much college as she had. Just as good. Now I have more."

"It's not college, honey. It's all the little shit you're raised up with, or not. People in The South call it 'breeding.' It's not that; it's culture, confidence, experience, relatives, looks and history. I don't have what she has either. I'm as low as you but out of a different pit."

"Their good stuff tends to play out after a couple of generations," Becker said. "It's like using the same coffee grounds over and over. They regress to the mean."

"Like The Governor," she said. "Still, they never forget they have some blood in them that once made something out of nothing. That floats them over their own shallows. They also get breaks, often from each other."

"She never made it an issue," Becker said.

"She never would," Julie answered. "You can fascinate each other with the little class-and-culture differences for a couple of years, but over time they drive a wedge between you. Opposites attract but sames have an easier time sticking it out. What were her parents like?"

"I met them in a restaurant once. Her mother, Jane -- she's called, Boo -- is a very polite, very proper Quaker gadfly. Patrician pacifist. She hasn't missed a Bake Sale for Peace in three decades."

"I'm sure she wore sensible shoes," Julie said.

"Determinedly orthopedic before she needed them."

"My Oberlin roommate's mom was like that."

"Her Dad's way of dealing with privilege and prosperity was to be dutiful to his wife and kids, act honorably and live plainly. Boo was bossy, but Walton could be tougher than nails."

"I'll say. Shooting Tony Bruno dead in the street!"

"It was a public service," Becker said. "I wish I had the balls to do it."

"It wasn't balls," Julie said. "It was family defense."

"Boo could push him around on little things, but you didn't cross him on big stuff. I tried to stay out of his line of vision."

"Didn't much like you messing with his daughter, did he?"

"Let's say he was traditional when it came to matters of tradition. I remember him being upright like Gregory Peck. He was bemused by our life in a tepee the summer we graduated. We were helping to remodel an old farmhouse with friends."

"Tearing down the old; building the new; learning by doing. How wonderfully revolutionary."

"It fit with the times," Becker said.

"All that suburban liberal back-to-the-land shit struck me as a miniature control trip. Alienated, young, middle-class intellectuals couldn't stop the War, eliminate racism, stop sexism or reverse the assassinations. But by God, you could build a yurt in Vermont and let your hair grow."

"We were retreating in the face of getting nowhere."

"Those were not retreats," she said. "They were land grabs and secessions. I heard my Oberlin classmates talk about moving to Vermont and 'taking over.' I never heard that at WVU."

"I heard the same. I wasn't comfortable with it."

"Was Allyson nice once upon a time?"

Becker drifted back, rummaging in his memories. "Once upon a time, she was a force. Smart, quick, funny, pretty and irreverent. Quaker centeredness. Civil rights, then peace. Nice? Not exactly. I was intrigued."

"'Was?'"

"I don't know," he said. "Maybe still. But she changed during The Grimness. Those years—the late '60s, early '70s. Those times killed 'nice.' 'Nice' was self-indulgent, bourgeois, weak. If you wanted justice, you had to go to war. Nice was a casualty. She became a prisoner of her own goals. I was the same; just as bad in some ways."

"I take it you were more than friends," Julie said.

"We were a lot of things. 'Friends'—sure, but that wasn't the most of it at least from my point of view. At the end, I'm not sure what we were. Critics. Enemies. Puzzles. Mutual obstacles."

"She dumped you hard, huh."

"You're stating."

"It's sort of obvious. Boys aren't complicated. You're not an onion."

"She left me with a bye-bye note in a tepee on a farm in Massachusetts. A stupid volleyball game triggered it."

"Sounds like a good story," Julie said, kindly. "What did you do? Hit her ball?"

"As a matter of fact, I did. Maybe, I'll write a book about it some day."

Julie raised her eyebrows. "Maybe I'll buy it. Volleyball? She wanted to be a spiker like the boys but couldn't jump high enough with the net raised. She didn't want to set all the time like the girls. So she…?"

"Left. Volleyball was a…"

"…metaphor. You know, Becker, even for as fevered a feminist as she probably was in those years, you hitting her ball doesn't sound like enough to break up a relationship that had some entangled roots. There had to be something more."

"She said I wasn't her Prince Charming." He saw himself going back without wanting to.

Julie broke up. "You're kidding me! She said that! No one is that dumb, that mind-fucked!"

"I guess she wanted the perfect match that would lead to The Happy Ending," he said. "It's an impossible standard. I wasn't manufactured in the Disney studio. I was 'displaced.'"

"'Displaced?' By someone else?"

"No. Not by a person."

Julie considered Becker's answer to be rich in information.

"Ah women's liberation," she announced. "Wacko-Left version. Late Sixties."

"Some women went a little nuts for a while," Becker fumbled. "That didn't come out quite right. That's not what I meant, exactly."

"Surely a bright lawyer can find accurate words," Julie said, mocking him gently.

"Men have oppressed women," he began.

"You haven't messed up so far," she said.

736

"Give me a chance."

"She really did put you through boot camp."

"I started as a volunteer."

"Speaks well for your instincts," Julie said.

"I didn't like being defined as 'The Enemy,'" Becker said. "Her Enemy."

"Who would? It dehumanizes you. Didn't give you much room, did it?"

"It legitimized treating men the way women said they were treated."

"Bad for the goose and bad for the gander," Julie said.

"I'm not defending how men treated women. I understood what she was saying."

"No one is defending men. You're just whining about being one."

"I'm 'whining' about labels. I'm 'whining' about herd instincts. About being stuffed and sealed in a box. About not making distinctions. It was a kind of McCarthyism. Guilt by association and birth."

"Guilt by gender. I'm sure your opinion made you popular in the ol' wigwam with The Princess."

"I wasn't perfect. I had attitudes that she changed. I'm a better man for feminism. But there wasn't room, space or time to figure it out. Sisterhood was too powerful."

"Sisterhood was a drug," Julie said. "It freed us to do whatever we wanted regardless of the consequences."

"Allyson's women's group at Bryn Mawr called her a 'closet heterosexual.'"

"The group I was in met once a week," Julie said. "We burned each other out in a year. No marriage survived. Half of us decided we were lesbians, because that was the remaining alternative. I remember the unbearably weak tea and potluck suppers. I haven't eaten a lentil since."

"I guess all of us had to go through it," Becker said.

"A lot of wreckage," she said. "Some justified; some needless."

"I think Allyson liked discovering that she could finally claim membership in a victimized class. She could feel bad for being a mistreated woman and feel good about it at the same time. She didn't have to piggy-back on blacks and others of The Oppressed. She was no longer just a privileged rich girl; she was a victim of systemic discrimination."

"A lot of people have a Purple Heart from The Sixties."

"Allyson never expected to be nicked," Becker said. "Then she poured all her feminist energy into being a reporter. As long as she wasn't pursuing anything as gauche as money, she felt free to let her ambition run wild."

"Why didn't that work for her?"

"From what she told me, The <u>Post-Gazette</u> tolerated her. Stuck her on the labor beat and let her be the house feminist. But they wouldn't give her the inches she wanted for what she wanted to write. Without good clips, she couldn't jump to a national daily. She was trapped—a predicament she had once thought only ensnared the powerless. She reacted, she said, by acting like all the guys she hated. Anything went, as long as she was fighting male chauvinism."

"So Becker are you now or were you then a pig? Did you have a curlicue in your tail?"

"I was moving up a learning curve. Willingly. Equality has to be equal. It doesn't mean you reverse roles. I have regrets. But I tried."

"You boys were the sacrifice generation," Julie said. "We had to establish a beachhead, be the 'firsters.' We all paid the dues for the next generation of men and women. We'll win when women say they don't need to be feminists anymore, because everyone is."

"I was salvageable."

"I guess you weren't as bad as most of the other one-eyed trouser snakes."

"How generous."

"So you're still in love with the memory of the tepee princess?"

"Nostalgia is inoperable," Becker said.

"So you drag her around like a curse. Why would I ever want to take you in?"

"If you put it that way…."

"She's gone, Becker. But maybe reality counts for nothing with heart-love."

"You're right, of course," he said.

"I guess that's enough 'reality' for one night."

"Agreed."

"You ought to go celebrate," Julie said, "even if you decide to blow up everything in the cold light of day. Don't forget—always duck the first punch."

"Sorry you and I didn't go anywhere."

"You shouldn't be. Better for both of us that we never started," Julie Cogswell said as she walked out of his office and closed his door.

Becker resumed mulling. Deciding whether or not to make a decision seemed a more achievable goal on this night than actually making a decision.

Susie and Willie Rutherford were getting ready for bed after the long, up-and-down, twisty drive from Charleston. They had accepted praise and returned congratulations to those who had worked for the Miners for a Democratic Union.

Willie sat on her quilt, unstrapping his right leg. He had been getting more comfortable in the socket that bore his weight. He thought he'd gotten beyond most of the depression that followed the roof collapse but the sense of vulnerability persisted. He had been attacked and violated, conquered. He had not defended himself and was now even less capable of doing so. He couldn't defend Susie if that need ever arose. And going down his front steps on an icy morning risked catastrophe even after Susie shoveled and scattered salt. Maybe, he thought, they should move to a house with no steps, one with a carport next to the kitchen door. At least, he thought, he had stopped grieving for the lost leg. He was alive, no diabetes, no bad black lung yet. He could still move around and even drive. Susie told him it didn't matter about the leg, and she was true to her word. And maybe this Delucci would even do some good.

"You were quiet comin' home," he said.

"It's a hard drive to make at night," she said. "I had to pay attention. Didn't want to fall asleep or get hit by a drunk drivin' home from a bucket-o'-blood joint."

"You did a good job, drivin'," he said.

"I was thinkin'," she said.

"Me, too," Willie said.

"Did Jeep talk to you 'bout a safety job like he promised?" she asked.

"No. I didn't ask about it."

"Me neither," Susie said.

"Give the boy some time," Willie said. "Maybe he do right. Maybe he stand by his words."

"Sure," she answered without conviction.

"Every miner he ever shook hands with is gonna be askin' for a desk job," Willie said.

"That ain't no excuse to back out of what he promised when he wanted our help," she replied.

"No, you right. It ain't."

Susie paused: "I sort of got used to causin' jes' a little trouble."

"You and the ladies gettin' pretty good at it," he said.

"Here's another thing. I don't want to hear nothin' about Wanda. Leave her be."

Willie had to smile.

"Jingle!" he said. "Jingle Bell?"

"Well, they did know each other in school," Susie said. She hoped the gravity of her tone would smear a little normalization over the matter. "He was up there tonight. She was up there. They both had a little to drink. He said he'd drive her home."

"Tomorrow," Willie said as non-judgmentally as he could.

"Well."

"Her business, not mine," Willie said. "Pins, he gone. She ain't. Young woman."

"It was him -- that Jingle -- who protected her," Susie said, "after the rock came into her house."

739

"He after her money," Willie said.

"No," Susie said, "I think he after *her*, money or no money. Wouldn't be the first white boy who had a taste for brown sugar."

"What in it for her?" he asked.

"She liked him in high school," Susie said, "Sometimes you can't explain why people like each other. Times are gettin' different. White and black, they can be together now. Even here."

"Man, I want to be at that weddin'," Willie chuckled. "You got Kluxers on one side of the dance hall scowlin' and brothers on the other lookin' hard."

"Same boys who went to school together and work in the mine next to each other," she said.

"If they got enough lubricants in the punch bowl, everybody get along okay. Or not."

"She and him would put the word out: 'If you all comin' to my weddin', you come peaceful or you stay away.' You, Willie. You don't say nothin' to her 'bout Pins. It's her life. Yesterday is done; can't do it different."

"Pins...he..."

"Pins, he dead. She ain't. And Willie...same goes for Linda Faye."

"That boy she went off with from Ohio, he look married to me," Willie said.

"That 'boy' look like he in his 50s, and she be only in her 40s."

"Late 40s," Willie said. "Real late."

"Don't matter if she 140."

"She's lonely," Willie said. "Folks do stupid stuff when they're lonely. Mike is laid up bad. Don't think he'll last much longer."

"Ain't yo' business or mine," Susie said. "But I might ask Miz Estep to say a word to her."

Willie swung his good leg onto the bed and pulled the covers up.

"So after I go," he said, "you lookin' next for one leg or two now that you tried both ways?"

"Don't recall that a leg is what a lady most interested in," Susie said.

"I couldn't have done better than you," Willie said.

"Glad you know that," Susie said, as she turned off their light and rolled toward him.

Chapter 52

Pittsburgh, December 6, 1975

Art Greiner drove into Highland Park toward the Rhododendron Shelter close to Carnegie Lake where kids were skating late on Saturday afternoon. He wondered how they could see the puck. And then he remembered playing hockey there *after* dark. He just had to be able to see enough of what he needed to see.

Greiner pulled into the Shelter's near-empty parking area and kept the engine running and the heat about half way. He was driving an official Pittsburgh Bureau of Police Chevy Impala sedan with black sidewalls, black paint job and the cheapest trim available. He could be made a mile away, which suited Art Greiner fine. If anyone asked, he was probing into the Bruno murder. He didn't think it likely anyone would ask why he was meeting Jerry Multirosa.

Jerry pulled his wife's Plymouth station wagon next to Greiner. He got out and opened the Chevy's passenger-side door.

"Nice wheels, Jer," Greiner said.

"It's Teresa's ride as if you didn't know. Gettin' colder," Jerry said, as he got in. "Fuckin' winter. Ya got Thanksgivin', Stillwers, Christmas and then fuckin' January and February."

"January and February—they are months to look forward to."

"Why's that?"

"They build persistence in our character," Greiner said.

"Artie, your brains are scrambled like an omelet," Multirosa said. "Frostbite don't build persistence. Frostbite builds blue toes that turn black. I know about cold feet. I was stationed in Alaska for a while."

"What's goin' on?" Greiner asked.

"Angelo Gigliotta's the new number one," Jerry said, taking off his gloves and lighting an unfiltered Pall Mall. "He took over this morning. No muss, no fuss. Can you believe this shit? Some old-fuck lawyer takes out Tony Bruno dahntahn while Chuckie DeFelice is sittin' in Tony's car twiddlin' his dick."

"It's hard to know who the bad guys are these days," Greiner said with strained sympathy.

"Yeah, Chuckie is on Angelo's to-do list."

"I can only imagine," Greiner said.

"This lawyer is a stone-cold murderer," Jerry said. "He's a bad guy, worse than me. Does Jerry Multirosa go around blastin' the shit out of people dahntahn in rush hour? Does Jerry Multirosa whack a Boss on a public sidewalk where citizens are standin' around like sittin' ducks? No,

Jerry Multirosa don't do that! I'd give this lawyer the chair and throw away the key. He's a menace to society."

"I'll recommend you for the first opening on the bench, Jer," Greiner said. "The prosecution always needs friends in black robes."

"You can be damn sure, Artie, I wouldn't let criminals like him run wild in the streets."

"I'll keep in mind your interest in a career change."

"I heard his shotgun is some antique. Worth 50 grand, or more. Who the hell uses a piece like that to do a job? And then he hands it over to a bank guard nice as you please. Who gives his smokin'-hot murder weapon to a cop? Not me! No offense intended, Artie."

"He wasn't a pro, Jer. Like you."

"Any jag off knows you go steal a 10-gauge and hack the barrel at 12 inches. Put a one-ounce slug in the right side and 00 shot in the left. Fire one, then the other. That'll do anybody."

"I'm sure it would and has," Greiner said.

"Or you do him with a .45 slug. I can swing this way or that," Jerry said with reflection. "I mean I don't want to seem…uh…."

"One-dimensional," Greiner said.

"Yeah, one-credential," Multirosa said. "Then you throw the piece off a bridge. Pittsburgh's got a lot more bridges than rivers in case you haven't noticed. Throw it into the Mon. Don't this guy know nothin'? Cops couldn't find their own noses in that muck. No offense."

"Maybe you could teach a crime class at Pitt for college credit."

"You think? I bet Angelo would tell the young guys to sign up."

"You might get an old Philadelphia lawyer enrolled."

"Aw, you're jaggin' me off, Artie."

"I need you to give Angelo a message for Frankie."

"For Frankie. Frankie Fagano?"

"Right. Tell him the reporter, Allyson Pickering…you remember her, Jer?"

"'Course I remember her. You squirreled up my contract on her! How could I forget? Pickerson."

"Pick-er-ing. …and Jeep Delucci's campaign manager, Becker, Jeffrey Becker, want me to meet them on Grant Street on Monday after lunch."

"So?"

"At the Donut, Jer."

"Yins havin' a late breakfast or what?"

"What's across the street, Jer? At 700 Grant?"

"The fuckin' feds!"

"That's right. The U.S. District Attorney for Western Pennsylvania."

"Jeez! Are them two goin' up there to talk about Tony?"

"My guess is that's what they want to talk over with me."

"Jeez! You want me to take 'em out before they go flap-flap?"

"No! I want *you* to tell Angelo to get this information to Frankie. Tell Angelo to tell Frankie that the best thing to do is do nothing. Let it ride. Don't hit either Pickering or Becker. Don't whack her father. Cool all the moves. Come back to them later if you need to. You got all that? I ain't gonna write it down."

"Sure I got it. No whacks. Sit back, Cool the moves. Come back, maybe. See, I got it."

"Good."

"But that ain't right," Jerry said. "We can't have people goin' around whackin' us whenever they get an itch up their bonnet. We're supposed to do the whackin'."

"Special circumstances, Jer."

"Naw, they ain't. They hit us; we hit back. You know that's how it goes. What happens if we don't even it up? Who'd be scared of us then?"

"Listen to me, Jer. There are bigger fish fryin' than Tony."

"Bigger than Tony? What kind of fryin' fish is bigger than Tony?"

"Trust me, Jer."

Jerry Multirosa frowned in thought. "Artie, which side are you on?"

"My side."

Jerry didn't know exactly what to make of that answer. "Josephine, she's real upset. The kids, too. Even their dog. Josephine was sayin' something about Protestants can always get away with killin' us Catholics. Like Italians don't count for nothin'. This no-whack rule ain't the way it's supposed to be. I object!"

"Duly noted. Remember, old man Pickering *is* in jail,"

"Temporarily," Jerry stressed. "Sure, they got a dozen witnesses on what he done to Tony. How's this Pickering gonna walk away from murder one? How do I know? Do I look like a legal beagle? But he'll walk believe you me."

"Sit tight, Jer," Greiner said. "Hey. You got Christmas plans?"

"Yeah, I told Teresa I'd take her to Miami Beach like always. Been goin' to Christmas at The Fountainblue since the late '50s. I try to meet guys who might remember me when they need a job. We'll see Sinatra."

"He likes it there," Greiner said. "Good place to make connections."

"That's right. I talked to Skinny D'Amato there five, six years ago, before his 500 Club in Atlantic City burnt down. I seen everybody--Kid Cann Blumenfeld, Joe Fischetti, Jimmy Blue Eyes Alo, Sam Giancana, Trafficante, Roselli and Meyer Lansky—I seen 'em all. Dagos and Jews. Hardly ever saw a regular white person there, like you."

"So I've heard."

"Lansky lives a couple of blocks away, but he uses the hotel for business because its lobby pay phones ain't tapped. Plays cards. Always comes with his stupid little Shit Zoo. Bruiser, he calls him. Dog craps wherever. Ben Novack, the Jew who runs the place, told his maintenance to follow the mutt when Lansky shows up."

"Nice of him to do that, don't you think?"

"Italians wouldn't let their own dogs crap on their hotel rugs, even their motel rugs," Jerry said. "Do you think a Shit Zoo is some special breed just for them people?"

"It's a Chinese breed, from Tibet originally," Greiner said.

"Naw, Artie, it can't be. It barks like my Doberman, except higher. Chinese don't carry their dogs around like purses. They use Chinese eatin' sticks on 'em."

"It's *Lansky's* dog," Greiner said. "You gonna tell Lansky where his dog can shit?"

"Well, when you put it that way, I guess not. Lansky, he says hello when he sees me, but he don't know my name.

"I like to sit where I can look through the glass wall at the broads swimmin' in the pool. But most broads stay out of the water. Sun themselves like snakes. You can see 'em dry, and you can see 'em wet."

"The boys like the place," Art said.

"Yeah, it's classy. Got poodles in a bar. Not real barkin' poodles. Dog faces on the wall, paintings. They got a Staircase to Nowhere just for broads walkin' down showin' off their ice and shit."

"Can't beat classy," Greiner said rolling his eyes.

"Teresa likes it. She shops. She thinks I'm a swell guy."

"You have a kind and loyal heart," Greiner said.

"Kind and loyal. That's me," Jerry said.

"Okay, Jer, I think we're done. You got the message straight?"

"Yeah, sure. Don't do nothin' to the old man. That's the important part, ain't it?"

"Right, you got it. Sit tight. No whackin' him or anybody."

"You're puttin' me out of business, Artie."

"So go into something straight."

"You mean like loansharkin'?"

"Something like that, Jer."

"Yeah. Maybe. I'd be good at something like that."

Becker arranged to meet Allyson at 12:45, 15 minutes before Art Greiner was expected.

He entered Dunkin' Donuts out of a falling snow, stomping flakes off his topcoat and wingtips. He grabbed a paper napkin from the counter and patted wetness off his hair. He skipped the rhubarb special donut and the blueberry cake in favor of the lower-calorie, chocolate-chip cookie, which he considered a poor third to the other choices. He wore a dark blue suit and a white dress shirt with a red-and-blue repp tie. He folded the topcoat and placed it next to him in the booth. He kept his tie tight and cleaned his glasses on another napkin. He carried his leather briefcase. Becker was dressed to be a lawyer; he left his gun at home.

As the lunch crowd cleared, Allyson entered, tramping in winter messiness. She did not stop at the counter. She wore fitted jeans. Her leather boots were made for fashion not walking. She unbuttoned her down jacket and took off her knit cap. She shook out her hair over a white, turtleneck sweater. She sat opposite Becker and placed a large over-the-shoulder bag next to her.

"Want something?" Becker asked.

She laughed silently, with a little toss of her head. "Yes, is the answer, but they don't sell it here."

"Sorry about your Dad," Becker said.

"I feel like I've been shot, perforated. I did this to him."

"No...well, some," Becker said.

"Well, *but for*, as you lawyers say. *But for* me, Daddy would have died of old age, respected and honored. Now?"

"Now," Becker said, "Walton's an American hero. He took out a Mafia boss who tried to murder his daughter. He'll plead justifiable homicide in defense of another. The tricky part is to show that he acted reasonably, that killing Bruno was reasonable force and the threat of great physical harm to you was imminent. He'll also have to get the jury to jump over the hurdle of premeditation, which he obviously did. The law is against him, but I'm betting a jury will free him with an invisible pat on the back."

"God, I want you to be right," Allyson said, looking into Becker's eyes with hope. "I've been thinking hard."

"About?"

"Law school."

Becker tried to maneuver that maverick thought into a familiar corral. "Okay," he managed.

"I applied to Pitt in October. I took the LSAT before all of this. I guess I knew I needed to leave reporting."

"You never liked lawyers or what they do," he said. "Present company included."

"Journalism is bad for me. It plays into my worst instincts. It magnifies my weaknesses. I became less of the person I want to be. Law is better even though I won't like it."

"But you were right about Delucci and the Mob's money. You were right about Joe Hunt killing Gallagher. Your instincts were right."

"Doesn't matter," she said. "My process was wrong. I was writing guesses. I just happened to guess right. I can't put myself in a position where I would be tempted to do that again. The main thing is I don't want it anymore—the recognition, fame, call *it* whatever."

"What kind of lawyer do you want to be?" he asked.

"Women's stuff. Hopeless criminal defense."

"Most lawyers make a living, no matter how inept," Becker said. "The smart ones are amazing; many are decent and competent. And then there are the others. You'll do fine."

"I'll take that as a cautious endorsement," Allyson said.

"Coffee? Cookie? Doughnut?" he asked.

"No. What am I doing here?" she asked.

"What would you think of walking across the street and giving what we know to the U.S. District Attorney?"

"All of it?" she asked.

"All of it."

But not really *all* of it, Becker thought. Not Roberta Magnelli's buried body near his house. And not pointing a finger at Weez Draney who'd saved his life. Or Rooky Gondleman who got him into this jam.

"Including Jeep's role, whatever you think it was, with Biggie and the car wreck?" she asked.

"That one is up to you."

"You, too."

"We'll see," Becker said.

"Why do you want to shoot yourself in the foot?" she asked. "The good guys have finally won something. Why take it away? Why blow up what you've worked for?"

"If we don't, Jeep will have to steal the money from Union funds to pay back the Mob and Biggie's loan. There's no other pocketbook. That will get him in deeper and deeper. Then it will be too late to get out. They'll pull him under and let him have just enough air to do what they want. The feds can stop this before Jeep unwillingly takes the Union down the toilet. They can force the Mob to sell the Bank."

"You should give Delucci a chance to make it better, to put things right," she said. "He earned it. You earned it. Biggie paid for it. To make things better for the miners. Isn't that why you joined his campaign?"

"Yes."

"If you take down Delucci, the Union will disintegrate," she said. "It will be worse for the rank and file. Give yourself a win, even a compromised win. Didn't you want to set up a model for changing other unions?"

"Yes."

"Then don't be a prig about this."

"But...."

"If Delucci corrupts the Union, let the feds fix it. If you point the finger at Jeep now, who will ever trust you again?"

"Probably no one. I'll go back to being a walk-up-to-the-second-floor lawyer over a peanut shop. Or maybe get a fresh start. Like you."

"Scraps?" she said.

746

"Work for my Dad, yes. Take over the business. Recycling Pittsburgh's trash. It's honest work. It's not morally ambiguous. It's useful."

"Scraps may be your destiny," Allyson smiled.

"After Earth Day, Dad renamed the business, 'Materials Recycled, Education and Development'—MR. ED," Becker grinned, "after himself."

"Dear Mother—a talking horse. Well," Allyson added, "my mother *was* a serious equestrian in college. Maybe she has a soft spot still. Should work better than Chief Running Bare, B-A-R-E."

Where is she heading with that? Becker wondered.

Becker closed his eyes and then opened them: "Pick, why did you leave? It couldn't have been over volleyball."

Allyson started and then exhaled. "I was pregnant."

Becker, blinked and bowed his head. "Did you have the baby?"

"No," she said.

"Why didn't you tell me?"

"Because."

"Because?"

"I put the diaphragm in with the spermicide facing the wrong way. I misread the little picture."

"Why didn't you tell me?"

"What was there to discuss? I wasn't ready to have a child. I wasn't ready to be a mother. We weren't ready to be married let alone parents. What was the point of telling you anything?"

"Simple courtesy? Don't you think I should have known, had a say?"

"No," she said. "It was my responsibility, my failure, my decision. My body."

"Bullshit!" Becker whispered with the force of an oath.

"It's over. You don't get to do yesterday a second time."

"Where did you go?"

"A lady in Philadelphia. She had done Bryn Mawr 'gulls' before."

"Who went with you?"

"Nobody."

"Where did you go after?"

"I took a room at the Alexander Inn in Center City."

"Complications?"

"I can't have kids. Bled a lot. Went to the ER at Pennsylvania Hospital in a cab sitting on three stolen bath towels."

Becker put his hand to his forehead. "I'm so sorry. Does your boyfriend, your fiancé, know?"

"Kennedy? Not yet. Not sure that he's still even a friend. He pressured me to stop digging into the ACMU election after his boss and a Mob lawyer from New York leaned on him."

"That was sensible advice," Becker said. "You would have been killed if Greiner hadn't stepped in. Don't screw up your relationship, because Kennedy was trying to protect you from yourself."

"It *was* sensible advice, like the sensible advice I just gave you. I should follow it. I've changed. Daddy shooting Bruno did that. This is too big for me. I was angry that Kennedy didn't support me."

"I sure as hell wouldn't have supported you, and didn't and don't."

"Look, Becker, you couldn't have done anything about the pregnancy. It wasn't your fault."

"Why didn't you have the kid and place it for adoption?"

"I was starting journalism school in September. It was just, well, inconvenient in my circumstances. And I'm not sure I could have let it go. My life would have become very complicated as a single mom. I wasn't ready."

"You...your family had enough money. You could have made day-care arrangements. I would have married you."

"I wasn't ready for that either," she said. "You, me and the papoose. That would have been the wrong reason to get married."

"Come on. We could have made it work."

"I'm sorry you asked," Allyson said, "and I'm sorrier that I answered. It would have been better had you never known."

Art Greiner walked in wearing a black-plaid raincoat and a gray herringbone fedora. He took them off and hung them on a hook by the booth. She got up at his suggestion and let him sit next to the window where he could keep an eye on the street.

"It's snowing harder," Greiner said. "It always smells good in here. You know what's across the street on the seventh floor, don't you?"

Becker nodded. He was having trouble shifting back into the question that had brought the three together.

"You goin' over?" Greiner asked. He sensed something wasn't right between them.

"What do you think we should do?" Allyson asked.

"Are you thinkin' a RICO case will go all the way up to Fagano?"

"Yes," Becker said.

"If you go over, Allyson, Frankie will whack your Dad," Greiner said with a certainty that startled her. "The City jail is an open sewer. Any stone junkie will gut him for a $5 fix. They sharpen toothbrushes into shivs."

"Won't we be able to get Daddy out on bail before the bad guys learn we crossed the street?"

"What makes you think the LCN don't have someone on the seventh floor feedin' them information?" Greiner asked.

748

"Her Dad isn't a witness -- an informant -- against them. We are. Why would they go for him?" Becker asked.

"Well, Mr. Becker, for one thing he did kill the boss of the Pittsburgh family," Greiner said. "That's a hard one for the wise guys to forgive and forget."

Becker felt foolish.

Allyson felt desperate.

Greiner went on: "Angelo Gigliotta's the new head Pittsburgh guy. He'd get to your Dad before you could bail him out. That's assuming the judge would even set bail for a cold-blooded, high-WASP assassin -- nothin' personal, sweetheart -- which I don't think he could do politically. The best thing for your old man is for you both to keep your mouths shut and pay the jail boss of the blacks to protect him. The whites are under the Italians. The blacks might protect a white guy if the money's right. "

"I'll keep quiet," Allyson said. "I have the money."

"The other reason they'd go for Mr. Pickering is to send a message to you two to not testify against them. If they think you'll testify, they'll take you out. That's old school. They put seven bullets into Sam Giancana in June to keep him from talking to the Church Committee about the LCN and the CIA. Sam's in his basement frying sausage for some 'friend' who then did him from behind. I'm just explainin' you the facts of life, and I do mean *life*."

"Can I make a deal with Gigliotta?" Allyson asked.

"Something like Allyson forgets she ever heard about coal miners, a Washington bank and wise guys and, in return, Daddy sleeps like a baby during his incarceration."

"I'll take that deal in a heartbeat," Allyson said. "Can you get word to Gigliotta? I'll give him my files and keep quiet to keep Daddy safe?"

"Are you absolutely sure?" Greiner asked.

"Yes. Definitely," Allyson said. "Immediately."

"That's how they always operate," Becker said. "Intimidation, extortion and fear."

"Very high-minded, Becker," Allyson said. "I've done enough to hurt my family."

"I'll get Angelo your message," Greiner said. "I think he'll give your father a pass to keep the lid on this toilet. Now about Mr. Becker here...."

"I can disappear. But my Dad is vulnerable. He runs a scrap yard on the South Side...."

"...off East Carson at South 24th," Greiner said, "I know."

"You know!"

"I did a little checkin'. Professional habit. Cops have lots of ways of finding out about citizens. Nothin' personal. You grew up at 1435 Hawthorne Street in Stanton Heights. Your Dad, Ed, has a guy, Jimmy Fabio who runs the grapple."

749

"Sure, Jimmy Fabio," Becker interrupted. "I've known him since I was a kid. He showed me how to cut steel with an acetylene torch. He taught me how to work the crane."

"His sister, Teresa, is married to Jerry Multirosa. He's the guy who came after Allyson a week back."

Becker was stunned. He also knew Stella Fabio, Jimmy's wife. "Mrs. Fabio always brought a baked mostaccioli casserole with sausage and ricotta-cheese cookies to Dad's Christmas party. I couldn't eat them fast enough."

"Small world, huh," Greiner said.

"Mrs. Fabio said she knew a nice Italian girl for me when I was a senior at Peabody. '*Di alta classe*,' she said. A girl named Laurie Mascaro. Funny name, that's why I've remembered it."

"Fights would be easy to make up," Allyson said.

Becker grimaced at the wordplay. "I never followed up on it."

"I know her," Greiner said. "Pretty girl. Smart. Laurie is money and moxie."

Art Greiner wondered how people like Becker ever got through life on their own. "Your loss. She's a quality girl."

"Thanks," Allyson said.

Greiner felt it was not worth trying to decipher the mixed signals he was picking up from these two.

"It would work like this," Greiner said to Becker. "Jerry Multirosa asks Jimmy Fabio about your Dad's schedule. Jimmy would have to make a choice at that point—his own well-bein' or your Dad's."

"Multirosa would kill his brother-in-law?" Becker asked.

"He might get someone else to do it," Greiner said matter-of-factly, "if he was delicate. On the other hand, Jerry has never been squirmy when it comes to business. You don't get to pick and choose who you do and who you don't do after you've been made."

"So why wouldn't Gigliotta just come after me. That's what I've been led to believe," Becker said.

"By whom have you been led to believe that?"

Becker sensed something in Art Greiner's question that made him protect John Corelli.

"Oh, you know, just from what I've read about the Mafia. The Godfather, that kind of information. They kill informers, not the families."

"They want you O-U-T of Delucci's business with the Union," Greiner said. "They want you shut up about what you know. They threaten families to get potential informants to stay silent. People are more protective of their families than themselves. Smart people take the hint. But every so often somebody in a civilian family needs to be hurt to make sure all the other civilians in the future understand that a warning sent has to be a message received."

750

"So what should I do?" Becker asked.

"If it was me, I'd finish my cookie, walk out the door, marry this girl sittin' next to me and start over together, somewhere a long way from here. Forget about what you've done and what you've heard over the last six months. If you stay away from Delucci and keep your mouth closed permanent, maybe I can keep both of you alive."

"That is a plan," Becker said neutrally.

"Becker doesn't love me," Allyson said.

"Right," Greiner said.

"He has told me so," Allyson said. "Several times."

"Right," Greiner said.

"He has a right not to love me," she said.

"Right," Greiner said.

"He thinks I'm a bad person," she said.

"Right," Greiner said. "So let me hear you tell her you don't love her."

Becker looked at Allyson.

"Jeffrey?"

Becker tried not to look dumb.

"We're waitin', cupcake," Greiner said.

"Maybe," Becker allowed. "It's complicated."

"Jeez-us!" Greiner said. "Lame, lame, lame!"

Becker looked at her: "I want those five months again. 1968. The tepee. I want to feel that way again."

"I do, too," Allyson admitted, more to herself than to him, "but it's gone. And it probably wasn't as good as you remember it."

"You made me better," Becker said. "It was the best time of my life."

"I was unsettled, unfocused," she said. "We have to think about what we could be now with our history. If we don't try, I suppose we'll never know."

"If we fail, I'll feel worse," Becker said. "You will, too."

"You people!" Greiner laughed. "Too much fuckin' college! This ain't a chess game. Either there's shit on the biscuit or there ain't. If there ain't, you eat the damn biscuit."

"Greiner, you're elegant," Allyson laughed.

"Anyway," Greiner said, throwing up his hands, "why did you ask me to meet you here? To go with you across the street?"

"Yes," Becker said.

"So are we goin' over?"

Becker looked at Allyson.

"No, not right now," Becker said. "She and I need to talk over a few things."

Allyson laughed. "A few!"

"Right," Greiner said. "Hope this is the last time I see either of yins. You want my opinion?"

"Yes," Becker said.

"Do what I said. Drop it here. You got four of them out of the picture—Little Louie, Bonk, a girl named Roberta Magnelli and Tony Bruno. You lost Biggie Stover. You go to the feds, Fagano will even the score—he'll get Mr. Pickering, you and you. You can count on him. You won't have no happy ending."

"I'm dropping it. Here and now," Allyson said.

"I…" Becker started.

Greiner glanced out the window. In the reflection, he caught a glimpse of two people walking toward his end of the restaurant.

Wearing a dark coat and a black shawl around her head, Josephine Bruno walked toward their booth with a cup of coffee. She pulled her dead husband's pistol from her pocket.

She threw the coffee in Allyson's face. Allyson screamed. Her white sweater turned brown.

Becker moved faster than he thought possible. Getting free of the booth, he knocked Josephine to the floor as she fired. Then he threw himself over Allyson. They collapsed against Greiner, pinning him.

"NO!" Greiner cried, as he tried to get to his pistol.

Jerry Multirosa fired at Allyson, hitting Becker. He fired again, missing her neck by an inch. He fired a third time, grazing Greiner's head by mistake.

"Fuck it," Jerry said. "Didn't mean it, Artie. This gun ain't no good!"

He pulled Josephine to her feet, grabbed her pistol and got her out the door fast.

Allyson felt Becker's weight heavy against her. She wrapped her arms around him.

"Not again, please, not again."

He didn't move.

"Stay with me, Becker," she whispered.

752

71429560R00424

Made in the USA
Middletown, DE
24 April 2018